Evelyn Hood was born and raised in Paisley. She now lives on the Clyde coast with her husband.

Praise for Evelyn Hood

'Hood is immaculate in her historical detail'
The Herald

'An extremely good read'
Historical Novels Review

'Evelyn Hood has been called Scotland's Catherine Cookson. Unfair. She has her own distinctive voice'
Scots Magazine

EVELYN HOOD OMNIBUS

A Stranger to the Town

The Shimmer of
the Herring

sphere

SPHERE

This omnibus edition first published in Great Britain by
Sphere in 2007
Evelyn Hood Omnibus copyright © Evelyn Hood 2007

Previously published separately:
A Stranger to the Town first published in Great Britain by
William Kimber & Co. Limited in 1985
Published by Warner Books in 1999
Reprinted 2000
Copyright © Evelyn Hood 1985

The Shimmer of the Herring first published in Great Britain in 2000 by
Little, Brown and Company
Published by Warner Books in 2001
Reprinted 2001 (twice)
Reprinted by Time Warner Paperbacks in 2004
Copyright © 2000 Evelyn Hood

The moral right of the author has been asserted

A CIP catalogue record for this book is available from the British Library.

ISBN 978-0-7515-4023-9

Papers used by Sphere are natural, recyclable products made from
wood grown in sustainable forests and certified in accordance with
the rules of the Forest Stewardship Council.

Printed and bound in Great Britain by Clays Ltd, St Ives plc
Paper supplied by Hellefoss AS, Norway

Sphere
An imprint of
Little, Brown Book Group
Brettenham House
Lancaster Place
London WC2E 7EN

A Member of the Hachette Livre Group of Companies

www.littlebrown.co.uk

A Stranger to the Town

To the people of Paisley,
past and present

Prologue

The Town Hospital had been built in 1752 to house Paisley's poor. It seemed to Elizabeth, as she tried in vain to scrub the scuffed parlour floor in 1828, that nobody else had attempted to clean it in the intervening seventy-six years.

The scrubbing brush was a poor mess of bristles and wood, the water she worked with cold and scummy, adding its own dirt to the filthy floor. The soap, harsh yellow stuff made in the hospital kitchen, had vanished.

'Teenie!' She sat back on her heels, pushed lank hair from her eyes, glared at the elderly woman kneeling beside her. 'Give me that soap!'

Teenie worked on, scrubbing as though intent on wearing her way through to the foundations of the building. But Elizabeth's sharp eyes had seen the yellow lump in Teenie's almost-closed fist. The woman was a known thief. She took everything she saw, and if she couldn't sell it for a few pence, she hid it in the garden.

'Give it to me!' Elizabeth launched herself at Teenie, who was caught by surprise. The two of them rolled on the wet, dirty floor, Teenie squawling in childish outrage, Elizabeth silent, fighting with tooth and nail, feet and fists. If the soap went missing it would mean yet another punishment. This time, surely, she would be made to spend an hour in the cells where the insane folk were kept. The thought of it made her skin crawl, and redoubled her efforts.

She had just gained hold of the precious soap when fingers dug into her scalp, dragging her head back as tears flooded into her screwed-up eyes. The soap slid from her hand and she and Teenie were separated.

'Elizabeth Cunningham!' Mistress Jamieson, matron of the hospital, glared down at her. 'I might have known it! Get to the kitchen this minute and wait for me!'

'She stole the soap, and—'

'I never did!' Teenie shrieked, then fled to the corner of the empty, gloomy parlour as Elizabeth rounded on her.

'That's enough!' the matron rapped, then another voice, low and calm, spoke from the doorway.

'And how old is this lassie?'

'Fourteen years, Mistress Montgomery.' The matron released her grip on Elizabeth, who stood where she was, Teenie forgotten.

'Old enough to go into service.' Mistress Montgomery came further into the room, lifting her skirts to keep them away from the muddy floor.

'She's of some use in the kitchens and with the younger children. And most folk feel she doesn't have the looks or the proper manner to be a servant.'

Elizabeth's cheeks flamed and she opened her mouth to protest that she wasn't an animal to be discussed as though she had no feelings. Then she remembered the cells, and closed her lips. Two hours at least, for a girl who had the audacity to answer back before a visitor.

Instead, she tilted her chin defiantly, determined that she wasn't going to lower her head. To her surprise, her brown gaze met grey eyes filled with warmth and interest. There was even sympathy there, though it was an emotion she hadn't seen often before.

Mistress Montgomery wore a fine dark red silk gown and a feathered bonnet. Greying brown hair framed a pretty face that looked as though it smiled easily. About her shoulders was one of the beautiful, intricately-patterned shawls woven on Paisley looms and famed throughout the world.

'Is your mother in the hospital?' The question was directed at Elizabeth herself, subtle reproof to the matron, who drew in her breath with a faint hiss, but said nothing.

'She's—' Elizabeth swallowed hard. 'They – died of the smallpox, my mother and father and – and—'

And Davie, and the laughing baby. In the seven lonely years since, she had demanded of Mistress Jamieson's God, over and over again, why she had been made to stay alive without them.

Her face coloured again as she saw the woman's eyes travel over the scar that stretched from one corner of her mouth to the angle of her jaw. Many people in Paisley carried smallpox scars, but Elizabeth felt as though the uneven, puckered groove she bore was the ugliest ever seen.

'But you survived it. You were meant for a long life,' Mistress Montgomery said gently. 'Tell me, Elizabeth Cunningham, would you be willing to work for me?'

Mistress Jamieson moved forward swiftly. 'I really think you should see the girl I've selected for you—'

Mistress Montgomery held up an elegant hand, her eyes still on Elizabeth's face. 'I require a girl who can learn to manage a household, and perhaps become my companion. Would you like that?'

'Aye.' The word was no more than a strangled gasp, but it spoke volumes. A smile told Elizabeth that the woman understood.

'Someone of a more placid disposition—' the matron tried to intervene, and the smile deepened.

'My dear woman, a more placid disposition would be quite bewildered in a household of men,' said Mistress Montgomery crisply. 'I require some-one with some spirit – and I think we'll both be well pleased. You can send her to the High Street tomorrow. And I think, under the circumstances, that it would be a kindness to forget today's misdemeanour.'

She swept out with a rustle of silk, followed by Mistress Jamieson with a clank of keys. The soap vanished within the folds of Teenie's greasy, shabby gown and she gave the bucket a sly kick, setting the floor awash with spilled water, soaking Elizabeth's worn shoes. Elizabeth didn't care.

On the following morning she stood in the Town Hospital's front hall, her face scrubbed until it glowed painfully, her hair washed and screwed into plaits and hidden beneath a respectable white linen cap. Her sole possessions, a change of clothing and a Bible, were in the bundle she held.

Mistress Jamieson surveyed her from every angle before coming to a standstill before her.

'I want you to know, Elizabeth Cunningham, that Mistress Rachel Montgomery is the wife of one of Paisley's most important manufacturers. You must never, never—' a large-knuckled forefinger wagged before Elizabeth's nose '—never do anything to anger her or her man. If you bring shame on this Institution by your bad behaviour or disobedience or impudence, the Lord himself will strike you down. Do you mind me?'

Elizabeth, too overcome to speak, nodded violently.

'May He go with you,' the matron finished, in a voice that said plainly that she was sure He had more to do than go with the likes of Elizabeth Cunningham, orphan and trouble-maker.

The hospital doors opened. Elizabeth took a firm grip on her bundle, and walked out to face a new life.

I

Rounding the corner from New Street into High Street, Elizabeth staggered and gasped as the wind caught at her cloak. She staggered again when an elderly woman pushed by her roughly, intent on getting out of the gale – in some ale-house, to judge from the smell that hit Elizabeth's nose in the passing.

The summer of 1831 was whirling itself out of existence with ill-tempered grace. Well it might, for it had been a bad summer for Paisley. Scotland's most successful weaving centre had too many looms lying idle and too many hungry weavers seeking work.

'Mind the stour, lassie—' A plum-coloured arm with lace at the wrist swept out to hold Elizabeth back from the gutter, which swirled with filthy water. The man smiled down at her as she regained her balance and stammered thanks, then

1

he disappeared into the tide of folk sweeping along the High Street in both directions. The footpaths were packed with housewives, bare-footed children oblivious to the cold, plump businessmen with gold chains looped securely across ample stomachs. The narrow roadway too had its traffic – carts and carriages, mail gigs, men on horseback swearing at pedestrians who crossed beneath the very noses of the horses.

It was just as well, Elizabeth thought as she looped the basket more firmly over her arm and battled on her way, that she hadn't much further to go. And there it was – the fine solid oaken door proclaiming in the gleam of its handle and knocker that it belonged to a prosperous man.

It swung open under her hand then closed behind her, shutting out the noise and the wind. As always, she felt a faint thrill of pleasure when she stood in the hallway of Rab Montgomery's fine house. It had an air of opulence that she had never known until three years before. Normally she would have scurried down the narrow passage that led down the side of the house to the back door. But now and then, when she knew her employer wasn't at home, she permitted herself the luxury of using the front door and pretending that the house belonged to her.

In reality the only part that could be said to be hers was the kitchen. Elizabeth enjoyed her moment of pride then crossed to the door set in the shadows beyond the staircase.

The kitchen of the Montgomery house was a large room, stone-flagged and, at that moment, rich with a mixture of aromas from pots bubbling on the range. The big scrubbed wooden table that took up most of the floor space was packed with platters carrying crisp golden tarts, sugared cakes, cold meats and loaves crusty and hot from the oven. Such a banquet had to be prepared for that night that several neighbours and one of the baker's shops nearby had been called on to lend their ovens for the occasion.

It was a sight guaranteed to gladden the heart of any housewife. But Elizabeth's attention was immediately taken from the table by the noise of Tibby's scolding and Jean's sobs.

'What's amiss?' She found a stool to hold her laden basket, and unfastened her tartan cloak.

'Well you might ask!' Tibby, a small shrew of a woman, rounded on her, hands tucked into her skinny waist. 'It's thon stupid big lump of a lassie. Why you keep her on here's beyond me!'

Jean, huddled in a chair with her apron over her face, howled like a banshee. Cold terror caught at Elizabeth's heart.

3

'She's gone and let the beef burn! Jean, did I no' tell you time and again to keep your eyes on that beef!'

'It's no' the beef.' Tibby made it sound as though burning the beef counted as a very small sin.

'What then?' Elizabeth anxiously studied the table as Jean bayed to the smoky ceiling like a dog serenading the moon. 'The puddings! What happened to the puddings?' The perfect house-keeper, she was more concerned over her employer's favourite foods than anything else. Rab Montgomery had spent days ordering this meal and he was a hard taskmaster if he was crossed.

'The puddings havenae come from Mistress McNair's kitchen yet. This daft gowk – you cannae leave her to do anything!' Tibby nudged Jean, bringing another howl from her. Elizabeth, now almost beside herself with worry, dragged the apron down and revealed a swollen, turkey-red face.

'Then what's she done? In the name of reason, Jean, will you just tell me what's gone wrong?'

'Oh, Miss Eliza – lizabeth!' Jean gulped, sniffed, and was about to slip into a fresh bout of keening when a look at Elizabeth's face made her change her mind. 'I c-cannae mind if I salted the b-br-b-broth or no'!'

'Is that all?'

'All?' Tibby squawked self-righteously. 'And me standing at that table for near on two hours chopping and cutting so that they'd have the best broth ever put on a table to welcome a wanderer home?'

'Did you think to taste the broth?'

They stared at her blankly and Elizabeth found a wooden spoon, dipped it into the huge pot on the 'swee' that held it over the range, and blew the soup cautiously before tasting it.

'Aye, you salted it, Jean.' She waited, unkindly, for the first look of relief to spread over the scullery maid's face before going on, 'Twice. Now see here—' she added swiftly as Jean's face screwed up again and Tibby opened her mouth for another scolding '—crying'll no' cure it, tears are salty too. Away and get more water for the kettle while I see to this.' She seized a cloth, lifted the heavy kettle that was always simmering on the range, and tipped some of it into the broth pot.

'You'll ruin it!' Tibby danced about the kitchen in a frenzy. Elizabeth tasted the mixture again.

'It's still got a good flavour to it, and there's enough to drink if the salt makes them thirsty. They'll no' complain.'

Tibby jerked a white-capped head in the direction of the open back door. 'Why you keep that

5

lassie on here's beyond me. She hasnae got as much sense as would fill a flea!'

'She can manage well enough when she's no' being hurried,' Elizabeth raced to the maid's defence. The truth was that Jean, like herself, had been brought up in the Town Hospital. Orphan must help orphan. Elizabeth knew well enough that Tibby, who worked in her brother's butcher's shop, would have preferred Jean's job and never missed the opportunity, when helping out, to show up the girl's shortcomings.

Jean staggered in from the darkening night with a stoup of water from the outside well in each hand. Elizabeth directed her to refill the kettle and to wash her tear-stained face, then hurried to the parlour, rolling up her sleeves as she went, to make sure that everything was prepared for the evening's celebrations.

The room was a flickering patchwork of light and shadow in the firelight. She drew the heavy curtains, lit a taper at the fire, and attended to the lamps. The parlour was large and well furnished with good pieces chosen by Rab Montgomery's late wife. The carpet, soft underfoot, was in muted shades of blue and green and brown. Elizabeth crossed the hall and peeped in at the door of the dining-room, nodding her satisfaction over the big table's snowy starched covering and the discreet glitter of glass and silverware. This room was hardly ever used; since Rab had been widowed almost a year before, he and his sons preferred to take their morning meal in the kitchen and their evening meals at the small table in the parlour.

The knocker rattled importantly and as soon as Elizabeth answered it Christian Selbie swept into the hall on a gust of cold air and a handful of rain. She divested herself of her fur-trimmed cloak, revealing a lilac silk dress with a lace-edged ruff about the neck, and full lace-trimmed sleeves.

'Well, Elizabeth—' She unfastened her bonnet strings and took the hat off, patting the fine lace cap that hid most of her grey-streaked dark head. 'Is everyone at home?'

'Mister Montgomery's gone to meet the coach.'

Christian tutted and smoothed the skirt of her gown with a beringed hand. She was a small plump active woman, warm-hearted and generous, quite unlike her dour cousin, Rab Montgomery.

'No doubt he'll catch the pneumonia and Adam'll find he only came home to attend a death-bed. Mind you, he'll probably be cosy enough in Sadie's tavern, waiting for the coach in comfort, with a drink in his hand. What about Matthew and James?'

'Not home yet.' Elizabeth allowed her fingers the luxury of a swift wriggle in the thick fur that lined the cloak Christian had handed to her. It would be dreary in the big warehouse by the river on a stormy night like this. She could picture the lamps casting weird shadows in the corners and on the high ceilings above the bundles and bales. Matthew and James Montgomery would be the last to leave as usual – Matthew with his brain buzzing over the figuring he hated, James in a dream of his own, working out a new poem or a new design in his head.

Christian brought her back to her own business with a bump when she said briskly, 'Well, we'd best be seeing to things—' and bustled off to the kitchen.

'Ma'am – Mistress Selbie—' Elizabeth scurried after her. 'Would you no' be more comfortable in the parlour?'

Christian tutted. 'Lassie, mebbe I'm here to preside over this party for Rab, but you'd surely never expect me to sit alone in the parlour till the folk come?' She threw the kitchen door open. 'Good evening to you, Jean – you're here too, Tibby?—' In a moment she had cast an eye over the table, swung the broth pot out from the fire and peeped inside, muttering to herself all the time.

Born to money and widowed by a well-to-do husband, Christian had inherited the character of her grandmother, a weaver's wife. She was used to servants, but she had no time for a woman who knew nothing of the workings of a kitchen or the right way to apply a poultice or darn a stocking. Her father had been a surgeon, her brother a lawyer, her husband a banker. It was Christian's belief that she could have bettered any of them if she had not had the misfortune to be born a woman.

'I see the fatted calf's been killed for the prodigal son,' she observed dryly, unfastening her sleeves and rolling them back to expose rounded, capable forearms. 'Elizabeth – a clean pinny, if you please!'

A rap at the back door heralded the arrival of Mistress McNair's small maid with the sweet puddings. Suddenly all the last-minute arrangements became essential and by the time everything was ready Elizabeth had reason to be grateful for Christian's calm, efficient organisation.

'You're on the young side to be giving orders to the likes of Tibby.' Christian brushed words of appreciation aside as she led Elizabeth back to the parlour, fastening her sleeves again. 'She's lazy and she needs someone who's ready for her. It's foolish of Rab to expect you to see to everything. He should have had the sense to employ an older woman.' Then, realising that her words sounded critical, she added kindly 'After all, poor Rachel engaged you to be her companion, not the housekeeper.'

Rachel Montgomery, Rab's second wife and mother to James and Matthew, had died several months earlier, and Elizabeth missed her warmth and her guidance bitterly. But there was no time to think of that now. The front door opened and closed and Christian, tidying her hair in the mirror above the mantel, whirled round.

'They're here! Rab? Adam—?' Then her voice flattened with disappointment. 'Oh – it's you, James.'

James Montgomery, youngest of Rab's three sons and twenty-one years of age, blinked in surprise at his cousin.

'Are you here already?'

'Already?' she screeched at him. 'The guests arriving at any minute and Adam late? Have you no idea of the time? James Montgomery, get upstairs this minute and get yourself into a decent coat and cravat, else your father'll have something to say when he gets home!'

Placid James, who always gave the impression that his thoughts were elsewhere, gave her his sweet, warm smile and turned away obediently.

'Wait – where's Matthew?' she rapped, and he looked around as though slightly surprised to realise that he had come home alone.

'Oh yes – he's calling in at Shuttle Street,' he remembered.

His kinswoman raised her eyes to the ceiling. 'Does he have to go courting tonight of all nights? Off you go, James—' she added, shooing him across the hall as though he was a stray chicken. Then she bustled back into the parlour. 'Mind you, I see no reason why Isobel couldn't have been invited here tonight with Matt. Nobody ever ended something by pretending it wasnae there. Isobel's a fine lassie. Rab's a fool – his son could find a worse wife.'

The knocker banged and Elizabeth hurried to the hall, rushed back to the parlour in answer to Christian's squeak of horror, caught the rejected pinny as the older woman tore it off and threw it to her, then ran back to open the door.

She returned to the kitchen just as the back door opened, frightening the life out of Jean, who had been leaning against it.

'Beth!' Matthew seized her hands in an icy grip, his nose red from the cold wind. 'Are they here yet?'

'No, but due any minute. Your cousin Christian's entertaining the Blairs in the parlour. You're awful late, Matt—'

His light brown hair was windswept. 'I saw the Blairs at the door, so I came down the side passage. I'll get upstairs and get ready.'

He picked up a pastry, ignoring her angry 'Matthew Montgomery—!' and slid like a shadow through the inner door. Tibby, stirring the broth, sniffed.

'That's no way for a young gentleman to behave. Stealing through his father's back door like a thief. Mind you, there's some say that he's no' keeping the right company these days—'

'You can see to the potatoes now.' Elizabeth found a new hardness in her voice to make the woman subside. Christian was right, Tibby did need to be bullied before she would mind her sharp tongue. Elizabeth had a soft spot for Matt, for she knew he was unhappy working as his father's warehouse foreman. And Isobel Gibson, Matthew's love, was a friend of Elizabeth's.

Isobel's father was a silk weaver, now old and unable to do much work. Isobel herself worked for the Montgomerys, trimming shawls for one shilling and threepence a day. Rab had made it clear that he didn't consider her a good match for his son.

The door knocker thumped again. And again, and again. Matthew and James, both neat and well groomed, appeared among the guests. The parlour was full, the meal ready, but still Rab Montgomery and his eldest son, Adam, the guest of honour, were missing.

'I mind Adam was never good at arriving anywhere on time,' Christian remarked to Mrs Andrew Blair as Elizabeth went into the parlour for advice. 'He took three days to his own birth, and his mother never survived it, poor flower. What's amiss, Elizabeth?'

The meat was amiss, beginning to sizzle ominously in its own shrinking fat. And the potatoes were ready for eating.

'Could I serve the meal now, ma'am?'

'You cannae put the food on the table before the master of the house is here, no' to mention—' Christian's head lifted sharply 'Did I hear the front door? They're here!'

Her shrill voice caught everyone's attention. It was too late for Elizabeth to slip back to the kitchen, so she had to stay with the others and await Adam Montgomery's entrance. He had been away from home for some years and Elizabeth had never set eyes on him. She would have preferred to be well out of the way for his re-introduction to Paisley.

All heads turned towards the door and Rab Montgomery, arriving on the threshold of his own parlour wet, cold and in a very bad temper, found himself the centre of some two dozen pairs of eyes.

'You can all stop staring,' he informed his guests curtly. 'He's no' here.'

'No' here?' Christian, a miniature Moses, divided the throng with little effort, clawing a path to her cousin. 'The stage didnae arrive?'

Rab let his damp coat fall to the floor and scowled at the gathering. Mrs Andrew Blair gasped and fluttered a hand to her throat. She was known to be a highly-strung lady.

'Here? Of course the stage is here, woman!' Rab snarled. 'A good hour late, and with Adam's boxes on board.'

'Mercy,' quavered Mrs Andrew Blair. 'He's fell off!'

Rab gave her a withering glance and pushed his way to the small cupboard where the whisky was kept. Ignoring the buzz of speculation that rose about his ears he poured himself a generous glassful and drained half of it before speaking.

'He left the coach on the outskirts of the town. It seems that some drunken fool of a man let himself fall under the horses and Adam undertook to tend him. As to where he is—' His small blue eyes, bloodshot and bright in his round red face, were like glass as he looked at them all over the rim of the tumbler. When he lowered it again he went on '—I have no idea. And damn me if I care!'

'We'll have the dinner now,' Christian's voice cut decisively across the babble of shocked, alarmed voices. 'Elizabeth—'

Everyone turned with relief towards their hostess. Everyone except Rab, who emptied his glass and picked up the bottle.

'Aye, off you go to the trough,' he told his guests with his customary surliness. 'That's what you came for, was it no'? For myself, I'll just have a wee dram—'

His arm was seized by a plump, determined fist. Its partner took the glass from his hand.

'You'll just come through and sit at the table with the rest of us, Rab,' Christian ordered. 'For you're more in need of hot food than of drink on a stormy night like this.'

She was the only person, now that his wife was dead, who could make Rab Montgomery do anything against his will. The two of them warred whenever they met, but Christian kept Rab's household going, and his life in order. Muttering beneath his breath, he allowed her to lead him to the dining-room, followed by the people who had come to welcome Adam home.

The meal was more like a wake, with Adam's empty chair reproaching them all. Some of the guests, who had indeed come for the food, gave a good account of themselves. Rab, a big man who had never been known for his cheerfulness, and who had become even more soured since Rachel's death, picked morosely at the contents of his plate and devoted more time to the wine, not opening his mouth to anyone. He had planned this evening to the finest degree, and by missing it Adam had spurned him.

Matt, deeply disappointed by his brother's absence, also picked at his food. As she bustled round the table, serving people and making sure that all was in order, Elizabeth caught his blue eyes, and was rewarded by a smile. She knew that Matt was wishing that Isobel could be at his side.

James worked valiantly to entertain the guests, though all he wanted was to get away to the peace of the small room he shared with Matt. He, too, had dreams; in James's case they were about books of poetry, or fine shawl designs. Like Matt, he found that his ambitions were scorned by his father.

The guests didn't stay for long once the meal was ended. Christian was the last to go.

'I have it in mind to hold a wee gathering for some of the younger folk soon,' she murmured to Matt as he escorted her to her carriage. 'I'd like fine if Isobel would come to it.'

His face flushed and he beamed at her gratefully. 'I'd – she'd – that'd be fine!' Gratitude hampered his tongue.

Rab and James were in the hall with Elizabeth when Matt went back indoors. 'I'll wait up – mebbe Adam'll come home tonight.'

Rab rounded on him. 'You'll go to your room and get a good night's sleep! There's plenty to be done at the warehouse in the morning and I'll have you ready for it, no' sleeping over the books because your laggardly brother saw fit to go off with some drunken fool. He can sleep at the house-end till the door's open in the morning!' Rab locked the door firmly. 'That might teach him a lesson – if he troubles himself to come home at all!' And he stumped upstairs, dragging the leg that had been injured during the riots eleven years earlier. Matt and James, exchanging looks, followed him.

Tibby and Jean helped Elizabeth to clear the table and set the house to rights. A great deal of food had been left over and Tibby went off home with a bundle beneath her shawl, her shrill tongue sweetened at last. As Elizabeth shut and bolted the back door behind her she thought of the missing Adam Montgomery. The wind was still strong and it was raining heavily.

She sent Jean off to sleep in the cupboard-like bedroom off the kitchen and decided, tired though she was, to sit up for a little longer just in case Adam Montgomery arrived home. She couldn't bear to think of him having to huddle in the shelter of a wall till morning. After all, Rab Montgomery hadn't forbidden her to stay up.

The rest of the house was in darkness now, but the kitchen was lit, and cosy. The kettle simmered quietly on the range. Rain tapped now and then at the window and the wind howled round the trees in the garden. Elizabeth's lids drooped, lifted, drooped, and settled.

She woke with a start, bewildered to find herself in the kitchen, confused by the noise that identified itself, as she blinked drowsiness away, as a thunderous attack on the front door. Still not fully clear as to why she wasn't in her bed she snatched up a lamp and scuttled into the hall, the light chasing shadows before her.

Someone was pounding the solid oaken door with determined fists, and adding a kick now and then. Elizabeth, hurrying to answer, recalled the fiasco of a few hours before and the missing man. She set the lamp down on a carved straight-backed chair and reached up to slide back the bolt at the top of the door.

As soon as the bolts were drawn and the latch lifted the door was thrown back, Elizabeth staggering with it. Then the handle was torn from her fingers as the door was slammed shut again, closing out the wind and rain. A large shape, a man in heavy coat and tall hat, his chin tucked close to his chest, and his coat collar pulled well up, surged into the hall.

'God's teeth!' boomed an angry voice as the door slammed shut, 'is everyone deaf in this place? Must a traveller take the very walls apart before he's heard?'

Flickering lamplight stilled and grew as the air settled again. Its glow illuminated Rab Montgomery's slippered feet and bare ankles below his night-shirt as he stopped on the third bottom step of the staircase. His own candle, held high, lit his face and his night-capped head. Behind him Elizabeth could hear Matt and James in the shadows.

'Adam!' Matt whooped, but Rab's sturdy body blocked the way down as he stood still, glaring at his errant son.

Adam Montgomery took his hat off and tossed it onto a table, peering up into the candle-lit area above. 'Matthew. Father. James,' he acknowledged his family crisply.

In the uncertain light Rab's face was drawn into a malevolent scowl. 'So you found your way back home after all,' he said sourly, making no move to come down the last few steps.

'I was – detained.'

'We heard. No doubt I'll see you in the morning – if you've nowhere better you'd rather be,' Rab sneered, and turned to go back to bed. When Matt and James stood back to let him pass, he barked at them, 'I'll have no family reunions at this time of the night – get to your beds! You can speak to your brother in the morning!'

Reluctantly, the two were driven before him to the upper floor, leaving Elizabeth and Adam in the hall.

'Well – do you mean to let me stand here all night?' he turned on her. All she could see of him was a face set in lines as uncompromising as Rab's, and broad shoulders that shone wetly. Hurriedly, she bobbed a curtsey and led the way to the kitchen. He ducked his head to follow her through the door, then looked round as he unfastened his caped travelling coat.

He let it drop to the floor, in a gesture similar to his father's earlier, and went to spread large, long-fingered hands before the range, shivering.

'Is there food in this place?'

She realised that she had been standing gaping like a fool.

'Of – of course. There's broth I'll heat for you, and some cold fowl, and—'

He tore a handful of bread from a loaf on the table, delved into the butter crock, and spread the bread liberally.

'And hot water – I'm in sore need of good hot water,' he ordered thickly through a mouthful of food.

Nervously Elizabeth fetched a piece of her own soap and a basin, which was promptly tossed into a corner.

'A decent wash, woman, not a dipping of my fingers!' he barked at her. 'Is there no bath in this God-forsaken house of my father's?'

She opened a door and dragged out the tin hip bath, struggling with it to the door.

'Now what are you doing?'

'I'm – I'm taking the bath to your r – room—' Her tongue wouldn't shape the words properly.

'You'd have me wash in a cold room on a night like this?' The bath was taken from her and deposited before the fire. The steaming kettle was emptied into it, followed by a pot of water that had been sitting on the range. There was about two inches of hot water in the bottom of the bath.

'God save us – there's enough for a sparrow!' he said in disgust.

'There's the water heating in the wash-house for the morning's washing—' she ventured, hanging the soup pot on the iron swee and swinging it over the fire.

'Then hold the light for me—' Adam opened the back door and plunged out into the night, Elizabeth close behind him. The wash-house, which held the big copper boiler, was built at right angles to the back of the house and had its own door, close to the kitchen door. He picked up two buckets, scooped warm water from the boiler, and returned to hurl their contents into the bath.

By the time he was finished the boiler was almost empty and the kitchen was fragrant with the aroma of hot broth. Adam grunted with satisfaction as he surveyed the hip bath, half-filled with warm water.

'Will you eat first?' Elizabeth had set a corner of the table with cutlery and food. He studied it hungrily, then looked down at his own untidy, mud-splashed figure.

'I'll take the edge off my appetite, for the hunger's gnawing at me,' he decided, flicking a contemptuous finger at the bottle of his father's prized brandy she had set out for him. 'You can take that away. Get me a jug of good Scots ale, woman!'

She ladled out broth, fetched the ale jug, and ran to put a warming pan in his bed. Adam was to use the small room at the far end of the upstairs passage.

When she returned with towels he had emptied the soup pot and the jug. He indicated to her to bring more ale, then she retired to a chair by the fire, waiting for his next instructions.

He ate swiftly, greedily, with his eyes fixed on his plate, and after a moment she dared to look up at him. His clothes were good; a dark red coat, a yellow satin waistcoat, fawn trousers and sturdy boots, with a black cravat at his throat. The boots and trousers were covered in muddy streaks, the coat splashed with darker stains which could have been blood. His dark hair was neither dressed nor powdered, but left free to curl strongly about his forehead and the nape of his neck.

His face was square, rugged, handsome, though set in forbidding lines, his eyes—

His eyes, she realised with sudden confusion,

were looking straight into hers. Flustered, she fluttered her fingers together in her lap.

'And what do they call you?'

'Elizabeth.' Her voice came out in a gasp.

He pushed his chair back and stood up. 'Well now, Elizabeth, you may have saved my very life with your broth.'

He moved to the fire, leaving her free to go to the table to begin gathering up the used dishes. 'You sleep here in the house?'

'In the attic.' She nodded to the door of Jean's little room. 'The scullery maid sleeps in there.'

He dropped his stained coat onto a chair, began to unfasten the buttons of his waistcoat. 'She must be a heavy sleeper tonight – if she isn't dead.'

'Once her eyes close Jean wouldnae know if the house fell down about her ears.' Elizabeth attempted a laugh, but it died before the unsmiling scrutiny from the man who stood in the kitchen as though he owned everything in it. The cravat dropped from his nimble fingers, followed by the waistcoat.

'Mebbe it's time you were going to your own bed, Elizabeth.'

'But—' It didn't seem right. This was no welcome for a man who had been away from home for so long, and had travelled so far. But

Adam, it seemed, was as uninterested in convention as his father. He was unfastening the pleated cuffs of his shirt, popping buttonholes from neck to waist – then the shirt, too, was tossed carelessly to the chair. His smooth, muscular torso gleamed in the lamplight as he let the garment fall and straightened up again.

'Unless—' he suggested as his fingers moved unhurriedly, but with purpose, to the buttons at the waistband of his tight-fitting trousers, 'you have some notion of giving me your own welcome home? You must forgive me if I devote myself to my bath first. Or are you gifted like those famous geisha girls of Japan—?'

Elizabeth didn't wait to hear any more. With a scandalised gasp, realising that he had no intention of letting her presence prevent him from stepping naked into the tub, she scooped up a lamp and fled to her room.

She tiptoed up the main staircase to the first floor, then up the second, narrower flight of stairs to the attics high above the street. One room was used as a store-room, the other was Elizabeth's – her first private room and her pride and joy. Here, on a shelf Matt had made for her, stood a few books that Rachel Montgomery and Christian Selbie had given her. There on the wall was a picture painted by James. This was where Elizabeth kept her few clothes, her hairbrush, her mirror.

It was the middle of the night. In a few hours she would have to be up again. She swept the lawn cap from her light brown hair and let the long, heavy tresses tumble down her back. She brushed it out as she used to brush Rachel's hair, then took off her apron and gown and underclothes, putting them away neatly before slipping into bed in her shift.

She knew that she would never be able to sleep. There was too much to think about.

She blew out the lamp, then opened her eyes to the sound of the first risers moving about in the street below. It was time to get up.

II

The house was silent as Elizabeth hurried down to the ground floor. She was always first up and it was her duty to have the housework started and breakfast ready before the men of the house arrived in the kitchen. She and Jean would normally have started work on the washing first thing, but the copper had been emptied for Adam Montgomery's bath. This meant that work would be behind-hand all day.

Trying to reorganise the day in her mind she went into the kitchen, put the lamp on the table by the remains of Adam's meal, then turned and caught her breath. He was still there, fast asleep by the range, which now glowed dully. He had dressed himself again in his shirt, open at the neck to expose a strong throat, and his trousers. The stained jacket was thrown over his shoulders and his bony bare feet sprawled untidily on the mat before the range. The hip bath had been put out of sight.

She lit a second lamp and put it on the shelf above the fire. Its light fell across his face but didn't disturb him. He looked, she thought, very uncomfortable. His long frame spilled over the chair, his head lolling on one shoulder. Even in sleep the set of his mouth was uncompromising, though the dark lashes brushing his cheeks were surprisingly long and silky. His hair was disordered, and she saw in the light that there were threads of silver among the black curls over his temples. One arm lay across his body, the other was over the wooden arm of the chair, his fingers dangling in mid-air. He had fine hands, she thought enviously, aware of her own work-reddened fingers. But then, Adam Montgomery was both a physician and a surgeon, where she—

She suddenly realised that it was almost six and nothing had been started. She was torn between reluctance to wake him and the urgency of her work. Nervously she spoke his name but he didn't stir. Her hand reached out towards his arm, hesitated, withdrew, and finally settled. His body was strong and hard beneath the soiled material of the shirt.

She shook him slightly, saying his name in a

louder voice, and his dark blue eyes suddenly flew open. For a moment he stared uncomprehendingly at the hand on his arm, then he said sleepily 'Who—?' and lifted his chin to look up at her.

'Oh – it's you.' He rubbed a hand over his face. 'What is it?'

'It's nearly six, sir. I have to clean the range and get the meal ready.'

He brushed her aside and got to his feet, yawning, stretching till his knuckles almost touched the ceiling, then looking with distaste at the clothes he wore.

'Did my boxes arrive?'

'Aye, sir, they're in your room.'

He nodded, picked up his jacket from the floor where it had fallen, and went to the door. Then he turned, supporting himself with one hand on the frame.

'How do you address my brothers?'

'By their given names.'

'Then you'll call me Adam,' he said, making an order of it, and walked out.

Jean was buried in blankets, her hair a rumpled black mass on the pillow, mouth open, eyes tightly shut. Elizabeth shook her awake with a lot more vigour and a lot less sympathy than she had used on Adam and dragged her, protesting, to the cold floor. Then she hurried back to the kitchen, where she scooped up the remains of the late meal, cleaned out the grate with noisy speed, and set the fire. Jean shuffled in, sleepy-eyed and yawning, and was ruthlessly ordered to wash her face in a bowl of cold water.

'And stir yourself, girl, for there's the porridge to make and the front doorstep to clean – and see you get a good polish on that door knocker! Set out the dishes first – I'll have to see what can be done about the washing!'

The flurry of orders set Jean in action, and Elizabeth hurried across the yard, still dark and cold. As she whirled through the wash-house door she realised with surprise that the place was warm. Someone had stoked up the fire beneath the boiler during the night.

She lifted the top of the boiler and found that it had been refilled, and the water was steaming gently, ready for the morning's wash.

When Adam joined the family for breakfast he had changed into dark trousers, strapped beneath the foot, and a clean white shirt under a red patterned satin waistcoat. He looked as though he had enjoyed a good night's sleep.

Rab was distant towards him at first, obviously still angry at being forced to return home alone to face his guests. If he had hoped to shame his son into an apology he didn't succeed. Adam greeted them all cheerfully, and launched into answers to his brothers' clamoured questions without giving his father a second look.

Elizabeth, apparently busy about her work, listened avidly. Adam had been a naval surgeon for the past six or seven years, and the stories he had to tell filled her with astonishment. She was vaguely aware that there was a world outside Paisley, but never before had she heard a first-hand account of beaches of white sand, dark-skinned peoples, continuously blue skies, tremendous heat, or the sight of the sea stretching to every horizon. She could visualise each picture as he described it.

'And where did you get to last night?' Rab finally asked.

'The coach knocked a man over in the dark. I saw to it that he got home, and dressed his injured leg.'

'A drunken fool, I've no doubt.'

'Aye, he was drunk. But a man in drink can bleed and suffer as much as an abstainer once he's been hurt.'

'And I was left to explain your absence to your friends!'

Adam raised those compelling dark blue eyes

from his plate. 'Your friends, father,' he corrected calmly. 'I'm sure you managed fine without me.'

'You're as ill-mannered as ever you were. Have you learned nothing in those seven years?' Rab barked at him.

'I learned that no man's my inferior or my superior unless he can prove it to my satisfaction.'

There was a brief silence as he and his father eyed one another, Adam serenely, Rab cautiously. Then the older man said, 'You've picked up a fancy English way of speaking, I hear. Too proud to use your good Scots tongue?'

Adam shrugged. 'We've to learn to speak the way they do, else they'd never understand what they're being told. And a surgeon has to be understood.'

'I can follow the English tongue well enough,' Rab said shortly. As a shawl manufacturer he visited London markets now and then. His eldest son darted a glance at him from beneath thick black brows as he concentrated again on the food before him.

'Aye – but that's because we've got a sharper ear for a turn of the tongue than the English.'

'What was life like on board ship?' James butted in, unable to keep silent any longer.

'It wasnae pleasure trips I was on. I saw little of

what went on above decks. As for between them –
I saw sights I'd as soon no' have had to face.'

'What about India—' James urged, then
coloured as Matt dug him in the ribs. Adam's
face, Elizabeth noticed, tightened slightly, though
his voice was still calm. She had heard that the
girl he was to marry, the daughter of an Army
officer, had died in India before the wedding
could take place.

'Hot and barren, what I saw of it. And folk are
folk wherever you are, even if they do speak differently.'

Rab pushed his chair back and got up, moving
awkwardly to get past the table. A big-boned man,
he had put on weight in middle age. His bad leg,
the souvenir of his hot-headed younger days,
when he was quick to support political activities,
made him awkward in confined spaces.

'You'll be coming to the warehouse, Adam.'

'I've things to see to first, but I'll be down when
I can.'

Rab's ruddy face took on a deeper hue at the
casual words, and he turned on the other two.

'I'd appreciate it if you'd break your fast as soon
as you can. There's plenty of work waiting for you.
A shipment of silk yarn's coming in, and the
weavers are waiting for it!'

'Father—' Matthew half rose. 'Will you see John Gibson today?'

'How often do I have to tell you I've no time to listen to Gibson's fancy plans?'

Matthew reddened. 'But I've seen the new yarn. It's good. All he needs is a manufacturer who's willing to commission enough for one shawl!'

'Aye – a fool that'll throw his money away on a daft ploy, when there's trouble enough making ends meet. And we know good and well why you're favouring the likes of John Gibson,' his father sneered. 'I'll be no party to it – and let that be an end to your arguing. I dinnae pay you to encourage the likes of John Gibson!'

Elizabeth winced as she went ahead of Rab to the hall, where she waited with his coat, his tall hat, and his silver-knobbed stick. This time, she hoped, Matt would realise that there was no sense in calling his father's anger down on his head by persisting. John, Isobel's brother, was partner in a small thread and silk factory, and Matthew wanted his father to commission work using a new thread that John had spun.

Rab's mouth was still tight with anger as he came into the hall, checked that his spectacles were safely in his pocket, took his coat, hat and stick from her, and went off with a brief nod.

'And James has drawn a fine design – we could manufacture a shawl that would be the envy of the town,' Matt was telling Adam when she went back to the warm kitchen. 'But he'll try nothing new. The order books are busy, and that's all he cares about. Now John'll have to find another manufacturer and we'll lose the chance of getting that new yarn.'

'And the chance of pleasing Isobel and her father,' James put in slyly and Matt's fair skin, a torment to him, flushed rosily.

'James, it's time we were off. There's more work waiting than I can manage as it is, and the London shipment due in—'

Adam tipped his chair back, thumbs hooked into his waistcoat. 'You sound like father. Have you turned into a money-minded creature as well?'

The flush deepened. 'I have not! Damn it, I'm a silk weaver, and no notion to be anything else. But thanks to you and your physicking I'm the one that's going to have to take over the business one of these days. I'm the one who's had to give up his trade and spend his time sitting in a draughty office working with numbers!'

'James has to work there too,' Elizabeth pointed ut and Matt gave his younger brother a withering

35

glance. 'Ach, he's happy enough designing his patterns and scribbling poetry when he thinks nobody notices. It's me that was born to work with my hands, no' my head!'

Adam, unruffled by the outburst, unfolded his long body from the chair and followed the other three into the hall. 'Then it's time you told father that you want to get back to your trade, surely?'

'Man, the hot sun and all that salt water to look at must have addled your brain,' Matthew said flatly. 'When did you ever know my father listen to reason? And he's got worse in the past twelve-month. James, will you put your hat on and come with me?'

James stopped at the open door, his eyes fixed hopefully on his half-brother. 'Did you read those poems I sent you?'

'I did, but I could make nothing of them,' Adam said bluntly, and the younger man's face fell. 'James, we all see things differently. For Matt here, beauty's in his Isobel's smile—' Matt's face, now bobbing outside the door in the lightening September morning, flamed again. '—for Elizabeth it might lie in a copper of hot water, ready for the washing—' Adam's eyes glinted blue fire at Elizabeth. '—for you it's words, for me it's the sight of a clean, healthy stump I've operated on.

But I left the poems in London with a man I know. He's sending them to a publisher of his acquaintance,' he finished, and the disappointment in James's dark eyes flowered into delight.

'Come on, James!' Matt crowed impatiently, reappearing behind his brother.

'Come with me to the theatre tonight, Adam—' James asked.

'I will, if I havenae caught my death from standing at this open door.' Adam slammed it shut in his brother's face. 'God's sakes, Matt's going to be as dour and difficult as my father in another ten years' time if this Isobel of his doesnae save him.'

Elizabeth couldn't stand by and let Matt be criticised without taking his part. 'Someone's got to run the warehouse – mebbe he's dour because he's no' happy!'

Adam looked fully at her for the first time in an hour. 'You sound more like a sister than a servant lassie.'

Colour rushed to her face and she scurried to the kitchen, teeth sinking deep into her lower lip. She had defended Matt against his arrogant brother, but as he had just reminded her, they were in his father's house, and she could not defend herself.

If he knew that he had hurt her he gave no indication of it, following her into the kitchen instead of going to the parlour, or his own room.

'How did you come to work here?'

Busying herself as a pointed reminder that she had better things to do than talk – and also taking the opportunity to keep her face hidden from his gaze – she explained briefly that Rachel Montgomery had found her in the Town's Hospital, had seen to it that she was educated at Hutcheson's Charity School, and had brought her to High Street to become her companion.

'It can't have been long ago. And instead of being a lady's companion you found yourself acting as nurse in her last months.' She could feel his eyes on her, but refused to meet them. 'I mind now that she mentioned you in her letters. What are you doing working in the kitchen when you were meant to sit in the parlour and talk about ribbons and scandal?'

The man was a fool! Without realising what she was doing she looked up, straight into those pene-trating blue eyes.

'Your father didnae have much need of a lady's companion,' she said tartly, 'but he did require someone to see to the running of the house.'

He laughed, but persisted, 'Are you content with – this?' One hand indicated the range, the sink, the dishes she was taking from the table.

'Content enough.' It was all right for the likes of him, she thought resentfully as she swept crumbs from the board. It would never enter his head that if his father had put her out of the house after his wife's death she would have had nowhere to go, nobody to turn to. She was grateful for the rough kindness that had allowed her, young as she was, to take over the running of the big house. Nobody knew how often she longed for Mistress Montgomery, with her humour and her wisdom and her ability to soften her husband's hard ways.

'I'd have thought—' He stopped, then went on briskly, 'Is there plenty food in the house?'

'A lot left over from last night.'

'Put some into a basket – a big basket – and put your bonnet on. I've work for you elsewhere.'

'But my work's here!'

'The lassie can see to that, can't she?' he asked impatiently, on his way out of the room.

'Jean? She cannae lift a hand without me telling her how to go about it. There's the washing and the rooms to be seen to, and the parlour fire to be set in case you want to sit in the room—'

'I've more to do with my day than sit in a parlour, woman! It's time the girl learned how to manage. Where is she?'

'In the wash-house. But I cannae—'

He caught her hand, dragged her, protesting, behind him as he strode out of the back door and into the wash-house. Jean, wreathed in steam from the hot water, blinked uncertainly as the two of them burst into the small room, and the clothes she had been sorting fell from her fingers.

'Jean, you're to listen well to what you're told, for you're to see to things on your own this morning,' Adam said firmly. 'Elizabeth, it'll take no more than half an hour to instruct her and get yourself ready.' He consulted the watch on its chain across his flat stomach. 'I'll expect to see you in the hall in thirty minutes' time. And make sure there's nothing but good nourishing food in that basket.'

Jean squawked as the door closed behind him. Elizabeth began to marshal her thoughts and decide what Jean must manage on her own and what could be left until later. She had no liking for Adam Montgomery's ways. They might be all very well on board a ship, but they were not going to do in Paisley.

There was something about him, though, that made it impossible for her to defy him. Exactly thirty minutes after he had left her in the wash-house she was in the hall, wearing her cloak and bonnet and carrying a basket filled with Rab

Montgomery's food. Adam, dressed for the street and carrying a shabby leather bag, came downstairs as she arrived, and cast a critical eye over the basket's contents before nodding.

'It'll do. Come on.'

He forged a way ahead on the busy footpath, putting a hand beneath her elbow now and then when the crowd was thick. The previous night's rain had stopped but the weather was still unseasonable, with the sky heavy and the air damp.

As they hurried west towards the fringe of the town the crowds thinned and the going was easier. Down Maxwellton Street Adam strode, Elizabeth hurrying after him, the basket bumping against her hip. They were going to Maxwellton village, she realised. It consisted of a huddle of weavers' houses, formerly built for men employed by manufacturer Humphrey Fulton. Until fairly recently the hamlet had been separated from Paisley by grassy land, but now the two were linked and Maxwellton was being drawn into the town's claws. Many of the inhabitants of the cottages now worked at the thread manufactory built at nearby Ferguslie by the Coats family.

Moisture dripped from a row of low thatched cottages and the aroma of wet, rotting straw tickled Elizabeth's nose. She divided her attention between Adam's broad back and the narrow path she walked on. A step too close to the houses meant drips landing on her from the thatch; a step too far away from the walls risked the greasy puddles edging the road.

When Adam stopped and thumped at the door of one of the houses she almost bumped into him. The door opened a crack and he swept it wide with one hand, taking off his hat with the other, not so much from good manners as from a need to bend his head as he went into the house. Elizabeth, clutching her basket and quite bewildered, bobbed in after him.

The smell of rotting straw was in the cottage, mingled with the stink of people living in close, insanitary conditions. She recognised it from her dimly remembered babyhood and tried not to wrinkle her nose against it. Not that it mattered if she grimaced. There was little light allowed into the room through the dirty, patched little window, and the people already in the house were watching Adam, not her.

'Have you no candle?' he wanted to know, taking his coat off and tossing it over a rickety chair. There was a scuffling in the shadows then a small wavering flame helped to brighten the place as the stump of a candle was set on the table.

'Right, man, let's see how the leg is—' Adam seated himself on the edge of a wall-bed and Elizabeth saw that there was a man lying there, propped against a sagging, split pillow. His face was grey, his eyes suspicious as he watched the visitor. Adam pulled the blanket aside, unwrapped the man's leg, and moved his fingers over it gently. The sick man flinched.

'As I said last night, you're fortunate the bone wasnae broken.'

'Aye, but look at the size and colour of it.' The man's voice was a thin whine. 'And me no' able to put a foot on the floor.'

'You're able enough,' Adam said dryly. 'It's whether you're willing enough that matters. It'll take a while to mend properly, but you'll no' be crippled, be grateful for that.'

The only furnishing in the room was a table, two chairs, and a truckle bed. The fire was unlit and the earthen floor thinly scattered with straw. A woman near the bed watched patient and physician anxiously. Her clothes were patched and her apron, the good housewife's emblem, was dirty and torn. There was a baby in her arms and two small children held tightly to her skirt.

'What about my loom?' the weaver was asking.

'You'll no' get back to it for a day or two. The

next time you take a fondness for ale you'll mebbe watch what you're about on your way home. Though I'm thinking the silver would be better spent on caring for those bairns of yours,' Adam told him. His accent, Elizabeth noticed, had lost its slight English flavour. He spoke to the weaver in the broad Paisley tongue.

'A day or two? How are my family to live in the meantime?'

There was faint disgust in Adam's voice now. 'You're a wee bit late in thinking about their comfort, are you no'?'

He got to his feet and reached for his coat, while the sick man raised himself on one elbow.

'D'ye expect them to live on air while I'm away from my loom? Or on the charity of neighbours? We're none of us rich folk in Maxwellton, mister. Nobody's got food to spare for another man's weans. Would you stand by and watch—'

'Elizabeth—' Adam cut across the lament, his voice like the crack of a whip. She had moved obediently forward before she could stop herself. 'The lassie here's brought some food to help you out, and there could be more if you do as I tell you instead of lying there pitying yourself.'

He swung the basket to the table for her then turned away and left her to unpack it. The woman, her fear forgotten in wonder, edged forward, eyes gleaming in the candle's light. They widened as she looked at the bread and meat and cheese being lifted from the basket. A long-nailed dirty hand reached out to touch a quartern loaf.

'Oh – God bless you, mistress!' she whispered, and to Elizabeth's embarrassment her hand was caught and carried to the woman's lips.

'Stop havering!' Adam barked. 'See to your bairns and make sure your man gets onto his feet before that leg goes stiff.'

The door opened, bringing a welcome waft of cold damp air and a glimpse of daylight to the stuffy room. A child backed in, dragging a bundle with it. It turned out to be a girl, in clothes that had obviously once belonged to an adult. They bunched around her, trailing on the ground. Her wrists and ankles poked out like dry sticks and her head was a tangled mess of hair, probably alive with vermin. She let the bundle go and turned, blinking in the light, seeing but not understanding the food on the table. Her face was gaunt but her eyes were enormous, reflecting and throwing back the light, as brilliant as diamonds.

Adam, putting on his jacket, stopped.

'What's amiss with this wee one?'

'Nothing,' the weaver's wife said swiftly, too swiftly. 'She's fine!'

Adam lifted the candle and moved round the table to the child, holding the light so that it illuminated her. When his fingers touched her shoulder she jumped, seeming to waken from a trance, and cowered away, one arm thrown over her face.

'I'm not going to harm you, lassie.' It was a voice Elizabeth had not heard from him before, gentle and reassuring. 'See, come over here for a minute and let me look at you.'

Reluctantly, eyeing her mother's expressionless face, the child allowed him to lead her to where light filtered through the window. He pulled a chair towards himself and sat down, drawing the girl forward to stand between his knees, talking gently to her all the time. Suddenly the flint and iron were gone, and Elizabeth watched, astonished, as the child began to relax under that voice, and his touch. Even the blue gaze, so penetrating, so quick to sharpen in anger or exasperation, bathed the dirty little girl in its warmth.

Elizabeth had never known anyone as different as Adam Montgomery. His step-mother and her sons had spoken highly of him, and she knew a little from them, but nothing that had led her to expect this strange, outlandish man. Adam, born to Rab's first wife, had been apprenticed to a Paisley apothecary, had then studied at a Glasgow medical school, and had opted to finish his medical training in the best way, as a surgeon with the navy.

He had recently left the service, and his visit to Paisley had originally been planned to introduce his new wife, the girl who had died in India.

'There's nothing wrong with her!' The weaver's shrill voice broke into Elizabeth's thoughts as she watched Adam. 'Look at the lassie – she's got better colour than the rest of us!'

'She has that,' Adam agreed under his breath, smiling at the nervous child as his eyes noted the red patches high on her cheeks. 'D'ye keep well enough, lassie?'

'Whiles she has a cough – but nothing to fret over,' the mother said anxiously. It was clear to Elizabeth that the man and his wife wanted Adam out of the place.

'And how old are you, my wee bird?'

The child whimpered deep in her throat and it was left to her mother to supply the information that she was seven years old.

'What sort of work does she do?' Adam persisted. His voice was still soft, but now Elizabeth recognised steel beneath the velvet tones.

'She helps to pay her way. That's only right, is it no'?' The weaver was getting angry, twisting round in the bed to glare at this interfering stranger. 'The lassie runs errands and helps with the cleaning in some of the big houses. And she helps her mother with washing for the big houses too. And some mending.' He nodded to the bundle she had dragged in. 'If we sent her to work in one of the manufactories the way some do, she'd work harder than that – and have the walk there and back too.'

'What food does she get? And what caused these?' Adam turned the child round to face her parents, holding the candle so that it lit her. Elizabeth could make out dark stains beneath the general dirt on her face and neck.

'You've done what you came here to do, mister – now get back to your fine friends and leave us be!' the child's father flared, his voice cracking in its pathetic attempt to bluster and bully. The child shivered violently and would have run to hide in her mother's skirts like the others if Adam hadn't kept a restraining hand on her shoulder. He got to his feet, his head almost brushing the smoky ceiling.

'The bairn's overworked, and it's my suspicion that she's had some ill-treatment as well. No doubt

I could find bruising on the others if I looked for it.'

The woman shrank back, her grip on the baby tightening, her free hand pressing the other two children against her legs. Her husband raised himself up in the bed. 'It's no concern of yours!'

Instinctively Elizabeth moved to stand by Adam, putting a hand on the little girl's arm. She could feel a frantic pulse banging beneath the hot dry skin. And she could sense the effort that the man beside her was making to guard his tongue. The weaver was right; there was little Adam could do, and the man's anger would probably be taken out on the children later.

When Adam spoke again, it was in a level, reasonable voice. 'Listen to me. Your daughter's sick and she has to rest for a while. She needs good food to build up her strength.'

The weaver sneered at him openly. 'And where do the likes of us get good food from? How can we live at all while I'm unfit to work and she does nothing to earn her keep?'

'I told you I'd see to it that your bairns would have food till you were back at your loom—'

'If there's any work to be had,' the man interrupted sullenly. 'There's plenty waiting to be taken on in my place.'

A muscle jumped in Adam's jaw. 'Then you'll

49

need to make sure that you're back at work as soon as you can instead of lying here making yourself out to be an invalid. You can begin by getting out of that bed and putting the lassie into it. And she's to stay there until I tell her to get up, d'you understand me?'

He slipped a hand in his pocket, leaned forward, and flipped a coin onto the table. The dull ring of it on the scored wood brought an immediate change in the weaver's attitude. He scrambled from the bed, dragging his bandaged leg behind him, and the bewildered child found herself taking his place. She lay with eyes wide and body rigid with fear, obeying her elders without understanding what was happening.

'I'll be back often to see her,' Adam warned as he and Elizabeth left. The woman hurried out of the cottage after them and clutched at his sleeve.

'We've no money to pay for a physician,' she said anxiously.

'For God's sake, woman, d'you think we all worship silver—?' He stopped as she flinched under the barrage of angry words, then went on gently, putting a hand over the fingers on his arm, 'There'll be no payment needed, however many times I visit the bairn. If there's an account, she's already paid it in full herself. Now – go back inside and see to her.'

'I've no doubt the lassie'll be dragged from her bed in the morning and put to work,' he added bitterly as he and Elizabeth walked towards Broomlands Street. 'I'd have dearly liked to lift her and carry her away from that place to where she could be looked after.'

'What's wrong with her?' This time Elizabeth didn't have to run to keep up with him. He walked slowly, eyes on the muddy ground.

'Consumption. A destruction of the lungs. I thought it would do you no harm,' he added with a return to his former arrogance, 'to see for yourself how these folk have to live. A far cry from my father's fine house in the High Street, is it no'?'

Anger sharpened her voice as she retorted 'You've no need to complete my education – I was born in a cottage like that, and raised in the Town Hospital as a pauper.'

He spun round, dark eyebrows climbing. She had never noticed people's eyebrows before but Adam's were thick, well-shaped, and strangely attractive. 'You?'

He waited for more information, and she regretted having spoken. But it was too late.

'We moved to the hospital when I was small,

51

after my father lost his work as a farmhand and we had to leave the cottage.'

'Where do your family stay now?' They had reached Broomlands Street.

'I'm the only one left. There was smallpox in the hospital one year and they – they—' It was still difficult to talk about it.

'They died of it,' Adam said crisply. 'And you lived – although it left its mark on you.' His fingers, surprisingly warm against her cold face, lifted her chin. His eyes studied the scar from her mouth to her jawline and she felt herself redden under that gaze.

'How old are you, lassie?'

'Seventeen.' She tried to pull away but those firm fingers forced her to stay where she was, face raised to his.

His brows tucked together thoughtfully. 'You've nothing to be ashamed of in a wee scar like that. You're bonny enough with that pretty brown hair and those wide brown eyes of yours.' A faintly teasing note crept into his voice as she closed her eyes against his look. 'Long dark lashes, too. Many a lovely lady would like to steal those lashes from you. And many a young gentleman would try to steal a kiss if you fluttered your lashes at him like that.'

She opened her eyes at once, started to indignantly deny any such ploy, and was unable to speak because he refused to release her chin. He grinned at her embarrassment.

'There's gold flecks to those eyes—'

She tore herself free with undignified haste and turned to hurry on, the basket bumping against her hip.

'We all carry scars,' Adam caught up with her. 'Whether they're on the skin or below it, they're there. Paisley's scar is that family we've just left and others like them. D'you know what I mean?'

When she shook her head he sighed and walked on, lengthening his strides so that she was forced to run to keep up. She was shocked to hear that he was misquoting the Bible when she reached his side. Furtively she looked around, worried in case he was overheard.

'Lord, forgive them,' Adam was declaiming as he passed through the crowd as though it was made of mist. 'For they know fine what they're about.'

III

A carriage passed, throwing muddy water from its wheels. A voice screeched from within and the coachman drew the horses to a standstill. A bonneted head emerged from the small window and the screech was heard again.

'Adam! Adam Montgomery! And Elizabeth,' Christian Selbie added with some surprise. 'I've just been to the house to look for you, Adam.'

He kissed the gloved hand she held out to him. 'Well, cousin, I'd have known that voice if I'd heard it in an Indian bazaar,' he drawled.

'So you found your way home after all. Not that I ever doubted you would.' The door swung open. 'Come and take tea with me – both of you.'

Elizabeth began to shake her head, thinking of the housework and Jean's lack of efficiency. Without looking at her Adam said, 'We'd be pleased to—' and bundled her into the carriage, while Christian moved along the well-padded seat to make room.

Adam, opposite them, had to take his tall hat off in the confined space and rest it on his knee. Christian immediately demanded to know what had happened on the previous night, and Elizabeth left it to Adam to talk to his cousin while she herself gave her attention to the window. She had not been whirled through the town in a carriage since Rachel Montgomery's illness had confined her to the house, and this short journey was something to enjoy and treasure. The horses turned to take the steep climb up Hut Brae to Oakshawhill and she clutched nervously at the strap, certain that the harness would break, catapulting the carriage backwards down the narrow hill.

But the leather held, the horses managed the climb without difficulty, and they disembarked before the large, square house where Christian Selbie lived.

Adam eyed the building fondly. 'You're still rattling round in a house that's far too big for your needs, I see.'

'Only because I'm too busy to find somewhere more suitable – and I'm no' one to rattle, I'll have you know,' she told him severely. 'Though the window tax alone fair destroys me. The Council seems to think I've nothing to do but pour good silver into their purses.'

'It must be a sorry plight, having so much wealth to fret over,' her kinsman agreed solemnly, eyes twinkling. It was already clear to Elizabeth, following Christian into the entrance hall, that Adam and his cousin shared a deep affection, well smothered in sarcasm.

In the handsome drawing-room Adam declined tea from the fine silver tea-service, and chose to pour himself a generous helping of brandy from a crystal decanter.

'At this time of day?' Christian clucked. He took his place before the fire, glass in hand.

'And why not?'

'You've learned some strange habits abroad. But all the same—' her faded blue eyes travelled over him with open approval '—you've grown into a fine figure of a man.'

He returned the scrutiny. 'And you're as you've always been – a fine figure of a woman.'

She smoothed her skirt, tidied a strand of hair back beneath her lace cap. 'I've worn well,' she agreed smugly. 'Go on with your story about the man that was hurt by the coach – but keep the nasty bits out of it, for I cannae be doing with talk of blood when I'm at my tea.'

Adam gave her a graphic description of the cottage, the poverty, the sick child, turning to Elizabeth now and then for confirmation.

'It seems to me, cousin,' he finished, 'that you could take on the task of helping the family, for Elizabeth here's doubtless got enough to do looking after my father's house and trying to get some work out of that lassie in the kitchen.'

'So you think time hangs heavy on my own hands, do you?' Christian snorted. 'You've been away too long, my lad. I could show you a dozen families living in the same misery, not a stone's throw from here. We cannae molly-coddle each and every one of them. Have some sense!'

His hand tightened on the glass he held and his brows knotted together. 'You could do more for them – you and my father and all the other well-to-do folk in this town.'

'We're no' exactly unaware of the need for improvements,' Christian told him stiffly. 'But it's the way of the world, Adam. There's aye been folk that find it harder to make their way through life than others. Mebbe some of the fault's their own. Mebbe they just don't strive in the way our family did.'

'Don't try to confuse me with words,' he told her bluntly. 'I'm talking about the one lassie. Seven years in this world, just – that's twenty-three years less than me, and she's dying of old age. She's been starved and beaten and worked till the heart's gone out of her. She'll no' live to see eighteen thirty-two – though some might say that that's no loss to her. All I'm asking you to do is to see that the last few weeks of her life are made a bit easier than the first seven years!'

Christian looked thoughtfully at him. 'I could see about getting her into the House of Recovery.'

His laugh was harsh. 'And have her die of fear and loneliness within two days? Mebbe her family's no' much, but it's all she's had. Poor wee soul, she should at least end her days with those she knows.'

Elizabeth's cup rattled slightly as she set it in its saucer. 'Adam, I'll keep an eye on the bairn for you—' she began, but Christian interrupted her.

'Tuts, lassie – you've enough to do. I'll see to the child and her family. And that's the thing decided. And you needae smirk like that, Adam, I'm no' saying you've won, I'd have done it anyway.'

The smile on his handsome face widened. 'I know that. I was counting on it.'

'In return I'll expect you to attend a wee gathering I'm planning.'

He paused in the act of putting his empty glass on the table. 'Ach, I was never good at those social fripperies, Christian.'

'James and Matthew and Elizabeth'll be there,' she went on, ignoring him. 'And Isobel, of course. And Helen – you have mind of Helen, surely? Rab never forgave you for going off to sea instead of marrying her.'

Exasperation clouded his eyes. 'We were never more than friends, me and Helen, and my father knew it.'

Christian shook a forefinger at him. 'I have a feeling Helen herself would have been willing to marry you at one time. But now she's Mistress Alec Grant and living in his parents' big house in Barrhead. As bright and bonny as ever, for all that she's got a wee girl of her own. You should meet Helen again, now that you've come back to Paisley.'

'I'm only here for a visit. For a few weeks, mebbe.'

Her brows rose. 'They must have paid you well in the Navy if you can afford to live like a gentleman of leisure for all that time. Surely you don't expect Rab to support you while you're here? He'll put his hand in his pocket for nobody.'

'I know that. I have the money I earned those

past years. There's little use for money on board one of His Majesty's ships, unless it's spent on gambling or drinking, and I never cared for either of them as a pastime. I can pay my way for a wee while, then I have it in mind to settle in England.'

'There's a good living to be made by a surgeon in Glasgow. My own father did well enough for himself in this district.' Christian looked complacently about the fine drawing-room. The house she lived in had once belonged to her parents, Margaret Montgomery and Gavin Knox.

'Your father pandered to the society folk. My work's with those who might have most need of me. I've no interest in money.'

Christian shrugged off the insult to her father. 'So Paisley's no' good enough for you?'

'I've no quarrel with it. I just don't care to live in the place. That's why I wouldnae take up the loom as a trade.'

She barked a laugh at him. 'Man, it was the loom that refused you, no' the other way round. Highlanders are all thumbs, and you inherited your hands from your Highland mother, God rest her soul.'

The smile caught again at his wide mouth as he held out his broad, capable hands. 'So I turned to surgery because I was too handless to be a weaver?'

'Weaving,' Christian told him crushingly, 'is an art, and don't you forget it, Adam Montgomery!'

The delicate clock on the mantelshelf tinkled out a peal of bells indicating the time, and Elizabeth jumped, her mind flying at once to the work that waited for her at the High Street house. Christian's sharp eyes caught the movement.

'But no doubt I'm keeping you both from your business,' she said, making it possible for Elizabeth to get to her feet.

They were at the front door when Christian put a hand on Adam's arm. 'Adam, I was right vexed to hear about your Caroline's death.'

His face stilled suddenly. 'My father and my brothers did me the service of not mentioning her,' he said flatly. 'I'd be obliged, cousin, if you'd do the same.'

'Men—' said Christian as the door opened to reveal the coachman waiting to take them back to the High Street, 'have never learned to handle bereavement.'

At dinner that evening Adam asked his father abruptly 'Do you know of a man named Patrick Hamilton?'

Elizabeth, who usually dined with the family,

felt her stomach constrict beneath the blue silk of her gown. Rab, supping his broth, shook his greying head.

'He knows of you, father.'

'There's no' many folk hereabouts havenae heard of me.' It was a simple statement, not a boast. Matthew scraped his bowl clean and pushed it away.

'I know the name. He's a weaver. He's worked for us.'

'I want you to offer him work again,' Adam said bluntly.

'So—' Rab surveyed his eldest son. 'You're giving orders to the warehouse, are you?'

'I'm asking you to give a man work. He has need of it.'

Rab laughed. 'Man, if we offered work to everyone in Paisley who needs it this day, we'd have more webs than we could sell.' He turned his attention to Matthew. 'What d'you know of him?'

Matthew looked embarrassed. 'He's a slow worker and we found him to be unreliable.'

'You see? There's plenty of good skilled men ready and grateful for work without entrusting it to the likes of that. I've neither the time nor the money to spend on a man who'll no' do his fair share. Find some other manufacturer to look after

'our lame dogs for you,' Rab told Adam, and went
back to his food with an air of dismissal.

Elizabeth saw Adam's jaw stiffen. 'Why should
go cap in hand to another manufacturer when my
own father's one of their number? Mebbe the
man's no' one of the best workers, but he's got a
amily to care for and a dying child that's been
orced to earn her own keep from the time she
could toddle.'

'Be damned to that, sir,' Rab's irritation was
growing rapidly. 'You seriously expect me to squander hard-earned money on a useless worker just to
please you?' One thick thumb stabbed at his own
chest. 'Look at me – I served my time at the looms
and so did my father before me. I'd be a weaver yet
f I hadnae been crippled while I was marching in
the name of better conditions for working men. I
could have given up then and let you and your
brothers live in poverty in some hovel—'

'I know well enough how hard you've worked!'
Adam interrupted. Everyone knew of the struggle
Rab had had to rebuild his life after his leg was
shattered. He had clawed his way into the manu-
facturing industry, and had finally raised enough
capital to start his own business.

'Then let Hamilton stand on his own feet and
support his own bairns, as I did!'

The soup bowls were empty. Elizabeth gathered them together and helped Jean to serve the meat course. Then she despatched the girl back to the kitchen and sat down again, nervously picking at the food before her. Rab had started on a well-worn lecture about independence and laziness. The words rolled about Elizabeth's down-bent head. It was foolish to challenge him when he was in a mood like this, but Adam had either forgotten that, or didn't care about tact.

'You're forgetting something,' he cut into his father's lecture at last. 'When your father and your grandfather were making a good living as weavers a man could hold his head high and shape his own life. But it's different now that the manufacturers have a grip of the weaver by the back of the neck. They're the ones that make the money now. How much can a weaver expect to earn today?'

Rab spluttered, and glared over cheeks bursting with blood when Matthew supplied the information.

'If he's in steady work he can make about six shillings a week. A year ago it might have been seven or eight shillings in the week.'

'You see, father? The weaver's dependent on the manufacturer to advance the cost of setting up his loom now. And he's got rent to pay, and the use of

64

the loom if it's in someone else's shop. Is the fine lady paying less for her shawls? Oh, no – it's just that the manufacturers – you and the others – are never out of pocket. It's always the weaver who has to take the loss and worry about how he's going to make ends meet until he gets his money from the manufacturer. And there's no assurance of that, either. There's lazy manufacturers, and there's truck trading—'

Rab's fist crashed onto the table and dishes clattered. A potato rolled from James's plate but nobody except Elizabeth noticed it.

'There is no truck trading done by my warehouse!' Rab said thickly, his eyes almost bursting from his head. 'And no son of mine is going to accuse me of it, by God, or I'll—'

'Nobody,' Adam told him coldly, 'said such a thing, and you know it. I just asked you to find it in your heart to give work to a poor man with sore need of it!'

'Now here's a bonny man for you!' Rab sneered, and Adam's lids drooped to half-cover eyes that had darkened with anger, Elizabeth noted. 'He thinks himself too grand for the likes of Paisley, and yet he's more than ready to make use of the folk that helped to give this town its proud name. The day I tell you how to do your bleeding and your cutting, mister, you can tell me who should bring their webs to my warehouse!'

His anger, almost out of control, was a frightening sight. Matthew started to speak, but Adam put a restraining hand on his brother's arm.

'Finish your food, Matt.' He had been holding his knife in a white-knuckled grip; he put the utensil down carefully beside his untouched plate and stood up.

'I have your answer, father, and it seems that the matter's closed. James – I'll meet you at the Saracen's Head later. Elizabeth—'

He nodded briefly in her direction and turned towards the door.

'Sit down, man, and finish your meal!' Rab barked, rising.

'I have no appetite for it. And I'm no company for the rest of you tonight,' said Adam, and walked out, straight-backed.

In the silence that followed Rab Montgomery reseated himself and glared belligerently round the table. Matthew's lips parted, and his father's hand immediately swept up to stop the words.

'There'll be no more talk at this table!' he said harshly, adding after a moment, 'It seems that travel's done little for your brother's manners!'

Elizabeth would have been happy to escape to

the kitchen as soon as the meal was over, but for some reason of his own Rab insisted that she should keep him company. James went off to meet Adam and go with him to the theatre, Matthew disappeared, no doubt on his way to Isobel's house. Elizabeth fetched her sewing and spent the next few hours working, while Rab stared morosely into the fire.

When his sons had returned home for the night, Rab signalled to Elizabeth to bring out the big family Bible, which was read every evening. Tonight he chose to read from Paul's epistle to the Colossians exhorting them to obey their parents in all matters. As Elizabeth listened to his deep, rich voice rolling the phrases around the room she thought, as she had thought before, that surely Paul himself must have lost some of the beauty of his own words, being unable to deliver them in Rab's good Scots tongue.

When the Bible was closed, Rab wished everyone goodnight, in the same doom-filled tones used during the reading and limped upstairs. Jean, who had started one of her interminable colds, sniffed her way to bed, and the three brothers, freed from their father's presence, noticeably relaxed.

'My God!' James threw himself into Rab's special armchair, eyes dancing. 'Did ye hear the way his voice rose over that passage about paying heed to parents?'

'And the way it dropped right down when he reached the bit about how fathers shouldnae provoke children?' Matthew grinned. Adam shrugged and poked at the coals in the grate, sending a final burst of flame leaping up the chimney.

'It was in my mind to quote the Good Book right back at him,' he said dryly. 'Thon bit about supporting the weak, and it being more blessed to give than to receive. But since I near brought him to apoplexy already today, I thought it better to hold my tongue. Matthew – surely you can find some way to give Hamilton work?'

'Nobody tells father what business the warehouse gives out. He knows each and every one of the folk we use, and nobody else has the power to give out work.'

'You could talk to him about it.'

Matthew flushed. 'Adam, it's no' that easy! I'm trying to find the right time as it is to tell him that I want to wed Isobel.'

'For any favour, man!' Adam exploded at his younger brother, 'Are you so afraid of the man that you cannae even choose your own wife? What's amiss with the lass? Her father's been a respected weaver all his adult life, and her own brother supplies silk for the Montgomery house, does he no'?'

James sighed with exaggerated impatience. 'You never learn, Adam. It's no' a question of man marrying woman with the Montgomerys now. Matt's going to take over the warehouse one day. He's expected to find a wife among his own sort. A warehouse marries another warehouse – a London agent's daughter would be even better.'

'You're no' serious!' Adam stood tall before the fireplace and Elizabeth, finishing off the hem she was stitching, realised how unlike his home-based brothers he was. Adam had gone out into the world and his values were completely different from theirs. He found it hard to understand how they could meekly accept their father's rules; unlike him, they were conditioned, and so was she, to a life that was now alien and out-dated in his eyes.

'I mind the days when my father was a weaver himself, like old Gibson. And he'd no' have allowed any man to consider him inferior,' he said.

'That was before the riots and before he lost his trade trying to get better conditions for his fellow-workers,' Matthew pointed out. 'It wasnae just his leg that mended wrong, it was his faith in folk. He's crippled inside as well as outside.'

'That sounds like some of James's romantic thinking,' Adam sneered at him, and Matt's round face flushed. To her surprise, Elizabeth found herself saying hotly, 'It's no' romantic nonsense! Unhappiness can twist folk up inside.'

She blushed as they all looked at her, James and Matthew with warmth, Adam with amusement.

'Elizabeth's right,' Matthew defended her. 'I know that if I lose Isobel it'll break something inside me. And as for you, Adam—'

Adam's face was suddenly expressionless, as though smoothed over by an invisible hand. 'I've no' forgotten the bitterness the old man must have felt,' he said swiftly, his voice harsh. 'But I see no reason why he should let it warp him for the rest of his life.'

'He's fair enough with the workers,' James spoke up in his father's defence. 'He doesnae try to break the table of wages like some. And he'd never go in for truck trading. There was one manufacturer in court for it no' that long ago. A man by the name of Dunn. He was charged with paying a weaver a shilling only, and the rest of the payment in potatoes. The case was found to be not proven.'

'Justice is the same as anything else,' Matthew added bluntly. 'You get it if you can afford to pay for it.'

Adam surveyed his brothers. 'And you accept that?'

'We cannae alter it.'

'You can have a damned good try,' Adam said forcefully.

'And have our legs broken and our hearts twisted?' Matthew asked in a rare burst of cynicism. He yawned, stretched. 'I'm away to my bed. It's too late to start trying to change the world.'

Elizabeth made sure that the doors were locked and the kitchen range banked so that it could be poked into life in the morning. When she went back to the parlour to rake out the fire and put a screen before it she found Adam there, frowning down into the embers. He blinked at her, then rose from his chair.

'Sleep well, Elizabeth.'

'Adam—' She stopped him as he was leaving the room, lamp in hand. 'Adam, what were those lassies you talked of last night – from Japan?' The name of the country, so pretty and so alien, had been echoing in her head all day.

He raised an eyebrow. 'The geishas?'

'That was it. What do they do?'

'I've only heard about them, for I've never had the fortune to visit their country. But it's said that

71

their work consists of singing and dancing and – pleasuring the menfolk.'

She was confused. 'With the singing and dancing, you mean?'

A slow smile curled his wide mouth at the sides. 'That – and all manner of other ways, I've heard.'

'Oh!' She felt her face burn.

'Mind you,' said Adam thoughtfully, 'I never did find out the truth of it for myself – I'm vexed to say.'

As he went into the hall, she caught the faint sound of a chuckle.

It was left to Christian Selbie to find employment for the weaver with the sick child. She called in one afternoon to report to Adam and Elizabeth on her visits to the Maxwellton cottage. She settled in the parlour like an exotic bird, in her beribboned bonnet, bright blue gown, and colourful Paisley shoulder shawl with its deep borders of blues, scarlets, and greens.

'As far as I can tell the man's attending to his work well enough. That poor stick of a wife he's got fairly glows with pleasure about it.'

'What about the bairn?' Adam was drinking tea today, but Elizabeth was sure that it was in order not to hurt her feelings rather than an honest interest in the beverage.

Christian put her bonneted head thoughtfully to one side, emphasising the similarity to a bird. 'She's been in bed each time I've called,' she admitted, 'but since there's aye a right scuffling about the door when they see me coming it's my belief that she's up and working most of the time, and they push her into that bed as I step through the door. Her mother tries to do the right thing by the bairns, but she's just no' what I'd call a good manager.'

'I suppose we're doing all we can,' Adam said absently, frowning at a bunch of flowers on the wallpaper behind his kinswoman's head.

'Well, I'm certainly doing all I can,' she told him. 'And I'm expecting you to keep to your side of the bargain. Next Friday evening at my house – and you can escort Elizabeth there, just to make sure you don't forget!'

When the appointed evening arrived, though, Elizabeth went to Oakshawhill with James. Adam had gone off in the morning to visit friends in Renfrew, promising faithfully to be back in time.

'Aye – well, he'd better arrive soon, or he'd better stay in Renfrew out of my reach,' Christian said when Elizabeth reported his absence. 'There'll be trouble for Master Adam if he thinks he's going to stay away from my gathering! Come in, come in,

73

the pair of you, and don't look so guilty, Elizabeth. You're no' responsible for the big useless lump of a man.'

Without doubt the most beautiful woman in Christian's parlour that evening was Helen Grant, Elizabeth decided with admiration rather than envy. Helen alone had dared to spurn the pastel shades that were in vogue and had dressed in a deep red gown cut in the latest fashion, with off-the-shoulder puffed sleeves and a daringly low neckline. The dress emphasised her full bosom and tiny waist. Her large brown eyes sparkled and rich auburn hair blazed round her lovely face. She looked far too young to be the mother of a toddler.

Elizabeth knew that she looked well enough in her home-made pink muslin gown, with her brown hair pinned up and allowed to curl at each side of her face. Her figure was pleasing, she assured herself in a hasty glimpse into the mirror while going through the hall to collect something from the kitchen. Her small breasts, not nearly as fine as Helen's, rose with becoming modesty from the square neck of the gown and her flushed cheeks gave her added beauty. But – her hand went up to the scar on her face, then was pulled down out of sight as her sharp eyes registered the rough red skin and broken nails – she could never match Helen for looks or for charm.

Alec Grant complemented his wife perfectly. Since their marriage he had left the army to work on his father's estates, and had put on weight. His handsome face had rounded and taken on a rosy tinge that spoke of fondness for the bottle rather than fresh air. Some said that he was too fond of the gaming tables, and evenings spent with his cronies, but there was no doubt, seeing them together, that he and Helen were deeply in love with each other. Alec wore a silk jacket of the same shade as his wife's dress, with a yellow waistcoat and white cravat and trousers.

As the evening wore on Elizabeth saw her hostess glance now and then at the clock, her brows tucked together disapprovingly. There was still no sign of Adam.

She was in the kitchen, refilling the punch jug, when knuckles beat at the front door.

'I'll see to it,' she said hurriedly, and the maid settled back in her seat with a sigh of relief.

Elizabeth put the heavy jug down carefully on a small table and, candle in hand, opened the door.

'It's yourself, Elizabeth.' He stepped inside, closed the door quietly, and put a delaying hand on her arm as she was about to lead him to the drawing-room.

'Is there a crowd in there?'

'Aye – and all waiting for you. Your cousin's getting more long-faced by the minute. You promised, Adam!'

He screwed up his nose. 'I know I did, but – ach, I was never one for reunions. All those folk peering at me and asking questions and treating me as though I was in a side-show.'

'They mean it kindly.'

He began to take off his coat. 'It's their very kindness that sticks in my throat.' As he turned to slip the coat off a draught from the sleeve blew out the candle, leaving them in darkness. The coat dropped to the floor with a rustle, and Adam cursed.

'I'm feared to move in case I knock over one of those daft ornaments Christian sets such store by! Elizabeth—'

'Here—' She captured his flailing hand in hers. Her eyes were becoming used to the dark quickly, and she had located the thin line of light beneath the drawing-room door. '—Just come with me, I know where to go.'

Their fingers entwined, then his tightened and drew her back towards him.

'Ach, I'm in two minds about this. It's all a palaver! Could we no' skip out quiet-like, you and me, Elizabeth—' His free hand found her shoulder, drew her closer, a fellow conspirator. She could feel his breath warm on her cheek, feel herself being drawn into the spell of the words murmured into her hair. 'We'll go off back to the High Street and sit by the kitchen fire, and I'll tell you about India, and the sun, and the strange animals, and the fine clothes—'

It sounded so tempting. She had to bite back words of swift acceptance and make herself say sternly 'We'll do nothing of the sort, for your cousin's waiting for you to attend her party!'

'Women were always nags!' he grumbled, then tried wheedling again, 'I thought you were different, Elizabeth.' His lips were brushing her ear now, setting up shivers throughout her body. She felt the breath flutter in her throat like a trapped butterfly, and knew, as his fingers tightened on her shoulder, that he knew very well what was happening to her. 'Lass – come away with me—'

The drawing-room door was thrown wide and Elizabeth swung away from him, suddenly aware that in the light from the door they might be mistaken for an embracing couple. She had forgotten in her confusion that anyone coming from a lighted room would be unable to see the hall clearly. Beside her, Adam swore softly beneath his breath.

A slender, graceful figure hesitated in the lit doorway and one slim arm reached back for a lamp on a nearby table.

'Is that you, Elizabeth?' a clear voice asked, half nervous, half amused. There was a note or two of soft musical laughter. 'Elizabeth! Don't fright me like this!'

Elizabeth's lips parted immediately to call out but her voice was silenced by the tremor that ran through Adam's body, down his arm to the fingers that clasped hers. His grip tightened sharply then loosened, fell away. She heard him catch his breath, sensed the lift of his head towards the doorway, the way his eyes widened.

The woman silhouetted against the light raised the lamp she held so that its glow travelled from her slim waist to her breasts, her white throat and shoulders, and at last to her face, eyes wide, lips parted, skin like the sheen of a flawless pearl. It was Helen Grant.

'Elizabeth?' she said again, and moved a tentative step or two into the darkened hall. Now the lamp she carried dazzled her own eyes, and if Adam hadn't gone forward swiftly, freed from his trance, and caught her arm, she would have blundered into a small carved chair.

'Be careful—' he said, as though her safety was

the most important thing in the world. The lamp illuminated his face and Helen's mouth curved into a sudden delighted smile.

'Adam? Is it really you, after all this time? Oh – welcome home!' With the unselfconscious grace of an old friend she caught his shoulder, raised herself on tiptoe, and kissed him. 'D'you not know me?' she added with that musical laughter bubbling again in her voice.

'Helen?'

'Of course it's Helen – and not nearly as changed as you are. You're so handsome, and so tall – come and meet everyone!'

Laughing, talking, asking questions and too excited to notice that he was too busy looking at her to answer, she linked her arm through his and pulled him into the room, leaving Elizabeth to follow, alone and forgotten.

Adam's reluctance to become part of the gathering melted away. Helen demanded to hear about his life as a naval surgeon and her word was his command. His unexpectedly poetic tongue brought the heat and dust of India and the roar and crash of a sea-storm into the Scottish drawing-room and captivated his listeners. Only Elizabeth was apart from the crowd, only she was too pre-occupied with her own thoughts to pay much attention to what he was saying. Nobody, including Adam, noticed her silence.

'Now you're going to stay with us, in Paisley?' Helen asked. He let his eyes linger on her face for a few seconds.

'I've no plans at the moment.'

'Have you had experience of this cholera?' Alec wanted to know. Adam nodded.

'I've seen it.'

'Is it as bad as they say?'

Adam's dark blue eyes were fathomless. 'From what I hear you'll have the chance to find out for yourselves.'

Helen shivered and reached for Alec's hand. 'It's no subject for a time like this,' she said firmly. 'Anyway – the cholera'll never get as far as Paisley.'

Looking at her, Elizabeth almost believed what she said. It was impossible to think that anything as terrible as a cholera epidemic could touch the world Helen Grant lived in.

'I hope you're right,' was all Adam said.

Even his sharp-eyed cousin seemed to be unaware of the sudden passion he felt for Alec Grant's wife. To Elizabeth, who had been with him when he first saw Helen, it was obvious, as though a finely-spun rope of pure gold stretched between

Adam and Helen. When she was at the other end of the room and Adam, his back towards her, was immersed in conversation with someone else, awareness of her presence radiated from him.

And yet, watching Helen closely, Elizabeth realised that even she was not conscious of Adam's new feelings. She was happily married, she was used to male admiration, and to her Adam was merely a childhood friend who had come home after a long absence.

The intensity in his gaze as he once, thinking himself unobserved, allowed his eyes to rest on Helen for a full thirty seconds, struck a chill in Elizabeth. She knew instinctively that he was not a man to love lightly.

She was afraid of the result of his passion, if he couldn't overcome it by himself. And she found herself wishing with a passion of her own that Adam Montgomery had never decided to return home to Paisley.

IV

Isobel Gibson was pale, red-eyed, but deter-minedly cheerful as she sat at the kitchen table in the High Street house, Elizabeth by her side.

'I can manage fine on my own,' she insisted tremulously for the third time since Matthew had brought her in. 'Whatever happens I don't want to be the cause of trouble between Matt and his father. I'd never want to come between them.'

Matthew, staring out of the window, seeing nothing of the laundry decorating the bushes in the garden, gave a sardonic bark of laughter.

'You flatter yourself, lass. There's little love lost between me and him. The man's changed out of all recognition since my mother died. He's a stubborn, difficult old—'

'He's lonely, Matt!' Isobel automatically came to the defence of the sour old man who disapproved of his son's love for her.

'So there's all the more reason to believe that he'll welcome a grandchild,' Adam, the fourth member of the group, pointed out. 'It's the best thing that can happen – another Montgomery to carry on the family name. I take it that you intend to marry Isobel?' he asked his brother bluntly, and Matt flushed to the roots of his hair.

'Of course I do – what d'ye take me for?' he asked angrily. At the same moment Isobel said swiftly, 'He doesnae need to marry me!'

'Don't be daft!' her sweetheart told her harshly, and she subsided, her fingers twining nervously together. Elizabeth reached out and put her own hand over her friend's and Adam, leaning back against the dresser, looked with a hint of impatience from his half-brother to Isobel.

'Then the matter's settled, surely. What's all this fuss about?'

'It's no' as easy as that!' Elizabeth said angrily. She wished that he would learn to look at a problem from every angle instead of cutting, with the efficient ruthlessness of the surgeon, through every argument as though it didn't exist.

He stared down at her, contempt in his dark blue eyes. 'A man, a woman, a bairn on the way, a wedding. That's not easy?'

'You're forgetting about your father.'

'He'll be grateful enough that Matt's found himself a good wee wife.'

'Aye, but—' Matt stopped short and darted an embarrassed look at Isobel. She wasn't afraid to say what he and Elizabeth were thinking. Her gaze met Adam's with nothing to hide.

'Your father's a manufacturer with a big house. Mine is a weaver with a rented cottage. And I clip shawls for the Montgomery company. It's no' what anyone could call a fine marriage for the likes of Matt.'

Adam's eyes darkened, his mouth took a downward droop. Elizabeth had come to recognise the signs of anger in the few short weeks he had been in the house.

'If Matt's satisfied with his choice, it has nothing to do with my father,' he said curtly. Matt ran both hands through his thick brown hair. He looked utterly miserable, torn between fear of his father and love for Isobel. Elizabeth's heart went out to him and she felt anger of her own at Adam. Surely he should show sympathy towards the younger man instead of refusing to see Matt's difficulties.

'He pays my wages, that's what's bothering me,' Matt blurted out. 'If he sees fit to put me out then how can I support Isobel, let alone the child?'

'Rubbish!' Adam rang the word out, and

Elizabeth was reminded of the way he had tossed a coin onto the table at the Maxwellton weaver's cottage.

'Look at this—' Isobel indicated the kitchen. 'I know nothing of fine houses like this. One day Matt's going to own the warehouse, and I know as well as Mister Montgomery does that I'd make a poor wife for a manufacturer, me living in a cottage all my days.'

Now Adam's anger was there for them all to see. 'Are you going to stand there like a loon and let the lassie lower herself with talk like this?' he barked at his brother.

Matt shot him a glance of loathing and put his arms awkwardly about Isobel. 'Hush, lass, I'm no' shamed to take you for my wife before the whole town, have I no' told you that time and again?'

Adam moved from the dresser and leaned both fists on the table. Since arriving home he had taken to wearing the plain clothes favoured by the local men – linen shirt, patterned waistcoat, brown trousers, and a cravat tied loosely about his throat. Even so he retained that air of confidence and authority that set him apart. Now, as he looked down at his brother's sweetheart, his anger was tempered with warmth.

'Listen to what I have to tell you, Isobel. Our

great-grandfather, Duncan Montgomery, came from Beith with nothing but his trade and his new wife. His son Robert was a weaver, and proud to be one. And his son, the same Rab Montgomery that owns this house, would have been at the loom all his days if he hadnae damaged his leg and had to give up his chosen trade. You and Matt come from the same stock, and whether he goes back to the loom or takes over the warehouse he'll always be proud to call you his wife. Am I right, Matt?'

'Of course he is,' Matt rushed to assure Isobel. 'He's just got a better way of putting it than I have.'

'Oh – Matt!' Isobel got up and held him close. Over her head he gave Adam and Elizabeth a look that was half-embarrassed, half-belligerent.

'It'll be all right. If my father doesnae take to the idea of a marriage I'll leave the warehouse and go back to my own trade, as Adam says.'

The words were brave, but Elizabeth wished that Matthew himself had been the first to reassure Isobel instead of leaving it to his brother.

'If you ask me,' Adam was saying, 'getting out of that warehouse would be the making of you, Matt. A man sickens when he's doing work he hates. All you have to do is face him with the truth of the matter. He'd never be foolish enough to turn you out. It'll never come to that. He'll admit defeat.'

Matt looked pityingly at him. 'You might have learned a lot while you were away from home, Adam, but it seems to me you've forgotten as much again.'

Elizabeth agreed with him, though she had the sense to keep her thoughts to herself. Adam didn't take kindly to opposition from a woman.

She herself shared all of Matt's misgivings, and added to that, she was worried about Adam's passion for Helen Grant.

Helen had been a favourite of Rachel Montgomery's, and after the older woman's death she had continued to visit the High Street house. She and Elizabeth were firm friends, and on several occasions Helen and Alec had shown her special kindness – a small present, an invitation to join them at the theatre, a sharing of confidences. Elizabeth didn't want to see Adam trampling on all that they had in their marriage, and she had a feeling that he wasn't a man to love silently and selflessly for long.

There was the scandal to consider, too. Rab was an important man in Paisley, Matt and James well thought of. If Adam made a bid for another man's wife in his home town, the place would rock with the result. The world, as she knew it, would come to an end.

While she watched and worried Adam and the Grants walked together, dined together, rode together, attended theatre performances and assemblies together. When Adam was preparing for one of those occasions he was cheerful; when he had to spend a full day without sight of Helen he was morose and silent. Rab, concerned with his own business worries, seemed quite unaware of his son's preoccupation, and James worked at his writing, oblivious to the rest of the uneasy household.

And each day the threat of the cholera epidemic moved a little closer. Walls in the town erupted in a rash of notices giving warnings and advice on how to tackle the disease. Meetings were held, arrangements made to dispense disinfectants and medicines if necessary. Under Adam's direction Elizabeth stocked a cupboard with powdered mustard and castor oil, spirit of turpentine, spirit of hartshorn, tincture of capsicum, laudanum and opium, ether and calomel. She put flannel strips aside, ready to be heated and wrapped about affected limbs.

Each time she looked at the cupboard she shivered at the thought that one of the people within those sturdy walls might need such attention. She agreed with Helen when, on a visit with her mother, that young woman announced that thinking of the cholera must surely be worse than experiencing it.

'Only yesterday Alec made me sit down and read through the latest notice so that I might recognise the illness at once – and I experienced every symptom as I read it!'

She screwed her nose up in a grimace of self-mockery. Her hair was like flames against the black bonnet and black-centred shawl she wore and her gown was a rich blue. She looked radiantly healthy.

'Chills and aches and cramps and other things I wouldn't mention! It isn't possible that one illness could do all that. Adam—' her brown eyes swept up at him from under long gold lashes '—tell me that they're trying to fright us!'

But he refused to be drawn. 'They can't print the truth of it. It's the devil's punishment on earth. You must promise me, Helen—' his voice was intense '—that you'll take great care, and avoid those places where the air might be unclean.'

'Really, Adam!' Helen's mother said sharply, her nostrils quivering with outrage. 'Cholera is known to affect only people of low habits and lack of

Christian feeling. I scarcely think that my daughter could be in any danger!'

A spasm of sheer anger flickered across his face and was gone almost at once. 'That's what they say,' he drawled from where he leaned elegantly against the mantelpiece, 'but I have no reason to believe that it's true. Besides, there's some would say that Christianity and piety might not be the—'

'You'll have some more tea, Helen?' Elizabeth said deliberately, knowing what was coming next. Adam had already scandalised his father with his cynical observations about folk who thought that they could buy their way to Heaven, and Helen's parents were staunch supporters and benefactors of the High Church.

'Elizabeth—' he said, with a coolness in his voice, but she pretended she hadn't heard.

'You must bring wee Catherine to see me soon. Is she on her feet yet?'

Catherine's mother and grandmother, eyes shining, immediately launched into the latest stories of the baby's exploits. Adam was quite forgotten.

'My knuckles were fair stinging with the rap your tongue gave them,' he said dryly when the guests had left. 'I've noticed, Elizabeth, that for all your youth you seem to rule the roost where Matt and James are concerned. I have no memory of telling you that you could do the same with me.'

She coloured, but stood her ground. 'I've heard enough of your views on religion to know that they'd not have been well received – and you'd never want to upset Helen.'

'So you think folk should be sheltered from the truth?'

'Why fright them when they can do nothing about it?'

Irritation sharpened his gaze, honed the edge of his voice. 'Of course they can do something about it! They can realise that folk get diseases because they live in filth and despair. They need help instead of contempt. And if folk like Helen's father and her father-in-law can't aid those wretches, God help humanity!'

'You can't change the world, Adam.'

'You sound like my cousin Christian,' he said in disgust. 'I only seek to change Paisley – let the rest of the world take care of itself.'

She stacked cups and plates on a tray. 'You'd have a better chance if you started with the rest of the world, for this town has a fine conceit of itself, and one man'll no' make it any different.'

'I thought you were more of a fighter than that,' he challenged as he opened the parlour door for her.

'I know my place.'

'That you don't,' said Adam. 'Or you'd never be content to stay in my father's kitchen.'

She waited until she had deposited her burden on the kitchen table then faced him.

'There's nothing wrong with being in the kitchen!'

'There is when you're too intelligent to stay there.' His eyes took in her neat figure and face with a dispassionate sweep. There was a great difference, she realised, in the way he looked at Helen and the way he looked at her.

'My brain's my concern!' she rallied.

'Not when it's wasted on puddings and porridge.'

She rattled dishes angrily. 'I'm proud to be able to earn my keep!'

That maddening grin tickled at the corners of his mouth again. 'Meaning that it's time I started earning mine?'

She didn't dare meet his eyes any more. 'I'm surprised you're no' finding life tedious, with nothing at all to do.'

'There's enough to keep me busy.'

'They do say that Satan finds mischief for idle hands,' she retorted, and could have bitten her silly tongue off.

'Do they, now?' he asked softly. 'And what does Elizabeth say, since she's such a fountain of knowledge all at once?'

'You're talking riddles!' She plunged her hands into the dishwater, head lowered. She had gone too far.

'And so are you,' he told her, his voice cool. 'Look to your own business, Elizabeth, and leave me to worry about mine.'

Matt came in the back way late that night when Jean was out and Elizabeth sat alone in the kitchen. His face was set, his eyes blazing with purpose.

'Is my father alone? Right—' he said, when she nodded. 'See that we're not disturbed, Elizabeth. I have something to discuss with him.'

It took a moment to get up, spilling her sewing from her lap. By the time she caught up with him he was halfway across the hall.

'Matt!' She snatched at his arm, halting him. 'Not tonight – he's in a temper and best left alone!'

'What I have to say cannae wait any longer. Let me be, Elizabeth!' Matt tore her fingers from his sleeve as the parlour door was thrown open and Rab Montgomery's bulk appeared.

'What's that noise?' he barked.

'I want a word with you, father,' Matt said crisply.

'Aye – well – I can do nothing to stop you.' Rab stumped back to his chair and Matt, without another look at Elizabeth, followed him into the room and closed the door, shutting her out.

There was a small carved chair in the hall; she sank onto it, knees weak. She had no plans to eavesdrop but she couldn't go back to the kitchen and leave Matt alone to face his father.

For a moment, there was only the soft murmur of Matt's voice then silence. Rab's reaction came clearly to her ears.

'You senseless, moon-eyed fool! Have you no idea at all of the ways of the world? Am I made of money, that I'm expected to support this lassie and her bairn? That is—' there was a change of tone '—if it's yours. Have you been daft enough to accept responsibility?'

'I'd no' think of denying it!' Matt's voice, too, had risen. 'I'm no' asking any favours of you. I'm just telling you that I'm going to marry Isobel and I'll expect her to be accepted into this family as my wife!'

'You what?' Rab roared. 'Laddie, you might have lost your wits but you can scarce expect me to do the same. I'll have none of this nonsense and you'll get no help from me if you go on with it!'

There was a thud and the rattle of glass and

Elizabeth, now on her feet and clutching at the chair-back, knew that Rab's huge fist had crashed onto the table.

'I'm no' asking for your help,' Matt said angrily. 'I'll support my wife myself!'

There was a derisive laugh from his father. 'What with?'

'We'll manage with my wages from the warehouse and the little she earns.'

This time Rab's voice was a bellow. 'D'ye expect me to keep you on as my foreman when you defy me as my son? I'll be damned first! There's no room in your life for a wife just now – and when there is, you'll make a good marriage with a lassie who can bring a dowry. And that's my last word on it, so you can get to your room and thank the good God that you've been brought to your senses before it was too late!'

'You old devil!' Matt's shaking voice was almost unrecognisable. 'You dare to expect me to turn away from Isobel and my own bairn like that? Is this the thanks I get for giving up the loom and spending day after day in that damned warehouse of yours, putting up with your black moods and your foul temper—'

'You impudent pup—' Rab screamed. A hand touched Elizabeth's arm. James had been drawn from upstairs by the noise. His face was ashen.

'—I'll teach you how to speak to your father!' Rab shouted, and there was the crash of fire irons.

'Get in and put a stop to it!' Elizabeth pushed James towards the door, but he hung back.

'They'd never listen to me!'

'Then I will—'

He pulled her back as her fingers touched the door-handle.

'For God's sake, Elizabeth, he's likely to kill you if you get in his way now!'

'We can't leave Matt to face this on his own!' She caught James's hand, reached out to open the door. 'We'll go in together!'

The street door opened and Adam stepped into the hall. Before Elizabeth could open the parlour door he had taken in the situation, and swept her and James aside.

'That daft gowk – I told him to wait for me before he told the old man,' he said, and threw the parlour door open. Peeping round his shoulder Elizabeth saw Rab by the fire, face mottled, eyes starting from his head. He clutched the heavy poker. Matt grasped the hand that held the poker and the two men were locked in a struggle.

'For God's sake!' Adam stormed into the room, dragged his father and brother apart, and stood between them, eyes bright with anger. The poker was thrown back on the hearth. 'Have you no thought of the folk living round here? D'you want them to hear your business down at the Cross?'

'They're welcome to hear mine, for I've nothing to hide!' Matthew threw himself towards the door, his face dark and distorted with rage. A livid scarlet welt stood out down one side. Adam caught at his arm and was cast aside with murderous fury.

'Leave me be!' his brother warned him and raged from the house without stopping to take his hat and coat. The front door crashed back on its hinges and was left open to the night until James closed it.

'Let him go – all of you!' Rab ordered thickly, spittle drooling down his chin. His eyes were bloodshot, his face a bluish colour. 'He's no son of mine from this day on!'

'Stop your wild talk and get a grip of yourself, man!' Adam ordered, forcing his father into a fireside chair. At first Rab resisted, then something about the steely fire in his eldest son's blue eyes made him think better of it. With a grunt deep in his throat he subsided.

'Elizabeth? Damn you, girl, stop staring as though I was some curiosity in a side-show—' He peered round Adam at her. 'Fetch the whisky!'

'You'll have a little brandy, just, with water. And you'll sit quietly until I tell you that you can get up.' Adam's voice was crisp. 'James, tend to the fire.'

He put his fingers to the pulse that fluttered at Rab's temple, and the older man beat him away with flailing hands.

'Let me be! I'll tell you when I've need of a physician!'

Elizabeth brought his drink, noting the tremor in the hand that snatched the glass from her. For a long time there was silence in the room apart from the fire's crackle and the noise of Rab sucking brandy and water through loose lips. James fiddled uneasily with the curtains, Elizabeth stood behind Rab's chair, and Adam, seated opposite his father, watched him with narrowed eyes.

'I'd advise you to go to your bed,' he said when the glass was empty.

'I was going!' Rab barked at him. 'Elizabeth, help me to my feet!'

'James, you'll take charge of the warehouse tomorrow,' he said at the door.

'You'd be best to wait until the morning, when your temper's cooled, before you make such decisions,' Adam said levelly, and his father glared at him.

'It'll all be the same in the morning – unless thon fool of a brother of yours does as he's told!'

They were all in bed when Matt came home. In the morning he stayed in his room until his father and James left the house.

Elizabeth set Jean to work in the dining-room, where she was safely out of the way, and returned to the kitchen.

'Should you not go upstairs and talk to Matt?'

Adam, still lounging at the table, shook his dark head.

'Leave him be. If he's no' man enough to handle this business without my help, he's no' worth worrying over. What were you thinking of doing when I came in last night?'

'Putting a stop to the scene before Matt and your father killed each other.'

He gave her a sardonic look from beneath thick dark lashes. 'All on your lone?'

'James was with me.'

'James is a poet, never a warrior. Lord's sakes, Elizabeth, the old man would have split you in two with that poker, the mood he was in. Have you no sense?'

'I could hardly stand by and—' she began hotly, then Adam's eyes suddenly slid to a point beyond and above her, and she turned.

Matt stood in the doorway. His face was grey, apart from the ugly black and blue and yellow bruise that showed where his father had struck him. His eyes were sunk in his head and there were lines that showed how he would look in old age. Elizabeth was shocked to see how like his father he would look in some forty years' time.

She hurried to fill a bowl with food, but he shook his head, coming to sit at the table. 'I'll eat nothing under his roof.'

'Then you'll be away to skin and bone within the week, man,' his brother said sarcastically. 'My, thon's a bonny bruise.'

Matt ducked his head away from the surgeon's probing fingers and looked at Adam and Elizabeth with dead eyes.

'You're wrong. I'm going to stay with Isobel and her father today, and never setting foot in this house again.'

Somehow Elizabeth had never believed that it would come to this. Neither, obviously, had Adam. While she stared in dismay at Matt, his brother said angrily 'Don't be a fool, man – the whole business can be sorted out tonight with a wee bit of sense from the pair of you!'

But Matt's normally cheerful face was set in stubborn lines. 'There's nothing to sort out.

Isobel's father needs her to look after his house. He's fair crippled with the rheumatics, and I'm to take over his loom. I'm finished with the warehouse, and I'm finished with the whole business!'

'Matt – it's no' easy to find work, and your father—' Elizabeth couldn't bring herself to finish the sentence. Matt did it for her.

'—My father might make it difficult for me? Aye, he might well try,' he held up a hand to stop Adam's words. 'You've got a strange faith in folk's duty, Adam,' he told him, and for once their roles were reversed. When it came to Paisley, and to Rab Montgomery, Matt knew more than Adam. 'He'll mebbe try, but I'm going to follow my own plans.' His eyes brightened slightly. 'I talked to Isobel's brother about it last night, then to James when I got home. I'm going to find a manufacturer who'll help me to set up my loom for a new shawl, using John's yarn and a design from James. I'm going to weave the shawl my father refused to consider. And I'm going to show him that it'll work!'

An hour later he paused in the hall, his possessions in one bag, and took a last look round the home he had known for most of his life.

Adam, unable to get him to change his mind, had finally walked out in a temper, so there was only Elizabeth to see Matt leave.

'It's no' too late to change your mind, as Adam says.'

He shook his head and, unexpectedly, bent to kiss her cheek. 'I'll never talk with him again, or set foot in his house, without an invitation. You'll dance at my wedding, Elizabeth?'

She nodded, lips trembling, then he was gone.

The town buzzed for a few days with the news, but Rab Montgomery paid the gossips no heed. Matt's name was never mentioned in his house.

James made some protest about being promoted to the post of foreman in the warehouse, but being of weaker material than either of his brothers, he gave in before his father's mounting anger. His hopes were pinned, now, on the poems that were with the London publisher.

'If they sell,' he told Elizabeth, 'I'm going there whether my father likes it or not. All I need is for one poem to be published, and I'll know where my path leads!'

A day or two after Matt walked out Adam returned home in a black mood. 'Can you read?' he asked Elizabeth abruptly.

'You know fine I can. I told you that your step-mother had sent me to the charity school.'

'Then look at that.' He threw the latest edition of the *Paisley Advertiser* on the carpet before her as she black-leaded the parlour grate. There was an announcement on the page that fell uppermost, to the effect that as Matthew Montgomery no longer was employed as warehouse foreman for the company of Robert Montgomery, Forbes Place, the said Robert Montgomery, shawl manufacturer, was not responsible for any of the said Matthew's debts or liabilities.

Rab was dining out that day. Adam was out for a while after the evening meal, and when he returned the paper was tossed onto a table by Rab's elbow, without comment. Rab glanced at it.

'I've seen it.'

'By God,' said Adam, white-faced, standing over him, 'You're a bitter, twisted old devil!'

James caught his breath with an audible gasp. Elizabeth stabbed her finger with her needle and didn't notice until later that blood stained the shirt she was mending. After a long, angry pause Rab looked up. Small pale blue eyes set in a lattice of red met and locked with furious dark blue eyes.

'And by God—' said Rab at last, picking up the newspaper and ripping it across as though it was a piece of flimsy lace, 'I learned in a harder school than you or your brother'll ever know!'

He tossed the newsprint carelessly onto the fire, and turned away from his son. Adam swung round on his heel and walked out. Sent to fetch him for the Bible reading five minutes later, Elizabeth found him in the hall, gripping the finely carved banisters.

'The wee lassie in Maxwellton died tonight,' he said without looking round when he heard the rustle of her skirts. 'You'd best burn the coat I was wearing. There's – blood on it.'

She put a hand on his arm, but he didn't seem to notice. 'Adam, your father's waiting with the Bible—'

He drew a deep, ragged breath, expelled it slowly. Then his shoulders straightened and he turned, eyes hooded, face carefully expressionless.

'I might as well,' he said bleakly. 'Whatever happens we must never forget to thank the Lord for the day he's given to us.'

Matt wasn't the only young man in the area to be at odds with his father. For some time rumours had been flying about Alec Grant, Helen's husband, and his fondness for the gambling tables. His father, a staunch Presbyterian, was opposed to games of chance, and the gossips who predicted trouble between father and son were proved right.

Helen's growing unhappiness was obvious. She spent a lot of time at her parents' Paisley house, and visited Elizabeth frequently.

'I could never tell my mother the whole truth of it,' she said wretchedly, twining her white fingers together. 'Even when Alec and his father aren't quarrelling about money and Alec's duties, the house rings with the echoes of, it seems to me. Mistress Grant's a poor, purse-mouthed woman, so there's no help for us from her. Alec should never have left the Fusiliers, that's the truth of it. He was happy as a soldier, and he only left for my sake, when we wed. He's so unhappy, working for his father as estate manager. He sees his friends often because he needs to be with folk that take him as he is. But they're never away from the tables or from the bottle—'

Elizabeth felt helpless in the face of such misery. 'Is there no way he can leave Barrhead and make a new life for himself?'

Helen shook her red head. 'What could he do? He was raised to go into the Army and it was always understood that he'd work for his father after that. He's dependent on the old man. Thank God it's a daughter I have, and not a son!' she added bitterly.

One day when she found Adam at home she appealed to him to talk to Alec about his increasing dependence on drink.

'You must have seen his restlessness yourself,

coming about the house so much, and being a close friend of his.'

Elizabeth felt, rather than saw, the way he winced at the words. Obviously Helen saw his presence at Barrhead as friendship for her husband alone and had no idea that she was the reason.

'I know he's unhappy. I've often seen that look on board ship, when a man was raging inside to get away from duty and live his own life.'

Helen's mouth trembled. She looked swiftly down at her own clasped hands, and missed the sudden, brief movement Adam made, as if preventing himself from going to her. 'And he's getting into debt too. I'm that feared his father'll find out! Adam—' she looked up again, pleading with him. 'Could you mebbe talk to him? You know more about the world than any of us, and he'd listen to you.'

'And lose – his friendship?' Adam's voice was thick, strangled deep in his throat. He turned away abruptly and the hand Helen put out to him dropped to her side, rejected. 'Helen, a man who's bent on going his own way doesnae take kindly to advice.'

'You're my only hope, Adam. Please – for his sake, if you'll no' do it for mine!'

It seemed inconceivable to Elizabeth that Helen

didn't know how much she was torturing the man who stood staring out of the window, his back to the room. She began to speak, trying in clumsy fashion to help him out of the agony he must be enduring; but before she had said more than a few words Adam had turned, his face like a carving in stone.

'I'll do my best – since you ask me,' he said, and the smile that illuminated Helen's face made the tears in her eyes sparkle like diamonds.

Surely, Elizabeth thought, watching that radiant smile, Adam must realise that despite everything, Helen loved Alec deeply, and there was no other man for her. If he did, he gave no sign of it.

Matt married Isobel Gibson at the end of October. Their wedding party was held in her father's house, a cottage in Shuttle Street with the living quarters and the four-loom weaving shop separated by a through-passage from back to front of the house.

Elizabeth, Adam and James all attended. Isobel, noticeably stouter, glowed with happiness, but Elizabeth felt there were shadows on the bridegroom's round face, and his smile wasn't as ready or carefree as it had once been.

'He's grown up at last,' Adam dismissed her concern. 'It's past time – he's twenty-three years old.'

The weeks since he left his father's house hadn't been easy for Matt. Rab had used his powers in the town to block several work opportunities for his rebellious son. But Matt proved to have the tenacity of a bulldog. He had found the goodwill of a manufacturer indifferent to Rab's wishes, and the man had agreed to finance the new shawl. Matt's meagre savings had gone into the venture and he had found more work as a weaver to support himself and Isobel and her father, who had given up his loom to Matt, while the shawl was worked on.

Being a plain weaver himself, Matt could only provide the centre of the shawl. His search for a skilled man to weave the more intricate patterned border had brought him to Daniel McGill, a harness loom weaver of considerable talents, but also a notorious character.

Dan, a tall, lanky, shabbily dressed bachelor, was at the wedding celebrations, his fiery red hair like a beacon above every other head.

'I hope you know what you're taking on, with Dan,' James said apprehensively as he watched the man down a tumblerful of whisky as though it was water. Dan was one of the most skilful weavers in the town. He was also the least trustworthy, always ready to forsake his loom for the gaming tables and the tavern. He could have found work with any manufacturer he chose, but because money meant nothing to him he was continually in debt and seldom employed.

'I'll see to it that he works well on this shawl – and I'll see to it that my father's made to acknowledge his mistake,' Matt vowed, and Isobel's hand slid into his as the last words took on a bleak note.

Her smile had faltered, and her clear eyes were worried. Rab Montgomery no longer bought yarn from her brother's small factory, and she herself had found the warehouse door closed to her after Matt left home. Her entire family had been affected by her love for the wrong man.

Matt was quick to sense his young wife's mood. 'Ach, we'll manage just fine, you wait and see,' he said cheerfully, but as he looked round the small room with its low smoky ceiling and the little wall bed where he and Isobel would sleep Elizabeth knew that he was comparing it with the home he had known.

She fretted over Matt as she and Adam walked back to High Street later. There was no doubt that he loved Isobel, but there was a new restlessness in him that reminded her of an animal in a cage. All his hopes and ambitions were centred on the success of the shawl he planned. If that failed, what would become of Matt?

Adam's thoughts were occupied with more pressing matters.

'Did you see the newspaper today?' He put a hand beneath her elbow to guide her round a stagnant puddle. 'The cholera's reached Britain. A man named Sproat died of it in Sunderland.'

'It might not be the blue cholera.' That was the name given to the terrible death that had swept the globe from India.

'It is. The paper listed his symptoms. I'd know them anywhere.'

'It might not reach Paisley.' She was clutching at straws and Adam mercilessly snatched them from her one by one.

'It will. There's no doubt of that.' His voice was harsh. 'They have no real notion of what's coming to them, Elizabeth. They talk about sobriety and a respectable, pious life – they suck at cholera sweeties and call the epidemic God's punishment on the wicked. They've got no notion!' he repeated in frustration as they turned off High Street to go down the dark passageway that led to the back door of the Montgomery house.

She wished that she could change the subject, yet there was a morbid fascination in this disease that had killed thousands, and couldn't be stopped.

'Have you seen it, Adam?'

'Seen it? Aye, I've touched it, I've fought with it, and I've been defeated almost every time. Win or lose, I've never known whether a patient died because of my treatment, or whether a patient who lived would have survived anyway. It's an evil thing, cholera, and I'd no' wish my worst enemy to see it at work.'

She was suddenly racked by a shiver from head to foot; he stopped speaking and turned, as they reached the back door, to put his hands on her shoulders. The long garden was in darkness, bushes and trees black against the dark blue of the sky. Beyond the drystone wall fields stretched to the hills. It was a pleasant garden by day, but at night there was something sinister about it, Elizabeth thought for the first time.

'You're right, Elizabeth – cholera's no' a pleasant subject for young ladies like Helen and you.'

'I didnae say you shouldn't talk to me about it,' she protested, and he laughed.

'D'you no' consider yourself a lady, then?' His hands still held her shoulders. Jean had left a lamp in the kitchen window and its pale glow caught the lines and shadows of his downbent face and made his eyes glitter. 'Mebbe someone should take you in hand – someone like my cousin Christian Selbie.

It's time you began to think of your own future, Elizabeth.'

'It'll be here, in your father's kitchen.'

'Ach, he can employ a fat old wifie any day of the week to run the house and see to his meals. You've more to do with your life. Marriage, for one. Surely there's some young man who calls on you?'

She was glad that he couldn't see the colour rush to her face. 'Don't make a fool of me, Adam!'

'I'm not. Is there nobody? Or have you mebbe got thoughts about James? You're just a year or two younger than he is, when all's said and done.'

'Of course I've no thoughts of James, or him of me!' She tried to pull free, but he held her.

'It's time you considered marriage. There's plenty of good men right here in the town who'd be proud to wed you. You should be mistress of your own home, not keeping a clean hearth and a good table for a cranky old creature and his quarrelsome sons.'

'Who'd take me?' Her hand flew up to touch her scarred cheek, but almost at once it was caught in his fingers and drawn away. Then he cupped her chin, tracing the line of the scar with a gentle thumb.

'You're bonny enough – you've no need to worry about that. A man worth having looks for more than a pretty face, did you never learn that? He wants a woman with a ready smile and a happy nature and a kind heart. And you've got all of those, Elizabeth.'

Unexpectedly, he bent towards her. His lips brushed the line of the scar, then moved to settle for a brief moment on her mouth. Then he straightened up and added crisply, 'But what are we doing standing out here when there's a good warm house waiting for us?'

She was glad when he strode through the kitchen and on into the hall, leaving her alone to take off her cloak and fuss about the kitchen, setting oatmeal to soak for the morning porridge, damping the fire down, cleaning an imaginary speck of dust from the grate.

Her hands trembled slightly and her mind was in confusion. Adam's kiss, if it could be called that, had succeeded in sweeping away the chill fear brought by talk of cholera. Her body tingled, from toes to lips, where his kiss still throbbed and burned. She had never been kissed before, and had never felt the loss of it.

Now she realised what it must be like to be really close to someone, to be loved, to have someone to depend on, someone confident and invincible like Adam Montgomery.

Jealousy had never been part of Elizabeth's nature. But as she put the lamps out and made sure that the front door was locked before going silently to her little attic room, she envied her friend Isobel, who from that day on had a man of her own to call husband.

V

Adam was not one to let a matter alone once his mind had fixed on it, Elizabeth discovered.

A few days after Matt's wedding, he wandered, bored, into the kitchen where she was alone, finishing off the week's ironing. The room was hot and stuffy, a fire burning fiercely in the range to keep the irons hot. Elizabeth's face was crimson and strands of damp hair escaped from beneath her cap as she worked.

'Did James ever tell you of his friend Thomas?' he began. 'Buried his sweetheart on the very day before their wedding. And him with a nice wee house all ready for his bride, and a good job as a cobbler—'

'And a temper that made some folk think that mebbe his sweetheart was as well under the ground as in his kitchen,' Elizabeth cut in. 'If you're thinking of marrying me off to that man, Adam Montgomery, you can think again.'

She glared at him and thumped the flatiron viciously onto the shirt she was ironing. 'I'll find my own husband in my own time. And it seems to me that you should be thinking of your own heart, and the way it's running away with your brains!'

She stopped, horrified. After a brief, terrible pause Adam said softly, 'And what of my heart?'

She swallowed hard. She had gone too far to retreat now. 'Helen Grant's a good friend to me, Adam, and I'd never want her to be unhappy.'

He drew in his breath with a hiss, and caught at a chair, swinging it round so that he could straddle the seat, hands gripping the back. Now he was below her and within her vision. His eyes were blue chips of ice beneath hooded lids.

'Mind your own business!'

She completed a full sweep of the iron. 'It is my business when it concerns folk I know well. What will your father have to say about this pickle you've fallen into?'

'To hell with my father!' he said through tight lips.

'And what about Helen herself, and Alec, and their bairn?'

'That's no concern of yours! Even Helen knows

nothing of – God knows how your sharp wee nose smelled it out!'

'I was there – the night you met her.' She heard an unfamiliar bitterness in her voice. 'I wish you'd never set eyes on her again.' She put the iron back on the range. 'Go away from Paisley now, and leave Helen to her marriage.'

'At your bidding?' he asked mockingly.

'I know you, Adam Montgomery. You're not a man to hold your tongue for ever. You'll only cause trouble and unhappiness. And it'll be wrong, all of it!'

'Helen—'

'Helen loves her husband, do you no' realise that?'

He got to his feet in a clumsy movement that sent the chair crashing to the floor. Adam made no move to pick it up. His face was a mask, lit by glittering narrowed eyes.

'She doesn't know what love is!'

'It means different things to different folk. Let her be, Adam, she's no' meant for you.'

For a moment she shrank back, convinced that he was going to strike her. But he stayed where he was, the impulsive move forward checked.

'Keep your tongue and your thoughts off my concerns, Elizabeth. You're the housekeeper here, no' my conscience. By God, Fate's already done its worst with me – nobody's going to take Helen away from me!'

'Adam, she's no' free to belong to you!'

The intensity in his voice was frightening. 'She could win her freedom. Wait and see, Elizabeth, wait and see. One day Helen's going to be my wife!'

The door crashed shut behind him. Stunned by the force of their quarrel, dazed by angry voices and by Adam's last words, Elizabeth righted the chair, smoothed another garment onto the table, and reached for a fresh iron, only to draw back with a gasp of pain as her bare fingers touched the hot handle.

No more was said about Helen. Adam's behaviour towards her was more guarded, and he stopped strolling into the kitchen to talk to her during the day, to her relief. She buried herself in work and tried not to worry about his plans.

As it happened Alec Grant went off to Edinburgh on business a few days later, depriving Adam of the chance to visit Barrhead. Helen called to see Elizabeth now and then, and Adam usually managed to be at home for these occasions, hungrily watching the young woman when he could.

It seemed to Elizabeth that one problem no sooner quietened than another wakened. She was almost knocked down as she left the house on her way to the shops one morning.

'Sorry, Elizabeth – is Adam still at home?' James asked breathlessly. 'Good – come on!' He seized her hand and swept her back into the house, yelling his brother's name.

'Is there a fire?' Adam wanted to know, appearing at the parlour door with a book in his hand. At the same moment Elizabeth, in sudden fear, asked 'Is it your father?'

'Him? What could ever go wrong with him?' James asked with the astonishment of one who believed that Rab would survive for ever. 'No, it's worse than that. It's Dan McGill – Matt got word to me to tell you, Adam – he's been put into the jail!'

'Dan?' Adam's dark brows swept to his hairline. James, breathless after his rush from the warehouse, bobbed his head vigorously.

'Lucky my father wasnae in the warehouse when the word came. I'll need to get back there quick. Matt's trying to find the money to pay off Dan's debts.'

'Ach – Dan's always in debt,' the surgeon shrugged. 'Why should they imprison him this time?'

'That's just it!' James almost choked in his excitement. 'The flower-lasher that set up his loom for the shawl wants to be paid right away. And Dan and Matt havenae got enough to clear the debt.'

'But that's the way it always is,' Elizabeth protested. 'The man'll get his money when the shawl's finished and sold, surely?'

'Exactly. But things are different this time. The flower-lasher we're talking about does a fair bit of work for the Montgomery warehouse. And him and my father were right friendly in the coffee-house yesterday. I saw them with my own eyes.'

'Damn him for an old dog!' Adam said softly. 'He's had Matt's weaver taken away to stop work on that shawl!'

'He'd no' do such a thing!' Elizabeth said at once. But at the same time she was beginning to realise, with sick reluctance, that Rab Montgomery might be capable of just such a piece of deceit to punish his independent son.

'He'd do it, all right. What's owing, James?'

'A fair amount. It's a difficult design, and it took a lot of work to set the loom. That was one of the reasons my father'll never use one of my designs. And there's other money owed to the same man by Dan. Matt's gone to speak to old Peter Todd, but if

he lends the money it'll take time. You know Peter
– aye wants to think about things.'

'What about Christian?'

'You know fine Matt would never ask her. She's
a woman – and besides, it would come between
her and my father.'

'If I had it, I'd give it to Matt here and now. I'd
like fine to see that old man taught a lesson.'

'Matt never asked this, it's my own idea – would
you talk to him, Adam? Ask if he'd advance the
money himself, as a loan?'

'I'd no' ask him for help if I was at the gates of
Hell!' Adam said viciously.

'It might be the only answer.' Elizabeth's fingers
were clasped as though in prayer, her eyes fixed on
Adam. 'What could you do to teach him a lesson
anyway? He knows more about the shawl business
than any of you – give in, Adam, and talk to him,
for Matt's sake.'

But his long, capable fingers were rubbing his
chin thoughtfully. 'Wait a minute – he might know
more than me about business, but there's things I
know about—' His voice trailed off, then he sprang
into life, blue eyes snapping fire. 'James – get word
to Matt that he's got to persuade Peter to make that
loan, whatever the terms. We can worry about high
interest later. And tell him that the two of us'll visit

Dan tonight. Elizabeth – the key of the cupboard the medication's stored in. Come on, lassie, don't just gape at me, I've work to do!'

James, mystified but unenlightened, galloped back to work. Elizabeth was whisked into the kitchen, fumbling in the bunch of keys about her slim waist. Adam opened the cupboard and let his fingers dance along the collection of bottles and packets. A small package was slipped into his pocket.

'What are you doing?'

'This town's jumpy over the cholera,' he made for the hall, caught up his hat and coat. 'If the jailer thought that Dan was sickening for something like that, he'd no' be keen to keep him, would he?'

'Adam, you'd no'—' She caught at his arm as he opened the door. 'Adam! It's criminal!'

The grin on his face slipped and his eyes hardened as he looked down at her. 'So's trying to destroy your own son when he's struggling to prove that he's a man,' he said, and the door closed behind him.

The ground floor of the new prison by the river was given over to a howff where debtors and their visitors could talk over a glass of porter or ale, sold by Mr Hart, the jailer. The Paisley people always felt that this was a civilised Scottish custom, and at the moment it suited Adam's purpose very well.

Dan's long face brightened when he saw his visitor waiting with two generous tumblers of porter.

'You don't look well, man,' Adam told him cheerfully.

Dan took a large mouthful of drink, wiped his mouth on his sleeve, and said that he was fine.

'But I'm vexed for Matt. This has never happened to me before.' He gazed about the place, his brow wrinkled. The debtor's prison had always been a threat over his red head, but he had never expected anything to come of it. Usually, he paid his debts at the last minute, then set about making new ones. 'That flower-lasher knew fine he'd get his money – he always has!'

'Mebbe he's been talking to the wrong folk. You're sure you're well?' Adam peered at the other man. 'What did you have for your dinner?'

'Tripe.'

Adam tutted. 'I'd never touch the stuff, myself. Matt's trying to raise the money to pay off your debt. But it might take time. And in the meantime, what about this web on your loom? Matt's fair anxious to see it finished.'

Dan took another long drink. 'As God's my witness, Adam, I've been working hard at that web. But what can I do now? They'll never let me bring it into the jail to work on.'

'So we'll have to get you out.' Adam leaned across the table and refilled Dan's glass. 'Tell me – d'you ever have a ringing sound in your ears?'

'Like a bell?' Dan was perplexed.

'Just so. And then there's a feeling of giddiness, and a bad stomach. They'd no' want to keep you in here for another minute if they ever thought you'd caught something dangerous, like the cholera—'

'What?' Dan's voice rose sharply and a few heads were lifted. His eyes rolled in a suddenly white face. 'God sakes, man, don't joke about a thing like that! I never felt—'

'Shut your mouth and listen to me!' Adam hissed at him, and he subsided. 'Now – if you were to be a wee thing unsteady on your feet when you leave here, and for the rest of the day too, and if you complained tonight about a ringing noise in your ears—'

Understanding was beginning to dawn in the green eyes opposite. 'They'd think I was – oh, but it'd take worse than that to make them put me out.'

'I can see to that for you.' A small packet found its way beneath the table into Dan's hand. 'Put that in your pocket. When dusk comes, swallow it down and throw the paper away. It'll make you awful sick, but it'll no' kill you.'

'Aye, but—' Dan swallowed nervously, '—they'll send for the physician, and he'll know it's nothing bad.'

'I'm a physician myself, man – and I've seen the cholera. If I'm visiting you at the time they'll be happy enough to take my word for it that you should be kept away from folk. Me and Matt'll take you home and keep you alone for two days. That'll be long enough for Matt to find the money.'

'Are you sure I'll get better?' Dan eyed him suspiciously.

'There'd be no point in getting you out of here if I couldnae get you back at your loom within a few hours. All you'll need to see you right's a tot or two of whisky – and I'll have that waiting for you,' Adam added swiftly, and the weaver's eyes brightened.

'Wait a minute, though – if I'm as sick as all that my drawboy'll no' come near me. I cannae work without someone to operate the harness.'

Adam wasn't in the mood to suffer obstacles. 'Matt trained as a drawboy, didn't he? He'll work with you, and I'll see to the money. Will you do it, Dan?'

It took a little persuasion, but Adam could be

very persuasive when he put his mind to it. When he left thirty minutes later, he was gratified to see Dan stagger on his way back to the cells, knocking over a respectable town councillor who was visiting another prisoner.

Dan was spectacularly ill when Matt and Adam called on him that evening. The anxious jailer was only too pleased to see him carried into a carriage under the supervision of a medical man. Dan was then whisked off to his house, where he was put to bed, moaning and convinced that he had been poisoned.

A few generous doses of whisky revived him enough to work up a rage as he watched Adam and Matt fumigating his house, scrubbing walls and floors with disinfectant, and washing his clothes.

'There's nothing wrong with me, you know that yourself – and will you put my best coat down!' he bawled from the wall-bed.

Adam, bent over a tub of water and strong lye soap, straightened his back and winced. 'We've to be seen to be taking all the proper precautions, you daft loon,' he said, and plunged the coat into the water. 'Think yourself lucky we're no' scrubbing you too.'

'First he tries to kill me, then he ruins my best

coat,' Dan mourned, clutching the whisky bottle for comfort.

'Kill you? You'll be better than you've ever been by the morning. A good purging never did anyone any harm,' Adam told him callously. 'Jings, Matt, I had no notion that washing was so hard. I'd rather have a full day walking the wards in some hospital than a morning as a laundrywoman!'

Elizabeth, anxious to hear what happened, sat up late into the night waiting for Adam to come home, then went to bed, her curiosity unsatisfied. The next morning she found him sprawled across his bed, fully-clothed and fast asleep, reeking of disinfectant. She closed the door, and told Jean to keep away from the upper floor in case he was disturbed.

He arrived in the kitchen at noon, demanding food and looking fresh and rested. He was like a schoolboy, she thought with a mixture of exasperation and affection, as she set a place at the kitchen table for him. The escapade with Matt had put new life into him, and in his eagerness to tell the story he swept aside the coolness that had lain between them.

'You're nothing but a pair of silly bairns, you and your brother!' She felt years older than him when she looked at the sheer mischief in his eyes.

'How long d'you think a daft ploy like that's going to fool folk?'

He grinned and bit into a thick slice of bread with white teeth. 'Long enough.'

'If you find yourselves in the jail along with Dan tomorrow don't look to me for sympathy,' she scolded.

His hand caught at her wrist, turning her to look down at him as he sat at the kitchen table.

'Who else would I look to? You're a sharp wee thing, Elizabeth – too sharp for your age. But for some reason beyond my understanding,' his eyes held hers in a level look, 'you'd never want me to fall into bad ways.'

It was the nearest he had come to referring to the quarrel they had had over Helen.

Elizabeth, embarrassed, jerked her hand away. His look, his touch, set up a confusion in her that was hard to understand.

'You'll always worry about me and watch over me,' he finished smugly, going back to the bread.

'I hope you never have cause to find out if that's so,' she snapped, to cover the turmoil within.

'Anyway, who can blame me for being cautious about Dan's health, with the cholera on its way? I'll discover tomorrow that it must have been bad tripe he ate yesterday. And who'll be any the wiser? In the meantime, folks are scared to go near him and prove me a liar.'

He laughed, reaching for a scone. 'There's a corporal posted outside his door to see that nobody but me goes in or out, so Dan and Matt are free to get on with their work in peace.'

The smile faded slightly as he inspected his hands, reddened by scrubbing. 'And on top of that, Dan's house has never been cleaner!'

'And what if one of the other physicians wants to see Dan?'

Adam winked. 'I've already had a word with them. Those that couldn't be told the truth were happy enough to agree that I should deal with this case myself, and call them in if the patient got worse.'

When he had eaten he hurried to the weaver's cottage where a police officer stood on duty, seemingly unconcerned by the steady thump and clack of the loom within. Obviously he believed in doing as he was told, and he hadn't been ordered to see that the possible cholera victim didn't work.

Matt and Dan were both drawn after hours of toil. The cloth, face down on the rollers, was a misty confusion of coloured threads to Adam's unpractised eye, but the other two men knew exactly what the pattern on the other side looked like, and they kept their gaze fixed on the work as they talked, each of them automatically registering the tension of the material and the number of lines still to be 'shot'.

'I'm no' sure how you'll get on with Peter Todd, Adam. He's an honest soul, but awful careful when it comes to parting with money. He always wants time to sleep on it.'

'He's had that – which is more than I can say for you two,' Adam eyed them with swift sympathy. 'I'll sweeten my tongue when I talk to the old miser,' he promised blithely, and departed with a suitably grave expression, having left a fresh bottle of whisky and some food with the prisoners. He knew, as he looked at the little knot of people hurrying by on the far side of the road, that he was playing a cruel trick on Paisley; but loyalty to Matt came first.

Like Rab Montgomery, Peter Todd had given up weaving and had become an employer. Peter had made a comfortable fortune in Paisley's flourishing thread industry, enough to ensure a pleasant retiral. He was a bachelor, and he and Matt had always been friendly. Peter's grandfather had employed Adam's great-grandfather when he first came to Paisley, and Matt had been Peter's drawboy many years before. There was a family link that Peter cherished.

Even so, Adam tapped the brass door-knocker meekly, quite sure that he'd have to curb his usual brusque tongue if he wanted to win the old man over. But he was pleasantly surprised. Peter greeted him with a smile, and poured out glasses of claret before saying, 'You'll have come about that wee matter for Matthew.'

'That's right.' Adam took a sip of claret. It was excellent.

'Well, I've been thinking about it—' Peter tucked his hands beneath his tails of his coat. 'For old time's sake, and because I know he's a hard-working man, and honest, I'm prepared to give him a loan – but mind you—' he swung round, finger raised, '—I'm just covering six months, and I'd be looking for a good return on the money.'

'You'll be repaid – every penny of it, within the time,' Adam promised recklessly, elation bubbling up in him as he watched the old man writing out his personal note for the Provident Bank.

'There you are, then—' The slip of paper that meant so much to Matt was put into his brother's hand. 'You'll have another wee glass,' Peter added and Adam, longing to get to the bank and pay in the note, hesitated, smiled, and said that he'd be happy to drink another wee glass. It was, after all, the least he could do under the circumstances.

'Emmmm—' Peter delayed him again on the doorstep. 'You're a man that's travelled a lot, and seen a lot, they tell me. What's your opinion of this venture your brother's embarked on? D'ye think he's going to get this fine shawl, when all's said and done?'

Adam looked down on the grey head and lined face of the man. 'I think, Mister Todd, that I'd have to travel a sight further and see a lot more, before I'd meet a man as honest as my brother. Your money's safe with him – and a good return you'll get, that's a promise.'

Then, at last, he was free to go plunging down the street, and just managed to get to the bank, housed in the Chamberlain's office, before it closed for the day. Dan was freed from the threat of cholera and Matt's brave new future was secured again.

Rab Montgomery made no sign that he knew anything of Adam's part in the whole business. He had remained carefully aloof from Dan's arrest, and he could not show any reaction to his release.

'But I'll wager he's eating his heart out over it right now,' said James the next night when Rab had limped up to bed. 'D'you think he'll try anything else?'

Adam, in his father's favourite chair, put one

heel on the footstool Rab scorned, and swung the other foot on top of it with the air of a man who had done a fine day's work.

'He's no' a complete fool. He'll leave it at that. But man, it was one of the finest operations I've carried out since I don't know when!'

'And you didn't lose a patient!' James gave him a mock salute.

A grin cracked his brother's face wide and his blue eyes danced. 'No – but for all that I managed to amputate my father's intentions skilfully,' he said, and he and James laughed until the tears ran down their faces.

Watching them, trying without success to look disapproving, Elizabeth realised that Adam's laugh was a natural, free sound that must have been heard often at one time. She wondered how many times he had permitted himself to laugh since his fiancée's death.

'We've shocked poor Elizabeth,' he warned his brother.

'I'm no' shocked, I just—' she began, then Adam started laughing again, James was set off once more, and she was laughing with them and wishing that the fine house could ring to the sound of young happy people more often.

As though echoing her thoughts Adam said,

when the hysteria had died down, 'You don't laugh often enough, Elizabeth.'

'It's this house.' James mopped his face. 'The folk in it never have anything to feel joyous about.'

Adam was still looking at Elizabeth, his eyes brilliant, taking on an intent look. 'You're young and bonny – I wish I could tell you, as a physician, to make sure that you laugh at least once a day.'

She flushed. 'That would be daft. Most folk never have occasion to laugh every day!'

He stood up, stretched, yawned. 'I'm off to my bed. But I think you're wrong – most folk just never think of looking for cheeriness. Mind what I said.'

She wondered, as she got ready for bed in her attic room, if Adam had ever considered taking his own advice. It would do him good too, she thought, remembering the pleasure of hearing his laugh. But all thought of that was swept aside the next day when Helen Grant arrived at the High Street house, white-faced and with tears in her brown eyes.

'It's Alec – he's ill—' she burst out as soon as Elizabeth opened the door. 'I had to bring Catherine over to my mother's, for there's nobody

134

in Barrhead can care for her day and night. I came to tell you—'

'Is it bad?' Elizabeth tried to lead her friend into the parlour but Helen stayed where she was, just inside the door, shaking her head when Elizabeth held out a hand for her cloak.

'I can't stay – I've to get the next stage-coach. It's smallpox. Oh, Elizabeth, I'm so frightened for him! I'm going to try to get the Edinburgh coach when it comes through at two o'clock, else I'll have to go to Glasgow first—'

'You can't go!'

Elizabeth and Helen swung round and looked up at Adam, who was standing at the bend in the stairs. He came swiftly down, his eyes fixed on Helen, his face set. 'You can't go!' he repeated.

'Adam—' she caught at his sleeve. 'Did you hear what I said? Alec's ill in Edinburgh. I must get there!'

He ignored the fingers on his arm and gripped her shoulders. 'Don't you understand? Were you ever inoculated against smallpox?'

'Adam—' she began, then as he shook her slightly she submitted. 'No, I wasn't – there was a lass near us went weak in the head after she was done and my mother would never let them touch me.'

'Then you could catch it!' He shook her again. 'You could die of it, Helen! You could – be blinded, or go mad, or—'

Elizabeth's hand flew to her face to touch the mark there. She could see the horror in Adam's eyes as he looked down on Helen's beauty and imagined it scarred as she, Elizabeth, was scarred.

'What does that matter to me?' Helen was demanding fretfully. She pulled away from him.

'It matters! Stay here, where you're safe—'

She was angry now. 'You think that my safety matters more to me than my husband's life? He's sick, alone – he needs me. We belong together, me and Alec – I'm his wife!'

The last three words were low-voiced, intense, and Elizabeth saw them strike Adam with the force of a thonged whip.

Helplessly she watched him flinch, saw his hands drop, empty, to his sides. Helen added gently, 'It's kind of you to be concerned, Adam, but you must see that if I could save him by taking the sickness on myself, I'd do it gladly. Elizabeth, you'll visit Catherine while I'm away? And if I should—' She stopped herself, then went on, 'I'll be home as soon as I can bring Alec with me.'

'Of course I'll visit Catherine, and your mother. I'll walk part of the way with you.' Elizabeth turned to fetch her shawl as Adam went back upstairs without another word.

He scarcely ate a mouthful that night at dinner. The following morning he announced that the time had come for him to go to England.

Elizabeth stirred automatically at the food she was simmering over the range. Adam had admitted defeat. He was going away, leaving Helen and Alec to their marriage.

The second thought came hard on the heels of the first. Adam was going, and a cold hand touched her heart. Life would be less perilous without him – but very bleak.

'Why not?' Rab grunted dourly. 'My sons never seem to realise when they're well off. I'm thankful for James here – at least he's got the sense to be content with what he's got.'

James, who was waiting impatiently every day for good news from the London publisher, flushed scarlet and attacked his porridge with great concentration.

His father didn't notice. 'And when do you plan to go?' He scowled at his eldest, and most exasperating, son.

'As soon as I can make arrangements.'

'It's a pity you had to decide to leave now,'

Christian said later when she called in to talk about Alec Grant's illness, 'You could have set up an office. We could always do with another good medical man.'

Adam stared moodily out of the window. 'I couldnae do anything for you – nobody can if the cholera comes.'

Christian tutted and smoothed the fringe of her shawl, a striped pattern known as Zebra. 'And they say women are fickle. All this fuss about whether you should stay or whether you should go – you belong here, when all's said and done.'

'I don't!' he said curtly, and stamped out.

'Tuts! There's something amiss, but nobody could ever get a secret from Adam,' was all Christian said.

Daniel McKinlay, a surgeon with a practice in New Street, gave Adam a letter of introduction to a former colleague who worked in St Thomas's teaching hospital in London, and he began to make plans for his departure.

There was a cloud over the house. Rab was in a bad temper over Adam's desertion, and Adam himself, deprived of Helen's company and wounded by her devotion to Alec, scarcely had a word to say to anyone.

The days leading to his departure seemed to

whirl by. While he made his farewells and began to collect his belongings together Elizabeth shut herself in the kitchen, baking and cooking and washing and ironing until she fell into bed exhausted each night.

She didn't want to have time to think, and she didn't know why. She told herself that all the changes – Adam's arrival, his imminent departure, James's plans to go to London if his poems were accepted, Matt's marriage – had unsettled her. She needed to find a routine again.

She visited Helen's mother's house and played with little Catherine, and she spent as much free time as possible with Isobel, who was lonely.

Since the time when he had had to borrow money from Peter Todd Matt had become obsessed by the desire to defeat his father. He worked at his loom late at night, lamplight turning the other, silent looms into grotesque creatures watching over his efforts. When he wasn't working, he was with Dan, watching the shawl grow, or with Cassidy, the manufacturer.

'He comes home at night so tired he can scarcely get into his bed, and in the morning he goes back to the loom half-asleep,' Isobel said wistfully. 'I never see him to talk to.'

Elizabeth took the other girl's hand in hers.

'Wait until that shawl's finished. Matt'll make you so proud of him one day.'

'I'm proud of him now,' Isobel hurried to say. 'I always was. But it would be nice to walk up the street with him, the way it used to be.'

Adam's departure rushed closer. He was looking through a pile of books in the dining-room one day, ignoring Elizabeth, who was waxing the big table, when Jean erupted from the kitchen, still wrapped in the shawl she had put on to do the shopping.

'Mind your dirty feet!' Down on her knees by the table-legs, Elizabeth saw with horror that Jean's feet were still in her outdoor, muddy boots. They advanced, and their owner, cheeks red with cold and excitement, pushed the dining room door further open. From where Jean stood Adam, in a corner by the window, wasn't noticed.

'Did you hear the news? I was in the cheese market a few minutes ago and a woman told me that Lieutenant Grant of Barrhead died of the smallpox in Edinburgh! That poor young wi—!'

She stopped short as she saw Adam. A rough, chilblained hand fled to her mouth.

'Get out of here with your boots on, you stupid gowk!' Elizabeth knew that she was shrill, screeching like a fish-wife, but she had to get the girl away from the sight of Adam, ashen faced and motionless. 'And stop tattling – have you no' been told that before?'

Jean whirled and ran, but not before protesting. 'It's the truth! I met someone else on the way home and she says it's right enough!'

As the kitchen door banged Adam, a book still in his hand, turned to look out of the window, his broad back to Elizabeth.

'If – if it's the truth, Helen's going to be in a fair taking, poor lass—' she said at last.

'Aye.' It was like a long-released sigh. 'Poor lass. Poor Alec.'

'Adam—?' A strange unease was stiffening Elizabeth's throat. He turned very slowly to face her, and as he spoke she knew what he was thinking; knew, too, why she was uneasy.

'Would you say,' asked Adam very quietly, 'that it would be reasonable enough to leave a young widow such as Helen for a full year to mourn, before making her a proposal of marriage?'

Elizabeth moistened her lips, the polishing cloth dropping from her fingers.

'I'd say that it's a terrible thing to think of a wedding when you're in the presence of death. I'd say you should think shame of yourself for talking like that!'

His eyes glittered at her. 'It's well seen, Elizabeth, that you have no notion of the grip love can have on a man.'

'Promise me you'll say nothing to Helen!'

'I promise you this – I'll say nothing of it to her for a year and a day. And you'll say nothing to anyone about what you know.'

He smiled at her faintly, and his face was like a weird mask, with its bright, narrowed eyes and its thin-lipped, humourless smile.

'I never wished ill on Alec – but I did tell you, did I not, that one day Helen would be my own wife?' said Adam, and began to put the books back on the shelves, one by one.

VI

It was considered seemly for a widow to wear black from head to toe and shut herself away in mourning for a year. But within a few weeks of Alec's death, Helen Grant moved to her parents' home with her baby daughter and, chin high, set about taking up the reins of her life again.

'My mother's fair shocked at me, but sitting in that big house with only Alec's family for company would have driven me to the grave myself!' she declared stubbornly, arriving at the Montgomery house one day with the baby.

'Tell me you're no' shocked, Elizabeth,' she begged. Elizabeth was shocked, but a look at Helen's lovely face, thinner and sharper since she returned from Edinburgh after burying her young husband, told her that the widow was fighting grief in her own way, the tears not far behind those wide, luminous eyes.

'Of course not!'

Catherine, angelic in a blue woollen dress and pantalettes, snarled balls of wool contentedly on the hearth between them, quite unaware of the tragedy that had hit her life. She picked up a ball, toddled to her mother with it. Helen received it with a brilliant smile.

'You see, Elizabeth, Alec was so full of – of life. I could never betray him by sitting in that dark house, letting Catherine here feel the misery of it all around her. I'm not going back. I'll stay here, in Paisley.'

'What about Alec's inheritance?'

Helen blinked rapidly. 'I'll not buy it with my baby's happiness. It was the finish of her father, and Alec's brothers can take it for all I care. I'll support my bairn and myself in my own way. It's a ploy I was thinking of before – before Alec went to Edinburgh. A way of getting the three of us back to Paisley. A sweetie shop.'

As Elizabeth stared at her, stunned, she burst into shaky laughter.

'You should see the look on your face! I'm serious, Elizabeth. I was always good at making confectioneries. It's the only thing I'm good at. There's a wee shop for rent in George Street, and if my father'll lend me the money to start, I might be able to pay my way.'

Her brown eyes, darker than Elizabeth's, were fixed imploringly on her friend. 'I need to keep myself busy,' she sounded almost desperate. 'I know fine that my mother thinks I should have hopes of finding some other man to support me and Catherine after a suitable time. But how could there ever be anyone else for me but Alec?'

Her voice broke on his name, and she fought to control her trembling mouth. At that moment Adam, who had come in unnoticed, said from the doorway, 'Helen!'

Helen's face blurred, dissolved. Tears filled her eyes and she stood up, said, 'Oh – Adam!' and went to him. His arms were waiting for her.

Catherine's rosebud mouth drooped uncertainly, she gave a little whimper. Elizabeth scooped her up, holding the warm solid little body close as she watched Adam and Helen over the baby's fair curls.

Adam held Helen tightly as she wept into his shoulder. He murmured soothingly to her, with that rare tenderness he had shown in the Maxwellton house, when he was reassuring the consumptive child.

But now there was a hunger, a male longing that fluttered Elizabeth's heart and dried her throat.

Catherine's whimper broke into a wail, and she struggled to reach her mother. Helen drew away from Adam and his arms released her with great reluctance. Smiling through her tears, she took the baby and sat down, searching in her reticule for a handkerchief.

Adam seated himself close to her, his face taut with concern.

'I promised myself I'd not cry like that.' Helen mopped her eyes vigorously. 'It was seeing you, Adam, and minding the times the three of us had those past few weeks. Well, mebbe it did me good, just this once, but no more!'

She put the handkerchief away and pinned the bright smile on her face once more. Weeping didn't redden her eyes or blotch her skin. Her dark eyes were dewy and her mouth soft.

'Adam, I'm glad you arrived, for I'd like your opinion of my plans as well.'

Elizabeth watched him closely as Helen spoke about the shop and her determination to support herself and her daughter. Shock and anger raced across his face, and when Helen had finished he said explosively, 'A shop? You? For any favour, Helen, you're far too – fragile – to take on such a responsibility. If it's money you need—'

His reaction swept away the last trace of tears.

146

Helen's red hair seemed to take on a fiery look, her mouth firmed.

'Adam Montgomery, you're as bad as the rest of them. There's no reason why I shouldn't work for my money, like Elizabeth.'

'Elizabeth,' said Adam icily, without looking at her, 'is used to it. It's different for her.'

'And why?' Helen asked before Elizabeth could start to defend herself indignantly. 'The only difference between us is that she's got more courage and sense than I have. Whether you like it or not, Adam, I'm going to have my wee shop. And you needn't feel obliged to patronise it!'

'Wait a minute!' he said swiftly as she put Catherine on the floor and started to rise. 'If your heart's set on this ploy then I'd never want to stop you. It's just—' He put his hand over hers. 'Will you promise me one thing? If it's too much for you, will you tell me and let me help you?'

Helen paused, the anger dying out of her face. She removed her fingers from beneath his and patted his hand lightly.

'Of course I will. But I'm determined that it'll work. I hear that you're planning to stay on here after all?' she added as she scooped her daughter up and prepared to go.

'You're not the only one to make a fresh start.

I'm looking for an office in the town – for a while, anyway.'

'I'm glad,' Helen said sincerely. 'It'll be good to have friends near me at a time like this.'

The door had scarcely closed behind her when Adam said savagely, 'How much of this stupid idea came from you?'

Elizabeth stared at him, anger bubbling up in her.

'If you mean the shop it was Helen's idea, not mine. She's well able to think for herself!'

'But not able to take on work like that!'

'I don't see why not!'

They were still in the hall, glaring at each other.

'Just because you're too independent to contemplate marriage with a mere male it doesnae mean that Helen has to be encouraged to think the same way!'

'Helen has a mind of her own. It's time you realised, Adam Montgomery,' Elizabeth told him tartly, 'that some women do, in Scotland!' And she flounced off to the kitchen, leaving him to his own thoughts.

There was little reason for Paisley people to celebrate the start of 1832. There were still too many skilled men out of work, and each day, it seemed, a cholera cloud was rolling across the grey skies towards the town.

Edinburgh's first case was reported in January. The capital was a considerable distance away but it was said that the disease travelled through the air, which meant that it could travel faster than a horse or a boat.

Adam, still searching for a suitable office, put his name onto the town's medical register. Subscriptions were being raised so that those who couldn't afford to pay for disinfectants, medicines, and medical treatment could get help. Adam, working in the hospital, would receive some form of payment from these subscriptions and the poor-rates, though it would be little.

The only cheerful, optimistic member of the household was James, who had been invited to send more work to the London publisher. He was waiting for a letter from the man, and as the only person he could confide in was Elizabeth a lot of his spare time was spent in the kitchen, where he talked and she patiently listened.

'It's the waiting that's bad. I'd leave for London tomorrow if I got just one poem accepted.'

'And what would you live on?' She chopped vegetables with practised speed.

'I'd live on crusts and water, and sleep on the

pavements if need be,' the young poet said dramatically.

'You're daft!'

He laughed. 'Just ambitious. Writers have to suffer a bit to make them better at their craft. A wee bit starving would do me no harm. I've never suffered in my life, now that I think of it. Look at poor Rob Tannahill.'

Tannahill, a weaver and the most famous of the town's many poets, had drowned on the town's outskirts some twenty years before.

'From what I heard, he was a lonely soul, and crossed in love.' Elizabeth sniffed as the onion she was slicing stung her eyes.

'I've never even been in love – not really.' James sounded gloomy. 'I'll have to break my heart – and suffer a bit into the bargain. Then I'll write my best stuff, or mebbe even paint a fine picture.'

'Your father would just think it a waste of time – and leave that bread alone!' She slapped his fingers from the warm loaves from the oven.

'My father'll be proud of me once I'm a well-known literary figure. And you can be my house-keeper, if you like.'

He went off to his duties in the warehouse, whistling cheerfully. Elizabeth finished the vegetables and began to roll out pastry, her mind on

James. She had no doubt that he would succeed as a poet. He was the gentlest of the family, but he had the Montgomery determination that dominated his father and brothers.

'What a place!' Adam threw the inner door open and erupted into the kitchen, scowling. 'I was just in the Coffee Rooms at the Cross, and one idiot with all his brains in his paunch had the impertinence to tell me that Paisley could never be affected by the cholera. An industrious, pious town, he called it. A God-fearing community protected from harm by Divine right!'

He hurled his big frame into a chair, and Elizabeth sighed inwardly as she realised that her peaceful afternoon was to be interrupted again.

'They only need to open their eyes and look around—' he ran his fingers through his hair. 'The streets are filthy, half the folk not fed properly, a fair number of them in rags – and the river's a sewer. D'you know what I heard of yesterday? Nine folk living in one room in George Street. No furniture, no blanket – scarcely any rags between them. How can they miss any disease that arrives, poor devils!'

Adam had a way of making Elizabeth feel that she should be able to improve the town single-handed. Scattering flour on the table, thumping the dough into a ball, she said defensively, 'But you've got to remember that to the Council and the gentry, there's no place in the world but Paisley. They'd never acknowledge its faults. I sometimes think that the Bailies believe that when the Lord himself dies he'll come to Paisley—'

She stopped, her own words ringing in her ears, and dropped the bowl of flour, clasping her hands to her scarlet face, horrified by her own blasphemy.

After an astonished look at her, as though he hadn't been able to believe his ears, Adam howled with mirth, deep genuine peals that rolled about her shamed head as she stood rooted to the spot, flour all down her apron and the bowl, still intact, rolling by her small feet. He laughed until he had to mop the tears from his cheeks, while Elizabeth scrabbled for the bowl and keened over the mess on the floor, half-convinced that she was going to be struck down by a bolt of lightning for her impudence.

'There's still hope for you, lassie – for all that you live in a mausoleum like this.' He wiped his eyes and took the bowl from her. 'God, Elizabeth, you're a certain cure for a sore heart!'

'Look at the floor!' Her voice shook and she turned away hastily, fumbling for the broom in the corner. Adam took it from her.

'You'll just make flour fly all over the place. Here – I'll see to it.'

She stood looking down on his dark head as he knelt and deftly blotted up the flour with a damp cloth. Then he straightened and began, gently, to brush the clinging powder from her clothes. His touch was light and efficient, but suddenly she realised that her skin was burning beneath the sturdy, plain material that separated it from Adam's fingers. Warmth rose to her face and she tried to pull away, confused and embarrassed. He caught her shoulders and made her stand still, his eyes intent as he worked. Then he looked at her face, and his own features crinkled into laughter again.

'Lassie, you're like a barber's pole with half your face white from flour and the other half red. Stand still, now—'

She closed her eyes as his finger-tips moved over her mouth. Then to her horror she felt two tears ease their way beneath her lowered lashes.

'Elizabeth?' His voice was warm, concerned. 'There's no need to take on like that over some spilled flour. The bowl's no' even broken.'

'It's not – it's—' How could she tell him what was wrong, when she didn't know herself? How could she explain that since he had arrived in the

153

house she was no longer sure of herself or anyone else?

Adam, typical man, misunderstood. 'It's about what you said?' He folded her into his arms and for a precious moment she leaned against his shoulder, savouring the wonder of close contact with another human being, the hardness of his chest beneath her cheek, the strength of him, the rumble of his voice just above her head.

'Elizabeth, the words weren't spoken in malice. You'll have to learn that a quick wit's a blessing, no' a sin!'

Then, too soon, he was holding her at arm's length and laughing again, this time at the white smear her cheek had left on his green jacket.

The comfort of that embrace was stored away in her memory, together with the light kiss he had given her on the night of Matt's wedding. Adam, that abrasive, impatient, quick-tempered man, had somehow managed to show her that close contact with another person was sweet. He had set up a restlessness in her, a yearning that could bring her nothing but dissatisfaction; she had the sense to realise that. Perhaps one day she would find some- one to fulfil the new need in her – in the meantime, she tried hard not to think of it.

Soup kitchens were set up, and she volunteered

her help in the kitchen near the Montgomery home, at Town-head. She was shocked to find how much need there was for charity in Paisley. Each day there was a long line of men, women and children waiting patiently, and Elizabeth grew to be ashamed of her own rounded face and clear, healthy skin as she served bowls of broth to people with grey faces and helpless, hopeless eyes. She began to realise why Adam was so bitter in his attacks on well-fleshed citizens.

In the second week of February a hawker living near the river fell ill and died of cholera the following day. A woman living nearby was next to know the dreaded symptoms. Then a warper fell sick – a carter – a flesher's assistant – another carter. All at once Paisley was under attack and panic raced through the streets.

Flaming tar barrels flickered eerily on house walls at night as they were carried through the streets to cleanse the air. The street cleaners fought to keep the gutters clear, but the familiar stench of rotting waste remained, now mingled with burning pitch. Suspect houses were white-washed, clothes fumigated, the bodies of cholera victims sprinkled with vinegar before burial. The Council decided that a large open stretch of land at the Moss, on the outskirts of Paisley, should be used for cholera burials.

Almost at the moment the disease struck Paisley the House of Commons was deliberating an Anatomy Bill which would, if carried, permit anatomists to use dead bodies. Reports of the Bill fuelled rumours that local doctors were allowing poor people to die of the disease so that they could dig the bodies up from the Moss and dissect them. Now and then mobs of terrified people prevented physicians from reaching patients, or stopped the funeral van on its way to the Moss. One woman was said to have paid some boys to dig up her sister's body as proof that the physicians hadn't substituted a coffin weighted with stones. Some three years earlier the notorious Burke and Hare case had electrified Edinburgh, and in Paisley suspicion and terror prowled the streets hand in hand.

'Fear gives folk strange notions,' Adam said wearily as he dragged himself from his bed after a few hours' sleep. 'They'd be better advised to think on what causes the sickness and how they can stop it.'

His face, in those terrible, hurried first days, was bleak and furrowed with new lines carved into the flesh. Elizabeth, scarred by her work in the soup-kitchen, could understand why he felt increasing bitterness towards those who had more than they needed and ignored the fact that others not a stone's throw away were in desperate straits.

'You're all lucky that they're too ignorant or too defeated to think of doing something about it,' he said one night when he and his father had been arguing over the supper table. 'Want can make a man dangerous. Look at France.'

Rab's mouth twisted. 'The time for that's long by. I should know – I was one of those who thought that if most of the people wanted reform, they'd get it. I was a hot-headed fool. What have I to show for it? A crippled leg, and the country no' much better, for all the fine talk in London.'

'It'll happen again. And the next time mebbe the workers'll be better led and more able.'

'You're havering!' Rab snapped, and Adam subsided, though there was a cynical look in his blue eyes.

Frost whitened the ground and set Jean crying over the pain of chilblains on her toes and fingers. Elizabeth was busy rubbing them with chalk dipped in vinegar one grey afternoon when Rab, who had come home early and settled himself in the parlour, crashed without warning into the kitchen and out again, on his way to the outside privy.

Jean screamed, startled, and knocked the bowl

of vinegar over. Mopping up the mess and scolding the girl, Elizabeth was aware of a trickle of ice down her spine. It wasn't like her employer to sit at home during daylight hours. He had refused food, and had chosen to huddle by the parlour fire, which was lit for him, with a bottle of brandy by his side.

He was gone for so long that she was almost out of her mind with worry by the time he came back into the house, his big red face now greyish and fallen in.

'Are you all right, Mister Montgomery?'

He glanced at her with bloodshot eyes. 'You mean, have I got the cholera?'

Jean whimpered, and he rounded on her. 'Hold your noise, girl! And you too—' he whirled back at Elizabeth, breathing hard. 'You know fine that the sickness wouldnae come to a house like this! It's only in the old part of the town they're visited by it!'

That wasn't true, and they all knew it. Cholera had already begun to poke an inquisitive finger into areas where cleanliness and comfort reigned. But neither Jean nor Elizabeth had the courage to say so.

Rab swung his lowered head from one girl to the other and Elizabeth was reminded of an old bull at bay. 'I've got a chilled stomach from standing talk-ing too long in the street,' he said ponderously, then added, 'I'll away to my bed. You can bring a hot bottle and a basin – and more brandy!'

The door slammed behind him.

An hour later Elizabeth was really frightened. Rab was undeniably worse, though when she tried to question him about his symptoms he roared at her to get out of the room.

'No wonder I'm ill with the likes of you pester-ing me!' He clutched at the blankets and looked alarmingly small and insignificant in the big marriage bed. 'Out – and dinnae come back! I'll cure myself!'

She fled to the kitchen and drew a shawl about her shoulders.

'Jean, I'll have to go to the hospital to fetch Adam.'

The girl's normally blank face was ashen and filled with fear. 'Is it—?'

'Of course not!' Elizabeth managed to put conviction into her voice. 'It's a chill, as he says. But he's getting old, and it's best to let Adam deal with him. Now – keep an eye on that soup pot and see to the potatoes. I'll be back soon.'

Cold air stung her face as she ran, slipping on frosty stones, to the cholera hospital at Oakshaw. It

159

was an uphill journey and her breathing tore at her throat by the time she got there. The ambulance wagon was rattling and bumping away from the door when she arrived, and there was a constant stream of people passing in and out of the hospital.

She had never been inside before. There was a chilly ante-room, where a few people stood talking softly, some weeping. The place smelled of vinegar and turpentine and spirits of camphor, all used to fumigate the town. There was nobody who could direct her, so Elizabeth went on through the double doors and found herself in a huge room packed with beds.

The smell of death and disease was new to her. So was the noise – a continual chorus, strangely muted, of moans and harsh breathing and sobs, with now and then a voice suddenly lifted in delirium or anguish. A group of men stood talking near the door, and she saw to her relief that one of them was Adam.

As though her look had disturbed him he glanced at her absently and turned away. Then his head was raised sharply and he looked at her again. With a swift word to the others he made his way among the beds to get to her.

'What do you think you're doing here!' Without waiting for an answer he seized her arm and ran her from the ward into the ante-chamber. She had only time to glimpse one blue, skeletal face on a grey pillow as she was hurried past. A brief glimpse, but one that she would never forget. The eyes were sunken and the mouth hung open. She had heard Asiatic cholera described as the blue cholera. Now she knew why.

Mercifully, she wasn't given time to dwell on what she had seen. Adam stopped, swung her to face him, his eyes blazing down at her.

'You've got no right to be here! You could catch the sickness just by being in here, d'you no' realise that?'

'It's your father!' she almost shouted at him, and the blood drained from his tired face.

'God help us! Wait here, I'll be back.'

She waited, watching the flow of relatives, physicians, ministers and priests. She turned away when a patient was brought in, arms and legs lolling. A young woman, screaming and cursing, her face wet with tears, clutched at the sick man and had to be pulled away. Elizabeth swallowed hard as the ward doors closed behind the small party. She hadn't realised that people like Adam spent hour after hour in such a place. Even her vivid imagination hadn't prepared her for this brief sight of reality.

He re-appeared and hurried her out of the hospital into fresh air, dragging her after him so fast that her feet stumbled over the rough footpath and she had to clutch at him to remain upright. As they went he shot out questions and she managed to find the breath to answer.

'And did you manage to give him anything?' he asked as they finally reached the house.

'Thirty drops of laudanum in brandy and water, as you told me.'

'That's good.' They went into the hall and his hand rested briefly on her shoulder before he raced upstairs. She leaned on the newel post at the foot of the stairs to regain her breath and calm the trembling in her knees. It was a full minute before she realised that the house smelled of burning food.

The soup pot was still on the fire, black and sticky. Jean had disappeared. Almost in tears, Elizabeth peeled the potatoes and began to clean the burned pot.

She was still working at it, attacking it viciously and wishing that it was Jean she had between her hands, when James arrived home.

His cheerful smile died when she told him about his father and he was on his way upstairs before she had finished speaking. He came back a few minutes later and dropped into a chair at the kitchen table, staring at the scrubbed, grained surface intently.

'Adam says there's nothing I can do. I felt so useless and helpless, standing there. The old man looks – he looks as if he's dying—' His voice trembled.

'He probably looks a lot worse than he is,' she said, as much for herself as for him. 'James, the dinner's wasted, but if you wait a half hour I'll have something ready for you.'

He shook his head. 'I couldnae eat a thing.' One finger went out to trace a crack in the table. His head was still lowered. 'It's funny – I've miscalled him so often, and now I wish I'd cut my tongue out instead. Ever since Adam came back I've been thinking and talking of moving to London. I've never given my father a thought. I never realised that with Matt away, he needs me.' He attempted a shaky laugh, and failed. 'This is a fine time to start feeling guilty – when the man might be at death's door—'

The words shot up a few notes and he stopped abruptly, covering his eyes with his hand.

'James—' She went over to him and he rested his head on her shoulder with a natural movement, his arms going about her.

'I've been selfish. I'll promise you this, Elizabeth

– if he gets better, if he escapes the cholera, I'll stay and I'll work in the warehouse for as long as he needs me! And I'll never complain about my life again!'

'You're over quick to go promising your youth away for his sake,' Adam said dryly from the door, where he stood surveying them.

They jumped apart like guilty lovers. 'Is he—?' There were tears in James's eyes, and he made no effort to hide them.

'He's ill – but I've no way of knowing yet just what's wrong with him.'

'What about Matt?' Elizabeth suddenly remembered. Adam gave her a swift glance.

'If the man upstairs has the cholera, then for Isobel's sake as well as his own Matt should stay away. If he hasnae got the cholera, there's no sense in frightening Matt. We can fetch him later, if we need him. James, I thought you were going off to some literary meeting?'

'I'll stay here, just in case he wants me.'

Adam lifted an eyebrow. 'He's never wanted any of us much in the past, and he's no' likely to begin now, for all that he thinks he's on his death bed. You're too soft with him, waiting about here for news.'

James looked at his brother challengingly

through a curtain of tears. 'Haven't you got a theatre appointment yourself?'

Adam's brows came down and his gaze, for once, faltered before his brother's. 'Aye – well, I'm a physician. We're noted for our stupidity,' he said gruffly. 'Elizabeth, do you think you could have some food on that table within the hour? I'm starved.'

When he re-appeared he threw the meal down his throat without seeming to notice what he was eating, then disappeared upstairs again. Elizabeth and James kept each other company, scarcely speaking, and listening intently for sound from above, until late at night Adam reappeared, looking exhausted.

'I think the old fool's right – it's a chill and mebbe something he ate as well,' he announced. A radiant smile broke over James's face.

'By God – we might have known that the cholera wouldn't dare to set foot in Rab Montgomery's house!' he whooped, and threw his arms around Elizabeth, lifting her off her feet and whirling her round. Adam watched unsmilingly.

'I'll sit with him for a wee while—' Elizabeth offered hurriedly when James released her.

'No, I'll do it, Adam.'

'I'll do it myself, just to make sure that he's all

right. I'll call the two of you if I need you. Where's the lassie?'

'She's gone, and I've no notion where.'

'She's probably taken to her heels at the first thought of the cholera in the house.' He locked the back door. 'She'll no' be back tonight. Get to bed, the pair of you.'

They went, obedient as two well-behaved children. As she went upstairs Elizabeth heard the bolts being shot on the front door. Brushing out her hair, staring solemnly into her own mirrored eyes, she felt a sense of security. Adam was under the same roof, and nothing could go wrong. She yawned, and the glass reflected a pink tongue, small white teeth, a face pretty in its contentment, framed by thick brown curls of shining hair.

Adam was eating bread and butter in the kitchen when she went downstairs in the morning. He had changed his clothes, and looked rested. He had lit the fire and the kettle was steaming softly.

'He's well,' he assured her before she could speak. 'He had a chill that might have carried off a weaker man, but he'll be fine after a day in bed. You're going to have trouble getting him to keep off the drink and eat the right food.' He grinned. 'I don't envy you. Make me a decent meal before I get back to the hospital.'

He sat down to breakfast with enthusiasm, after making sure that his father was still sleeping.

'I chapped James's door on my way down. He'll have to get to the warehouse soon if he's going to take over from the old man.' He attacked a huge bowl of porridge, well salted and awash with milk. 'It's all right for laddies like him, lying abed till all hours. Away and tell him I'll be up with a stoup of cold water if he's no' down by the time I finish this.'

Smiling, Elizabeth went upstairs. James was well known for his dislike of early rising. She tapped on the door, then opened it slightly and put her head round it.

'If you don't get up now Adam's going to—' The words died on her lips. In the glow of the lamp she carried James looked ghastly as he struggled to sit up in bed. The sheets were tangled about him, the pillow on the floor, and his eyes were large and bright in a waxen face that was only a poor copy of the James that she knew.

'Elizabeth—' his voice was a harsh whisper. 'I'm – I'm feared I'm no' very well this morning—' said James, and fell back, his body suddenly convulsed in a spasm that made the whole bed rattle on the floor.

Clutching the lamp in numbed fingers and

remembering, even in her panic, that she mustn't waken her employer, Elizabeth flew downstairs, her feet skimming the treads. She didn't have to speak when she opened the kitchen door. Adam looked up, smiling – then the spoonful of porridge on its way to his mouth dropped back onto the plate and he pushed past her, out of the room while his chair was still rolling about the floor.

There was no doubt at all about what was wrong with James. Elizabeth, back in the bedroom and holding the lamp for Adam, could tell by the flat hardness of his eyes that he held out little hope for his young brother.

He worked swiftly, efficiently, giving crisp orders to Elizabeth, who followed them without stopping to think. She brought cans of hot water, emptied pails, soaked strips of flannel in warm water and helped to wrap them about James's limbs, now racked by cramps.

'You shouldnae be here,' Adam said once, suddenly noticing her as their hands met across the bed. 'You could catch it yourself.'

'I'll be fine,' she rapped back, then straightening to push a lock of hair from her damp forehead with the back of her wrist she remembered the other invalid. 'What about your father?'

'I forgot about him.' Adam massaged his

brother's hands, his gaze fixed on the sick man's face. 'You'll have to see to him – get word to Christian to come and look after him. And let Mister Stewart know about this. James is his patient when all's said and done.'

'Will I tell your father about James?'

'Tell him the truth – there's no sense in molly-coddling the man!' he suddenly flared irritably, and she fled.

Rab was still asleep, and looking a little better. Elizabeth found a passing youngster willing to carry messages, and Christian and the doctor were there before Rab woke.

Christian demanded to see James, but Adam refused to let her go upstairs.

'There's enough of us in danger,' he said from the top landing, his shirt rumpled and his big hands hanging helplessly by his sides for the moment. 'You'd be of more use if you'd take my father off to your own house and leave us in peace.'

'What about Matt? Have you thought to tell him?'

Adam rubbed a hand over his face. 'Mebbe you could see to that too, Christian. But tell him to keep away – he's got enough to worry him without taking sick and passing it to Isobel.'

'He'll want to see his brother!' she objected, and his eyes sparked blue fire at her.

'Damn it, woman, James isn't wasting away prettily of some easy condition! I doubt if Matt would want to see what the cholera's made of the laddie. And you can tell him that if he sets foot over this front door before I send for him I'll throw him back out myself!'

'Well!' squawked Christian in outrage, and flounced into the parlour.

'You'd no cause to speak to her like that!' Elizabeth said hotly, halfway up the stairs. He rounded on her and she stood her ground. 'She's only trying to think of the right thing to do.'

The heat went out of his eyes. 'Mebbe. But she has no idea what's happening up there.' He jerked his head in the direction of his brother's room. 'You should go off to Christian's house too. You'd be safe there.'

His shoulders lifted in a slight shrug when she shook her head. 'It's your own choice. Best see to the old man, then,' he said, and went back into the room where Allan Stewart, the family physician, watched over James.

Elizabeth thought at first that Rab was going to collapse when he heard the news. He stared at her, his face reverting back to the grey sheen it had had the day before. Then he swore and tried to push past her to the door, still in nightshirt and bare feet.

'Adam says you cannae go in, Mister Montgomery—' She caught at his arm and he threw her off, roaring:

'You'll no' tell me what to do in my own house, you slut! You'll take orders from me alone, or you'll go back to the poors' house you came from!'

'Hold your tongue!' an icy voice interrupted him. Adam, eyes wild in a stony face, filled the doorway. 'D'you no' think the lad's got enough trouble without you screaming all over the house?'

Rab's grey hair was standing up in stiff peaks and his cheek-bones burned like red lamps, incongruous against the pallor about them. 'Take James to the hospital – now!'

Adam's chin came up and he spread his arms, putting a hand on each side of the door-frame and physically blocking his father's way. 'He'll stay here. I'll no' allow anyone to take him to that place if I can help it. I can tend him myself.'

'Damn you for a wooden-headed idiot – will you do as I tell you!' Rab roared, trying to force his son aside. But he was weak from his own illness, and Adam was determined. He stayed where he was and Rab, after a futile, humiliating struggle to move him, had to fall back, coughing and gasping with weakness and rage.

'You're a manufacturer, father, no' a medical man. You didnae like it when I tried to tell you who you should employ.' There was open contempt in Adam's eyes. 'Now you can keep your nose out of my business.'

'You—' Rab's voice broke. To her horror Elizabeth saw tears glisten on his cheeks. Adam was unmoved.

'Get dressed, and get yourself out of here. Christian's waiting for you, and you're only a hindrance to me,' he said curtly. 'You're sick and you're raving, and you're too damned old and pig-headed to be of use at a time like this.'

A finger jabbed him in the back, and he jumped, startled, and stepped aside. Christian Selbie swept into the room and went to Rab, her arms going around him much as Elizabeth's had gone around James a few hours earlier.

'Rab – you're no' well, and you're upset.' Her voice was surprisingly gentle. 'Put some warm clothes on, and you and me'll drive up to Oakshawhill – leave the physicians to see to James.'

He turned away, head down, and fumbled for the clothes over the back of a chair. His shoulders shook, and he moved like a very old man. Christian pushed Adam and Elizabeth out of the room and closed the door. Her faded blue eyes were sharp and hard as she looked up at her young cousin.

'If you're going to tell me I should have stayed down below, save your breath,' she snapped. 'Rab needs someone of his own generation with him now. I'll wait here until he comes out, then I'll take him away. And I'll tell you this, Adam Montgomery,' she added, the ribbons on her bonnet trembling with anger. 'You're a hard-tongued, merciless man. May God forgive you for talking like that to your own father!'

A curious blankness came over his eyes. The anger disappeared, and all at once looking at him was like looking into windows made of dark blue glass that reflected what they saw, and showed nothing of what was on the other side.

'If you saw James now, you'd know that God's forgiveness doesn't exist,' he said, his voice flat, and turned away.

Christian sighed as the door of James's room opened just wide enough to admit Adam, then closed.

'What's happening to this family?' She looked years older now that the anger was gone. 'Is James bad, Elizabeth?'

'Aye.'

Christian blinked fast. 'Adam's wrong – there is a God, but at times I find him a difficult sort of creature to follow. You'll send word if anything—'

Her voice faltered. 'Aye, I will. You'll mind that Mister Montgomery should just eat mild foods today, and keep away from spirits?'

'I'll take good care of him. You've got a generous heart, lassie.' Her hand patted Elizabeth's cheek. 'You'd need it – to take on James and Adam at the moment. I'm glad Adam's got you by his side. He mebbe seems strong, but the strongest men are the very ones who need someone when the bad times arrive.'

Mister Stewart agreed with Adam. James was as well in his own home, and there was nothing more to be done apart from the treatment Adam was giving. Adam steadfastly refused to try cold baths, blistering, or bleeding.

'He's suffering enough, and I know they do little to help. I'd as soon try to keep him comfortable, if I can.' He looked down at the figure on the bed, and the older man picked up his bag.

'I've got my own doubts about those fancy cures. You'll call me if I'm needed?'

After that they were alone, the three of them – and the cholera. Elizabeth found herself thinking of the disease as a being, an entity that occupied its own space as surely as she occupied hers. It was a personal enemy, and it had chosen James as its battlefield.

They watched over him throughout the day. Life was an island, with only the three of them on it; but James scarcely counted as a person now. He had gone, leaving a small, shrunken, old effigy of himself in his narrow bed.

Going into the parlour to get more brandy at some time in the day Elizabeth glanced from the window at the unreal life outside the house, and saw Matt. He stood huddled against a doorway opposite, trying to keep out of the wind, waiting.

She went to the front door, moving quietly so that Adam didn't hear her. Matt hurried across the street, skipping in front of a cart-horse. His face was blue-red with cold, his teeth chattering: he could hardly speak.

'Is it bad?'

'Adam says it is.'

'Can I no' see him?' he begged.

'You could catch it yourself, or infect Isobel. Adam's right, you have to keep away.'

For a moment she thought he was going to push her aside and force his way into the house.

'Think about Isobel, and the bairn, Matt. Think what you might take home to them!'

He stopped with one hand on the door, then nodded and turned away. At the last moment she saw the tears welling into his eyes. He went back across the road, moving slowly and stiffly, and she closed the door.

As the afternoon drew on James quietened and seemed to become easier. Adam had at last agreed to snatch a few hours' rest, and Elizabeth watched alone over the invalid, noting that the cramps had gone, and his moaning breath was calmer.

She began to hope for a recovery, but when Adam came back into the room he took one look at his brother and shook his head.

'It's just the next stage. His body's collapsed. At least he doesnae feel anything now.'

'He can still get better?'

He gave her the ghost of a smile. 'Poor Elizabeth. He's as good as dead now.'

She got up, fists clenched, ready to fight tooth and nail for James's life.

'How can you know?' she hissed at him, and he lifted his shoulders again in that faint, tired shrug.

'I've seen it more than once. D'you think I haven't hoped for a miracle, just like you? But I've learned that it won't happen.' He stood by the bed, looking down at his brother's still figure. 'My own fiancée died just like this. That's when I learned that hoping's for fools.'

'Adam—' Her immediate reaction was one of sympathy. She reached out a hand towards him, then drew it back as his face hardened and his eyes narrowed.

'I've no time for sympathy! Folk die, and that's all there is to it!' His voice was a barrier, shutting her out. 'Go to your bed, Elizabeth, it's late, and there's no sense in us both being tired. I'll give you a shout if I need you.'

Rejected, she went to the door. Working together, fighting for his brother's life, they had been drawn together. Now, they were strangers again.

'You'd best sleep in my room—' he ordered as she was going out. 'Then you'll be close at hand.'

She fetched her night clothes, and lay awake in the strange room before sleep rolled in like a black cloud and enveloped her.

She awoke in a fright. The room was lit by a lamp and someone was standing by the bed, looking down at her. With a whimper of fear she sat up, and a hand touched her shoulder.

'It's all right, Elizabeth – it's me.'

She remembered, and pushed the bedclothes

aside, sweeping her long silky hair free of her face, ignoring the fact that she wore only her night-shift. 'Is he worse—?'

He sat on the bed. 'It's all right, lass, there's no more you can do for him.'

She sat still, one hand still smoothing a curl, unable to understand him. Realisation came slowly, probably because she didn't want it to be true. James was a poet, an artist. He deserved something better than an early, terrible ending.

'Can – can I see him?'

Adam's mouth twisted briefly. 'He's gone. I had to send for the funeral cart at once. The rest of them can be told in the morning. I—' He hesitated, then went on, 'I don't want anyone to know just yet.'

'But you cannae just let him—'

'Do you not understand, woman? Folk who die of the cholera have to be buried as soon as possible. There's no time for moping over a bonny-looking corpse!'

He was right, and she was being stupid, she realised that as the last traces of sleep left her mind. She must be practical.

'I'll get his room scrubbed out—' The floor was cold beneath her bare feet.

'In the morning.' His voice was drained of emotion. 'I cannae face any more – I'll have to sleep.'

She could see that he was almost at the end of his strength, emotionally and physically. 'I'll go to my room, and waken you in the morning.'

'Aye.'

At the door she paused. He was still sitting on the bed, his head sunk between his shoulders. His hands, she realised, trembled slightly. She spoke his name softly, afraid to leave him like that, but afraid, too, of provoking one of his outbursts.

He looked up at her, his eyes dark and blank again. His lips parted, just enough to let the words squeeze out, as though against his own inclination.

'Don't – don't leave me on my lone.'

She put the lamp down and went to him, smoothing the tangled black hair back from his brow. His face was cold and clammy with sweat as it was lifted to her. He closed his eyes, put his arms about her, and held her as though afraid that he would be lost forever if he let go.

The early morning street sounds, louder on this floor than they were in the attic, woke her before dawn. She and Adam were clasped closely together on his narrow bed, and her limbs were stiff and cramped.

He was still deeply asleep, and didn't waken when she eased herself slowly and gently from his grip. She rubbed her sore shoulders as she stood looking down on him.

He stirred, mumbled something, threw an arm out so that his fingers touched the floor, but didn't wake. He was still fully dressed. They hadn't spoken after she went into his arms. They hadn't even kissed, she remembered with vague surprise. They had lain on the bed together, Adam's embrace painfully tight, his face pressed into her hair, and they had stayed like that while the trembling in his hands transmitted itself to his whole body, shaking as though he was in the grip of a fever.

Then, slowly, it had eased, his body had relaxed, though his arms retained their hold, and she had been able to tell by his regular breathing that he was asleep.

Soon she would have to waken him. But not just yet. For one thing, she wanted to be respectably dressed, her loose hair brushed and tucked beneath her cap, before she faced him again.

Elizabeth went noiselessly from the room towards her attic, passing the closed door of the room where James Montgomery had once dreamed of a future in London.

VII

Elizabeth could find no tears for James. The horror of his final hours seemed to dry her eyes and polish them into hot stones in her head.

She drew down the blinds in every window but Adam's, muffled the door knocker with black cloth, and went back indoors, ignoring the inquisitive stares and whispers of the few early passersby.

It was only after she had set the table for the morning meal that she realised that there were four places, one for Rab, one for each of his sons.

She was staring stupidly at the cutlery when someone began to pound on the front door. Shocked at such an intrusion on a house of death she hurried to answer.

Matt crashed into the hall, white-faced. 'Is it true what they say? Let me by, Elizabeth, let me see him—'

He pushed her aside and was halfway up the stairs when Adam appeared on the landing. He had brushed his hair and changed into a black coat and dark red trousers.

'There's nothing to see. He's gone to the Moss.'

The cool, clipped tones stopped Matt's headlong rush. He stared up at his brother, then began to retreat down the stairs, step by step, as Adam advanced.

'You should have sent for me! You should have let me be there at the last!'

'For what?' Adam asked with frightening control. He didn't glance at Elizabeth. 'So that you could have talked with him? He wouldnae have heard you. So that you could have seen him? Best remember the way he was. As for self-pity – I'd enough to do caring for James without having a handful of mourners weeping over the living corpse.'

'Where are you going?' Elizabeth asked sharply. He turned, one hand on the door. His eyes were withdrawn, surveying her as they would a stranger.

'To the hospital. There are living folk still waiting for help. You'd best get back to your wife, Matt, instead of grieving round here.'

'Damn you for a cold-blooded—'

'Matt – no—!' Elizabeth tried to catch his arm as he moved swiftly past her, murder in his eyes. He brushed her off, and made for his brother.

Adam side-stepped, ducked, and suddenly Matt was held in an iron grip, cursing furiously as he struggled to free himself.

'You learn all sorts of things on board one of His Majesty's ships,' Adam said breathlessly. He let his brother go, stepped back. Matt stood where he was for a moment, then his hands came up to cover his face.

Elizabeth moved towards him, but Adam stopped her.

'Come on, Matt,' he said, putting one hand on his brother's shoulder and opening the front door with the other. 'We'll walk to Shuttle Street and see Isobel. There are a lot of ways to mourn, you'll learn that in time.'

The door closed behind them, and Elizabeth was glad to be alone as her tears at last began to flow.

With three and four deaths in the town each day from cholera alone, grief was a luxury few families could afford. James had gone, Elizabeth still had to run a house, Adam was busy in the hospital; Rab, grey and sullen when he came back from Christian's, had even more to occupy him at the warehouse, now that he had no sons to share the burden. Routine claimed them all with shocking speed.

Nobody else in the household came down with cholera, but even so Jean refused to return to the Montgomery kitchen. Tibby, the shrew who had assisted Elizabeth on the night of Adam's return, was taken on in her place.

Her triumph was short-lived. Her habit of always being underfoot when she wasn't wanted infuriated Rab.

'I'd like to walk out of a room in my own house without falling over that besom,' he snarled at Elizabeth. 'Mebbe we've got the best polished keyholes in the town since she came here, but keyholes are meant for keys, no' for eyes!'

Elizabeth was glad to oust Tibby. The woman was meddlesome and sour-tongued, and the kitchen buzzed like a bee-hive when she was in it.

It was decided that Elizabeth should choose a girl from the Town Hospital to be trained into the ways of the household. To her relief, Christian agreed to go with her on her errand.

'See and pick a lassie who'll handle the work and keep her opinions to herself,' the older woman advised as the carriage rolled to a halt before the building.

As she stepped into the gloomy entrance hall,

onto the floor she had scrubbed many a time, Elizabeth felt the years falling away. It was a surprise to be greeted with a smile by Mistress Jamieson, instead of being scolded for some misdemeanour. Her past crimes were apparently quite forgotten and she was treated with almost as much deference as Christian, who took charge of the situation.

'An able-bodied lassie, one who knows her Catechism and can keep a still tongue in her head,' she said briskly, as though buying sausages in a butcher's shop.

Her brows rose when Elizabeth opted for a thin, shy girl called Mary.

'There's no' a pick on the lassie!' She eyed the girl's skinny arms.

'She'll manage. And she doesnae need to know her Catechism to know how to bake a good pie,' Elizabeth said firmly, and saw Mistress Jamieson's nostrils flare slightly at her impudence. Christian laughed.

'Well – if you're certain, that's all there is to say. It's your kitchen.'

Elizabeth was certain. There was something about Mary that reminded her of herself on that day Rachel Montgomery had rescued her. Now it was her turn to rescue Mary. She owed somebody something for her good fortune, she thought in a confused way, aware of the envious glances the inmates gave her good blue gown and red-bordered shawl.

Mary arrived the following day, complete with Bible and change of clothing, and Elizabeth set about training her, glad to have a companion now that Rab and Adam were rarely at home.

Cholera still held the town in its grip, and seemed likely to stay for many months. The smell of burning tar barrels was everywhere and not a day went by without the cholera bier being trundled at least once to the Moss for a hurried burial.

Rab, bereft of his two sons, was in sole charge of the warehouse, and had to work long hours. He took to eating his meals in the Coffee House near the river, and when he was in the house every room seemed to be filled with shadows.

Hutcheson's Charity School, where Elizabeth had received her education, had been turned into a cholera hospital, and work was underway on a new hospital in Bridge Street, near to the Dispensary and House of Recovery. Adam was out almost all the time too, and he became obsessed by the need to find out what caused cholera, and how to cure and prevent it.

His training as a physician and as a naval surgeon gave him the right to make up prescriptions, and he began to set up a small laboratory in his bedroom where he could work. He had no time for the pious belief that cholera was sent from Heaven to chastise those who had fallen from grace.

'Nobody's going to tell me that folk like James deserved a punishment like that,' he said, and filled his small rooms with bottles and flasks, jars and packets. Elizabeth and Mary were forbidden access to the room, and they were happy to obey orders. Elizabeth was convinced that he would either burn down the house or poison them all with the strange-smelling, bubbling liquids she sometimes glimpsed over his shoulder if she took food to him. He worked most of the day and then came home and worked far into the night.

He had nothing but mocking scorn for the fast days held throughout the country because of the cholera.

'It would make more sense to give the folk bread, not hunger. It's all very well for the King and those with fat bellies to make a display of fasting to appease the Almighty. They want to think of those who have to do that day in and day out. And what reward do those poor devils get? They die of the cholera,' he said sourly, and was accused by his father of forgetting his Christian upbringing.

James's death seemed to have forced Adam and Rab apart, instead of drawing them together. Elizabeth, a silent, concerned observer, knew that there were times when Adam, exhausted and embittered as he was by the sights he had to endure each day, made an attempt to behave well towards his father; but each time, he was rebuffed.

'Confound the old fool!' he exploded to Elizabeth after Rab had stormed out of the room on one occasion. 'If he wants my civility from now on, let him crawl for it – I've more to do than wonder what's up with him!'

Two weeks after James was laid beneath the cold earth at the Moss Elizabeth was shocked to see his name on a small bundle delivered by the letter-carrier. She stood in the hall staring at the familiar words written in flowing black letters. Tears suddenly stung at the back of her eyes.

Rab was eating his breakfast in the kitchen. She knew that the parcel should be given to him along with his own letters. But as she crossed the hall she thrust it into the pocket of her apron. All morning it lay heavily against her thigh, then Adam came home at noon to write some letters, and she handed it to him.

His mouth tightened as he stared down at his

dead brother's name. 'Should you no' have given this to my father?'

'I couldnae bring myself to do it.'

He shot a swift glance at her. 'You're over thoughtful about hurting his feelings,' he said dryly. 'Wait—' as she turned to the door. She watched as he slit the packet open. It contained a bundle of papers tied with tape, and a letter, which Adam scanned hurriedly.

'It's from that London man. He's returned James's poems. He says they're well written, pleasing, but not quite what's needed.' His mouth grimaced into a mirthless smile as he balanced the bundle of poems on the palm of one large hand. 'The man says he hopes James'll continue to write, and send some of his more mature work one day.'

'He'd have been awful disappointed,' she said without thinking. 'Are you going to give them to your father?'

In answer he bent suddenly and picked up the poker. Before she could stop him he had thrown the bundle into the parlour fire and was holding it down firmly. Even as Elizabeth caught his arm and was shrugged off the paper burst into flames.

'Adam – no!' It was a cry from the heart, unheeded. She watched, horrified, as the sheets curled and peeled away from each other, the tape burned through, and the poems that had taken hours to write disappeared in seconds, turned to ash.

'They belonged to James – you should have kept them!' She could have flown at Adam in her anger.

He dropped the poker and kicked the coals with the toe of his sturdy leather boot. They collapsed inward, covering the last fragments of his brother's work.

'Kept them? For what? Until they turned yellow and old? Who would read them? He had to keep them secret from my father, and poems are wasted on the likes of Matt and me,' he said savagely, his face turned away from her as he stared down at the fire. 'I'll remember James in my own way. I'd as soon destroy the sickness that killed him as sit in comfort and read pretty words!'

On the following day she got back from the market to find him at home, in the room James and Matthew had shared. She stood in the hall, gaping through the door that had not been opened since James's death. 'Adam Montgomery, what do you think you're doing?'

He straightened from the task of pulling the two cots to the back of the room and grinned at her, brushing dust from his hands.

'I'm clearing the place. Fetch a pail and brush, the floor needs scrubbing.'

'But—' She went into the room and watched, open-mouthed, as he began to clear the top of the chest of drawers, stacking books onto the beds.

'I need more room for my laboratory work,' he explained patiently, as though speaking to a child. 'And I need a clean room. There's too much stour in here. Get me some hot water.'

'Did your father say you could do this?'

He gave her a look of sheer exasperation. 'Elizabeth, this room isnae used, so why should he object? And I'll see to him,' he added as she opened her mouth to protest. 'Go and get that pail and brush when you're told, woman!'

It was the voice that reminded her that she was, after all, a servant, and he was her employer's son. Humiliated, frustrated, she did as she was told. For the rest of the afternoon the two of them scrubbed and cleaned until he was satisfied the room was fit to use. Then she began to help him to bring in his glass tubes and bottles, gingerly handling the scientific equipment.

Intent on their work, neither of them even knew Rab had arrived home until he spoke from the doorway.

'What the blazes do you two think you're up to?'

Elizabeth jumped, almost dropping the flask in her hands. Adam took it from her, unmoved by his father's sudden appearance.

'I need more room to set up my laboratory.'

Rab's face set in mulish lines. 'You've already got a room in this house. Be content with that.'

'It's more like a cupboard.'

'If you're no' taken with the accommodation I give you—' Rab began ominously. Elizabeth edged towards the door, but he stood there, unmoving, blocking her way.

Adam's voice was quite easy. 'My own room's fine – for sleeping in. But I need more space for the work I'm doing, and this place is empty. It might as well be put to good use.'

Rab's eyes moved about the room. 'This is my sons' bedroom, no' a laboratory.'

Adam's face flamed, then paled. 'Neither Matt nor James has use for it as a bedroom now.'

Rab's nostrils flared and his cheeks took on a deeper shade of red. 'Well now, Elizabeth—' His eyes fixed on her. 'And you agree with my son here?'

She stared at him, unable to speak. Adam said swiftly, 'I ordered Elizabeth to help me, this has nothing to do with her. You've surely got no objection to me using the place?'

To Elizabeth's relief, her employer's gaze slid from her, back to the surgeon. 'Why not? When the fox digs himself a lair he should be allowed to lie in it, eh?' His voice, soft to start with, ended on a snarl.

'You're speaking in riddles.'

'So – the clever surgeon cannae figure out what I mean? I mean, sir, that you're the one that cleared this room. Matt was contented enough here until you came back with your high ideas. You're the one that encouraged him to go off and marry that lassie. You're the one – and you neednae deny it, for I've got informers all over this town – that got Dan McGill out of the jail and back at his loom. And you're the one—' his voice suddenly shot up, out of control, '—that let my son James die!'

Elizabeth heard herself cry out, but neither of the men looked in her direction. Adam's eyes, sapphires set in white marble, flared wide then narrowed to become blue slits. He spoke through tight, colourless lips.

'You old fool – you're insane!'

'Am I, by God!' Rab lashed out. His stubby fingers closed round the neck of a flask, and he threw it at Adam, swinging blindly so that the missile went nowhere near its target. Instead it hit the wall near Elizabeth, exploding into greenish fragments with a noise that tore through her head. As it struck, Adam's arm flew out, caught her, and swept her across the front of his body to safety, away from the tinkling shards of glass. She was tossed onto one of the beds where she stayed, watching as Rab advanced on his son, one forefinger stabbing the air before him.

'I told you, did I no'? I told you to take that laddie to the hospital when he fell sick. But you saw fit to defy me, the way you've always defied me!'

There was anger, now, in Adam's voice. 'He would have died just the same! And he would have died in the noise and the misery of the place instead of in his own home. You'd have done that to him? You'd have condemned him to a place you've never seen? You don't know what you're talking about!'

Foam flecked the corners of Rab's mouth. His rage filled the room, threatened to burst the walls. Elizabeth, huddled on the bed, could scarcely breathe because the very air was charged with fury.

'Some recovered after they were taken to the hospital. James could have been one of them, if you'd given him the chance!'

'Aye, some recover – but most die, and we've no

way of knowing why. That's why I want to get on with my work!'

Rab's laugh was a weird cackle. 'It's a bit late for that, is it no'? Your brother died of your so-called healing. And now you want to use his room, to try to save the rag-tag out in the streets? D'ye think I give a damn what becomes of them? It's James you should have saved – James! No' these swilling, carousing scum from the gutters!'

There was a moment's silence before Adam spoke. 'So – that's the truth of it, out at last.' He sat down on the other bed, ran his hands over his face. 'That's why you've never been able to look me in the eyes those past two weeks. You thought I'd let my own brother die. All this time, you've let your suspicions fester in you, poison you. Man, you're in sore need of healing yourself.'

Rab's eyes bulged. 'Aye, it's out. You killed him as sure as Cain killed Abel, and I curse you for it, Adam Montgomery. I curse the day you first drew breath!'

'But nobody could have saved James!' Adam said in a sing-song voice, as though to din the fact into a child. 'He had the worst form of the sickness. Nobody's survived it.'

'What gave you the right to decide that while there was still breath in his body?'

Elizabeth saw that there were tears in the old man's eyes. Rab, who had never shown any warmth towards his youngest son in the time she had spent in the house, was totally bereft by his death. If only, she thought drearily, James had been given an indication of that love when he was alive.

'I know fine what I'm talking about.' There was fire in Adam's voice. 'I've seen other people taking the path James took. That's what happened to Caroline.'

If he had hoped for pity, he was disappointed. Rab fixed on the name, used it to punish his son further.

'My, my, Adam, mebbe you're in the wrong profession after all. First your bride, then your brother – you've been letting the folk you love die like fleas, while you—'

The words became a gurgle. Adam surged up from the bed to grip his father by the lapels and lift him, heavy as he was, onto his toes. He shook Rab like a rat, then released him with a contemptuous push. Rab, choking, reeled back as Elizabeth scrambled to her feet.

'Damn you—' said Adam thickly, and swept a box of glass bottles off a nearby table with a wide swing of one arm. The crash echoed through the room and left behind it a tense silence, broken only by Rab's efforts to catch his breath again.

When he did, he ordered, 'Elizabeth – clear up this mess and lock this door!'

'Father—' Adam's clear voice halted him on his way out. 'You think James could have been saved? You didnae see him, towards the end. Tell him, Elizabeth, what it was like.'

'Adam – let it be!' She caught at his sleeve, shaking his arm, but his blue gaze raked her mercilessly before returning to his father.

'Since he's got his own opinions he should know more about it. You'd as soon hide away from the truth about sickness, wouldn't you, father? You know nothing of the cramps, and the convulsions, and the pain that's like a sword being drawn through the body – handle and all—'

Rab's turkey-red face took on a grey tinge. He went into the hall, and Adam, ignoring Elizabeth's tugging at his sleeve, followed him. The surgeon's voice went on mercilessly describing the illness in detail, as Rab went down the stairs to the hall clumsily, catching at the banisters and tripping over the bottom step. Adam stayed at the top of the steps, raising his voice to make sure that his father heard every word. He didn't stop until the front door slammed shut behind Rab.

Then, with the bang of the door, the clear voice was cut short and he stood still, knuckles clenching the wooden rail, head lowered as though his strength had suddenly given out.

Below, Elizabeth heard the kitchen door open and Mary's frightened voice calling her name. She ran down to reassure the child and set her to work on the evening meal that would probably not be required.

Adam wasn't on the stairs when she ventured out of the kitchen. She went into the parlour to make up the fire before tackling the mess in the upstairs room, and found him slumped in Rab's favourite chair, his eyes fixed on the cold, empty grate.

She began to retreat, then made herself stop, twisting her fingers in her apron. 'That was a wicked thing to do to an old man.'

His mouth twisted. 'So you're going to take his side, are you? And what d'you think he did to me?'

'He's grieving. He's no' able to show his sorrow like other folk. He should be pitied.'

'Sometimes, Elizabeth, I think you're wise, and sometimes I think you're a fool. I've never in my life met a mystery like you.' He stood up slowly, stiffly, in a way quite unlike his usual supple movement. 'So you agree with him.'

'I said nothing of the sort! I know fine what you did for James. I was there.'

He considered her for a moment, then the ghost of a crooked smile touched one corner of his wide, well-shaped mouth. 'Aye, you were there.'

Neither of them had ever referred to that night spent in Adam's room. Now, recalling it, she flushed. If Adam thought of it, or saw the sudden colour in her face, he gave no sign.

'That man drives us all away one way or another. I'm leaving, Elizabeth.'

A chill gripped her. 'Where are you going?'

'There's places – I can get a bed at the hospital for the night, or mebbe Christian would take me in.'

His eyes had taken on a curiously smoky grey-blue colour. 'I'm getting out, Elizabeth, and so should you. You'll grow old here, you'll die long before your heart stops beating. You'll be forgotten and you'll become as soured as he is, if you stay with him.'

Her lips were stiff. 'I have no place else to go.'

For all his caring about those less fortunate than he was, Adam knew little about them, she thought. Domestic servants were no longer bound by law to their employers, but they were expected to stay where they found work, unless they were put out. Rab Montgomery was well known in Paisley – his housekeeper would find it hard to get a good place in any other house in the area if she deserted him.

'Poor lassie,' Adam said with sudden gentleness, as though reading her mind. His hand caressed her scarred cheek gently, the palm warm and strong against her skin. 'I'll take you to Christian. Come with me now if you value your happiness.'

She wanted to lean her cheek against the comfort of that warm hand, wanted to walk out of the house with him. But she drew back, shaking her head.

'I made a promise to your step-mother in her last illness. I told her I'd not leave the house. And your father kept me on after she died. I couldnae walk away from him.'

The smoky haze in his eyes hardened to flint.

'My step-mother had no right to make a young girl like you promise her life away!'

'She asked for my word and I gave it to her!'

'He'll never thank you for it!'

'I'm no' looking for thanks. I couldnae live with myself if I broke a promise.'

He laughed shortly. 'So – you'd as soon martyr yourself as break a promise? You know fine the woman was dying. Probably not in her right mind!'

The torment was more than she could bear.

'I've had little kindness in my life—' she rounded on him and saw his eyes widen with surprise. 'So I cannae afford to forget it! Mistress Montgomery was good to me, and I gave her my word knowing what it meant. Mebbe the likes of you can forget a promise, but I never will! And that's an end to it!'

There was a long pause before he spoke again. When he did, his voice was remote.

'Well – you've made your bed. Let you lie on it. Or mebbe that's what's in your mind already?'

She stared at him, puzzled.

His gaze was cold, angry. His voice hardened, ripping and slashing at her. 'Is it the promise you're thinking of, or your own future? A wealthy, lonely man – one son dead, the other two driven away. You could do worse than become a third wife.'

The colour rose slowly, burningly, to her face. She could have struck him down in her rage. Instead she moved back, opened the parlour door.

'You have a foul tongue, Adam Montgomery. Get out of this house – now!'

For the moment his anger matched hers.

'You're a thrawn, stubborn fool of a lassie!' he said, and walked past her. She stood very still until she heard the front door slam behind him, then she wrapped her arms tightly about herself, trying in vain to stop the trembling, and the chill that his going had brought.

Rab made no reference to Adam's departure. On the following morning Elizabeth set the breakfast table for one, and he fed himself silently, as though used to being alone.

She discovered later that Adam had taken himself off to Christian's house on Oakshawhill. Later that morning when she was on her knees busily polishing the hall woodwork he came back for his belongings.

After one quick, impersonal glance at her he led two labourers up the stairs, telling them over his shoulder 'Mind how you step in this house – the mistress is particular.'

Almost spluttering with frustrated rage, she whisked into the kitchen and stayed there with the door shut, listening to the tramp of feet on the stairs as Adam's possessions were taken out. Only when the front door closed with a definite sound did she venture to investigate.

His books had gone from the shelves in the dining-room and all his medical apparatus was cleared from his small room and from the room he had planned to use.

It was as though Adam had never lived under his father's roof.

'What made Adam move into Mistress Selbie's house?' Helen Grant asked with mild curiosity a few days later. She and Elizabeth were hard at work, cleaning up the tiny shop that Helen had found.

She was on her knees, sleeves rolled up, scrubbing a floor for the first time in her life, and enjoying it. Elizabeth was working on the small, dirt-encrusted window panes.

'He needed more room for his work.' Nothing would make her tell the truth.

'He's a strange man, Adam. He comes in here if he's passing, and has a word with me.' She sat back on her heels and scrubbed a dirty hand across her face. 'We might have got wed once, did you know that? But all he could think of was medicine.'

Elizabeth saw Matt hurry past, head down and eyes unfocused as he occupied himself with his thoughts. He was gone before she could tap on the glass.

'I wonder what would have happened if he'd stayed in Paisley?' Helen was musing. 'He was a fine looking lad – not as hard as he is now. But he's had sorrow in his life since then. We all do, sooner or later—'

Her voice trailed away, her head drooped on its long slender neck; then she looked up again, and went back to her work.

'I'm going to have shelves put up over there, and a table about here for serving customers. And my mother's agreed to let me make the sweets in her kitchen just now – uugghhh, beasties!' She snatched up a broom and used it to crush a nest of spiders that she had disturbed in a corner. Watching her, Elizabeth decided that Helen was a more capable and independent young woman than Adam realised.

She didn't see him in the first three weeks after he left his father's house, and as the days went by her anger ebbed away. To see his fiancée and then his brother die so horribly, to be unable to save them, and then to be accused by his father, must have driven him wild with helpless rage.

But his final words on that day echoed again and again in her mind. He was right – she could grow old and soured in the Montgomery house, now a silent and dismal place. Everyone had a future – Helen with her shop, Isobel with her baby, Matt with his work. Only she, Elizabeth, saw her days stretch ahead to the grave without change.

She and Adam finally came face to face in Matt's home just after his son was born. When Elizabeth went to see Isobel on the day after the baby's birth Matt was there, taking time from his loom to gloat over his child. Isobel lay in the wall-bed, the shawled bundle in her arms.

'Be careful—' she admonished anxiously as her husband took the baby. He grinned confidently.

'D'you think I'd ever let anything happen to this wee lad? See, Elizabeth – look at his fingers—' he marvelled over the baby, a doting father.

Elizabeth took the warm solid bundle into her own arms, cradling the sweetness of him against her breast. 'What name do you have for him?'

'I thought it should be Robert,' Isobel began at once, but Matt interrupted.

'And I said I'd never have that man's name in my house! He's to be known as Duncan,' he said firmly. 'It's Isobel's father's name, and it was my great-grandfather's given name too.'

The passage door opened and a familiar voice called.

'We're here, Adam—' Matt shouted back and the baby jumped in Elizabeth's arms at the sudden noise, his alarm masking hers.

Adam's eyes met hers briefly as he appeared in the doorway. 'You're here, Elizabeth,' he said easily, and dropped an unexpected kiss on his sister-in-law's cheek before slapping Matt on the back.

'He's a Montgomery – poor bairn.' He poked a finger at the baby's cheek, his breath stirring Elizabeth's hair as he stood close by her. 'Well, Matt – that's one of your ploys safely seen to; how's the shawl?'

Matt beamed. 'Another two weeks and it'll be ready. Mister Cassidy wants me to take it down to London with him.' He glowed with happiness on that day. There was no more restlessness, no bitterness. Matt had found his place in life.

'You could warm your hands at him,' Adam said as he and Elizabeth left the young family. 'I knew that getting out of the warehouse and marrying Isobel would be the making of him.'

'Do you think Isobel looks too pale?'

'We didnae deal much with childbirth in the navy,' he said dryly. 'She seems fine to me.'

He himself looked well, she thought, darting sidelong glances at him as they walked. Despite his hard work his eyes were clear, his shoulders straight, now that he was away from his father's house. He wore a claret-coloured coat with ruffled shirt and blue striped waistcoat. There were good Hessian knee-length boots of soft black leather on his feet and a smart beaver hat rode his dark head.

He was less discreet in his study of her.

Elizabeth flushed and stared down at the path as he turned and looked her over.

'You're pale yourself. You don't get out enough.'

'I'm out every day.'

'But never for pleasure. I told you, did I not, what would become of you if you stayed in that house?'

She stopped, glared up at him. 'You told me – and I'll hear no more of it!' she said, and walked on, quickly.

He laughed, his long easy strides keeping up with her. 'You're as nebby as ever, anyway. You looked bonny back there, with the bairn in your arms. Have you no notion of children, Elizabeth?'

When she didn't answer, he laughed again. They were passing the little sweet shop Helen had bought, and he automatically stooped and peered through the window. The shop was deserted.

'Are you still angry with me?' he teased, catching up with her again.

'Why should I be?'

'Did you know that when you're in a rage that wee nose of yours quivers?'

She clapped a hand to her face, and he laughed.

'Just a wee bit. It suits you, but when you're trying to be high and mighty it spoils the effect.'

To her relief, they reached the corner of the

street, and their ways divided. Adam put a hand on her arm as she was turning away.

'Remember – I'll always find somewhere for you if you decide to leave that old devil.'

She pulled back from his touch. 'I'm no' a piece of furniture to be shifted from one house to the other by the likes of you – and I'm no' interested in your opinions of a possible marriage for me either!'

Surprise widened his blue eyes.

'Aye – well – I deserve that, for the things I said that night. My apologies, Elizabeth. I was angry with the old man, and angry with you for your loyalty to him when I thought you should have come away with me. But I worry about you.'

'I'm no concern of yours!' she almost shrieked at him. 'I'm a person, can you not understand that? And I'd as soon be a dry old maid in a garret as live with the sort of man you'd choose for me. I have no faith in your tastes!'

She turned to stamp back to his father's house, then whirled back.

'And you can just keep my nose out of your conversation!' she said in a final, confused burst of rage, and saw his astonishment begin to dissolve into amusement before she rushed off, furious with herself, and with him for putting her into such a state.

Christian was delighted to have Adam as a lodger.

'It gives the house a bit of life, having a man about the place,' she crowed to Elizabeth. 'His glass stuff does well enough in the wee conservatory, where my own father kept his tubes and bottles, God rest his soul. Men aye need something to keep them occupied, or they get into mischief.'

She sighed, and scratched her head with one of her knitting wires. 'Whiles I take a wee peek at the stuff, when he's out. I'd have been interested in work like that if I'd just been born a man.'

James used to say that if all Christian's ambitions had been realised she would have been the most experienced and talented Jack of all trades in history.

Matt and Dan finished the new shawl in the middle of March. The new design and new thread excited a lot of interest in the town, but Rab Montgomery remained aloof.

Elizabeth had never seen such a beautiful shawl. The borders were stitched on in reverse, so that when the cloth was folded its jewel-like colouring could be seen to best advantage. The thread was fine, silky, and yet strong and warm. The centre, woven by Matt, was black, and Dan's skilled hands had created deep borders of rich red exotic design, shot through with deeper red, black, green, and tiny flowers of vivid blue.

'It's beautiful, Matt!' Standing in the loom shop she let him drape the shawl about her shoulders. It lay there, wrapping her in luxurious folds, making her feel more elegant and beautiful than ever before.

'And to think that my father could have been the man to have this, if he'd only listened to me,' Matt exulted, then his smile faded, and he said what had been in Elizabeth's mind. 'I just wish James could have seen it – he'd have been proud.'

Isobel came through from the living-room where she had been settling little Duncan in his crib. Matt's sunny smile broke through again at the sight of her.

'But we should only look forward, eh, lass? Did I tell you, Elizabeth, that old Cassidy asked me to come into his warehouse as foreman?'

Reluctantly, she took the shawl off. 'Are you going?'

'He wants to stay at the loom,' Isobel said, her eyes fixed on Matt, her voice soft.

'That's right. We're weaving folk, and that's the way we'll stay. Now that I've proved myself and paid my debts and got a son to follow – I've no need of anything more.'

Laughing, he hugged Isobel then draped the shawl about her and stepped back to admire the way its soft folds covered her shoulders.

But it seemed to Elizabeth that the rich colours only served to make Isobel's skin look paler, her eyes more sunken in her face, and her once rounded, sturdy body thinner.

VIII

I sobel's health continued to deteriorate, and Matt's trip to London was cancelled.

It was as though the baby, large and rosy and healthy, was sucking the life from his young mother along with her milk. Isobel was always tired, she lapsed into long silences, and soon a wet nurse had to be found for Duncan because she couldn't give him enough nourishment.

Matt, desperately worried over her, and behind with his work, had to look after Isobel and the baby as well as his father-in-law, now badly crippled by rheumatism and becoming vague. Elizabeth spent every spare moment at Shuttle Street, caring for Matt's family so that he could snatch some hours at his loom.

Rab Montgomery was as bad-tempered and cantankerous as ever. The only person who could do anything with him was Christian. She, as she told him outright, persevered when any other woman would have given up.

'You've no need to call on me if you've better things to do,' he growled at her.

'Someone has to keep an eye on you. You've made your wealth and your name – be content with that, and sell the business.'

'Sell it – after all the work I've put into it? Woman, you're a fool!'

'And you're a heathen if all you can do is worship money and the making of it. You've years of pleasure ahead of you. A fine wee grandson for a start, and you never clapped eyes on him yet!'

He glared. 'If that's all you've come to say – you can get out!'

She bristled. 'I'll go when I'm good and ready! I swear, Rab, you'd try the patience of a saint.'

'I wouldnae ken about that,' Rab said pointedly, 'since I've never met one.'

'Mebbe you have, but you're too coarse to recognise her,' his cousin rapped back tartly. It was a conversation they had every week; usually Elizabeth and Mary heard most of it in the kitchen, for both Rab and Christian tended to get louder as they grew more exasperated with each other.

Adam took to calling at Matt's home often, and no longer brushed Elizabeth's anxiety aside.

'I'm hoping it's no' childbed fever,' he said gravely as they left the cottage together one afternoon. Her heart turned over.

'It could just be the worry they've had, and her father's health, and the cholera here—' she said swiftly.

He shrugged. 'We'll hope so. When she can get out into the sunshine again it could make a difference.'

Though his mouth smiled at her, his eyes were serious.

To Matt's surprise old Peter Todd refused to take repayment of the loan he had made when Dan was put into prison.

'They say Tom Cassidy's invited you to go into his warehouse.' He looked at the young man shrewdly.

'He did. But I'm just weaving for him.'

'Still – he's no fool, is Tom. I'm thinking that there's a good future for you with him, if ever you decide to leave the loom again. I'll tell you what I'll do – I'll take the interest on my loan, and I'll leave the original amount in your hands. You can give me your signature on a promise of another six months' interest.'

Matt was astounded. Peter wasn't known for his willingness to trust others with his money. The renewed loan gave him the opportunity to employ another plain silk weaver, and as Dan agreed to stay with him, Matt was able to guarantee plain work for the Cassidy house as well as another elaborate shawl to follow the first, which had been snapped up by a London dealer.

The only cloud on his horizon was his wife's health, and that cloud grew until it began to darken his life. Daily he prayed for an improvement, and daily the laughing, plump girl he had married became more of a stranger to him. At times she seemed to be better, but those days grew scarce, and most of the time Isobel barely acknowledged him or her father and baby.

Her first spate of violence took him completely by surprise. Elizabeth and Adam, summoned on a rainy morning, found Matt pale and drawn, and Isobel sleeping peacefully in the wall-bed.

'Mister Falconer's bled her and given her some opium. I was frightened out of my wits during the night.' He rolled up the sleeves of his linen shirt to show them the angry scratches and purpling bruises on his muscular forearms. 'I had to cover her mouth in case her father heard the noise – I damned near smothered her.'

It was hard to believe the story, looking at his wife's calm, pale face on the pillow.

'I got John's wife to take Duncan and the old man in case Isobel woke up in the same mood. I just said that she'd had a restless night and needed to sleep. I couldnae tell the truth—' Matt's mouth softened, trembled, and he rubbed a hand fiercely over his face. 'Adam, if she goes on like that—'

They all knew what it would mean. A room in the Town Hospital, and a strait-jacket. Matt's eyes were filled with nameless horrors as he contemplated such a future.

'I'm at my wit's end – Adam, what am I to do?'

Adam's face was grim, but he tried to sound reassuring. 'There might be a good hospital in Glasgow where they'd help her.'

Matt set his lips stubbornly. 'I'll no' let her be taken from me. It would kill her for sure. D'ye think I could take her and the bairn away to some quiet place? She's aye been fond of the braes, has Isobel. If I could find work on one of the bleach-fields, or a farm—'

'And give up everything you've worked for? Man, you'd never be content!'

'What would that matter?' Matt asked his brother fretfully. 'As long as it cured Isobel – we could come back, later.'

Adam took his shoulders and turned him away

from the bed. 'Listen to me. She's quiet enough for the moment, so mebbe it's all by and she's going to get better. You go off and work your loom. Elizabeth'll stay with Isobel for a while.'

Reluctantly, stopping to touch Isobel's fingers gently, Matt went. Adam's hand brushed the sick woman's wrist, lingered.

'Somewhere in there's the answer. But we have no way of knowing what it is!'

'You're doing your best, Matt knows that.'

Adam scowled at the patient. 'It's no' enough, though, is it? Mebbe this sickness lies in a woman all her life. Mebbe it's in the blood, waiting to be roused. I don't know.' His blue gaze sharpened, studied Isobel as though trying to see beyond the skin to the mysteries beneath. 'All I know is that some can have bairns without any bother, and others take the fever. Fine lady or weaver's wife, it makes no difference. If we only knew why!'

When Matt came back Isobel was awake and perfectly calm. Clearly, she had no memory of what had happened during the night. Elizabeth left husband and wife together and hurried back to the High Street, noticing as she went that more doors were adorned with papers on which the word 'Sick' was printed to warn callers. The cholera showed no sign, six weeks after it had arrived, of leaving them in peace.

A noisy crowd pushed past her as she went towards the Montgomery house and she was hustled into the roadway. In the late afternoon light their eyes were like slits, their mouths gaping as they shouted a meaningless jumble of words. There was a menacing air about them. She had no sooner stepped back onto the footpath again than Tibby, the local gossipmonger, grabbed at her arm.

'Have you heard? They're going to the Moss to dig up the graves!' Her nose was bright red with excitement and her bonnet, thrown on in her haste to get into the street, was squint.

'To dig them up?' Elizabeth echoed the words stupidly.

Tibby's thin-lipped grin was that of a hunter after a fine specimen. 'Someone found shovels and a rope with a hook. They've been put on show in a shop window for all to see. It's grave-robbers at work! It proves what they've been saying—' her voice rattled on, scarcely stopping for breath, '—the physicians are taking the poor dead corpses and cutting them up. Denying them decent Christian rest. The folk are going to look into every coffin buried out there, to make sure—'

Bile stung the back of Elizabeth's throat. She

wrenched herself away from Tibby violently and ran the rest of the way home, trying to close her mind to the picture the woman's words had printed in her mind. The thought of James disturbed from his final sleep by rough hands shot her night's sleep through with bad dreams.

The mob appeared in the streets on the following day. Elizabeth was choosing trimming for a new dress in Peter Brough's shop in Moss Street when they passed.

This time there was a lot more of them, jostling their way along the street, pushing under the very noses of the cart horses and causing chaos.

The angry shouting took Elizabeth and the shop assistant to the window. Men carrying shovels led the way, with a gaggle of women and children following.

'It's a disgrace!' muttered the assistant. 'A rabble – where's the magistrates? I've heard that they're going to lay hands on the physicians if they find any coffins empty.'

Elizabeth had only a moment to feel concern for Adam's safety when her eyes were caught and held by a face in the crowd. She stared, then ran to the door, ignoring the assistant's warning to stay where she was until danger was past.

Outside, she picked up her skirts and scurried

through the scatter of children following the crowd until she managed to catch at the arm of one of the women.

'Isobel!'

A familiar and yet strange face turned and smiled uncertainly at her. 'I have to hurry—' Isobel slid from her grasp.

'Come back – you have no business here!'

Isobel eluded her grasping hand. 'I have to go to the braes—' Her light voice floated back to Elizabeth as she hurried on, to be lost in the gathering crowd.

Elizabeth started to run after her, but just then a huge man burst from a close-mouth and sent her spinning.

'We'll learn those Burking spalpeens!' he bellowed, and sped off towards the Moss. Someone caught Elizabeth up out of the path of a carriage and pulled her to the wall of a house. By the time she had gathered her wits the mob had gone, taking Isobel with them.

Muddy, bruised on the stones of the road, Elizabeth fought her way back up Moss Street against the flow of people hurrying towards the Moss. She wove in and out like an eel, using her elbows and her well-shod feet when she had to.

Matt's loom shop was tranquil. Linnets chirruped

in wicker cages and the men's voices murmured beneath the steady clack of the looms. When Elizabeth broke in on the scene five faces gaped up at her – Matt, the other three weavers, and old Mr Gibson, sitting by the fire enjoying his pipe.

'It's Isobel—' She leaned against Matt's loom, dragging breath into her lungs. The skirt of her gown was torn and muddy, her bonnet hanging down her back by its ribbons.

'She's in by,' Matt was perplexed. 'The bairn's with John's wife, and Isobel's sleeping, so I thought I'd just—'

She all but tore him from the loom in her urgency. 'Matt – she's up and dressed and away to the Moss with the crowd! I couldn't stop her, she's deranged—'

His face changed colour. 'Dear God!' he said, and pushed past her. She heard him throwing open the house door at the other side of the passage, calling Isobel's name, then he was back, gathering his fellow weavers, shouting to her over his shoulder to take the old man to a neighbour's and fetch Adam.

Adam was at the hospital. For the second time she ran through its doors, and this time he was in the ante-room on his way out, so that she was spared the sights of the ward beyond.

'Go home or go to Christian's house,' he ordered when she had gasped out her story.

'I'll stay with you.'

'I've no time to argue – though you're mebbe taking your life in your hands, being seen with a surgeon this day,' he threw the words at her as he strode through the hospital gates and down the narrow road. She had to run to keep up with him.

He led her without hesitation through a maze of narrow alleys and backlands that she had never seen before, then lifted her bodily over a tumble-down brick wall, across a greasy, slippery yard, and into a foul-smelling dark close.

'We're in Moss Street—' he began, then stopped and pressed her against the wall behind him as a dull murmur in the street beyond began to swell to a roar.

'I doubt we're too late. They're coming back into the town. If you value your skin stay still and keep your mouth shut!'

Huddled close to him in the damp, narrow passageway, she peered from beneath his shelter-ing arm at the grey oblong of the close-mouth. It darkened and flickered in a series of erratic pictures as the mob began to surge past on their way back up Moss Street.

The ground shook to the tramping of hundreds

of feet. She heard, for the first time, the voice of a mob, high and shrill, filled with hate and hysteria. Faces blurred into a collection of mouths, fists stabbed into the air, some carrying ropes or shovels. Mercifully, nobody turned to look in the dark close as they passed, and she and Adam, motionless, weren't seen.

Elizabeth had never thought that she could be so frightened in her home town. Many of the people going by only a few yards away, screaming hate, might have brushed past her in the street again and again. Today, each person was part of one frightening animal, a dragon that shouted and stormed up the street, accompanied now and then by the brittle sound of a window smashing or a door being kicked in.

Something flashed past the oblong of light, long and dark, carried high. She thought that she could make out a chant in the midst of the noise.

Then the people were gone and Adam was hurrying her back the way they had come.

'They've brought an empty coffin into the town,' he said breathlessly as they ran. 'That means they'll be looking for the physicians. I'll have to get back to the hospital before they get there.'

As they gained Oakshawhill again the sound of the approaching mob rolled up towards them. The district had once been a Roman camp, and it rose above the rest of Paisley. The crowd would just be starting the uphill climb to the hospital, as Adam had predicted.

'Listen to me, Elizabeth—' He stopped, whirled her about to face him. 'Get to Christian's house and stay there, no matter how long you have to wait, do you hear me? Stay safe until I come to take you home.'

'I won't!' She tried to hold onto his coat. She didn't want to be separated from him while he was in danger. He shook her hard, tearing her fingers from his lapels. Her hair, released from the lace cap, flew about her face and whipped against his shoulder.

'Listen to me!' he shouted into her upraised face. 'Get to that house and wait for me or by God I'll strangle you where you stand and save the mob the trouble. Go on!'

He released her with a violent push that sent her headlong to the ground. She scrambled to her feet, sobs choking her throat, to see him striding away without a backward glance.

At first she didn't think she was going to get into Christian's house. That lady had gone off in the morning to visit friends outside Paisley, and the cook and Effie only opened the door after

Elizabeth had convinced them, through its sturdy panels, of her identity.

The two of them wrung their hands and exclaimed over her wild appearance and torn clothing.

'I kenned these wild rag-tags from the gutters would get up to something wicked!' wailed the cook, an elderly lady who was as thin as a stick, but had a superb talent for preparing food.

They brought hot water and towels for Elizabeth, then settled her in the parlour and gave her tea, properly served in one of their mistress's best tea services.

Distracted with worry over Adam and Isobel, she couldn't even sip the hot liquid, but left it to cool in the cup while she paced about the room, longing to go outside but afraid to disobey Adam.

An hour after he had left her a fringe of the mob came straggling along the road. Cold fear struck into Elizabeth as she peered from behind the curtains and saw a dozen or so men stop and eye the house.

'There's one of the thieving spalpeens lives here—' she heard a voice say, then a man stooped, an arm went back, and a large stone crashed through the drawing-room window, landing almost at her feet.

Splinters of glass dropped from her skirt as she ran through the hall to the kitchen, meeting the two women on their way out and bundling them back.

'They're here – they might try to get in—' In a frenzy she slammed the door to the hall, threw herself at the heavy dresser beside it. 'Help me to pull this over. And make sure that the back door's locked!'

Breathless, terrified, they turned the kitchen into a fortress and huddled together, waiting. There were shouts from the front of the house and glass crashed twice more, but nobody tried to force the front door, or came in through the walled back garden.

After a long silence, they decided that it was safe to venture out, and had just begun to draw the dresser clear of the hall door when fists began pounding on the front door.

Effie screamed and threw herself into a corner. The cook pulled her out and slapped her face, and a familiar voice roared, 'For the love of God, Christian, will you let me in!'

Elizabeth's feet couldn't carry her across the hall fast enough. Adam stormed in as soon as the handle turned and made straight for the side room where he had his laboratory. He emerged almost at once, nearly knocking her down on his way across to the drawing-room.

'If they thought to do damage they failed. A broken window or two, but the apparatus isn't broken. Is my cousin at home?'

'She's in Elderslie—'

He stopped short in the drawing-room, looking at the smashed window and the glass lying on the rich carpet and over the furniture. 'She'll be in a fine taking about this when she sets eyes on it.'

'Adam, are you all right?' Elizabeth was surprised by the steadiness of her own voice.

'Me?' He frowned at her, puzzled, then glanced into a mirror. 'Oh – they broke down the hospital gates and made off with the cholera bier, the daft loons. It's just a wee disagreement I had with a man who was all for taking the patients as well.'

His clothes were as torn and muddy as hers. There was bruising round his left eye, which was half-closed, and dried blood, apparently from a shallow cut on one cheekbone, crusted part of his face. Looking at him reminded her of the picture she must make herself. She pushed her long, tangled hair back, tried without success to pull together a tear in her sleeve.

Then she remembered. 'Have you heard anything of Isobel?'

'I've been no further than the hospital. I'll get

down to Shuttle Street now. Likely Matt found her
and took her home safely.'

Effie, red-eyed but obviously fighting to restore
normality, appeared with a tea-tray set, again, with
attractive china and a silver teapot.

'You'll take some tea, Mister Montgomery?'

'Tea?' Adam asked as though he couldn't
believe his ears. 'Tea?' His voice rose to a bellow.
'Brandy, woman – for any favour, brandy!'

She put the tray down carefully, with a slight
crunch of broken glass underfoot, clasped both
hands to her mouth, and fled. Adam marched to
the corner cupboard, snatched out a large glass
and a bottle, and filled the glass to the brim. Then
he swallowed half of it in one movement of his
strong throat.

'What's up with the old besom?'

'I think—' Elizabeth said carefully '—that she's a
wee thing upset, Adam. She's no' used to riots and
folk breaking windows. And to tell you the truth—'
All at once her composure had begun to slide
away, like a wayward coverlet on a bed. It was a
strange feeling. '—To tell you the truth, I—'

He shot her a short, puzzled look over the rim of
the glass. Then it was put down and Adam was
across the room, gathering her into his arms, holding her close, and she was clutching him tightly

because she didn't ever want him to move away again.

'Elizabeth—' he said softly into the brown hair spilled over his shoulder, '—lass, was there ever a more thoughtless fool than I am?'

It was then, despite the fear and misery, that Elizabeth realised that she had come home. She knew, with a clarity that almost stopped her heart dead then set it pounding faster, that she didn't care how thoughtless or bad-tempered or intolerant he was, there would never be anyone in the world for her but Adam Montgomery.

She couldn't tell him about it. She could only cling to him and be grateful to him for holding her until the trembling stopped and the dry-eyed sobbing was over. Then he smoothed her hair back, made her sit down, and gave her some brandy, which tasted terrible.

'You're no judge of spirits,' he teased, the ghost of a smile lighting his blue eyes, when she pushed the glass away with a grimace. 'Thon's Cousin Christian's best liquor you're turning your neb up at. Now – I'm going to take you to the High Street, for it's time you were safe home.'

'I'm coming with you to Shuttle Street. I have to know that Isobel's all right,' she insisted as he began to shake his head.

'My father'll no' be pleased at you being out when he gets back.'

She folded her hands in her lap. 'Isobel's my friend,' she said, and he gave in.

The town was in an uproar and it wasn't easy getting to Matt's house. The militia were on their way, they were told as they came down from Oakshawhill to find a trail of broken fencing and smashed windows. The cholera bier had been wrecked then carried through the town. Doctors' homes had been attacked. Now the mob, its first thirst for vengeance dulled, had broken into sullen groups, muttering in corners.

Tibby pounced on them as they made for Shuttle Street. Her mouth was working and her eyes glistened.

'There you are, Elizabeth – and Mister Montgomery too. My, what a state you're in!' She drank in the sight with a blink of her eyes. 'Is it no' terrible what's happened?'

'It's a bad day for Paisley,' he agreed shortly, his arm about Elizabeth's shoulders as he tried to hurry her past the woman. But Tibby was determined to have her say.

'Paisley? Oh, aye – but I was talking of the accident.'

'What accident?' Adam snapped at her, and she

flinched back, then rallied.

'Down at the Moss – poor Isobel—'

Adam released Elizabeth and almost snapped Tibby's thin arm off at the shoulder in his impatience to find out what she was talking about.

'I'm trying to tell you!' She snatched the crushed limb back, rubbed it, glaring at him. But bad news was of more importance to her than a bruised arm. 'She got caught up in the rabble at the Moss and got hit on the head with one of the shovels, poor bairn. They took her to the Town Hospital—'

A carriage belonging to one of the town's bailies was standing nearby, out of the way of the rioters but near enough to make out what was happening. Adam whirled Elizabeth up into it and followed her without a pause. Fortunately, the occupant knew who he was, and was willing to drive them to the hospital.

They had to take a roundabout route to keep clear of trouble. Adam was on the ground before the wheels had stopped turning and Elizabeth was almost pulled headlong from the door. With a swift word of thanks for their benefactor, Adam ran into the building.

Matt was closeted in a small ground floor room with the hospital master, Mister Crichton. On a table lay a shrouded figure. Adam lifted the edge of the sheet, looked, dropped the cloth.

'Who did this?' he asked, low voiced, murder in the tones.

Matt shook his head. He was dazed, his voice a dull monotone. 'Nobody knows. It was an accident, just. I met them when they were bringing her back. She was – it all happened at once, they say. Just an accident. She was there, the place was crowded, she got in the way of a shovel—' His voice dropped, rose again. 'If there's anyone to blame, it was me. I thought she'd be all right on her own, for a minute. I just wanted to finish a wee bit of work—'

Tears rolled down his waxen face, one after another, and Adam took him in his arms as though he was a child.

As he was being led out to the carriage that was to take him home Matt raised his head and gazed round the high-ceilinged hall.

'I mind I said I'd no' let her come in here.' He tried to smile. 'Poor lass – it's as well we never know what's ahead.'

It was dark when Adam and Elizabeth made their way to High Street. John Gibson was with Matt and Adam planned to go back and stay the night at the cottage. There was an uneasy, brooding air about the streets. The mob had returned to the cholera hospital and had forced the doctors to flee for their lives. The magistrates had appeased them by promising to investigate the coffins in the Moss, and the rabble had retired for the night, hungry beasts waiting for the dawn.

Adam insisted on going into the house with her, but she refused to use the front door while his father was home, and he had to follow her down the side passage.

Mary almost hugged Elizabeth in her relief at seeing her but hung back shyly when Adam, still ragged and bloody, stepped into the kitchen.

'Is Mister Montgomery home?' Elizabeth marvelled over how normal the kitchen seemed after the events of the day.

'These two hours past.' Mary's eyes were like saucers. 'And he was awful angry when I said you hadnae come home. I was frighted, Elizabeth—'

'There's no need,' Elizabeth said automatically. 'Away to your bed now and I'll talk to you in the morning.'

The hall door flew back on its hinges.

'So you've decided to come back, have you?' Rab asked belligerently, then his eyes narrowed as Adam stepped into the centre of the room. 'Keeping strange company, too.' He ground the words out.

'I have to speak with you, father.'

For a moment Elizabeth thought that the older man was going to ignore his son's presence, then curiosity won the day.

'You know where to find me,' he said curtly and turned into the hall.

'Elizabeth—' Adam made it an order, waiting at the door as though she was a lady, his blue eyes weary but compelling as they held hers. She walked before him to the parlour where Rab waited, legs straddled before the fireplace, hands behind his back and chin up in his most arrogant stance.

'Well?'

'Sit down, Elizabeth,' Adam commanded, then deigned to look at his father at last.

'Elizabeth's been in Christian's house, hiding from the mob. And then she was with me, at Shuttle Street. It's through no fault of hers that she wasnae here earlier.'

Rab's eyes flickered over them both. 'You look as though the mob got you.'

'I'm a physician, father. Today this whole town shares your feelings about us. We kill folk, it seems. You'll no doubt be pleased to see that somebody tried to do something about it.' He indicated his bruised and swollen face.

A muscle jumped in Rab's cheek, but he said nothing.

'I brought Elizabeth home, for it's no' safe for a lassie to be in the streets on a night like this. And I came to tell you that Matt's wife died today.'

There was a slight pause, then, 'Aye?' Rab asked enigmatically.

'I thought you might feel it your duty to go and see the man.'

The muscle jumped again. 'If Matt has anything to say to me, he can come here, as you've done,' Rab said harshly. 'I'll no' seek him out.'

Adam drew a deep, ragged breath, and Elizabeth could see that it was costing him a lot to keep his temper in check. She willed him to remain calm. An outburst now would only be turned to his father's advantage.

'Am I to go back and tell him that?'

'You can tell him what you damned well please! And you can leave my house!'

Their eyes locked, and Rab's shifted almost at once. Adam walked to the door. Elizabeth rose to show him out and he said swiftly, 'I'll manage fine.'

Rab, who had opened his mouth to bellow an order at her, closed it again with an audible click of teeth.

'To think—' Adam said very softly, but with a chill in his voice that almost froze Elizabeth's blood '—that I ever wanted to come back to this town, and this house.'

'To think—' his father's guttural voice followed him as he walked out '—that I ever thought to welcome you back! I rue the day you set your accursed foot in this place!'

The front door closed quietly, and he dropped into his chair, watching Elizabeth from beneath lowered lids, daring her silently to utter a word.

She stood before him, head high, hands folded before her, and in her heart she hated him with all the force she could muster.

'Go to your bed,' he said at last, and she went, leaving him alone with his thoughts.

IX

Just after he buried his wife in the churchyard near her home Matt Montgomery began working in the Cassidy warehouse, as foreman. Without Isobel he lost his ambition to stay at the loom, and turned a new corner in his life.

'If my father had acknowledged her as my wife I could have cared for her better,' he said savagely to Elizabeth. 'She might be with me today.'

She settled a large shawl about her shoulders and scooped the baby expertly into its folds. His warm little body nestling against her breast seemed natural.

'Matt, Adam says the sickness that took Isobel could have been with her no matter how she lived.'

'Mebbe so, but I could have given her more – we could have spent more time together. I'll never forgive that old devil in his fine house!' His face hardened, grew older. Then he touched the baby's cheek gently with the back of one finger. 'You'll fetch him to see me tomorrow, Elizabeth?'

'Aye, as soon as I can get away.' Isobel's father had moved in with John Gibson and his wife; the baby had been farmed out to neighbours. Every day Elizabeth carried him to the weaving shop so that Matt could spend some time with him.

'I'll need to find someone to look after the two of us so that I can bring him here, where he belongs.' He looked about the cottage. 'Or find somewhere else to stay.'

'That takes money.'

His jaw set. 'Then I'll find the money. I've nothing else to do with my time. I tell you this, Elizabeth – if it's anything to do with me, that wee lad's going to have all the comforts his mother never lived to see!'

It was as though the bitter blow he had suffered had cracked the old shell open and released a new man, forged of stronger material than ever. Within weeks of Isobel's death he had started on the road to success. He won the right to have more say in the Cassidy house than he had ever known in his father's employment. He managed to secure a loan from the Union Bank, and took on a new harness loom weaver to increase the shawl output.

The man and his family moved into the Shuttle

Street cottage and Matt rented a new house for himself, in St George's Place. It was near the warehouse and separated from the weaving shop by a communal drying green at the back, enabling him to keep close contact, day and night, with the work under his supervision.

He found a capable widow to act as housekeeper and summoned Elizabeth to inspect the house. It consisted of a downstairs kitchen, and a small room where the baby and the housekeeper could sleep. Upstairs there was a bedroom for Matt and a small, but perfect, high-ceilinged parlour, a room designed on airy, graceful lines, with two large windows, one looking out onto the cobbled Place and the majesty of St George's Church, the other overlooking a lane, with a glimpse of walled gardens opposite.

'It's so – elegant,' she said in wonder, gazing at the carved fireplace.

'It'll do. The devil of it is, what do I put into it? I'll have to buy chairs and tables and suchlike.'

'Not a great deal. Curtains, and a desk there, and mebbe a sofa, but nothing big or dark for this room,' she began, and was interrupted.

'Just as I thought – you've got the right idea, Elizabeth. How would it be if I was to leave it to you to choose the right pieces?'

She realised too late that she had fallen into a trap. 'But, Matt—!'

He looked as though a load had been taken off his shoulders. 'Anything'll do, just so long as I can get the place fit for Duncan and Mistress Mackay. Wallpaper – something on the floor – whatever you think best, lass.'

She left the house in a daze, her mind so full of chairs and tables and sofas that she didn't look where she was going, and cannoned into someone as she turned a corner.

Elizabeth, the smaller and lighter of the two, staggered across the path, bounced off the wall of a house, and landed in the arms of her assailant.

'You daft gowk,' she lashed out, 'you nearly had me in the dirt!' She twisted in his grip to examine the skirt of her good mulberry-coloured gown. The wall had been soft with age and damp, and as she had feared there was a stain on the cloth.

'Look—' She caught a handful of the material and dragged it round to study it. 'Look what you've done to my best gown!'

'Forgive me, ma'am – it was my fault entirely, I confess it!'

She looked up swiftly as she heard the clipped English voice, then reddened. The man before her was immaculately dressed, stylish in a dove-grey

coat over black trousers, white shirt, blue satin
waistcoat and blue cravat. He was half a head
taller than herself, his hair was the colour of corn
in sunlight, and his eyes, wide with horror as he
looked at the stained dress, were dark brown. He
looked, her numbed senses told her, like one of the
noble heroes in the romantic novels she was fond
of reading.

'Your pardon – it was clumsy of me—' His voice
was deep, beautiful. She realised that she was
gaping, and blinked rapidly.

'It's nothing, sir.'

'But your gown—' He stepped to one side to
examine the damage and Elizabeth, scarlet with
embarrassment, whisked round like an animal at
bay, one hand smoothing the marked skirt behind
her, out of sight.

'Ach, it's fine. I'll put it to soak in a tub of water
when I get home, and it'll be as good as new.'

'You're not hurt, ma'am?'

Nobody had ever called her 'ma'am' before. The
splendour of it almost took her breath away.

'Ma'am?' he prompted, anxiety entering his
voice, and she realised that she was too caught up
in admiring him to listen properly.

'Oh – I'm fit as a – quite hearty, thank you, sir.'

'I'm glad.' She felt his gaze like a touch, travelling

241

over her, and was pleased to recall that she had put on her new bonnet, the one that framed her neat face and brown hair to advantage. If she could have thought of something else to say, to prolong the meeting, she would have said it gladly. But her stupid tongue couldn't utter the words that would keep him there. He bowed, she sketched a clumsy curtsey, and they turned to go their separate ways.

'Ma'am—'

She spun round. 'Aye, sir?'

The dark brown eyes were like treacle. She was lost in them. 'Could you perhaps direct me to the Montgomery warehouse in Forbes Place?'

She beamed at him. 'It's just across the street and down a bit towards the Cross. I'm—' the lie tripped off her tongue easily 'I'm going past that way myself.'

She saw him raise one eyebrow slightly and glance in the direction she had been walking, away from the Cross. But he had the grace to say nothing, except, 'Then I'm delighted to accept your assistance, ma'am,' as he offered her his arm.

She skimmed across the street as though walking on a cloud. 'I look after Mister Montgomery's house. My name is Elizabeth Cunningham.'

He stopped on the opposite footpath, sketched a

bow. 'Jeremy Forrest. Your servant, ma'am.' Then he tucked her hand back into the crook of his arm and they walked on.

'You're new to Paisley, Mister Forrest?'

'This is my first visit. My father has a business in London. I've been sent up to buy merchandise and to meet the people.'

They reached the warehouse all too soon, making their way through the usual cluster of people about the doors; weavers carrying away new webs in clean white linen bags, women bringing back finished shawls or collecting yarn to be wound, carters delivering new materials. Rab was inside, haggling with a weaver over the price of a shawl.

'Well, girl?' he asked shortly when he glanced up and saw her. His manner changed when Jeremy Forrest introduced himself. He shook hands, beaming, ushering the young man towards his tiny office.

'You can go off home,' he said curtly to Elizabeth, and his eyebrows shot up in astonishment as Jeremy Forrest took time to bow over her work-roughened hand and say, 'Your servant, ma'am. I hope we may meet again.'

Elizabeth's ears were still singing with the excitement of it all when she presented herself at

Christian's house twenty minutes later for advice about Matt's house.

The older woman eyed her closely. 'You're in a right state about a few sticks of furniture,' she commented dryly. 'Roses in your cheeks, and a shine to your eyes that I've never seen before.'

Elizabeth opened her mouth to tell Mistress Selbie about her meeting with the young Englishman, then thought better of it. 'I'm just worried I'll choose the wrong things,' she said lamely.

'He'd no' notice if you filled the place with boxes. And I'm quite sure you'll do a grand job. It'll be practice for you, for when the time comes for you to furnish your own wee house.' She looked up, her eyes sliding beyond Elizabeth. 'It's yourself, Adam. Will you have some tea?'

'I will not,' he said, 'I'll have what I need.'

Christian tutted, but did nothing to stop him as he took a generous ration of whisky from the bottle in the cupboard.

Elizabeth hadn't seen much of him since Isobel's funeral. The cuts and bruising he had received on the day of the riots had gone, but he looked thinner, paler. As though reading her mind, Christian said, 'D'you not think he looks awful tired, Elizabeth?'

He emptied the glass. 'I've told you, cousin – I can take care of myself.'

'Is it bad at the hospital, Adam?'

He looked at Elizabeth, his eyes dark and smoky, as though he didn't really see her. 'Bad enough, for the five poor souls that died in the past week. There's some recovered, mind.'

The smokiness cleared. 'But you're looking well, Elizabeth. Have you found a secret of health that poor physicians like me would like to learn?'

'She's just keeping herself busy. Matt's asked her to furnish his new house.' Christian's knitting wires clicked busily.

'There's an honour for you. See to it well, now – my brother's going to be a man of importance in this town before he's done. Did you know—' he took his eyes from Elizabeth and turned to Christian '—that old Peter Todd's added to the amount he's loaned Matt?'

She raised her eyebrows. 'Has he now? Well, well, the laddie must be giving a good account of himself. I told Peter he was worth trusting when he first asked me if he should lend Matt money.'

Adam, about to pour another drink, put the bottle down. 'You told him?'

Christian took advantage of his surprise to take the bottle from his unresisting hand and put it back into the cupboard. 'Peter always asks my advice.'

'And what would you know of money matters?' her kinsman asked with ungracious bluntness. She looked smug.

'More than you ever will. Did I no' marry a banker? And did my own brother, poor skelf of a man that he was, no' take up law? I've got a good tongue in my head, and a good mind as well. It was a simple enough matter to pick their brains.'

Adam shook his head. 'You're full of surprises, Christian. Tell me this – do you charge poor old Peter for all this advice you give him?'

She picked up her knitting again, gave him a withering look. 'As if I would! Wasn't his father Jamie fair dying to marry my mother at one time? As Peter sees it, we're nearly brother and sister, him and me.'

'I have it in mind to have a wee bit of a gathering,' Rab Montgomery told Elizabeth on the following day as she waited by the front door with his coat and stick. He shrugged into the coat, a lightweight garment now that June had arrived. 'A few folk, just. On Friday.'

She felt her knees tremble beneath her dark gown. 'For their dinner, Mister Montgomery?'

'Aye, for their dinner.' He snatched the silver-knobbed cane from her fingers. 'You ken what dinner is, don't you? It's when folk sit down and stuff their bellies with someone else's hard-earned silver, that's what it is. You'd best find something to please them, even if it bankrupts me. And you'll sit at the table yourself,' he finished crustily, and opened the door to an early morning filled with the promise of a hot day.

'How – how many would there be?' she quavered, dry-mouthed.

'About half a dozen, I suppose. I've not got it in mind to feed the entire town.' The door swung to leaving her trembling in the hall.

It was the first social event to be held in the house since Adam's homecoming. Elizabeth sank down onto the bottom step of the staircase, terrified at the thought of catering for a dinner party. She immediately thought of running to Christian Selbie for help, then thought better of it and went to the kitchen to break the news to Mary.

'We'll manage fine, you and me, will we no'?' she finished, with more confidence than she felt.

'D – d'ye no' think it would be a good idea to ask Mistress Selbie—?' the little maid said doubtfully.

'Shame on you! D'you think I cannae do anything for myself? And isn't it my place to teach you what to do?' Elizabeth's mind was beginning to function again. 'Listen – we'll have beef, and mebbe a goose, and I'll teach you how to make a fine pie.'

The thought of baking and cooking again, after weeks of supplying sketchy meals for Rab, began to appeal to her. As the day wore on she worked out a menu, and her confidence grew.

Christian Selbie appeared at the door the next day.

'I'm told that I'm expected to attend a dinner party here on Friday,' she announced almost accusingly, flouncing into the parlour. 'No' as much as a please or thank you, mind you. Anyone would think a body had nothing else to do but run after Lord Rab Montgomery!'

Elizabeth, who had now set her heart on taking responsibility for the dinner, grew pink with agitation.

'We can manage fine, Mary and me. I'm just away to the butcher's, then the bakery, and I thought Helen might—'

'Tuts, lassie, no need to go on like a burn rushing to the sea!' Christian flapped a hand at her. 'I know you're taking to do with it yourself and I've no mind to stick my nose in unless it's asked for. It's another matter I'm here about – something I'm sure you've never thought of.' She tilted her head to look Elizabeth over. 'What are you going to wear for this grand occasion of Rab's?'

Elizabeth gaped, then rallied. 'My pink muslin.'

'Just as I thought. It's pretty enough in its own way, but never the thing for Friday. You'll have to get a new gown.'

'There's no need.'

'Get your bonnet and shawl and come with me now to a wee seamstress I know,' Christian swept on. 'You can bring your basket and go to the shops after I've done with you.'

Meekly Elizabeth obeyed. It was easier than arguing.

'I'd have liked to take you to a woman in Glasgow, but Rab's not left us much time,' Christian said as they drove to the old bridge, where the seamstress had her little shop. 'I'd enjoy to see you dressed like a lady, Elizabeth, for I think you'd carry the clothes well.'

The dim room, its window overlooking the river below, glowed with colour from materials carelessly tossed over the wooden table. Christian and the seamstress scooped their hands into the cloth, arguing, agreeing, rejecting, selecting. Elizabeth submitted to being measured and pulled about, her mind on the food she must prepare for Friday. When Christian finally led her from the shop she had only a vague idea of the dress that was to be made for her.

'She's a good wee soul,' Christian said as they separated on the footpath. 'She'll have that gown ready on time, even if she has to work late at night to do it. See and be ready at four on Friday.'

True to her word, she was on the doorstep as the parlour clock chimed four on Friday afternoon. Elizabeth was bundled into her shawl and whisked back to the old bridge, calling last minute instructions from the carriage window to Mary. The little maid, running a few steps from the front door to catch her orders, nodded vigorously. Then she was out of sight and Christian was saying, 'Ach, she'll manage fine, don't fret about things.'

Elizabeth couldn't help fretting. The dinner party was the greatest challenge she had faced so far. In the little shop she let the two older women strip her brown dress off and put her in the new gown, while she went over lists and plans in her head.

She paid no attention to the new dress until she was pushed before a long mirror and ordered to look into it.

All thought of the dinner went out of her head at once.

'But – you've made a mistake!' She gaped at the

250

woman reflected in the glass, her voice rising to a shocked wail. 'My shoulders! I can see my shoulders, Mistress Selbie!'

Christian nodded smugly, as though she had made them herself. 'And very pretty they are, too.'

On anyone else, such as Helen Grant, Elizabeth would have agreed that those smooth rounded shoulders were fine, and worthy of the froth of pale blue lace that cupped them. But shoulders like those, the soft full breasts and elegant throat – they couldn't belong to her, Elizabeth, the charity school girl, the little housekeeper. They couldn't!

'Mistress Selbie—' she quavered.

'Take a good look at yourself, and not a word until you've done it!' the older woman commanded. Elizabeth swallowed her protests and turned back to the mirror obediently.

She was wearing the most beautiful dress she had ever seen. It was of periwinkle blue satin with a pale blue lace frill around the low bodice and pale blue ribbons across the front of the full, graceful skirt. Her arms were left bare and the snug-fitting bodice emphasised her ripe breasts even while it gave them a demure mystery with its drift of lace.

Elizabeth's wide eyes moved down to the skirt then up again, past the slender waist, the pale shoulders, the white column of the neck, surprisingly long and slim – then they met their own stunned reflection in a pink-cheeked face.

'It's bonny,' Christian said with satisfaction, and the seamstress chirruped agreement.

'It's bonny, but—' Elizabeth threw out her red hands with their short, sensible nails. 'It's no' for the likes of me!'

'Of course it is! We'll buy slippers – you've got neat wee feet, always a sign of a lady—' Christian whisked the skirt up, revealing the feet in question, and slender ankles. '—And you'll have long gloves, and since my Effie's to help serve the meal, I'll bring her early and she can help to dress you. Effie's good with hair. I've got a necklace that would go with that dress—' Then she stopped herself. 'No, it'd be a crime to put anything round that bonny white young throat. You'll stay unadorned, and all the prettier for it.'

A few hours later Elizabeth was again studying her own reflection, this time in the long mirror in the upstairs hall of the Montgomery house. Effie's nimble fingers had pinned her hair up in an elegant sweep of shining gold-brown with three ringlets nestling in the curve of her neck on the left. Pale blue gloves to the elbow made the most of her small-boned hands and hid the red, rough skin.

Soft slippers caressed her feet and made her feel as though she was walking on a cloud. Her cheeks were bright with excitement and her blue eyes sparkled.

Her throat had been left unadorned, as Christian had decided, but tiny blue pendant earrings swung from her lobes when she moved her head.

'If they hurt, it makes no difference,' the older woman had said as she clipped them on. 'A bit of pain's nothing if a lady looks right. You carry yourself well enough, and if you're no' sure of anything, watch me.'

She herself was magnificent in deep red with gold lace trimming. Rab, standing before the parlour fire, almost choked on his glass of whisky when they entered.

'You're no' bad – both of you,' he said grudgingly when Christian had thumped him on the back.

'The lassie's a picture, and you know it!' said his cousin tartly, then added, 'And I'm bonny, myself.'

Elizabeth had hoped, when she saw how lovely she looked, that Adam might be among the guests. Rab hadn't troubled to tell her who had been invited, and she hadn't liked to ask. As it turned out Christian was the only blood relation at the dinner. A prominent local manufacturer and town bailie appeared, together with his wife, and shortly after that the last guest arrived. Elizabeth felt her heart stop, then flip over and beat hurriedly as Jeremy Forrest, handsome in a claret-coloured coat with dark green facing, high white collar, green cravat and pale grey trousers, came into the parlour.

He came into the room quickly, bringing with him the fresh vitality of youth, and looked swiftly round the people already there. His eyes lit up when they reached Elizabeth, and he made his way over to her as soon as the introductions were over and he was free.

'Mistress Cunningham – I hoped to meet you again.' He raised her gloved hand to his lips, and she prayed that he wouldn't sense the thrill that ran through her.

She had dreaded the meal, but with Jeremy at her side everything became an adventure, a challenge she met with skill. Now and then she glanced across the snowy tablecloth at Christian, and each time met with a small approving nod.

With Effie's practised guidance Mary served the meal correctly, and Elizabeth was able to relax and even permit herself the luxury of laughter now and then.

When the men joined the ladies in the parlour after port, Jeremy sat by her on the sofa.

'I hope you don't feel that I'm stealing too much of your company, Miss Cunningham?'

'Oh no, I—' She stopped short, remembering just in time that the ladies in the romantic novels were never too enthusiastic. 'I enjoy talking with you.'

He leaned closer, lowered his voice. 'The other ladies are charming, but not as enchanting or as beautiful as you are. That dress—' his warm brown gaze moved slowly over her throat and shoulders and breasts before settling on the satin skirt '—is quite the most perfect I've seen in years. The material is very fine.'

She glowed. 'Isn't it? And the ribbons are – oh!'

She sat upright, eyes wide with horror. Jeremy, fingers daringly within inches of the skirt folds, snatched his hand back as though she had just bitten it.

'I do beg your pardon, Mistress Cunningham, I had no intention of—'

'It's no' you – it's me!' She had forgotten to watch her tongue in this moment of terrible realisation. 'I never even asked how much the gown would cost – I havenae paid for it, and here I am sitting in it like a lady!'

Bewilderment crinkled his face, and was swiftly followed by blazing amusement. 'You—' he began, then went into a fit of coughing, jumping to his feet.

'Did a crumb go down the wrong way, Mister Forrest?' Christian enquired politely from the far side of the room, and he shook his head.

'Thank you – I'm quite all right,' he said at last, voice shaking. 'Mistress Cunningham has a very dry sense of humour.'

Then he caught Elizabeth's hand and drew her up to stand beside him. 'Come and look out of the window.'

She was still absorbed in the horror of her situation. She worked for little more than her keep in the Montgomery house. It would take years to pay for such a fine dress. 'There's nothing to see but the houses across the street,' she said fretfully as she was drawn across the room.

'I don't care what I see. I find that looking out of a window is a very good way of recovering one's composure,' the English voice drawled, his breath tickling her ear.

Side by side, in silence, they stared from the window for a while, Elizabeth frantically going over sums of money in her head.

She was scarcely aware of the sidelong glances her companion gave her now and then.

'I don't care whether you've paid for the gown

or not, Mistress Cunningham,' he murmured at last, 'It becomes you very well.'

'But—'

His voice became firmer. 'Besides, a great many young ladies in London never pay for their gowns until long after they've worn them and thrown them away.'

'That's stealing!'

'Not—' he turned her to face him, and she saw laughter in his eyes, tugging at the corners of his mouth. '—Not if they're ladies of fashion. And you, Mistress Cunningham, were born to be a lady of fashion. I think—' there was faint regret in the words '—that we have neglected the others for long enough. Shall we join them?'

Christian's sharp eyes were on them as Jeremy led Elizabeth to a seat near the fire. 'I was just saying, Mister Forrest, you'll no' have travelled on our fine canal yet? I'm taking a journey to Johnstone on Monday, and I could go by water if you'd care to travel with me?'

He bowed. 'I'd be honoured, ma'am. Perhaps Mistress Cunningham would join us?'

Monday was laundry day. Elizabeth began to shake her head, the little pendant earrings dancing in the light. To her surprise Rab said, 'Havers, lassie, you can manage to take a day from your duties, can you no'? You'll go with my cousin and Mister Forrest.'

He made it plain that he had given an order. Elizabeth bit her lip and saw Jeremy's eyes darken, his brows tuck down as he shot a sidelong look at his host.

'The choice lies with Mistress Cunningham, of course,' he said coolly. 'I would not wish her to take part in this outing if it's going to bore her.'

'Of course it won't.' Rab snapped. 'But by all means, Elizabeth – tell us what you think of my cousin's invitation?' There was mockery in his imitation of the Englishman's courtesy, and the frown deepened on Jeremy's forehead.

'I'll be happy to go,' Elizabeth said quickly, embarrassed by the sudden attention from her employer's guests.

When they had all left, Jeremy with a soft, 'Until Monday, Mistress Cunningham—' Rab stopped at the foot of the stairs on his way up to bed.

'Thon Londoner seems to like your company, Elizabeth. His father's a good man to do business with. Mind that when you're on the canal with him.'

'Mister Montgomery!' She stopped him as he continued on up to the landing. The newel post was hard and smooth beneath her fingers; she gripped it tight for comfort as she glared up at the insensitive man above her.

'Mister Montgomery – I'm your housekeeper. I was never employed to attract men to your warehouse doors!'

He came down two steps, but she held her ground, anchored to the newel post. Rab stabbed a finger at her.

'You—' he said, with level emphasis on each and every word 'are my employee. My servant. The cloth on your back and the food in your belly and the cot you sleep on are all thanks to me. I have the power, if you displease me, to send you back to the paupers' house you came from and make sure no decent folk ever give you work in this town again. Just think about that before you decide whether or not you'll do my bidding, my girl!'

He stumped back upstairs and disappeared into the shadows of the upper floor. Alone, Elizabeth uncurled her fingers with difficulty from the polished wooden post and went back to the kitchen, clashing pots about in her rage.

He was right, she knew that. The doors open to her were of little comfort – she could defy him and return to the Town Hospital in shame, she could leave the town and go elsewhere, alone; she could accept Adam's offer of help and be beholden to him for the rest of her life.

'I'll not dance to that old man's tune!' she vowed to herself as she brushed out her hair before going to bed later. 'I won't!'

She set off for Oakshawhill as soon as she was free on the following morning. First, she had to talk to Christian about the cost of the new gown; then she would turn down the invitation to join Christian and Jeremy on the canal. After that – she shelved the terrible thought for the moment, refusing to start worrying until she had to – she would decide what to do if Rab kept his threat and put her out.

Christian, in a voluminous dressing-gown and big cap, was still having breakfast.

'What a fuss to make over a bit of cloth and a few ribbons!' she said scathingly when her visitor started to explain why she had arrived. 'I know fine Rab doesnae give you enough money to buy decent clothes for yourself. By rights he should pay for the gown, for weren't you playing hostess at his table? But I decided from the start that it would be my own gift to you, so that's an end to the whole matter. It was worth the money just to see you enjoying yourself for once. Now – about the canal—'

Elizabeth opened her mouth to speak, but wasn't given the chance.

'—I've made up my mind that we'll make an outing of it altogether. I'm going to see if Helen'll come – she needs a rest from that shop of hers – and I have it in mind to ask Matt as well. Adam's already said he'll honour us with his company.'

Elizabeth shut her mouth again. She hadn't seen Adam for several days. Although she would scarcely admit it, even to herself, she missed him.

She would go on the canal trip after all – but not to please Rab Montgomery. She had her own reasons now.

X

Rab Montgomery was away from home for the entire day, so after leaving Christian Elizabeth was free to visit a cabinet-maker's shop in Orchard Street. She would have liked to have plenty of time to select furniture for Matt's new home, but he was impatient to move his son and the housekeeper in.

She wasn't entirely displeased with the pieces that the man had to show her. There were some graceful chairs, delicate and yet sturdy, and an elegant wall cupboard.

She was reluctant to make the final decision on her own. She found Matt in the loom-shop and dragged him, protesting, back to Orchard Street.

'I'll no' have you saying something displeased you once it was in the house.'

'I told you – anything'll do!' He was like a peevish child lagging half a step behind its mother. The thought made her smile as she looked up at his powerful body, looming over her, then the smile died on her lips as a familiar voice said, 'Mistress Cunningham!' and she and Matt came to a standstill before Jeremy Forrest.

She was instantly reminded, as she looked at his beaming face, of Rab's plan to use her to gain orders for his warehouse. With this in mind her nod was cool, and Jeremy's eyes clouded over.

It wasn't his fault any more than it was hers, she reminded herself, and immediately regretted her coldness. Jeremy's look of relief as she smiled was quite radiant.

'I dined at your father's house last night,' he shook hands with Matt when Elizabeth had introduced them. 'I'm sorry you weren't with us.'

'My father would as soon break bread with a mad dog as sit at the same table as me,' the weaver said bluntly.

'Matt!' She tugged at his arm, shocked and embarrassed. 'That's no way to speak of your own father!'

'I was never one for pretty words, Elizabeth.' He looked levelly at the Englishman. 'I'm sure Mister Forrest knows that shared blood doesn't always mean shared affections.'

'Indeed,' Jeremy grinned. 'My own father and I

have our quarrels. I think I was sent to Paisley because he was tired of the sight of me.'

'You're on business?'

'I'm buying shawls.'

Matt's eyes narrowed but he only said, mildly, 'You've come to the right town for that. You'll be staying long?'

'Another ten days, perhaps. I'm lodging in the Abbey Close with Mistress Mackay. If it was left to my own discretion—' for a warm moment his eyes rested on Elizabeth, '—I would stay longer. But my father says that time means money.'

'God, he's right about that,' Matt was suddenly reminded of his own work. 'Come on, Elizabeth, I've got to get back to the weaving shop. Good day to you, Mister Forrest, we'll mebbe find our paths crossing again.'

He bustled her off to the cabinet-maker's, approved of all she had selected with one impatient glance, and was off to the loom shop before she could catch her breath. Time did indeed mean money to Matt Montgomery these days.

He was certainly far too busy to spare time for Christian's outing on Monday. Helen, fresh and pretty despite her hard work in her new shop, was there with Adam in close attendance.

To Elizabeth's astonishment, the sight of Helen

didn't draw Jeremy from her side. He made certain, as they were handed aboard the gig-boat in the canal basin, that he obtained a seat beside her. Helen seated herself with Christian and began to chatter about her new business, and Adam was left to his own devices. He chose to sit alone, astern.

It was a warm, still day, and the boat, built to seat about one hundred passengers, was more than half filled. The helmsman aft and the lookout in the bows loftily ignored the bustle of humanity embarking on the trip. Christian scorned the covered cabin, and made sure that her charges got good seats at the side, where they could look down on the water, but where the awning would protect them from the sun. She cast a glance at Adam, apart from the rest of them, but left him to his own devices.

Two patient horses drew the boat from the basin and out onto the canal proper. A small boy, filled with self-importance and brandishing a whip made from a branch, sat astride the hind animal, but the horses knew their way along the tow-path well enough. Wallowing slightly in the shallow, calm water, the boat obediently answered the tug of the tow-rope.

The first part of the four-mile journey took them

past private property on the fringe of the town, then they moved at a stately pace into the surrounding countryside. At intervals they passed close to the road to Johnstone and were stared at enviously by pedestrians and carters. For most of the journey they sailed between fields where their only audience was cows, placidly chewing and unimpressed by the familiar gig.

Grassy banks vividly patterned with wild flowers framed the canal. White yarrow, red and purple knapweed, neat yellow meadow buttercups and marsh marigolds, white and red clovers, dandelions and deep pink ragged robins flourished. White and pink convolvulus twined through the hedges, their bell-like flowers at odds with their groping, choking stems.

Foxgloves rose behind the smaller flowers in stately ranks and delicate shell-pink wild roses massed the hedgerows. Elizabeth felt her anger with Rab melt away.

On a day like this she could forgive anyone.

They arrived all too soon, slipping into the basin at Johnstone half an hour after leaving Paisley. The gig bumped gently against the quay and the travellers were helped out onto dry land.

'Now, Mister Forrest, you must come with me and meet my friends,' Christian ordered. 'They're quiet folk and an Englishman'll be a novelty for them. You too, Elizabeth. And of course, Adam and Helen—' She looked about for the rest of her party as Jeremy's amused eyes caught and held Elizabeth's in shared, secret mirth.

'Tuts, they're off on some ploy of their own,' Christian said irritably, and Elizabeth turned in time to see the two of them, Adam's hand beneath Helen's elbow, disappearing along the path that led away from the small community.

'Well, we'll manage without them,' the older woman said. 'Adam gets fidgety if he's asked to sit still for long anyway. Now, follow me—' And she bustled off in the opposite direction while Jeremy offered Elizabeth his arm.

During the visit Elizabeth's thoughts kept straying to the missing couple. The year that Adam had spoken of wasn't yet over but there had been a growing tension about him, as though his patience was running out. As yet Helen had shown no interest in him other than as a friend, in Elizabeth's opinion. She was enraptured with her shop, and close friends like Elizabeth herself well knew that under her cheerful exterior Helen still grieved deeply for Alec. It was unlikely that any proposal of marriage, even the suggestion of one, would be well received.

To her surprise, the two of them were already waiting at the basin when Christian, Jeremy and herself arrived there.

Adam was swishing at grass heads with a stick, and Helen was staring down into the water, her face still.

She greeted them with a relieved smile. The gig was ready to leave, but as they were going aboard Adam said abruptly, 'I want to stretch my legs – I'll walk back.'

'But—' Christian gaped after him as he strode off with only a slight nod to them all. 'Now what's got into the man this time?' his cousin said in exasperation. 'Helen, do you know?'

'I havenae the faintest idea,' that young lady said shortly, and almost flounced into the boat.

'I trust young Mister Forrest had an enjoyable day,' Rab said heavily that evening.

Elizabeth ladled broth carefully into his bowl. 'He seemed to get on well with Mistress Selbie's friends.'

'Be damned to Christian's friends – did the man get on well with you, is what I'm asking?'

She gave the pot to Mary and nodded to the girl to take it back to the kitchen. 'As to that, I couldn't say. I've no way of knowing how to tempt a young man. I wasn't brought up to it!'

'Eh?' He lifted his head from his food and glowered at her. 'Don't be a fool with me, lassie! Did you smile at him and invite him to sit by you?'

She could feel her face burning. 'I was polite to him, as I was polite to Adam and to—'

'Adam?' Rab barked. 'Was he there? You've no need to waste your time being pleasant to that one, for he'd no' recognise good manners if he supped them from his porridge plate with his own spoon. Ach – away and leave me in peace!'

She went, thankfully, telling herself that she was as bad as he was. While he wanted to know what had transpired between her and Jeremy Forrest, she was longing to find out what had been said between Adam and Helen.

Helen herself brought up the subject when Elizabeth had an excuse to call in at the shop a day or two later. Wiping her hands on her apron, frowning thoughtfully after her last customer, she said abruptly, 'Elizabeth, what do you make of Adam?'

Startled, Elizabeth almost dropped the scale weights she had been fiddling with. 'What do you mean?'

'He's changed in the time he's been home.' Helen's lovely face was perplexed. 'He's become so serious – and downright domineering. He was on at me, that day in Johnstone, to give up the shop and stay home where my father could look after me. You'd think I was Catherine's age instead of a grown woman! Look after me, indeed!'

'He – worries about you. He cares – about your well-being.' Elizabeth had to choose her words as though they were sweets from the colourful jars on the shelves.

Helen's brown eyes were cool. 'He has no need. I know what I'm about and I made that quite clear to him. I'm tired,' she added with a firmness that would have worried Adam if he had heard it, 'of folk who try to make me behave like some soft-handed female with no notion of how to do anything for herself!'

Her chin jutted out and she thumped on the counter with a determined fist. At that moment she looked very capable indeed.

Matt's furniture was moved in, and at last the baby and the housekeeper took up residence. Matt decided to mark the occasion with a small dinner party, and informed Elizabeth bluntly that he must have her help.

'Mistress Crombie can see to the food, for she's a fine cook. But I'm looking to you to sit at the table with me and tend the other guests.'

'And what would your father say to that?'

'How's he to know? I'm inviting the Cassidys, and Adam, and mebbe someone else to make up the numbers. I have the right to ask you to dine at my house, and you have the right to accept. So we'll have no more argument about it, or I'll be forced to come and escort you there myself.'

She marvelled at his confidence. He was happy in his work, he had a home of his own and his son was with him again. Matt had a firm grasp on the ladder and his feet were impatient on the lower rungs.

As it happened, Rab was in London on a rare visit to the exporters when Matt's dinner was held, so she had no trouble in getting a free evening. She hesitated over her fine new gown, then decided that it was probably too grand, and settled instead for her pink muslin. Mary brushed her hair until it shone and crackled, then pinned it up with nimble fingers, getting a reasonable copy of the style Effie had given her before.

Adam called for her. It had been a hot day, but a pleasant breeze had sprung up by the evening, ruffling the 'Sick' notices on house doors.

'Will the cholera ever go, Adam?' It was becoming difficult to remember a time when it had not been part of the town's life.

'It'll tire of us one day.' He shivered. 'God, this place oppresses me!'

'Why don't you leave?' she asked at once, and sensed his side-long glance.

'You're the only person that knows the answer to that.'

They had reached St George's Place. She stopped by the church railings and turned to look up at him.

'Adam, Helen's contented enough with the life she's got. How can you be sure that she'll want to wed you when the time comes?'

His eyes darkened, his voice was scathing. 'Contented? That shop's like a new toy to a bairn. It's the wrong life for a woman like Helen. She'll find that out soon enough – and I'll be waiting.'

'You still think that all a woman needs in life is a man?'

'I know Helen. Give her a full year and she'll turn to me. Then I'll give her such happiness, such love, that—' his voice sharpened. 'Are you all right, Elizabeth?'

She had never known that emotion could act like a blow. The intensity of Adam's voice and his eyes as he talked about Helen and their future together had made her gasp and clutch at the church railings for support. She felt the blood drain from her cheeks and rush to her heart.

'I'm – a stone moved under my foot.' She

released the railings, walked on, pulling away from the hand he had put beneath her elbow for support. She couldn't bear him to touch her, just after he had mentioned Helen's name with such open passion.

She and Adam were the first to arrive. They went straight to the kitchen, to admire the baby.

'You should marry again, Matt, and give this bairn a mother,' Adam said with the bluntness born of affection. 'You're the sort of man who needs a woman by his side.'

Matt shrugged his broad shoulders, clothed in a smart new dark green jacket. 'I'm too busy to go courting, and I cannae think of anyone fit to take Isobel's place. Look to your own interests – is it no' time you were settling down yourself ?'

His brother smiled enigmatically. 'Mebbe I'm no' the marrying sort. Elizabeth – the gown becomes you, but my Cousin Christian was telling me what a fine lady you were when she dined with my father. I'd hoped to see you in that dress tonight.'

She blushed. 'It's a thing too grand for me. Who's expected, Matt?'

He gave Duncan a final hug and laid him down in his crib. 'The Cassidys and their two daughters, and thon Englishman – Forrest.'

She had no time to say anything. The knocker rattled and Matt bustled out to answer it, leaving Adam and Elizabeth to follow.

The Cassidys, husband and wife and teenage daughters, were all plump and rosy and cheerful. They squeezed up the narrow staircase and flowed into the elegant parlour, fingers fluttering, mouths opening and shutting like fish as they admired the well-chosen and carefully placed furniture, the pale grey wall-paper with its delicate floral pattern, the deep red curtains.

The knocker clattered again and Jeremy was there, in pale blue coat and well-cut grey trousers, his eyes once again searching for Elizabeth and holding her in their gaze.

'I'm indebted to Mister Montgomery for bringing us together once more,' he murmured in a stolen moment together. 'The gown is delightful – paid for or not!'

Over his shoulder, she caught sight of Adam's thoughtful blue gaze on them both.

'Mister Forrest—' She moved slightly so that his body blocked the sight of Adam. 'I'd be obliged if you'd be careful no' to let my employer know that you met me in this house.'

His brows lifted. 'Why should he object?'

Coming from a big city – and another country,

when all was said and done – he could have no understanding of the Paisley ways. Rab had thought to use her to attract Jeremy's business; instead, without realising what she was doing, she had introduced the young buyer to Matt. It was clear to her now that Matt had followed up that first meeting with the intention of obstructing any arrangements between his father and Jeremy's company.

If Rab found out about the part she had played in the affair his full anger would come down on her. But she couldn't begin to explain all this to Jeremy.

'Matt and his father don't get on,' she said, lamely.

Jeremy frowned. 'But surely your employer wouldn't object to you visiting a friend—' he began, then shrugged. 'However, if it's your wish – not a word shall he hear of it, I promise you.'

He left with the Cassidys at the end of a successful evening. Adam tossed Elizabeth's shawl carelessly about her shoulders and the two of them went out into the clear mild night.

'I'd never have known Matt was so good at business if I hadn't seen it for myself,' Adam said after a long silence between them. 'While you ladies were inspecting the bairn after dinner he set about young Forrest with all the skill of a politician – or a surgeon. He's got a sharp brain, and a smooth tongue when he wants to use it.'

'Did he get an order?'

'More or less. I'm thinking that he could be Cassidy's junior partner before he's much older. That'd stick in my father's throat,' Adam said with relish.

Then he added with an abrupt change of tone. 'He's no' for you, Elizabeth.'

'Who?'

'The Englishman. Oh, he's pretty enough, and he has a fine way with him,' said Adam condescendingly, 'but you need someone with more to him than that.'

She felt her face burn. 'Adam Montgomery, are you at your black-footing again? I've told you before—!'

'I know what you've told me. I'm just saying that Forrest's mebbe a bonny diversion, but you'd be well advised no' to let him sweep you off your feet altogether. He's a toy – a plaything,' said Adam, and chuckled when she tossed her head and flounced ahead of him along the path.

Matt, at his parlour window, looked out onto the quiet night long after Adam and Elizabeth had turned the corner and disappeared from sight. He felt elated by the success of the evening and by the business deal he had just snatched from his father's very fingers. He had never realised, during those long dull years in the Montgomery warehouse, how invigorating business could be when a man was given the chance to think, and use his brain.

He sat down, gazed complacently about the room, then got up again at once and began to pace the carpet's length. He tingled with energy and the need to talk, or to work. The housekeeper was a civil soul but useless as far as conversation went. Matt wasn't one to spend his time in local howffs, drinking and gossiping – but tonight he needed company. With a brief word to Mrs Crombie, nodding by the kitchen fire, he went out and began to walk.

As he turned into George Street, with some idea of strolling round the streets before stopping somewhere for a drink, a woman hurrying towards him tripped over a stone and the large basket she carried fell from her hand, spilling some of its contents.

Matt was near enough to leap forward and catch her before she fell full-length. She was surprisingly light in his arms, a soft bundle of material and flesh that gave itself to him for safe-keeping then immediately struggled for independence.

'Och, those stones!' said a pleasant voice. 'One of these – it's yourself, Matt!'

He peered through the summer darkness. It was a long time since he had seen Helen Grant, but her wide eyes and red hair were unmistakable.

'It's a while since we've met.' She was upright now, but balanced on one foot, still clutching at his arm. 'Did you see my shoe anywhere?'

He located it, and managed to reach for it. She stuck one shapely little foot from under her skirts. 'Would you put it on for me?'

He obliged clumsily, then the two of them crouched in the dusk, gathering up packages that had spilled from the basket. Helen clucked over each one.

'There's no harm done,' he reassured her as the last parcel was retrieved.

'I had them packed in the right order—' She poked among the collection. 'Now look at them!'

He took the basket from her. 'It's over heavy for you, is it no'?'

'I'm no' helpless!' she said at once, tartly, and he grinned.

'I'm sure of that. But I'd be willing to carry it for you – I've nothing better to do,' he added as she hesitated.

She put her head on one side, considering him,

then said, 'Come on, if you're coming,' and set off without another glance.

For an hour he followed her about the streets, both in the old town and in the new town on the other side of the river. When the basket grew lighter and Helen announced that she could finish the work herself he shook his head. 'It's getting late. I'll see you to the end of this and walk to your father's house with you.'

To his surprise he realised that the restlessness had disappeared, and that he was talking more freely to Helen than he had to anyone since Isobel's death. In return, she spoke honestly about Alec's gambling and the last few months of their marriage. Matt, who had always dismissed her as a frivolous female, realised that under the lovely, cheerful exterior was a young woman of considerable courage and great determination.

On the way home Helen stopped outside the Shuttle Street loom-shop.

'Can I see the cloth your weavers are working? It's been a long time since I was in a loom-shop.'

He led her through the passage, beating a light tattoo on the living-room doorway to let the family know that he was there. His fingers found the candle that was kept just inside the loom-shop door for his regular evening visits.

Light flickered over the looms, casting their shadows grotesquely over walls and ceiling. Then as Matt lit a lamp the room was touched with soft gold and the shadows disappeared. A linnet stirred in its cage and cheeped sleepily. Helen's neat nose flared as she drew in the remembered smell of the shop – yarn, linseed oil, the lingering traces of tobacco smoke, the scent of the flowers on the deep sills.

'It's strange to see looms at rest.'

'It's sad.' Talking about Isobel had set up a keen hunger for her. As he stood there, it ached at his body and his heart and his soul like a rotting tooth.

'It's only sad if there's no work for them. But these looms are resting. There's a waiting about them, a promise for tomorrow. You and me need to know about that, more than most.'

'What was it like, the first six months?' he asked bluntly. The question didn't seem to surprise her at all.

'A terrible loss. I put on a cheery face, and I worked and worked to dull my mind. At night, alone in the shop—' she said softly, remembering '—I'd talk to him, say the things I'd never got round to saying. And I'd cry for him.' She laid a small hand lightly on a loom as though feeling for the stilled life within it. 'And after a long while, I began to discover that I can go on living, even though it's never the same.'

'Aye.' He put his own hand, big and confident in the loom, near hers. The pain began to recede slightly, eased by Helen's understanding.

'You'll do well, Matt.' Her voice fell into the golden stillness of the room; her face was like a water-lily within a pool of red hair. 'And so will I. But for now I'll have to get home, for I've to be up early tomorrow.'

'Do you have many late deliveries?' he asked diffidently when they reached her parents' house.

'Quite a lot.'

'I'll mebbe take a walk round to the shop now and then, to help you with your basket.'

Helen studied him with warm brown eyes, then smiled.

'I'd like that. Good night to you, Matt.'

She went indoors, and Matt strolled home, whistling, and slept like a child till morning.

On the evening before he was due to return to London Jeremy Forrest took a box at the theatre and invited some people, Elizabeth included, to visit the New Tontine Theatre with him.

The play was a melodrama, *The Warlock of the Glen*. The drama and pathos of it absorbed Elizabeth from the moment the curtains swept aside to reveal the castle of Glencairn. She leaned over the edge of the box Jeremy had taken, soaking in every moment of the first act, and when the interval came she was stunned to find herself in the small crowded theatre instead of the Scottish glens.

'It's a lovely story!'

Jeremy smiled down at her. 'I wouldn't know. I'm too busy enjoying your pleasure to listen to mere actors.'

She blushed. 'You should pay heed to what they're saying. At five shillings for the seats it's a waste to sit and look at me!'

'On the contrary, every penny was well spent. I'm sorry to be leaving Paisley, Mistress Cunningham. May I pay my respects when I'm next in the town?'

'You're coming back?' The news brought a flutter of excitement to her voice, and she could tell by the lift of his eyebrow that he knew it.

'Certainly. I've bought goods from the Cassidy warehouse and I want to see more of their work next year.'

She felt her heart sink. 'You didnae buy from Mister Montgomery?'

'I'm sorry to disappoint your employer, but I must spend my father's money where he can be sure of the best return. I'm impressed by Matt

Montgomery, and grateful to you for introducing us.' Then his eyes lifted from hers and moved to a spot behind her. 'Isn't that his brother?'

Elizabeth turned. People were beginning to take their places for the next act. There were a few men standing in the box opposite and Adam was among them, watching Elizabeth and Jeremy. He bowed and she saw, quite clearly, the mocking lift of his dark brows as his eyes met hers.

She pinned a bright smile on her face, inclined her head graciously as she had seen Christian do, and turned back to Jeremy, laughing up at him and chattering about the play.

It would do Adam good to see that his opinions about Jeremy mattered not one jot to her.

Jeremy Forrest went back to London and Rab grew more morose with each day that passed. Although she could no longer find a shred of liking for her employer, Elizabeth pitied him. She heard the rumours that were floating from mouth to mouth, whispering that the Montgomery warehouse was failing, the work no longer satisfactory, buyers going elsewhere because of Rab's churlish behaviour.

When Matt crowed to her about his success in

snatching the Forrest business from under his father's nose, Elizabeth's pity for the old man made her say hotly, 'Have you no feelings at all? He's alone now, with nobody to turn to!'

But Matt had learned to be hard.

'He's alone because he drove everyone from him. His new foreman's a dishonest fool and his designer's no' much better,' he said shortly. 'Let him suffer – it's no' before time!'

Only Christian stayed true to Rab, visiting him several times a week, even although the only time she could be sure of finding him at home now was to call late in the evenings.

Elizabeth welcomed those visits. Rab still insisted on her presence in the parlour after supper and she hated every silent moment of it, the old man sunk in his thoughts in one chair, while she sat stitching or knitting in another.

But even Christian could do nothing with Rab.

'Sell off the business and be done with it, man!'

He stood before the grate, glass in hand, and glowered down at her. 'I'll be damned if I will! I've given twelve years of my life to that warehouse and I'll no' let it go now!'

'You've as much money as you'll ever need. You should settle down and enjoy the time that's left to you.'

He gave a harsh bark of laughter and drained the glass.

'There's nothing else that'll interest me. Talk sense, woman! Elizabeth – more whisky!'

'And that's another thing—' Christian nagged as Elizabeth obediently laid down her work and scurried to the kitchen '—you drink too much. One of these days you'll do for yourself. As for talking sense – I never stop, but you're too thrawn to listen to me!'

The rumours grew and took on a sinister note. It was being said that the once-proud Montgomery warehouse was indulging in truck trading, the practice disreputable manufacturers had of paying weavers with unwanted goods instead of with the money the weavers needed.

A man who tried to cheat the workers in Paisley only brought down trouble on his own head. Elizabeth couldn't believe that Rab would be so foolish. But there was no denying it, once the word ran like wildfire through the town, from one coffee house to another, from the Cross to Broomlands, and in all the howffs where men gathered to drink.

'They're making an effigy for old Montgomery—' The story spread as swiftly and as dangerously as the cholera.

Elizabeth had never witnessed the weavers on

the march with drum and fifes; even so, her blood ran cold when she heard about the effigy. Everybody in the town knew what it meant.

If a 'cork' – a manufacturer – tried to undercut the fixed price table, or tried in any other way to cheat his workers, the weavers marched to his door at night carrying before them an effigy of the man for all to see.

Manufacturers had been known to flee the town when they heard that their effigies were being prepared. It was a form of condemnation that few could survive.

As soon as the malignant whisper reached her ears Christian swooped down on her kinsman's house. She and Rab had a furious scene when he refused to find some business to take him elsewhere until the matter had been forgotten, and Christian slammed out of the house, thwarted for once.

Rab continued about his business, face closed, eyes cold, apparently oblivious to the stares and the murmurs about him. It was as though he couldn't believe that the weavers would carry out their intention to shame him, the son and grandson of highly respected local men.

Adam's impatient fist thundered on the street door the day after Christian and Rab quarrelled.

He pushed past Elizabeth without a word and strode into the parlour, where his father sat at his supper.

'It's tonight,' he announced crisply. 'The men are going to march – and it's your door they're coming to.'

Rab picked up a piece of bread, broke it, and dropped the fragments into his broth. 'Get out of my house.'

'For pity's sake, man, are you deaf?' his son asked impatiently. 'Do you think you can take on the whole town and win? I'm no' here for your sake, mind. I wouldnae let Christian come back to face you. Will you do as she says and go off to Helensburgh or some such place till the thing's died down? I can have her carriage here in minutes.'

Rab looked up, his eyes malevolent. 'I'll run from nobody, let alone ragged wastrels with a wooden doll!'

'You're whistling in a gale – there's nobody left to admire your bravery!' Adam shouted at him, enraged beyond endurance. When Rab said nothing, and picked up his spoon to continue eating, the younger man turned on his heel, brushing clumsily past Elizabeth. His face was black with rage.

'Adam—' She hurried after him, caught at his sleeve.

'Let the old fool be shamed before the whole town,' he gritted at her. 'I've done as Christian asked, and I'll do no more!'

Then the anger faded and his eyes focused on her.

'Come with me to Christian's house – you and the lassie. You shouldnae be exposed to such ugliness – not you, Elizabeth.'

There was a look on his face that she had never seen before. It was as though he was seeing her clearly for the first time.

'I've told you before – I cannae just leave him.' Her voice trembled on the last few words. Adam cupped her face with one hand, and without thinking she put her own hand over his, holding it against her cheek.

'By God, Elizabeth—' he said softly, with wonder. 'I've never met your equal. If it wasnae for—' Then he stopped as his father bellowed her name from the room behind them. The hard warmth of Adam's palm left her skin, the door opened and she was alone, her heart crying out for him.

'Tell the lassie to get to her bed – and away to your own room,' Rab ordered harshly when she went to him.

'You've still to take your meat.'

He pushed his half-empty plate away. 'I'm no' interested in food. Just get yourself and the girl out of my sight for today!'

The weavers came later that night, as Adam had said. Lying awake, listening for them, she heard the chant of voices in the distance, the piping of fifes, the deep boom of the district drum.

She slipped out of bed and stood at the window. The street outside was narrow, and her attic room only allowed her a view of the attics and roofs of the houses opposite. Even so, she could imagine the scene below as clearly as though she was watching.

There would be torchlight flickering eerily on walls and turning the men's faces into grotesque, open-mouthed masks. The street would be filled, from house-wall to house-wall, with folk drawn from hearth and howff to watch the spectacle. There would be a taggle of bare-footed, ragged children and noisy, excited drawboys, and there would be the effigy, the centre of attention.

The noise swelled, and she knew that the marchers were outside Rab's front door. Jeering voices floated up to where she stood shaking with cold and terror. She was vividly reminded of the day when the coffins had been dug up and Matt's wife had died, and she listened for the crash of breaking glass and splintered wood.

But the angry weavers had no intention of breaking into the house. There was a sudden cheer, then the voices began to ebb, the drum gave out a final hollow note, and the fifes piped once more then fell silent. The marchers went home, their work done. There wasn't a sound anywhere in the house.

Elizabeth dozed through the long night and was up early in the morning. Even so, the outside door was swinging on its hinges when she reached the bottom of the stairs, and Rab's hat, stick and coat were missing.

She went to close the door then stopped, staring, one hand at her mouth to stifle the scream that came to her throat. For a terrible moment, she had thought that it was Rab Montgomery himself who dangled against the house-wall across the street, hanging on the end of a strong rope that had been thrown about a chimney.

The effigy had been made by someone with a clever talent for detail. In height and breadth it was identical to the man it represented. The men had even managed to get their hands on clothes very like Rab's – dark tailcoat, fawn trousers, a white shirt with a black silk band about the high collar, a top hat on the lolling head.

The mask they had put on it for a face was a parody of Rab's square, ruddy features, and the sightless eyes gave it a ghoulishly human appearance. There was no need to read the label pinned to the figure's breast to tell who it portrayed. A few early risers were standing staring at the hanging creature. Attracted by movement at the door they turned and gaped at Elizabeth, and it seemed to her that their eyes held the same round blankness as the effigy's.

Her empty stomach heaved. She slammed the door and sank down into a heap against it, her knees like water.

She was still there when fists pounded at the wood and Mary came running, sleepy-eyed and frightened from the kitchen.

With the girl's help Elizabeth got up and opened the door, her eyes averted from the wall opposite.

The white-faced man panting on the step was Rab Montgomery's new foreman. He had been the one to find his employer in the vast, half-empty warehouse, hanging from a sturdy beam, with a length of good strong Paisley yarn about his neck.

XI

It was as though the town felt that Rab Montgomery had paid sufficiently for his misdemeanours. Even though he was a suicide, he was given a brave funeral, with a long train of sober-faced men following his coffin.

Matt and Adam led the mourners. At first Matt had strongly resisted his brother's efforts to get him to attend.

Elizabeth, still stunned by the horror of the effigy and the shock of Rab's death, was in Christian's drawing-room when the brothers faced each other, both determined.

'It would be hypocrisy if I was seen there,' Matt said scathingly. 'And to tell the truth, Adam, you'll be a hypocrite yourself if you go!'

Adam gave him an icy blue stare. 'Has the man no rights at all? We owe him some courtesy – family quarrels have no place at a time like this, with the whole town looking on!'

'What's all this noise?' Christian interrupted sharply from the doorway, and the brothers had the grace to look embarrassed as she came to stand between them.

She had acted with her usual efficiency when she heard of Rab's death, sending Adam to the house to bring Elizabeth and Mary back to Oakshawhill with him, seeing to it that a place was found for the maid with friends of hers. Now, Elizabeth thought, the older woman was beginning to show the strain. Her black dress highlighted her pallor, her face was drawn, her eyes blank. But her spine was as ramrod straight as ever and her voice had a bite to it.

'Of course you'll walk behind your father!' she snapped at Matt. He flushed, but shook his head.

'Not even to please you, cousin. There was no love lost between the two of us, and everyone knows that. I've got more to do than stand arguing about it!' he said, and walked out.

'Leave him be!' Christian raised a hand and Adam stopped on his way to the door, his face like a thundercloud.

'Christian, it would be best if we just had a quiet burial, if it's leading to trouble between Matt and me. Who's going to care anyway?'

Small though she was she seemed to expand with sheer rage.

'Who's going to care, is it? Who's going to care? You impertinent upstart,' she flared at him, while he and Elizabeth stared at her in astonishment. 'I'm going to care, that's who! My own kinsman – your own father. He'll go to his final resting place in style supposing I'm the only mourner—'

'You know fine it's not done for a woman to attend a funeral,' he interrupted, but her voice rose above his.

'Don't you presume to tell me what I should do, Adam Montgomery! I'm head of this family now that—' she choked slightly '—now that Rab's gone. If I want to hire the militia band and bury the man with my own two hands I'll do it without interference from the likes of you! He'll have a fitting burial, and you'll be there – and you'll mourn him!' she finished on a note of fury, and swept from the room, leaving Adam and Elizabeth in total bewilderment.

'I pity Matt when she gets to him,' Adam said at last.

But when Christian rattled loudly on Matt's fine door-knocker she discovered that her errant cousin had changed his mind about the funeral. Cheated of her victory, Christian never found out that it was

Helen who had changed Matt's view during one of their walks by the river at night, when the town was settling to sleep and the long working day had finished for them both.

'You'll do what you think's best, Matt,' she said quietly in the near darkness. 'Just remember that you've a son of your own now. Would you want him to see you to your grave when the time comes?'

Suddenly it made sense to Matt, viewed from that angle. He had grown dependent on those meetings with Helen; her easy relaxed presence and tidy, practical mind had helped him to solve more than one problem. With her help he was becoming used to life without Isobel. And still nobody knew about those meetings, which made them all the more precious to him.

After the funeral Christian invited Elizabeth to stay on in her home, as her companion.

'It's lonely now that Adam's found that wee place in Barclay Street. I got used to having someone else around – and after all didn't Rachel, God rest her, mean you to be a companion anyway?' she said sensibly.

Adam had set up his sign at a tiny surgery not far from Helen's sweet shop, and had found himself rooms nearby. The house in High Street was up for sale.

Even in the turmoil of Rab's death Elizabeth found time to wonder over that brief moment when Adam had cupped her face in his hand and looked at her with a new awareness. She hadn't seen that look since, for he was too busy with the funeral and his moving to be more than courteous to her when they met.

Christian insisted on taking Elizabeth off to Edinburgh for a few days to choose new gowns.

'I couldn't be doing with those dull dresses Rab expected you to wear day in and day out,' she said as the carriage jolted over the roads. 'No point in having some bonny young thing about the house if she's wearing dull clothes. Besides, you've more chance of catching Adam's eye with better clothes.'

Elizabeth gaped at her and the older woman chuckled, delighted with herself.

'Did you think I never saw the way you brighten up when he walks into a room? Don't look at me like that – the man has no idea of your feelings for him. Montgomerys were always slow on the uptake when it came to romance. But it's my belief that you'd make a fine wee wife for a young surgeon.'

'Mistress Selbie! I'm a person, no' a cow for sale in the market! And anyway I'd never be Adam's preference.' Elizabeth swooped from indignation to gloom as she finished. Christian clucked her tongue.

'I'm no' talking about his preference, but about what's good for him. And it's my opinion that you're the right lassie.'

'He might have other views.'

'Not at all,' Christian said, so sweepingly that Elizabeth knew she had no idea about Helen. 'You're the one, and the sooner he finds that out the better.'

'If you tell him I'll – I'll—'

'What in the name of goodness do you think I am?' Christian asked, innocently. 'Not a word he'll hear from me.'

But the gleam in her eye said that Adam might receive a nudge in the right direction now and then, and Elizabeth was uneasy for the rest of the journey.

Edinburgh swept everything else from her mind. The streets were packed with people, the new town was a wonder of wide roads and elegant squares, and the dressmakers' shops and milliners' shops and hatters' shops and haberdashery shops were palaces compared to anything she had set foot in before.

'It's a relief to get out of Paisley for a day or two,' Christian said on their final evening as she toasted her toes at the fire in their lodgings. 'Especially at a time like this. I'm glad we had a reason to get away.'

'You're going to miss Mister Montgomery.' Elizabeth watched her closely.

'It's a thought when folk you knew all your life go off and die,' the older woman admitted, staring into the flames, her face averted. 'There's never anyone to take their place. He was an old rascal, but I'll admit to having a fondness for him.'

Then, still watching the flames dancing, she added, 'In fact, there was a time when I might have been his wife instead of Adam's mother, God rest her.'

Elizabeth held her breath and let the silence lengthen until Christian broke it again.

'Och – that was when we were too young to have sense. Rab was all for marriage, but my sights were set higher than a weaver in Paisley. And I did what I set out to do, I wed a banker and had more money than Rab could ever have given me. Not that money matters much when you get older and begin to think clearly.'

A smile twisted her mouth for a moment.

'By the time I came back to Paisley as a well set-up widow Rab was married for the second time. And when Rachel died – well, old bodies never talk of marriage, do we? I thought of putting it to him once or twice, plump and plain, that we should visit the minister and get the thing decided. But Rab would never have agreed to that, and I'd my pride. Mind you—' she added after another pause, '—I've been fair tormented by the thought that if I'd pushed him into marrying me, old bundle of bones that I am now, he'd be alive today. Still, we cannae turn the clock back, can we?'

She sniffed, blinked, and smiled at her new companion.

'Just mind this, Elizabeth – when happiness turns up, grip hold of it with your two hands. Never mind your pride. It never yet kept old bones warm.'

'Mind thon white kid glove you misplaced when you visited, a week or two before he—' Elizabeth said hesitantly.

'Aye?'

'I have it back at Oakshawhill. I found it among his possessions when I was clearing the house.'

Christian smiled, a radiant, bright-eyed smile.

'The daft, sentimental old devil!' she said, a youthful lilt suddenly in her voice, though it shook. 'You'll not forget to give it back to me when we get home, will you, Elizabeth?'

*

The High Street house was sold and the money split between Adam and Matt. Matt bought a partnership with Cassidy, and persuaded the old man to take over the Montgomery warehouse in Forbes Place. He paid a swift visit to London and came home filled with enthusiasm.

'I met up with Jeremy Forrest,' he told Elizabeth on a rare visit to Christian's house. 'He asked after you, and hopes to visit you when he comes to Paisley next.' His eyes twinkled. 'I told him what a fine young lady you'd become – and how bonny you've grown.'

Adam, sprawled over a chair, said nothing, but his eyes caught and held Elizabeth's, and she heard him say, as clearly as if he had spoken aloud, 'He's a toy – a plaything.'

She flushed and wrenched her gaze back to Matt, who had gone on to talk about the work he'd won for the new partnership among the London markets.

The cheerful, rather placid young man who had wooed and won Isobel Gibson had become an adventurer, a gambler with a sane streak that ensured the success of his gambling. Cassidy was trusting enough to let Matt have his head, and the new partnership was thriving from the start.

'You're like a coachman with a team of horses, every one of them going its own way,' Adam told him. 'You know what happens then – the coach ends up in the ditch and the coachman falls into the mire.'

Matt's grin was supremely confident.

'I've got the reins in my hands, and I know fine how to handle them. Besides, if I get hurt, my brother the surgeon can patch me up.'

Throughout October the cholera cases began to decrease at last. At the beginning of November, as the town excitedly prepared for the first municipal election under the new Reform Act, the disease came to a standstill. Well over eight hundred people in Paisley had fallen sick in the previous ten months, and more than half of them, James Montgomery included, had died.

In another month Helen would have been widowed for a whole year, Elizabeth remembered every morning when her eyes opened on a new day. She watched Adam and saw a spring in his step, a squaring of his shoulders, as his long self-imposed silence drew to its end.

Matt decided to put looms into the old Forbes Place warehouse, a move that caused a stir in the town.

'It's the done thing in England now, and it makes sense, having folk working under the one roof,' he argued when Christian criticised him.

'But there's no need for it. It's different in manufactories where there's machinery, like the thread mills at Ferguslie. But looms don't need steam.'

'It'll bring the weavers together instead of having to carry their webs to the looms and carry the work back to the warehouse when it's done. It gives weavers without their own looms a place to work, and it gives me a chance to see that the work keeps on during the day.'

'That's the part of it I don't care for. Handloom weavers have always worked their own hours. As long as the work's done nobody stands over them. Your warehouse is a step nearer the manufactories where women and men and bairns all have to work long hours, with no time to live like human beings.'

His jaw set in familiar, stubborn lines, and once again Elizabeth was reminded of his father.

'I'd never do that. Anyway, times have to change, cousin – and I'd as soon be the man making the changes as the man following along behind, always one step late.'

Then the elections were on them, and for a while nobody thought of anything else. The Paisley folk were highly political, and they had fought hard for the new Reform Bill, which gave them more say in the running of their town. They weren't going to let this election slip past unnoticed.

A day or two after it was all over Matt and Helen swept into Christian's parlour, both bright-eyed and rosy after a walk up the hill on a sharp November evening.

Adam, who was leaning against the mantelpiece talking, looked at once at Helen, Elizabeth noticed. The young widow was a sight to gladden any heart, with her glowing hair offset by a dark green cape and yellow gown.

'Mercy me – here's a surprise.' Christian jumped to her feet. 'Did you two meet on the doorstep?'

'We walked up the hill together.' Helen let Adam take her cape and sat by the fire, her hands held out to its blaze.

Matt stayed on his feet, bathing them all in a wide grin. 'We called at your lodgings, Adam, and your landlady said she thought you might be here.'

He rubbed his hands together, and Christian eyed him closely.

'You've got a plan in your head, Matt.'

The grin almost split his face. 'You could say that.'

She seated herself in her favourite tapestry chair. 'Well – out with it. Is it another new cloth?'

'It's better than that. It's a new wife.'

Elizabeth knew that the shock on Christian's face must be mirrored on her own. Before either of them could move Adam was shaking his brother by the hand, face alight.

'Man, that's the best news I've heard in a while! And I didnae know a thing about it. Well – who's it to be?'

Matt walked to where Helen sat, drew her to her feet, put his arm about her. 'Here she is. We're to be married at New Year,' he said, happiness shining out of his eyes as he looked down at her.

The world stopped. Elizabeth dragged her head round, away from Matt and Helen, past Christian's excited face, until she was looking at Adam. The hand that had clasped Matt's was falling slowly, slowly, to his side. Elizabeth seemed to be deaf, unable to hear anything though she knew somehow that Christian and Matt and Helen were talking all together. In stopping, the world had lost all sense of time. She was able to watch the expressions chasing each other across Adam's face – shock, horror, heartbreak. She was able to stand helplessly and see the colour draining from his features as though a grey veil had been pulled slowly down from hairline to neck.

His step back, away from the happy trio by the fire, was probably swift, but Elizabeth saw it as the languorous movement of a drowned man on the seabed, moved here and there by the tide.

Then all at once the trance shattered; she was back in the parlour, seeing and hearing, and the world was moving at its usual pace again.

'And I hadnae the slightest suspicion!' Christian was quacking joyfully. 'When did this come about?'

Helen's smile was radiant. 'We had no notion of it ourselves until last week. We just met now and again, walking home, and we talked. Then—'

'Then last week,' Matt cut in. 'We just – knew.' He hugged Helen. 'It's mebbe a bit soon, after Isobel and Alec, but we've got bairns to think of, and we're sure of our feelings—'

'Then it's the sensible thing to get wed,' Christian told him briskly. 'Mercy – a wedding, and me with nothing at all to wear—'

It might have been all right if Adam had been left alone to recover from the shock of the news. But Matt left the women to talk about weddings, and turned to his brother.

'Well, Adam – I took your advice. You'll be pleased—'

Even Elizabeth, watching Adam with her heart in her mouth, didn't realise what was going to happen. Matt, one hand held out to his brother, was quite unprepared for the fist that smashed into his face.

Helen screamed as Matt reeled back, tripped over the carpet, and fell against a small table. Wood splintered and glass tinkled as he crashed to the floor.

Adam caught Helen, spun her to face him. 'It's not true!'

She tore herself free and ran to Matt, who lay dazed on the floor. Blood trickled from the corner of his mouth and she used the skirt of her lovely gown to staunch it. Her head turned and her eyes blazed up at Adam.

'Are you insane?' she hissed at him. He moved towards her and she gathered Matt's head in her arms as though determined to defend him with her own life.

'Helen – it was always you and me—'

'Not in many a long year, Adam Montgomery. I'm a woman now, no' a little girl to be owned, can you no' understand that? Your brother can. Leave us to our own lives!'

He stepped back as though she had hit him, his face like marble. When Christian, finding her voice, asked, 'What do you think you're doing? Attacking your own brother, and in my house—' he gave her a strange, formal bow.

'Your pardon, cousin, I'll go before I can offend you further.'

'Adam – wait!' Matt said from the floor, but Helen cut in swiftly.

'Let him go, Matt – let him go away and leave us to our happiness!'

Adam's head came up swiftly at her words but he continued on his way to the door, shutting it with frightening gentleness behind him. Elizabeth wrenched it open, calling his name, and followed him to the front door.

He turned there, his face a mask, his eyes burning.

'You knew! You knew and you didn't tell me!'

'I swear I didn't!'

He walked out, leaving the door swinging. She ran after him and the cold air bit into her at once. Adam lurched onto the road and disappeared into the darkness with long furious strides.

Christian and Effie were in the hall. Christian issued swift instructions about warm water and soft cloths, then turned to Elizabeth.

'Did you know about this?'

She nodded. 'He's hoped, ever since Alec died, that one day she'd turn to him.'

Christian's mouth tightened. 'The daft, mis-guided creature! Did he never realise that Helen needed a man who'd treat her like a human being instead of a kitten? Where are you off to?'

Elizabeth pulled her cloak about her shoulders. 'I'm going to look for him.'

'In every howff in Paisley? That's where he'll be headed. Then, no doubt, he'll pay a visit to the houses by the river.'

The slums by the river were home for local petty thieves and beggars, and for the prostitutes.

'Think on, lass—' Christian put a hand on her arm. 'You'll get no thanks from Adam, you know that well enough. The man's in hell right now, and like as not he'll drag you down there with him.'

'I cannae leave him on his own!'

Christian sighed, and stepped back. 'He's a bigger fool than I took him for, setting his sights on Helen instead of looking closer to home,' she said, and turned away.

There was a rowdy party going on in the ground-floor flat where Adam's landlord lived. The landlady knew who Elizabeth was, and let her go up to his shabby, sparsely furnished room. It was empty.

Elizabeth waited, wandering about the room, picking up books, putting them down again. She managed to get a fire going in the grate, and huddled close to its warmth. The noise of the party floated up through the gapped floor-boards.

After a time she thought that Adam might be in his surgery, and ventured down the rickety stairs. The street was fairly quiet, for most of the townsfolk were in their own homes by that time of night.

She knocked on the surgery door, but there was no answer, and no light showed under the door or at the small window. She wandered on, shivering, joining little knots of children waiting patiently outside howffs for fathers and, in some cases, mothers who were drinking inside. She didn't dare venture in to look for Adam.

A man lurched out of a low, lighted door and into her path. He caught at her to steady himself, then his grip tightened as he bent to peer into her face.

'And what's a bonny wee lassie like yourself doing out at this time of night?' he asked, his voice slurred, whisky fumes almost stifling her.

'I'm – I'm going home to my bed—' She tried to draw away but he pulled her back, close to him.

'Come on, lass – come home to my bed instead.' He began to drag her towards a narrow, dark lane. Struggling didn't help. Instead, she bent swiftly and sank her teeth into the dirty hand that clamped over her arm, biting deep, choking at the sour smell of him.

He yelled and let go. She whirled and picked up her skirts, then ran blindly, gasping open-mouthed for breath, bumping into people.

Someone reeled back with an oath as she crashed into him. Thrown back against a house wall, she raised her hands before her face defensively, but they were dragged down.

'Elizabeth?' Adam stared at her, his face pale in the uncertain light from the street gas lamps.

She was so glad to see him that she could have wept. 'Adam! Are you all right?'

His mouth twisted bitterly. 'No need to let that worry you!' He began to walk away, moving unsteadily over the footpath, and she had to run to catch up with him.

'Where are you going?'

'Down by the river,' he said sullenly. 'To see if there's a kind-hearted lassie and a bottle of whisky waiting for me. Have you any money, Elizabeth?'

He swung round on her, one hand held out.

'I've nothing,' she lied. 'Come back to your cousin's house—'

He laughed. 'After what I did? Mebbe somebody'll give me hosh – hospitality in exchange for my timepiece—'

She caught at his arm. 'There's drink in your room.' When he stared down at her suspiciously she hurried on, 'I took a bottle there myself, for I thought you might be sitting alone.'

Frowning, he considered her, then shrugged and turned back towards the street where his lodging was.

She followed as he climbed the rickety stairs. The party was still going on below. Adam threw the door open and lurched into the room. When Elizabeth closed the door and turned, he was staring blearily around the room.

'Where is it?'

She moistened her lips. 'It – someone mebbe took it downstairs. Adam—' She stood before the door as he moved forward. 'Adam, I knew nothing of Matt and Helen!'

He stiffened and for a moment the effects of drink fled from his face, leaving him clear-eyed and hard as rock.

'I'll thank you no' to mention their names to me – never, do you hear me? Now get out of my way!'

She stood where she was. Some instinct told her that if he went out again, into the dark streets, down to the hovels by the river, he would be lost for all time to her.

'Elizabeth—' he said threateningly, but she was

311

the one who moved forward, half afraid, half determined, going into his arms, drawing his head down to hers, holding him close.

'Stay with me, Adam—' The words fluttered from her lips, and she saw his dark blue eyes, close to hers, clear again then narrow.

'If I stay – and if I let you stay,' he murmured, 'you know what'll happen. I need a woman tonight – oh, God, Elizabeth, you cannae imagine how much I need a woman with me tonight!'

She felt a trembling in the arms that slowly closed around her, a bruising hunger in the mouth he lowered to hers, and for all her inexperience and fear, she found that there was a hunger in her that matched his, passion for passion.

There was no tenderness in his love-making. He wasn't interested in giving, only in taking. His demands were great, his burning need greater still, but Elizabeth, freed from everything that had happened until that moment, gave gladly, again and again, throwing inhibition to the winds and letting the pure female instincts buried deep within her carry them both on until Adam finally rolled away from her in the narrow bed, and slept.

The party downstairs was over, the house quiet. Elizabeth shivered as the heat gradually ebbed from her and the night air touched her skin. Adam had rolled himself in the blanket and rather than disturb him she got up, moving stiffly, and wrapped herself in her cloak. Then she drew the chair close to the bed and huddled on it.

Her upbringing told her that what had happened was shameful. She had allowed a man to make use of her with no tenderness or care for her at all. She was disgraced.

But Adam's touch had released a deep, hidden instinct within her. In the past hour she had matured, become her true self. She could only be glad, as she shivered in the dawn chill, that it had been Adam, and nobody else, who had brought this gift. If Fate decreed that he was to be the only man, and this was to be the only night, she would accept it and go her own way without complaint.

He woke and rolled over.

'Elizabeth?' He half sat up when he recognised her by his side, then fell back, rubbing a hand over his face. 'God help me – I thought it was all a dream.'

She touched his cheek lightly and withdrew her hand at once, unsure of his mood. 'It's beginning to get light outside. D'you want me to go?'

'You should never have stayed—' said Adam, and reached for her. She let the cloak fall to the chair and moved into his embrace.

This time he showed some compassion, giving her time to match the rhythm of his needs.

He only spoke once. 'I was never a gentle man, Elizabeth,' he whispered, half-apologetically. Then it was her turn to sleep, a deep, sudden sleep that caught her unawares while she still lay with her head on his naked chest.

It was full daylight when she woke and at first she didn't know where she was.

Adam was up, dressed in his trousers, pulling his shirt on.

'You're awake. We'd best go and see my cousin Christian,' he said tersely. She sat up on the cot, and his eyes darkened as they slid over her body. He tightened his lips, but said nothing. Frightened by the look in his face, convinced that in daylight he found her repulsive, she glanced down, and realised that several ugly bruises marred her white shoulders and the soft, youthful curve of her breasts.

As she got up, glad that he had turned away to give her some form of privacy, she winced. She felt raw and stiff. She reached for her shift, then his words made sense.

'Why should you go to see your cousin? I can find my own way back without your help.'

Adam fastened his cuffs, intent on looking out

of the window. 'I can hardly let you go back at this hour of the day without giving her some explanation.'

'I can see to that!'

'Don't be a fool,' he said coldly. 'I have to go to the office for a minute. Wait here. There's no food, but no doubt Christian'll be willing to feed you – though I doubt if she'll feed me.'

'Adam—!'

The door closed behind him. With trembling fingers she finished dressing as quickly as she could, tidied her tangled hair, peered into a cloudy glass, and was glad to see that Adam's passion hadn't marked her face, though she looked like a tinker.

As she scurried down the stairs, anxious to get away before he came back, the landlady was passing through the close below. She turned, looked Elizabeth up and down, and smirked.

Walking was decidedly painful. She moved like an old woman at first, then the pain began to ease and she was able to step out. Even so, Adam caught her when she was only half-way to Oakshawhill.

'I told you to wait for me!' he said harshly.

She turned, glaring up at him. 'And I told you – I can see to myself. Just because—' she stopped short, feeling colour rush into her face. '—you neednae think that you own me!'

His brows knotted between his blue eyes. 'Own you? It's time you stopped reading those romantic novelettes, lassie! Owning's for hounds and horses and cattle, no' for women!'

Nevertheless, he put a firm, possessive hand beneath her elbow and refused to let her go back to Christian's house alone.

Christian opened the door while Elizabeth, grateful for Adam's hand beneath her arm, was negotiating the step.

'Mercy, Elizabeth, where have you been?'

'With me,' Adam said bluntly before she could speak. He bundled her into the house, and headed towards the drawing-room. Christian, mindful of the half-open kitchen door, waited until she had followed them into the drawing-room before she said, 'All night?'

'All night, cousin. It's a pity that I couldnae offer the lassie any breakfast, but I hoped you'd find it in your heart to be kind, and feed us both.'

Christian glared at him. 'My, but you're a cool one, Adam Montgomery.'

He met her look. 'You didn't think that last night. It's thanks to this lassie here that I've got my common sense back. Are you going to feed us, or

316

are you going to throw the two of us out?'

'No need to be daft altogether,' the older woman said crisply and marched out to order food.

'Adam,' Elizabeth said swiftly. 'When you've eaten, will you go to Matt and—'

'No! I don't mind much about last night, but I mind telling you I don't want to hear his name or – hers, again. That's my last word on it!' he said fiercely.

'But you'll meet him again and again. You cannae just pretend he's no' there!'

Adam's chin jutted. 'I'll no' meet him in London. We're going there as soon as I can make the arrangements.'

'London?' So he was going away, out of Paisley, out of her life.

'We?' Christian said sharply, coming back into the room in time to catch his last words. 'What does that mean?'

'It means I'm done with Paisley, for the rest of my life. I'm going to work at St Thomas's hospital, the way I planned before. And Elizabeth's coming with me. Don't fret, cousin, I'll marry the girl and make it all legal.'

Elizabeth turned on him. 'And what makes you think I'd take you for a husband?'

'You'd be well advised to.' His face was

expressionless. 'There can be no love in it, for I've had my fill of such nonsense. But I need a wife, and God knows you need a husband—'

'I can see to myself!'

He ignored Christian, marched over to where Elizabeth stood, and shook her.

'Use your head, girl! If you could see to yourself so well you'd never have allowed yourself to be tumbled into my bed last night!'

'Oh, my!' Christian said from behind him, eyes sparkling.

'And don't tell me that you're used to men, for it was obvious that I was the first. You're so innocent that you'd end up in one of those river houses sooner than see to yourself!'

She tore free, wincing at the pain of her bruises, and fled to her room. If she thought that that meant refuge she was wrong. Feet pounded on the stairs, Adam's voice roared out her name, and the door burst open, slamming back against the wall. He stood in the doorway, glaring at her.

'For the last time, Elizabeth – will you see sense and wed me!'

'Adam Montgomery!' Christian puffed from just behind him. 'Is that any way to propose to a lassie?'

'It's the only proposal she'll get from me,' he

said grimly. 'Go away, Christian! Elizabeth—?'

Christian's bright eyes appeared round the side of his arm. 'Elizabeth – before you say anything I want you to try and mind where you found that fine white kid glove of mine—'

'For the Lord's sake, Christian—' Adam bellowed, rounding on his cousin, 'is this any time to start looking for a glove? Now – out of here and let me and Elizabeth discuss our business in a civilised way!'

With a small shriek Christian disappeared. The door slammed shut, and Adam and Elizabeth were alone.

'Well?'

'What have you to offer me?' she challenged, though now her mind was on that little white glove that had been tucked carefully away in a drawer in his father's room, a symbol of pride and loss.

'Is it not obvious? A good home, comfort, a place in society – independence.'

She tilted her chin. 'I'd hoped for love, one day.'

'You've surely got more sense than that,' he said sweepingly. Then he shrugged. 'Well, if you'd as soon stay here, with Christian, it's your own concern.' He turned to the door.

'Adam—'

He stopped, his back towards her. 'Aye?'

Christian was right. Happiness had to be caught and held. And whatever sort of marriage Adam had to offer, would be better than staying in Paisley, knowing that she would never see him again. Once more she faced bleak choices.

'I'll wed you – if that's what you want.'

He turned, watching her warily. Now it was his turn to be uncertain.

'It has to be your wish too. It's no' a light offer I'm making.'

She nodded, went to him, and felt his arms go round her clumsily, as though he was unsure of his reception.

'It's my wish too,' she said.

XII

The days between Adam's blunt proposal and their marriage passed in a blur of packing and shopping. If it hadn't been for Christian Elizabeth would have thrown her hands up in despair and taken to her bed more than once.

But at last the boxes were packed, and Elizabeth stood by Adam in the minister's parlour, with only Christian and one of Adam's colleagues for witnesses, and promised to live with him as his wife for the rest of her days.

His hands were warm and confident as he slipped the gold wedding band onto her finger. His mouth curved in a brief, reassuring smile as she looked up at him. It was done.

A few hours later they were on their way to London, putting distance between themselves and Paisley with each turn of the coach wheels. Elizabeth hadn't had time to say goodbye to anyone except Christian, and she hadn't seen Matt or Helen at all.

Their wedding night was spent in an inn, a place of stained plaster and shadows in the high corners. While Adam remained downstairs Elizabeth shivered her way into her nightgown and brushed her hair, wondering if any other bride had had to go to her new husband with goose-pimples all over her body. Her teeth chattered with cold and fright. She climbed into bed, at once felt marooned in its icy wastes, and jumped out again, convinced that nasty beasties lurked between the sheets.

Adam found her standing in the middle of the floor when he came upstairs. To her great relief, he didn't laugh when he saw her hopping bare-footed on the wooden floor, shivering and almost in tears.

'It's – cold—' she said, lips trembling, and he reached out his arms and drew her close to him.

'Poor Elizabeth—' he murmured into her ear. 'What have I done, taking you away from the only place you've ever known?'

Then he lifted her and carried her to the bed, where there were no beasties, and his strong body warmed them both. And this time, his love-making was tender and considerate.

She slept contentedly in his arms afterwards, but as they rode into London at the end of their journey her restored confidence began to crumble a little.

She peered, a country mouse, from the windows at the teeming crowds in the capital. The streets seemed to go on for ever, lined with shops and coffee houses. Rows of hackney carriages waiting for custom lined some of the wider roads and there were a number of sedan chairs, each emblazoned with a coat of arms, and heavily curtained.

People strolled the pavements in various stages of elegance. Ragged urchins darted in and out of the crowds, flower girls sat by the kerb in a blaze of colour provided by blossoms that had, like Elizabeth herself, been plucked from rural areas and carried off to the city.

A knife-grinder plied his trade at one corner, puffing serenely at his pipe, gnarled hands insensitive to the showers of sparks that flew about them from his stone. Another man pushing a long wooden barrow was glimpsed as the coach passed, his clothes in rags and his mouth a black hole in his face as he roared out his wares. The coach had left him behind before she could see what he was selling.

Then they were out of the bustle and had turned into the coach station. Adam helped Elizabeth down, but she had little time to look about her before she was being handed into a hackney carriage for the last part of the journey, this time to a graceful quiet road with a tree-lined park opposite long windows.

While she and Christian had been busy buying clothes, Adam had sent word to friends to find a suitable house where he could bring his bride.

To her horror, she saw a small group of servants on the steps outside the high, wide door.

'That's never the house you've taken!' she squeaked in panic to her husband. 'It's too big! And what about those folk – Adam, I cannae look after a house like this!'

The carriage had stopped, the driver was deftly unfolding the steps and opening the door. Adam's hand under her elbow gripped painfully.

'You can and you will. You're my wife, mind that. And smile – nobody's going to behead you!' he added in a steely undertone.

Smiling, panic-stricken, she descended from the carriage.

It was difficult not to burst into tears and demand to be taken home. With growing concern she surveyed the large drawing-room, the lofty hall, the small but imposing dining-room. With each moment that passed Adam, who seemed to be quite at home in his new surroundings, became more of a stranger to her. The warmth he had shown on their wedding night ebbed away as he began to plan ahead to his hospital work.

'There's nothing to be afraid of,' he said a trifle impatiently on their first morning in the house. He leaned against the window sill, studying the street below, and Elizabeth, sipping a cup of hot chocolate, was left alone in the middle of the vast four-poster bed. 'Get dressed and I'll take you to visit the friends who found the house for us. Lucy can tell you all you need to know about life here.'

'I'll learn,' she hurried to assure him. 'With you to help me at first I'll learn—'

'Me?' He laughed shortly. 'My dear girl, don't depend on me for help. I'll have more than enough to do with my own work. Lucy can see to you,' he added carelessly.

Elizabeth was mortified to discover that one of the maids had been detailed to help her to dress. She had been used to fending for herself from the time she could toddle, and in her confusion she made matters worse by trying to assist the girl. Buttons slipped in buttonholes and back out again several times, ribbons were knotted clumsily by two pairs of hands, and hooks simply gave up and refused to co-operate with anyone.

The carriage was waiting and Adam was pacing

the hall restlessly by the time she went downstairs. During the journey he answered her questions tersely, and all she could grasp was that Henry Worthing had been stationed at the army base where Adam's ship called regularly, and he and his wife Lucy now lived in London.

It was obvious by the huge house they went into that the Worthings were moneyed people. Adam handed his hat to the footman and strode into the vast drawing-room without wasting a glance on the magnificent panelling and exquisite furnishings, but Elizabeth stared about her as she followed him, convinced that she had been dropped into some exotic treasure cave.

'Adam! Dear, dear Adam!' Lucy Worthing swooped on him as soon as he appeared.

'What a surprise you gave us!' She kissed his cheek lightly then stood back, to study him, her hands still in his. 'A wife, indeed! And no warning that you'd given your heart away. How dare you keep such a secret from me?'

'I thought you relished secrets. Elizabeth—' He freed his hands, brought Elizabeth forward. 'This is my wife. Elizabeth, may I present my dear friend, Lucy Worthing.'

Lucy was just as beautiful as Helen, Elizabeth noted with a strange, sinking feeling. She had silky fair hair and wide green eyes. Her flawless figure was dressed in a pale green gathered muslin gown that made Elizabeth's pink dress look young and plain.

'Adam, she's lovely!' Lucy's gaze skimmed her face and Elizabeth saw, from the slight tremor of the eyelids, that the other woman had noted the hated scar. 'Come and sit here, my dear, and tell me all about your marriage to this exciting man!'

Her eyes darted from one to the other of them, coquettish when they touched Adam, calculating when they brushed against Elizabeth. It was only natural that Adam's friends would be surprised by his sudden marriage, she thought uneasily as she was led to a satin divan. There was no reason why she should distrust Lucy on such short acquaintance, and yet—

A flibbertigibbet, Christian would have said. She had no time for what she called 'kittens in petticoats'. And Lucy certainly seemed to fit that description.

'I must apologise for the servants – I had little time to find them. I shall find a suitable ladies' maid for you this very afternoon.'

Elizabeth knew sudden panic. 'But I don't need any more servants!'

The other woman's eyebrows arched. 'My dear,

how else are you to see to your hair, and your clothes?'

'The lassie – the girl I have can do it well enough. And I dress my own hair.' Her Scottish tongue sounded heavy and clumsy in this lovely room.

The green eyes swept over her brown hair with a glance that said enough, and roused Elizabeth to defensive anger.

'If I think I need more maids, I can find them myself. Besides, servants cost money, and—'

To her gratitude Adam came to her rescue. 'My wife is quite right, Lucy. Mere surgeons can't afford to run a large household. We don't all come of wealthy stock. Is Henry not at home?'

Lucy's mouth had a downward droop that marked her as a woman unused to being crossed. 'He's making plans in the country with his father. He's to go into Parliament.'

'You didn't travel with him?'

Her nose wrinkled. 'Norfolk in November is dismal. Besides, I wouldn't have been here to welcome you if I'd gone with Henry. Aren't you glad that I stayed here instead, Adam?'

Adam took up a stance before the fireplace. He looked quite at home amid this splendour, Elizabeth realised, although his clothes were plain. 'So – Henry is to go into Parliament?'

'There's nothing else for him to do. It's Parliament or the Church, and of course, I could never be a parson's wife!' Lucy sighed. 'If only he'd left the army before this terrible Reform Bill was passed, he would have had no trouble in getting a seat. Papa says that the Bill will ruin the country, and rob him of all his money.'

'In Paisley—' Elizabeth blurted, then bit her lip.

'Yes, Elizabeth?' her husband asked gently, and she saw the glint of mischief in his eyes. 'You were saying?'

The words came reluctantly. She felt that he was making a fool of her, emphasising her clumsiness before his elegant friend. 'In Paisley, we feel that the Reform Bill will be more just – as you well know, Adam!' she finished with a bite to her voice.

Lucy raised an eyebrow. 'How strange,' she said vaguely.

'You seem to think highly of Mistress Worthing,' Elizabeth said on the journey home.

'She's a charming lady, do you not think so?'

'And very beautiful.'

'Naturally.' There was faint surprise in his voice. 'She was taught to make a career of being beautiful. It's her only asset – that and her father's money. Learn from her, Elizabeth. She'll introduce you to society, and fill your days.'

329

Elizabeth's days overflowed with Lucy Worthing, and were denied Adam. He became immersed in his work at St Thomas's, spending very little time at home.

Lucy introduced her to crowds of people, took her to the theatre, the opera, dinners, and balls. Sometimes Adam was with them, but more often he excused himself, pleading pressure of work. When Elizabeth tried to turn down invitations, however, he insisted that she go without him.

She quickly realised that Lucy's gossip was almost always motivated by envy and malice. She usually talked about people who had something that she coveted, and as the days dragged on Elizabeth grew to suspect that Adam was one of the items the beautiful woman would have liked for her own collection. She was usually surrounded by young men and her husband, a chinless, silent creature, was quite unruffled by his wife's entourage.

Eventually Lucy's chattering tongue led her to the subject of Caroline, Adam's dead fiancée.

'Such a romantic story – Caroline sailed to join her family in India on the ship Adam served in. And as fortune would have it, he and his fellow officers often paid visits to the area. He was quite besotted with her – I swear I've never seen a young man so in love, before or since.' Lucy's green eyes flicked sideways at Elizabeth. 'We were all in a flutter, preparing for their wedding, when the cholera came. Adam was one of the naval surgeons detailed to work in the district, but of course none of us dreamed that poor Caroline would fall ill. She died in his arms, you know, and he was beside himself with grief. I thought that he would never get over the loss.' Then her voice changed subtly, and she said, in sweet tones that would have made Christian Selbie sniff, 'It gives me such pleasure to see him happily married, after all.'

'Is there nothing I can do with my days? Nothing useful?' Elizabeth appealed to Adam on a rare moment together.

His brows rose. 'You look after my house, you entertain, you lead a busy social life. What more can you want?'

'The housekeeper runs your house. I sit and talk – and talk, and talk. I listen, and I never hear anything worth listening to. And I do nothing useful!' She paced the drawing-room, catching sight of herself in a long mirror – well-dressed glossy brown hair, a neat figure in a stylish dress of deep blue silk, white shoulders bare. 'Can't I be of some use at the hospital?'

Adam sprawled in a tapestry chair, watching

her. 'I couldn't allow you to set foot in the place. It's filled with despair and disease and human misery – can't you see that I need to know that you're here, safe and comfortable?'

She didn't realise until much later what he meant. At that moment she was too wrapped up in her own boredom to weigh his words. 'Surely I could contribute something, even if it was just visiting sick folk, talking to them – helping with their families, mebbe?'

'The women who work in the hospitals are either sisters of mercy or slatterns who sell themselves to patients and doctors alike for the price of drink. You'll not set foot in that place,' he repeated.

'Then what can I do?'

'Lucy seems to be contented enough with her life,' he said, and a curtain came down over his eyes, putting an end to the conversation.

There were happy moments, sometimes whole days when he stayed at home, resting, wanting nobody around but her. On those days he ruthlessly cancelled all her engagements, turning a deaf ear to Lucy's objections. They talked, or explored London in the carriage. They talked about his work, about Paisley, about Elizabeth's opinion of a play she had just seen. They never talked about themselves.

She still had the ability to make him laugh, and he still, when he was relaxed, teased her unmercifully.

In bed, the only place where they could truly be alone, he was sometimes demanding, often courteous and considerate, but always formal. She sometimes wondered, with an hysterical giggle that had to be suppressed, if he was going to call her 'Ma'am' when he made love to her. But he never spoke, and she was oddly shy, too shy to say the endearments she longed to speak aloud.

She loved him deeply, but she wasn't happy. Since it was what he wanted, she worked hard at learning from Lucy. She changed her accent, learned to develop good dress sense, overcame her shyness and mastered the art of polite conversation. She even started giving dinner parties. Winter gave way to spring, and Elizabeth learned to exist within the comfortable glass prison that Adam had made for her.

Christian's letters were a lifeline to her. The older woman wrote every week – a general letter for them both, and a private letter for Elizabeth, which Adam passed to her without comment.

In those private notes she put all the little morsels of gossip that Adam would have frowned on, as well as news about Matt and Helen. Adam knew nothing of their New Year marriage, the Townhead house Helen's father had given them as a wedding present, Matt's continued success, Helen's pregnancy.

'The old warehouse is filled with looms, and every one of them working,' Christian wrote. 'Though I still have my doubts about the whole business, Matt's doing well for himself. I see him very like his father; it's a mercy that he's got Helen to sweeten the hard streak in his nature.'

In April Elizabeth was stunned to see a familiar grin among the throng in the foyer of a theatre. Her hand was seized and shaken warmly.

'Elizabeth! Mistress Cunningham!' Jeremy Forrest's face glowed with pleasure. 'I can scarce believe my eyes! Are you down here on a visit?'

She was so pleased to see him that she could have kissed him in front of all the people. 'I live here, with my husband. I married Adam Montgomery.'

He looked for a moment as though she had struck him, but rallied swiftly. 'I remember him, but I – is he here with you?'

He wasn't, but Lucy swept up to them, eager to find out why her protégée and a handsome stranger had greeted each other so warmly. Her narrowed eyes moved thoughtfully from one to the other, her charm flowed over Jeremy.

'As you and Elizabeth are such – old friends – you must come to a social evening I'm holding next week, Mr Forrest.'

'I accept with pleasure.' His eyes held Elizabeth's. Lucy's beauty hadn't affected him at all. 'Eliz – Mistress Montgomery and I have a great deal to talk about.'

He became a member of the Worthings' circle and life brightened for Elizabeth. He offered sincerity among a sea of false charm, and affection when she felt starved of it.

Lucy saw to it that Adam heard about Jeremy, but he only said casually, 'As I recall, that gentleman was always a particular admirer of Elizabeth's. But not one to be taken seriously.'

When Matt Montgomery came to London on business in June Elizabeth heard of it from Jeremy.

'I'd like to invite yourself and Adam to my father's house for dinner – but Matt tells me that Adam will have nothing to do with him,' he said awkwardly.

'I would be pleased to accept for myself.'

'But you'd not come alone?'

She put her hand briefly on his arm. 'If Matt was to be my escort – oh, Jeremy, I want so much to see him, and I can't invite him to my own home.'

He looked doubtful. 'What would Adam say if he heard that you were dining with us?'

'Adam,' said Elizabeth, 'need never know.'

It was the happiest evening she had spent in London. The Forrests' home was similar to Christian's – large, plain rooms filled with honest, straightforward people. And in their midst, arms outstretched to hug the breath out of her, face split by a huge grin, was Matt.

When he finally released her he stood back and stared. 'My, Elizabeth – you're a lady now!'

'No, I'm still myself. How's Helen?'

'Bonnier by the day, and fairly looking forward to the bairn coming.'

He was Paisley itself. His face, his voice, his very actions transported her back to her home town. She was proud to see how comfortable he was among the English merchants, and how they paid keen attention to his views.

The Forrests and their other guests tactfully left them alone in a corner of the drawing-room after an excellent, plain meal. Questions poured from Elizabeth faster than Matt could answer them.

'Christian writes such news of you, Matt! You're doing well.'

'Well enough.' He hesitated, then broached the subject they had both avoided. 'How's Adam?'

'Working all the time.' She looked down at her hands. 'He seems to like the hospital, though.'

'Does he ever talk of me?'

She shook her head. 'I'd like fine to ask you to dine with us, but—'

'Aye. He must have cared deeply for Helen. If I'd had any notion—'

'You've got as much right to your happiness as he has.'

'And he's got you – what more could a man want?' Matt asked. 'Does Christian ever mention her own health?'

'Never. She's no'—?'

'She's fine. Just a wee turn during the winter. I wondered if she'd told you, that's all. I think she misses you – both of you.'

It was hard to say goodbye to him at the end of the evening. On the way home she made up her mind to speak to Adam, to insist that he invite his brother to his house. She had had enough of the one-sided quarrel and all that it had led to. But Adam was still out when she got home, and he had risen early and gone out again by the time she wakened in the morning.

He arrived home in the afternoon. She was in the drawing-room, alone, when he stalked in.

'Where were you last night?' he asked at once,

and a tremor of fear ran through her. She suppressed it.

'I dined with friends.'

'Indeed?'

'I often do when you're at the hospital.'

'Last night I wasn't at the hospital. I came home because I thought that my wife might like my company at the theatre. When the housekeeper said you had already gone I took it that you had gone on with Lucy. So I followed.'

She moistened her lips.

'Lucy said that she had no idea where you were. Jeremy Forrest was also missing from the group.'

'And Lucy drew that to your attention, I've no doubt. She's over fond of causing mischief.'

'Perhaps – but she has sense enough to know that secret assignations between a man and a married woman are most unwise!'

'You think that I had an assignation with Jeremy?' she taunted, half frightened, half amused. He caught her arms, lifted her out of her chair. His eyes blazed at her.

'Where were you?'

'I was dining at Jeremy's father's house, with Matt.'

The name caught him off balance. He blinked, repeated foolishly, 'Matt?'

'Your brother. He's in London on business, and Jeremy thought that I would like to meet him.'

'You have no right to accept invitations without informing me!' Adam let her go and she stood still, refusing to be intimidated.

'I have every right! Matt's a friend of mine – and so is Helen. It's time you ended this nonsense, Adam. I want to invite your brother here.'

'No!' He swung away from her, almost fell over a small chair, and gripped the back of it. 'I've told you – I'll have nothing to do with him. As my wife, I expect you to respect my wishes!'

'Adam, do you no' see— ' in her agitation her Scottish accent took over '—that as long as you're bitter towards Matt, our marriage is empty? This love for Helen's between us all the time!'

He turned. 'Helen? You think I still love her? You know fine that love has no place in my life – certainly not where Helen's concerned.'

'Without love we have no sort of marriage, can't you see that?'

If he had taken her in his arms then, everything would have been all right. For a breathless moment she thought he might. She moved a step towards him, her heart thumping. But the flicker of doubt in his eyes disappeared and his face was mask-like again as he said stiffly, 'Perhaps you'd prefer to make an end to it?'

'Would you be happier if we did?'

'I made a marriage contract with you,' he said with icy formality. 'I intend to honour it for the rest of my life, if that is your wish. But I must be assured that you'll respect my feelings.'

He strode towards the door, turned as he got to it.

'If you're not prepared to accept those terms, Elizabeth, then you are free to leave. I promise that I'll make no effort to stop you.'

XIII

Elizabeth didn't see Matt again. She and Adam lived for a week in a state of armed truce. He worked long hours at the hospital, came home late, and made no effort to touch her, day or night.

They only spoke when they were with other people. After the first week, life slowly got back to normal, but it seemed to Elizabeth that the pretty glass case she lived in was shrinking and suffocating her.

Three weeks after their bitter quarrel a letter arrived from Scotland, addressed to Elizabeth in a round, unfamiliar hand.

'It's from Helen—' she said without thinking and Adam, sunk in his own thoughts across the breakfast table from her, lifted his head sharply.

'Why would she have anything to say to you?'

'Your cousin Christian's ill.' For the first time in weeks she looked fully at him, and saw how tired

341

and drawn he was. 'It seems that she neglected a chill and it turned to pneumonia.'

He was giving her his full attention now. 'Is she bad?'

Elizabeth's eyes fled along the lines of script. 'She's recovered, but very weak. Helen thinks she'd be the better for seeing us.'

'I have no time to go to Scotland just now,' he said at once. 'But if you want to—'

'Without you?'

'Why not?' He pushed his chair back and stood up. 'God knows we're poor company for each other these days. And it might be as well for you to go where there's no mischief brewing.'

She stared up at him blankly. 'Mischief?'

His mouth twisted. 'You were born with innocent eyes. You know as well as I do that I'm talking of young Forrest and the way he pines after you.'

'How dare you speak like that about my friendship with him? What do you know of him, since you're never with us? I suppose Lucy has been tattling again?'

He ran a hand irritably through his dark hair, now well streaked with grey.

'I've told you before, Elizabeth – he's a pretty enough bauble for you to amuse yourself with, but I have no intention of being cuckolded by a fop!'

Rage brought her to her feet. She faced him across the forgotten meal.

'I'm not a possession to be treated like this!'

'You're a wife,' he told her coldly. 'You made your marriage vows before a minister. And that gives me the right to say what I think about your behaviour.'

She gave a strangled laugh. 'And you made vows on that day too. Why should I remember, when you've forgotten?'

Adam's eyes were narrow shards of ice in a set, pale face. 'I'll not discuss this any further, Elizabeth. Go to Paisley, for that's where your heart is. God knows it was never here, where it should be!'

'Was it ever needed here?' When he said nothing, she swept on. 'And what about my duty as a wife, since you're so set on preaching about it? If I go off to Paisley, who's to see to your comforts and obey your wishes?'

'I'll manage well enough with the servants to look after the house,' he said icily.

'And Lucy to see to your own comforts, as she's always wanted?' she jeered. 'I'm not blind, Adam!'

'I swear that you've dipped your tongue in vinegar. Malice doesn't become you nearly as well as it becomes Mistress Worthing,' Adam told her.

He picked up his blue coat, shrugged himself into it, and began to walk out of the room.

'Adam—' Her voice stopped him, though he didn't turn round. '—If I go to Paisley without you,' she said to his broad back, 'I'll not come to London again.'

Adam adjusted his collar, touched the lace at one wrist.

'I'm aware of that, Elizabeth,' he said, and walked out, leaving her alone.

There was nobody to turn to but Jeremy. She finally found him in his father's warehouse by the docks. Terrified by the bustle of the place, almost knocked off her feet several times as she fought through crowds of burly men carrying crates or rolling barrels to and from the high-masted ships, she almost wept with relief when she saw him.

'Elizabeth!' He caught her by the arm and whisked her out of the path of a trolley. 'This is no place for a woman!'

Her hands were shaking so badly that she could scarcely take the money from her purse. 'I want you to book a seat for me on the next coach to Glasgow, Jeremy. I have to get to Paisley quickly, for Mistress Selbie's ill and needs me.'

'But—' he took the money, perplexed. '—but surely Adam should arrange all that for you?'

'Adam's – he's—' She had intended to say that he was busy, that an urgent message had just arrived from Paisley and she had been unable to trace Adam. Instead the tears that had been unshed during the past terrible weeks broke through, and Jeremy's bewildered, friendly face blurred and disappeared.

He took her into a tiny cubicle where, unseen by anyone, she could cry to her heart's content, wrapped closely in his arms, his fingers stroking her hair. Between sobs, the whole story came out.

'Elizabeth—' he said wretchedly against her forehead, his lips warm. 'How could anyone treat you so badly?'

She mopped at her face, already regretting the words that had spilled out, betraying Adam. 'It's no' the way it seems – he's had so much unhappiness, and I thought I could make up for it. But—'

His fingers brushed her cheek. 'I never thought he was the man for you. When I heard that you'd wed him – oh, Elizabeth, if you'd just waited until I went back to Paisley!'

'Jeremy, you'll help me to get home?' she interrupted, in no state to deal with the declaration of love that seemed to be on its way.

He did everything he could. Elizabeth was put into a carriage and sent back to her house, where she packed a few things and wrote a brief, formal note for Adam. Then she returned to the warehouse, and Jeremy escorted her to the stagecoach depot and saw her on her way back to Scotland.

Her spirits rose as she crossed the Old Bridge on her final lap home. She breathed in the air, devoured the narrow streets and old buildings with her eyes. She was home.

Christian was frighteningly withered and grey-faced, but as full of spirit as ever.

'You should never have come all this way just to see me,' she scolded almost at once. 'Adam has more need of you than I have!'

'He can manage fine for as long as I'm needed here, so that's final,' Elizabeth retorted, and could tell, by the older woman's acceptance of what she said, that Christian was happy to see her.

She slipped back into Paisley life with such ease that after two weeks it seemed that she had never been away. She was busy running Christian's house and seeing to her comfort, and although she sat down several times to write to Adam, she could think of nothing to put on paper. They had said more than enough to each other before she left. That life, the life they had shared uneasily for a short time, was over.

Helen, happily pregnant, welcomed her with open arms.

'I've missed you – and you look so grand! But too pale, you need to get out more.' Her lovely face shadowed. 'Matt says he didnae see Adam at all when he was in London. I wish he'd come north with you.'

'He's too busy just now,' Elizabeth said mechanically, and repeated the words, like a charm to hold Adam's presence at bay, each time she was asked about him.

Christian's health improved from the moment Elizabeth arrived, and three weeks later she was her old self.

'You've a natural healing way with you, lass, but I'm vexed with myself for keeping you from Adam for so long.'

Elizabeth concentrated on the rose she was embroidering. 'He's too busy to miss anyone.'

The cloth she was working on was whipped from her hands.

'I'm not a fool,' the older woman said. 'Adam's too busy to visit his sick cousin, too busy to claim his wife back – even too busy to put quill to paper. What's amiss?'

'You said I'd be welcome here if I found that I'd

done the wrong thing. That's all there is to it.'

'I said you'd be welcome, and I meant it. But I didn't say I'd ask no questions,' Christian said firmly.

It was better to get it over with. Elizabeth gave Adam's cousin a brief, crisp outline of her disastrous marriage, ending with, 'And I'm not going to discuss it with anyone.'

'Except Adam.'

'As he'll never come here to speak to me, I'll never be able to discuss it with him.' Elizabeth said shortly, and reached for her sewing.

'So—' It was warm and still in the garden where they sat. Bees murmured round a flowering bush, a butterfly investigated Christian's patterned dress then moved on, disappointed. 'You just left him in London, did you? With that empty-headed trouble-making minx?'

'If that's what pleases him—'

'Tush! You know fine and well you should never have given her the satisfaction of seeing him deserted by his own lawful wife!'

'I'll not discuss it!' Elizabeth snapped, and accidentally drove the needle into her finger. At least it gave her an excuse for the tears that had arrived in her eyes.

At the beginning of August Jeremy Forrest came

back to Paisley on business. Although there were only two months to go before Helen's baby's birth, she and Matt entertained often, and so Elizabeth and Jeremy met several times.

'That young Englishman's fair taken with you,' Helen remarked when she and Elizabeth were alone in the Townhead house. 'He's gentleman enough to try to hide it, but it's there for a sharp-eyed woman like myself to see.'

'He's just—' Into Elizabeth's mind floated a well-remembered voice, saying '—a toy, Elizabeth.' She pushed it out of the way. 'He's just a dear friend.'

'Is he now? Elizabeth, would I be right thinking that you're in no hurry to go back to Adam, and he's in no hurry to come and seek you out?'

She looked up at her friend's compassionate eyes. 'There's no sense in denying it.'

Helen sighed. 'I'm no' over surprised. He's a strange man, Adam. I could never have settled with him, and I've no idea why he thought I would.'

'He's an unhappy man, and I was wrong when I thought I could help him.' Elizabeth kept her voice steady.

'If you couldn't, of all people, then he's hard to please. Now – Matt's taking the bairns to the fair on Friday, but I've no wish to go through these crowds like this—' she patted her swollen belly. 'Would you like to go along with them? I'd better tell you that Jeremy's going to be there.'

The first day of the annual fair was given over to the farmers, who crowded the town with livestock, machinery, and themselves. The second day belonged to the people, who flocked in their thousands to St James' racecourse to see the stalls and side-shows, the waxworks, and races and Wombell's Menagerie of caged animals.

It took three adults to keep up with young Duncan and Catherine as they scampered through the crowds, demanding to be shown everything. Catherine tackled the merry-go-round and swings with enthusiasm, but Duncan, still a baby and not long on his feet, clutched at his father, wide-eyed with frightened excitement.

The waxworks came next, then the tumblers and the trained pigs and the menagerie. The whole town was in holiday mood and the atmosphere was exhilarating. On the way back to the swings, Elizabeth was side-tracked by a small tent.

'Look – a fortune teller! I've never had my fortune told!'

Matt disappeared through the mob with the children, but Jeremy lingered beside Elizabeth.

'I could tell your fortune for nothing, if you'd listen to me.'

'You've got the gift?' She laughed up at him. The handsome face above hers was serious.

'Enough to know that your happiness lies with a fair-haired Englishman – like me, if you'd only admit to the truth.'

'You're teasing me,' she said swiftly, and turned away towards the tent so that she wouldn't see his expression. 'Oh – my wedding ring – she'll know I'm married.'

'Give it to me, then.' He held out his hand. Elizabeth shook her head.

'I'll no' bother. It'll be a pack of romantic nonsense,' she said lightly, and ran after Matt. She couldn't bring herself to take off the ring Adam had put on her finger. Only one person had the right to do that. Until he did, she would wear it.

'You've never once asked me about Adam,' Jeremy said on his last day, when he came to say goodbye and found her alone. His eyes searched her face intently.

'I have no reason to ask about him.'

'I never see him anyway. Nobody does – and I stopped going to Mistress Worthing's gatherings when you left London. A beautiful woman, but an empty one. Will you write to me, Elizabeth?'

'I was never a good hand with letters.'

'Write to me all the same,' he insisted, 'and when I come back we'll talk properly, you and me.'

'Safe journey – mind me to your family.' She held out her hand, but instead of shaking it formally, he used it to draw her into his arms.

She put her hands to his shoulders to push him away, then his mouth was on hers, warm and firm, and suddenly Elizabeth found herself holding him, responding to his kiss eagerly.

They were both breathless when they drew apart. Jeremy's eyes glowed, and he released her reluctantly.

'I wish I had found the courage to do that earlier,' he said huskily.

When she was alone she went out into the garden, stunned by her reaction to his kiss. For the first time in six weeks a man had held her, and her starved body had responded immediately, giving itself away.

It was the underlying reaction that frightened her. She hadn't been satisfied, in those few moments when Jeremy had held her. He had brought her back to life – and had also wakened the deep need for someone with more strength, more vitality, more – arrogance.

She sank down onto a stone seat, staring in

dismay at Christian's immaculate rose-bed. She wanted Adam, she missed him, and her body told her clearly that she would rather be used by him than loved tenderly by a hundred Jeremys.

'God help me!' she said aloud, appalled by her thoughts, and by the tingle that was still travelling along her veins, quickening her pulse, tensing her breasts.

'Why?' said Christian from the door. 'What have you done?'

Elizabeth jumped up guiltily. 'Nothing.'

'Then mebbe He should help you, for you're too young and too healthy to sit about doing nothing,' the older woman said briskly. 'I just met thon Englishman of yours at the gate. He tells me he's away home – but he's coming back. I don't think it's shawls he'll be after next time.'

'What else could it be?' Elizabeth moved about restlessly. Her body was glowing now.

'It's you. He's a nice enough laddie, and moneyed, I hear. What's up with you – you're like a hen on a hot griddle.'

'I'm fine.'

'Aye – well – mebbe he is the right man for you, when all's said and done. Polite, treats a lady like a lady. Whereas Adam—' it was almost as though Christian knew about the torment building up inside Elizabeth '—Adam, now, is no gentleman when it comes to womenfolk. Altogether too conceited, and demanding, and—'

Elizabeth made some excuse and went to the little room where she slept. She threw herself down on the bed, fingers digging into the top coverlet, and whispered Adam's name over and over, consumed by such longing that it hurt.

Adam filled her mind for the next two days. She had become a woman that night in his shabby lodgings, the rowdy party going on below them, but it was only now that she began to mature emotionally, going over their unhappy marriage in her mind, paying attention to small details.

She remembered him refusing to let her work in the hospital, saying to her, 'I need to know that you're here—'

Now she knew what he meant. She had been his hold on reality, his refuge as he worked among suffering and misery. And she had deserted him, knowing full well that his pride would never allow him to ask her to stay.

Who looked after him now? The servants could keep him fed and clothed, but who was there now to share his life and his bed?

With sudden insight, she knew that only she could do that, and that only Adam could ease the ache that had tormented her from the moment she had been in Jeremy's arms.

'I'm going to London,' she said flatly when she and Christian were at dinner. The older woman almost knocked over a glass of water.

'What brought that on?'

'I have to talk to Adam.'

To her surprise, Christian said, 'Are you sure you're wise to rush off like that? Wouldn't you be better to think it over for a week or so?'

'Do you think I'd be doing the wrong thing, seeking him out?'

'I didnae say that. I just think you should turn it over in your mind before you make the move.'

'I've turned it over. I'm expected at a dinner party in Helen's house the day after tomorrow. I'll leave the following morning. I'd best get it over with now I've made up my mind.'

Christian tutted. 'My, Elizabeth, but you're as tender and romantic as that man you wed!'

Although Elizabeth had resolved her marriage in her own mind, she was not at all sure that Adam would agree with her. She steeled herself for a cold rejection, and knew that she might well come back to Paisley in humiliation. But before she did take the journey north again, she vowed to herself, Adam would take the ring from her finger, and she would return as a free woman.

On her second last evening, she stayed up late, stitching at a skirt she was making for herself. Christian and the servants went off to bed, leaving her in peace.

Towards midnight, when she was thinking of giving up the fight to get the skirt finished, someone pounded at the front door.

The material fell to the floor as she jumped up, convinced that there had been some disaster. Or – the thought sent her hurrying through the hall – could it be Matt, to say that the baby was coming early?

She fumbled with the bolts, lifted the latch, and was almost knocked over as a cloaked figure burst into the hall.

It was like taking a step back in time. She wasn't in Rab Montgomery's house, the tall, dark man confronting her wasn't a stranger, his black hair wet with rain; but the scowl was the same. There was even a candle on the stairs, the murmur of sleepy, wondering voices – female, instead of male.

'Adam!' Christian said triumphantly from behind the candle. 'Man, I thought you'd never get here in time!'

'In—?' Elizabeth began to repeat, confused, but Adam's hand closed on her arm, and he steered her to the parlour, saying over his shoulder, 'Get back to whatever you're doing, Christian, and let me talk to my wife in peace!'

He unloosened his cloak, dropped it onto a chair, went to warm his hands at the fire. 'It's a God-forsaken town still. I thought I'd never get an answer at the door. Are you all deaf?'

'They're in their beds, and I was just going to mine,' she said half-apologetically, still unable to believe that he was really here, filling the quiet room with his crackling presence like a thunderstorm.

Then he swung round from the fire and glared at her, brows knotted, and she knew that it wasn't a strange dream.

'In their beds?' said Adam, astonished.

'It's midnight! And this isn't London, remember. Folk here go to their beds at a respectable hour – and rise at a respectable hour too.'

'It's well seen you've settled back in fast enough.' His gaze raked her. He looked thinner, his face drawn, but his vitality was as strong as ever. 'I was right when I said you belonged here.'

'You're always right, are you no'?' They were quarrelling again, not two minutes after he had arrived. All her good intentions and her determination to be reasonable and understanding had flown at once. 'What sort of time's this to arrive on anyone's doorstep?'

'One of the horses cast a shoe and we had to wait until some lazy fool of a blacksmith could be found. Though why I was in a hurry to get here, I cannae think. I'd forgotten about your sharp tongue, woman. Is there any whisky?'

She put herself between the cupboard and his tall, lean body. 'When did you last eat?'

'I've no idea.'

'Then you'd be better with food than drink.' She flounced off to the kitchen, hoping for a few minutes to collect her thoughts, but he followed her, and leaned against the dresser, watching her while she put out bread and meat and ale.

'You've lost none of your skill in the kitchen.'

'It's where I belong,' she said bitterly. 'I leave the drawing-room for fine ladies like Lucy Worthing. She's well, I hope?'

'The last time I saw her, she was blooming.' He pulled out a chair and sat down, reaching for the ale jug. 'You never wrote, Elizabeth.'

'Neither did you. I took it that you were too busy with Lucy.'

Adam eyed her slowly, taking his time, and she felt her skin tingle as though he had touched it.

'Lucy Worthing,' he drawled, 'can be dealt with in only a few minutes of any man's time. It's no wonder that Henry looks as though he's got nothing to do.'

She almost threw the food on the table before him. 'There you are – I'll be getting to my bed now!'

'You'll be sitting down here and keeping me company,' said Adam, nodding at the chair opposite. 'And you neednae look at me like that,' he added as she sat, glaring at him. 'Would you prefer me to lie and say that I'd had nothing to do with the woman?'

'I'd never have believed you, for she was setting her cap at you right under my nose! And men were never any good at resisting temptation!'

'It was Eve that ate the apple, though Adam choked on the core – my namesake, I'm talking of. I was never one to let things stick in my throat. Besides,' he went on with a sudden edge to his voice, 'my own wife had gone off and left me. A man needs a woman around, I'll grant you that much. Come back to your rightful duties, Elizabeth.'

She blinked. There was no pleading in his voice, only an order.

'I will not!'

'You've found someone who can suit you just as well as me?' he asked mockingly.

'I'd no' have to look far to find someone better!'

Adam reached over and took her chin in his hand before she could stop him. He turned her face to the lamplight.

'You don't have the look of a woman who's being pleasured,' he said, and she pulled her face away, blushing.

'There's more to life than a man!'

'There's more to life than a woman – but it's the seasoning that makes the difference at a banquet. It seems to me that we could both do with some seasoning, Elizabeth.'

She got to her feet. 'I'd not go back to you if you asked me on your bended knees.'

He laughed with pure amusement. 'You'd have to wait a long time for that. Now where are you off to?'

'To get some fresh linen. You can have the wee room across the hall.'

'Be damned to that,' said Adam. 'I'll sleep with my wife – the Lord knows I've spent enough time in an empty bed those past weeks.'

She planted her hands on her hips. 'Sleep in my bed? Indeed you'll do no—'

'Hold your tongue, woman,' he said, and pulled

her down onto his knee. Her flailing hand knocked over the ale pot before he managed to capture it and bind it against his chest. She fought against him, then as her lips parted and his tongue teased its way round hers she felt the ache of the past few days dissolve into liquid warmth.

When his arms relaxed their hold she reached up to run her fingers over his hair, stroking the silver above his temples then moving her hand down to hold his face. He was really there, and she was home again. She knew that as surely as the moment she had first realised it, the day Adam held her in Christian's parlour after the cholera riots.

'I love you, Adam Montgomery,' she said, and felt him tense for a moment in her arms. Then he laughed against her hair.

'You drive a hard bargain. But if love's being exasperated with someone till you want to choke her, and if it's wanting to be with her every day, even if it's only to quarrel with her – then I suppose I must love you, Mistress Montgomery.'

It was as much as she could expect from him, and it was enough.

'Oh, Adam—' she sighed, then sat upright on his lap. 'What did Christian mean when she said she thought you'd never get here in time?'

'She's wandered.' Adam reached out for her, but she held him back.

'The truth, now!'

He shrugged, looked slightly guilty. 'She wrote and told me that if I had a brain in my head I'd come up here and talk to you. But I was about to come to Paisley anyway,' he added hurriedly as she opened her mouth to speak, 'for I was going out of my mind in that house without you.'

Then it was his turn to frown. 'I don't know what she meant by me being in time, though – were you planning something?'

'Since you've told me the truth, I might as well tell you. I had a seat booked on the London coach for Friday.'

'So I could have saved myself the bother?'

She struggled to get up. 'Indeed you could not! If you think I was going to come to London just to ask you to take me back, you're—'

His mouth stopped hers. 'D'you want me to help you fetch the linen for the wee room?' he whispered after several minutes.

'The bed in my room's awful narrow—'

'So was the bed in my lodgings, but we managed fine,' he said, and grinned when she blushed. 'And it seems to me that thon big bed in London made us strangers to each other. So—' He stood up, lifting her easily into his arms. '—We'll just have to make the best of that narrow cot, for I've waited long enough to love my own wife!'

She wakened in the morning to find him propped on one elbow, studying her. He bent to kiss her, then drew back again, his eyes warm.

'Now – that's what I'd call the look of a woman who's been pleasured,' he said softly.

'What time is it?'

'Gone nine.'

She sat upright, almost knocking him off the edge of the bed. He recovered, and pushed her back.

'Adam, it's time I was up!'

'You're not a housekeeper now.'

'But what's your cousin going to say to us spending half the day like—' She indicated the tousled sheets, his clothes and hers strewn over the room where they had been impatiently thrown the night before.

Adam was calm. 'We can tell her that we had a lot to discuss,' he said solemnly. 'And now I come to look at you—' his eyes slid over her shoulders, down to the swell of her breasts peeping from the sheet '—I can think of something I'd like to discuss with you right now.'

XIV

C hristian was most put out by Adam's refusal to stay in Paisley any longer than he had to.

'Folks are going to be displeased,' she sniffed, but he was unmoved.

'I was never one to let folks get in my way. I've business in Glasgow today, and I hope that Elizabeth and I can be on our way back to London tomorrow.'

'So I'll be expected to travel all the way down there, will I, if I want to have a decent conversation with you?'

He stood before her parlour fireplace. 'Mebbe there'll be no need for that. My business in Glasgow concerns a post in Edinburgh, at the University. Elizabeth, what would you say to living in Edinburgh?'

'Are you not happy in London?'

'Happy enough. But now that the Anatomy

Bill's gone through Parliament and physicians can work with more freedom I've a notion to turn to anatomy. I'd like fine to try to find out what killed folk such as James and Isobel. There's a place for me in Edinburgh.'

Later, when they were alone, he said, 'Come with me to Glasgow.'

'I'd as soon stay here and get ready to go to London, Adam.' She took his hand. 'I'm dining with Matt and Helen tonight. They'll be pleased to see—'

His hand slipped away from hers.

'You know full well that I'll not go with you,' he said coolly. 'I'd be obliged if you'd make your own apologies, and stay with me.'

Her heart sank, taking with it the glow she had been feeling all day.

'So you still care for Helen,' she said dully.

'You can say that to me after what was between us last night? You know very well that it's no' Helen!'

'Matt's your brother! It's time you made your peace with him!'

'Am I to have no understanding from my own wife!' he said angrily. 'Let Matt live here and carry on the family name, and let you and me start our own lives elsewhere, without this nonsense.'

'Not until you face the truth,' she told him steadily. 'You're angry with Matt because, for once, he was the better man. He took what you wanted – and even now you'll not forgive him for it. That's no start to our future!'

'It seems to me that instead of me bringing Helen between us, it's you that's bringing Matt!'

'He's my friend, and so's Helen, and if I can't invite them into my home I'd as soon not share it with you!'

It was hard to understand how a man who had loved her so tenderly a few hours earlier could look at her so coldly now.

'Keep your nose out of this, Elizabeth. It's a family affair!'

He turned away and she caught at his arm and dragged him round to face her again.

'A family affair? Haven't I been part of your family those past three years? Haven't I taken their name for my own, and the worst of them for my husband? God help me, I'm a Montgomery now – and I'll be no party to family squabbles!'

They stood glaring at each other, Elizabeth with clenched fists buried in the skirt of her gown, Adam cold and expressionless, his eyes burning with rage.

'Elizabeth—' he put his hands on her shoulders

'—we're in danger of finishing it here and now.'

It would have been very easy to step forward, towards him. She knew that he wanted to hold her as much as she wanted to be held. But the price was too high. If she and Adam were to take up their marriage again, it must be without any barriers.

'I'm going to Matt's house tonight, as I promised,' she said, low-voiced.

'You'd let him come between us?'

'Matt has no quarrel with you. It's the coldness you feel towards him that'll be the ruin of us. I could never be sure that it wouldn't turn on me one day.'

He stared. 'That's nonsense!'

'It's what I feel.'

'Are you coming to Glasgow with me now?' he insisted.

'No.'

His hands fell away from her shoulders. His face was dark with sudden rage.

'Then be damned to you. You can stay in this town until you rot. I'll go to Glasgow without you – I'll return to London without you – I'll take up residence in Edinburgh without you, and may we never meet again!' said Adam, and slammed out of the room and out of the house.

'Mercy, lassie,' clucked Christian when she

arrived home and heard the news. 'You've driven the man too far this time.'

'I'll not deny Matt and Helen as my friends just to please Adam. That's what was wrong with his father – nobody ever had the courage to make him see his own faults.'

'If you were so set on marrying a perfect man you shouldn't have chosen that one for a start.'

'I never wanted a perfect man!' snapped Elizabeth, and burst into tears.

Helen's bright face clouded over when Elizabeth arrived for dinner on her own.

'We heard that Adam was in Paisley. We hoped he might be with you,' she said hurriedly, delaying Elizabeth in the hall. The murmur of voices came from the drawing room, where the other guests were gathered.

'He was only here on business. He's gone back to London.' Elizabeth's stormy tears had washed her clean, left her feeling very calm, as though she had just been widowed, or was recovering from a long and dangerous illness. She had no doubt that there would be a lot of pain later, but for the moment she felt strangely protected from grief, and apart from other people.

Helen looked at her closely. 'Are you feeling well?'

'I'm fine,' Elizabeth assured her serenely, and swept into the busy room.

She wasn't hungry, but she managed to eat enough to satisfy Helen's watchful gaze. The rest of the night, alone in the great empty spaces of her small bed, loomed ahead, but for the moment she was surrounded by people, and safe from her own thoughts.

Peter Todd trapped her in the drawing-room after the meal so that he could talk at great length about his beloved prize carnations. A stir at the door caught her wandering attention.

Adam, still wearing his dark travelling clothes, stood there.

'Mercy!' Elizabeth thought in a panic, and tried to shrink behind Peter, away from the blue gaze that scissored through the crowd of people between them.

Helen's tawny head swam towards him, followed by Matt's brown mop. Peeping over Peter's shoulder, Elizabeth watched fearfully. If Adam caused a scene in this house, before Matt and Helen's guests, then he would live to regret it, she vowed, swallowing back terror and trying to bolster herself with anger instead.

As though they had met just the day before, Adam shook his brother's hand absent-mindedly, looked down at Helen's lovely face and swollen figure with brief recognition, then his eyes swept up again, scanning the other people there. They found what they sought and he marched across the room just as Peter, suddenly aware that he had lost Elizabeth's attention, turned.

'What's this? Elizabeth didnae tell me that you'd be here, Adam.'

A formal smile flickered about Adam's mouth, and was gone.

'Good evening, Mister Todd. I'll have a word with you before I go. In the meantime—' his hand closed over Elizabeth's elbow, firmly '—I must speak with my wife.'

She was whisked off to the window, pinned against the curtains by Adam's big body, which effectively blocked her way back to the others. Attack was the best form of defence.

'Adam Montgomery, if you make trouble for Matt and Helen and me, you'll live to regret it!'

He glowered down at her. 'Stop clucking like a chicken that's lost its way, woman! I already know that I'll live to regret this evening's work without your threats. I've done as you wanted – I've shaken Matt's hand, and I've come into his house. And you and me leave for London tomorrow morning, if I've to tie you into the stage-coach myself.'

'If Christian put you up to this, you can go back and tell her to keep her nose out of my business!'

He looked as though he would like to shake her hard. 'I've not been to Oakshawhill – I came straight here from Glasgow. I knew fine that my wife would never think of obeying my wishes. Now – we're to take up residence in Edinburgh in six weeks' time, and there's plenty to be done before then, so we'll just get back to Christian's house and—'

'I don't trust you!'

The beginnings of a smile trembled at the corners of his mouth. 'That's the way I prefer it, Mistress Montgomery. I'm going to see to it that this is the last time I dance to your tune. From this night on, you'll do the dancing. Now—' his face softened, his eyes bathed her in their blue light, and her knees weakened at once '—how soon can you and me get out of this place and be alone?'

'Another hour, at least. Folk'll want to talk to you—'

'I'll never be able to keep my hands from you for as long as that,' he said, low-voiced, and she felt her body tighten with desire.

'Adam—'

'Elizabeth—' he said, and the word was a caress that tormented her with its sweet promise. 'To hell

371

with them all. We've travelled a long hard way to find each other. We'll go now and leave them to their own ploys.'

She firmed trembling lips, shook her head. 'We will not,' she said, and the sharpness in her voice was more for herself than for him. 'You're one of them, and they have the right to talk with you while you're here.'

She put a hand on his arm, her fingers keenly aware of the hard, lithe body beneath the cloth, and he sighed and turned so that they faced the room together.

'You're a bully, Elizabeth,' he murmured. 'And you're wrong. I never was one of them. I was always a stranger to this town. Are you willing to come with me and be a stranger here from now on?'

There was no decision to make. Now that she and Adam understood each other, she would be a stranger to any community that didn't hold him.

She pressed his arm lightly, and knew that he understood.

Side by side, they moved forward to make their farewells to Paisley.

The Shimmer of the Herring

This book is dedicated to
Isabel M. Harrison and Peter Bruce,
both of Buckie, and both descended from Moray Firth
fisher-folk. It is my pleasure and my privilege to know
them as good friends.

Acknowledgements

My thanks to Isabel M. Harrison, poet and historian, who generously gave me access to her own Buckie history collection; to Peter Bruce, who provided the title for this book; to Carol Thornton for her assistance in gathering research; to Sheila Campbell, chief librarian at Elgin Library; and to Ian Leith, chief librarian at Buckie Library. My thanks, too, to the volunteers who staff the Buckie and District Fishing Heritage Museum, the staff at Buckie and Elgin Libraries and the staff of The Drifter Museum in Buckie.

I am also indebted to the staff of the Scottish Fisheries Museum in Anstruther, Fife, particularly Alan Whitfield, model-maker at the museum, who helped me with research into details of pre-First World War steam drifters.

Without all those people, this book would not have been possible.

1

‘You know your trouble, Weem Lowrie? You’re lazy, that’s what. Bone idle! Always were and always will be, and God forgive me for ever takin’ you on as a husband,’ Jess railed. ‘Lyin’ there and leavin’ me to deal with all the worry of your own bairns – and me gettin’ too old for the task. And look at the state of ye – am I never tae be done runnin’ after you and tidyin’ up your mess?’

She plucked irritably at the single weed that had dared to plant itself on the grassy green mound and put it into her pocket to dispose of later, then clambered to her feet and rubbed vigorously at the gravestone with the cloth she had brought specially.

A year after their carving the letters stood out clear and strong, claiming the six-foot rectangle of ground before them for William James Lowrie, fisherman of the parish of Buckie, born 1870, died 21 July 1911, beloved husband of Jess Innes and father of James, Bethany and Innes.

Her work done, Jess stepped back and surveyed the grave, head to one side. There was not a speck of dust on the stone, not so much as a fallen leaf on the grass. The mixed bunch of flowers she had brought from her tiny back yard had been arranged neatly in a glass jar and for the moment, at least, her man was neat, tidy and seen to.

‘You’re fine here, aren’t you, Weem, where I can tend tae you?’ Her voice was anxious, and she bit her lower lip as she glanced at the fields surrounding the small graveyard. It would have been more fitting for a man who had spent most of his life on the sea to be buried within sight and sound of its waves, but since the small fishing town of Buckie did not have its own graveyard, the Buckie dead had to be buried in Rathven Cemetery, on the hill high above their own small part of Buckie with its huddled houses and narrow cobbled streets. Jess took comfort in the thought that on days like today, with the high grey clouds scudding across it like ghostly sails, the great stretch of sky above the graveyard could well be likened to the ocean.

'Aye, you're fine.' She answered her own question. 'I just wish to God that your bairns could be put tae rights as easy as you are, Weem.' Even as she spoke she knew that there was no sense in talking to him about such matters, for he had always left the worrying to her.

She sniffed, used the cloth she had brought for the headstone to mop at the tears that had spilled over of their own accord, then put it back into her bag and brushed at the skirt of her coat.

'I'll be back next week, same as always.' Picking up the bag, she made her way out of the graveyard, straight-backed and with her head held high.

Fields of young corn to each side of the road rippled and swayed in waves beneath the wind; again, the similarity to the sea was obvious, but deep in her heart Jess knew that similarities would mean nothing to her Weem, for he had never had much time for the land. As she came within sight of Buckie, nestling on the shores of the Moray Firth and clustered for the most part round the harbour, guilt tramped alongside her as it had done since the day she had claimed her husband from the sea and laid him in the black earth.

Jess lifted her chin higher and quickened her step, trying to appreciate the bright yellow magnificence of the broom bushes by the road and the delicate beauty of the pink and white wild roses. The decision to bury her man in the ground instead of letting their son James return him to the huge rolling sea had been hers, made in the full knowledge that she must live with the consequences for the rest of her life. She had not realised, then, that it would cause such a deep rift between herself and her first-born, the son who was so like Weem in nature.

She had intended to go straight home, but when she reached the town she hesitated, then turned towards the huddle of houses known as the Catbow. As she neared her daughter's house a small, brown-haired tornado detached itself from a group of children and hurtled towards her, crashing into her knees and locking itself there with sturdy little arms.

'Granny Jess!' Rory Pate yelled up at her, his blue eyes wide and angelic in his dirty face. 'Where have ye been?'

'Tae London tae see the Queen.'

'Did she send me anythin'?'

'Aye, a facecloth and a bar of soap,' she retorted, rummaging in her bag. 'But I must have left them behind, so you'll have to have this instead.'

Rory's eyes lit up at sight of the liquorice strap and he released her knees to snatch at it with one hand.

'Is your mother busy?'

'No, she's just talkin' to Aunt Stella. I was playin' with the bairns, but they all got too tired and went to sleep. They're too wee to play,' four-year-old Rory said scornfully.

He accompanied her to the door then darted off again, leaving her on her own. 'Are you in, then?' she called, tapping gently at the door before lifting the latch. Most local women were free to walk into their own daughters' homes without having to announce their arrival. But then most local women did not have a daughter like Bethany.

All day Bethany Pate had dreaded a meeting with her

mother. She had been trying hard, without success, to
keep thoughts of her once-adored father at bay on this
first anniversary of his death, but despite all her efforts
he had pushed himself into her mind at every opportunity.
To make matters worse, her sister-in-law Stella had been
sitting in Bethany's small kitchen since early afternoon,
talking about Weem Lowrie.

'I'm just glad that James is away at the fishing, for
I don't know what he'd have been like if he'd been
home today.'

'He'd not have let it make any difference.' Bethany
had little time, even when she was in a good mood, for
Stella's assumption that because her twins weren't much
older than Bethany's step-daughter Ellen the two women
had a lot in common. It never seemed to occur to Stella
that Bethany, not having given birth herself, might not be
interested in continuous talk of bairns and domesticity.

'You don't know what he's been like since his father
went. He's not the same man at all. I never know what
way to take him.'

'James was always difficult. It's in his nature. It's a
family thing.' In Bethany's hands the knitting needles
flew along the row, turned and flew back, the points
stabbing into the thick wool. She was knitting a jersey
for her husband while Stella worked at a jacket for one
of the twins.

'Innes is a good civil soul, and your mother's the
same.'

'James inherited his nature from our father, same as
me.' It was all Bethany could do not to throw the knitting
into Stella's bland face. No wonder James was difficult at
times, she thought with a stab of pity for her older brother.
Having to spend his time ashore with a woman who could
talk of nothing but bairns and cooking, and bairns and
mending, and more bairns would turn any man morose.
And James had been moody to start with.

'But you'd think . . .' Stella began, then stopped short

as they heard the tentative tap on the outer door, and the voice from the street. 'It's her . . . your mother!' Her brown eyes, guileless as a child's, flooded with concern.

'I know my own mother's voice.'

'Should I say something about . . .'

'No!' Bethany put the knitting aside and got up to fetch a cup as her mother came into the kitchen, crooning at the sight of the three infants drowsing, exhausted from their games, in an intertwined, boneless heap on the hearth rug. They woke at the sound of her voice, reaching stubby arms up to her and chattering like a nestful of baby birds.

Jess sank on to the chair Bethany had vacated and managed to gather them all into her lap. 'Aren't ye the bonniest bairns in the whole of the Firth?' she asked them. 'And I'd not sell one of you for a thousand pound!'

'You'll not be able to take your tea now,' Bethany said irritably from the stove.

'I'll manage fine. I'm used tae bairns climbin' all over me.' With difficulty, Jess tucked sixteenth-month-old Ellen and fifteen-month-old Sarah and Annie into the crook of one arm and reached out with her free hand for the mug of sweet black tea.

'Sit nice now, my wee birdies, for Granny Jess.' She drank it down swiftly and handed the cup back. 'That was good. I'd a thirst on me.'

'Have you been walkin' to Rathven and back?' Stella asked.

Jess shot a look at Bethany, who devoted all her attention to washing her mother's empty cup. 'Aye, pet, I just took a stroll up the hill.'

'On your lone? Me and the bairns would've gone with you if you'd asked.'

'I'd not have you walking that distance when you're so near to your time.' The children were squirming to get down now and Jess was glad of the diversion. She lowered them to the floor, then pulled her own knitting wires from the leather pad known locally as a whisker, slung from her belt. Buckie women never let a moment lie idle, and if there was nothing of greater urgency for their hands to do there was always knitting or darning. 'How are you keeping, Stella?'

'Well enough. Wearying for the time to come.' The girl hesitated then said shyly, 'If it's a boy I thought to call him Weem, after his grandfather.'

'But is that what James wants?' Bethany asked tartly, returning to her chair.

'I've not asked him yet, I wanted to speak to Mother Jess first.' Stella beamed at Jess, who hesitated, glancing over at her daughter. Bethany, head bent, was intent on her knitting.

'It's a kind thought, lass, but I think James should have the final word on the matter.'

Stella's mouth drooped a little. 'He wasn't interested in naming the lassies.'

'If it's a laddie that'll change.' Bethany's voice was brittle. 'Sons count more than daughters. Sons can carry on the family tradition and the family name. Daughters aren't of much use.'

'You think so?' Stella asked nervously, eyeing her little daughters and placing a protective hand on the great swell of her belly. Then, putting her knitting needles away, she began to ease herself up from her chair. 'I'd best go. The bairns'll be gettin' hungry.'

'I'll come with you, and help you with the wee ones,' Jess offered.

Outside Stella said, 'Bethany's in a right black mood today. She snapped at me more than once before you came in, and I can't think what I did to deserve it.'

'It's not your fault, pet. We've all got our ups and downs.'

'Aye, I suppose so. I just thought it would be nice for the two of us to spend some time together. Even with my father and the bairns tae see to, the house seems awful empty when James is at the fishin'.'

'Aye.' Jess felt sorry for the girl, knowing full well how hard it was to be head over heels in love with a man who did not possess a grain of romance in his soul. 'Why not come along to my house for a wee while?'

'Best not, my da'll be ready for his cup of tea.'

'How is he?' Mowser Buchan, a former fisherman, had been in poor health.

'Not too bad. The worst of his troubles is the way he's still pinin' for the sea, even though he's been ashore these three years past.'

'My own father was the same when he got too old to go out on the boats. Once the sea gets them it never lets go.' The words were out of Jess's mouth before she realised it and, as she walked the short distance to her own house after parting with Stella, they came clamouring back, filling her head until her ears rang. Worse still, they were being shouted not in her own voice, but in Weem's.

'Once the sea gets them, it never lets go.' How could any woman who knew the truth of that have kept her man's body back from the sea, which had been more dear to him than anything else?

'For love, Weem, for love,' she muttered, and didn't realise she had said it aloud until two little girls scurrying towards her hand-in-hand hesitated, looked at each other, giggled and gave her a wide berth as they ran past.

'Hello, Innes.'

'Zelda . . .' Innes Lowrie, intent on the piece of machinery on the bench before him, greeted the newcomer brusquely without turning to look at her. Unabashed, Grizelda Mulholland found a corner where she was out of his way and waited. She enjoyed watching Innes at work; she liked the gravity that overlaid his normally cheerful face, the narrowing of the dark eyes, the way his strong, long-fingered hands moved deftly among what to her were lumps of metal, but to him were objects of beauty.

After a few moments he straightened, wiping his oily

hands on a rag then turning to give her his usual broad grin. 'What brings you here?'

'Johnny had to bring one of the carthorses to be shod and wee Peter wanted to come to the smiddy to see the work being done.' Zelda was employed as a maid at a farm in Rathven, helping the farmer's busy wife to tend the hens, make the cheese and see to the house and the large family.

'Again? Wee Peter's been here that often to see the horses shod that he must be able to do it himself by now.'

'Bairns like smiddies.' She hoisted herself up to sit on the rough wood of his workbench, swinging her legs. 'You're not complaining, are you? If I'm in your way just say and I'll be off.'

'I'm not complaining a bit, Miss Grizelda.' Innes leaned on the bench, enjoying the way the girl pouted at the mention of her full name.

'Don't say that! Is it my fault my family have long names? When I have . . .' She stopped short, flushing and looking up at him from beneath her lashes, 'If I have bairns they'll be given proper names like Ann and Mary and John.'

'I think Zelda's a fine name.' Innes wiped the sweat from his face with the rag he still held. Because the blacksmith who employed him had his furnace positioned against the brick wall between workshop and smiddy, both places were always hot to work in.

'At least it's better than Grizzel. That's what my aunt's called.'

'That wouldn't suit you, not with your bonny nature.'

Zelda flushed with pleasure at the compliment, then poked a finger at the metal he had been working on. 'What's that? Part of a motor-car?'

'Just a bit from a reaper. I wish it was a motor-car,' Innes said longingly. 'We don't see many of them hereabouts.'

'Zelda!' A small boy appeared in the doorway, face flushed with heat from the blacksmith's fire. He stamped in and clutched at the maid's hand. 'I want to go home. I don't like it here!'

'Yes, you do.'

'I don't!' Peter insisted. 'You know I don't. Why do we have to keep coming?'

'Don't you be cheeky . . . And what are you laughing at, Innes Lowrie?' Zelda snapped, flustered by the little boy's revelations.

'Nothing at all.'

'That rag you wiped your face with has left dirt all over your cheek,' she said and flounced out, towing Peter behind her. In the doorway she turned. 'Will you come up to the farm for me later?'

'I can't tonight, my mother'll mebbe want me to go to Rathven cemetery with her. It's . . . it's been a year since . . .'

The girl took a step back towards him. 'Oh, Innes, I forgot about your father. I'm sorry.'

'It's all right. I'll come up tomorrow night?'

She beamed and nodded, then hurried off, leaving Innes to return to his work.

Jess was stirring the soup when the youngest of her three children arrived home from work. 'Are you all right?' he asked as soon as he came in the door.

'Why wouldn't . . .' she began, then changed it to, 'Aye, lad, I'm fine.' Then, eyeing his dirty overalls, 'Get yourself washed, now, your dinner'll be on the table in a minute.' She had never become used to the streaks of oil on Innes's dungarees, or the smell of it. 'Your clean shirt's over the back of that chair.'

Unlike her own mother, Jess had the luxury of a cold-water tap in her kitchen, but Innes, a thoughtful lad, always insisted on washing the day's grime off at the big sink in the outhouse. Whistling, he went out the back with a kettle of hot water while Jess rattled the pots busily on the stove.

Although she had always tried not to favour one of her children over the others, her last-born was more precious to her than his older brother and sister. For one thing, he was still under her roof and therefore in her care: for another, he was the only one of the three with whom she felt comfortable. Innes had been a loving and giving soul from the moment of his birth, whereas James and Bethany had both shrugged off embraces from an early age. Now that they were grown there were times when she felt quite uncomfortable with them, while with Innes she could say and do as she wished without fear of being laughed at or criticised.

'I thought the two of us might take a walk up to Rathven after,' he said casually when he returned to the kitchen, sleeking his wet hair back with both hands and reaching for the shirt.

'It's all right, laddie, I went to see your father this afternoon.'

'On your lone? Did Bethany not think to go with you?' he asked when she nodded.

'I didn't ask her. Would you mind just having your own company when you go there later?'

'I'll stay in with you instead. To tell the truth, I paid my respects this morning before work. Mebbe Bethany went on her own, too.'

'Mebbe.'

'Then there's James . . .'

'He'd be too busy catching herring to remember.' Jess put the soup bowls on the table and sat down. 'James has his own life to live now.'

Weem had always predicted that he would die at sea and rest there, but in actual fact he had died of a sudden, massive heart attack on board the *Fidelity*, the steam drifter that he, his brother Albert and James jointly owned. James had wanted to honour his father's wishes by putting the body over the side there and then, but Albert had insisted on leaving the final decision to Jess.

Despite James's arguing and, eventually, his pleading, she had settled for a burial, unable to face the thought of losing her man completely to the sea, with no grave to visit. Since then James had scarcely had anything to do with her. It was as though she had lost a son as well as a husband.

2

When her step-children were in bed and asleep and the dishes had been done Bethany pulled a shawl over her head. 'I'm just going down to visit my mother.'

Gil Pate, settled by the fire with his pipe and the newspaper, reached up and caught his wife's hand as she moved past his chair. 'D'you have to go out?' His strong fingers caressed the soft skin on the inside of her wrist.

'I feel that I should. It's a year to the day since my father went. She gets lonely.' It was an excuse she had often used in the past months, when she needed to get away from the house to walk by herself in the fresh air, away from the cloying domestic responsibilities.

'She not on her lone, there's still Innes at home.'

'He's never there – you should know what laddies are like.'

'Laddies have to go out looking for companionship,' Gil said, his fingers stroking and stroking. 'But a man has the right to find it there at his own hearthside.'

'You won't miss me for an hour. You'll have your nose in the newspaper for longer than that and the bairns'll not be any trouble. They're sound asleep and they'll stay like that till the mornin'.'

'I like to know you're sittin' on the other side of the fire, knittin' away, all bonny and contented,' he sulked.

'Just an hour, that's all.' She drew her hand away gently but firmly.

'If you must, you must . . . but don't take all night about it. It's time Jess realised that you're a wife now, and that's more than a daughter.'

Once over the doorstep Bethany drew the night air deep into her lungs with a great, shuddering sigh before walking briskly down the hill towards Cluny Harbour. At that time of year most of the Buckie fleet was fishing the waters round Shetland, Orkney and Caithness, and the few boats left in the harbour rode high in the water, occasionally nudging against each other. For a moment she drew the peace of the place into her soul. Then, turning away from the water, she moved in the opposite direction from her mother's house, keeping her head down and her shawl drawn close about her face.

The road to Rathven was quiet and all too soon the larger monuments in the cemetery were outlined against the cool blue-grey of the evening sky, then she had reached it and the iron of the gate was cold and hard beneath her fingers. She knew exactly where her father's grave lay; she could even see his stone from where she hesitated, clinging to the gate.

Over the past year she had often walked up the hill to this place, but she had never been able to take that first step into the cemetery. It was the same story tonight; before peace could be made with her father's memory she would have to come to terms with the conflicting emotions within her own soul. She would have to relinquish something – either the deep love she had had for the man from her earliest days, or the bitter rage born of knowing that he had used her love and trust to further his own interests, trapping her in the process with a man who meant nothing to her.

Bethany's fingers tightened painfully on the gate. Letting go of the rage meant that she must resign herself to becoming what Weem had made of her: a wife and mother with no other identity. And she could not do that. Not yet, perhaps not ever. She turned away from the graveyard and started back down the road towards home.

Once in sight of the Firth she could see the lights of a group of sailed fishing boats sliding out of the harbour below. Although its fishing fleet was second to only that of Lowestoft in size, Buckie was badly situated for the large fishing grounds, and during the busiest seasons its boats were obliged to stay away from home for weeks at a time, discharging their catches and re-coaling in more accessible ports. The sailed boats, smaller than the steam drifters and dependent on wind and weather, were less able to reach the big fishing grounds and concentrated on line fishing in the deeper waters of the Moray Firth. The boats below, passing in stately procession though the harbour entrance with their masthead lights twinkling in the gloaming, would be back in the morning with their catches.

Once out of the harbour they dipped and bounced, moving apart and picking up speed as the wind caught their spread sails. Bethany watched hungrily, longing to be on board and heading for the open sea with no thought for the land falling away behind her.

Back in the town she returned to the harbour, standing at the very edge, looking down into the deep, still water where as a bairn she had swum with the lads, heedless of the future. She had certainly never anticipated that it would bring marriage and a ready-made family. While the other lassies had played with dolls and as they grew from childhood dreamed of their own homes and their own men and their own bairns, Bethany had had other plans. Even though she knew that women did not crew on fishing boats she secretly hoped that her father, who could deny her nothing, might break the unwritten rule specially for her. But Weem was as superstitious as any fisherman and, on leaving school, Bethany was set to work in one of the smokehouses, then became a 'guttin quine', as the fisher lassies were known in the area.

Frustrated, she had then come up with another scheme. The guttin quine, employed by fish curers, coopers, or buyers, worked in three-woman teams, with two gutters and one packer to each team. Once brought ashore, the fish were emptied from baskets into the farlins, wooden troughs similar to the deep sinks used for washing clothes. Salt was scattered over the herring to make them easier to grip, and in seconds the gutters' sharp knives slit the fish open and scooped the entrails out. The gutted fish was tossed into a tub on one side of each gutter and entrails into a tub on her other side. The packer arranged the fish in the barrels; an outer ring and an inner ring, with a space between each fish to avoid damaging them. The layers were separated by handfuls of coarse salt.

The work was hard, and when the fishing was good the guttin quine might work at the farlins for twelve or fifteen hours, with only short breaks for meals. For this they were paid threepence an hour, plus tenpence per barrel, to be divided between the three women in the team.

It had occurred to Bethany that an ambitious, hard-working woman could take over the running of the teams, renting their services out, bargaining with the curers and coopers and possibly earning more money for the teams and for herself . . . money that, carefully and patiently hoarded over the years, might eventually enable her to buy her own boat one day and pick her own crew to work it.

With this secret aim in mind Bethany had set herself to work hard at the farlins. Once the herring were landed they had to be gutted, sorted, salted and packed as fast as possible. Usually there were one or two experienced women working alongside the teams, ready to step in and take over if someone had to drop out for any reason. Bethany, her hands as fast as her mind, had swiftly learned the art of gutting and by being in the right place at the right time she had become a supervisor.

The next step had been to gather the women together

and persuade them to consider working for themselves instead of for the menfolk, but while she was waiting for the right time, fate – in the form of her beloved father – had stepped in and ruined everything.

Since childhood Bethany had had striking looks. Her curly hair was long and thick, brown like her father's, but with a rich mahogany glow to it that came from her mother's colouring. She possessed her mother's good bones and her father's clear grey eyes, which, in Bethany's case, could change in an instant from warm velvet to the hard, cold grey of slate or become as stormy as a wild sea or glitter like silvered spray. Full-grown, she was slightly on the tall side for a woman, with a body that was feminine yet sturdy. Like her older brother James she was never short of admirers, but while James, in his bachelor days, enjoyed the attentions of blushing lassies, Bethany had no time for the youths who sought to court her.

Her natural ability to supervise others, combined with her youthful good health and her striking looks, had caught the eye of her employer, a cooper by the name of Gilbert Pate. Although Gil already had a wife, he would have bedded Bethany willingly if she had shown any signs of being agreeable to it. The other women at the farlins had joshed her about Gil's interest, some with amusement and others (the younger ones who thought the cooper a good-looking man) with a certain amount of jealousy. Unfortunately, James had heard of it and had teased her unmercifully in their father's hearing, something that Weem Lowrie remembered when Gil's wife died in childbed, leaving him in sore need of someone to look after his home and his two children.

Gil was ripe for the picking and Weem Lowrie had never been one to let a chance go by. Only months after burying his first wife Gil had taken Bethany as his second, and Weem and Albert Lowrie had secured an arrangement to sell all the *Fidelity*'s future catches to Gil and his brother Nathan, a curer, at a price that suited all four men. Nobody had asked for Bethany's views on the matter. And now, she thought bitterly, it was too late to do anything about it. She had made her bed . . .

The unfortunate but apt phrase reminded her that time was passing all too quickly while she stood there, still as a figurehead, lost in her own thoughts. And time was no longer hers to squander. Shivering in the cool air, she wrenched herself away from the sea and went slowly back to the cottage where Gil was asleep in his chair, legs stretched across the hearth, his newspaper spread across his deep chest, his mouth open and snoring.

As Bethany closed the door he choked in mid-snore and struggled upright in his chair, wiping drool from his chin and glancing at the clock. 'You were a good while.'

'We got to talking.'

He reached up and touched her fingers as she went by his chair. 'You're chilled.'

'I went down to the harbour to look at the boats on my way back.' She picked up the poker and bent to stir life and warmth into the glowing range, but he put his paper aside and got up to take the poker from her.

'Leave it.'

'I'm cold.'

'I'll warm you in the bed,' Gil said huskily, his hands busy.

'The bairns . . .'

'There's not been a murmur from them all the time you've been gone.' He pulled her to him, one arm about her waist, his free hand catching hers and pushing it against his swelling crotch. 'They have your attention during the day. The night-time's mine,' he said into her neck.

'I'll just make sure they're settled, then I'll be back,' Bethany said and escaped to the small room at the back of the house, just large enough for two cribs. Rory and Ellen were both sound asleep, Ellen on her stomach and Rory on his back, arms and legs spread like the tentacles of a

starfish. They were good bairns and she was fond enough
of them, but in the same way she tolerated all young
things such as kittens or puppies. Watching Stella and
the other women she knew that she lacked their maternal
feelings. Perhaps if she had children of her own . . . but the
very thought made her flesh creep. Gil, who fortunately
seemed content with the two bairns he already had, had no
knowledge of the ways in which his young wife guarded
herself against an unwanted pregnancy.

'Bethany?' Gil, already in his long night-shirt, said from
the doorway. 'Come on, woman, I want my sleep.'

'I'm just going out to the privy first.' She lingered
there, in the smelly, spidery dark, hoping that he might
fall asleep, but knowing he would not. Young and healthy
and with a natural appetite for life and all it had to offer,
she had enjoyed her bridegroom's attentions at first, but
after a few months her duties as a bedded wife had become
tedious; why, she had no idea, but she suspected that it
might be because Gil was not of her own choosing.

When she returned to the warm, dark kitchen, lit only
by a faint glow from the range, Gil was awake and too
impatient to wait until she had brushed her hair out and
put her night-gown on. Bouncing rhythmically on the
mattress, her scalp pierced by straying hairpins, Bethany
stared beyond her husband's head at the ceiling and
thought of her father, who had engineered this marriage
to suit his own purposes.

Weem had been unable to understand why his beloved
daughter had become so withdrawn from him after her
marriage and it had hurt Bethany to see his bewilderment.
She had always assumed that one day, when the hurt had
eased and she was ready to forgive him for pushing her
into this marriage, they would become close again. Then
suddenly Weem was dead, and it was too late.

As Gil rolled on to his own side of the bed and began,
almost to once, to snore, she stared at the dull glow of the
fire and wondered if the continuous seething restlessness

within her would have eased and vanished if she had been able to make her peace with her father.

Busy as James Lowrie was that day, his father was not out of his thoughts all through the journey to the fishing grounds off Caithness. It was a relief when they were ready to shoot the nets not long after darkness fell, for it was an exercise that involved every member of the crew and gave them little time to think. In the rope locker, an area little more than a cupboard below-deck, the ship's lad feverishly paid out the messenger – the thick, tarry rope that held the nets. At the same time the huge nets themselves were being fed carefully from their hold on to the deck, where one man attached the corks that kept the nets suspended from the sea's surface, and the buoys that would indicate their position, while another passed the netting strop-ropes to James, who made them fast to the messenger and sent them on their way overboard – on the starboard side of the boat, since it was considered bad luck to shoot the nets to port.

'I'll stand watch,' James said two hours later when the others stretched cramped, weary limbs and looked longingly towards the galley, where the deckhand who doubled as a cook was already starting to prepare their supper.

The boat had been brought round head to wind and the mizzen set to hold her there. Below the surface of the water, their presence indicated by floats at regular intervals, some two to three miles of drift-nets spread out from *Fidelity*, hanging in curtains, waiting for the herring to swim into the trap set for them.

Albert Lowrie, square-built like his late brother, though without Weem's height, narrowed his eyes as he stared out into the darkness. 'It's a quiet enough night, she'll not move much. I doubt if we'll need any more swing-rope. You get below, Malky can stand tonight,' he told his nephew, but James shook his head and repeated with a bite to his voice, 'I said I'll watch!'

Albert shrugged then nodded to the other men, who tumbled into the galley at once, eager to get out of the wind that chilled now that they were idle. It was a relief to James when his uncle followed them. He was in no mood that night to be shut up with the others, listening to their endless talk. He lit a cigarette, drawing the tobacco deep into his lungs. It was dark apart from the carbine lamp fixed forward of the wheel-house and the oil lamp at the mast. Around him, he knew, a vast fleet was scattered over the fishing grounds, tossing on the heavy but regular swell, though in the darkness all he could see was an occasional masthead light and the quick froth of a wave-top now and again.

Like his father and sister, James loved the sea more than anything else. He loved its contrary moods – the worst of them as well as the best. He loved the sight and sound of it, its salty kiss on his lips, the harpy screaming of a gale in the rigging. When first he went to sea he had been taught his craft by his father on one of two sailed Zulu fishing boats owned by Zachary Lowrie, his grandfather. A shrewd and ambitious man, Zachary had put one boat in the care of Weem, the older of his two sons and the better fisherman, while he himself was skipper of the other with his younger son Albert as mate.

The arrangement had worked amicably until Weem, shrewd and ambitious as his father, set eyes on one of the first steam drifters in Lowestoft during an English fishing season. He had done all he could to persuade his father to sell both Zulus and invest in steam, but Zachary would have no truck with the newfangled 'steam kettles'. James could still remember every word of the quarrels that flew between them each time they met.

'D'you know the cost of one of these things? Three thousand poun' and more! I've never been in debt in my life, and I'll not be in debt in old age,' Zachary had thundered.

Weem stood his ground. 'You're well enough known

and well enough respected to get a good loan from the North of Scotland Bank. The sale of the two Zulus would pay off some of the money . . .'

Zachary took his pipe from his mouth and gobbed a mouthful of phlegm into the fire. 'They'd fetch next to nothing compared to the cost of a steam drifter!'

'. . . and once we're able to reach the fishing grounds in all weathers without fear of being becalmed,' Weem ploughed on doggedly, refusing to be diverted from his dream, 'we could soon make up the rest.'

'And there's you and Albert and the rest of the crew to be paid, and an engine driver and a trimmer to feed the furnace,' the old man pointed out. 'I'm fine as I am. Once I cover the cost of my sails the wind's free. So hold your tongue, Weem, for I'll not have any more of this nonsense, and that's final!' He humphed and bit so hard on the stem of his pipe that James expected it to snap in two, then he took it from his mouth to add, 'When I'm gone you'll probably win Albert round, for you always were a silver-tongued bugger and he's a fool, more interested in fathering bairns than makin' sensible decisions. But you'll never get me to change my mind.'

The door of the galley clanged back on its hinges and Jem, the younger of the two bastard sons Albert had brought on board the *Fidelity* as crew members, arrived on deck with a mug of hot tea and a sandwich big enough to warrant the title of doorstop.

'My da says I've to take over the watch if you want to go below.'

'I'm fine where I am,' James told him shortly and the lad, recently promoted from ship's boy to deckhand, shrugged and ducked back into the warm fug of the galley. As the door opened James heard the low rumble of voices from the cabin below, and the soft strains of his cousin Charlie's mouth organ. The rest of the crew would be clustered round the table in the small, pitching cabin, smoking and drinking mugs of strong tea sweetened with condensed milk. They were welcome to it . . . Give him the open air and the sea and his own company any day.

He ate and drank without tasting the food or noticing the scalding sting of the tea, then hunched into the shelter of the wheel-house to light another cigarette, sucking the smoke deep into his lungs, blowing it out again on a long, shuddering breath.

Zachary Lowrie had been right. Almost as soon as he was in his grave Weem had talked his easy-going brother into agreeing that they should replace the Zulus with a drifter, which they would crew together, with Weem as skipper and Albert as mate. There was one snag: as the old man had pointed out, steam drifters cost a lot of money. Between them the Zulus only cleared one-third of the cost of a steamboat and although both Weem and Albert were prepared to take on a hefty loan from the bank, the debt would have been crippling.

That was when James became important to his father's calculations. When he closed his eyes he could still see the pub that the three of them had visited after inspecting the *Fidelity*, which was up for sale and lying in Fraserburgh harbour.

'She's a grand boat, we're all agreed on that,' Weem had said, and the other two had nodded vigorously. 'But the cost of her – the bank won't lend us all that money. Who'd have thought good Zulus would raise so little?'

'The value of sailed boats has gone down, Da, because more and more folk like us want to turn to the steam drifters.'

'Aye.' Weem tugged thoughtfully at his beard, then said, 'Another Zulu to sell would make all the difference.'

'We've not got another.' Albert's eyes were on the barmaid's round backside as she bent over a nearby table.

'No,' Weem said; then slowly, with emphasis on the second word, 'No, *we* don't, but I was speakin' to Mowser Buchan the other day. His chest's that bad that he's havin' to give up the fishing, poor man, and him with his three lads drowned two years back and nobody left to sail his boat out for him. A fine Zulu lying idle in the harbour with neither a skipper nor a crew.'

'Mowser's surely not wanting to come in with us at his age?' Albert asked.

'No, no, the sea's done with the man, poor soul. But there's other ways. James, fetch more drink for us.'

'I'll go,' Albert offered swiftly, but his brother clamped a hand on his arm when he made to rise from the table.

'You'll bide where you are and leave that lassie alone. We're not looking to start trouble with the Fraserburgh men over any barmaid. James . . .'

Waiting for his turn to be served, James saw his father and uncle deep in conversation, heads close together. Once he was back at the table Weem said, 'I was just saying to Albert here that Mowser's daughter's not spoken for.'

James took a deep drink from his tankard and summoned Stella Buchan to mind. She had been in his class at the school: a quiet sort of lass, brown-haired and brown-eyed, not interesting enough to attract his attention. 'What about it?'

'A young fisherman like yourself could do a lot worse than buying a share in a fine steam drifter. Just think of the fish we could get to the shore in that beauty we saw today.'

'Me? I only earn what you pay me. How could I buy a share in any drifter?'

'If you'd a sailed boat you'd make enough from the sale of it to buy a share in that very drifter we saw less than an hour since.'

James choked on his drink. 'Are you talking about me offering for Stella Buchan?' he spluttered, wiping his mouth with one sleeve.

'She's a bonny enough lassie,' Albert put in, adding hurriedly, 'Not that I've had any dealings with her myself, you understand.'

'You hear that, James? Who's a better judge of women than your uncle, eh? Famed the length and breadth of the Moray coast.' Weem slapped his brother on the back and Albert grinned. Although he had never married, every one of his large brood had a different mother.

'I've no thought of marrying yet!'

'Have you no sense in your head at all? If you want to be in that bonny drifter when the next herring season comes round you'll get a ring on that quine's finger before some other young lad comes up with the same thought. I know Mowser would be proud to see the two of you settled together.'

'You've spoken to the man behind my back?'

'To clear your way, just. And it would suit him fine to know his lass had a good hard-working man to look out for her.'

'And what does Stella say to it all? I suppose you've spoken to her behind my back and all?'

'Don't be so daft,' Weem said in his most reasonable voice. 'All the lassies of marriageable age have their eyes on you, and Stella Buchan's no different. If you're half the man I think you are you'll welcome a wife with such a fine dowry.'

James, footloose and fancy-free, had fought against the idea, but in the end he came to realise that his father was right when he said that selling off three Zulus instead of two was the only way to raise enough money to buy the *Fidelity*. And he wanted the drifter just as much as his father and uncle did. He had wanted her from the moment he first saw her in the harbour at Fraserburgh. So he had married Stella Buchan, and the Zulu was sold within a week of the marriage. A week later he was a shareholder in the *Fidelity*.

'Albert giving up his own Zulu gives him the right to be mate,' Weem had explained to his son, 'but his heart's not in the fishing, like ours. He'd far rather be in bed with a woman than out on the boat, and once we've cleared our debt with the bank you and me can buy him out. Then you'll be mate, and follow me as skipper when I give up the sea . . . or when it takes me.'

But the bank loan was still outstanding on the boat when, in a cruel twist of fate, Weem's heart gave out one morning just after they had finished hauling in the catch. If only the man could have been struck down while working the nets moments earlier, James thought, sucking hard on his cigarette, he might have toppled over the side and been dragged to the seabed by the weight of his boots and his clothing. Instead he had collapsed on to the deck planks almost at his son's feet, and as a result he now lay in rich farming earth, away from the sound and taste and feel of the Firth he had lived on for most of his life.

'It's only natural for her to want to know where he is,' Stella had tried to explain to James before the funeral. Her three brothers had drowned during a bad storm and the misery of not knowing where they lay had tormented her mother for the rest of her life.

'It's not her right at all,' he railed back at her. 'He always said that when his time came he'd be with the sea!'

But she had not understood. And why should she, James thought wearily, reaching for another cigarette. She was only a woman, with no understanding of fishermen and the ways that were important to them.

3

James's hand had been stinging for some time before he realised that the glowing cigarette butt was clenched between two fingers, burning into the skin.

Cursing, he threw it overboard as the moon ripped another hole in the ragged clouds and peered at him, its light picking out the wintry-white glitter of spray on the crests of the heaving, tossing waves. A wind had come up and the boat was beginning to dance restlessly. He knew that he should call the others on deck, but he also knew that in the calm depths below the stormy surface the silver darlings were tangling themselves into *Fidelity*'s nets. If Albert Lowrie, sleeping soundly in his bunk at that moment, was made aware of the worsening weather he would head for shore, abandoning the catch. So James did nothing.

By dawn the sea was worse, and the first of the light showed that some of the boats in the distance were getting up steam and hauling in their nets hurriedly, preparing to run for shelter. The rest of the crew arrived on deck, pulling on jerseys and sou'westers as they tumbled out of the galley.

'Damn you, James, why didn't you call us up sooner?' Albert was having difficulty in knuckling the sleep from his eyes.

'It's just a wee swell. Plenty of time to get the nets inboard.'

'A wee swell?' Albert barked, staggering and grabbing for a handhold as the *Fidelity* reared up like a nervous horse. 'You damned young fool, you'll not be content till you drown the lot of us!' As he roared down to the engine driver and trimmer to come up on deck and lend a hand, and the steam capstan leaped into action, James grinned to himself, throwing away his half-smoked cigarette and moving to the starboard bulwarks, where he held on with one hand and leaned precariously over the side, heedless of the waves thundering in on the boat.

It was there, glimpsed beneath the water's foaming surface as the first net was coaxed slowly and steadily upwards . . . the faintly milky tinge that quickly became a silvery shimmer. Although he had seen that same glimmer rising towards him from below the waves on countless occasions, James's body still tingled with a surge of elation and excitement. It was what he was born for, what he and the others risked their lives for over and over again.

'It's a good shot today, lads!' he shouted over his shoulder to the rest of the crew, waiting in a line along the deck. 'Didn't I tell you when we got here that I could smell the herring?'

'You and your bloody nose,' his uncle grunted, his own eyes fixed on the dark sky above. The weather was closing in fast now, but as the seas raced in on her from all sides the boat fought back, twisting and rolling and righting herself every time, only to stagger as another huge wave crashed towards her, then rally and begin the struggle for survival again. Each time she rolled to port the deckhands dug their feet firmly into the angle formed by bulwarks and deck, twisted their hands into the thick wet mesh emerging slowly from the water, and leaned back with all their weight. The trick was to hold tight to the net, which was being lifted from the sea by the rolling action of the boat itself. Over she went, until she was close to lying on her port side, the men almost horizontal on the steeply sloping deck, teeth gritted hard and muscles screaming with the effort of pulling the net along with them. The capstan roared as it hauled in the great messenger rope inch by bitter inch.

When she had rolled as far as was safe the *Fidelity* hesitated, as though making a choice between living and dying; then, deciding, she began to reverse the roll.

The men came upright with her, then as she began to pitch to starboard, threatening to take the emerging nets with her, they leaned forward, clawing at the mesh, their fingers slipping among the tightly packed fish. The steam capstan spun faster now, gathering in foot after foot of the messenger, then as the vessel reached the furthest edge of her roll the net exploded on to the decking among them, filling up every inch and forcing them back towards the gaping maw of the hold while it spilled out its catch, until the crew were knee-deep in hundreds, thousands, of leaping silvery fish.

Now they began to work as one, each man concentrating on his own given task. Jem caught up a wooden shovel and began to scoop the herring towards the hold, as another man deftly disconnected the netting from the messenger rope. Two more detached the round canvas buoys and tossed them into a corner of the deck, out of the way. In the soaking dark rope locker the lad feverishly coiled the dripping rope, while in the hold Charlie and the three other men used their wide wooden herring shovels to scoop to the sides the torrent of fish descending on them in order to make room for the herring following on. When the net was freed from the messenger it, too, went into the hold, where the men disentangled those fish still caught by the gills in the mesh, before bundling it up and clearing it out of the way. Later it would be shaken out and folded and properly stowed, but in the meantime the fight was already on for the next length of netting.

'The weather's gettin' worse . . .' Albert shouted.

'There's time yet, and fish.' James tossed the words

brusquely over his shoulder. All that mattered was getting the fish aboard. Even with the assistance of the steam capstan, the job of bringing a good catch inboard was back-breaking work. Spray and sweat mingled to run down the crew's faces, their necks, their backs beneath the layers of warm clothing. Their oilskins dripped salt water and their feet skidded on the slippery fish scales.

Albert roared an oath as he almost fell after his heel landed on a lump of jelly-like substance that had fallen from the net. 'Watch what you're about, man,' he barked at a young deckhand who had just managed to free a hand and was about to scrub some spray from his face. 'There's scalders in the nets – touch your face and you'll burn your eyes out!' Scalders were a type of jellyfish that covered the fishermen's hands with a toxic stinging slime, which passed to anything they touched. The only solution to the agony of burning eyes or mouths was to wash the afflicted areas with fresh water, but when the nets were coming inboard there was no time for such niceties.

A wave larger than the others caught the boat, lifting it up, then letting it slide down a long, steep flank. It rolled sickeningly and a mass of green water poured inboard. Down and down the boat went, dropping fast enough to leave James suspended almost knee-deep in the sea. For a long, breath-stopping moment he hung on to the net, waiting, then the deck came back up with all the strength of the next wave beneath it, slamming against the soles of his iron-nailed boots with a solid thud that vibrated right through him to the top of his skull. He grinned, relishing the stomach-churning thrill of the experience. One of these days he and the boat might well part company in such a sea, and he would either topple forward into the net, among the thrashing fish, or be carried straight to the seabed far below by the weight of his iron-studded boots. If that should happen he would not struggle, for it would be what fate had intended for him all along.

The next time the boat rolled Albert, too, was left

suspended in the water for long seconds before the deck heaved up beneath him, sending him staggering. He immediately announced that they were heading back.

'But the hold's not full,' James yelled against the banshee howling of the wind.

'I'm not minded to lose the boat for the sake of a few more cran of herring. We've enough fish. Jocky, Claik, down below with ye and get these engines going.'

'When did a fisherman ever have enough!' James shouted, and was ignored.

As they passed those boats still fishing the great stretch of the bank, every vessel heeling over sharply as its crew wrestled with the nets, James felt humiliated to be heading for safety. In his father's day, he raged inwardly as he and the others stored the buoys and, retrieving the nets from the hold, piled them to one side after the last of the fish had been shaken free, the *Fidelity* had been known to wallow back to port with her hold filled to capacity and her decks piled so high with baskets of fish that she was more often below the water than above it. To his mind it was a crime to own and skipper a good steam drifter like *Fidelity* and not use it properly. Albert, damn him, might as well own a wee rowing boat and a few lobster pots, for he'd no proper understanding of the way to treat a good vessel.

Davie Geddes came to mind, a man in his early sixties, still wiry and strong but beginning, by his own admission, to slow down. 'A man has to be fast on his feet and quick with his thinking if he's to face the sea on its own terms,' he had said when he and James met in the public house a few days before. 'Although the Lord's been good to me, I believe He's decided that the time's come for me to spend more of my energy on doing His work instead of my own.'

'You're looking for another crew member?' Unlike most fishermen, James was not a strong Christian and sometimes he found such talk confusing.

'I'm looking for a mate, lad. Johnny's the same age as myself, and to my mind there's nob'dy else in the crew ready to take on such responsibility yet. Since the Lord never saw fit to bless the wife and me with sons, I'm looking for a good man to sail with me during the next season so's he can get to know the boat, then he'll take it over when I leave. A man like yourself, James, though I doubt if you'd want to leave the family boat.'

Davie raised his brows when James said that he might be willing to make the change, but merely said, 'No hurry. We'll both think on it and pray for guidance, and when the answer's been given to each of us we can talk about it.'

It was a good offer; Davie's boat was sailed but sturdy, with years of good use in her yet. However, James knew that there would be a third member in the partnership – the God that Davie introduced into almost every sentence he spoke. James had heard that the old man led his crew in prayer before the nets were shot, and after they were hauled, no matter how great or small the catch. Davie's mate and partner would be expected to be a regular church-goer, which would please Stella, who had tried in vain when they first married to persuade her husband to attend Sunday worship with her.

Then there was the prospect of leaving *Fidelity* and giving up all hope of being her master. Putting a hand briefly on the mast as he straightened from working on the nets, James felt the heart of the boat throb and sing through the timber beneath his palm. His father had fallen in love with her at first sight, wooed her like a lover and bonded so strongly with her that flesh and wood had become one. James ached to do the same. It would be hard to leave her.

Once the work was done it was James's turn to rest. Bone-weary though he was, he tossed in his narrow bunk, the thud and judder of the engines echoing through his

skull. Although the steam drifters were faster and their
engines removed the punishing physical work of hoisting
and trimming sails, they were not as comfortable as the
sailed boats. Steam drifters tended to pitch and jar, while
the constant noise from the engine made sleep difficult.

He sighed and crossed his arms behind his head. The
bunk was narrow and uncomfortable, but at least he was
alone in it. At home Stella would be asleep in their
marriage bed, her soft rounded body heavy with their
coming child. Or she might be awake, tending one of the
twins or making a hot poultice for her father's chest. She
had a sweet, caring nature but she was not the right woman
for James Lowrie. He had never met the right woman, and
perhaps he never would.

'There's times, Jess, when I fair envy you with your bairns
and your grand-weans,' Meg Lowrie said as Innes went to
the back yard to change out of his dirty overalls and get
washed. 'Times I cannae help thinking that if things had
been different I might have had young ones of my own.'

'Life treated you badly, Meg.' Jess touched her sister-
in-law's large knuckly hand. Meg's young husband had
been lost at sea just two weeks after their wedding and,
since his body had never been recovered, she had never
had the chance to say her last farewell or to have him laid
to rest in a decent Christian fashion.

'Ach, it's the way things go.' Meg, never one to brood,
shook off the sympathetic touch. 'At least I've always had
my health and my strength. But I'd not have minded a
nice laddie like your Innes. It was a great disappointment
to Weem when the boy refused to crew on his boat.'

'He didn't refuse, Meg.' Jess fought to keep the anger
from her voice. 'He did his best but he was so sick after
those two voyages that I couldn't let him try again. If
anyone was in the wrong, it was Weem for taking it
so badly.'

'Everyone gets sick at first. It passes.'

'Not the way Innes was. If I'd let him go back to sea the way Weem wanted, the laddie might have died! And it's not as if he's a failure,' she insisted to Weem's sister, just as she had insisted it to Weem himself over and over again. 'Look how well he's done since, apprenticing himself to the blacksmith in Rathven, then being set up in his own wee workshop.'

'Aye, well, there's no sense in hashin' over the past, nor in you and me falling out over what might have been. I'd best be off, for I've got my own things to get ready for Yarmouth.' Meg groaned as she heaved her bulk from the chair, clapping a hand to the small of her back when she was upright. 'Packin' herrin's awful sore on the back. I'm fine when I'm sittin' down and I'm fine when I'm on my feet, but see that bit in atween? I feel as if someone's been usin' my spine to poke the fire!'

'D'you want me to come along tonight and rub some liniment on your back before you go to bed?'

'Would ye? That would be awful good of ye,' Meg said when Jess nodded. 'That's the worst of living alone – there's nob'dy tae give me a good rub when I need it.'

'You should be thinking of giving up work at your age.'

'Away you go . . . What would I do with myself if I wasnae at the farlins durin' the fishin'? Anyway, when we're away from home and livin' a'thegether in lodgings, there's aye someone there to rub my sore joints for me.' Meg laughed gustily. 'You should see us some nights, all standin' round in a circle with every one of us rubbin' away at the woman in front of her. We must be a sight!'

She was still chuckling wheezily when the latch was lifted and James walked into the kitchen. 'Is Innes about?'

'He's out the back. He'll be here in a minute.' Jess was flurried at the sight of her first-born, who only came to her house when necessary, now. The way he had breenged in as though he owned the place reminded her painfully of his father.

'I'm just sayin' to your mother, James, it's been good fishin' so far,' said Meg, seemingly unaware of the tension between mother and son.

'Aye, it has.' His grey eyes studied the air around the two women, never settling on one or the other.

'You'll be glad to get back to your own house for a wee while,' Jess put in. In the two months since the anniversary of Weem Lowrie's death the herring shoals had moved south to the Moray Firth, which meant that the Buckie men were able to work out of their home port for a short time before following the fish down the east coast to England. 'How's Stella, and the new wee bairn?'

'Fine.'

'I'll have to go and see them. What did you cry the wee one?' Meg wanted to know.

James's mouth opened then shut again, and it was left to his mother to supply the answer. 'Ruth. You're all right with the name, James? Stella said you'd not settled on one before you went to Caithness, and since she'd to get the wee one baptised . . .'

'It'll do,' James said. Then as Innes came into the kitchen, 'I've been waitin' for you,' he snarled, clearly relieved to be spared any more conversation. 'Come on outside for a minute.'

'What in the name's up with that man?' Meg asked as the brothers went through the street door.

'He's vexed at fatherin' another lassie.'

'There's nothin' wrong with lassies, I'm one myself,' Meg said vigorously, booted feet planted apart on the floor. She didn't look very feminine, being as sturdy and square-built as her two brothers, with a froth of grey curls rampaging over her head and round her weather-beaten face. 'And he should mind that every lassie that's birthed could be the mother of another good fisherman one day, not to mention becomin' a bonny worker at the nets or the farlins when she's old enough.'

'I know that, but after the twins were born Weem took

to jibing at James, and telling him that he'd not be a man until he'd fathered a son . . .'

'Ach, Weem's been dead and gone more than a year since! James is never still frettin' about it?'

'Things fester with him.'

Meg peered into her sister-in-law's face. 'God save us, Jess, you're not tellin' me that he's still angered with you because you put our Weem in the ground?'

'You surely saw for yourself just now that he can scarce bear to look at me, let alone talk to me.'

'That's nonsense!'

'But it's true that Weem always said the sea would take him in the end . . .'

'Aye, he did, but when his end came the sea thought otherwise. I'll have another cup of that tea if you don't mind, but I'll stand to drink it, for sittin' down again's not worth the bother. If the sea had wanted my brother it would've taken him and that's all there is to it,' Meg went on as Jess hurried to refill her cup. 'Just as it's wrong to claim a body back from the sea, it's wrong to put one in unwanted. James should know that.' She sucked noisily at her tea.

'Sometimes I think I made the wrong decision, Meg, but I couldn't bear the thought of being left with no grave to visit.'

'I know what you mean and you're quite right.' A shadow passed over Meg's face then cleared away as she said, 'It's time the lad let bygones be bygones.'

'You'll not say anything to him, will you? He's still missing his father and I don't want things to be made worse.'

'That's another thing he'll have to get over . . . and the rest of them as well. To tell the truth, Jess, I never thought it right for a man to be as caught up with his bairns as our Weem was.'

'He loved them, and they worshipped him!'

'That's what I mean. Birthin' and raisin's a woman's

job. It's the man's task tae provide for them, then set them to work when they're old enough.'

'Weem did provide for them, and very well too.'

'I never said he didnae.' Meg set her empty teacup down. 'But it sometimes seemed to me that everyone in this house was daft over the man, and he revelled in it for he was aye fond of himsel', was our Weem.'

'With good cause, for there were few men on the Moray coast to match him. And there was no harm in his children loving him, surely.'

'Fathers are for mindin' and respectin', no for lovin'. Albert's young ones never fussed over him the way Weem's did.'

'That's because Albert never raised any of his bairns, being a bachelor,' Jess pointed out a trifle tartly. 'They were all reared in different houses by their own mothers.'

'Aye, but at least he acknowledged every last one of them, and those two lads that work on the *Fidelity* with him are a credit to him. Just as your bairns are a credit to you, Jess,' Meg hastened to add. 'Give James time. He'll settle down and become his own man once he's got this nonsense about his father out of his head.'

'He'll have to,' Jess agreed. Her sister-in-law's words had hurt and worried her more than she was prepared to let on. It was true that Weem's children had adored him from birth, and he, unlike most men, had always found time for them. Jess had more than once consoled herself with the thought that even if her restless, energetic, handsome man ever tired of her – and she used every womanly wile she knew of to make sure that that didn't happen – he would never turn his back on his beloved children for the sake of another woman and another bed.

She had had no inkling, then, of the problems that would come later, as James, Bethany and Innes grew up and Weem, an ambitious man, began to use them to suit his own ends.

4

'Why me?' Innes felt as though an icy hand had reached deep into his body and caught his bowels in a painful grip.

'Who else?' James asked impatiently. 'You're good with engines . . . better than Jocky, for all that he thinks he's the best engine driver in the whole fleet.'

'I work with farm machinery and delivery vans, and mebbe a car now and again, not with drifters.' Innes, who had thought the September day mild until then, shivered and wished that he had had the sense to take his jacket from its hook as he followed his older brother out of the house.

'God's sake, man, an engine's an engine and you'd not want us off down the coast to Yarmouth with a faulty boat, would you?' James peered into his brother's face then gave a short bark of laughter. 'Is it being on the water that worries you? The boat's moored, and there's that many drifters crammed into the harbour with her that she couldnae sink even if the keel was ripped out of her. You'll be safe enough.'

The jeering note in his voice didn't bother Innes, for he had been so used before his father's death to hearing it day in and day out, every time Weem spoke to him. What bothered him was knowing that he couldn't refuse to go aboard the *Fidelity* and see to her engines, because she was the family's boat and he, together with his uncle, brother, sister and mother, was part-owner.

'Well . . . will you do it?'

'Aye, I'll do it.' The words came out with an effort, for his tongue felt as though it had swollen in his mouth. 'When d'you want me there?'

'Good man.' James's big hand landed painfully on his shoulder. 'Now's as good a time as any.'

Now! Innes swallowed hard, though there was nothing to swallow since his mouth had gone bone-dry. 'I'll . . . I'll have to get my jacket.'

'I'll see you down there, then.'

'Come in and wait. I'll not be a minute.'

'I've got things to do,' James said, and hurried off. The irony of the situation wasn't lost on Innes and, if he hadn't been so upset and worried, he might have been amused at the realisation that they were both scared: he at the prospect of going on board *Fidelity* and James at the thought of having to return to the house and make conversation with their mother.

Going back through the low doorway, Innes ran up against Meg's bulk on the way out and had to skip aside like a rowing boat giving way to a steamship. As she passed she gave his shoulder an affectionate pat, her hand as heavy and as strong as James's.

'I'll see you afore I'm off to Yarm'th, Innes,' she said, and went striding down the street, her steps as long as any man's.

In the kitchen Jess had set the flat-irons to heat on the range and was kneading the dough that had been left to rise. 'Where are you off to?' she wanted to know when her son, who had gone through to the back yard without a word, re-appeared in his oil-stained work overalls.

'James wants me to have a look at the *Fidelity*'s engines.' His tongue still felt as though it belonged to someone else.

Jess looked up, consternation in her face. 'Is that what

he was here for? Will you be all right?' she asked when he nodded.

'I'll be fine. The boat's in the harbour, just. I'll mind and jump off if they start putting to sea.' He tried to make a joke of it, but knew as he felt the smile falter and tremble on his lips that he had failed miserably.

'Innes . . .'

'Keep my dinner hot, I'll be back for it,' he said swiftly and went out before she could say anything else. He had sheltered behind her skirts before, as his father had never tired of reminding him. Now he had to stand on his own two feet.

It wasn't easy. With every step of the short walk to the harbour the days, weeks and months seemed to fall away from him. He went from being an eighteen-year-old garage mechanic to a bairn in the old battered perambulator that had had the life knocked out of it by James and Bethany before he ever drew breath.

He had been too young at the time to put a sentence together or to toddle more than a few faltering steps, but even so he still remembered that bonny summer's day on the shore as vividly as if it had happened the week before. He remembered James hauling him out of the perambulator, clutching him round the waist, lugging him over the rocks to a little inlet where the water waited, lapping gently. Normally when older brothers and sisters tossed them into the sea the local bairns spluttered, floundered, then instinctively began to swim. But for some reason this instinct was lacking in Innes, who had spluttered, floundered, then gone down like a stone.

He could still recall with painful clarity the sea's dark-green chill and the way he had been imprisoned in it as though stoppered in a bottle made of thick, cold glass. He remembered the salty bite of the water flooding mercilessly into his mouth and his eyes, and filling his lungs when he tried to suck in air. He remembered the flashes of red light before his bulging eyes gradually dimming into blackness, and he very dimly remembered James, kneeling on the rocks and reaching deep into the waves, catching hold of him and hauling him out by the seat of his rompers.

He had been slung face down over a rock and his back pummelled until water rushed from every orifice in his body and, at last, his traumatised lungs managed to suck in their first breath of air. He had then been tossed into the perambulator by his irritated brother and trundled home, soaking and shivering, curly black hair plastered to his round little skull, too shocked to cry until James wheeled him into the kitchen and Innes caught sight of his mother, his beacon of safety. Then the floodgates had opened.

Innes had never again gone swimming, even when he was much older and all the other lads stripped off on hot summer days to plunge in from the rocks, or from moored rowing boats in the harbour.

'Ach, it's no loss,' his father, sorry for him at first, had said when James and Bethany jeered. 'What use is swimmin' to a fisherman anyway? If you go off the boat, the sea fills your boots and takes you down whether you can swim or not. You're better to go peaceably.'

His rough kindness only made things worse for Innes, for the words burned themselves into his brain through all the years of growing up. Like his brother and his father, and his forebears for generations before him, Innes was destined to be a fisherman when he turned fifteen. There was no question of getting out of it. And he knew, through the days and years, that when the time came he would, sooner or later, feel the cold, salty water rushing into his heavy, nail-studded boots as he went down and down into the green bottle that had been waiting to reclaim him.

As he turned the corner and saw the harbour he stopped short, the breath leaving him. All four basins were crammed with vessels, mainly steam drifters but with a sprinkling of the sailed Zulus that had been the mainstay of the Scottish fishing industry before steam arrived. There were so many of them that it would have been difficult to squeeze in a toy yacht – every one of them swarming with men painting, or cleaning out the holds, or storing the great drift-nets aboard.

The very sight of the boats brought a rush of sour bile into Innes's mouth and he had to turn his head aside and spit it out against a wall. His first terrible trip to sea had been at the opening of the season, and from the moment the engines started, the stench of fish and stale sea water from the bilges had set him vomiting even before they cleared the harbour entrance.

'Ach, it's always like that when the boat's been lying idle,' his cousin Charlie had told him as Innes hung over the side, retching. 'It's a filthy stink, but once she's been washed through by a couple of good hard seas it'll clear.'

It was true that by the time she was halfway to the fishing grounds the boat smelled much sweeter, but that stink had lingered on in Innes's memory for all of that voyage and all of the next, and for months after his father had given up on him as a seaman. Now the sight of the boats cramming the harbour vividly brought back the memory.

He would have turned tail and run for home there and then if James, who had been waiting for him on the harbour, hadn't grabbed at his arm. 'Come on, then.'

'Where is she?'

'There, can you not see her at the other side? We were lucky to get her by the harbour wall. We'll go across the other boats.'

Innes shied back. 'I'll walk round.'

'Oh, for . . .' The grip on his arm tightened, forcing him towards the nearest boat. 'It's quicker this way. Don't worry,' James said, the sneer back in his voice, 'I'll see that you don't get your precious feet wet!'

To James, who would have swum the harbour without a second thought, crossing it by scrambling from boat to

boat was no trouble at all; but Innes – his stomach lurching
with every faint movement beneath his feet, every rasp of
hull rubbing against hull, every glimpse of black water
below – felt as though an eternity passed before he finally
arrived safely on the deck of the *Fidelity* to be met by his
uncle Albert Lowrie and the engine driver, who was black
with oil.

'I've tried everythin' but I'm no sure that I've got it
right,' the man said. 'You'd best come below and see for
yersel'.'

Engines, Innes told himself as he scrambled down into
the boat's bowels. Just think about the engines. Sure
enough, at the sight and smell of the compound steam
engine everything else faded into the background and the
mechanic in him took over.

Half an hour later, when his uncle Albert said, 'You're a
grand clever lad, right enough,' Innes, on his knees among
the engine parts, lifted a hot, oil-streaked face and grinned
up at him. The problem had been found and resolved and
he had enjoyed every minute of the work.

'It wasn't that difficult.'

'You'll come and have a drink with us.'

'Of course he will.' James, who disliked the smell of
oil and the cramped conditions of the engine room, was
in a hurry to lead the way back on deck.

Following him, no longer occupied by thoughts of the
machinery, Innes suddenly became aware of the slap and
thud of water against the wooden hull only inches away
from where he stood, and of the slight motion of the
boards underfoot. Memories rushed back, swamping and
paralysing his mind. All at once the low-roofed space
he stood in was no longer the engine room but the rope
locker, a tiny cupboard immediately below the forrard
deck, where the messenger warp had to be coiled as it
brought the nets inboard. Whenever he thought of Hell he
visualised it as that little cupboard where he had crawled
round and round in the cramped darkness, wretched with

sea-sickness, tugging at the thick, wet, slimy rope that smelled of the sea's depths and fought against him, almost as though it wanted to return there, pulling back out of the slot it had been fed through, slithering over the deck and splashing into the waiting waves and down to the seabed. And the worst horror of all was that it seemed to Innes as he wrestled with it that the rope wanted to take him with it.

Hour upon hour he had struggled, his arms feeling as though they were being wrenched out of their sockets, his lungs labouring in the stuffy, smelly atmosphere, his clothes slick and filthy with grease and dirt. It had been like being buried alive; the stamp and clatter of feet on the deck just above his head as his father, his brother and the rest of the crew fought to drag the big nets, heavy with sea-harvest, inboard had become the sound of people jumping on his coffin lid to hold it down and keep him imprisoned within. And all the time the boat rolled and tossed, throwing Innes against the wooden walls and then, before he could gather his wits, hurling him back, to sprawl against the coiled rope that took up more and more of the limited space as it continued to slither in.

The mercy, if there was any at all, was that he had already emptied his stomach long since, so although he retched continuously there was nothing left to bring up. Had there been, he would have had no option but to crawl through it.

As he now followed James out on to the deck the nightmare of remembering went on. Once the nets had finally been hauled aboard and he was allowed to stagger on to the deck to breathe in some fresh air, the sight of the tossing sea, the desperate leaping of the silver herring as the last of them were shaken from the nets into the hold, and the frosting of fish-scales and blood on his fellow crew members' hands and clothes, faces and hair had set Innes's tormented stomach off again. He remembered his father's big hands plucking him off the deck where he sprawled and holding him over the side of the boat, suspended above the sea while the icy spray was tossed into his face with each roll of the drifter. And even worse than the conviction that he was going to fall from his father's grasp and be sucked down was the contempt in Weem Lowrie's voice from above Innes's head, 'For God's sake will ye behave like a man instead of a wee lassie? I'm sick with shame over ye!'

Aware of the familiar clenching in his gut, desperate to get off the boat and on to solid land, Innes now strode across the deck, almost falling headlong over a rope being coiled by his cousin Charlie, Albert's oldest by-blow.

'Mind out,' the man said, amiably enough, but the only voice Innes could hear in his mounting panic was his father's. 'Call yourself a son of mine? Call yourself a Buckie man? If ye cannae go to sea ye might as well go to Hell!'

Fortunately the boat's holds were empty and she was riding high on a full tide, which meant that the deck and gangplank were more or less level with the harbour wall. Even so, halfway along the narrow plank Innes stumbled and almost lost his balance. Arms flailing, he looked down and, at the sight of the water below, his mind froze with sheer terror.

'Not so fast, man,' his uncle admonished from far away, then a hand thumped him between the shoulder blades, propelling him willy-nilly along the last section of plank to stumble on to the flagstones. 'You were takin' it like a bull at a gate,' Albert Lowrie said amiably, fetching up alongside his nephew. 'That's no way to do it.'

James, scorning the plank, balanced a foot on the bulwarks and gained the harbour with one long stride. 'Aye, Innes, you shouldnae be showing off like that,' he chimed in as he landed lightly beside them. 'You might have fallen in and got yourself all wet.'

He too sounded amiable, but Innes knew without having to look that his brother's grey eyes were glittering with contempt, an expression that he well remembered. Even Bethany had looked at him like that, bitterly resenting the fact that her younger brother should hate the sea when she, who loved it, was denied his chances just because she was a girl.

Innes clenched his fists in his pockets and wished that he had the courage to knock the sneer from James's face. 'I'll have a drink . . . if you're putting a hand in your pocket to buy it for me,' he told his brother grimly.

'Good man. Charlie, Jem, you're comin'?' Albert hailed his sons. 'And fetch Jocky and the rest along with ye.'

The small public house was filled with fishermen standing shoulder to shoulder, as close-packed as herring in a barrel. Used as they were to living in crowded conditions at sea, none of them was bothered about the darkness and the lack of space; at first Innes was keenly aware of it, but his first pint, hurriedly downed, hit the pit of his stomach and sent a calming glow through him, easing tense muscles. When Albert insisted on buying another round, Innes nodded and held out his empty tankard, aware of his brother's watchful eyes, knowing that James fully expected him to turn tail and run for home as soon as he could. After what he had been through, he needed a good drink.

When Innes and his drinking cronies emerged two hours later night had fallen. Bidding the others an affectionate farewell, he reeled and lurched along Main Street, weaving from one side of the narrow road to the other. He had done it. He had gone on board the *Fidelity*, and he had repaired her engines and had drunk shoulder to shoulder with the fishermen. Taking two shots at the latch before managing to lift it, he gained entry to the house in a fine mood.

It was well past the dinner hour, but Jess said nothing as her son wafted into the kitchen on an alcoholic cloud. This had happened so many times in her life with Weem

and James, who worked hard, pitting themselves against
the might and moods of the sea and were entitled, in her
view, to take their ease in their own ways when they
were ashore.

'You fixed the engines, then?' she said calmly, putting
his dinner on the table.

'Aye.' He had slumped down in a fireside chair, heedless for once of his dirty overalls, and was making a stab
at taking his boots off. 'James and Uncl' Al . . . Uncl'
Albish took me for a wee drink after.' He belched, gave
up on the boots and leaned back in his chair. 'I'll see to
these later.'

'It was the least they could do, since you were such
a help to them.' Jess knelt down and unlaced his boots
with practised skill. When she stood up she saw that
he had fallen asleep, his head lolling against the back
of the chair, one arm hanging over the side, his mouth
wide open.

She covered his food and put it back in the oven, then
picked up her knitting, marvelling at the way grown men
could revert to the innocence of their childhood when
relaxed in sleep.

He gave a slight snore, then came another, louder this
time, while Jess's hands flew over the wool on her lap, the
knitting growing fast. Soon she would walk along the road
to Meg's single-roomed home and rub her sister-in-law's
aching back, but for the moment it was pleasant to sit
quietly with only the ticking of the clock and her son's
snoring for company. It was a bit of a worry about her
good chair and his dirty overalls, but she was reluctant
to disturb him.

She didn't grudge him the drink or the dinner, carefully
prepared and now ruined, for she knew what an effort it
must have been for him to go on board the *Fidelity* that
afternoon to see to the engines. Although every fisherman,
even Weem and James, suffered from sea-sickness when
they first began their trade, it had been different with

Innes. Weem had refused to listen to her when she voiced her fears after the boy came home from his first trip, tense and nervy, his eyes little more than haunted pits in a white face.

'We all have to find our sea-legs, and he's no different,' Weem had insisted, and Innes was dragged off on another voyage. This time when he returned he was unable to eat or sleep, waking the rest of the family from their own much-needed slumber with his nightmares. Noting how he jumped and quivered at every sound, especially his father's voice, and seeing the way his hands and mouth trembled when they should have been in repose, Jess had refused to let Innes return to the boat. It was one of the worst quarrels she and Weem had ever had, but she had won, though he never forgave her for coming between him and his son. Although Innes had then found work in the garage and had done well for himself, Weem had never stopped thinking of him as a coward, hiding behind his mother's skirts.

At least, Jess thought, getting up to fetch the ointment needed for Meg's sore back, she had made sure that Weem – who had loved his children so deeply when they were small, and had used them with such a lack of understanding once they reached adulthood – did not manage to destroy Innes the way he had destroyed James and Bethany.

5

'James thinks this year's fishing'll be just as good down in England,' Stella said as the Lowrie women – Jess, Bethany, Meg and Stella herself – mended the nets.

'It's to be hoped so.' Meg plied her needle busily. 'We could all do with a good bit put by for the winter.'

The four of them were in James's net loft, sitting cross-legged with a great stretch of net spread over the floor between them. From below, where old Mowser had been coaxed into keeping an eye on the five children, they could hear the continuous murmur of Rory's voice. As they worked, the women frequently wiped their hands on their aprons, and Stella had set two buckets of fresh water within easy reach, for the men had seen a lot of scalders among the summer catches. When the nets dried, fragments of jellyfish still adhering to them turned to a powder that stung the hands and burned like pepper if it got into unwary eyes.

September was a busy month, for the English winter fishing was about to begin and provisions had to be arranged, nets checked and mended, engines overhauled or, for those who still used the graceful, efficient Zulus for their fishing, sails readied in preparation for the journey south to Grimsby, Lowestoft and Yarmouth.

Jess had always found net-mending a soothing occupation and she loved the companionship and the bustle at this time of year. Once, she had gone south too as one of the guttin quine, until the year when Weem Lowrie first noticed her in Yarmouth. A year later, when he left in his father's sailed Zulu for the fishing grounds, Jess had had to wave him goodbye from the harbour wall, with small James straddling her hip and the tears choking her at the thought of being without her man for weeks.

'We'll have a cup of tea,' Meg suggested, putting her needle aside. She made to get up then stopped, wincing, one hand flying to the small of her back.

'Is that lumbago bothering you again?'

'Just a wee twinge. That salve you put on it made a difference.'

'Sit where you are and I'll see to the tea.' Jess put her own needle down and went to the ladder. The children, bored with their games, greeted her with yells of joy and Mowser, brightening at the sight of her, got out of his chair remarkably quickly. 'I'll just take a turn for you,' he said, and made for the ladder, pathetically eager to play his part in the preparations.

Growing old was a terrible thing, Jess thought as she measured tea into the big pot. Bad enough for a woman, but worse for a man who had once fought the sea as a living, only to find himself eventually reduced to the status of child minder. Mowser Buchan had been a fine, handsome man in his time, but the loss of all three of his sons in the one storm, followed within a twelvemonth by the death of his wife, had taken a heavy toll on the man. Years of hard work had carved themselves deeply into him, and now he was bowed, slow-moving and suffered badly from bronchial problems. The luxuriant moustache that had given him his nickname was still there, but nowadays it was yellow from the pipe Mowser smoked and dominated the shrunken face behind it.

The womenfolk, normally never allowed to set foot on a fishing boat for fear that they would bring bad luck and poor catches, came into their own when the boats were

being 'rigged out' for the journey south. Then they were
allowed to go on board, armed with buckets of water and
scrubbing brushes, to turn out cupboards and clear every
corner of dust and dirt. It was a matter of pride with
them to keep the Scottish fishing boats free of diseases
that thrived in dirty conditions.

For once, working together at the net-mending and then
cleaning out *Fidelity*, Jess and her daughter were freed of
the awkwardness that had crippled them since Bethany's
marriage. They even laughed at times as they carried the
long sacks of chaff that served as mattresses up on deck
to air them, before giving the cabins fore and aft a good
redding out.

Slipping sidelong glances at her daughter as they brushed
and scrubbed, Jess knew that this was where Bethany was
happiest, on board the *Fidelity*. Like her father and her
elder brother she was a child of the sea, treating it with
respect but without fear. Jess would never forget the day
a neighbour had come to her door to ask if she knew that
three-year-old Bethany was swimming off one of the creel
boats in the harbour with the laddies. Rushing from the
house with Innes in her arms, Jess had discovered her
daughter, stripped to her drawers and semmit, balancing
precariously on the edge of the boat while James and some
other boys cheered her on, treading water. As Jess watched
in horror, Bethany had leaped into the deep black water,
surfaced, paddled like a dog to the mooring rope, then
moved deftly hand-over-hand along it back to the boat,
where she clambered aboard, punted up from behind by
two of the boys, and went through the whole process again.

To Jess's fury Weem, coming back from the fishing
grounds to find Bethany moping and scowling because she
had been forbidden to swim again, scooped his beloved
daughter into his arms and told her that she was a fine
wee lassie and her daddy's pride and joy. He even gave
her permission to return to her swimming and, as she
scampered off, barefoot and wearing one of Jess's pinnies

pinned between her legs in place of her underclothes, he shrugged off his wife's protests.

'She's got courage, that one. I'm right proud of her.'

'She's only a baby yet. She could drown!'

'If the sea takes her it'll be because she belongs to it,' Weem said calmly. 'You know that, Jess. We don't want to mollycoddle the lassie.'

By the time she started school Bethany was an accomplished swimmer and more of a daredevil than most of the boys. Most of her time was spent at the harbour, and when her father was home she hung on his every word.

It was a pity, Jess thought as they shook the chaff mattresses out on the deck, then dragged them below to the bunks, that Bethany hadn't been born the boy and Innes the girl. It was a cruel twist of fate that had given him such a fear of the sea and her such a love of it. When she was grown, the girl had tried repeatedly to get her father to take her on a fishing trip, but without success.

'Women don't belong on the boats,' he said each time she asked, coaxed or demanded. 'It would bring bad luck, same as meetin' the man in black . . .' The word 'minister' was never mentioned in Weem's house, let alone on board his boat, for fear of bringing bad luck to the fishing.

'Why should James get to go to sea and not me?'

'Because you're a girl,' taunted James, now out of school and sailing with his father.

'I'd be better than you!'

'You'll still be part of the fishin',' her father had tried to console her. 'You'll work at one of the net factories, and when you're old enough you can go to the farlins with your Aunt Meg. And that's an end of it,' he added sharply as Bethany opened her mouth again. Later, he had told Jess, 'That lass of ours is gettin' too big for her boots. You've spoiled her.'

Jess, knowing her man well, had not bothered to argue.

'At least the cabins smell a sight better than they did,' she said now, as they climbed back to the deck.

'Aye, for a wee while. You go on ahead,' Bethany said as they were about to cross over the intervening boats to get to the harbour. 'I'll just give the wheel-house another going over.'

Alone in the small wheel-house, she put her work-reddened hands on the wooden spokes, settled her feet firmly into the decking and closed her eyes, giving herself over to the gentle motion of the boat and the soft thud of water against the hull. For a long time she stood there, motionless, and she might have stayed all afternoon, heedless of her duties ashore and of the children, waiting for her at Stella's house, if booted feet hadn't thudded on to the deck.

'Still here?' James asked, surprised, as she emerged from the wheel-house. 'I thought you'd be done long since.'

'I was just finishing. That's you ready to go south, then?'

'Aye, if Uncle Albert can be persuaded to stir his fat carcass.' His mouth took on a sour twist. 'If it was left to him, the boat would never leave harbour.' He looked restlessly around the deck, then at the other boats crammed into the harbour. 'And if it was left to me we'd be at sea all the time.' He gave her a quick, conspiratorial grin. 'I never was one for the fireside and bairns.'

'Neither am I,' Bethany said sharply, irritated by what she saw as his smug attitude. 'But some of us have no other choice.'

The grin faded. 'What's wrong with you now?'

'Think it out for yourself,' Bethany snapped, scorning the point where the next boat rubbed gently against *Fidelity*. Instead she moved to a spot where there was quite a gap to cross, then placed one foot on the gunnels and leaped out across the black water below, her skirt swirling about her legs. Running across the deck, she repeated the leap a few more times until she had crossed the other boats and gained the harbour.

As she reached the street a cart passed with several chattering children perched on its load of nets. The carter, a man who had often let Bethany and James ride his cart on top of the piled nets when they were younger, called out, 'Want a lift, lass?'

All at once the thought of going back to Stella's house to collect her step-children was more than Bethany could bear. She almost ran to clamber up on to the narrow seat by his side, then common sense prevailed. It would not be the done thing for Gil Pate's wife to behave like a foolish bairn in public.

She shook her head, then stood in the middle of the road watching the cart trundle away towards the cutching yard, where the nets would be dipped in tanks of boiling water and tannin to season and strengthen them, then spread out or hung up to dry.

Then, slowly and reluctantly, she made her way back to Stella's house.

James, watching his sister storm off the harbour, saw her pause when the carter called to her. For a moment, as her lithe body lifted and half-turned on her toes, he thought that she was going to run to the cart and climb aboard the piled nets. But instead she settled back on her heels and stood watching as the cart went on its way. When it was out of sight she turned and walked slowly away, head lowered, all the fire and anger quenched.

He tried to fathom out the mystery of what had happened to Bethany as he went below to the fore-cabin, which smelled strongly of soap and disinfectant underlaid by the odour of fish and bilge water. Once she had been as good as any lad, clambering over the rocks without a thought of danger, swimming off the boats in the outer harbour basin, climbing trees and fishing, playing kick-the-can and football while all the other lassies were contented with their dolls and peevers and skipping ropes. She had been a bonny fighter too, had Bethany. Nobody ever picked a fight with her more than once. Even James himself had had his nose bloodied by her small, sharp-knuckled fists.

It had been a grand childhood, but in growing up they had also grown apart. He had been too busy making the transition from laddie to man, too cock-a-hoop and full of himself to give much thought to his sister.

His mouth twisted derisively at the memory of himself only a few years ago, swaggering about Buckie in his good blue jacket and his cheese-cutter cap, enjoying the way the lassies fluttered their eyelashes at him when he went to the dancing. He had had his pick of them in those days, and he had made the most of his popularity. And now look at him!

It had all gone sour since the very moment of his father's death. James groaned and slumped back on the narrow bunk, remembering Weem, washed and dressed in his good suit by the womenfolk, then laid out in his coffin quiet and still, with two pennies to close his eyelids and a patterned kerchief tied about his jaw.

The neighbours had crowded in to pay their respects, bringing with them dishes and bowls of food, and when they were gone and Jess had been persuaded to rest, James and his uncle and Innes and Gil Pate had kept Weem company. All through that long, silent night James had been unable to take his eyes from the open casket or close his ears to the clamour of his father's voice, reproaching him for bringing him back from the sea and forcing him to be the centrepiece of this circus of ritual mourning, when he should have been beneath the waves, at one with the fish that had been his livelihood.

When James had returned to the house after the funeral, uncomfortable in his best suit with its stiff collar and his shining, tight-fitting black shoes, Bethany had opened the door to him, her mouth hard and her grey eyes glowing like two hot coals as though she, too, blamed her brother for not having had the courage and the wit to bundle their father's body over the side of the boat when he died, even if it had meant locking his arms about the corpse and going down with it. She had stepped back without a word and he had walked past her and into the kitchen, coming face-to-face with his mother and turning away at once, unable to look her in the eye and forgive her for the wrong she had done Weem Lowrie.

The chasm that had opened between him and his mother was one thing, but Bethany's rejection was another. It bothered James, who was sorely in need at times of someone to talk to openly and honestly. Innes, having turned his back on the sea, did not count, but Bethany might well have been that person if she hadn't changed so much.

It might not just be him that she disliked now, he reasoned. She tended to glare at everyone these days, even poor Gil Pate, a decent enough man and a good, providing husband. Women! Stella and his mother and the bairns and Bethany . . . the sooner he was off to Yarmouth, the better.

Back home, he went up to the net loft after he had eaten. There was nothing left to do . . . *Fidelity*'s nets were all mended and neatly stacked for the trip down south, and the ropes checked and coiled, but he enjoyed pottering about the place inhaling the smell of ropes and creels and baskets and canvas, free of the need to make conversation.

'Can I give ye a hand, son?'

James felt his heart sink as old Mowser came wheezing and gasping up the narrow ladder.

'I was just having a look at the lines.' In an attempt to look busy James dragged out a basket of the long lines used for catching white fish – cod, ling, skate, whiting, haddock and halibut – in the early part of the year before the herring began to run, and pretended to be inspecting it closely.

'I'll see to them while you're off in Yarm'th, never worry about that.' Mowser settled himself on the scarred old box that had once carried all his clothes and personal possessions when he was at sea, scrabbling in his pocket for his pipe, matches and baccy pouch. When the pipe was packed and lit and drawing to his satisfaction he blew a long stream of pale smoke towards the rafters, gave a thoughtful 'Aye . . .' and launched into a monologue of memories, as he always did whenever he caught James's attention for a moment.

The smell of the tobacco mingled pleasantly with the other aromas in the loft and the old man's wheezy voice, interrupted now and then by a bout of coughing and spitting, was not intrusive. He didn't need to be listened to, for he was quite happy to ramble on without any contribution from his audience. Gradually James gave up the pretence of work and settled on the floor with his back against the wall, elbows on knees and hands idle for once, letting Mowser's creaky voice wash over him without bothering to listen.

Below, he could hear the twins squealing and giggling as Stella bathed them before the kitchen fire. The baby began to cry and was hushed, and after a while he heard his wife singing a lullaby, an indication that the twins were in their bed and close to sleep.

'. . . one of the worst storms I ever encountered.' Mowser's frail voice drifted in the air like his pale-blue tobacco smoke. 'Three boats lost from this coast on that one night, one of them takin' my uncle and two cousins with it. And me just a laddie new to the sea, certain sure that I'd be down deep among the fishes come the morn . . .'

James felt a stab of pity for the old man, dependent on his daughter's husband for bed and board, with nothing to do but while the long days away down by the harbour, where he exchanged memories with old fishermen like himself and watched younger, fitter men take the boats through the entrance and out towards the horizon.

But at least Mowser had food and shelter, a fireside to sit by at nights and money for baccy. Unlike Weem, he had reached a good age and survived a lifetime spent at the whim of the sea. One day if he lived long enough, James reasoned, he himself would be in the same position. And it might well be the very same position, for the way things were going there would be no sons to be taught the way of the fishing. He might well have to live under a son-in-law's roof as Mowser did now, feeble and dried up and dandling grand-bairns on his knee.

He scrambled to his feet, suddenly anxious to get out of the house, then said diffidently, 'D'you want to come down to the pub for a drink?'

'Eh?' Mowser blinked at him, then his lined face lit up. 'Aye, son, I'd like that fine.'

Albert, at the bar, greeted them noisily and insisted on buying their drinks. The three of them retired to a table, but half an hour later Albert announced that he had to go.

'A wee matter of business,' he said, with a wink and a leer.

'Daft bugger,' Mowser said blandly when Albert had gone. 'I had him as a deckhand on my own boat once, as a favour to his father. Albert wasnae long out of school at the time, and he'd already got a lassie in trouble. Since her father was on the same boat, and he was too good a man to lose, I took Albert till the fuss died down.' He shook his head. 'I was glad to get shot of him – a useless loon, and lazy intae the bargain. The only part of him that was willin' to work was in his trousers.'

'He's not changed.'

'Why d'you put up with him then?' Mowser asked bluntly.

'I've not much choice, seeing it's the family boat and he's older than me.'

'Did your own father's share not go to you?' the old man asked, and James shook his head.

'I already had a one-third share, from selling . . .' He stopped short, and Mowser nodded.

'I know, lad, from selling my boat. A bonny Zulu, she was. The way things have worked out you might have been better keeping her and turning your back on the *Fidelity*.'

James looked at him with new respect. 'Aye, I should have, but we never know what lies ahead. Anyway, my father's share went to the rest of them – my mother and Bethany and Innes.'

'And that's why you're stuck with Albert. I've often wondered.' Mowser drained his glass noisily and set it down. 'Have you never thought that if you could get the three of them to go along with you, you'd have two-thirds of the boat? Then you'd be able to put Albert in his place.'

As James stared at him in dawning realisation, Mowser sniffed, scrubbed the back of a knotted hand across the underside of his thick yellow moustache and pushed the glass across the scarred table. 'I'll have another pint, son, since you're in a buying mood.'

'It was nice of you to take Da out for a drink,' Stella said when the old man had gone off to his bed. 'He fairly enjoyed it.'

'He's good company.'

She smiled at him across Ruth's head as the baby sucked noisily, starfish hands the size of seashells spread over the blue-veined curve of her mother's full breast. Suddenly sated, she fell asleep, her slack mouth falling away from the nipple; Stella used one corner of her shawl to wipe a dribble of milk from the little chin.

'You're fretting to get to Yarmouth.'

'The sooner we go, the more herring we catch and the more money to see us through the winter.'

'Aye.' She gave a little sigh, and he knew that she was thinking of the weeks ahead, without him. But that was the way it was for a fisherman's wife. 'Are you coming to bed?' she asked, drawing back the curtain that hung by day across the wall-bed, and reaching in for her night-gown.

'In a minute.' James poked the fire into a red glow, half-aware of the soft sounds of his wife undressing. Then he got abruptly to his feet and reached for his jacket.

'You're not going out at this time of night, surely?' In the long gown, with her hair loose and falling about her shoulders, she looked like a lassie just on the verge of womanhood, rather than the mother of three children.

'Just for a wee while.'

He knew, as he went out of the door, that she would still be awake when he returned, unable to sleep until he was home. The knowledge that she cared for him so much was one of the many burdens he had to carry.

6

Gil had every right to go out in the evenings. Men who worked hard to support their families were entitled to relax once the long day's work was done, their stomachs full of good food cooked by their womenfolk, a pint mug in their hands, in the company of other men. It was what Bethany's own father had done almost every evening when he was ashore and, until her own marriage, she had taken that male right for granted.

Now, throwing down her knitting and staring round the kitchen's four walls, she asked herself if it was fair. It was true that her man had been working all day, but so had she: cooking and cleaning and washing and ironing, blacking the range and scrubbing the front doorstep and seeing to his two children. And where was the relaxation for her? Here she was, bored and alone, with no chance of getting out of the house for a breath of fresh air and nobody to talk to. Not that she wanted any more of the sort of talk she got from the likes of Stella, all about bairns and recipes and knitting patterns.

Rising to pace about the small room, she thought longingly of the days when she had been free to earn her own money and live her own life. It had been hard work, in the net factory during the winter months and at the farlins during the summer and autumn herring fishing, but it had been good, too, specially at the farlins, with the fishermen and coopers and curers and buyers all around, and the other women, with their lively minds and quick tongues. At the end of the day, hands stinging and back aching, she had slept soundly, drugged by the fresh air and happy in the knowledge that she had done a good day's work and earned a day's wage. Now, although she was kept busy from morning to night, she had lost the deep, almost exhilarating exhaustion of the old days and her sleep was continuously broken by demands either from Gil or from one of his children.

By the time he rolled in through the door, flushed and smelling of beer and in high humour, she was almost at her wits' end with frustration.

'I'm going to take a turn down by the harbour.' She reached for her shawl.

'At this time of night? I'm ready for my bed . . . and a bonny, willing wife to share it.' His voice and his look were both heavy with meaning.

'In a minute. I'll not be long.' She put a hand to the door latch, anxious to get out before he delayed her further. He had had a lot to drink; she estimated that he would be asleep and snoring in ten minutes, which would suit her fine.

'Make sure of it.' He collapsed into his usual chair and made an unsuccessful stab at untying his shoelaces. 'Give me a hand with them before you go, pet,' he begged plaintively, and when Bethany left the door and went to kneel before him he put a hand on her bright chestnut hair, his fingers slipping round to stroke her cheek. 'My wee birdie,' he said thickly, then, 'I was speakin' to your James tonight.'

'And drinking with him, I'll be bound.' One shoe was off, but the lace of the other was knotted. Bethany pulled at it, cursing below her breath.

'Your Uncle Albert's fair driving him mad. He thinks he could do better.'

'He probably could. He's a good seaman, James.' But

not as good as she would have been, given the chance, she thought, fiddling with the obstinate lace.

'You know how James owns a third share in th' boat, an' you an' yer mother an' Innes hold another third between ye . . .' Gil paused, brow knotted, trying to puzzle out the next part of the sentence.

'Aye, and Uncle Albert has a third share. What about it?'

'Well, James thinks . . . and so do I, mind, so do I,' Gil slurred solemnly above her head, 'that if he'd control over the other third – the shares you an' yer mother an' Innes have – that would make him a maj-majority holder. Then he'd be able tae give Albert the orders for a change. D'you see what I'm trying to tell ye?'

'Of course I see, I'm not stupid.'

'I knew you'd understand, lass. You always had a good head on your bonny shoulders.' Gil reached down to caress the shoulders in question. 'So I told him he was welcome to make use of your share.'

Bethany left the knot and sat back on her haunches, staring up at him. 'You told him what?'

'That he could have your share of the boat. That way he's got a bit more say in the run . . .' He stopped as she jumped to her feet.

'What right do you have to say a thing like that? Behind my back, too. How could you!'

'Eh?' Her husband peered myopically up at her through a drunken haze.

'James already has a share in the *Fidelity* and he's not having mine as well. It's all I've got, d'you not see that?'

'But you'll still get the money, pet, I made sure of . . .'

'You daft gowk, it's not the money I care about, it's the boat! Here.' Bethany stooped, picked up the shoe she had just taken off his foot and tossed it at him. It cracked against his shin and bounced to the floor. 'You can just put that on and go and tell him you'd no right to make decisions for me!'

Gil rubbed at his leg. 'I'll do nothing of the sort. D'you think I want him to see me as a weakling who takes orders from his wife?'

'He can see you any way he likes, but he's not getting my share of the *Fidelity*!' Knowing that if she stayed a moment longer she would probably strike him, Bethany stormed out of the house, ignoring Gil's shouted order to stay where she was. As she slammed the door behind her she heard the wail of a child wakened abruptly from sleep. Let him see to his own bairns for once, she thought, striding off into the night. She had had more than enough of domesticity.

Although most of the houses she passed were in darkness, a light still burned in James's kitchen window. Bethany raised her fist to give the door a hefty thump, then paused. She was in the mood for a good quarrel, but if she started one in front of Stella and her father she would upset them, not to mention rousing the children. Best to wait until the next day and catch him on his lone. There was no fear that her anger would cool completely in the interim; it glowed in the depths of her mind like a fire that had been banked up to nurse its heat for hours and burn brightly again when needed.

She turned away and went on along the coast road, making up her mind to walk until she was too tired to think. That way she would be sure to stay out until long past the time Gil was asleep, which suited her, for the thought of being fondled and used by him that night was beyond bearing.

Heartened by his conversation with Gil the night before, James went first thing the next morning to the smiddy – an apt place, he thought as he heard the jingle of a harness and the nervous stamp of hooves in the blacksmith's shop, for wasn't he here with the intention of striking while the iron was hot?

There was a smile on his face as he marched into the

adjoining workshop to put his proposal to his younger
brother, but it faded when Innes, having heard him out,
said uncomfortably, 'I don't know, James.'

'Why not? We all know that you've no interest at all
in the boat.' James could have bitten his tongue out as
he saw the colour rise in the younger man's face. 'Not
that that's wrong,' he hastened to add. 'Each to his own.
And I give you my word that if you put your share of
Fidelity in my name I'll see to it that you get your money
just the same.'

'I'm not bothered about the payment, for mine all goes
to Ma.'

'Well then! You're a landsman, Innes, and I'm a seaman. I earn my living and support my family from my
work on that boat, and that's why I need to have more
say in the way she's used.' James swallowed and ran a
finger round his collar. 'How can you stand the heat in
here? And there's scarce room to move. It's like being
buried alive.'

'I'm used to it. Here . . .' Innes poured water from a
jug into a chipped mug. 'You need to drink plenty, it
makes the heat more bearable.'

The water was lukewarm and tasted stale, but at least
it moistened James's dry throat. He drained the mug,
wondering what sort of man Innes was to want to spend his
days in this place. To his own mind the cramped, wet rope
room below the *Fidelity*'s foredeck held more appeal.

Innes fidgeted nervously with a spanner. This workshop was his own private world, where he was happiest,
and now James, who had never before entered this place,
was destroying the peace he always found there. He
wished that his brother would just go, but instead James
wiped his mouth with the back of his hand and returned
to his argument.

'When the boat was first bought, Da and Uncle Albert
and me were equal partners, all of us free to speak our
minds and have our say. But now that Da's gone and

Albert's running the boat his way there's wrong decisions being made. Albert hasn't got half the brains Da had.'

'Or you have?'

James flushed at the note in his brother's voice. 'I'm a good fisherman and there's plenty folk would tell you that,' he countered sharply. 'And I've more sense than Albert, for my father taught me well. Bethany's already agreed to give me her share, and with yours and Ma's I'll own more of the boat than Albert does. Then I'll be the skipper and he can go back to being the mate. He'll not mind that – it's always been easier for him to let others make the decisions.'

'If that's the way of it, why don't you get him to give you his share and be done with it?'

James's face reddened further. 'Don't be daft, he'd never do that. I'd have to buy it from him, and where would I get the money? We're already owing the bank more than enough.'

'So Uncle Albert would want paying, but the rest of us wouldn't?'

'You're closer kin than he is and I've already said that you'll still get your share of the catches, so it'll make no difference to you. Stop playing the fool, Innes, I've got work to do. What d'you think?'

Innes gave him a swift sidelong glance. 'Have you spoken to Ma about this ploy of yours?'

'I thought it right to come to you first, seeing as you're the only other man of the family now.'

'But you spoke to Bethany.'

'I saw Gil; it's the same thing.'

'I'd like to see what Ma thinks before I make my mind up.'

James fought to keep his irritation from showing. 'She'll tell you just what I'm telling you.'

'I'll give you my answer tomorrow.'

'Once you've asked Ma's permission?' Tools rattled as James, his patience nearing its limit, thumped his fist down on the bench. 'Innes, you're eighteen years of age, you're a man now! D'you still have to consult your mother before you so much as wipe your own backside?'

His brother's face tightened. 'I just want to know her views on the matter. You look out for Stella and the bairns, and Bethany's got a husband to care for her and see to her interests. Ma's only got me.'

'You?' James gave a scornful laugh. 'She doesn't need you to look out for her. It's more likely to be the other way round, for when it comes down to the truth she's twice the man you are.'

'That's enough, James.'

'Prove me wrong. Make your own mind up here and now.'

'In my own time, I told you that.'

'In Ma's time, you mean.'

'Get out of here,' Innes suggested, his voice level.

James felt his hands curl into fists. He yearned to give way to impulse and give his brother the thrashing he deserved, but as Innes picked up the spanner again, tapping it against the palm of his free hand, common sense prevailed. A brawl between them would not bring him the shares he needed.

'Gladly,' he said with an effort. 'I've no liking for the air in this place. How any man can work in a black hole like this I don't know!' And he stormed from the workshop, blundering into the blacksmith on his way in.

'What's the matter with him?' Tam Gordon asked his employee.

'Nothing.' Innes turned back to his work.

'We could hear the two of you in the smiddy. A quarrel, was it?'

'Just brothers talking,' Innes said levelly, and after a moment Gordon shrugged and returned to his own work.

He should never have gone to Innes first, James told himself angrily as he stormed back into the town. It had been

THE SHIMMER OF THE HERRING

courtesy on his part, a belief that the menfolk of the family
should settle the matter of the shares between them, without troubling the women. But how could anyone expect
a coward to understand the importance of a good fishing
boat? His father had been right when he said that Innes
was only half a man; and to be honest, James had been
relieved when his mother had interceded and refused to
allow Innes to go to sea for a third trip, thus putting an end
to the embarrassment of him. Although their father was
convinced that eventually Innes would find his sea-legs,
it seemed clear to James that he never would.

And now this useless brother of his had refused him the
shares he needed, which meant that he must now confront
his mother, something he had hoped to avoid.

He smoothed down his jacket, set his cap more firmly
on his head and drew a deep breath. Since it had to be
done, best to get it over with now.

Jess was calm enough on the surface as she sat at the
kitchen table and heard her elder son out without inter-
ruption, her expressionless face and folded hands giving
no indication of her inner turmoil.

James was having a hard time of it, stammering and
stumbling over the words he had clearly tried to prepare
before coming to her door, his own hands locked tight
together on the scrubbed table, his eyes travelling all over
the kitchen but never coming closer to hers than the edge
of her ear or the point of her shoulder.

When he finally came to a halt there was a long silence,
so long that he eventually had to ask, 'Well?'

'James, I'll not give you my share in the boat.'

For the first time he looked full at her, shock in his
eyes. He opened his mouth to speak, closed it, then tried
again. 'Why not?'

'Because it's mine and I don't want to give it to anyone,
not even you.'

His eyes turned to chips of ice. 'It's because I wanted

to put my father in the sea, isn't it? Because I wanted him to have a proper ending – the ending he wanted for himself. But that would have put him out of your reach, and you couldn't bear to let that happen.'

It was the first time in a year that he had spoken to her so harshly and Jess felt as though each word was being used as a stick with which to beat her. 'As far as I'm concerned,' she said slowly and clearly, 'that business is over and done with and not to be mentioned between us again. I told you . . . my share is mine. It's all I have of the *Fidelity* and I want to keep it.'

'But I've said that you'll get your money at the. end of each season, just like now. D'you not trust me?'

'Of course I trust you,' she flashed back at him, roused to sudden anger. 'The whole world can trust you, for you're mine and Weem Lowrie's son. This has nothing to do with trust.'

'Until I can stand face to face with Uncle Albert as an equal I'm nobody on that boat, just another crew member,' James argued desperately. 'The man's not fit to skipper *Fidelity*. You know that when my father ran the boat we were the first to reach the fishing grounds and the last to leave. If any vessel went into port loaded down to the gunnels with the fish spilling out of her holds and over her decking, it was the *Fidelity*. That never happens now, for Albert's too lazy to make his crew work and at the first sign of poor weather we're hauling the nets in and running for safety every damned time. If there was any justice my da would have made sure that all of his share went to me, as the head of the family after him.'

'If the Lord hadn't seen fit to take him so suddenly he might have done that. But it happened differently, James.'

'You know fine and well that some of the money that went into her came from the sale of old Mowser's boat.' James jumped to his feet and stormed about the little kitchen.

'Aye, I know that. That's why you got your own third share of the drifter.'

'That was the only reason I married Stella, to get the boat as her dowry.'

'God forgive you for saying such a thing, for she's a good wife to you, James Lowrie, a loving wife and the mother of your three bonny bairns.'

'My three bonny lassies – not even a son to call my own – and oh, did my da not make a joke out of me because of that, after what I did for him!' James glared down at his mother, who sat still, hands locked together on the table before her. 'You were as bad, for you stood by and let him push me into a marriage I never wanted, just so's he could get his hands on Mowser's sailboat.'

'My heart hurt for you then and it still sorrows for you now, if the truth be told, for it was wrong of Weem to use you and Bethany as he did. But when were you or me, or any of us, able to make that man change tack when he was set on a course of his own plotting?'

James spat out a contemptuous laugh. 'You managed it well enough for your precious Innes!'

'He was ill and getting worse. The fishing was going to kill him.' Her voice shook slightly and she firmed it with an effort. 'If he'd done one more trip, it's a body you and Weem would have brought back to me, and I couldn't let that happen. Marrying Stella didn't kill you, James, but it's made you into a bitter man, and that's not my blame. Mebbe it's time you learned to appreciate what you've got instead of hungering after what's passed you by.'

There was a short silence, during which the air between them simmered with James's rage. The only noise was the rattle and rustle of coals in the grate and it seemed to Jess that they were shifting nervously, as unsure as she was of his next move.

Then James said, low-voiced, 'If you care anything for me, Mother, you'll save me the way you saved Innes. You'll let me use your share in the boat.'

Jess longed to give him what he wanted. It might help to atone for the harm that Weem had done the lad; it might even heal the great rift between herself and her first-born. But on the day she had pledged before the minister to cleave to Weem Lowrie for the rest of her life she had made a commitment that, in her eyes at least, would last to the grave and beyond.

The *Fidelity* had been Weem's life, and relinquishing the small part of it she still retained would be like letting his memory slip through her fingers. She couldn't do that for anyone.

'No,' she said, and heard her son's boots scuff across the stone-flagged floor. The door opened, letting a draught of cold air into the kitchen.

'I wish to God that I'd put the man into the sea when I had the chance, for you didn't deserve to have him,' James said bitterly before the door closed.

7

The *Fidelity* slumbered in the harbour, rocking slightly to the rise and fall of the water, snug among the other boats. Most of them had crewmen aboard, freshening up the paintwork, seeing to the engines, checking the gear in preparation for the English fishing trip, but James was alone on the *Fidelity*, working with the nets in the small, claustrophobic net room.

The lack of space didn't bother him, for he saw the drifter as far more than just a boat; she was mother, sister, friend, lover, wife and child, filling all those roles better than Jess and Bethany, and Stella and his three little daughters, ever could. Every time he put to sea he entrusted his life to his own skills and to the drifter, and in all weathers and situations she had looked after him and brought him safely back to harbour. Now he was letting her strength soothe him and ease the emotions roused by the jarring encounter with his mother.

When someone jumped on to the deck and a voice yelled his name, he cursed and would have stayed where he was if Bethany hadn't shouted again.

'I'm here.' He began to crawl out of the net room, but yelped in shocked surprise as Bethany caught at the front of his jacket, dragging him the rest of the way, then releasing him so that he landed clumsily on the deck.

'Ye daft bitch, what are you doing?' He scrambled to

his feet, painfully aware of laughter from the men on the adjacent boats.

'Me? It's you that's up to no good, James Lowrie!' It had been years since he had last seen his sister in such a rage. 'What d'you think you're doing, taking over my share in this boat without so much as a word to me?'

'Folk can hear you!'

'I'm not bothered.' Bethany deliberately raised her voice. 'Let the whole town know how my husband and my brother plotted to rob me!'

'To what?' He grabbed her arm and hustled her along the deck to the galley. 'If you're going to talk nonsense, then talk it down in the cabin where nobody can hear you.'

She glared, then flounced to the top of the vertical metal ladder leading to the cabin. He followed her down, scorning the rungs and descending by the uprights, his open palms and the insides of his ankles controlling his slide.

In the cabin he said angrily, 'I've stolen nothing from you.'

'You talked Gil into saying you could have my share when you know fine it's not his to give away. That's theft.' Bethany's voice had dropped – always, James recalled from the time when they were youngsters together, a bad sign. He remembered his cousin Charlie warning a newcomer to their circle, 'Watch Bethany, she might just be a lassie, but when her voice goes down her fists come up.'

'But Gil's your husband and we agreed that . . .'

'I'm not a dancing bear with a rope round my neck and no voice of my own. I'm part-owner of this boat, not Gilbert Pate. He'd no right to speak for me!'

'You'll still get your money, I promised that to Gil . . .'

'You're not having my share!' Her eyes, grey like his own, had the same cold, threatening, leaden look that James had seen in the sky and the sea just before a bad storm came shrieking over the horizon.

'Will you listen to me? Just sit down there for one minute and listen,' he insisted as she stood her ground, glaring.

For a moment he thought that he was going to have to take her wrists and force her, then she eased herself to the edge of a bunk, her back straight and her chin up.

'Now, I've lost count of the times this past season we've run for the harbour with the holds only half-full, just because Uncle Albert saw the weather getting a wee bit rough. We've all lost money because of that man . . . you've lost money! Weem Lowrie would've gone down with the boat sooner than turn back to land while the fish were still coming into the nets.'

'We all have to put up with fools now and again – why should you be any different? At least you can change things if you must.'

'That's what I'm trying to do, but there's not one of you willing to help me!'

Her eyes narrowed. 'You mean that Ma and Innes won't let you have their shares either?'

'They don't understand, but I thought you would.' He sat on the opposite bunk. 'You understand the ways of fishing more than they do. I can only get the better of Albert if I've more say in the boat than he does. Can you not see that?'

'Why should I help you when you never helped me?'

'Helped you how?'

'When I left the school and wanted to crew on the boat, you made a fool of me!'

'For God's sake, Bethany, how could a woman be part of the crew on a drifter? I'll grant you,' he added hurriedly as her eyes darkened, 'that if things had been the other way about you'd probably have been as good a seaman as me . . .'

'Better!'

'. . . but it didnae happen that way,' James forged on. 'Listen.' He leaned forward, elbows on knees, his head

close to hers. 'We can work together on this, you and
me. Let me use your share, and make Ma and Innes see
sense, then mebbe between us we can buy Albert out once
the boat's paid up. That's what Da planned, only he never
lived to see it.'

'The two of you were going to buy Uncle Albert out
and share the boat between you?'

'That's right,' James started to say, then realised that
he was walking into trouble. 'I mean, it would still have
been the family boat, but . . .'

'But you'd have been the skipper.' She got to her feet.
'And no doubt you'd have made sure that the rest of us
had no share at all then.'

'That's nonsense!'

'You should know, for you talk plenty of it.'

'Ach, Bethany!' He caught at her arm as she made for
the ladder. 'Another two years of good fishing should see
us clear of the bank – less than that, mebbe . . .'

'If you'd wanted my help you should have asked me,
not gone to Gil behind my back.' She wrenched her arm
free, eyes blazing. 'You can just keep your thieving hands
off my share of this boat, James.'

'You bitch!' he spat at her as she grasped the sides of the
ladder. She tossed a cold smile at him over her shoulder.

'I've been called worse,' she said, her skirt belling out
briefly as she floated up the narrow rungs. Her booted feet
clattered across the deck, then the boat shifted slightly as
she jumped on to the harbourside.

Alone again, James hurled every curse he knew at the
opposite wall, then scrabbled in one of the cupboards and
brought out a half-empty bottle of whisky. He had believed
Gil's assurances that Bethany would not mind handing her
share over to him, had convinced himself that – of all the
family – she, his childhood companion, would understand
his frustration. He had even been relying on her to talk his
mother and brother round. And now she had betrayed him.

When the bottle was empty he crawled into one of

the narrow bunk beds (more like coffins, some said, but adequate for a crew that spent most of its time on deck anyway) and fell asleep.

When Innes came home from work, his normally cheerful nature subdued and his eyes wary, Jess decided not to beat about the bush. 'James visited you today, didn't he?'

'You too? Did he ask for your share in the boat? And did you agree?' he wanted to know when she nodded.

'No, but you must make your own decision.'

'I'd as soon give my share to you, then you could use it as you wish.'

'I don't want it.'

'Neither do I.'

'Then give James the right to use it as he asked.'

'If you believe that, why didn't you give him yours?'

'I'm keeping my part in the boat because of what she meant to your father. It's different for you. Sit down to your dinner now. You'll be going out afterwards?'

'I said I'd meet Zelda at the farm.'

'If you take my advice,' Jess told him, 'you'll put James and the boat out of your mind and just think about that bonny wee lassie of yours. There's no need to hurry with a decision, whatever your brother says.'

James woke in darkness. Someone was shaking him violently, pulling and dragging at him. 'James . . . James, you fool, wake up!'

He tried to sit up, bumped his head on the underside of the upper bunk and realised that he was on the boat. 'Wha' . . . who . . . Is it time to haul the nets?' he asked, bounding out of the bunk, then clutching at his aching head.

'We're not at sea, you daftie! It's me, Charlie.' A match scraped, its flame searing into his eyes. He screwed them tightly shut and when he opened them again, cautiously, the lamp on the table had been lit.

His cousin, dressed in his best clothes, blew out the match and put it in the tobacco tin kept for that purpose, before bending to lift the empty whisky bottle from the floor. 'God sakes, man, we could hear your snores before we even came on to the boat.' He wrinkled his nose. 'And the place smells like a pub. How long have you been sleeping?'

'Not long.' James rubbed hard at his face with both hands. His head felt twice its usual size and his throat and tongue were swollen and dry. 'We? Who else is here?'

'Just me and . . . a friend,' Charlie said evasively.

'A lass? You've brought a lass on board?'

'There's no harm in it when we're in harbour.'

'That depends on what you're up to.'

'Nothing worse than what you've been up to. Go on home to your wee wife and leave me to my own business.'

James straightened, holding on to the top bunk for a moment until his head stopped swimming. 'You must be desperate. These bunks are narrow for sleeping in, let alone what you've got in mind.'

'Mebbe so, but the table's just fine.' Charlie winked, then said, 'Go on now, she's waiting on the deck and I want you out of here before she decides to go home to her ma and da.'

On deck, the girl was nothing more than a pale, blurred face hovering in the shadows, and a faint nervous giggle when James, about to leap on to the next boat as usual, missed his step and went floundering. He would have fallen overboard if Charlie hadn't thrown an arm about him.

'Easy now, Jamie. Over we go.' He escorted his cousin to the harbourside then leaped back on board to where his companion waited.

As James made his unsteady way along the harbour, bumping into the sea wall one minute and perilously close to the water's edge the next, a ribbon of giggles followed from the *Fidelity* – the unknown girl's light and musical trill mixed with a deeper undertone, sleepy yet sensuous. Charlie was his father through and through, James thought blearily. Even down to the lassies and the laugh.

'Are you sure you should go?' Jess asked anxiously.

Meg Lowrie, sitting on a small three-legged wooden stool in her back yard, her skirts kilted over her knees and her legs spread wide so that she could plant one foot on either side of the large tin box that she and Jess were packing, shaded her eyes against the sun and squinted up at her sister-in-law.

'What else would I do with myself?' she wanted to know. 'Sit at home and order the serving lassies about? Or mebbe starve to death, since there's no money comes into this house bar what I earn myself? Were those two clean semmits where I told ye?'

'Yes.' Nothing in Meg's one-roomed house was ever where she expected to find it but Jess, who was good at running lost objects to ground, had found the vests beneath the extra winter blankets. 'I'd look after you, you know that well enough,' she said as she knelt on the piece of old carpet brought out to protect her knees from the stone flags. 'I just don't think you should be going off to Yarmouth with your back still troubling you the way it is. What do you say, Bethany?'

Bethany, busily stuffing fistfuls of clean fresh chaff into a large sack that had been washed and re-washed until it was soft and pliant, paused for a moment and rested on her haunches, running the back of one hand over her hot face. It was a perfect early-October day, mild and golden and soft as silk. 'I say she'll do as she pleases no matter what you say about it. At least I've made you a comfortable bed to ease your back when you're not at the farlins, Aunt Meg.'

'Thanks, lass, I'll bless you when I'm lying on it.' The three of them were preparing for Meg's departure for Yarmouth. Now she peered into the trunk. 'I think that's my kist packed and ready now.'

'I put in that roll of flannel: don't forget to wrap it round you underneath your bust bodice for added warmth. And get someone to pin it so's it keeps right all day. And there's three jars of that liniment that does you so well.'

'Aye aye, I'll be fine. Don't fuss me, Jess!'

'You're too old to be working with the herring, you know that.'

'If you want me to give it up you'll have to find a young husband willing to keep me in comfort.'

'You'd not want the trouble of a young husband, Aunt Meg.'

'Mebbe not, but I'd no' mind findin' that out for myself.' Meg chuckled wheezily then put her hands on the edge of the open kist and began to lever herself up. 'Time to make a cup of tea. We've earned it.'

'Sit on where you are and enjoy the sun a bit longer.' Bethany got to her feet, dusting her skirt down. 'I'll see to the tea if you sew up the end of the mattress, Ma.'

'Give the nice china an airing for a wee change,' Meg called after her as she went into the house, a single dark room crammed with the possessions that her aunt had collected during her lifetime. On a hot day like this the two small windows and the street and yard doors were all open wide to catch any fresh air there might be. Ellen still slept, slumped at one end of the horsehair sofa in the boneless way of cats, dogs and young humans, while Rory, at peace for once, sat on the floor near the open yard door, intent on threading a collection of buttons on to a length of fishing line.

The best china was kept in the corner cupboard, cups and saucers and plates and ornaments all lavishly hand-painted, with most pieces gilt-edged and bearing the name of one of the fishing ports Meg had worked in. Bethany chose the one that had been her special favourite from childhood, a cup and saucer covered with fat red and pink roses, with *A Present from Lowestoft* inscribed round their rims. For her mother and aunt she selected presents from Grimsby and Whitby.

'Me too,' Rory clamoured as she poured the strong tea. She put a little into a mug and topped it up with water, and he went out into the sunny yard clutching it to his chest while she followed with the fancy cups, crowded together with a battered tin teapot on an equally battered tin tray.

For a while the women sipped at their tea in silence, enjoying the peace and warmth of the afternoon, then Meg, never one to stay quiet for long, said thoughtfully, 'I'd miss it if I didnae follow the herring. To tell the truth I don't know what I'll do with myself when I get too old for the work.'

'You'll stay home and keep me company. There's plenty going on when the boats and the fisher lassies are away,' Jess told her robustly.

'Mebbe, but there's far more where we are.' Seeing Meg's eyes grow vague, Bethany knew from her own experiences that already her aunt's heart was moving south, towards the busy English harbours. 'All the folk from every place in the country, and the friends you met last year . . . And the crush of boats, and the gulls screamin' for the fish guts and the gossip from all the different ports. And the folk from further away too – the Russians and the Germans and the Hollanders, and dear knows who else.'

She chuckled, digging her niece in the ribs. 'D'ye still mind what it's like, Bethany, walking down King Street in Yarmouth on a Saturday night with the week's work done, all of us dressed in our best?'

'Of course I mind it. I've not been away from the farlins that long, Aunt Meg.' Bethany's voice had an edge to it and Jess, always alert for trouble where her daughter was concerned, glanced at her apprehensively. Meg was too busy with her own thoughts to notice anything amiss.

'And the mission. I love the mission,' she said dreamily.

'Singing away at those lovely hymns and listening to the pastor's sermon, then the men comin' back afterwards tae the lodgin's for a cup of tea and a good gossip . . .'

In the shaded room behind them Ellen woke and began to cry, frightened at finding herself alone in an unknown place. Bethany got up and went in to her and Rory followed, clamouring for something to eat. The little party in the sun-washed yard was over.

Meg's talk of Yarmouth had stirred memories in Jess as well as in her daughter. It was a bonny evening, and when her work in the house was done Jess walked out along the shore road towards Portessie, where she had been born and raised.

The evening was still, the water grey-streaked and velvety. A soft mist blurred the horizon, and the sky was pewter, lightened towards the west by the last rays of the hidden sun. Portessie's huddle of cottages, their windowless gable ends facing towards the Firth, were like a group of old wifies settling down for the night. Everything was calm, until suddenly the dolphins appeared, swimming up the Firth as they did every evening, their sleek bodies breaking the surface of the water as they played. She went down on to the shore and sat on a rock to watch them frolic. When they had gone and the surface of the sea had stilled again she sat on, her mind filled with those days at the farlins in the bustling English port, the Saturday evenings when, their work done, the lassies walked along King Street arm in arm.

It was in King Street that Weem Lowrie first spoke to Jess, skilfully separating her from the others, walking her back to her lodgings, kissing her in the soft shadows of a house end . . .

Her middle-aged body quickened now, remembering, and her eyes filled with tears. Alone on the shore, in the soft grey gloaming, she sobbed out her longing and her hunger for Weem.

8

In the weeks before the Scottish fishing fleet, more than 1,200 strong, went south Gilbert Pate and his workmen toiled from dawn to dusk on the barrels that would be needed as soon as they reached Yarmouth. Once there they would be required to produce a further sixty barrels a day to hold the herring, most of which were salted and packed on the quayside for consumption in Germany, Russia and the Low Countries.

As well as the men working in his cooperage, Gil employed ten teams of gutters and packers, a total of thirty women in all to be hired and transported to the accommodation arranged for them in Yarmouth.

Here, Bethany was invaluable to him. Calmly and efficiently she dealt with the women, getting each of them to sign on with the Pates for the season in return for a small advance payment known as 'arles', seeing to it that their chaff mattresses were uplifted and taken to Yarmouth by cart and arranging their accommodation in the two lodging houses Gil always used. The women themselves would be driven by lorry to Aberdeen; from there they would travel by rail to their destination.

The *Fidelity* was one of the first boats to leave Buckie on the journey south. Stella stood by her mother-in-law on the harbour wall holding the twins, and even the baby, up in turn to see their daddy go off to England. The twins waved energetically and Stella wagged Ruth's little hand to and fro, while James gave a terse wave in answer before turning away to get on with his work.

As the drifter slid through the harbour entrance and dipped a demure curtsey to the open sea, Jess knew without having to look that her daughter-in-law's eyes were damp.

'If the herring keep running the way they have this year, we'll all be well set up for the winter when the boats come home,' she offered.

'Aye, but a good season means they could be away for longer than usual.' Stella's voice was muffled.

'Lassie, your own father was a fisherman; you know what the life's like. I mind how much I missed my Weem when he first sailed away and left me at home,' she prattled on, collecting a twin in each hand so that Stella was left in privacy, hampered only by the baby, to scrub the tears from her eyes. 'But you've the bairns to see to, and your father as well. And there's always some neighbour or other in need of a helping hand. The time'll pass fast enough, then there's the homecoming to look forward to.' She smiled, remembering past homecomings.

'My father always looked forward to coming home to us,' Stella said, then, hurriedly, 'I mean . . .'

'You don't have to watch your tongue in front of me,' Jess assured her. 'I know fine that my James is never content unless he's on the sea.'

'He went about like a bear with a sore head when his uncle refused to take the *Fidelity* to the fishing off Northumberland in September,' Stella confided.

'As I mind it, Albert had other things on his mind,' Jess said drily. Half the town knew that during September Albert had been paying a lot of attention to a well-set-up middle-aged widow in Buckpool. 'It fairly put the man's nose out of joint when that woman settled for a farmer in Fochaber. Though from what I hear, she made the most of Albert's attentions before comin' to her decision.'

Stella hesitated, eyeing her husband's mother, then said

in a rush, 'James is thinking of working for someone else when he comes back from Yarmouth.'

Jess stopped in her tracks. 'He'd never leave the *Fidelity* – she's the Lowrie boat.'

'I don't think he'd be happy away from her. I'd not want him to make a mistake he'd regret.'

Guilt swept over Jess. If only she had given James the right to use her share in the *Fidelity* when he asked; if only she had persuaded Innes and Bethany to do the same . . . But what was done was done, and she had learned early on in her married life that there was no sense in fretting over the past. The only way was forward.

'He's probably thinking the better of it already. I'll walk back with you and have a wee visit with Mowser,' she said briskly.

Stella followed Jess along the road, wondering if she had said too much. The one thing she had not disclosed, and never could disclose to anyone, was her constant fear that one day she might lose James. Not to the sea – as a fisherman's daughter she could cope with that if she had to – but to another woman.

She knew well enough, for she was no fool, that he had only married her to help his father buy the *Fidelity*. She hadn't minded being part of the bargain, for since they were both at school she had secretly adored James Lowrie, hiding her passion behind her clear brown eyes and serene nature as she watched him courting the prettier, bolder girls in the area. She had never dreamed of becoming his wife, but when it happened – not because of her beauty or charms, but because of her father's sailboat – she had been the happiest girl on the Moray coast.

She had believed, naïvely, that once they were man and wife James would grow to love her, but instead he had become even more distant. Even when they lay together, even when he was inside her, part of her body, she knew that for him their union was no more than the satisfaction of needs, both material and animal.

Here, in Buckie, where everyone knew everyone else, and there were no secrets, she was more sure of James. But each time he followed the herring up north or down the English coast Stella worried and fretted until he came back to her.

Normally easy-going, though he had a fiery temper when roused, Gil had driven Bethany mad with his fussing and panicking and it was with a sense of relief that she stood on the harbour wall, Ellen straddled over one hip and Rory's hand firmly in her grasp despite his efforts to wriggle free, and watched her husband leave Buckie.

As the boat, its holds crammed and its deck piled perilously high with barrels, went through the harbour entrance into the open sea, she suddenly scooped Rory up, tucked him under her free arm and began to run, chanting, 'Ride a cock horse, to Banbury Cross . . .' with both children clinging to her and giggling helplessly as they were jostled and swung around. By the time she gained the street her tawny hair, pulled free of the loose knot at the nape of her neck, flew in curly strands about her face and her skirt clung to her pistoning thighs.

Older women, sedate and proper in black, hair trapped beneath the shawls and scarves most of them wore, even in the house, tutted and raised their eyebrows, whispering their disapproval as Gil Pate's scandalous second wife raced by. But Bethany paid them no heed, panting out the rhyme about the lucky lady with her fine white horse again and again; she timed it so that, as she reached the house and swung sideways to allow Rory to lift the latch, they burst inside to 'To see a fine lady . . .' and ended up in a heap on the wall-bed with '. . . upon a white *horse*!'

The three of them rolled together on the bed, tickling and screeching and kicking their legs until finally, worn out by the fun, they collapsed in a tangled pile. At times like this Bethany enjoyed her step-children; they reminded her of puppies, smelling of sun and fresh air and soap, and something that could only be described as the sweet perfume of babyhood innocence. They were soft-covered bundles of wiry energy with the ability, at a second's notice, either to spring into action or collapse in limp, vulnerable sleep.

But such moments were all too few. Apart from the fact that Gil didn't like to see his wife behaving like a wild bairn, too much of her time and energy were taken up by the constant drudgery of feeding, washing and having constantly to keep watch over the children. From now on there would be no solitary walks by the sea for her, for there would be no Gil sitting by the fire, reading his paper and smoking his pipe and available, albeit grudgingly, to keep an eye on his son and daughter for a precious half-hour. Rory and Ellen were in her sole charge now and their needs would fill her every moment, sleeping as well as waking.

Even as the thought came to her, Ellen, worn out by the fun, began to grizzle and Rory pulled at Bethany's arm, chanting, 'I'm hungry!'

When the children were in their beds and she finally had a moment to herself, Bethany found it impossible to settle with her knitting and her mending. It was always the same when Gil was away from home, and yet it wasn't as though she missed him. On the contrary, she relished her freedom. For a month at least she would be able to lay down the burden of being a wife, freed from the need to have his food on the table at exactly the right time; free to sprawl bonelessly, like the children, from one end of the bed to the other if she so pleased, and to sleep the night long without being plucked and groped at, or wakened from dreams of freedom and the sea to satisfy his sudden urges.

Prowling around, she suddenly realised that the house itself was the cause of her unease. It was Gil's home, not hers; it bore his stamp at all times, and Bethany's place in it was only on sufferance, as his wife. Even when he was away for any length of time, as he was now, the house refused to be hers, subtly reverting instead to the days when it had been the domain of her predecessor. The pictures on the walls had been chosen by Molly Pate and the fancy curling shells and the gold-edged hand-painted dishes in the parlour's glass-fronted corner cabinet had been brought home by Gil for Molly's pleasure. Molly's hands had crafted the rag rug that lay before the fire and the cushions on the two fireside chairs. Molly had chosen the wallpaper and had even stitched the patchwork quilt that covered Bethany and Gil every night. She had birthed the two children now asleep in the tiny bedroom, and she had died through Ellen's arrival in the world.

Every day Bethany dusted Molly's wedding portrait, which stood at one end of the kitchen mantelshelf, and her own at the other end. Both prints were strikingly similar; the bride seated and Gil standing, a big hand clamped on his new wife's shoulder in what was probably meant to be a protective gesture but looked, to Bethany, more like a public declaration of ownership. In the first likeness he was youthful, with a full head of dark hair and a curve to his cheeks and chin. Molly's thin shoulder seemed to be weighted down by his hand, while her neat features were solemn and somewhat anxious, as though she had just become aware of the responsibilities she had taken on.

Moving to her own wedding portrait, Bethany noted the distant expression on her pictured face and the way her body was poised on the chair as though planning to leap up, throw off the restraining paw from her shoulder and dart out of the picture entirely. This, she thought, was understandable, given that the marriage had been arranged by her father and had not been her own wish. In this second portrait Gil's hair had shrunk to a thick fringe skirting a bald head and the youthful chubbiness had given way to the onset of middle-aged fat; although still in his mid-thirties, he was the type of man who had a brief youth and a prolonged middle-age.

Bethany sighed and turned both portraits to the wall. She could, of course, have made changes about the house to suit her own taste. Gil had suggested this when they first wed, but she had done nothing, having no interest in domestic virtues. As a result she now had little option but to continue to live as an interloper in her predecessor's home.

Returning to her chair, she picked up her mending then put it down again, still too restless to settle to it. Instead she opened the door and stood leaning on the frame for a long time, her face lifted up to the dark night, eyes closed, drawing the salt air deep into her lungs. The chill wind made her shiver, but she wrapped her arms tightly about her body for warmth, refusing to go back into the house. She would have given everything she had to be where Gil was now, out on the water, facing away from Buckie and looking towards new adventures.

'It's awful cold,' Zelda was saying at that moment, up on the hills above Buckie. 'I'll have to go in before I'm chilled to the bone.'

'Am I not keeping you warm?'

'You're certainly trying hard enough – you're near squashing me to death.' She wriggled out of Innes's arms and sucked in a deep breath. 'That's better.'

'There's always the barn . . .'

'And have me going into the house with straw all down my clothes and in my hair, so's the mistress can tell what I've been up to?'

'I'm not saying we'd get up to anything, I just mean that we'd be away from the wind in the barn.'

'What's the sense,' Zelda wanted to know, as contrary as any other woman, 'of us going into the barn if we're not going to get up to anything?'

'Then we will, if that's what you'd like.' Innes clamped an arm about her and tried to ease her towards the great dark shape at the other side of the farmyard. 'I'm willing enough.'

'I know you are, Innes Lowrie, but I'm not. Not yet.'

'Och, Zelda!'

'It's not the right time or the right place.'

'If it's marriage you want I'm more than willing.'

'Really?' She peered up into his face. 'You mean it?'

He touched her cheek with his free hand, loving the curve of it against his palm. 'I'd marry you tomorrow if I could.'

'It's not just the – you know – the need for me that's got your tongue, is it?'

'Zelda, my need and my tongue aren't so close together that one can rule the other.'

'Oh!' She bounced away from him. 'You're coarse, Innes Lowrie!' she accused, her voice rippling with shocked laughter.

'Mebbe, but I'm honest too. And I mean it . . . we'll get married if you want to.'

She came back to him, close enough to play with the buttons on his jacket. 'Where would we live?'

'There's room in my mother's house.'

'I couldn't!'

'She'd not mind. She likes you.'

'But I couldn't . . . you know. Not in the same house as your mother!'

'What then?'

'We'll have to save, both of us, until we can afford a wee place of our own.'

'That'll take a long time.'

'The sooner we start, the faster we'll save.'

'And in the meantime there's always the barn.'

'There is not! I'm not going to roll in the straw like any common slut!'

'Zelda . . .' he pleaded.

'I'll have to go in, it's time,' she said as the bells of a church clock splintered the chilled air.

'Not till you give me a proper kiss,' Innes insisted, and pulled her into his arms. She melted against him for a moment, her mouth softening beneath his, then as the fire kindled in his loins and his hands became more urgent, she pulled away.

'I'll see you on Saturday afternoon?'

'Aye.'

'And we're agreed to start saving?'

'We are.'

She flitted away from him, then returned to brush his mouth again with her own in a soft butterfly kiss. 'I love you, Innes Lowrie,' she said.

He waited until the farm door opened, spilling a flood of lamplight over the flags, then closed again before turning for home, striding out not only because it was too cold to loiter, but because the burning, throbbing swelling between his thighs made great steps essential. He didn't mind the discomfort at all because it was part of being a man and the cause of it had said she loved him, and they had committed themselves to a future together. And the fishing fleet had gone, taking James and his cool contempt with it. And tomorrow a man who lived in one of the big houses was bringing his motor-cycle into the workshop for repair. Life was very sweet.

As he marched homewards Innes began to whistle.

9

'You should never have tried to pull that kist out from below the bed, not when it was all packed, Aunt Meg. You knew I'd see to it for you if you'd just let me know.'

'I'm not in my dotage yet, Innes,' Meg Lowrie snapped. 'I can still do things for myself.'

'So we see.' Jess's voice was dry and her sister-in-law flounced from her in high dudgeon. It wasn't easy to flounce when huddled in a chair, but she achieved it by tossing her head and turning away slightly. Even that movement caused her to draw her breath in sharply. 'See here, Meg, there's no sense in us arguing about what's over and done. We need to get you right again, so Innes is going to fetch the doctor to you.'

'He'll do nothing of the sort! We're leaving tomorrow – all I need is some ointment and mebbe a hot toddy to comfort my bones, and a good night's sleep.'

It was obvious to both Jess and Innes that Meg needed more than ointment and a night's sleep. Her face was drawn with pain and she winced with even the slightest movement. They had both come running, leaving their dinners half-eaten on the table, after a summons from a neighbour who had heard Meg's shouts for help and found her lying on the floor.

'If you'll just give a hand to get me into my bed, and give my back a wee rub before you go . . .'

'You'll sit where you are until we hear what the doctor has to say.'

'I'm not spending my hard-earned silver on a physician!'

'Nobody asked you to. I'm paying the man and to my mind it's money well spent, for it'll buy me peace of mind. Innes, off you go.'

'I'll not see him!' Meg roared. Innes, at a loss to know what to do, hovered by the door, looking from one woman to the other.

'You've little choice. He's coming and I doubt if you're up to hiding from him below the bed, alongside that heavy kist of yours,' Jess shot back.

'You're a right thrawn bitch, Jess!'

'I'm a Lowrie . . . we're all thrawn. Innes, do as you're told. Now, is there anything you need before the doctor comes?' Jess asked as her son escaped, glad to be away from the arguing.

Meg remained silent until the door had closed behind Innes, then she said, her voice suddenly shaky, 'You could mebbe bring the chamber-pot out from below the bed. I couldnae say anything about it in front of the laddie, but I was tryin' to fetch it when my back went. I just didnae feel up to going out to the privy in the yard.'

Tears of humiliation glittered in her eyes and Jess felt a great wave of compassion for this strongly independent woman, who was suffering as much from the shame of having to depend on others as from her pain. 'Oh, Meg!'

'Never mind "Oh, Meg",' came the sharp rejoinder from the old woman huddled on the chair. 'Just fetch that damned pot, will ye, for I'm wetting my breeks like a bairn at this very minute. I thought Innes would never leave us!'

'I'm sorry you've got this landed on you the very day before the lassies go off to Yarmouth, Bethany, but the doctor'll not hear of Meg leaving her bed just now. Not that she can, poor soul, for she's twisted like a hairpin. I think it's the end of her days at the farlins.'

'She must be in a right taking about it.'

'She's bellowing like a bull gone daft The sooner she realises that shouting doesn't mend anything, especially old bones that have been hard treated for years, the better,' Jess said feelingly. 'The thing is, I was trying to think who you could get to replace her. There's Isa Thain – her bairns are up in age, and her mother lives with them, so she can see to them all while Isa's away. I know she'd like to earn a bit more money,' she added, then as her daughter stared past her shoulder, her eyes like grey mist and her fingers worrying her lower lip, 'Bethany? Are you hearing me?'

'What?' Bethany blinked, then said with an attempt at a casual air, 'Isa Thain. I'll go and see her now. I was just thinking,' she added diffidently, 'that mebbe I should go to Yarmouth myself.'

'You? But you've got the bairns to see to!'

'Gil's mother would take them . . . or she could come here, instead of them having to go to Finnechtie.'

'And what d'you think she'd say about you running off and leaving them?'

'Ach, that woman finds fault no matter what I do. She can't see past Molly's memory,' Bethany said bitterly, 'and she's never thought I was good enough for her son and her grand-weans. Anyway, if I'm not here I won't be troubled by what she says.'

'Mebbe not, but I'll have to listen to her.'

'Ignore her. She's not worth bothering over.'

'But Meg's a packer and you're a gutter. How could you do her work?'

Bethany hesitated for only a second before saying, 'I'll still hire Isa if she's willing, then I can supervise and help out with the gutting like I used to. Isa's got a sharp tongue in her head and some of the other lassies might not get on with her, so it would be as well for me to be there to keep the peace. Gil's no use with the women, he's got the wrong manner entirely – I should know, I worked for him myself – and since Aunt Meg's not going to be there to keep things right he'll need me.'

'He won't like the idea of his wife working at the farlins alongside the other quine, like any common fisher-lassie,' Jess said, but realised that she had made a mistake as soon as she saw the sudden spark in her daughter's eyes, the lift of her chin and the way her shoulders straightened.

'Why not?' Bethany demanded. 'I am a fisher lassie, one of the best. And Gil can say what he likes. He doesn't own me and neither does his witch of a mother. I'm going to Yarmouth and that's an end to it.'

That night when the children were asleep she climbed the wooden stairs to the loft, which was filled with all the accoutrements of the cooper's trade. The tin trunk she had used in her days at the farlins was in a corner, stowed beneath a bench. Bethany manhandled it down the narrow staircase into the kitchen, where she knelt to open the lid.

The deep trunk was almost empty, apart from a few items covered by a folded length of canvas, which she opened out and spread over the floor. Moving the kist to the middle of the canvas she began to unpack it: a small tin box for her soap, facecloth, hairbrush and comb; a bundle of clean rags, held together with lengths of twine and used to safeguard her fingers against injury from her own knife or from sharp herring bones; her long waterproof apron and sturdy leather sea-boots, both kept in good condition by regular applications of linseed oil. And at the very bottom, carefully wrapped in a piece of oilskin, was her gutting knife, honed and polished.

Bethany took it out of its wrapping and turned it about so that the blade caught the light. She hefted it in her hand, loving the way the handle fitted with easy familiarity into her palm and handling it with the respect it demanded, for although it had not been used for a year the blade was still razor-sharp. Then she wrapped it up again and laid it back in the trunk. Time was moving on, and the trains carrying the guttin quine south were due to leave the day after tomorrow.

Isa Thain had agreed to travel to Yarmouth. Tonight Bethany planned to do most of her packing, and tomorrow morning she would walk to Finnechtie to see Gil's mother. She had no doubt at all that the woman would be pleased to have her grandchildren to herself for several weeks, and even more delighted to have a grievance against her son's second, unsuitable wife.

Once the arrangements were made she would spend the rest of the day cleaning the house from top to bottom. Whatever else the older Mrs Pate might have to say to the neighbours about Bethany in her absence, she would not be able to claim that Gil's young wife kept a dirty house.

While lamps were being blown out in the neighbouring houses and her neighbours were settling into their beds, she flitted about gathering clothing, toiletries, a long, thick woollen scarf to put about her head when she worked on the open harbours, warm stockings and underwear to keep the worst of the Yarmouth early-winter winds at bay. She tore up more clean rags to protect her fingers and packed sewing needles and threads, scissors and thimbles, her knitting wires and wool.

When they followed the boats north to places such as Lerwick, the fisher lassies even packed wallpaper and curtains into their kists in an attempt to make the long, dreary huts where they lived more homely, but in larger ports such as Lowestoft, Grimsby and Yarmouth, where they lodged in houses, there was not the same need. This meant that Bethany had room for her best dress and a lighter, pretty scarf for Saturday nights, when the fishing – for the Scots crews at least – ended until after midnight on Sunday. On Saturday evenings the fishermen and the lassies socialised.

When the kist was full and she was quite certain that she had remembered everything, she threaded a large needle with thick, strong thread and gathered the ends of the canvas sheeting together. In and out the needle flashed and when she was done the kist was protected by a snugly fitting canvas jacket. Rising stiffly to her feet, she inspected it from all sides, nodding her satisfaction, then undressed and fell into bed where, snug beneath the quilt made by her predecessor, she nursed her new-found sense of freedom.

When the motorised lorry blared its horn outside the house two days later Rory, who often embraced adult knees but was too manly to approve of hugging and kissing, clamoured to be lifted up. When Bethany obliged he put his arms tightly round her neck and whispered into her ear, 'You'll not be long, will you?'

'I'll be as quick as I can,' Bethany lied. The children both liked their grandmother well enough, but it was clear that the little boy was not at all certain of being left in her charge. Putting him down, Bethany took Ellen from the older woman's arms and buried her face in the child's silky hair for a moment. She had never loved them as much as she did now that she was deserting them. 'Be a good lassie now, for your grandma,' she told Ellen.

'Of course she will, I'll see to that.' Mrs Pate took the little girl back and captured Rory's fingers with her free hand. 'Tell my son he can rest assured that his children will be properly fed while they're in my care. And I'll give the house a good redding out too.'

'I see to it every week.'

'Mebbe so, but I've my own ways and I like to observe them wherever I may be,' the woman said inflexibly, then nodded towards the lorry with its cargo of excited guttin quine. 'You'd best be off, since you insist on going. You can tell Gilbert I'll be writing a letter to him directly.'

Bethany could make a shrewd guess as to the contents of the letter, and she was certain that Gil would disapprove of her actions just as strongly as his mother did. But the die was cast and she was escaping from her life in Buckie for a while, and that was all that mattered.

The driver clambered down from his cab and ambled over. 'Here, Bethany, I'll take your kist for you,' he offered.

'You will not! If I can't lift my own kist, how d'you think I can manage with the barrels at the farlins?' She bent and caught the heavy tin trunk in exactly the right grip, remembered from earlier days. There was a cheer from the women standing on the back of the lorry as she hoisted it up and began to walk towards them, grateful that there was only a short distance to cover.

When she reached the lorry, willing hands reached down to take the kist from her and carry it to the back to be stacked with the rest, while other hands seized hers and hauled her up. The driver helped her on her way by cupping his own hands over her backside and pushing, grinning at the remarks the women were yelling down at him.

'I'm just bein' a gentleman,' he protested in mock-innocence. 'Just doin' my duty by the ladies.'

'Duty? The last man that put his fingers where you put yours when you punted me up, Walter Lochrie, had tae marry me,' a hefty middle-aged woman boomed back, and as the lorry-load erupted in gales of laughter Bethany saw her mother-in-law, her face the picture of outrage, whisking the children into the cottage out of earshot.

As he was dragged in, Rory twisted round for a last look and a final wave before the door slammed.

Although weeks of hard work in harsh conditions lay ahead of them, all the women were in high spirits, waving and calling to passers-by and singing whatever came to mind – hymns, choruses, even popular nursery rhymes – as the lorry covered the miles to Aberdeen, where the railway station was thronged by fisher-lassies from all over the area, crowding on to the special trains awaiting them. Once on board they found seats, gathered their possessions about them, took their knitting needles from the padded leather whiskers strapped about their waists and settled down to knit and gossip the hours and the miles away.

'Here . . .' Isa, sitting beside Bethany, offered her a screw of paper, 'have a sookie sweetie. Your Gil's surely not going to be pleased to see you working on the farlins again,' she went on as Bethany prised a sticky humbug free of the lump and popped it into her mouth. 'He surely thinks his wife's too grand to mix with the likes of us.' The spiteful undertone that accompanied so many of Isa's remarks, and which had more than once led to ill-feeling when she worked at the farlins with the other women, could clearly be heard.

Bethany licked her sticky fingers. 'That's my business, Isa, and his. All we want you to do is work hard, the way you can when you put your mind to it.'

'All *we* want?' The woman emphasised the second word. 'So you're comin' along to make sure your man gets his money's worth out of us, is that it?'

'I'm going to Yarm'th to work, the same as the rest of you, and to make sure that we're all of us getting our money's worth,' Bethany said lightly, aware that all those within earshot were listening with keen interest. 'Thanks for the sweetie, Isa, it was kind of you.'

When they finally arrived in Yarmouth Bethany was taken aback to find Gil himself waiting on the platform for his teams. She had not expected to see him until the next day at the farlins and had given herself up to enjoying the noisy journey, instead of planning what she would say to him.

She thought at first that his arrival was simply bad luck, but when he came striding straight towards her down the platform, scattering women to left and right, she realised that he had already known she was on the train.

'Look at the face on him,' Isa whispered into her ear. 'I told you he'd not be pleased!'

'Right, there's carts waiting, get your boxes out as fast as you can,' Gil told the other women roughly, then he grabbed his wife's arm and pulled her aside. 'What d'you think you're doing here?'

'I suppose you got a letter from your mother? She didn't waste any time.' The woman must have been writing her letter even while Bethany was walking back to Buckie after asking her to look after the children.

'She did her duty as she saw fit, and she was right to do it. I wrote at once to tell you to stay where you belong. Did you not get my letter?'

'It must have arrived too late,' Bethany said, thanking the fates for their timing.

'Well, you can just go home tomorrow.'

'I'll do nothing of the sort! I've come to work at the farlins.'

'I will not have my wife working along with the guttin quine!'

'Why not? I'm one of the best, as you well know. I'm here because my Aunt Meg's ill with a bad back, so I had to ask Isa Thain to take her place, and it's lucky for you that she was able to do it at such short notice. She's a good worker, for all that she's got a tongue sharp enough to gut the herring with if she ever lost her knife, and can cause trouble among the other women . . .' Bethany babbled on, trying to prevent Gil from talking, then as she looked up at him and saw the anger in his eyes she finished lamely, 'Anyway, since Aunt Meg's usually the one to keep an eye on the teams, and I used to do that myself before we wed, I thought it best to come here in her place.'

'I hope you got the payment back off your aunt now that she's not working for me this season.'

'I told her to keep it, since she's bad enough to need a doctor.'

'You did, did you? So how d'you think I can afford Isa if I don't get my money back from Meg Lowrie?'

'I paid Isa her seven shillings from your wee bank,' Bethany told him, and his eyes bulged. His wee bank was a large treacle tin hidden in a far corner of the house loft.

'That's my money and it's private!'

'Not from me – I'm your wife. And Aunt Meg's had my share, since I didn't pay myself any arles.'

'That's as well, for you're not staying.'

'I am, Gil. You're going to need me at the farlins, and the bairns'll be fine with your mother until we get back home at the end of the season.'

'But the town's packed with folk from all over. I don't know if I can find somewhere for us to stay.'

'No need for that; you'll lodge with your men the same as always and I'll bide with the lassies.'

'But . . .'

'There's no but about it, Gilbert, I'm here and I'm staying. And we're all worn out after the journey. If you want us at the farlins tomorrow morning in time for the boats coming in you'd better take us to our lodgings and no more arguments!'

10

Yarmouth's vast harbours were packed and still the boats came up the river on their way back from the 'brown ledges', as the nearest fishing ground was called. The steam drifters, with smoke belching from their tall, narrow stacks, were first at the quayside, with the benefit of their engines, but the first of the sail boats with their great dipping lug sails hauled in and their high mainmasts lowered were close behind. All the boats were low in the water, weighed down by the fish known as the silver darlings; all were impatient to open up their holds and get the fish ashore in great baskets. Buyers and sellers were just as impatient, and as each catch was landed men swarmed to inspect it and bargain over it.

The Buckie guttin quine had settled into their new lodgings the previous evening with the ease of women well used to setting up home wherever they happened to find themselves. They had been allocated two former sail lofts in adjoining houses, which together formed a great long space below the sloping roofs of the two-storey buildings. Iron-framed cots were lined down each side, two stoves in the middle provided warmth and the means of cooking, and there were double stone sinks at either end and three long narrow tables, flanked by a collection of wooden kitchen chairs and stools, down the centre of the room. The beamed lofts were claustrophobic, with little space for movement, but since the women would spend most of their time at the harbour this was not a problem.

Their chaff mattresses had already been delivered and it had not taken the women long to make up their beds with the blankets and quilts they had brought in their kists. The kists themselves served as bedside tables, while the food they had brought with them was handed over to their landlady to be stored in the cool, stone-flagged pantry on the ground floor. Not that there was much danger of foodstuffs being spoiled at this time of year; the women knew that most nights they would be obliged to sleep with all their clothes on for warmth, and it was not unknown for water left in basins or jugs overnight to be frozen hard in the morning.

Bethany slept well on that first night and by half past six the following morning she and the others were preparing the farlins: the gutters positioning the fish barrels to one side and slightly behind them at the long wooden troughs, while the tubs where the offal was thrown were put to the other side; the packers checking the big tubs of coarse salt and bringing up empty pickling barrels. Usually farlins consisted of long, shallow tables, but this year the Scottish women were working at the deep farlins, tubs some three feet in depth, each of them only long enough to take four gutters.

Despite her announcement to her mother and to Gil that she was going to be there to lend a hand wherever needed, Bethany had managed to persuade one of the older gutters to change places with her. Now she was on a three-woman team with Isa as the packer and Kate, a young woman on her second season, as her fellow gutter.

When the coopers arrived a short time later Gil made no attempt to speak to his wife, although she was aware of his gaze following her every movement. At one time she had been one of his best gutters but now, she knew, he wanted her to fail, to be forced to admit that she had lost her old skills and to return home where she belonged.

She was damned if she would give him that satisfaction, she thought as she wrapped clean rags round her fingers, deftly using her teeth to knot the twine about them. Catching his gaze on her, she deliberately faced him for a long moment, her eyes holding his, then she turned her back and went to help one of the other women manoeuvre a tub of salt into place.

Waiting for the fish to arrive was the most tedious part of the women's work and the hardest for Bethany. Like the others, she took her knitting wires from the leather whisker slung as always at her waist, but all the time she was knitting, her stomach churned with nerves beneath her thick jersey and her oilskin apron, and inside her sturdy boots her toes curled and uncurled restlessly.

It wasn't just Gil who bothered her, it was the other women as well. Once she had been their equal, but things had changed now that she was married to their employer. She knew from the sidelong glances being cast in her direction that some of them resented her and suspected that she was in Yarmouth as Gil's spy.

It was a relief when the clanging of a bell signalled the arrival of the first boats from the fishing grounds and the women put their knitting wires away, hurrying to their places. It wasn't long before the first carts appeared, piled high with baskets of herring. As the silver stream spilled into the deep farlins and the packers scattered double handfuls of coarse salt over them for easier handling, Bethany tightened her hold on her sharp knife and prayed behind set lips that the old skills had not deserted her.

She needn't have worried, for almost as soon as she slid the blade into her first fish it was as though she had never been away from the farlins. In four seconds the fish was split and gutted, the offal tossed with a twist of the wrist into the barrel slightly behind her and to one side, and the prepared fish put into a tub on the other side; then the knife was into the next fish and she had settled into the old, practised rhythm.

By the time daylight came, bringing with it the buyers and the carriers, Bethany and Kate were working as an effective team while, behind them, Isa scooped the gutted fish from their barrels and packed them in tiers consisting of two circles – inner and outer – laid in such a way that the fish did not come in contact with each other. Then she threw generous double-handfuls of salt over each layer before starting the next. A cooper assigned to their section was on hand to inspect each barrel as it was started, to make sure that the fish were being properly packed, then he covered the barrel when it was full and rolled it off to one side. After a few days, when the fish had settled, the salt brine would be run off through a bunghole, the barrel opened and topped up with more layers of herring, then more brine would be added before it was finally sealed.

Someone further down the line began to sing a popular hymn in a rich, clear contralto and Bethany joined in along with the others, singing her heart out as her hands flew about their task, feeling as though she had come home after a long absence. The hours flew by and one hymn followed another as basket upon basket was emptied into the farlins in a never-ending silver stream.

'This is going to be the best year yet,' Effie, gutting in the next team, called down the line.

Bethany looked up at the mountain of herring still waiting to be shovelled on to the farlins when space permitted. 'And the busiest,' she said, and Effie took a second to wipe the back of one hand over her brow, decorating her forehead with a mixture of glittering scales and fish slime.

'There's no harm in being busy. It makes it harder for the devil to put mischief into our hands.'

'He'd be a fool if he tried,' Bethany pointed out. 'The knives'd have his fingers gutted and into the barrel for packing before he knew what was afoot.'

The constant hard work kept the women reasonably warm and only when they began to walk back to the lodgings for their midday break were they aware of the stiff cold wind.

'There's somethin' to be said for that big wall of barrels all round us,' Isa said as they linked arms and ran for shelter. 'They fair keep the wind away.'

'But not the rain.' Effie looked up at the lowering sky. 'We'll get soaked before the day's done. Here, I'm fair ready for that soup!'

They had made two big pots of soup the night before and several of the women had been sent back to the lodgings earlier to heat it up and cook some fresh herring. After working all morning in the fresh air they fell upon the food as soon as they gained the big lofts, stuffing it into their mouths in a rush to satisfy their hunger before hurrying back to work. A long afternoon lay ahead of them, and judging by the pile of fish still waiting to get into the farlins, they would be working until late in the evening, too.

As they returned to the quay they met James, who stared when he spotted his sister among the others. 'Bethany?'

'Aye, it's me all right.' She stopped, letting the others walk on without her.

'What are you doing in Yarm'th?'

'What does it look like?' She indicated her oilskin apron and her boots with a sweep of the hand. 'Aunt Meg's not able for the work this time, so I'd to hire a new packer. I thought it best to come down to see how she settled in.'

'Gil said nothing about that when I spoke to him yesterday morning.'

'He didn't know. I only arrived last night.'

'What about . . .'

'The bairns,' Bethany said with a touch of irritation, 'are being well looked after by Gil's mother.'

'You'll be finding the work hard after being away from it for a year.'

'I'm managing fine,' Bethany retorted, and went on her way.

James watched her go, head high, shoulders squared and booted feet striding out across the stone flags as though she owned the place, then shrugged, yawned and hurried to catch up with the other men. It had been a long night and he was more than ready for a good sleep, then a meal and a drink with the rest of the lads before setting out to sea again.

The rain stayed away and the clouds cleared; as the afternoon wore on a knot of onlookers arrived to watch the fisher-lassies work, marvelling at the way their bandaged hands moved so fast that each movement blended into the next. The women were well used to these audiences and paid little heed to them, apart from occasionally involving them in their talk. Today a well-dressed middle-aged man caused great excitement among the crowd as he set up a tripod and camera.

'D'you fancy being one of these fillum actresses, Bethany?' Effie wanted to know as he began to take pictures.

'I'd as soon fill another barrel and get paid for it.' It was going to be grand to have her own money again, Bethany thought, her knife flickering and the barrel at her back filling steadily. Gil was generous enough, but he always needed to be told what every penny had been spent on and whether she had got value for money. Even her annual share from the *Fidelity* was banked by him. This was her chance to make some money of her own.

She was determined to avoid the trap some of the younger quine fell into – spending all their wages at the Yarmouth picture houses and theatres, or on clothes for themselves and gifts for family and friends back home. She intended to save every penny and enjoy for as long as possible the sense of independence that the money gave her. She was aware that Gil would do all he could to make sure that she would not get back to Yarmouth again.

As afternoon met evening and the sky darkened, the

photographer packed up his equipment, tipping his hat to
the fisher-lassies as he left. The buyers, having made their
deals, were long gone and the watchers began to drift off.
The women had another meal break and this time when
they returned to the farlins they trudged, where earlier they
had stepped out in linked lines. After almost everyone else
but the coopers had gone, they toiled on in the light of oil
lamps, for the fish had to be gutted and pickled while it
was still fresh.

With no more boats coming in, the level of fish in
the farlins fell rapidly, but for the tired gutters the work
became harder. Now they were required to lean into the
deep tubs, and by the time the last fish had been gutted and
packed, and the final barrel covered and rolled away, the
women were stiff and exhausted, longing for the freedom
to return to their lodgings.

The fishermen had landladies to cook their meals and, for
extra payment, wash their clothes, but the guttin quine,
being women, were expected to do all that for themselves
on top of the long day's work.

Once they had satisfied their hunger they divided by
mutual agreement into two groups, one taking on the
housework and the other, Bethany included, doing the
washing. Tired though they were, they laughed and joked
and sang as they scrubbed and wrung out the clothes before
putting them through the big mangle, glad to know that the
first day's work was behind them.

Trudging back upstairs with a bucket of damp clothing, Bethany was uncomfortably aware of a knot of
pain between her shoulder-blades. 'When the washing's
hung up I'll need to get one of you to rub ointment on
my back.'

'I'll do it, if you do the same for me,' offered Kate.
'I feel as if a carthorse has been dancing a reel on
my spine.'

'At your age?' one of the older women scoffed. 'Lassie,

you've got years ahead of you yet. Leave the sore backs to us old ones.'

'At least you're used to these deep farlins. My back's not had time to get accustomed!'

Arguing and teasing, they gained the top of the stairs and burst into the loft, where the washing lines still had to be strung from the rafters and the clothes draped over them. Bethany, anxious to be accepted by the others, caught up one end of the clothesline and stepped on to one of the narrow beds. Balancing precariously, she managed at her first try to toss the rope over one of the cross-beams that ran at intervals down the room. A bit of jiggling brought the end back down to her hand so that she could catch and tie it. Triumphant, she was about to jump down and repeat the process halfway down the room when one foot slipped and she only just saved herself from plunging on to the floor below, or, even worse, crashing on to the edge of one of the tables, by jerking her body up so that she could catch at the cross-beam directly over her head.

'Bethany!' Kate squeaked. 'Are you all right?'

'I'm fine.' Bethany, heart thumping from the fright, managed to get her other hand over the rafter to secure her grip.

'Hold on, I'll fetch a stool for you to stand on.' But when Kate came scurrying back with the stool, Bethany, both hands clamped on the beam, said breathlessly, 'Leave me be for a minute. This is the first time all day that my back's stopped hurting.'

'Don't be daft, lassie, come on down,' one of the other women ordered.

'I mean it.' She ducked her head between her upraised arms and grinned down at the knot of women below. 'It must be something to do with the stretching. It feels grand!'

'Here, let me try it.' Kate scrambled on to a table and, by standing on tiptoe and stretching her arms up,

just managed to take hold of the beam above her with
both hands. 'Oh here, you're right, Bethany. My back
feels grand.' She swung her legs to and fro. 'It's like
being a bairn again, playing at climbing trees.' Then,
peering down at the uplifted faces, 'You should try it,
it feels good.'

'Ach, why not? Give me a hand, someone,' Effie
ordered, kilting her skirts to reveal sturdy, slightly bowed
legs.

'Don't be daft, why would you want to be hanging
from rafters like a bat at your age!'

'If it takes the ache from my bones, Isa, I'll try anything.' With help, Effie clambered on to a chair, then on
to one of the tables and finally, to resounding cheers from
below, she managed to hook both hands over a beam.

'Catch me making a fool of myself like that,' Isa
sneered. 'You look like a monkey in a cage.'

'At least I'm a monkey with a contented spine. Try it,'
Effie urged, and within five minutes all the women except
Isa were hanging from the rafters, blissfully stretching
their aching spines.

'Like fish hanging from a pole in the smokehouse.' Isa
threw herself down on her bed and glared at them. 'And I
can see right up your skirt, Effie Jappy. I can nearly tell
what you had for your dinner.'

'You know what I had for my dinner – the same as you,'
Effie snapped back at her. 'As for the rest, I've nothing you
havenae got yourself, only it's in better working order.'

'And how are you going to get back down?'

'This way.' Bethany, her arms beginning to ache, edged
her way hand-by-hand along her beam. When she was
directly above one of the beds she let go, and although
the bed-frame squeaked alarmingly it took her sudden
arrival without collapsing beneath her. The younger and
more agile women followed suit, then between them they
managed to ease the older quine down.

'Oh my,' Effie gasped when she reached the floor, 'that

was as good as a party! I'm going to do it again tomorrow night, and so are you, Isa Thain, even if I have to hoist you up myself.'

'If you're going to hoist anything up you could start with the washing,' Isa told her sourly. 'It'll not dry by itself in those buckets.'

'I knew you'd be calling, Mistress Lowrie, to find out if the children are all right.'

'I know they're fine with you, Mrs Pate, and very well looked after,' Jess told the woman courteously. 'I only came to ask if I could do anything to help.'

'I raised my own five with no help at all, so two are no trouble. You'll have a cup of tea.' Phemie Pate made it sound more like a command than an invitation.

'I'd not want to put you out.'

'You're not. The housework was done by eight o'clock and the bairns washed and fed long before then. Have you got no manners at all, Roderick Pate? Say good morning to your Grandmother Lowrie,' the woman admonished Rory, who was looking unusually subdued.

'Gran . . .'

'What sort of word is that? Only lazy tinks use that. Say it properly now, the way I told you.'

'Good morning, Grandmother Lowrie,' the child muttered, giving a stiff little bow.

'Good morning, Ro . . . Rory,' Jess said firmly, ignoring the hissing intake of breath from the other woman. 'And good morning to you, Ellen.' Even the baby, she noticed with dismay, looked subdued. Both children were immaculately dressed, with not a crease or a dribble to be seen. 'Are you not going out to play today, Rory?'

'He's been doing his letters. But now that your Grandmother Lowrie is here I suppose you'd best get out from under our feet. Mind now,' Phemie warned as Rory made a bolt for the door, 'you've to stay close to the house, and no rough games, and keep your clothes clean. And mind . . .' She broke off as the door closed behind him, then sniffed and said disapprovingly, 'These children need to learn their manners.'

Jess felt her hackles rise. 'I've always found them to be very pleasant bairns. Did you say Rory was doing his letters?'

'Indeed.' The woman handed Ellen a rag doll. 'Play quietly with that, now, and don't make a mess. I made sure that Gilbert and his brothers and sisters were well on with their letters and their figuring by the time they went to the school, and it's stood them all in good stead. There's Gilbert and Nathan both with their own businesses, and my three lassies well married to good, hard-working God-fearing men. You'll have a scone, they're fresh made this morning.'

She split the scone, put a tiny scrape of butter on it and handed it to Jess on a plate. 'I'd expected you here before now.'

'I had to see to my sister-in-law before I could get out. I'm staying with her just now, because she's a bad back and can't do a thing for herself. Otherwise I'd have offered to . . .'

'I mean, I expected you here before today.' Mrs Pate set two cups of strong black tea down and settled herself in her son's seat at the head of the table. 'To make certain that the children were being well cared for.'

'I knew that without having to call in.'

'Gilbert knows it too. It's eased his mind, I've no doubt about that.' The woman sipped like a bird at her tea. 'Though it would have been best if his own wife had been here to see to his wee children. She's still very young, of course, I pointed that out to Gilbert when he first thought of taking her for his wife. And young women need a stern hand if they're to be taught to observe their duties. I know my daughters did. Ellen, stop sucking at that doll's hand, only dirty lassies do that.'

11

'I could do nothing but sit there and let her criticise my Bethany,' Jess raged to Meg an hour later. 'How could I speak up for the lassie when I know as well as Phemie Pate does where her duty lies? Anyway, I'd not want to quarrel with Gil's mother in his own house in front of his own children. But it was hard to keep silent, Meg, very hard.'

'Just mind that it's none of your business,' Meg advised. She was in her fireside chair with all of Jess's cushions stuffed behind her back, for Meg had none of her own. 'Let the woman have the pleasure of feeling like a martyr if that's her way. As long as the bairns are all right . . .'

'You could say so, if being all right means being fed and looked after, but the two of them looked as if they were in prison instead of their own home. Poor wee Ellen was scared to move. They'd been scrubbed till their faces were shiny. I should have taken them myself, but . . .' Jess stopped suddenly and her sister-in-law completed the sentence for her.

'But you'd me to look after.'

'Now don't you go thinking such a thing, Meg Lowrie. You're not able to see to yourself and I'm happy to do it. And if you were fit you'd have been down south at the farlins and Bethany would have been here, so I'd still not have been looking after the bairns.' Jess paused, realising that there was no sense to be made of her laboured efforts to keep Meg from feeling guilty about the situation, then rushed on, 'The whole place smelled of carbolic. I hope Bethany sees sense and comes home soon.'

'No doubt she will. You're probably fretting about Innes, too – you're a right mother hen, Jess.'

'Innes can manage fine without me for once. Look at your Albert, he's lived alone for years and it's done him no harm.'

'Our Albert and your Innes are nothing like each other.' Meg wriggled in the chair, then gave a contented sigh as she found a comfortable position. 'Albert's a randy pig and Innes is a nice quiet laddie. Our poor mother's heart was fair broken with Albert and his shenanigans . . . sometimes it seemed that every knock at the door brought some poor man to say that Albert had been misbehaving with his lassie. You're fortunate, Jess, you can trust Innes.'

'Are you certain sure it's all right?' Zelda whispered, staring round the kitchen as though she expected Jess to pop out from below the wall-bed or behind one of the high-backed fireside chairs.

'I told you, my mam's staying with my Aunt Meg at nights because of her bad back. We've got the house to ourselves.'

'If that's true, why are you whispering?'

'Eh? Ach, it's you,' Innes said aloud, irritated with himself. 'You're behaving like a cat on hot coals!'

'Well, no wonder. Just think how it would look if your mother came in and found us like this.'

'Like what?' he asked innocently. 'We're just standing here in the kitchen.'

'I doubt if that's what you brought me here for – to stand in the kitchen.'

'That's true,' he admitted, suddenly tired of the game. 'Oh, Zelda, you've got me so's I don't know whether I'm on my head or my heels. I can't concentrate on my work for thinking of you.'

'You think it's any easier for me? You're like the chicken-pox, Innes Lowrie: you've got me fidgeting and thinking about you all the time until it's hard to get my work done properly.' She side-stepped deftly as he reached for her. 'Listen!'

Innes froze, his ears stretched to their utmost, certain that Zelda had caught the sound of his mother's step on the path outside; but all he could hear was the slow, comforting tick of the pendulum clock that had been on the kitchen wall since before his birth, and the occasional whispering shift of a coal in the range. Nervously he eyed the girl in the middle of the room, head tilted back, so still that she might have been a statue.

'What?' he whispered at last, unable to bear the tension any longer. 'I can't hear anything.'

'That's what I mean.' She looked over her shoulder at him. 'It's so quiet in here!'

'Zelda, you gave me the fright of my life! Of course it's quiet, there's only you and me in the place.'

'You're lucky, Innes. You've seen for yourself what our house is like . . . so many folk crowded into it that there's never any peace to think.'

'Aye.' Zelda had taken him several times to the small tied farm cottage in which she had been born and raised. From the moment they stepped through the door she was claimed to calm a fractious toddler, nurse a crying baby, help a perplexed younger brother or sister with school homework, peel potatoes or wash the pots. The Mulholland house was a seething mass of bodies, no matter what time of day it was.

'And it's so nice, too.' She flitted about the small kitchen, looking at her own reflection in the gilt-edged mirror, stroking the neat folds of the curtain drawn across the wall-bed, peering in through the glass front of the display cabinet at the painted china dishes. Seeing her delight and pleasure in the things he had always taken for granted, Innes felt his very bones melt with love for her.

'We'll have a place like this ourselves one day.'

'Will we? D'you mean it?'

'I promise you.' He did mean it. No matter how hard he had to work, no matter what he himself had to do without, he meant every word.

'Oh, Innes!' She flew at him, holding him tight and covering his face with kisses. 'I love you!' Then, as his mouth became more urgent and his hands began to roam, she drew back. 'Where do you sleep?'

'In the loft.'

'Show me.'

Now that the prize was almost his, Innes hesitated, though his body ached for her. 'You're sure?'

She cupped his face in a work-roughened palm. 'I'm sure,' she said, and with trembling hands he lit a candle then led her up the narrow stairs to the loft area.

Since his father's death James had taken away most of the ropes, nets and lobster pots and the lines and tools Weem had used, but there was still a clutter of bits and pieces and the air still held a smell of sea water and tar and pipe tobacco. Although he feared the sea, Innes found the mixture of smells comforting, for it reminded him of his early childhood, when his father had been his safety and refuge, his delight and his god.

The candle flame flickered and danced as he led Zelda along the side of the loft, their heads bent beneath the slope of the house roof, to where one-third of the space had been partitioned off to form an extra room. This had been Bethany's bedroom before her marriage, but now it was Innes's domain. Apart from the bed, covered by a patchwork quilt of Jess's making, there was a small table, one chair, a cupboard where Innes kept his clothes and a shelf holding the few books he had managed to buy. The books were all about engineering and the walls were covered with pictures, cut from magazines and newspapers, of cars and lorries and motor-bicycles.

When the lamp was lit Zelda took in the entire room

with one swift glance, then went to look out through both windows, the one at the back overlooking the yard and the houses beyond, the one at the front showing a glimpse, over house roofs, of the Moray Firth.

'You've got this all to yourself?' Her voice was awed. 'I've never had a place of my own, or a bed of my own. There's always six or seven of us at home, and at the farm I have to share with the dairy lassie.'

'I shared with James until he got wed.' Innes felt the need to apologise for his good fortune. 'And there's only me left now. That's why I said we could get married and live here until we could get a place of our own. There's room up here for two of us.'

Zelda looked round enviously, then heaved a sigh and shook her head. 'I couldn't, not with your mother downstairs.'

He reached out and touched her lips with the tip of one finger, very gently. 'She's not downstairs now,' he whispered and a radiant smile lit up the girl's round, expressive face.

'No, she's not,' she agreed, and moved into his arms.

Now that she was sure they were alone her nerves had gone, and she returned his kisses with a passion that first astonished then excited him. In all the time they had spent together, always in the open, she had been willing yet reserved. Now, indoors and safe from discovery, she changed completely, sighing and moaning, pressing her soft body tightly against him, her mouth and hands just as adventurous and daring as his. When Innes, driven to distraction by his need for her, lifted her and carried her to the bed and began with trembling fingers to unfasten the buttons of her blouse, she didn't push his hands away as he had expected but reached down to unfasten her skirt before wriggling out of it like an eel.

The entire Mulholland clan was dark-haired and dark-eyed – a throwback, Innes had heard some say, to gypsy blood. Kneeling on the bed above Zelda, seeing her bathed in lamplight, he wished that he had the words to express the glowing skin shades before him. Her face and throat and arms could only be described in his limited vocabulary as being a soft golden colour, matched by the gold flecks that the light picked out in her dark eyes, while her smooth, plump body was the rich, creamy shade of the flowers that blossomed in hedgerows in early summer.

'Do I please you, Innes?' Her voice was suddenly uncertain.

'Please me? Oh, Zelda . . .' His voice shook and to his horror he felt unmanly tears prickling behind his eyelids. Now of all times, just when he felt more like a man than he had ever done! He raised a hand to dash them away, but Zelda pushed it aside and reached up for him.

'Come here, you silly,' she said, suddenly in complete control of the situation, knowing instinctively what to do. She drew his head down on to magnificent pillowy breasts tipped with large, dark nipples and held him there, stroking his hair, the nape of his neck and the length of his back through his shirt for the few minutes that his tears flowed. When he lifted his head again, sniffing, she kissed the last of the moisture from his eyes, then said, 'And now I want to see you.'

Once he was naked to her gaze it was Innes's turn to tremble and wonder if he was good enough, but only for a moment before she said, 'Come here, my handsome lad!' and drew him down on to the bed, turning over on her side so that they could lie facing each other, breath mingling and bodies touching.

'Have you ever . . . ?'

'No, have you?'

'Never once?'

'I never found a lass I wanted to lie with, till now. Are you certain . . .'

She gave his arm a little slap. 'You just be quiet, Innes Lowrie, and let me enjoy myself.'

'But you've told me more than once that you wanted to wait till our marriage bed, and this isn't it.'

'I know, but you can be very persuasive,' Zelda said comfortably, nestling closer and sliding her upper leg over his flank. The touch of her skin against his sent a tremor through his already trembling body. 'This is close enough. Women just know these things.'

Then suddenly, just as he felt that he had made sure of her, her soft body went rigid within the circle of his arms.

'What's that?'

'What?'

'That!' she hissed, and now Innes heard it too, the sound of the street door closing and movement in the kitchen directly below.

'Dear God, it must be my mother back home!'

'You said . . . !'

'I thought she was staying the night with Aunt Meg. She's been sleeping there for the past three days!'

'What are we going to do?' Zelda began to scramble over him in an attempt to get out of the bed, but he pushed her back.

'Stay still, then she won't hear us.'

They lay for a moment, two naked bodies locked together, but with all their sexual excitement drained away by the fear of discovery. There was more movement from below, then Jess called from the foot of the loft stairs, 'Innes, are you there?'

'I'll be down in a minute,' he yelled back, and Zelda jumped so violently that she almost tossed him off the narrow cot on to the floor.

'I thought we were supposed to be quiet?' she hissed, raising herself on one elbow as he leaped up and began to snatch at his scattered clothes.

'I had to answer; she might have come up to see for herself if I hadn't.'

'What are we going to do?'

'Stay still.' He dragged his jersey over his head, emerging to say, 'I'll be back as soon as I can.'

'I can't stay here all night. I have to get back to the farm.'

He turned in the doorway, a warning finger to his lips, then went out, closing the door behind him.

Down in the kitchen his mother was ferreting about in the large canvas bag she used to store all her mending and knitting things. 'I thought you'd still be out with Zelda.'

'Mrs Bain wanted her back early, so I thought I'd just go to my bed and get a good early start in the morning.' He had never in his life lied to anyone, but it turned out to be quite easy, given the right circumstances. 'Is Aunt Meg all right?'

'As all right as she can be. I just came back for some wool she needs. Here it is. You've not touched the pie I left in the oven.'

'I was looking something up in one of my books. I'll eat later.'

'Are you all right? You look flushed.'

'I'm fine. Really,' he added hurriedly as she reached up to put a hand on his forehead.

'I shouldn't be leaving you on your own like this.'

'Mother, I'm old enough to look after myself. And Aunt Meg needs you.'

'Well, don't study too much, and get to your bed early. And be sure to eat all of that pie for you're still a growing lad,' she said, and at last she took the wool and left.

Zelda had crawled under the blankets and pulled them over her head. When he drew them away she blinked up at him and mouthed the words, 'Is she gone?'

'Off to my Aunt Meg's for the night. She only wanted to fetch some wool she'd forgotten.'

The way her breasts lifted and tautened when she heaved a sigh of relief brought the warm tingle back to his loins. 'I thought she was going to stay here all night and I'd not be able to get out. I thought she was going to find me.' She raised herself on one elbow. 'What d'you think you're doing?'

'Taking my clothes off again.'

'You think we can . . . be the same as we were after the fright we've just had?'

'We're really alone now. And my ma says I have to get to my bed early.' He grinned down at her. 'She says I'm still a growing lad.'

'I can see that.' She reached out and laid a hand lightly on his groin, exciting him beyond bearing. 'Put the lamp out, then.'

In the darkness they kissed and touched, coaxing each other back to the heights they had reached before being interrupted.

'D'you know what to do?' Innes whispered, desperate for relief but not certain just how to achieve it.

'I've only ever seen animals together.'

'Well, what do they do, then?' Animals or humans, it was all the same to him at that moment.

'We'll work it out somehow,' Zelda said against his chest.

12

'Thank God that's the first week near over.' As one of the coopers covered the barrel she had just completed and trundled it out of the way Isa snatched a minute to drink from the bottle of cold tea she had brought to the farlins. 'I'm chilled to the bone. I wish I'd been born a cooper!'

She scrubbed the drizzling rain from her face and looked longingly over to where Gil and his men were hard at work beneath the shelter of a makeshift tarpaulin. In contrast to the shivering fisher-lassies, the men were sweating and stripped to their shirt sleeves, for they were in close proximity to a blazing fire that was used to bring tubs of water to the boil. The steam from the heated water was needed to shape the staves for the barrels. 'Why is it that men always get the best jobs?' Isa girned.

'Never mind, hen, the first week's the worst,' one of the other packers called over to her. 'You'll be bright as a linty once you've had a wee rest and a bit of a party. You know fine that Yarm'th's the great place to be.'

'I'm not so sure.' Isa squinted up at the heavy grey sky, then stoppered her bottle as one of the other lassies rolled an empty barrel to her. 'Here we go again . . . you'd wonder who eats all these fish.'

'Folk with sense. There's nothing like a good herrin' to keep a body fit and well,' Effie told her. 'Look at me for a start. You'd never guess that I'm really a hunner and thirty.'

'I'd have put you at nearer a hunner and thirty-five,' Isa said sourly.

'Ye're as old as ye feel,' Effie told her, then suddenly broke into song. '"Twenty-one today, I'm twenty-one today . . ."'

'"I've got the key of the door, never been twenty-one before,"' Bethany roared along with the others, her knife slicing through the herring with renewed vigour. It was Saturday morning and, as far as the Scottish men and women were concerned, there would be no work the following day, for Sunday was the Lord's Day and the Scottish boats would stay in the harbour no matter how well the herring were running. The fisher-lassies could have worked every day of the week, for they were renowned for their skills and in great demand, but they agreed with their menfolk – Saturday evenings and Sundays until midnight were sacrosanct.

Once the boats had been cleaned and made ready to go out immediately after midnight on Sunday, the crews were free to enjoy a well-earned rest, but the fisher-lassies, as women, simply exchanged one job of work for another. Before they sat down to their evening meal on Saturday buckets of water brought up from the wash-house were set to heat on the stoves; then, after they had eaten, one group went off to the shops with money contributed by all to buy tea, sugar and milk, bread and cheese, cold meat and a large selection of fancy cakes, while those left behind cleaned out the loft, scrubbing the two long tables as well as the great expanse of wooden flooring. The pots of water on the stove were constantly re-filled, and when the others had returned with their purchases they all turned to the task of washing clothes and bed-linen and cleaning the skylight windows.

'To think I was complaining about the cold earlier,' Isa puffed. 'The sweat's runnin' off me now!' By the time the loft was as clean and neat as they could make it they were all hot, sticky and uncomfortable, and more than ready to strip off their working clothes and take turns in the three tin baths provided by their landlady.

As they dressed in their best they discussed plans for the evening. Some opted for a visit to a music hall or to the cinema, but most planned to take the evening air and either meet up with the menfolk or enjoy a wander through the streets, peering in shop windows to see the wares on offer.

'I wish we could get a fiddler and an accordion player and have a nice wee dance to ourselves,' young Kate said regretfully. 'That's what I like about going to the islands.'

When they followed the fishing fleets north, to places such as Orkney or the Shetlands, the lassies lived in isolated wooden huts and had to make their own entertainment, which usually took the form of late-night dancing with the fishermen. In large, well-populated ports like Lowestoft and Yarmouth, where the lassies were under the eyes of landladies, there were no parties other than a fairly sedate gathering after the mission church services on Sunday.

'Away ye go,' Effie boomed. 'It's much nicer bein' able to look in the shop windows and visit the music hall.'

'At least in the islands you know where your man is when he's not at sea,' Kate grumbled. 'In Yarm'th my Charlie could be up close with any of these English lassies.'

'I don't blame you for frettin' over that,' Effie conceded, 'since he's Albert Lowrie's lad.'

'He's not like his father that way,' the girl flared, her face flushing, then the colour deepened as Effie immediately shot back, 'Then why are you worryin' yourself about where he might be when he's ashore? Anyway, the big ports are safer for you, lassie. More than one nor'-east bairn's been started in the islands during the herring season. Best for you young folk to be where the landladies and the rest of us can keep an eye on you.'

That night most of them ended up strolling along King Street, where they soon met up with their menfolk, smart in their blue suits and black jerseys. Arm-in-arm in groups or couples they promenaded in slow and stately fashion along the street, stopping every few yards to greet old friends. During the Yarmouth fishing season there could be as many as twenty thousand people in the town, and as they all followed the herring along the coast year after year, coopers and lassies and fishermen from all the ports got to know each other well.

It wasn't long before Gil fell into step beside Bethany, threading her arm firmly through the crook of his elbow. 'So how d'you feel after a week back at the farlins?'

'Grand. It's as if I'd never left. You'd see for yourself that I was keeping up with the rest of them.'

'I wasnae watching.'

'I noticed that,' she said drily, and he cleared his throat and walked on for a while in silence before saying, 'I've had some letters from my mother.'

'And I've had letters from mine, saying that the bairns are fine.' She didn't add that Jess thought the children were missing her and perhaps being too firmly disciplined. She had only skimmed that part of the letter and refused to let herself dwell on it.

'Of course they are, with my mother minding them. But she's not happy about you being here and neither am I.'

'That's too bad, Gil, because I'm staying.'

'Is it something I've done? Are you trying to punish me?'

'Of course not!'

'Then why d'you make a fool of me by going back to the farlins?'

'It has nothing to do with you. I'm making sure that everything's fine and Isa's settling in, that's all. And it's nice to be earning my own money again.'

'That's another thing – folk'll be thinking that my own wife has to go out to work because I cannae support her.'

'If they're daft enough to say that, let them. We both know it's not true.'

'Why d'you need to work for your own silver?' he burst out, stopping and turning her to face him. 'Do I not give you everything you ask for?'

'You do.' And he always wanted to know exactly what she wanted it for, too. 'It's just that I was always used to keeping myself and I miss having money of my own in my pocket. And it's nice to be back at the farlins, Gil.'

'It's . . . it's nice to see you there,' he admitted, turning to walk on. 'Looking so brave and so bonny, with that gutting knife in your hand and the pretty colour of your hair peeping out from under the scarf about your head.' His arm tightened so that her hand was wedged close against his side. 'It fair takes me back to the days before we were wed. I never thought then that I'd have you for my own one day.'

'Neither did I, Gil.' Young and innocent, enjoying her life and her work, she had had little idea in those days of the plans being hatched in her father's head. She shivered a little as the wind leaped out at them from a narrow lane as they passed. The ranks of the walkers were beginning to thin out as some couples slid quietly into the darkening night on private business of their own and others turned back towards their lodgings. 'I'm going back now,' she said. 'It's been a hard week and I'm tired.'

'I'll walk with you. I just wish we could be together,' he went on as they turned. 'I've been looking around, but there's not a room to be had in the entire place.'

'I told you I wanted to stay with the other lassies. If I moved into lodgings with you they'd say I was too stuck up to bide with them.'

'Never mind what they'd say,' Gil growled, squeezing her arm so tightly that pins and needles began to shoot through her fingers. 'It's driving me mad being without you, Bethany.'

'You'd have been without me anyway if I'd stayed home with the bairns.'

'That's different. It's seeing you every day that's unsettling me.'

'You're just saying that to get me to go home.'

'Back home,' said Gil, 'is the last place I want you to be right now.' Then as they reached the door that led to the attic stairs, 'Come here a minute.'

Before she realised what was happening he had deftly pulled her off to one side and into the narrow lane that ran up the side of the lodging house. High walls on either side cast deep black shadows and as Bethany's feet skittered and slid over the uneven, unseen cobbles he looped an arm about her waist to hold her upright, using his superior strength at the same time to urge her deeper into the darkness.

'Gil . . .'

He pushed her against a wall and slathered damp kisses over her mouth, all along her jawline, then down to her throat, one hand fumbling at her breast and the other tugging her skirt, pulling it up to her thighs. 'Bethany lass,' he mumbled through the kisses, 'I'm on fire for you . . .'

'Gil . . . no, Gil, not here. Not like this.'

He lifted his head and the dim light from a gas lamp in the nearby street glanced off his eyes so that they glittered down at her. 'This is all we have, thanks to you,' he said, arousal souring the edge of his temper. 'So this it has to be.'

'It doesn't have to be at all!' She pushed him away but he was ready for her, anticipating her attempt to slide along the wall and round the corner to the house door.

'Bein' in Yarm'th's mebbe good for the both of us,' he said breathlessly, his hands sliding inside her blouse, and up her thigh.

*   *   *

Bethany paused on the attic landing to pin up her hair, now straggling about her neck, and make sure that her clothes were in place before venturing in. It was not necessary, for although some beds were still empty all the women in the attic were already asleep.

She stripped swiftly and used her skirt to scrub at her face and body, rubbing Gil's touch away before rolling into bed, drawing the blanket right up to her ears and relishing the pleasure of being alone at last.

On Sunday morning the women were up early to put on their best clothes, make the beds, take down the washing lines and put the clean laundry out of sight. Then they made up piles of sandwiches and arranged them and cakes on the long tables, for on Sunday afternoon it was traditional for the fisher-lassies to entertain their menfolk.

When all was ready they pinned on their hats and went off to the morning service in the mission, which as always was packed with worshippers. The service was long, but Bethany enjoyed every minute of it, for it wasn't often these days that she got the chance to go to worship. Although most fisher-families were keenly religious, neither she nor Gil was a great church-goer, for he usually lay late in his bed on Sunday mornings, while Bethany had the children to see to and a big midday meal to cook. But in Yarmouth it was different, for the mission services were social as well as religious gatherings.

She saw Gil as soon as she went in, sitting with the other men and turning round each time he heard the door open. He grinned at her, the smug grin of ownership, and she gave him a brief smile and a prim nod. She was surprised to see James – who, to Stella's distress, had not set foot inside the church since the day of their marriage – sitting among the congregation, his hair sleeked back and his face impassive.

'I never thought you'd be here,' she said when she met him and Gil outside afterwards.

'I was with Davie Geddes. He sets great store by religion.'

'Why should you want to please Davie Geddes?'

Gil clapped a hand on the younger man's shoulder. 'It seems that Davie's looking for a mate for his boat.'

'You've already got a boat, James.'

'Uncle Albert has a boat, not me.'

'But . . .'

'Are we going to the loft or are we not?' Gil interrupted. 'All that hymn singing's made me hungry. You'll come back with us and have something to eat, James? Religion's great for the appetite!'

James hesitated for a moment, then shrugged and nodded, striding up the road ahead of them, the studs in his sturdy boots striking sparks from the cobbles.

'You were in a right hurry to get away last night,' Gil said low-voiced as they followed.

'I was tired, and you got what you wanted, didn't you?'

'Watch your mouth,' he hissed in a panic, eyeing his brother-in-law's broad back. 'D'you want the whole place to hear you?'

'Speaking for myself, I'm not bothered. And as far as the rest of our stay here goes, there'll be no more hiding up dark alleyways for me or you, Gil Pate. I'm not a loose woman and I'll not be treated like one. You'll have to wait until we get back to our own house,' Bethany said haughtily, and ran ahead to catch up with Isa, Kate and Charlie.

The loft was filled with folk all afternoon and Bethany had no chance to speak to James. She caught sight of him now and again, talking mainly to the other men, though at one point she saw him in conversation with one of the younger lassies. By the time she had managed to work

her way to the corner where she had seen them the girl
was on her own.

'Has our James gone already?'

Maggie, a known flirt, shrugged and pouted. 'How
should I know? I never thought he was all that fond of
Stella, but I didnae realise that he's got no time for any
woman at all.'

'If you'd taken the trouble to ask I could have told you
that my brother cares about two things: himself and his
boat,' Bethany said flatly. 'He didn't say where he was
going?'

'To the devil, for all I care.'

'There's plenty men in Yarm'th, Maggie, some of them
single. Don't waste your time on our James.'

Finding him at last by the table, picking through the
scattered remains of the food, Bethany took his arm and
towed him to an empty bench. 'That nonsense about Davie
Geddes's boat – you're not really thinking of leaving the
Fidelity, are you?'

'I'm a free man, I can do anything I choose.'

'What would Da think about it?'

'If he wanted me to stay on the *Fidelity* for the rest of
my life he should have left me his share, since I'm the
only one in the family to work on the boat.'

Bethany bit her lip. 'Mebbe I was too hasty. You can
have my share if it matters so much to you, and I'll talk
to Ma and Innes as soon as I get home. I'll write to them
now if you want.'

'It's too late, d'you not see that?' James glared at her
from beneath shaggy black brows, just like their father's.
'None of you cared enough about me – not him or you or
the others. I'd as soon go my own way.'

'You'll not be happy on another boat.'

'I'm not happy where I am, so where's the difference?
Stop fretting about what Da would want, Bethany. He was
never worth it and he didn't give a damn for you and me
when we were grown.'

'He did!'

'He used the two of us to serve his own purpose and he doesn't give a damn now for us or for the boat, because he's dead and buried in the earth and feeding the worms. And they're welcome to him!' James said savagely and walked off.

She stayed where she was, shocked by the strength and ferocity of his bitterness, but even more shocked by the realisation that she recognised and understood it, for it burned in her as well as in her brother.

'Bethany . . .' Gil arrived and drew her into the corner, away from the others. 'Listen, I've been speaking to a man who lives on the edge of the town, and he says that his landlady might have a wee room to rent.'

'How many times do I have to tell you that I'm biding here where I belong?'

'Mebbe I'll just take the room and find another lassie to share it with me, then. There's plenty of them about.'

'You're right, and no need to look far, either. Try Maggie,' Bethany suggested coldly. 'She's always looking out for a man.'

In Buckie, Jess continued to spend her nights with Meg, who found it hard to start moving in the morning without a good back rub. This meant that Zelda could spend her nights off in Innes's bed, with nobody any the wiser, since Mrs Bain, her employer, thought that she was with her parents; they, in turn, were under the impression that she was sleeping at the farm.

'My mother says that Mrs Bain should pay me more than she does, seeing as she keeps asking me to stay on,' she giggled into Innes's shoulder.

'And what did you say to that?'

'I told her that it was only for a wee while, until the bronchitis leaves Peter's chest, and it wouldn't be a good thing at all to anger Mrs Bain by refusing.'

'It'll be just for a wee while too,' Innes mourned. 'My mother's good with bad backs.'

Zelda, cosy in the nest they had made for themselves within the blankets, sighed. 'I'm going to miss being here with you, Innes Lowrie, all snug and warm. It wouldn't be the same in a draughty old barn or,' she shivered deliciously against him, 'a drystone dyke.'

'But you'd not deny me, surely?' he protested, alarmed at the thought. He couldn't get enough of Zelda's warm, silky body, with its exciting curves and hollows; for the first time in his life he felt truly alive and the thought of being without her loving was more than he could bear.

'I should . . . but I don't know that I could deny you, now,' she confessed.

Making a sudden deft move that flipped her on to her back with him poised above her, he grinned down at the pretty face on his pillow.

'The thing to do,' he said, 'is to make the most of the comfort we have now, and the time we've got left.'

13

With most of the boats at the English fishing grounds the village was achingly quiet. Mowser Buchan and the other old men, who spent most of their time down at the harbour, had nothing to look at but the horizon and nobody to speak to but each other. The womenfolk, once they had scrubbed and polished, and beaten rugs and told each other what a blessing it was to be able to get the work done now that the menfolk weren't getting under their feet, found time heavy on their hands for once.

Walking by Cluny harbour on her way from Meg's to her own house, Jess mourned to see the place so silent and empty, with only a handful of smaller boats berthed in one or other of the basins. The harbour had been built at the end of the previous century on the site of The Salters, an old boat haven, to cope with the rapid growth of the herring trade. The deep-water refuge, capable of sheltering hundreds of boats, looked quite desolate now that it was offering protection to only a few of the smaller fishing boats and a commercial sailing ship unloading its cargo of timber in the outer basin.

The tide was out and, in the last of the four inner basins, a few children had clambered down the iron ladders set into the stone walls to play happily on the mudflats. Smiling, Jess stopped to watch them climb in and out of the beached rowing boats, their voices ringing in the cold air. Rory was not among them – they were all

older than him, but the little boy had an adventurous spirit
and normally he would have shinned down the vertical
ladder with the best of them. Instead he would be at home,
poor wee mite, firmly under his grandmother's thumb and
hating every minute of it.

Jess decided that that very afternoon she would offer to
take both children off Phemie Pate's hands for an hour or
so. They would walk along by the shore and climb around
the rocks and look for crabs in the pools. Pleasant though
the outing would be, the thought of it already depressed
her, because of the looks she would no doubt see on their
two little faces when the time came to return them to their
grandmother. She wished with all her heart that Bethany
had never gone to Yarmouth, or that she would come home
early instead of waiting until the end of the season, but she
knew full well that having tasted freedom, her rebellious
daughter would not be in a hurry to return to the duties
of a wife and mother.

Perhaps if she birthed a bairn of her own, Jess thought . . .
then dismissed the idea. Bethany had never been mater-
nally minded and perhaps it was just as well that Gil
seemed content with the two he already had and showed no
signs of wanting to father more. Although Jess herself had
never had the desire or, thank God, the need to prevent a
pregnancy, she knew that some did, and she suspected that
her healthy, childless daughter was among that number.

'I only ever mind seeing you once with such a long
face, Jess Innes,' a voice said just behind her, 'and that
was the last day we set eyes on each other.'

She turned sharply to see a sturdy, squarely built man
not much taller than herself, his weather-beaten face dominated by bright sea-green eyes with a youthfulness in them
that denied the grey in the thick eyebrows above.

'Jacob?' Shock stole her voice away and the word came
out as a mere whisper. 'Jacob MacFarlane, is that you?'

'You mind me then?' The skin about his eyes crinkled
up in a huge smile and he seized one of her hands in

his. 'Och, Jess, it's grand to see you after all those years!'

'But . . .' A glance took in the silver-topped cane in his other hand, and the caped Ulster coat protecting him against the sharp wind. 'In the name of God, Jacob, where have you been?'

He gave a great boom of laughter that sent nearby seagulls, foraging for scraps among the crab pots, leaping for the sky with shrill screams of vexation, and made the children on the mudflats stop their play and stare up at the two figures high above them. 'Fishing out along the rocks with a pole and a string and a bit of bait on a pin, Jess. Begging a hurl on top of the nets being carted off to the cutching yards. Running a message for my mother,' he said in delight. Then, as she stared at him, uncomprehending, 'You said that just the way you used to say it when we were bairns playing together. It was for all the world as if we'd seen each other not an hour since.'

'And I'll say it again. Where have you been . . . all these years?' she added.

'Oh, such a lot of places, Jess. England, The Netherlands, Russia. Here and there.'

She looked again at his fine clothes, which could have been made specially for him. 'You'll have given up the fishing?'

'Long since, though I've stayed in the trade one way or another,' he said, then shivered as a particularly keen gust of wind swept along the harbourside. 'It's far too cold to be standing here.'

'I'll need to be on my way home anyway.'

'Then I'll walk with you if I may.' He took the shopping basket from her and turned to match his steps to hers.

She was still trying to come to terms with the shock of seeing him again. 'What are you doing in Buckie?'

'I've come to see you, Jess.'

'All the way from Russia and The Netherlands just to see me?'

'Not entirely,' he admitted. 'I'd to visit Aberdeen on a matter of business, so I stayed with my sister Minnie and her man. You'll remember Minnie?'

'I do indeed.' The MacFarlanes and the Inneses had been neighbours in the village of Portessie, just along the coast from Buckie, and their children had grown up together, more like brothers and sisters than friends. 'How is she?'

'Hearty. She asked to be reminded to you. It was Minnie that told me about Weem passing away,' he added soberly.

'I was sorry to hear it.'

'Aye, well – it comes to all of us in the end.'

'Somehow I never thought of it as happening to Weem Lowrie.'

'Nor did I,' Jess said huskily. Then, as she heard the intake of breath that meant that he was about to say something else, she jumped in quickly with, 'I always mind Minnie's lovely long black hair. She was a beautiful lassie.'

'She's a bit heftier these days, with not a bit of black left in her hair, though it's still as thick as ever. Just like my own.' Jacob took off his curly-brimmed bowler hat to reveal a healthy shock of grey hair. 'But she still has her looks. There's only the two of us left now, me and Minnie.'

'Is that right?' There had been five MacFarlane children; Jess knew that the other sister had died young, in childbirth, and that Jacob and his brothers had all left home as young men. She had not heard any more of them, not even of Jacob.

'Minnie managed to keep in touch with us all, and give us news of each other, though I never saw any of the others once we were scattered across the face of the globe.'

'Have you been along to have a look at Portessie yet?'

'I'm not sure that I want to. Some memories are best left in the past and the place has nothing for me.'

'It's not changed.'

'Mebbe I will take a look, if you'll come with me.'

'Surely, if there's time before you're off again.'

'There's time all right. I've taken a room in the Commercial Hotel, for I might be doing business in the area. And I'd welcome the chance to catch up with all your news.'

'There's little of that, since I've only moved a few miles from the house where I was born and raised.'

'There's different ways of travelling and I'm sure a lot's happened to you since we last met.'

They had reached Jess's door; she hesitated, then said, 'I'd ask you in, but my son's been staying on his lone in the house for a week or more and there's no knowing what state he left it in this morning. And I have to visit my grandchildren.'

'You have grandchildren, Jess? I wondered.'

'Five of them. Three belong to my son James and two are step-children to Bethany, my daughter.'

He handed the basket back, his eyes locked on her face, as though he was trying to absorb the look of her and hold it in his memory. 'Children and grandchildren. You see, Jess, you have travelled far in your own way. And I want to know all about your journeying.'

'You could come for your dinner tomorrow night about six,' she blurted out, made suddenly and ridiculously shy by the intensity of his gaze. 'You'll meet Innes, he's still at home with me.'

He put a hand to the brim of his hat. 'I'd be delighted to accept.'

'You've lost the Doric,' she accused.

'Fit like, Jessie quine?' The traditional north-east greeting was accompanied by a huge grin. 'Caal wither, is't no? My natural speech has had to bide quietly in the background, because I've spent most of my life talking to folk that would never have understood a word of it. But it's not left me, I can promise you that. I still use it for thinking.'

The house was tidy enough and Innes had even made his bed before going off to work that morning. Thinking herself lucky that it was her youngest who had been left to fend for himself, and not James or Bethany, Jess dusted the place and set the table, then started preparing the evening meal.

Her mind was so full of Jacob and his sudden arrival, after all those years when she had heard nothing from him or about him, that she had peeled three times the quantity of potatoes needed before she realised what her hands were doing. She clicked her tongue in annoyance. Now she would have to put most of them into a bucket of water in the wash-house, to use over the next day or two.

She had bought three plump herrings for the dinner, one for herself, one for Innes and one to be taken along to Meg, but on second thoughts she covered them with a plate and put them away in the larder, then retrieved some potatoes from the bucket and added them to the pot on the stove. They could be cooked today and fried tomorrow. Jacob would probably enjoy a traditional meal of fried potatoes and herring coated in oatmeal. Tonight she would use the mince she had bought for the next day.

Innes was surprised and disconcerted when he came home from work to find his mother bustling about the kitchen and the table set for two.

'You're not going to eat at Auntie Meg's then?'

'Not tonight. She's more able to move around now and I told her I'd take some dinner along after I got the pots washed.'

'So you're sleeping at her house tonight?'

'Aye, but I think this'll be the last time I'll have to leave you on your own, for she's well on the mend, providing she takes proper care of herself.' She lifted the lid from a pot and stirred its contents, then turned and flapped her hands at him. 'Off you go and get washed, the dinner's nearly ready.'

His mind was in turmoil as he went to the wash-house. Only one more short night with Zelda in his arms, one more morning of waking to see her hair spread over his pillow and her pretty, sleep-flushed face close to his. He washed hurriedly and put on clean clothes, then returned to the kitchen feeling like a condemned man who has just been told the date of his execution.

'Are you sure about leaving Auntie Meg alone at nights? I don't mind seeing to myself.'

'You're a good lad,' Jess said with a sudden rush of affection. 'You've not once complained about being left on your own, and you're the first man I've ever known to make his own bed without being forced to it.'

'Och, that? It's easy enough done.'

'To tell the truth, I'm hankering after my own bed and I think me and Meg are getting on each other's nerves. I'm sure she'll be as pleased as me to get back to her own ways, for it's never a good thing to have two women in one kitchen. Mind you,' she went on as she helped him to more potatoes, 'neglect hasn't done you any harm. You're looking right well these days.'

'I've not been neglected, Mother. You've left a good supper out for me every night.'

'And from now on I'll be here to put it on the table for you and eat it with you, too. Oh . . . there'll be a visitor coming for his dinner tomorrow night,' she added casually.

'Who's that?'

'Jacob MacFarlane, a man I knew before you were born. His family lived next door to mine in Portessie, but they all moved away once they were grown.' It was the simple truth; no need for Innes to know that she herself had been the cause of Jacob leaving the Moray coast.

'So what brings him back?'

'Some kind of business. We met at the harbour this

afternoon.' The tea was well mashed by now; she got up and brought the teapot from the stove to the table, pouring the liquid – black in the way the fisher-folk liked it – into two big cups. ''Are you meeting Zelda later?'

'Aye,' Innes said casually, reaching for his cup. 'I said I'd look in at the farm to see if she'd an hour off.'

On her way to Buckie, Zelda would pass an old ruined cottage where they sometimes met. Innes got to it in good time and waited, sheltering behind one of the better remaining walls. When he heard footsteps approaching he called softly so as not to scare her, then stepped out to meet her as she ran towards him, a small shape in the dark night. As he caught and held her he felt as though his heart was breaking, and she was just as dismayed when he told her the news.

'Oh, Innes, what'll we do?'

'I don't know, lass.' He buried his face in her hair. 'It's like being taken to the gates of Heaven, then having them slammed in your face just when you think you're going to be allowed in.' His voice was muffled.

'We'll have to save every penny we can for a place of our own.' She drew back slightly. 'You still want to wed me, don't you, Innes?'

'Want to? It's all I do want, but it's going to take so long to get our own place, Zelda.'

'It's like walking – you keep at it, and then one day you find that you're there.' She reached up and kissed him, her nose cold against his face. 'We'll just have to think about that all the time. What about tonight?'

'My mother was at the house when I left, but she should be gone by now. She's spending one more night with Auntie Meg.'

'And Mrs Bain says I can stay at home tonight, so we're all right.'

'For the last time!'

'Since that's the way of it,' Zelda said firmly, linking

her hand in his and pulling him away from the cottage's tumble-down walls, 'then we must make the most of it, my bonny lad.'

Once Innes had gone out, Jess swept and scrubbed and polished until the house was as clean as she could make it. Jacob, with his fine clothes and his elegant way with words, must have been in some grand houses in his time. Perhaps to his eyes the cottage she had shared with Weem and their children would seem very small and shabby, she thought, then caught herself up sharply. What did it matter what he thought? This cottage had served her and her man and children well. It was clean and neat, with not a thing in it that hadn't been paid for, and if Jacob MacFarlane had become too grand for the likes of a fisherman's dwelling place then that was his problem. If he had stayed in the close huddle of cottages that was Portessie this was just the sort of home he would have had himself, and he would have been contented enough with it.

If he had stayed . . . Jess sank on to her usual fireside chair, the duster still clutched in her hand, remembering. He would have stayed, would have been happy to stay and spend the rest of his life fishing the Firth and the seas around Britain, if it had not been for Weem Lowrie.

There had never been a spoken pledge between her and Jacob, but for as long as she could remember there had been an understanding between them as they progressed from babyhood to childhood, then to young adulthood. Even although Jacob, the shyest of the three MacFarlane boys, had never gone beyond a few sweet gentle kisses when they happened to find themselves apart from the others, Jess had been content in the knowledge that one day – when they both felt the time was right – there would be more than kisses.

But the future was never certain and for her everything changed unexpectedly, with a surge and a rush that had swept all sense from her head and her heart. Working

at the farlins in Yarmouth, she had met up with Weem
Lowrie, who had no time at all for gentle kisses. Weem
took what he wanted, and as soon as he set eyes on her
he wanted Jess Innes.

Even now, with her body thickened by childbearing and
a lifetime of hard work, the pit of Jess's stomach clenched
and she caught her breath sharply as she recalled those
Yarmouth nights when Weem had contrived to get her
on her own. She remembered the sweet confusion and
delight into which his loving had spun her, thrilling and
bedevilling her. She remembered lying awake in the
lodgings when the other lassies were asleep all about
her, savouring over and over again the precious moments
she had shared with him.

And she remembered with bitter clarity the day she had
told Jacob that she was carrying Weem's child.

She had expected him to turn from her, disgusted and
repelled, but instead he had stood his ground, those sea-
green eyes of his blazing. 'He'll not wed you, Jessie, his
sort never do. But I'll marry you gladly, bairn and all.'

'He's said he will. We've set the date.'

He had argued, begged, then when he realised that she
was lost to him the light had gone out of his eyes and he
had cried, standing before her, hands by his sides; cried
silently but with his head up, making no attempt to conceal
the tears. When she tried to offer comfort, appalled by the
hurt she had dealt him, Jacob had stepped back, shaking
his head, refusing to let her touch him. Finally he had
wiped the moisture from his cheeks with a rough motion
of one hand and said, 'You really think the likes of Weem
Lowrie can make you happy?'

'I hope so.'

'He'll break your heart,' Jacob told her in a flat, empty
voice. 'He'll never be able to love you as I do.' Then he
had gone to seek out Weem, who had laughed at him and,
when Jacob flew at him, had beaten him soundly down on
the harbour in front of a crowd of men.

The next day Mrs MacFarlane came to the door, distraught, to tell Jess that Jacob had gone. It was clear from the woman's voice, and from the bitterness in her eyes, that she knew why her son had left and where to lay the blame. Jacob had never returned and within a year both his brothers had followed him; one, Jess heard, to crew with him on a fishing boat out of the English port of Whitby, the other to join the Navy. By then Jess had married Weem and was settled in Buckie, with wee James to care for and Bethany on the way.

Jacob had probably been surprised to find out from his sister that the marriage between Jess Innes and Weem Lowrie had survived until death, she thought, rubbing absently with the duster at an imaginary mark on the polished table. And that Weem hadn't broken her heart after all.

Then, remembering the rift between herself and James, now that her husband's bones lay in Rathven Cemetery instead of at the bottom of the sea, and her own aching sense of guilt over what she had done to Weem, she wondered if perhaps Jacob had been right after all.

14

Jem, who had been left on watch overnight, was too inexperienced to read the weather signs properly. The sudden squall had arrived out of nowhere, giving Albert Lowrie no time to bring in his nets and run for shelter. When the crew – alerted by a wave that lifted the boat high, then slammed it down again, bouncing them out of their bunks – raced on deck, the wind, screaming out of the dark, slapped them hard and took the breath from their lungs.

'Ye bloody loon!' Albert screamed at his son as, with a rending sound only just heard above the scream of the gale, the mizzen ripped, to hang in tatters. 'Why did ye no' call me up long afore this?'

'I didnae think . . .' The words were ripped from the lad's mouth. His eyes were wide with the horror of what was happening, the shock of its suddenness.

'You'll have plenty to time to think when you're down below, lookin' up at them nets above ye!'

'Never mind that now,' James yelled. He had been thrown hard from his bunk when the first wave struck, and he could almost feel the bruising coming up on his right arm. Even so, he felt his body tingling, coming alive, joyously preparing to meet the sea on its own terms and win. 'Get the capstan started, stand by to haul or we'll lose the lot! Jem, into the hold with you.'

Lights from the other vessels strewn across the fishing

grounds were sparking out and in again as the boats slid down into the well of the waves, then fought their way back up to the crests. The grey-black water was lanced with ragged white flashes as the gale snatched at the tips of the waves, ripping and tearing them into foam.

The boat danced, bucked and shied, and the crew had a fight on their hands to bring the first net, well filled with herring, to the surface. Each time the *Fidelity* rolled hard to starboard, dipping beneath the water and taking in green seas that swirled round their legs, threatening to pluck them from the deck and hurl them into the deep, the men hauled back hard; they deftly pinned the messenger to the bulwark by one knee, so that when the boat lifted again her bulk and weight lifted the net a little further out of the water.

When the dawn light came it was cold and grey, and only served to reveal the full extent of the storm. At times it seemed that there was no sky at all, only great walls of water bearing down on the boat like hungry grey wolfhounds, their foam-white teeth bared and eager to crunch and smash the drifter and her crew into oblivion.

James wondered, during a brief respite while they braced themselves and waited for the roll of the boat to aid them in easing the nets a little further from the sea, whether the inland folk who enjoyed a nice herring for their breakfast or their dinner ever gave a thought to how it was caught. Then, as the boat lifted and he felt his muscles and sinews stretch to snapping point and his joints threaten to come apart under the terrible strain of holding on to the net, habit took over and all thought fled.

Yelling above the sea's thunder and the sharp whine of the winds, James struggled to spur the others on, while he himself worked harder than he had ever worked before, desperate to get all the fish in before his uncle's nerve went. But he did not manage to save the final net, for Albert insisted on emptying it so that it could be hauled in easily while the boat turned to run before the heavy seas,

leaving behind a great mass of dead fish tossing belly-up
on the mountainous waves.

'Bloody dogfish!' Albert grunted as he spotted several
great holes in the empty net. Dogfish fed on herring,
and when they found themselves trapped along with
their quarry they used their vicious teeth to tear their
way free.

'The nets'll mend, but there's no recovering the fish
we left behind,' James told him.

'We've got plenty.'

'We could have had more.'

'We could have been at the bottom of the sea . . . and
more likely would be, if you had your way,' his uncle
snapped at him and stamped below, leaving James to
clear the few herring that had been brought aboard with
the final net.

Disentangling a limp fish and flipping it into the hold,
he decided that he had no option in the next season but
to become a member of Davie Geddes's crew – a fisher
for the Lord, as Davie proudly put it. That part would not
be easy, for James had never been one for religion, but
he would have to learn to thole it. At least Stella would
be pleased, he thought morosely.

It would also mean making a move from steam to sail,
but that didn't trouble him for he had learned his trade
on the sailed boat that his father had skippered before the
Fidelity and some of his most exhilarating experiences had
happened there. James grinned, recalling one storm more
vicious than the one they were running from, when the
boat had been tossed on raging, white-capped seas like a
leaf being carried down a rain-flooded gutter. The wind
had screamed like a harpy through the rigging, causing
the sails to crack like thunder and belly out until young
James, half-thrilled and half-terrified, was certain that he
could see the powerful mast bending like a bow beneath
the strain of trying to hold on to them.

That voyage was his third, and as the storm grew instead

of abating, he became convinced that they were all – boat and crew – set for a watery grave and that he would never see land, or his mother or Bethany, again. The fear mounted until he wanted to scream it aloud, to beg the wind to go away and the sea to leave them alone. He wanted to demand that his father take him home at once and stop frighting him, but when he turned to look at Weem, steady as a rock behind the wheel, fighting to keep his boat afloat and get his catch home, James's fear ebbed, replaced by the knowledge that his father would not let him die. In any case, if drowning was the right death for Weem Lowrie, then it was the right death for his son, too.

When at last the storm let up and they had time to draw breath, Weem asked, 'Were you frighted, son?' And James had shaken his head violently. 'No.'

To his surprise, his father said, 'Well, you should have been, for it's only right for men like us to be afraid of the sea's tempers. You need to give her her place, James. She's like a woman, and you'll find out for yourself when you're older that women need to be respected sometimes, and gentled sometimes, and coaxed sometimes. Aye, and pushed sometimes too, but you have to be sure of them before you can go the right way about that. You'll learn.'

Learn he had, about the sea and about women too. And he had had more success with the sea, since the 'herring fever' – a burning desire to fish all the seas of the world in search of the silver darlings – was in his blood.

He would bide his time, and when he was master of Davie Geddes's sailed boat, James swore to himself, he would show all of them – Albert Lowrie included – how a real fisherman went about his business.

'Is that all the barrels you've filled?' Gil came storming down the line of women. 'What's the matter with the lot of you?' He pointed to the mountain of herring waiting to be shovelled into the farlins when there was room. 'There's more boats due in and more herring on the way, and I'm not minded to be kept on working here all night just because you're too busy chattering.'

'The work's being done all right.' Bethany took a minute to straighten her aching back and draw her forearm across her brow to clear it of sweat, which chilled as soon as it burst from the pores. 'We can use our hands and our tongues at the same time.'

It was almost midday, cold and grey with a sharp wind, and not many people lingered to watch the lassies work, but those who did pressed a little closer, interested in the promise of a quarrel. Ever since Bethany had refused to move into lodgings with him, Gil had been in a black mood, watching the women at the farlins like a hawk hovering over a dovecote, bullying and nagging at the slightest opportunity. They were all, Bethany knew, on a short fuse.

Even the buyers, eyes narrowed and faces absorbed as they studied the barrels already packed, mentally transferring the fishermen's and fisher-lassies' work into profit and loss, sensed the air of tension and drama and edged a little nearer so as to be in on any confrontation.

The other women had the sense to keep on working, though their eyes were watchful and their faces tight with a resentment that Bethany could feel as keenly as she could feel the wind trying to burrow beneath the layers of wool she wore below her big oilskin apron.

'Well, use your hands a bit more and your tongues a bit less. Wait . . .' Gil rounded on Isa, who had just finished spreading the first layer in her barrel and was scooping up a double handful of salt to scatter over it. 'Are you packing those barrels properly?'

The woman's face, reddened by the cold, took on a deeper hue. 'Of course I am.'

'I'll not have my customers getting short weight or having the fish spoiled because it's not packed right.' He elbowed her aside to check the barrel for himself. 'Fish that's been properly packed should stay right where it is, even if the barrel's shattered round it,' he blustered on, glaring round the farlins. 'Mind now, I'll not have poor workers in my teams!'

As he stalked away Isa made an obscene gesture behind his back and mouthed an oath, then glared at the others. 'There's nothin' wrong with my work!'

'Of course there isnae, lass. What's up with that man of yours, Bethany?' Effie wanted to know. 'He's been going round all this week with a face like a skelpit arse.'

'Asking for a skelpit arse, more like,' one of the women muttered and a peal of laughter rippled up and down the farlins.

'How should I know what's wrong with him?' Bethany bent again to her business, the knife in her hand flashing through one fish after another.

A gutter further down the line leaned forward to ask sharply, 'Have you been clyping to the man?'

'What would I have to clype about?' Bethany was enraged by the suggestion that she might tell tales. 'I'm here to work, the same as you.'

'So you say.' The muttered words were pitched just loudly enough to reach her ears. Despite the cold she felt her face burn.

'We could do the work better without his nagging. I've never known Gil Pate so bad-tempered before. It's not as if we're all that well paid for standing out here in all weathers, while the coopers stay warm by the fire.' It was clear that Effie, well respected among the fisher-lassies, was deeply offended. 'He wants to watch his tongue – where would he be if we decided to stop work?'

A murmur of agreement ran along the row of women and Isa chipped in with, 'I've a good mind to look for work with one of the other coopers.' She shot a venomous glance at Bethany.

'You'd not do that, surely. It was me who brought you

here to take my Aunt Meg's place.' Bethany's natural impulse was to tell the woman to do whatever she wanted, but if she did that they would all be against her. 'Stay for my sake, Isa.'

'I don't know. Fourteen years I've been a packer and nobody's ever shouted at me the way he did today.'

They were all good workers, tried and tested and loyal too, but Bethany knew that today Gil had pushed them to the limit, and one more contrary word from him would be enough to make them down tools and return to their lodgings. Unless something was done, and done quickly, he would lose not only his teams, but also the fish that must be pickled before it spoiled.

On impulse she pushed her gutting knife into her pocket and left the farlins, marching over to the great mountain of barrels that had been left to settle, then be topped up and covered in readiness for the carters. She tugged at one, but to her frustration it was too heavy for her to manage on her own.

'Duncan . . .' She beckoned to the nearest cooper. 'Over here.'

He came at a run. 'What is it, missus?'

'Give me a hand to take that barrel back to the farlins.'

'Eh?' He gaped at her. Then, as she roared at him, 'Do as I say!' he hastened to ease the barrel upright. The two of them manoeuvred it across to where Isa stood, then Bethany held out her hand.

'Now, give me your hammer.' Duncan automatically did as he was told. By now all the women had stopped work and gathered round, the loiterers pressing close behind them.

'Give me room,' she ordered, gripping the heavy hammer in both hands. The look on her face and the tone in her voice swiftly cleared a reasonable space around her.

As she hefted the hammer, wondering if she was going to manage its considerable weight, Gil burst through the growing crowd. 'What's going on here?'

'Since you're so set on finding out if Isa's packed the barrels properly, we'll do it the right way. You've said often enough that if a well-packed barrel fell apart the fish should stay in place without it.' Bethany lowered the head of the hammer and adjusted her footing in the mud. 'I'm testing Isa's work for you.'

'You're what? Stop this nonsense at once!'

She ignored him, glancing instead at the other woman. 'All right, Isa?'

'Aye . . . oh, aye. You go ahead, lassie. I've got nothing to worry about, and I doubt,' Isa flashed a malevolent glance at Gil, 'if that barrel needs much of a dunt to make it fall apart.'

Fidelity had outrun the sea storm, and now James, worn out from the night's struggle, was on his way to the nearest pub after making sure that her decks had been cleared and cleaned and all made ready for her next voyage. Noticing an unusual number of people hurrying across his path, seemingly heading for the farlins where the Scottish fisher-lassies worked, he slowed and hesitated. Then, as a cheer went up from somewhere beyond the clustered backs, he gave in to curiosity, pushing his way through the growing knot of folk until he came across his cousins Jem and Charlie.

'What's up?'

'It's your Bethany,' Charlie told him gleefully. 'It's as good as a turn in the music halls – she's taking a hammer to one of Gil's barrels and he's near havin' apoplexy.'

'What?' James used his square shoulders to carve a path deeper into the crowd, until he was stopped short by the fisher-lassies themselves who, their work now forgotten, were standing in a tight group at the end of one of the farlins cheering and shouting. Stretching to his full height, he had a good view over their scarved heads of Gil, who did indeed look as though he might collapse with a stroke at any moment, and Bethany, clutching

a large hammer. Between them stood a full barrel of
herring.

'Come on now, Bethany, you show him!' one of the
women shrilled, and as the rest took up the chorus Gil's
crimson face deepened to purple.

There was no going back now for Bethany. She straddled
her feet, shifting her hips to balance her body properly,
and began to heave the hammer up and back. The cloths
tied round her fingers to protect them during her work
helped her to grip the broad wooden shaft, and once she
had started the lift it gathered momentum.

'Bethany . . . !' Gil appealed to her, his voice almost
drowned in a burst of cheering from the onlookers as the
hammer-head swung up and back, forcing her to shift
her foothold again quickly in order to avoid being pulled
backwards by its weight.

Gil cast a despairing glance at his men, but although
they were as interested as anyone else they all made a
point of avoiding eye contact with him. None of them
was willing to try to get the hammer away from Bethany
or to fall foul of her supporters.

He looked back at his wife, then as the hammer set out
on its downward path, he shouted, 'Wait! Stop!'

It was too late to halt the hammer's momentum, but
Bethany managed to twist her body round slightly, just
far enough to avoid her original target, the upper rim
of the barrel. The hammer-head sliced viciously through
the air between husband and wife and thudded into the
ground, narrowly missing one of Gil's feet, before she
let the shaft slip from her hands and staggered back to
lean against the farlins, breathless. A roar of approval
burst from everyone but Gil; even the coopers standing
behind him, out of his sight, were applauding.

'You'll accept that Isa can pack as good a barrel as
anyone, then?' Bethany wheezed, one hand pressed tightly
to her chest.

'Aye, I suppose so . . . if it'll get the lot of you back to work. Come on now, or I'll dock your wages,' he bellowed, swinging round on the women. As they scurried back to the farlins he snatched the hammer up in one hand, as though it weighed nothing at all, and drove his own men, suddenly subdued, back to their duties by the brazier.

'That lassie's got spirit,' commented a man standing by James. 'She's a bonny fighter – and a bonny looker, too.'

'She's my sister,' James told him coolly, then pushed his way through the crowd to stand by Bethany. 'Are you all right?'

'What are you doing here?'

'Watching the circus act,' he said drily. 'I'm asking, are you all right?'

'I'm fine, though I think I've stretched my arms a good inch or so.'

'You could have done yourself damage trying to throw that thing around. It's over-heavy for a woman.'

'Gil had to be taught a lesson. He's been right crabbit all week and the women have had enough of him.'

'He's been taught, right enough. If you were a man I'd buy you a dram for what you've just done.'

She smiled wryly at him, the first smile he had seen from Bethany for many a long day. 'I wish I was a man,' she said, 'for I could fairly do with that dram.'

Word of Bethany's stand against Gil swept over the vast harbour and that night gutters and packers from the other farlins arrived at the Scottish fisher-lassies' lodgings, eager to hear the true facts of the story. As Isa said, the place was as full of visitors as it was on a Sunday afternoon.

'It's high time one of us stood out against the menfolk,' one of the local women said. 'They never think of the way we've to stand at the farlins in all weathers, or the back-breaking job and the hours we work. And what do we get for it?' She glared round at the great crowd of women filling the loft. 'A pittance, that's what. Tenpence for every barrel filled. Tenpence to be shared between three women.'

She put her huge hand on Bethany's. It felt as strong and heavy as a plank of wood and it was covered with scars gathered during years of hard work at the farlins. All gutters packed their cuts with a poultice made by chewing pieces of bread; it was an effective treatment, but as the edges of the wounds were kept apart it resulted in heavy scarring. 'If the man that employs you tries to make you suffer for what you did, pet,' the woman said, 'just you let me know. Sal Whitton's my name and everyone in Yarmouth knows where to find me. It's time we took a stand together and looked after our own.'

'He'll not do anything to Bethany,' Isa scoffed. 'He's her own wedded husband.'

Sal's eyes widened. 'You gave your own man a showing up in front of all those folk? You've more courage than I thought.'

'She has that,' Kate said proudly.

'Husband or none, I mean what I say – if he does bother you, then let me know. We'll not have any man causing grief to one of the fisher-lassies.'

'To be fair to Gil, he's not usually a bad employer,' Effie spoke up. 'But he's had some flea in his lug all this week. I don't know what's amiss with him.' She dug Bethany in the ribs with a sharp elbow. 'Mebbe he's missing his comforts, what with you biding in the loft with the rest of us. Men can get awful narky when they've to go without.'

'If that's all it is, tell him he can move in with us and welcome,' Maggie suggested. 'We don't mind the two of you being nice and comfy right here. We could do with a bit of entertainment at night.'

'That's kind of you . . . I'll tell him about it right away,'

Bethany shot back. 'And I'll mind him that while I'm a guttin quine I work in a team, so he'll need to take on Kate and Isa, too. That should put a smile on his face.'

It was a relief to hear the scream of laughter thundering up and down the length of the room and to know that she had managed to turn aside their animosity towards Gil. Bethany regretted the way in which she had humiliated him, but sometimes humiliation was the only lesson men like Gil understood. There had been no need for him to bully her fellow workers just because of his frustration and anger with her.

Some of the visitors had brought food and others had brought bottles; as time passed the evening developed into a party, with the women roaring with laughter as they vied with each other over what they would like to do to the men who worked them so hard and valued them so little. Sal in particular had a sadistic turn of mind and every time the door opened Bethany glanced over nervously, hoping that Gil wouldn't take it into his head to come looking for her. If he walked in on all those women in the mood they were in, there was no knowing what might happen.

15

Gil Pate sulked among the other coopers for the rest of the day and after work he went with his brother Nathan to the White Lion, a public house popular with Scots fishermen, to drown his sorrows. By the time James met up with them Gil, egged on by his brother, was in a surly mood.

'I suppose you heard all about it?' he grunted as soon as James sat down opposite.

'I did better than that. I saw it for myself.'

Gil, elbows on the table, glared up at his brother-in-law from beneath his eyebrows. 'What's the matter with that woman?'

'How should I know? She's your wife, not mine.'

'She's your sister.'

'We've scarce exchanged more than half a dozen words in the past year.'

'I've not heard much more than that from her myself. She's a sullen bitch, with a right temper on her.'

James shrugged and took a deep drink before saying, 'You must have known that before you married her, so why did you take her for your wife?'

'Because she's the sort of lass every man wants to find in his bed when he wakens in the morning,' Nathan suggested with a snigger. Gil glowered at him.

'You watch your mouth! I married her because my bairns needed a mother.' He started to lever himself to his feet.

'And you needed some comfort for yourself.' Nathan was undeterred. 'You cannae fool us, man. You couldnae keep your eyes or your hands off that lassie, even when your bairns had a mother.'

Gil had begun to move away from the table, but now he turned suddenly and leaned on the scarred wooden boards, bending so that his face was close to his brother's. 'I told you, Nathan, guard that tongue of yours. If you don't, I'll take it out of your throat and wrap it around your neck with my bare hands,' he said softly, menacingly, then elbowed his way through the crowd.

'Has he eaten anything?' James wanted to know and Nathan shook his head.

'He wasnae in the mood for eating, just drinking.'

'You should get some food inside him. The drink on an empty stomach's making him dangerous.'

'It's not the drink; it's that sister of yours that has him so's he doesn't know where he is. He's right, she is a sullen-tempered bitch.'

James thought of Bethany as he had seen her that afternoon, angry and determined, struggling to lift the heavy hammer up high enough to strike the barrel. He recalled the almost comic little dance-step she had had to perform in order to avoid the barrel as the hammer began its downward sweep and Gil roared his submission. He remembered her faint, wry grin and felt his own temper beginning to stir.

'I've got no quarrel with Gil when he miscries her, for she's his woman and he's got a right to say as he pleases. But I'll not take it from you, Nathan.'

The man shrugged indifferently, but said no more. Soon Gil rejoined them and James started trying to get him to go back to his lodgings, where his evening meal would be waiting. But his brother-in-law had other ideas.

'I'll not put a morsel into my mouth till I've sorted this business out with Bethany,' he announced, staggering to his feet again.

'Tonight? Best leave it until tomorrow, when you're rested and clearer in the head,' James said, alarmed.

'I cannae rest till I speak to her . . .' Gil set off towards the door with James in pursuit and Nathan tagging along behind. Outside, the fresh cold air hit the cooper and he reeled, clutching at a lamp-post for support as his knees gave way beneath him.

'I'll be all righ'. I'll be . . . all righ',' he said peevishly, swatting James away as he tried to help.

'You'd be the better for some hot food in your belly and a good sleep. Come on now, Nathan and me'll see you to your lodgings.'

At first Gil showed signs of going along with the idea, but they had scarcely peeled him from the lamp-post and set off, with Nathan guiding his erratic steps on one side and James on the other, like a couple of tugs assisting a big ship downriver to the open sea, when he changed his mind.

'Bethany bides this way.'

James caught him as he tried to change direction. 'I know, but you live this way.'

'We should be together, James. A man and his wife should be together, d'you not think so?' Gil clutched at him. 'It's not right for a woman to sleep apart from her own legal husband, not when they're in the same town.'

'Mebbe not, but your lodgings are nearer than hers, so come on.'

'I found a room for the two of us together, James, but she wouldnae share it with me. And I miss her! My wee Bethany – I miss her!' Alcoholic tears sprang to the cooper's eyes.

'You're daft, man. If your woman refuses to share your bed, you should seek elsewhere for what you want,' Nathan broke in. 'I know the very house – we'll get something to eat first, then you can come with me. The lassies that bide there know how to make a man welcome, for a price. You'll come too, James?'

'I've never had need of company I'd to pay for.' James felt his skin crawl at the very thought. His own marriage might not be what he wanted, but he thanked God that he had never been driven to lie with whores and prostitutes.

'It's just you and me, then, Gil. There's women in that house can do things you've never dreamed about,' Nathan said eagerly.

'I don't want other women, I want Bethany!' Gil wailed, but his brother lost patience with him.

'God knows why. There's my mother having to go to Buckie to look after your bairns because your precious Bethany won't do it. And here's you in a right state because she'll not share your bed. How can you speak of her like that, right after she made a fool of you in front of the whole harbour . . . ?'

'Leave it, Nathan,' James warned, but he was ignored.

'I'm telling you, Gil, you're best off without her. A decent woman wouldn't have done what she did to you today. If you must go to her then go, but for God's sake don't slobber over her. Give the bitch a good hiding and then mebbe she'll make a better wife.'

Nathan's tirade ended in a strangled squeak as the cooper's big hand caught at his throat. 'Up here, you,' Gil stormed, dragging the smaller man into a pend. 'I told you already that I'll not have my wife miscalled.'

'Gil!'

Gil paid no heed to James, for he was too intent on making his way along the passageway, reeling and bouncing off the walls as he went. Since he was still gripping Nathan's throat the curer, too, was staggering against the damp stone walls, yelping at every thud.

'Gil!' James dived after them and caught up with them in a dark back court. After a moment's determined wrestling he managed to free Nathan, who slumped against the wall of the court, choking and wheezing. 'Stop making a fool of yourself, man, and get off home!'

Gil, breathing heavily, concentrated on steadying himself. 'Home? My home's in Buckie with Bethany and my bairns, not in this place!'

'Get back to your lodgings, I mean. Things'll sort themselves out in the morning.'

'A'right, James, a'righ',' Gil held up his large hands in an appeasing gesture. 'Back to the lodgings. A'righ'.' He began to stagger towards the pend then added, just as James thought he was getting somewhere, 'But first I'm going to teach our Nathan to keep his tongue off my wife!'

'You'll not, for I'll not let you. There's been enough carrying on today as it is.' James moved to stand before Nathan, who was still bent double, catching his breath.

'Then I'll see to you first and him after,' Gil growled, and swung his arm up and out in a wide arc, using his big knotted fist like a club. James dodged to one side, hearing a shout of agony as his heel, in its sturdy, iron-studded fisherman's boot, landed four-square on Nathan's toes. He felt a breeze brush against his face as Gil's fist swept through the air then continued on its way. In his drunken state the cooper was forced to go with the swing of his arm, his feet slapping and stumbling all over the place in an ungainly dance until they tangled with each other and sent him down with a crash.

As James watched, ready to dodge again if need be, and Nathan hopped about on one foot, cursing, Gil began to pull himself to his knees. He had almost managed it when his stomach suddenly and violently rejected the drink he had been pouring into it all evening. For several minutes he spewed helplessly before toppling sideways, very slowly, to the ground.

'You damned near broke my foot,' Nathan yelped.

'Think yourself lucky, for Gil would have done worse if he'd managed to hit you. Gil?' James bent and shook his brother-in-law's shoulder. It felt slack beneath his grip. Gil began to snore softly.

'He did enough, banging me off that wall and trying to squeeze the life out of me. The bastard,' Nathan added, darting towards the inert mass on the ground. As the toe of his boot found its mark, Gil's body quivered and he grunted and tried to lift his head. Then it fell back and he started snoring again.

'That's enough! I'll not have you beating the man when he's not able to defend himself!' James put himself between the brothers for the second time. 'I hope you're fit, for we're going to have to carry him back to his lodgings. I doubt if he'll stir till morning. At least he didn't fall face first into his own vomit. If he had, he could have lain here all night far as I'm concerned.'

As he and Nathan laboured to get the big cooper on to his feet, James realised that at least he had achieved his original purpose. His sister would not be troubled by a visit from an irate husband tonight.

'That,' Jacob MacFarlane said contentedly, 'is the best meal I've had since I last tasted my mother's cooking.'

'It was nothing much, but I'm glad you enjoyed it.' Jess tried to hide her pleasure.

'Nothing much? If I could just know for certain that they serve fried potatoes and herring in oatmeal in Paradise, I'd go there happily when my time comes.' Jacob edged his chair back from the table and caressed his stomach with both hands. 'You're a fortunate man, Innes, to get food like this as often as you do.'

'Aye,' Innes agreed with a wan smile. Fortunate indeed, when his mother was going to sleep in her own house from now on, keeping him and Zelda apart.

'Are you all right, son?' she asked, peering at him. 'You're awful quiet.'

'I'm fine. I was just thinking, there's a job needs finishing back at the smithy. The farmer's coming to fetch it tomorrow, so if I could manage to see to it tonight . . .'

'D'you have to?' Jess asked as he got to his feet.

'Can it not wait until the morning? We've a visitor, Innes.'

'Don't mind me, lad, just you go ahead. Your mother and me have a lot of talking to catch up on.'

'Well, if it's all right . . .' Innes muttered, reaching for his coat. There was no job to be finished and no Zelda to cuddle either, for she was wanted at the farm that night. But his mind and his body were both in turmoil and he felt that if he didn't get out into the night air he would suffocate.

'He's a fine lad,' Jacob said when the door closed behind Innes.

'He's a good son and I think the world of him.'

'More like you than Weem, I would say.'

'James and Bethany were Weem's bairns from the start.'

'I'm looking forward to meeting them.'

'They're both in Yarmouth for the fishing and they'll not be back for a good few weeks yet.'

'I'm not in any hurry to leave the Firth.'

'Have you not got work to go back to? Or a family, mebbe?' she probed gently.

'I never married, Jess, and there's nobody waiting for me anywhere. As to the other, I work for myself now, so my time's my own.' He stood up and stretched luxuriously. 'And I've got some business in mind for the place where I was born.'

'Sit in at the fire while I see to these plates and make another pot of tea.' As she cleared the table and stacked the used dishes Jacob took his pipe and tobacco pouch from his pocket. There was a long silence as he tamped tobacco carefully into the bowl of the pipe, then she heard the scratch and fizzle of a match being ignited. It was so like having Weem back home again that her heart ached a little, and sang a little.

The pipe was going well and his head was wreathed

in sweet-smelling blue smoke by the time the tea was ready. Jess filled two thick cups and handed one over before sinking into her own chair, inhaling the aroma of the tobacco.

'What are you smiling at, woman?' Jacob wanted to know, smiling himself as he set his cup carefully on the hearth.

'I just can't believe that it's you sitting there, as large as life. I never thought to see you again.'

'You mean you'd put me out of your mind and forgotten all about me?'

'Never!'

'That's good to know, for I never forgot you, not for one single day.'

The intensity of his gaze was disturbing, but familiar. Even in childhood Jacob had had that strange ability to sit or stand for hours, just looking and looking at something that gave him pleasure – the sea, a bonny boat, her own face. She recalled, now, how he had been able to sit watching her, never seeming to tire of it. In those days it hadn't bothered her because she knew him so well, but now, after all those years apart, it was different. She reached for her knitting, anxious to have something to fix her own eyes on.

'Tell me what happened to Weem.'

'Another time, mebbe.'

'Then tell me about that lad's brother and sister.'

'James is mate to Albert, Weem's brother. You'll mind him?' she asked, then, when he nodded, 'He's skipper of the *Fidelity* now. She's the Lowrie boat, a steam drifter. Weem and Albert bought her a few years back.'

'A drifter, eh? That was a good move.'

'Bethany's married to Gil Pate, the cooper. One of his teams was a woman short this year, so she went down to work at the farlins. She and James are more like Weem than like me.'

'Thrawn, and determined to get their own way.'

'Aye,' Jess agreed and let the matter drop, relieved when Jacob began asking her about people he remembered from his childhood. When he rose to go he said, 'I hope I can call on you again, Jess.'

'Of course you can, and welcome. I'm glad to see you back,' she said on impulse.

'I should have done it a long time ago, but mebbe it's as well that I waited until now. Before might not have been the right time.' He stood in the doorway, looking out into the dark night towards the Firth, listening to the shushing of waves on the rocks. Then he looked back at her.

'You know, Jess, sometimes you have to leave a thing behind before you can find out how precious it is to you,' he said, then clapped his curly-rimmed bowler hat on to his greying head and disappeared into the night, while she was still wondering what he meant.

Gil took Bethany aside in the morning when she arrived at the farlins, drawing her behind a pile of barrels that afforded some privacy. She was aware, as she followed him, of the other women's watchful eyes.

'Well? Are they going to work for me today or are they going to tear me limb from limb?' he asked with a weak attempt at humour.

'They'll work for you, but you'd be advised to stop nagging them. Not that you're in a fit state to do any nagging today,' she added. He looked terrible. One side of his face looked as though it had been scraped along the ground, and his eyes, sunk into his head, were half-shut against the morning light. 'You've been drinking, haven't you?'

'Can you blame me? You made a right fool of me yesterday, Bethany!'

'I stopped you making a fool of yourself, more like. D'you not realise that if you'd pushed Isa any further the whole pack of them would have walked away from the farlins, and me with them, leaving you with no way of getting the herring into your precious barrels? You'd have had to go cap in hand to the English lassies for help, and that would have made an even bigger fool of you, man.'

'My teams wouldn't have walked out on me.'

'Look at them, Gil!' She threw her hand out to indicate the women huddled in groups near the farlins, all of them busy with their knitting wires but furtively watching their employer and his wife, trying to guess at what they might be saying to each other. 'Look at the place where we're going to be working for the next eight hours or more. We're ankle-deep in mud and sand and fish guts, and Maggie's had to go to the mission station so that the lady dresser can see to her hands. She scarce slept last night with the pain of the cuts and the ulcers she's got from working with the brine. And you think they'd rather be true to you than think of themselves? It was just fortunate I was here . . .'

'Fortunate, you call it? You nearly smashed one of my barrels, you damned near smashed my toes with that hammer . . .'

'I had to do something to turn their anger away. And just because I'm determined to stay with the other women, instead of sharing a bed with you, it's not right to take it out on them.' She peered up at him again. 'You've not been fighting as well, have you?'

He rubbed a hand over his face roughly, mashing his nose almost flat. 'I fell against a wall on my way home.'

'The wall fell against you, more like,' she said as the clang of a cooper's hammer against iron caused him to wince and bite his lip hard. 'You should be in your bed, sleeping it off.'

'I wish I could get back to my bed, pull the blankets over my head and never get up again. This is the best fishing season we've had in years, but for me it's the worst.'

'Just stop fussing at the women on the farlins and everything'll be fine. I'd best get back to work.'

'Wait.' He pulled a crumpled sheet of paper from his pocket. 'This letter came this morning. It's from my mother.'

Angular and grim-looking, ground deep into the texture of the paper as though written with a knife instead of a pen, Phemie Pate's handwriting was just like the woman herself. The children were well, she wrote, though she had found them sadly out of control and it had not been easy to train them into proper ways. The house had been cleaned from roof to doorstep and she herself was managing to hold her head high in Buckie, though it was not easy when the whole place was gossiping about her daughter-in-law traipsing off to Yarmouth without a thought for the well-being of the young innocents left in her care. The cold winds from the sea were screwing wickedly into Phemie's old bones and she would be grateful to her son if he saw where his duty lay and sent his errant wife home at once, thus enabling his mother to retire to her own house to recover from the burden of the duties thrust upon her, which she had accepted as the lot of a good Christian woman and devoted mother.

'I'm not going home until the work here's done.' Bethany pushed the letter back at him.

'But the wee ones . . .'

'I know from my own mother that they're fine. She takes them out most days to give Mrs Pate a rest and she'd be the first to tell me if anything was wrong.' She was heart-sorry for the little ones and felt guilty about the way she had landed them with their grandmother, but having read the letter she was more determined than ever not to return home in disgrace. 'She'll be having a grand time playing the martyr to the other old gossips. She doesn't want me back, she wants you to feel guilty. And it'll not do the bairns any harm to be with her for a few weeks. After all, she's the one that raised you and Nathan.'

'I know,' he said glumly. 'That's why I wish you'd go home.'

'I'm better here where I can look after your interests.'

'Look after . . .' Words failed him.

'You nearly had trouble on your hands yesterday, and it's not just the Scottish lassies that are getting tired of the way they're treated; it's all the women.'

'God, they're never satisfied unless they're causing bother!'

'That's not true! It's all right for you, under shelter and working beside your nice warm fire. We're out in the snow and rain and the bitter wind, and we work long, hard hours, Gil. Back-breaking work too, specially on the deep farlins.'

'Keep your voice down, they're all looking at us!'

'It costs nothing to look,' she snapped, but lowered her voice as she went on, 'I'm only here because Auntie Meg's got terrible pains in her spine from working at the farlins for years for just three or fourpence a barrel. Would you work for that amount?'

'You get wages, too.'

'A few shillings, just. And most of that goes to pay our lodgings and buy our food. Some of these women go back to their families at the end of the fishing with scarcely any money to show for their work.'

'If they were paid better they'd work less, it's always the way.'

'If they were paid better – and treated better by the likes of you – they'd mebbe be more willing. Have you never thought of it that way? I'm telling you, Gil, there's trouble in the air and that's why I'm not going back home until the English fishing's over!'

16

'I never thought to see this.' Jacob MacFarlane's voice was sombre. 'Poor Weem.'

'It comes to us all.' Jess had to fight the impulse to kneel and smooth the grassy mound over her husband, as she would have done had she been alone. She felt uncomfortable with Jacob there, but he had asked her to show him where Weem lay.

'Aye, it does, but Weem – there was something about the man that made you think it would never happen to him.'

'I wish . . .' she began, then shut her lips tightly against the next words.

'You wish you'd taken more thought before you decided to put him here? I'm not a mind-reader, Jess,' he added with a faint smile when she gaped at him. 'Your Meg told me about the stramash between you and your oldest lad when Weem died.'

'Meg's tongue's hinged in the middle. It's the fuss you make of her,' Jess scolded, 'it's turned her head!' In the few weeks since he arrived in Buckie Jacob had been accepted by the local people and had completely charmed several of them, including Jess's sister-in-law.

He laughed, a great hearty laugh that made a passer-by turn to see who could be finding humour in a graveyard. 'The man who could turn Meg Lowrie's head isn't born yet and probably never will be.'

'Then you're the closest there is to him at the moment. Not three weeks in the place and you've already got her telling you all the family secrets.'

'You don't mind me knowing about young James falling out with you over where to lay Weem to rest, do you? Meg knows that we've been friends since before we could walk, and there was no harm meant.'

Jess shrugged. 'There's no point in minding things and I'm sure she told you the right way of it. But I sometimes think mebbe I should have let him be taken back to the sea, Jacob. Most of all I find myself wishing that Albert had just let James have his way at the time, then I'd have been spared this misery of wondering and worrying over whether or not I'd done right by the man.'

He reached out to rest his hand lightly on her shoulder. 'You did what you had to do and, if I was you, I'd put the whole business out of my mind. Now, d'you think we should be getting back down that road? You promised to take Rory and Ellen out this afternoon. And,' he added, the laugh bubbling back into his voice, 'I need to have another wee practice at charming Mistress Pate.'

'You'll never manage it – not even you!' Jess had been amused at Jacob's fruitless attempts to break though Phemie's grim exterior.

'I'll keep on trying, though I'm wondering if there's anything at all behind that face and those folded arms, apart from a lump of granite or an iron pillar. Poor bairns . . . At least we can give them a happy hour or two.'

'It's good of you to spend so much time with them, Jacob.'

'Och no, I enjoy that wee laddie's chat.' He had managed to coax back some of the natural bounce and cheeriness that Rory had lost since his grandmother took charge of him. With the children Jacob behaved like a child himself, playing football with Rory and squatting beside him to study crabs and dead jellyfish – even buying him a little wooden boat that they sailed together in the rockpools. The four of them had walked for miles, with Rory scampering ahead and Ellen, when tired, being carried on Jacob's broad, comfortable shoulders.

'Were you content, you and Weem?' he asked as they set off down the road towards Buckie, leaving the graveyard behind.

'We had our quarrels, but I've no complaints.'

'Or regrets?'

'There's little sense in looking back along a road you've already walked.'

'If I'd stayed and we'd wed, I might still be a fisherman. Mebbe I'd have been father to your three.'

'Innes, mebbe, for he's a gentle, caring lad, something like yourself at his age. But never the other two,' Jess said emphatically. 'Never James and Bethany.'

'You worry about them, don't you?'

'Aye, I do that.' Jacob and Jess had spent a lot of time together since his arrival, talking and reminiscing, and getting to know each other again. There was no sense now in her denying the truth. 'They're hurting, Jacob, both of them. I can see it, but I can do nothing about it. They're neither of them happy. There's plenty who'd be content with what they have, but not James and Bethany. They've got such an energy about them. They're like . . .' she sought for the right words, 'like two bottles of fizzy drink that were shaken hard before they were opened. I've the feeling that one day the anger's going to burst out of them and the longer I wait for it to happen, the more I fret.'

'They're grown folk, Jess, not your worry now.'

'Don't be daft, man,' she snapped at him. 'Women can never walk away from their own bairns. The fretting just gets harder as they get older.'

They walked in silence for a few minutes before he said, 'I'm looking forward to meeting them.'

'They'd have been home by now if the fish hadn't been running so well.' Although it had been years since she herself was a fisher-lassie at Great Yarmouth, she vividly remembered the big harbours and the farlins. The fish supply would be slowing down now, close to the end of the season. There would be an air of finality about the place, as the days grew shorter and the weather colder, and people who had renewed old friendships prepared to say goodbye for another year.

In fact, rather more was happening in Yarmouth – events that Jess could not have begun to imagine. A few days later Meg, now completely recovered from her back trouble, came running to tell Jess that the impossible had happened. All the fisher-lassies in Yarmouth (English, Scots and Irish alike) had reached the end of their patience, and had gone on strike.

It was a splendid rebellion, fuelled by years of grievance among fisher-lassies from all over Britain's coasts. At first they were content enough to grumble among themselves as before, then the bolder women began to discuss ways of improving their lot. Finally the day came when a group of women stopped work and marched around the harbours, waving banners hurriedly made from whatever cloth came to hand.

That, as Effie said when the Scottish women raced back to their lodgings to root among their own trunks in search of lengths of cloth waiting to be made up, was the beauty of being women, with the ability to stitch and hem their own banners in no time at all.

As they paraded through the streets, singing lustily and waving their banners, the gutters and packers gathered quite a following, even among some fishermen. Female workers from the smokehouses joined them and in a few days, with the strike showing no signs of abating, union officials came hurrying from London to hold meetings with the lassies, then with the curers and smokers, who were all in a state of shock at what had happened.

With the farlins untended and the stockpile of barrels empty, the unsalted fish still on the harbourside had to be carted off hurriedly to be iced or eaten before it went bad. With nobody to gut, pickle or smoke their catches the fishermen were forced to cool their heels while their boats lay idle, crowded into the quays as tightly as matches in a box.

Since her husband was a curer and an employer, it was generally agreed (to Bethany's disappointment) that she should play no active part in any of the negotiations. She would have enjoyed the challenge and the excitement of it all – indeed, she would have welcomed a good confrontation – but Sal, who had become one of the women's leaders, put her foot down. 'When this is over and settled, as it must be one way or another, you've still to go back home and live in peace with your man. You've played your own part already; best leave the rest to us.'

So Bethany had to content herself with attending every meeting and rally, spending her free time in writing to her mother, her Aunt Meg and James's wife Stella. After a lot of thought she wrote a brief note to Rory, carefully avoiding any comments that might anger her mother-in-law, who would have to read it to the little boy. She wasn't even sure that he would know she had tried to make contact – it all depended on the woman's mood when the letter arrived.

She went to the shops and bought toys for the children; a soft rag doll for Ellen and a brightly painted train in a box for Rory. And she became so bored with her idleness that she began to wish secretly that the strike would come to an end. It was hard to hear the others talk, in the lofts, about the parades and the speeches when she herself was unable to take part.

But the strike dragged on, day following day with neither the fisher-lassies nor their employers giving ground. Mountains of stinking, rotting fish had to be carted away to be used as fertiliser in the Norfolk fields, upsetting for the women, who could scarcely abide the knowledge that good food was going to waste for want of their skilled attention. But as the strike leaders pointed out, if the lassies backed down now they would never win extra money or the respect of their employers.

Bethany had managed to keep out of Gil's way and he had not sought her out, but one evening when she was walking about the town on her own, trying to work off her growing restlessness and boredom, he stepped out of a public house just as she passed its door. They stopped short at the sight of each other and then, realising that flight would be undignified, Bethany said formally, 'How are you, Gil?'

The floodgates were immediately loosened. 'How am I? You must know how I am, woman! How could you do this to me?'

The genuine hurt in his face was hard to take. 'I've done nothing – it's all of us, all the lassies from right round the coast. We've struck because we've finally had enough, Gil. Have I not been trying to tell you that since I came here?'

'Never mind what you've been telling me; it's what you've been telling the rest of those bitches that I'm interested in!' She could smell the drink on his breath, and a fine mist of spittle sprayed across her forehead as he spoke.

'I've told them nothing. I didn't need to: they've got the sense to know when they're being treated wrong.'

'Oh aye? And even if some of them were too daft to know it, you made it very clear that day you threatened to break one of my barrels, didn't you?' he said savagely, then as she shrugged and made to turn away he caught at her arm. 'Why did you have to make such a fool of me in front of the farlins and all the rest of the folk there?'

'I told you before, I was only trying to save you from causing trouble. The way you were going that day it was a wonder the strike didn't start right there and then.'

'It's not just my livelihood that's being threatened by this senseless strike, d'you realise that? It's yours and the bairns' too, and Effie's and Kate's. Have you ever thought of Rory and the wee lassie having to go without, because of you and these other women?'

'I doubt if it'll come to that.'

'For God's sake, woman, you're my wife!'

'Let me go, Gil!' His fingers were digging painfully into her forearm and when he made no move to release her, Bethany stopped trying to pull herself away and suddenly swung in towards him, catching at one of his lapels with her free hand.

'I know I'm your wife, Gil,' she said into his face. 'I know it every minute of every day and every night. And I know that it's not my choice, it was yours and my father's.'

'Eh?' he said, bewildered and confused. 'How can you say such a thing? Did I not come out and ask you to wed me, fair and square?'

'And did you not speak to my father first, and arrange with him that you and your brother would buy all the fish the *Fidelity* caught from then on, if I agreed to have you?'

He thrust her away. 'Weem and me made a business deal. It had nothing to do with us marrying.'

'Mebbe you can make yourself believe that, Gil Pate, but not me. Never me. My father was clear enough about it at the time. He told me what to say when you came courting and I did what he wanted, because God help me . . .' it was Bethany's turn to sound bitter, 'I thought the world of the man and I always did as he said. You didn't win me, Gil – you bought me!' She spat the words at him.

It was out in the open; it was said and it could never be unsaid. She took a step back, then turned and ran.

It wasn't Gil she was escaping from, it was herself and the words that chased her, buzzing round her head like a swarm of angry bees as she ran through the streets and on to the harbourside, right along it to the entrance, with nowhere else to go other than into the River Yare below.

Briefly, staring down at the water sliding in and out of the harbour, she considered it, but the thought was rejected almost as soon as it arrived. Bethany had been born with a great hunger for life and a curiosity, always, as to what lay around the next corner. No matter what befell her she could never let go of her existence voluntarily.

She stood still, as motionless as one of the carved figureheads that had graced the old sailing ships, one hand clutching at the scarf that the wind tried to whip from her head, quite alone in the dark, windswept harbour. When her heartbeat had slowed and her lungs had stopped labouring she turned her back on the open river, walking to the other side of the harbour wall to look down on the great mass of boats, sailed and steam, squeezed into every available inch of space. Winter had arrived and soon most of the boats would be moving out of the harbours and into the open sea, homeward bound, while the lassies packed their kists and clambered aboard the lorries and carts waiting to take them to the railway station. Soon, whatever the results of the strike, she would have to go back to Buckie, back to being Gil Pate's wife. His wife, bought and paid for.

Bringing the truth out into the open did not change things after all.

The tide was out and the boats themselves lay quite a distance below her, dark and silent and empty, for after scrubbing down the decks and putting the fishing gear away there was nothing left for any of the crews to do but wait on shore until the strike was settled and they could put to sea again.

Bethany could tell *Fidelity* even in the dark; with a swift glance along the windswept harbour wall to make sure that she was unnoticed, she kilted her skirt and stooped to catch hold of the topmost rung of the iron ladder set into the stones. It was no trouble for her to cross the three intervening boats in the dark, but as she bridged the space between the third boat and the Lowrie vessel a wave swept into the harbour from nowhere, making the boats lift and dip and jostle together. Thrown off balance just as she was poised to jump, Bethany tumbled on to *Fidelity*'s deck, landing heavily on both knees. She rolled, cursing beneath her breath, then scrambled to her feet and limped into the small galley.

Closing the door, she felt for the big box of matches that was always kept by the stove, then made her way cautiously towards the hatch leading down to the fore-cabin.

The small space smelled strongly of wet oilskins, tobacco and herring, both fried and raw. At sea, when the crew were on board, the engine throbbing on the other side of the bulkhead and the stove in the galley above lit, the cabin would be stuffy, but tonight there was a bleak chill about it.

Even so, Bethany wriggled out of her jacket and hung it carefully over the porthole so that nobody happening to walk along the quay would see a telltale gleam of light from the vessel. Then she struck a match and lit the lamp. Replacing it on its hook, she sat down on the edge of a bunk and hauled her woollen stockings off so that she could examine her knees. They were both red; tomorrow they would probably be bruised, if she didn't remember to bathe them well before going to bed. She flexed and straightened them a few times to ward off the stiffness, then wriggled her way on to the bunk and rested her head on the hard, flat pillow, closing her eyes and drawing the boat's calm serenity into herself.

She was almost asleep, soothed and contented for the first time in many a long day, when the thump of boots on the deck above brought her upright, her eyes flying open. She waited, holding her breath and hoping that whoever it was had only come aboard to check on the nets or the pile of canvas buoys on the deck; then her heart plummeted as the footsteps crossed the deck and she heard the galley door open, then shut. Bethany put the lamp out, and as the new arrival began to come down the ladder to the cabin she huddled back on the bunk, pulling her stinging knees to her chin and locking her hands about them, trying to make herself as small and unnoticeable as possible.

17

It seemed to James Lowrie that the whole town was in turmoil, with not a corner to be turned without a man running into groups of morose fishermen, forced to cool their heels ashore, or fisher-lassies on the march with their flags and their shouting. The only place where he could get some peace and quiet, and time to himself, was on board the *Fidelity*. There was a half-bottle of whisky in the cabin and James was in a mood to get drunk.

He was irritated to find that whoever had used the galley matches last had not put them back in their usual place. James had no need of a light, since he felt more at home on the boat than anywhere else, but as he made for the ladder he promised himself that the guilty man would pay for his negligence in the morning. Uncle Albert was at fault again: a lax skipper meant a lax crew, and carelessness could easily cost lives on a fishing boat.

Sliding down the ladder to the cabin, he frowned as he heard a sudden shifting, scuttering sound from below. Although rats were seldom found on the Scottish fishing boats, where cleanliness was an unwritten and well-observed rule, the vessels in Yarmouth's basins were moored so closely together that it would be quite easy for vermin to travel from land to boat, and from boat to boat.

James deliberately dropped down on to the cabin deck with a great thump of booted feet, but the panicky squeaking and scampering he had expected failed to materialise. Instead, he was certain that the clatter of his arrival had been met with a sudden, soft intake of breath.

'Is that you, Charlie?' That was all he needed – the fool bringing a lassie back to the boat just when James needed some time to himself. 'Charlie?' There was no reply, but as his eyes became accustomed to the gloom he saw the glimmer of a face within the dark cave formed by the upper and lower bunks opposite. He lunged forward, and as his outstretched fingers closed on a shoulder he yanked back hard. 'Out of it, you!'

His prey kicked and struggled, fighting like a cat. Blows rained down on James's shins, but they were too light to have any effect. He thought the tussle won when he got a grip on the interloper's narrow shoulders, but then a sudden, painful and most unexpected crack on the chin jerked his head back and made him see stars for a second or two. Enraged, he shook his prisoner hard and a howl filled the small cabin.

'Let go of me!'

James stopped. 'Bethany?' he said into the darkness.

'Of course it's me!' She brought her hands up to push herself away from him and he heard a thud as she collided with the upper bench. 'Oh, my head,' she lamented. 'And you stood on my foot – you've broken it, you big daft fool!'

The salty taste of blood was strong in his mouth; he explored with his tongue and found that the blood came from a small abrasion, where the inside of his lower lip had been smashed against his teeth by his sister's hard head.

'Never mind your foot,' he snapped as he fumbled for the hanging lamp. 'Where did you put the matches?'

'Here.' Her voice was sulky. Groping in the dark, he located the box in her hand and managed to light the lamp. Its glow revealed Bethany, crouched on the edge of a bunk and nursing a bare foot.

'Let me see.' James hung the lamp up, then examined her foot, moving each toe gently. 'It's not broken, but it's going to be bruised. And so's my mouth.' He put a hand to his lips, but there was not enough blood to stain his fingers. 'You always did have a hard skull,' he recalled.

'It serves you right, sneaking on board and frighting me like that.'

Recalling his decision to get drunk, he stood up and took the bottle from the overhead cupboard, swilling liquid into a cup. 'I'm the one with the right to be here. You know fine that women don't belong on fishing boats.'

She glared up at him. 'I've a share in *Fidelity* too. I can go on board her any time I like.' She looked like a tinker-lassie, sitting on the bench with her skirt tangled about her bare legs, her hair wild and her grey eyes glittering silver malice at him in the lamplight.

James hesitated, then offered the cup to her. 'D'you want a swallow?'

'I wondered when you'd mind that you owed me a dram. At the farlins,' she reminded when he frowned at her, puzzled. 'You said if I was a man you'd buy me a dram.' She took the cup in both hands and drank deeply, choking on the raw spirit. He thumped her back as she coughed, and when the paroxysm was over she shook her head when he reached for the cup. 'Fetch another for yourself, I'm having this one.'

He did as he was told and took a long drink before sitting down opposite her. 'D'you not think that you and the rest of the lassies have caused enough trouble, Bethany, stopping work on the farlins and forcing us to keep the boats in the harbour, when they should be out at the fishing grounds?'

'Would you work for what we're paid?'

'That's different. You've got Gil to keep you.'

'There's plenty of women at the farlins have to keep themselves, and some have bairns to support and all,' she flared back at him. 'Most of these lassies are married to fishermen. What happens to them when their men are lost at sea? D'you never stop to think on that?'

James threw himself back into his own corner. 'Life's not easy for any of us. We have to make what we can of it.'

'Or what other folk make of it.'

'Listen, I came down here for a drink and a chance to think. If you want to talk, go and find someone else to natter to.'

She glowered at him but made no move to go, and when he reached for the bottle she handed her cup over silently, waiting for it to be re-filled. James wondered about the wisdom of letting his sister drink, then decided that since she was Gil's wife it was Gil's responsibility, not his.

As though reading his mind, she took a gulp from her cup then said suddenly, 'I met Gil in the street just now. I threw it in his face about the way we wed. I wish I hadn't, for it changes nothing.'

'What d'you mean, the way you and Gil wed?'

'You know . . . Da marrying me off in return for Gil and Nathan buying all the *Fidelity*'s catch.'

'You're havering.'

'I'm not. It was the same for you . . . marriage with Stella in return for her father's sailing boat, so that Father and Uncle Albert could buy the *Fidelity*.'

James shifted uncomfortably on the bunk. 'It's the whisky talking. You've had more than enough.'

'So you wanted her, then?' When he didn't answer she gave a soft, mirthless laugh. 'I was thinking, before you came in . . . D'you mind that time in Cluny harbour when Charlie dared me to dive off the wall and swim under one of the big Zulus?'

He remembered as clearly as though it had happened the day before. For a full minute he had waited and watched for her to surface from the dive; when another minute went by, then another, he began to picture himself running along the road, bursting into the kitchen to tell his mother that

Bethany was drowned. He had been on the point of hurling herself into the basin when she surfaced like a cork from a bottle, her face puce and her mouth gaping open for air.

Even thinking of it brought back the terror, the conviction that she had gone for ever. Aloud he said, 'I mind the smug grin on your face when you came up the ladder.'

This time her laugh was genuine. 'As soon as I got to the top you pushed me back into the basin.'

'No wonder, it was a daft thing to do in the first place.'

'Have you ever known me walk away from a dare?'

'You're saying that Da dared you to marry Gil?'

'No, but that's the way I felt at the time. I didn't realise that it was for the rest of my life. We're a sorry pair, James, caught in a net as tightly as any herring.'

'You don't know what you're talking about!'

'Do I not?' She had been leaning back on the bunk, but now she sat up, arms tight round her knees. 'Tell me you're contented with the thought of spending the rest of your days with Stella.' Then, as he said nothing, 'No use in it anyway, for I always know when you're lying, James Lowrie.'

He finished his drink and stood. 'It's time we were both out of here.'

'I meant what I said to you in the loft. You can use my share in the boat and I'll get Mother and Innes to agree to it too, as soon as we get back.'

'What difference would it make?' he asked wearily. 'Albert's older than me and he's got more experience, for all that I'm the better fisherman. I'd still have to dance to his tune. I've made my mind up to going to Davie Geddes's boat for the great line fishing. That's something else Albert won't do: take the boat out to catch the white fish before the herring run again.'

'You're young yet and Albert won't be going to sea for much longer. His heart's not in it.'

'And he might be thrawn enough to hand the boat

over to Charlie, or the two of us together. I'm best out of it.'

She slapped a hand down on the bulkhead by her side. 'But this is the Lowrie boat!'

'What difference does that make?'

'If I'd been born a man, I'd show you that it makes all the difference!'

'If you'd been born a man, it might be you and me quarrelling over her and neither of us any better off than we are now. It's time we were both out of here,' he said again.

'You go if you want, I'm staying for a while.'

'You're not.' She had ruined his moment of solitude and he was not of a mind to let her have hers. 'Where are your boots?'

'I don't know.' She huddled back into her corner as James knelt down and felt beneath the table until his hand came up against a leather boot.

He held it out to her. 'Put it on.'

Ignoring the boot, Bethany leaned forward and put her hand on his wrist. Her fingers were icy cold.

'James,' she said with sudden urgency, 'don't leave *Fidelity*. If you do . . .' She swallowed hard then said, low-voiced, 'It'll be the end of us all.'

'Of course it won't!'

'It will,' she insisted. 'There's something about the *Fidelity* . . . she's part of us and we're part of her. If you're not with her, then we'll just drift apart. We'll be like . . . like dead things.'

He had never heard her speak like that before. It was nonsense, but at the same time her words, and their intensity, sent a shiver down James's backbone. Looking up at her face, only inches from his as he knelt on the floor, he saw to his astonishment that her eyes were filled with a sparkling golden mesh of unshed tears. As he watched, one perfect tear spilled very slowly over her lower lid; leaving a shining trail behind, it navigated her high cheekbone, then began to slide down the soft curve of her cheek, glittering in the lamplight as it went.

Even as a very small child, scarcely able to totter across the kitchen floor without falling over, Bethany had confronted adversity and even pain with a scowl on her face and her two hands fisted by her sides. This was the first time he had ever seen her cry, and for some reason the sight of that single tear affected him so strongly that he could scarcely breathe, let alone speak. As it reached the corner of her mouth, James leaned forward, giving way to an impulse stronger than any he had ever felt before, the tip of his tongue sliding out from between his lips to catch the droplet. Drawing back, savouring the saltiness on his lower lip, he saw Bethany's silvery eyes widen.

'James . . . ?' she said, her breath warm on his cheek. Then the boot, forgotten, fell from his fingers while his free hand reached out to cup the nape of her neck and draw her close.

It was scarcely a kiss, more of a delicate, preliminary brush-stroke on an artist's virgin canvas, but as far as James Lowrie was concerned it was like a match put to a pile of dry straw. The mere sensation of her mouth against his, the smell of her skin and her hair, caused such a strength of emotion to flare up that he drew back hurriedly, startled and confused.

If Bethany had been as appalled by what had happened as he was, then perhaps his sudden, inexplicable lapse might have ended there, never to be mentioned again. But instead the astonishment in the wide clear eyes just inches from his turned to realisation and she leaned in towards him, kissing the corner of his mouth and then the angle of his jaw. James gasped with pleasure, then took her face between his two hands, claiming her mouth with his. And suddenly they were on the bunk, locked together, and the two fires had become one, all-consuming and not to be denied.

*   *   *

The fisher-lassies returned to Buckie from Great Yarmouth like warriors arriving home after a great battle, waving exultantly from the open-bed lorries to those who had gathered to meet them and heedless of the biting-cold December winds. For they had won; they had beaten the buyers and the curers who, in order to save the last of the winter's herring catch, had been forced to agree to pay an extra tuppence per barrel from then on.

'And I wasnae there for all the excitement,' Meg Lowrie lamented. 'All these years of workin' at the farlins and I wasnae there!'

'It can't be helped,' Jess tried to console her. 'Think of the extra money you'll make next year.' Meg had found work in a net factory, and when the line-fishing season came during the opening months of the new year she would work in a smokehouse. The fisher-lassies enjoyed the winter work; hard though it was, they were at least warm and dry and under cover

'You must come and tell me all about it,' Meg ordered her niece. By chance she, Jess and Jacob had been in the street when the cart carrying the women who worked for the Pates arrived from the railway station at Aberdeen, and they had intercepted Bethany as she alighted. Jacob had left the women to their talk, while he gave the lorry driver a hand with some of the heavy kists.

'There's little to tell, for I didn't do much more than marching with the rest of them and going to the union meetings.'

'Your man must have been in a right state about it all,' Meg gloated.

'Aye, he was. How have the bairns been?' Bethany asked her mother.

'Fine. Phemie's very conscientious.'

'I'm sure she is. But now I'm back,' Bethany straightened her shoulders and lifted her chin, 'she'll no doubt be more than ready to get back home. Walter,' she put a hand on the driver's arm as he returned to his vehicle, 'when d'you go on to Finnechtie?'

'After he's had a wee cup of tea at my house,' Meg said. Then, raising her voice, 'And the lassies, too, for I want to hear about Yarm'th.'

'She'll never have room for all these folk in her wee house,' Bethany said as the women flowed off the bed of the lorry to follow Meg along the street.

'She'll manage – and she'll get all the gossip she didn't get from you. Bethany, this is an old friend of mine, Jacob MacFarlane. He was once a Portessie fisherman.'

'And I don't know a single one of those lassies from the lorry.' Jacob came forward. 'Times change too fast, Jess. Mrs Pate, I'm delighted to make your acquaintance.'

'And I'm pleased to meet you, Mr . . . er . . .' Bethany cast a confused glance at her mother, then said hurriedly, 'If you'll excuse me, I've the bairns to see.'

'That,' Jacob said as he watched her hurry to her own house, 'is the most beautiful woman I have ever seen on all my travels . . . apart from yourself, Jess.'

'She's got Weem's looks.'

'I see a look of you there too.'

'Mebbe so, but in nature she's his to the very marrow.' Jess had been waiting anxiously for the day when the winter fishing ended and Bethany came home where she belonged, but now she wondered if things were going to settle down after all. There was something in her daughter's eyes, in the way she had scarcely noticed Jacob, that told Jess that the trip to Yarmouth had raised more problems than it had solved.

As soon as she stepped across the threshold Bethany knew that Euphemia Pate had stamped her own mark on every inch and thread of the house. Standing in the middle of the kitchen, waiting to welcome her daughter-in-law home, the woman was like a black-clad spider in the middle of a web.

'Gilbert's not with you?'

'He'll be back tomorrow or mebbe the next day. He'd to stay in Yarmouth on a matter of business.' After the fishing season came the bargaining and planning for the season to come, and the settling of accounts.

'The bairns havenae been too bad, I suppose . . . in the circumstances,' Phemie said dourly. 'And I gave the house a good reddin' for you from ceiling to floor. It was in sore need.'

'That was good of you.' Bethany spoke through stiff lips. The woman made her skin crawl. 'Rory, Ellen . . .'

She dropped to her knees, holding her hands out to her step-children, who hovered behind their grandmother. They stayed where they were, peering out from the shelter of Phemie's black skirt.

'You've not forgotten me, surely?'

'Bairns forget easily, that's why it's never a good idea to go off and leave them,' the harsh voice said, every word sounding like a condemnation in itself.

Looking at the little faces, sullen-eyed and withdrawn, Bethany shivered. Was it true that Rory and Ellen had forgotten her – or were children, in their purity and innocence, able to see further and deeper than adults? Could those four dull, narrowed eyes have looked right into her soul and seen there the shameful secret she had brought home with her?

'They'll get back to themselves soon enough,' she said with false cheeriness. ''Specially when they see what I've brought back for them.'

Even that failed to move them or warm the look in their eyes. Bethany put her bag down, rubbed her hands nervously together and said, 'It was very good of you to look after them for me, Mrs Pate. You must be wanting to get back to your own house.'

'I should mebbe wait for Gilbert to come home. After all, it's his bairns I've been entrusted with.'

Horror filled Bethany at the idea of spending one night,

possibly two, under the same roof as this woman – in the same bed, for there was no other place to sleep. 'No.' She put a steely edge on her voice. 'No, Mrs Pate, I'll not presume on you for one moment longer. Walter Lochrie's going on to Finnechtie within the hour and he said he'd call for you. We've time for a cup of tea before you leave.'

Hearing the older woman's sharp intake of breath, and seeing the way her nostrils flared and her eyes hardened, she knew that Gil would be told as soon as he came home how his wife had mortally offended the mother who had birthed and raised him, and who had given up weeks of her time to care selflessly for his motherless bairns. But Bethany didn't care. She desperately needed time to herself, time to think, before Gil came home. At that moment she would have taken Phemie Pate by the scruff of the neck and run her all the way home, if there had been no other way to get rid of her.

'I've no need of the tea. I'd not be able to drink it in a place where I'm not wanted!' Phemie said. Then, as Bethany stood silently before her, hands clasped over her skirt, head up, her eyes fixed on some point just beyond her mother-in-law's red-rimmed left ear, Phemie gave another offended snort and snatched her jacket up.

As the door closed behind her Bethany let her breath out in a long sigh of relief. The children were still where their grandmother had left them, holding hands tightly. Determined to break the ice, Bethany advanced on them and scooped Ellen up. At first the little girl resisted, clinging to Rory's hand, and when Bethany finally managed to lift her the small body felt stiff. Then all at once she threw her arms about Bethany's neck, holding her tight.

'There's my bonny lassie. You've grown since I went away, you both have.' Smelling the scent of baby skin beneath the aroma of carbolic soap, Bethany realised to her surprise how much she had missed the two of them. 'Well now, let's see what I've brought back from Yarmouth for my good wee bairns.'

She carried Ellen over to her usual fireside chair, collecting her bag on the way. It took a moment or two to loosen the little girl's arms, but finally Ellen consented to sit on her lap, one hand tightly clutching Bethany's blouse. Rory watched from a distance, unblinking, as she opened her bag and rummaged through its contents. She had never known him to remain still for so long.

'Here we are. This is for Ellen . . .' She pulled out a rag doll, made out of bright patches of cloth and with yellow wool for hair, and dandled it before the child's eyes. Ellen automatically began to put her free hand out towards it, then pulled it back again, started to stick her thumb in her mouth, screwed up her face and shoved the hand behind her back. Bethany retrieved it and arranged it firmly round the doll.

'There we are, I'll hold on to you and you hold on to your new babby. Is she not pretty? And what do we have for Rory?'

The little boy, still motionless, watched as she dipped into the bag and brought out a handsomely painted wooden engine. 'That's for being such a good boy for Grandma.'

She held the toy out, but to her astonishment Rory merely put both hands behind his back.

'Rory?' When he remained where he was, his small round face set hard, she repeated in a voice sharp with apprehension, 'Rory Pate, come here at once and take your new toy!'

He came in a furious rush, his face suddenly flushing as he barrelled across the small room at her and collided painfully with her knees. Snatching the train from her hand, he threw it across the room with all his might. When it landed harmlessly in Gil's cushioned chair the little boy rushed at it, grabbing it up and throwing it again, this time into the hearth, narrowly missing the meagre fire. There was a great jangling of fire-irons, and one wheel came off the engine and bounced into a corner as Rory made for Bethany again, punching and pummelling at her legs and arms.

'I don't want your toy!' he shrieked at the top of his voice. 'And she doesnae want that!' Rory snatched the doll from Ellen and threw it after the train before returning to the attack on his step-mother.

'We hate you!' he screeched as he pummelled. 'We don't want you here! This isn't your house. Go away, go away, go away!'

Ellen, screaming with terror, locked her arms round Bethany's neck again, kicking back at her brother when he took a handful of her skirt and tried to wrench her away from Bethany.

'Leave us alone!' he roared. 'Go back to your own house, this isn't your house!'

Appalled by the ferocity of the attack, Bethany could do nothing at first but let the punches and kicks land painfully on her shins, her arms and her feet. Then, feeling Ellen beginning to slide from her grasp, she tightened her grip on the little girl, while trying with her free hand to hold Rory at bay. But there was no denying him; it was as if he was determined to force her out of her chair and out of the house. Finally realising that pushing him away was not the answer, she managed to scoop an arm about him and drag him on to her lap, where he continued to punch at her, his small knotted fists landing painfully on her breasts and shoulders. A blow in the throat drove the breath from her and caused her to see stars; she ducked her chin down for protection while pulling him closer, too close for punching.

'Rory, Rory . . . !' The noise of his shouting and Ellen's terrified wails filled Bethany's head. She felt as though she had a whole cageful of monkeys on her knee, but she didn't dare let go. 'Sshhh, pet, hush.' She resisted the temptation to raise her voice above the clamour, lowering it instead to speak directly into his ear. 'What's wrong? You've never hurt me before, you'd not hurt anyone. Hush, Ellen, everything's going to be all right.'

At first it seemed that he couldn't hear her, for he kept fighting, tugging painfully at her hair when he realised that he could no longer draw his arm back far enough to hit her. Tears of pain rolled down her cheeks but she held on, talking and talking, refusing to let either of the children go. Finally, just as she was beginning to wonder if her own strength was going to hold out much longer, the little boy went limp against her, sobbing as though his heart would break.

'Rory?'

'I h-hate you,' he hiccuped. 'You w-went away and left us w-with Grandma Pate, and Ellen cried and c-cried and sh-she wanted you and you w-weren't there!'

'Oh, pet! Oh, Ellen! I'm sorry, I'm sorry!' The full enormity of what she had done to the children suddenly broke over Bethany and her own tears of pain gave way to a great flood of misery. The three of them clung together, weeping and rocking, united in their grief.

18

By the time the children were comforted all three faces were so swollen with tears that they looked, as Bethany shakily pointed out, like three canvas buoys that had been painted bright red. The idea made Rory laugh, the first natural chuckle she had heard from him since arriving home and the first, she suspected, that he had uttered since she had gone to Great Yarmouth.

She bathed their faces and her own, then filled bowls with bread and milk, scattering sugar liberally over each helping. After they had eaten she gathered them back into her lap, reading stories and playing with them until they were limp with exhaustion and ready to be carried into the smaller room and put to bed. Even then they both clung to her when she tried to go back into the kitchen and she had to stay with them until they fell asleep. Ellen succumbed within five minutes, but Rory fought sleep with the same grim determination he had used against Bethany earlier, never taking his gaze off her face and forcing his eyelids open every time they began to droop. When exhaustion finally took him she stayed by his narrow little bed for a long time, watching his swollen face and listening to his breathing, which was interrupted occasionally, like Ellen's, by an involuntary hiccup.

Back in the kitchen she tidied the place, then washed herself and changed into her night-gown before retrieving the brightly painted engine and hunting for the wheel. The wood was undamaged; she would ask Innes to repair it tomorrow. She sat stroking the engine, staring drearily into the fire. The toy would mend easily, but it would be much harder to repair the damage she had done to Rory and Ellen.

She should never have gone to Great Yarmouth. She had put herself first as always, abandoning the children to their grandmother's harsh regime, leaving them without a backward glance because, fond though she was of them, she always thought of them as Molly's bairns, not hers. But they were hers; by marrying their father she had undertaken to care for them. And instead of caring she had tried to recapture her own freedom, going off to Yarmouth to be a guttin quine, shaming poor Gil with that silly business about the barrel, not to mention . . .

Her thoughts veered sharply away from the scene in *Fidelity*'s cabin, but she forced herself to remember, to face the pain and the shame of it.

They had rolled and tumbled on the narrow bunk like wild animals, she and James, kissing and holding and babbling wordlessly, shameless in their burning hunger for each other. When at last they came to their senses it was too late.

'God, Bethany, what did we think we were doing?' Moving like a man in a dream, James had lurched on to the opposite bunk and buried his face in his hands. 'What did we think we were doing?' he asked again, his voice muffled.

'I don't know, but it's never going to happen again.' She was pulling her blouse straight as she spoke, tidying her hair with shaking hands. 'It was the drink, it turned us mad.'

She pulled on her stockings, pushed her feet into her boots, found her jacket and dragged it on. 'I'll go first and you stay here for a while so that nobody sees.'

At the foot of the ladder she paused, her back to

him. 'It was nothing, James, just a nonsense. It'll not happen again.'

'It will not!' he said, his voice hard. 'Away you go . . . hurry!'

She kept to the shadows as she moved along the harbour, the shame and horror of what had just happened choking her, so that she had to keep swallowing in a vain attempt to clear her throat.

She thought to walk the town's quieter streets until the other women at the lodgings had gone to their beds, for she couldn't bear the thought of having to look at them, speak to them, behave normally after what she had done. But when she reached the town itself she found the place abuzz with excitement and every street filled with shouting, singing, exultant fisher-lassies.

The strike was over, and they had won.

Bethany suddenly realised that she was rocking and keening to herself in her fireside chair in her husband's kitchen, fresh tears running down cheeks already rough and sore from earlier weeping. She got up and walked about the room distractedly. She and James had only seen each other once since that night and, after the first glance of recognition, they had carefully avoided speaking to or looking at each other, or touching. Above all, they must never touch again, they both knew that.

It would be years before she forgot that night; perhaps she never would. But it was in the past, she told herself firmly as she put the lamp out and got into bed. It was a mistake, but it was over and she must put it out of her mind in case, one day, Gil or her mother or Stella looked into her eyes, saw the memories there and guessed what she and James had done.

She stretched out in the empty bed and closed her eyes, worn out with travelling, with the confrontation with Gil's mother and comforting the children. Tomorrow Gil would be home, but tonight, thankfully, she was on her own. All she wanted was to sleep, but instead she tossed and turned in the big wall-bed, thinking, despite all her efforts, of James; of the sweetness of his mouth, the throaty murmur of his voice in her ear and the burning warmth of his lean, hard body beneath her hands.

Without realising what she was doing, she began to caress her own body beneath the demure folds of her gown in a desperate search for relief. And when at last it came to her, the man she gave herself to in her fevered imagination was not her husband.

The day the boats began to come back from the English fishing grounds was always a day of celebration in Buckie, just as it was in every fishing community up and down the coast. The menfolk were home again, and they would remain on shore for several weeks, since there was little fishing to be done now that the herring were gone. The turn of the year was a time to settle accounts and plan for the future, and with a good season behind them there need be no worries about food or fuel, or paying rent over the winter.

When the first boats were sighted the entire village turned out, including babes in arms and old folk hobbling with the assistance of sticks and crutches – even using brooms for support if there was nothing else to hand. They thronged the harbour walls, spurred on by the hysterical screaming of the seabirds that flew in their hundreds to meet the boats and escort them in.

Bethany and the children, exhausted by the traumas of the previous day, had slept late. When they woke she hurriedly did what had to be done about the house, then bundled Rory and Ellen into their warmest clothing and took them off for a long walk along the coast and up the fields to Rathven; she carried Ellen most of the way and Rory, too, in the crook of her free arm when he began to grizzle and complain. When they were hungry she gave them the bread and cheese she had stuffed into her pockets before she left home, and when they were thirsty there was cold tea to drink from a bottle.

From the fields above the village the three of them saw the first of the boats come in, nudging over the horizon in a line that gradually opened out as the boats came closer. More and more appeared behind the leaders until the Firth was dotted with a huge flotilla.

As they neared the coast some split off, making for other communities, but most headed purposefully towards Buckie, crowding the waters outside the harbour, waiting patiently at the entrance for their turn. One after another, all morning and afternoon, they came in, the men hurrying ashore to be greeted by their families. Tomorrow they would return to clean the boats and check the nets, the ropes and the buoys, but today there was no more work, only celebration.

As the *Fidelity* nosed her way past the lighthouse at the entrance to Cluny harbour, James felt his belly curl with apprehension. While the drifter moved into the first of the inner basins he busied himself about the deck, taking quick glances at the crowds on the walls above. He spotted Stella with the baby in her arms and the twins at her knees, and his mother, beaming her relief at seeing boat and crew home safely, and nodded to them before his gaze travelled on, searching for a head with hair the colour of beech trees in autumn sunlight.

To his relief his sister was not among the crowd above, but even so he remained on his guard, just in case he caught sight of her unexpectedly and gave himself away to those watching.

He was the last of the crew to leave the boat and, when he did, Stella was waiting at the top of the ladder. 'James . . . oh, James, we've missed you!' she said fervently, forcing herself to hold back, aware that James, like his father before him, believed that shows of affection belonged behind closed doors in the privacy of a man's own home.

'Here . . . give her to me,' he said gruffly, holding out his arms for his youngest daughter. 'You'll be tired holding her all this time.'

The baby, cocooned in so many shawls that she was like a large, soft clothes-peg in his awkward hands, stared up at him with startled eyes, then blinked twice before breaking into panic-stricken yells.

'She's too wee to mind who you are,' Stella apologised, taking the bundle back and joggling it soothingly. 'She's a wee thing strange with folk just now, it's only her age. But you know your daddy, don't you?' she added to the twins, who looked solemnly at James. All three of them, he suddenly realised, were like their mother. There seemed to be little of him in the children he had fathered.

'You're safe home, then.' His mother arrived, accompanied by a sturdy grey-haired man and smiling the tentative smile she had adopted since their quarrel over his father's burial. 'I hear the fishing was good.'

'Good enough.' James eyed the stranger standing just behind Jess; not so much standing, he thought with a sudden sharpening of interest, as hovering in a protective sort of way. 'Who's this?' he asked bluntly.

Jess drew the man forward. 'Jacob MacFarlane. His people were neighbours to mine in Portessie and he was a fisherman like yourself.'

'But not any more, eh?' James eyed the outstretched hand. It was broad and thick-knuckled and Jacob MacFarlane's face was weather-beaten, but James was willing to wager money that it had been a while since the man had had to do manual work for his living.

'Not any more, though I'm still in the business.' His handshake was firm and hearty. 'I'm a buyer now.'

'A buyer? Were you in Yarm'th?'

'I'd men there and I was at Lowestoft myself for part of the winter fishing.' His voice was cultured, but there were strong undertones of the Moray coast lilt. 'So . . .' His sea-green eyes studied James with interest. 'You're Weem Lowrie's lad. I can see the likeness.'

'You knew him?'

'Aye, I knew Weem well when we were about the age you are now. And I'll hope to make your better acquaintance too while I'm bidin' in Buckie.'

James nodded. 'For the meantime, though, I'd like fine to get home and have something to eat,' he said, and turned away to swing one of the twins up and offer his big hand to the other. She surveyed it doubtfully and then, urged forward by Stella, gingerly grasped one finger.

'Who is this Jacob MacFarlane?' James asked his wife later.

'I know no more than you do. He arrived a week or two back.'

'I mind him well,' old Mowser chimed in from across the hearth. 'The MacFarlanes lived in Portessie and they had three or four lads, all of them good fishermen. But they went off to other places one by one and I never heard what happened to any of them.'

'He says he knew my father.'

Mowser puffed at his pipe, sending a cloud of pale-blue fragrant smoke into the air above his head, then took the stem from his mouth. 'Everyone knew your father and, from what I mind, Jacob MacFarlane had cause to know him better than most.'

'What d'you mean?'

The old man chuckled. 'Jacob and your mother were sweethearts all the time they were growing from childhood, right up until Weem set eyes on her. That was the end of it for poor Jacob. I heard that they even fought over her, but your father was more than a match for most of the lads round here. Jacob was sent off with a flea in his lug and nob'dy heard sight or sound of him till he turned up again the other week, dressed like a gentleman and with a silver-handled cane too, someone said.'

'I saw it,' Stella said from the stove. 'And a bowler hat. He's a right handsome man when he's all dressed up. He's been spending time with your mother, James.'

'Mebbe he's courting her now that she's a widow,' Mowser suggested.

'Don't be daft, they're both far too old for that sort of thing!'

The old man laughed, a wheezing, choking sound. 'Age has nothing to do with it, lad, as you'll mebbe find out in your own good time. And Jacob still looks to be a lusty man.'

'That's enough now, Father.' Stella's voice was sharp and the colour rose to her cheeks. The old man wheezed once more, then pushed the pipe-stem into his mouth, like a baby with a comforter, and went back to staring into the fire and thinking his own private thoughts.

James got to his feet. 'I'll wash before we eat.'

'The outhouse is cold. You can wash in here for once.'

'There's nothing wrong with the outhouse.' He rummaged in a drawer for a clean shirt.

'There's water heating in the kettle. It'll not be a minute . . .'

'You can bring it out to me when it's ready.'

The outhouse walls were old and full of cracks that let in the wind. The only time the place was warm was on washdays, when the fire had been burning for hours beneath the boiler and the draughts blew steam off the water's surface. James pulled his shirt off and dropped it on to the stone flags before fetching the soap and bringing the old tin basin from its usual place, upturned over the empty boiler.

As he ran cold water into it from the tap, Stella came in with the heavy kettle clutched in both fists.

'You don't really think that man's courting my mother,

do you?' James asked as he took it from her and emptied it into the basin.

She had picked up his soiled shirt and was folding it neatly. 'That's just Da blethering, pay no heed to him,' she said. Then, after a moment, 'Though mind you . . .' She laid the shirt on top of the basket of clothes waiting for the next wash-day. 'She's young enough yet, your mother, and bonny in her own way. It might be a good thing if it was true.'

'Of course it wouldn't be a good thing!' James was appalled.

'Why not? Bethany has Gil and Innes has Zelda, and you and me have each other and the bairns. Why shouldn't your mother have someone to care for her?'

'Because . . . because she doesn't need anyone else! Come here, woman . . .' He reached for her as she opened her mouth to argue further, pulling her tightly against him and kissing her hard.

When he released her she was pink and flustered. 'What's got into you, James Lowrie? You've never done that in the wash-house before!'

'I've been away a long time, that's all. Are you complaining?'

She giggled, daring to stroke both hands down the hard, cool planes of his bare chest. 'Not a bit of it.'

'Good.' He kissed her again and this time she responded, clinging to him and reaching up to draw him closer. When he released her she would have moved back into his arms, but he gave her a little push towards the door. 'Off you go and see to the dinner, for I'm starved. I'll be five minutes, just.'

When she had gone he turned back to the basin, gripping the edges tight, staring unseeingly through the grimy wash-house window to the little garden where, in spring, summer and autumn, his wife and his father-in-law raised vegetables.

Stella's kisses had been warm and womanly, but she

wasn't Bethany. Holding her did nothing to rouse the fire that had consumed him only a few nights ago in *Fidelity*'s cabin. Nobody could bring that back, except . . .

Cursing, he emptied the hot water from the basin into the boiler, replaced it with cold water from the tap, then set to work lathering the soap. Scrubbing his face and neck, his chest and arms, and spluttering water all over the wash-house's stone flags, he pushed all thoughts of Bethany from his mind.

19

Gil Pate was in high spirits when he got home, for it had been a good season and he was in profit.

'And that's even after those damned witches you threw your lot in with forced me and the rest of the employers to pay them more.'

'Then it shows that you could well afford it. Be fair, Gil,' Bethany protested, 'we deserved that money.'

'Aye, mebbe so,' he agreed grudgingly. Then, always one to get in the last word if he could, 'It's just fortunate for all of us that the fishing was so good, else you and me and the wee ones would've been hard put to it to find food for our bellies this winter.'

She bit her tongue and said nothing. Gil and his brother were both known to be shrewd businessmen, comfortably off by local standards. There was little fear of them or their families having to go without.

It was common practice on the Moray Firth for fishermen who owned their own boats and gear to sell their catches to certain curers at pre-arranged prices. The curers advanced the money needed to equip the boats, and at the end of each fishing season it fell to the curers to work out the total earned from the catches. Once that was done and an amount allocated to each boat, the skipper and mate deducted the vessel's expenses – coaling, paint, oil, repairs and food – before dividing the remainder between their crew.

Since Gil and Nathan Pate were sole buyers for all the fish caught by a number of Buckie boats, Bethany had to put up with being plagued by a whole series of meetings round her kitchen table as representatives of each boat met to go through the books with the Pate brothers.

So harassed was she by the meetings, which seemed to take place one after another, that she quite forgot that eventually James would be involved. On the day she opened the door to find him on the step, her mind went blank and her knees turned to water. She clutched at the door frame to keep herself upright.

'What are you doing here?' she hissed, mindful that Gil, who had gone to the privy at the back of the house, could walk in on them at any minute. 'Have you not got the sense to keep right away from this house?'

He frowned at her. 'What are you havering about now? We're here for the meeting . . .'

'Don't stand there blocking the way in, man,' Albert's voice boomed from behind him. 'Get in, I'm freezing to death in this wind!'

He gave his nephew a hearty push and James was propelled in through the doorway, almost knocking Bethany down. She backed away hurriedly as Albert stamped into the kitchen and Gil came in from the back yard.

'Have you not offered our visitors a drink, Bethany? Sit down, sit down, Nathan'll be here by and by.' He bustled about, fetching a bottle and glasses while Bethany began to get the children ready to go out. All she could think of was getting away from the house, which seemed to her overheated mind to be filled with James's presence.

'I hope you're away to make your peace with my mother,' Gil said pointedly. There had been a coolness between them since he had returned from a visit to Phemie Pate the day before, his ears ringing with complaints about his wife's ingratitude and ill manners. Bethany had resented his instructions to apologise as soon as she could, telling him sharply that she would make her own mind up about it. Now, anxious to have a reason for her hurried flight, she said, 'Aye, that's what I had in mind. I'll be away for a while.'

'We can manage without you,' Gil told her indifferently. He was a man among men now, and for that afternoon at least Bethany had been relegated to the ranks of all women – handmaidens and servers, who got in the way at times like this.

Nathan arrived just as she was about to leave. Outside, Bethany took a long, deep breath of the cold December air, then gripped the handle of the perambulator tightly. She would go to Finnechtie and force herself to apologise humbly to her dragon of a mother-in-law. Perhaps the walk there and back, and the punishing treatment she would no doubt receive while there, would help to calm the turmoil that had leaped up within her when she opened the door to James.

'That's better,' Gil said when the door closed behind his wife and children. 'We couldnae settle to business with the bairns running about the place, and women are best kept out of these matters anyway.'

Nathan downed half the whisky in his glass in one swallow. 'You're right there. Let a wife know how much you're worth and she'll not be satisfied till she's got every last penny of it out of your pocket.'

'Why d'you think I never wed?' Albert threw in his contribution. 'Enjoy the benefits without sufferin' the pain, that's what I always say.'

'Are we here to settle the wages or just to give our tongues a good airing?' James asked sharply. His fists were clenched in his pockets and it was an effort to stay seated, when all he wanted to do was walk away from their silly bragging – especially Gil's.

'God save us, here's a man still new enough married to be missing his wee wife when they're apart,' Albert sneered, holding his glass out to be re-filled. The other two started to laugh, then as James half-rose from his chair the laughter subsided and Nathan reached out to put a hand on his arm.

'Sit down, lad, we're just about to start on the business. Are we not, Gil?'

'Aye, and fine business it was, too.' Gil opened the books he had written up, with much licking of pencils and muttering, and James settled back into his seat as the meeting started in earnest.

Once the *Fidelity*'s expenses were cleared and a sum set aside for the bank in repayment of the loan still outstanding on the boat the remainder was divided as usual into three parts – one for the crew, one for the upkeep and repair of the nets, and one for the boat, to cover loss, wear and tear. This year, since the boat did not require any major repairs, the third part of the money would mainly be used for a dividend payment among all the crew. As the nets had belonged to Weem, and had been bequeathed by him to James, he fell heir to the money set aside for them.

'What would have happened, Albert, if you'd had a bad season and you'd not been able to pay the bank?' Nathan asked as each man stowed his share away. 'You've not got a house to bargain with.'

Drifters like the *Fidelity* cost as much as £3,000 to buy and as bankers, unlike fishermen, were not obliged to take account of the weather or of the years when the shoals of fish simply did not appear as expected, they demanded their loan repayments even when the catches were poor. Most skippers on the Firth owned their homes, and many a good Moray man had lost the roof above his own and his family's heads because the loan could not be honoured, through no fault of his.

Albert winked. 'If ye don't have a house ye cannae lose a house.'

'Then they'd take the boat and sell her to cover their losses,' James said. 'Probably for less than she's worth.'

His uncle, who had been re-filling his glass from Gil's

bottle more often than the others, shrugged. 'They'd be welcome to her, as far as I'm concerned. At my age a man doesnae know how many years' work he's got left in him anyway, and at least I'd still have my snug wee lodgings and we'd be free of the loan . . . eh, James?' He clapped his nephew on the shoulder.

'And me and Charlie and Jem, and the rest of them, would be out of work.'

'Ach, you'd all be taken on elsewhere, no bother.'

'I don't see why that would worry you, James, since I've heard,' Nathan added with a sidelong glance, 'that you're of a mind to leave *Fidelity* anyway.'

'James? Never!' Albert finished his drink and swiped the back of his hand over his mouth.

James cleared his throat. 'Davie Geddes is looking for a mate.'

'You'd work for that pious creature? I've heard that he gets his crew together to pray before they shoot the nets,' Albert mocked, 'and again after they've hauled them in. That would never suit the likes of you, lad!'

'Davie's thinking of giving up the sea. He wants to keep his boat, and leave it in good hands.'

'So it's a fine skipper on a sailed boat you'd be?' Albert pointed a finger at his nephew. 'You stay with the *Fidelity*, laddie, she'll be yours one of these days. Patience, that's all it takes, patience.' Albert struggled to his feet, using the table-edge as a lever. 'You'll have to excuse me, gentlemen. I must convey my compliments to a certain lady further along the coast,' he said with a huge wink.

'And that's all he'll manage to convey to her, judging from the state he's in,' Nathan grinned when the man had staggered out.

It had been a difficult afternoon for Bethany. As soon as the children realised that they were on the Finnechtie road and bound for their grandmother's house, Ellen had set up a thin wail and Rory had stopped short and refused to go another step. Bethany had had to put up with their whining and squabbling all the rest of the way to Phemie's cold, immaculate house.

Once inside, the children had both stayed close to Bethany, holding on to her clothing and scarcely speaking to the older woman, who made plain her belief that as soon as she had arrived back from Yarmouth their stepmother had set to and speedily re-introduced them to her slovenly ways, removing all the training that Phemie had painstakingly instilled in them. She received Bethany's apology for her behaviour on her return from England with tightly pursed mouth and steely eyes, grinding out by way of acknowledgement, 'I'll say this for my Gilbert, he knows how to exercise control over his own household.'

It was so unfair, Bethany seethed as she walked home after a very uncomfortable hour, that even when she had choked out the required apology Gil had got the credit for making her do it.

To her relief he was alone in the house when they arrived, cheerful after his afternoon's discussion and mellowed by the bottle that he and the others had emptied while attending to their business. The children, whose spirits had risen with every yard that left Finnechtie further behind and brought Buckie nearer, rushed into the house to greet him with boisterous affection and in no time at all the three of them were scrambling about the floor in some energetic game.

'Your James is in a right strange mood these days,' Gil said thoughtfully that night when the children were in bed.

Bethany kept her eyes on her darning. 'What sort of mood?'

'He's never what you'd call the best of company, but since he came back from Yarm'th he's been downright thrawn. He found fault with almost everything that was said today. And mind he spoke of leaving the *Fidelity* and going to be mate for Davie Geddes when we were in Yarm'th?'

'That was just talk, he'd never do such a thing.'

'You're wrong there, for he's set on it. He spoke of it in front of Albert this afternoon.' Then Gil knocked his pipe out and stretched his muscular arms above his head, yawning. 'Ah well, we've all got to see to our-selves and leave others to their own ways. As long as we're comfortable . . . and we are that. Life's good to us, Bethany, and with you by my side it can only get better.'

Gil's good fortune, it seemed, was set fair. A few evenings later, not long after he had returned from his day's work, Jacob MacFarlane paid an unexpected call.

To Bethany's embarrassment, Gil was washing himself in the kitchen when the visitor knocked on the door. 'Come on in, man,' he said cheerfully through a faceful of suds. 'I'll be done in a minute.' Then, to his wife's horror, 'You'll take some dinner with us?'

'I'd like that fine.' Jacob's face was red with the keen wind that was blowing in from the Firth that night.

'It's nothing grand,' Bethany said automatically, her mind racing as she tried to work out how to stretch the food, 'but of course you're very welcome.'

'I can think of nothing better than a good home-cooked meal on a night like this. Thank you both for your kindness.' Jacob, unperturbed by his host's naked, hairy chest and the basin of soapy water on the table, stripped his coat off, sat himself down by the fire and lifted Ellen on to his lap. When she looked at him doubtfully, wondering if she should weep or smile, he gave her his fob watch to play with, and when Rory immedi-ately rushed over he was presented with a small multi-coloured pebble.

'That,' Jacob told him solemnly, 'is very, very special. It comes from Portessie and it's been all over the world with me, and you are to look after it while I'm in your house.'

As she worked at the stove Bethany heard his voice ramble placidly on, the sound of it punctuated now and again with questions or squeals of laughter from the children. Every time she glanced round she seemed to meet the man's bright-green gaze. While they ate, he appeared happy to answer all Gil's questions, telling them of the years after he left the Firth, working his way all down the east coast of Britain, crewing on boats out of Johnshaven and Arbroath, Anstruther and Port Seton, Grimsby and Whitby and Lowestoft and Great Yarmouth, never staying in any one place for much longer than a season.

'I was restless and I was young and answerable to nobody. I'd a mind to see the world.' From Yarmouth he had gone further afield, working for a Dutchman for several years.

'That job took me all over The Netherlands, and to Germany and Russia too, so I stayed with him for several years.'

'Always as a fisherman?' Bethany asked and his gaze, never far from her, returned at once.

'At first, then the man that paid me started using me as a buyer. That's how I got to know about the other side of the business – pickling and smoking herring. Eventually I'd saved enough and knew enough to set up in business for myself. As you well know, the Russians, the Germans and the Dutch all have a great love of pickled herring.'

'They have that, and thank God for it,' Gil agreed heartily, pushing his chair back from the table and slapping his stomach with both hands to indicate that it was full and satisfied. 'You'll take a wee dram, Jacob?'

'I will that. And you'll have a cigar?' The visitor brought out a handsome cigar case and both men moved to the fireside as Bethany set about the business of putting the children to bed. By the time they were tucked up and she was clearing the table, Jacob had got down to

the reason for his visit. He was looking for people who
could supply herring, both pickled and smoked, and where
better, he had asked himself, than from his own part of
the world?

'When Jess told me that you and your brother ran just
such a business between you, and that you were a cooper
into the bargain, I knew that I'd been right to come back
to my own birthplace,' he finished.

Gil's face was radiant. 'You could do no better than
me and Nathan,' he agreed eagerly.

'You'd probably need to expand. I know you already
take all the fish that the Lowrie boat can catch, and buy
from other boats too, but you'd need to be the sole buyer
for a good deal more. I could mebbe find the extra money
you might need as an equal third partner. Of course, I'll
have to see round the cooperage and the curing yard and
the smokehouse first, and take a look at your books.'

'That's no trouble,' Gil said at once, and Jacob got up,
holding out his hand.

'First thing tomorrow, then, at your yard?'

'I'll look forward to it.' Gil shook his hand heartily,
then Jacob offered it to Bethany.

'Thank you for a delicious meal, my dear. You're a
fortunate man, Gil Pate.'

'I know that!' Gil was so pleased with himself that
when the visitor had gone he paced about the kitchen,
unable to sit at peace. 'This could be the making of us,
lass. I'll be a rich man, you wait and see. You and the
bairns'll want for nothing . . . And mebbe I'll be able to
take you to one of these fine new houses they're building
in Cliff Terrace. You'll be the mistress of a grand house,
Bethany, with mebbe a wee serving maid for you to order
about . . .'

'Gil, will you just wait until Mr MacFarlane's had a
chance to look at the yard and the smokehouse?' she
protested. 'He might not like what he sees, or he might
change his mind.'

'Not a bit of it, he's a man of integrity. When he gives his word he'll keep it.'

'He didn't give his word tonight, he just spoke of what might happen.'

'He as good as gave it – and I've you to thank for that.' Gil lunged, lifting her right off her chair and into his arms.

'Me? Put me down, you daft loon!'

'I will not.' He danced about the room with her, jiggling her so vigorously that she had to wrap her arms about his neck to prevent herself being tossed to the floor. 'Yes, you. The man could scarce keep his eyes off you.'

'Don't be daft!'

'I know what I'm saying. And I can't blame him for it, for you're my own bonny wee dove,' he said into her hair. The generous tumblerful of whisky he had downed before bidding their host goodnight bathed her in fumes that made her eyes water. 'It's all thanks to you!'

At the same moment, in a farm stable near Rathven, Innes Lowrie was saying feebly, 'You're not!'

'You think I'd make up a thing like that?' Zelda's voice was thick with fear.

'But . . . how could it be?'

She made a sound that was half-laugh, half-sob, and pummelled at his chest with knotted fists. 'How d'you think? Have you forgotten that week I slept in your bed every night while your mother was looking after your auntie? Though devil the sleeping you did, Innes Lowrie, you randy bugger! And now you ask me how it could happen?'

'I didn't mean . . . I just thought that . . .'

'You just thought it was all fun, and now that there's a result you're trying to pretend that it was none of your doing?' Now she was kicking his shins as well, her booted feet landing sore blows. Tears ran freely down a face twisted with fear and fury. 'Well, I didn't force you, though if you keep on denying me I can always tell my father that it was *you* forced *me*. Then see what you'll get!'

'Zelda . . . Zelda!' he repeated as the blows and kicks continued to rain down. When she ignored him he was forced to use his superior strength on her, catching her wrists and trapping them above her head, then rolling his full weight on top of her and locking his ankles over hers to hold her legs still, so that she was held flat against the pile of straw.

Subdued, trapped, she went limp and began bawling like a child in her misery.

'No, Zelda, it's all right, lass,' Innes implored, kissing the wet face that tried to twist away from beneath him. 'It's all right! I'll marry you, of course I will. You surely didn't think I'd abandon you at a time like this?'

'You d-didn't believe me!'

'It was the surprise of it. Somehow I didn't think . . .' he began, then found the sense to stop before he made things worse.

The precious nights they had spent together had been a delight and a joy that he treasured and would always treasure, no matter what the future might hold in store for him. But somehow he had not associated them with the making of a bairn. That was a business for adults, and Innes had not yet become accustomed to thinking of himself as a grown man.

'I just never thought of it,' he said lamely.

She wriggled free and sat up, rubbing both hands over her tear-streaked face. 'Well, you'd better start, for I'm not facing my father alone over this!'

'You won't have to, I'll be with you. I'll always be with you, Zelda,' he said earnestly. 'You and me and our bairn – we'll be together no matter what.'

'But where will we be? Here?' Zelda threw out her arms to indicate the small stable.

A sturdy building with straw piled in one corner to

make a comfortable couch, it had become their favourite meeting place during the cold winter nights. It was already inhabited by two placid cart-horses, and their big bodies threw off enough warmth to make the place seem cosy in comparison to the bitter weather outside. It was private, too, for once the animals were bedded down for the night nobody came near the place.

'Mebbe a stable did Mary and Joseph well enough, but it's not what I want for my bairn,' Zelda warned.

'Of course you won't have to live here. I'll find somewhere,' Innes said desperately. 'I'll look after you, both of you.'

'Oh, Innes!' She threw her arms round him and kissed him.

'How long . . . I mean, when . . . ?'

'I'd say another seven months.'

'We've got quite a long time, then,' he said with relief. A lot could happen in seven months.

'No, we haven't, for I'll be showing soon. Mistress Bain's already suspicious. I've been ill in the mornings, and it was her questioning me about it that made me realise what was wrong,' Zelda explained. 'We'll have to wed as soon as we can, Innes, and to do that we'll have to tell my mother and my father.' Her voice faltered. 'You know what my father's like. He's going to be so angry with me!' The tears began to roll down her face again.

'If he's angry with anyone it should be me, not you.' Innes held her tightly, his cheek against her hair. 'When he knows that we're to be wed he'll not mind.'

'You think so?' Her voice was doubtful. 'And we still don't know where we'll live.'

'I'll see to that, too. I'll see to everything,' Innes promised. Even in the midst of sudden shock he was certain of one thing: that he loved her and would do anything for her. 'If you want, we'll go to your house and tell your father the truth of it right away.'

'Tonight?' She drew away from him.

'The sooner, the better.' Speaking for himself, he would rather get things over and done with.

'I'm not walking over there tonight! It's bitter cold outside and I've to be back in the farmhouse in an hour's time.'

'When, then?'

She bit her lip. 'A week or two wouldn't matter. Can we not wait until after Ne'erday's over before we tell anyone? That'll give us time to get used to the idea ourselves, and start making plans.'

'I'm not sure I can keep quiet for another two weeks.'

'You'll have to. Anyway,' her arms slid round his neck and her voice deepened slightly, 'there are other things for us to do tonight.'

'But, is it all right, with you . . . ?' Innes asked, bewildered at the sudden change of mood.

Zelda let herself fall back on the straw, drawing him down with her. 'It's as safe as it'll ever be,' she assured him throatily, the tears and fears forgotten now that she was sure of his support. 'The harm's already done and there's no reason why we shouldn't enjoy ourselves while we still can.'

20

After inspecting the cooperage and the curing yards run by the Pate brothers Jacob MacFarlane expressed his approval.

'It's only a matter of him having the papers he wants drawn up, and by Ne'erday we'll be in partnership.' Gil was so excited that he could scarcely keep still for more than one minute at a time.

'It's like having three bairns in the house instead of two,' Bethany complained as he came up behind her while she was peeling potatoes for his dinner at the sink, wrapping his arms about her waist.

'So you think I'm a bairn, do you?' His beard rubbed the soft skin below her ear and his hands crept up to toy with the buttons of her blouse, while his body pressed tightly into hers, forcing her against the stone sink. 'Do I feel like a bairn?' he asked, his breath hot on her ear.

'If you don't leave me alone your dinner'll be late.'

'I'm not bothered.'

'Gil!' She pushed his groping hands away. 'The wee ones are just in the next room. They could come in at any minute.'

'I'll be quick.'

'Not as quick as I'll be with this knife if you don't leave me in peace.' She tried, with great effort, to keep her voice light. 'You should know by now never to pester a fisher-lassie with a good cutting knife in her hand.'

For a moment she thought he was going to defy her, but just then Ellen came trotting into the kitchen. Gil sighed and stepped away from his wife. 'Tonight, then.'

'Tonight,' she agreed, glad that her back was to him and that he could not see her face.

The days when the fisher-folk of the Moray Firth celebrated the turn of the year with burning torches, and offerings of food and drink to the sturdy boats they relied on for their livelihoods, were gone. Now Ne'erday, the first day of the new year, was marked by more sedate customs. In the morning the children opened the gifts brought during the night by Santa Claus, the benign being who visited English children on Christmas Day, and at night families and friends gathered together to share their Ne'erday dinner. It had become a tradition for the Lowrie family – Meg, Albert and Mowser included – to eat at Weem's home on Ne'erday, and although he was no longer there Jess insisted on keeping the custom going. This year Albert was visiting with his latest lady love, but with Zelda and Jacob invited as well there were ten adults to cater for, as well as five children.

'Your mother's taking on too much, feeding us all,' kind-hearted Stella fretted to Bethany. 'We'd be better calling on her in the afternoon, then going back home to eat our dinners.'

'She'd not have it any other way.' Bethany had no wish whatsoever to be part of a family gathering, but she knew that Jess was determined. So was Gil, who planned to use the occasion to make an official announcement about his new partnership with Jacob MacFarlane. 'And it's not too much for her, she's as strong as a horse.'

'Right enough, Mr MacFarlane's done her the world of good.'

'You think so?'

'Oh yes. Since he's come back to Buckie the years have just fallen away from her.' Stella hesitated, giving her sister-in-law a sidelong glance. Bethany was not one for confidences, or gossiping, but after all Jess was her mother. Stella decided to risk it. 'I'm beginning to wonder if he's got a fondness for her.'

'For my mother?' Bethany's knitting dropped into her lap and she gaped at the other girl. 'You're havering.'

Stella smirked, delighted to have startled her cool, self-possessed sister-in-law for once. 'He scarcely left her side all those weeks you were in Yarm'th. They grew up next door to each other in Portessie, you know. My da says they were sweethearts once.'

'If they were, why did she marry my father?' Bethany scoffed.

'Because she loved him more, but seemingly Mr MacFarlane's never married. Mebbe when he lost her he decided there could be nobody else.' Before marriage and motherhood claimed all of her time Stella had enjoyed reading romantic novels; now her cheeks were pink with excitement at the idea that she might at that moment be watching a real romance from the sidelines.

'That's because he had more sense.' Bethany's knitting was in her hands again. Her needles raced along the row, turned, raced along the next row. 'There's other things in life besides marriage.'

'I can't think of any.'

'Aye well, you're lucky. You've got everything you want.' Bethany knew that her voice was too sharp, but she couldn't help it. She had not set foot in James's cottage since her return from Yarmouth and the two of them had made a point of avoiding each other. She would have preferred not to see Stella either, but the woman called in almost every day and the sight and sound of her, the way she talked incessantly about James, were almost more than Bethany could bear.

She was surprised now as her sister-in-law said hesitantly, 'I wish I did have everything I wanted. Then mebbe James would be happier. He's been like a different person

since he came home from England. He's got no interest
in anything.'

'It's always the same between seasons,' Bethany told
her shortly. 'The men don't have enough to do. He'll be
his old self once the boats start going out again.'

'I seem to be always annoying him these days and I
don't know why. If I just knew what I'm doing wrong
I could stop it, but I don't.'

'You knew when you married him that he was thrawn.
Mebbe you should have had more sense at the time.'

'Sense doesnae come into it when you love someone.'
Stella looked at her sister-in-law. 'I wish I was more like
you, Bethany.'

'Me?' Bethany felt a guilty flush rise up the smooth
column of her neck, and she began to look for an imaginary
dropped stitch as an excuse to keep her head bent.

'James admires you; he always has.'

'He thinks I'm an outspoken interfering bitch.'

'Mebbe that's why he admires you. I'm too . . . too
nice.'

'So I'm not nice?'

'I didn't mean it that way! If I could answer him back
and argue with him, the way you can, he might respect
me more. But it's not in me to do that. I think,' Stella said
miserably, 'that he'd be happier if he'd found a lassie like
you to marry.'

'For any favour!' Bethany shot out of her chair. 'I've
never heard such nonsense in my life.'

'You've dropped your knitting. Look, the stitches have
all come off one of the wires . . .' Stella fell to her
knees and began to gather up the bundle of wool and
wires that had fallen from her sister-in-law's lap. 'What
a mess . . .'

'Leave it, I'll see to it later.' Bethany snatched the
knitting from Stella's hands. 'Is it not time you were
home? You'll not sweeten James's temper by being late
with his dinner.'

When Stella had gone she went out to the wash-house at the back, where she paced up and down, muttering, 'Stupid bitch. Daft wee fool!'

No wonder James was short-tempered. Who wouldn't be, married to a simpleton like Stella? She raged at her brother for his stupidity in marrying the lassie, and at Stella for running to her, of all people, in search of advice and sympathy. Adding to Bethany's pain, reminding her day after day of what had happened at Yarmouth, and what could never happen again. And what might have been, if only Stella could have been his sister and Bethany old Mowser's daughter.

Sobs began to rise in her throat and she put both her hands tightly over her mouth to stifle them. But she couldn't stop the tears that, as she paced and turned, paced and turned, kept spilling over her fingers.

Thanks to the good herring season 1913 was welcomed in grand style along the Moray coast. The boat crews and the fisher-lassies had come back from Yarmouth with gifts squeezed into every spare inch they could make in their kists, and when the children rose before dawn on Ne'erday they found their home-knitted woollen stockings, normally the least interesting garments they possessed, stuffed with good things.

While they squealed their delight over apples and oranges, chocolate money and sugar mice and pigs, games and dolls and toy soldiers, their elders made preparations for the first day of the year.

From mid-morning at the latest the streets were busy with folk calling on their friends and relatives with gifts of drink, food and the essential lumps of coal, which signified a wish for warmth and prosperity for the household throughout the new year. All were welcome, though dark-haired men were in particular demand, with their special ability to bring luck to a house simply by being the first of the year to set foot inside the door.

Stella and Bethany went along in the morning to help Jess prepare the Ne'erday dinner. Vast quantities of potatoes and turnips, carrots and onions had to be peeled and chopped; pastry had to be made for the two large steak pies; and there was chicken broth to make. By the time they arrived, bringing their children with them, since James and Gil would not have dreamed of looking after their own families, Jess had already mixed the clootie dumpling, tied it up in clean sheeting and set it to simmer all day in a huge pot of water.

An hour later, deserting the oatmeal stuffing that she was mixing in order to rescue Stella's protesting baby from Ellen, who was trying to carry her about the kitchen, Jess secretly wished that she had been left to see to the entire feast on her own.

'We'll put her down on the rug, pet. She's happier there.' She found something else for Ellen to do, then used the back of her hand to wipe the sweat from her forehead before returning to her work. 'I wonder if I should have asked Albert's family for their dinner?'

'How could you, when none of us knows how many he's fathered?' Bethany asked tartly, and Stella gave a shocked giggle.

'I meant the lads that work with him and James on the boat. And I should mebbe have asked Nathan and Gil's mother.'

'You've got more than enough already to see to,' Stella pointed out, while Bethany snorted at the idea of sharing Ne'erday dinner with Phemie Pate.

'She'd just ruin the day for the lot of us, with her evil tongue and her black looks. She'd not have come anyway. We'll have to go to her in the afternoon, for a wee while just, but we'll be back in time for your dinner. Where's Innes?' Bethany asked as the children's noise rose an octave, shrilling through the adults' ears. 'We could fairly be doing with him here to keep that lot busy.'

'He's gone to fetch Zelda.'

'D'you think we're going to see a wedding this year?' Stella wanted to know.

'I'd not be surprised.' Jess would be more surprised if there wasn't a wedding, and the sooner the better. She was no fool and Innes, unlike his brother and sister, was an open book to her. A book that over the past few months had made interesting and disquieting reading. In the autumn, while the boats were all away at the English fishing grounds and she was looking after Meg, he had been so happy that he almost gave off a glow; but over the past week or two his exuberance had dimmed. He had started working all the hours he could and on the rare occasions when he was at home he either hovered maddeningly on the verge of blurting something out or was so absorbed in his own thoughts that he was no company at all. Zelda, too, had become more withdrawn, as though she was trying to shrink into herself physically and become small enough to escape notice.

Jess knew that feeling, for she had experienced it herself when she first discovered that she was carrying James. She, too, had tried to make herself unnoticeable until the day when Weem, by sliding a gold band on to her finger, had blessed her with marriage and respectability. Then, and only then, had she been able to walk tall, proud to be carrying her first child and happy in the knowledge that the bairn would be born within wedlock.

She longed to tell the young couple this, but she could say nothing, for the secret was theirs, not to be spoken of until they decided to confide in her.

Before the bowls of chicken broth were emptied that night Jess, eyeing her elder son's downbent head, was wondering if she had insulted him by inviting Jacob, an outsider, to share their Ne'erday dinner. She had been careful to seat James in his father's former place at the head of the table and put Jacob several places down at one side, crammed between Innes and Meg. Even so, it was Jacob who dominated the meal.

'This,' he said with satisfaction as he relinquished his empty soup bowl, 'puts me in mind of my mother's table in Portessie. D'you mind those days, Jess? It was a grand life, was it not?'

'And yet you went away from it,' Meg reminded him.

'And did better for yourself than you would have done if you'd stayed,' Gil added. A permanent smile seemed to be pinned to his flushed face and it was clear that he had had a fair drop to drink before his arrival. 'You've done very well for yourself.'

'Mebbe so, but mebbe I lost more than I gained.'

'Never! See's that bottle over here, James.'

'Don't you bother yourself, James, the man's had enough already,' Bethany said sharply from the stove, then bit her lip as her brother, paying her no heed, thrust the bottle at Gil.

'To tell the truth, Meg, now that I'm back I do regret all those years away. Young folk often have the wanderlust in them, but going away from your own folk can be a mistake.' Jacob leaned forward so that he could look along the table at James and Innes. 'If you two lads take my advice, you'll stay right here on the Firth where you belong.'

'I intend to,' Innes told him while James, slouching in his chair and staring at the table, said nothing. Bethany, safe in the knowledge that he would not look up, shot swift, anxious glances at him.

'At least I'd the sense to come back, even though I took so long about it. And now I'm in a position to be able to help some of my own folk.' Jacob eyed the steak pies that Jess and Stella were placing on the table. 'I tell you, nobody the world over knows how to welcome the new year in the way the Scots do.'

'You're right there!' Gil patted his wife's backside as she leaned across him, a bowl in each hand, to reach the table.

'D'you want these tatties set in front of you or emptied over your head?' she asked sharply.

'Ach, what's wrong with you, woman? It's Ne'erday, and surely a man can give his wife a wee cuddle now and again.'

Bethany clattered the bowl of potatoes and a bowl piled with mashed turnips, better known as chappit neeps, so hard on to the table that Jess feared for her good china dishes. 'Not in front of company.' Her face, already flushed with the heat from the stove, was scarlet and there was an ominous, steely gleam in her grey eyes.

'Now then . . .' Jess, anxious to draw attention away from the little domestic squabble, seized a knife and cut into the domed golden pastry covering the nearest pie, releasing a gush of aromatic steam. 'James, pass your plate down. Stella, there's more gravy in that pot over there, mebbe you'd bring it to the table.' If only, she thought as she piled wedges of pastry and chunks of steak and sausage on to plate after plate, they could all forget their differences and put a good face on it for Ne'erday, for her, for their guests.

But apparently not. James continued to scowl, despite Stella's anxious attempts to bring him out of his shell, and Gil's attentions had sent Bethany into a huff. She sat silently, picking at her food, and even Innes was quieter than usual while Zelda, close by his elbow, was like a little mouse.

By the time the clootie dumpling had been served and eaten Jess was worn to the bone with the effort of trying to pretend that this was a normal, happy family occasion.

Gil scraped his spoon noisily round his plate to trap any crumbs that might be lurking unseen, then re-filled his glass once again before pushing his chair away from the table and levering himself with some difficulty to his feet. 'Quiet now, I've an announcement to make.' His words were slightly blurred round the edges. 'I am proud to announce that me and Nathan and Mr MacFarlane here are setting up in business together.'

'In business?' Jess echoed, bewildered. She had heard nothing of any business deals. 'Jacob . . . ?'

'Aye, indeed we are,' he confirmed smilingly. 'I've need of good fish for foreign markets, and who better at catching and curing the silver darlings than our own local men? So from now on I'll be buying all the salted and pickled herring that Gil and Nathan can give me. And now that your announcement's been made, man,' he added easily to his new partner, 'I'd advise you to sit down before you fall down.'

Gil collapsed back into his seat, lifting his glass in a toast. 'Here's to 1913, and here's to your good health, Jacob MacFarlane.'

'And yours.'

'Well, I certainly wish the new venture success,' Jess said briskly when the toast had been drunk. 'Now it's time to get these wee ones to bed, then we'll have a cup of . . .'

'Since it's to be a formal occasion, I've a wee announcement of my own to make.' It was the first time James had spoken since his arrival and all heads immediately swivelled to where he sat, hands planted on the table and head up at last. 'You're not the only one who's starting the year with a new partnership, Gil. I'm thinking of doing the same thing myself. I might well be going to crew on Davie Geddes's boat.'

'What are you talking about?'

'Did I not say it clearly enough for you, Mother?' James leaned forward, his eyes – so like his father's – fixed on hers. When he spoke again it was directly to her, as though they were the only two people in the crowded room. 'Then I'll explain. I've finished with the *Fidelity*.'

'But . . .' Her head was beginning to ache and she was aware of Jacob, the stranger in their midst, following every word, bright-eyed with interest. 'This isn't a subject for our Ne'erday dinner. Bethany, Stella, help me to get the bairns to . . .'

'Don't be daft, man,' Meg boomed, ignoring her sister-in-law. 'The *Fidelity*'s a Lowrie boat. You cannae leave her, to crew for someone else.'

'I can do whatever I want,' James told her icily. 'Davie's looking for a good man to run his boat for him. And I'm looking for the chance to be my own man. I'll not have to work with Uncle Albert any more.'

'And who'll take on *Fidelity* after Albert's done with the sea?' Mowser had been concentrating on eating and drinking until then, leaving the conversation to others. Now that fishing was being discussed he began to take an interest.

'Charlie, mebbe, or Jem.'

'But they're nowhere near as good with a boat as you are,' Meg protested. 'Everyone knows that.'

'Albert doesn't, and I'm not waiting any longer for him to find out.'

'But James, what would your father . . .' Jess began, then stopped short.

'What would my father say?' James's face was as still and pale as marble in the gaslight; only his eyes were alive, glittering at his mother, mocking her. 'Ask him the next time you climb up that hill to keep his grave nice and tidy. Ask him – but I doubt if he'll bother with an answer, since he's done with both the *Fidelity* and the sea himself!'

'That's enough,' Jacob said quietly. 'You've no right to speak to your mother like that in her own home, or to run your father down when the man's not here to defend himself.'

James blinked, then rallied. 'And who are you, Mr MacFarlane,' he spoke the name sneeringly, '. . . to tell me how to speak in the house I was raised in?'

'A friend of your mother's and your father's from long

before you ever knew them. I don't like to hear them miscalled by anyone, so sit down, man, and let us end this evening in friendship, the way it should be.'

'James . . . ?'

Stella put a hand on her husband's wrist, but he pushed his chair back sharply, ignoring her, then grabbed his jacket and charged out of the house. As the heavy wooden door crashed shut behind him wee Ruth started to cry and the other children immediately joined in, without knowing why.

'Well!' Meg was outraged. 'What does that laddie think he's doing, behaving like that in his own mother's house?'

'He's upset, just,' Jess cut in swiftly, rising to her feet. 'And these bairns are worn out. Stella, Bethany, bring them to the back room and we'll tuck them up in the bed. Zelda, mebbe you'd make some tea while Meg butters the currant loaf and fetches out the wee cakes. Sit down at the fire, the rest of you, and we'll have our tea in just a minute.'

'I don't know what's happened to James,' poor Stella said, bewildered, when the younger members of the family had been tucked into bed like a row of rosy-cheeked sardines.

'Don't you fret yourself, pet, he never could abide family gatherings. He'll just be needing a wee while to himself, that's all. Would you go and help Meg and Zelda?' Jess suggested, and, when the young woman scampered off, glad of the chance to make herself useful, 'She's right, I don't know what's got into James. Do you know anything about it?'

'How could I, when we never have anything to do with each other? He's had enough of Uncle Albert, that's all, and mebbe enough of this place and everyone in it, just like me! But he's a grown man and he'll have to fend for himself – just like me!' Bethany said, and opened the door with such force that it would have rebounded against the wall if Jess hadn't caught it.

21

In the kitchen Zelda was making tea while Meg set out plates loaded with slices of currant loaf, biscuits and cake. Gil, Jacob, Innes and Mowser Buchan were smoking their pipes around the fireplace and the storm caused by James's outburst seemed to have settled.

Although everyone but Mowser, who had a prodigious appetite for a man of his age, protested that they were too full to eat another mouthful, the plates cleared quickly and the big teapot was re-filled several times. The rest of the evening passed uneventfully and ended when Stella and her father collected the three little girls and set off home. Meg went with them, and immediately afterwards Bethany and Gil left too, Ellen cradled in Bethany's arms while Rory sprawled bonelessly over his father's shoulder, still sound asleep. Then Innes took Zelda back to the farm, leaving Jess alone with Jacob who, after seeing the others out, settled down by the fire and re-lit his pipe.

She stood over him, hands folded across her waist. 'Jacob, James is my son and this is the house he was born and raised in. It was not your place to chastise him tonight.'

'Not my place? Someone had to say something, and since Gil kept his mouth shut it was left to me. It fair angered me to hear that lad speak to you as he did. Anyway,' he went on calmly, 'there was a time when I thought that it was going to be my place by rights; when I thought that your bairns would be mine as well.'

'Well they're not yours, and there's no sense in trying to rake the past up again.'

'I know well enough that they're Weem's, and not mine. I think of that every time I set eyes on them. And I regret it, Jess. All right,' he went on as she began to speak, 'I'm not going to keep hankering after what's gone, and I'm sorry if I vexed you in front of your family by speaking out of turn tonight.'

'It wasn't all your fault, I suppose. It's just James – there's never any way of knowing which way he'll jump.'

'D'you think he means it about leaving the *Fidelity*?'

'Mebbe. And mebbe he was just trying to upset me and Bethany . . . her more than me, for that boat means a lot to her. She should have been born a laddie, then she could have gone to the fishing and worked on the boat herself.'

'That would have been a waste of a beautiful woman.'

Jess gave him the ghost of a smile. 'Better not say that to her. Being a woman's a curse as far as she's concerned. Jacob,' she went on as he picked his pipe up again, 'I don't want to be uncivil, but it's been a long day . . .'

'And you need to get to your bed.' He started tapping the pipe out on the grate, just as Weem used to do. 'Of course you do and I should have realised that for myself. My only excuse is that I enjoy your company so much.'

He went, and at last Jess was free to restore her kitchen to order. When Innes came in she was still working.

'Are you not in your bed yet?'

'Is that not what I'm supposed to say to you?' she asked drily. 'Put that cloth down, you've got your work to go to in the morning.'

'I can't go to my bed knowing that you're still busy.' He picked up a plate and dried it as he spoke. 'Two of us can get the work finished in half the time.'

'Zelda got back to the farm all right?'

'Aye. She fair enjoyed herself.'

'Good. I thought,' Jess said carefully, 'that she looked a wee thing pale.'

'Did you? She's fine as far as I know.'

Tell me, Innes, Jess thought. Talk to me and between us we can work out what to do. But he said nothing and so she, too, had to keep quiet.

'Mr MacFarlane?'

'Mrs Pate.' Jacob turned from his contemplation of the *Fidelity*, lying at rest in the harbour, and touched his cap. 'Good morning to you. A fine brisk day, is it not?'

'Well enough.' The sky overhead was blue, with what clouds there were racing across it before the wind.

Jacob bent to chuck Ellen under the chin and shake hands with Rory, then straightened again. 'I was just admiring the lines of the boat. She's a fine vessel – your father did well when he bought her.'

'He was proud of the *Fidelity*,' Bethany acknowledged, falling into step with him as he began to pace back along the harbour wall. 'Mr MacFarlane, I was wondering if I could have a wee word with you?' Her heart was thumping hard and she was glad of the keen January wind that had given both children bright-red cheeks and noses, for its sting would help to explain the high colour rising to her own face.

'It would be my pleasure. What can I do for you?'

'Mebbe you'd come along to the house and have some tea? We can talk in comfort there.'

He cheerfully agreed and as they walked together he talked about his enjoyment of the Ne'erday dinner they had shared at her mother's two days earlier. Only when the children were settled with their toys, and the tea made and set out along with a plate of shortbread fingers, did he ask, 'Now then, what can I do for you?'

'It's about my brother . . . about James.' She almost had to force the name past her lips, and a sudden darkening of the green eyes holding hers and a discernible tightening of Jacob's lips beneath his moustache made her mission all the more difficult.

'Ah yes, your brother. And what might we want to discuss with regard to him?'

Bethany took a sip of tea, realising only when it scalded her lips and the roof of her mouth that she had forgotten to put milk in. Seeing her wince, Jacob tutted, then took his own saucer and poured some milk into it from the jug.

'Drink this, it will soothe the sting.' While she emptied the saucer hurriedly he poured milk into her tea and stirred it. 'Now, take your time.'

Bethany had never been fussed over in her life, and it did not help at all, but she had been planning this business for two days and two sleepless nights, and had seized her chance when she saw the man standing alone on the harbour wall. Having taken the first step, she must go on.

'It's about what James said at Ne'erday about leaving the *Fidelity*. It's not what he wants, Mr MacFarlane.'

'Your mother seemed to think that he didn't mean it. That he was only trying to upset her, and you.'

'He does mean it, and it's got nothing to do with upsetting folk. It's our Uncle Albert: he's not half the skipper Da was, and James can't stand to see the boat wrongly used.'

Now that she was into the situation Bethany found things a little easier. Leaning forward, her tea left untasted, she explained how she and her mother and Innes had refused to hand over their shares in the boat to James in order to give him more say.

'We were just being thrawn and none of us realised how miserable James has been with the way the boat's being run. When I did find out I offered to let him have the use of my share, and to talk to Mother and Innes, but by then it was too late. I think,' she finished miserably, 'that he felt we'd betrayed him. And so we have in a way.'

Jacob had been watching her with that disconcertingly intent stare she had noticed the night he came to talk business with Gil. Now he asked, 'And what has this got to do with me?'

She bit her lip, realising that the hardest part was about to begin. 'I thought, when you took Gil and Nathan on as partners . . . They use all the fish the *Fidelity* catches, and James is right when he says she would do even better with a good skipper. And I wondered . . . Uncle Albert likes money better than he likes working, and if someone offered to buy some of his shares I'm sure he would sell them. Someone sympathetic to James's ideas. He is a very good fisherman,' she added hurriedly, 'and if the person who bought Albert's share was willing to make him the new skipper I'm certain he'd do well.'

'And you think I could be that someone.'

'None of us could afford to buy Albert out.'

'My dear young woman, what would I do with shares in a Buckie fishing boat?'

'What would you do with shares in the Pate businesses?'

'I expect . . . I intend,' MacFarlane said with emphasis on the last word, 'to make a deal of money from that arrangement. And so will your husband, which should please you. But a few shares in one fishing boat . . .' He shrugged, spreading his hands out. 'I'm not sure they would be of much use to me.'

'You could give them to my mother as a gift,' Bethany said without thinking. 'I'm quite sure that she would use them to help James.' Then, realising that she was speaking out of turn, 'I mean, you're old friends and it's plain to see that you like her, so . . .'

MacFarlane settled back in his chair. 'Has Jess ever talked to you about me?'

'No,' she answered, then wondered when she saw a sudden blankness in his eyes if she should have been kinder and lied.

'We grew up together. We'd have wed if she hadn't met your father.'

'You and my mother?' She could scarcely keep the astonishment out of her voice. So Stella's romantic notions had been right after all.

He leaned forward. 'Is that so surprising? I was a deckhand on another man's boat, and Jess was very beautiful, even as a child. You're like her,' he said. Then, as she merely looked at him as though he was talking nonsense, 'Oh, you're Weem Lowrie's daughter all right. You've his eyes – and his nature too – but you're fortunate in having your mother's fine bones.'

He reached out and touched one temple lightly; she stiffened but held still, without flinching as his fingertips traced their way down the side of her face, over the cheekbone to the point of her chin.

'You have the best of both of them,' he said, more to himself than to her. It was a relief when he sat back in his seat again, his voice taking on a business-like note. 'To be honest with you, Mrs Pate, I'm not of a mind to do anything to help your brother after the way he behaved in your mother's house the other night.'

She bit her lip, then said, 'You're right, he spoke out of turn, when he should have had the sense to hold his tongue, but that's not the way he really is, as you'll find out if you stay on here for long.'

'He's very fortunate in having such a loyal sister.'

His piercing gaze was disconcerting, and Bethany busied herself with pouring out more tea. 'We were close as bairns, James and me. And if you knew what had happened to him once he grew up you'd understand him better,' she said desperately; then as Jacob raised his eyebrows, clearly waiting to hear more, she threw caution to the winds and went on to tell him of the way her brother had been married off to Stella so that Weem could gain ownership of Mowser Buchan's sailboat.

'So, that's why he has such a grudge against the world?' Jacob asked when she had finished. 'And what about you, Bethany? What did Weem gain from your marriage?'

'Nothing.' She got up and began to collect the cups together, knowing that she had already said too much. His hand landed on her wrist, gently but with enough pressure to ease her back into her chair.

'I believe that Gil and Nathan Pate made an agreement with your father to buy all the fish the *Fidelity* catches.'

'Yes.'

'An arrangement made round about the time of your marriage, I'll be bound. Eh? Weem,' Jacob MacFarlane said when she kept silent, 'was more astute than I've given him credit for.'

'He was one of the best fishermen and sailors on this coast, and my brother James is every bit as good, as you'll find if you buy into the boat.'

'I'm sure he is.' Jacob got to his feet and began to shrug his coat on. 'It has been an interesting talk, and I'll certainly think over what you have said. But it might take a few days before I can come to any decision.'

'You'll not let Gil or James know we've been talking, will you?'

He gave her one final piercing look as he picked up his hat. 'Of course not. Thank you for the tea, my dear, it was very warming on such a cold day. And it was very kind of you to take pity when you found me shivering in that cold wind.'

As soon as he had gone Bethany wished that she had chewed her tongue out rather than spoken to him. She wanted to help James, but instead she had probably made things worse. She had even told family secrets to this man who had suddenly appeared from her mother's past, and in return she had discovered that Stella's romantic notions about Jacob MacFarlane and Jess Lowrie had been right after all.

It was a pity that she would not be able to tell Stella that.

Innes trudged along the last part of the lane that led to the Mulhollands' cottage. Anxious to get the evening's business settled, he had started at a brisk jog, but had been forced to slow down as the lanes became steeper. Clouds had come in from the north during the afternoon and now icy, sleety rain danced at him from the darkness, stinging his face. Down on the coastline angry great waves were crashing on to the shore and even the boats in the protection of the harbour shifted nervously at their moorings, crowding together as though for warmth and comfort.

For the moment at least the lane's high banks protected Innes from the wind that had been buffeting the village when he left. It was with this harsh winter weather in mind that the fishing folk who lived at the water's edge had positioned their homes with the windowless gable ends facing the winds and the spray.

Despite the chill bite that reddened his face, Innes perspired inside his best clothes, from nervous anticipation as much as from hurrying uphill. Tonight he and Zelda were going to tell her parents about their marriage plans. He thought that the Mulhollands, who treated him civilly enough when he visited their home, would be willing to accept him as a member of their family. Even so, the prospect of facing his intended's father and asking formally for her hand was an ordeal for any young lad.

'And not a word about the bairn,' Zelda had impressed on him at their last meeting. 'They'll mebbe accept you well enough, but I can't let my father know what we've been up to.'

'You make it sound dirty, and it wasn't! Not for me,

anyway,' Innes protested, and she went into his arms, hugging him fiercely.

'Nor for me. It was the happiest, most wonderful thing that ever happened to me! But I doubt if my father would see it that way. He says that purity's the greatest gift a woman can offer to her husband when they wed. That's all me and my sisters heard from him and my mother when we were growing up.'

'You offered your gift to me and I'm going to be your husband, so what's the difference?'

'Oh Innes, if you don't understand that you'll never understand my father. Just say the right things and keep away from the wrong ones. And you'll have to promise that we'll go to the kirk every Sunday when we're man and wife.'

'I don't go to the kirk.' Having been raised by parents who were rarely away from their church, Weem had turned his back on religion as soon as he was old enough to control his own life. Meg attended Sunday services, as did Albert, held up as an example by Weem to his children. 'If a man like my brother, with his carnal tastes, can walk into a church without it falling about his ears, then there can't be much to this God business,' Innes had heard him proclaim again and again.

'You'll go with me when we're wed,' Zelda ordered. 'And once we get married it won't matter about him finding out about the bairn, for then I'll belong to you and not to him.'

The shepherd's house was a matter of fifty yards in front of Innes now; he could see the light from the kitchen window, a pale glow that winked and fragmented, then disappeared and appeared again as the wind-lashed trees round the small building tossed their branches about. He would be glad to get indoors and sit by the fire and drink some hot tea. And see Zelda again.

Footsteps scurried down the lane in his direction; as he peered into the darkness, hoping that she had come to meet him, a small figure ran full tilt into him and clutched at his knees for support. 'Innes? Is that you?'

'Daniel? What are you doing out on a night like this?'

'Ma sent me,' Zelda's small brother panted. His face was a dim grey blob in the darkness. 'You've to turn round and go home right now, she says.'

'Why?'

'I don't know, but Da's in a rage and he's leathering our Zelda. Ma sent me to tell you not to come . . . She said not to!' Daniel squeaked as Innes began to run towards the cottage, towing the lad by the wrist behind him.

'Never mind what your ma said!' All Innes could think of was getting to Zelda. He charged along the last section of the lane and started hammering on the thick timber door with both fists, yelling out her name.

22

Innes was so busy attacking the door that when it opened he might have fallen into the stone-flagged kitchen, had Mr Mulholland not caught him by the collar, dragged him inside, then pushed him against the wall so hard that the breath was driven from his body.

'You dare to come knocking at my door after what you've done to my daughter?' Mulholland's face, just inches from Innes's, was twisted and so engorged with angry blood that his eyes stood out in their sockets.

'Mr Mulholland . . .' Innes's stunned lungs were still fighting to fill themselves again, and his voice could scarcely reach above a whisper. 'I love Zelda. I'd never harm her!'

'And you think that getting her with child, shaming a wee innocent lassie who's never known the marriage bed, isnae doin' harm tae her?'

Innes had managed to catch his breath. 'But I want to marry her! I came here tonight to ask your permission.'

'Marry, is it?' Mulholland turned away from him, easing his grip without releasing it. 'Grizelda, ye shiftless whore that ye are, bring my belt through to me. And there's a gentleman here with a proposal of marriage for you! Are you not the fortunate lassie?'

As the man shifted position Innes saw beyond him to the rest of the small kitchen. Mrs Mulholland, expressionless, sat in a corner with the two youngest members of her brood on her lap, while the others, including Daniel, who had managed to slip through the door unnoticed, were gathered round her in a tight group. The children were wide-eyed and white to the lips, and one or two were weeping silent tears of fright.

Innes only had time to glance at them before the door to the cottage's other room opened and Zelda appeared, her hair wild and her eyes red. A scarlet mark blazed across one cheek; her two hands, clenched before her breast, held the broad leather belt, decorated along its length with brass studs, that her father always wore about his waist.

At the sight of her all Innes's inhibitions about retaliating against an older man, the father of his future wife, vanished. Rage gave him the strength to throw Mulholland off and, as the man staggered aside, he reached Zelda, pulling her into the room, examining the welt on her face with his fingertips. 'Zelda . . . What in God's name d'you think you're doing to her, man?'

'How dare you use your filthy mouth to soil the name of the Lord!' Mulholland thundered behind him. 'I know all about you!'

'You told them?'

Fresh tears welled up in Zelda's dark eyes and she shook her head, biting her lower lip hard to stifle the sobs that were beginning to shake her shoulders.

'She,' her father stated contemptuously, 'said nothing. It was the farmer's wife who was the one to tell me that my daughter – my own child that I raised in God's light, and fed and housed and clothed, and guided along the path of righteousness – had shamed me before the whole community and pledged her soul to the devil as a whore!'

'Don't you dare say that about Zelda! She's a decent lassie; she's been with nobody but me, and that only because we're to be man and wife.'

'So you're proud of what you've done to her?'

'No, I'm not,' Innes said between set teeth. 'I lost my

senses and I behaved badly, but we'll be wed within the month. Surely you can find it in your heart to forgive us . . .'

'Only the Lord can forgive the sins you've committed against me and my blood, and I'm certain sure that He never will. Get out of my house,' Mulholland ordered, jerking his head at the door. In desperation Innes looked at Zelda's mother, who had always welcomed him into her house and treated him kindly. She had, after all, sent young Daniel to warn him to stay away. But she looked back stonily, tightening her grip on her youngest, and he realised that when it came to discipline and punishment her husband ruled the family and she agreed with all that he said and did. He and Zelda could expect no mercy or understanding from anyone in this house.

'I'm going, but I'm taking Zelda with me.'

The man shrugged his heavy shoulders. 'She's no daughter of mine now, you can lie with her in the pig pen if you've a mind. She's not worth any better than that.'

As Zelda made a small choking sound and tears poured down her white face, Innes swallowed down his rage. The important thing was to get her out of here as quickly as possible. 'Come away with me, we'll go to my . . .'

Putting a hand on the girl's back to urge her forward, he felt dampness against his palm just before she winced and pulled away, the breath hissing sharply between her teeth. 'Zelda?' He took her shoulders and turned her about, then exclaimed as he saw the blood seeping through the material of her blouse. It was then that he realised the meaning of the belt that her father had left in the inner room. The belt that was never away from his waist unless he was sleeping – or chastising one of his children.

'Dear God!'

'I told you!' Mulholland took a step towards him. 'I'll not have His name in your vile mouth!'

'It's safer in my mouth than it is in yours. Call yourself a man of religion just because you go to the church every

Sunday and say your prayers every day?' Innes faced
him, feet apart and fists clenched. 'I'll tell you this,
Mr Mulholland, I'd rather be a blasphemous sinner than
worship any god willing to heed the prayers of a man
who bullies defenceless lassies in the name of religion!'

With a low roar Mulholland seized him by the upper
arm with one hand and snatched the belt from Zelda with
the other. As he was hustled out of the cottage Innes heard
the girl shout his name. Twisting round to look at her, he
saw that her attempt to follow him had been foiled by her
mother who, thrusting the little ones into the arms of two
older children, jumped up and pulled her back.

That was the last Innes saw of her before the door
slammed and he and her father were outside in the bitter
dark night.

Mulholland propelled Innes down the dark lane, their
booted feet scuffling and scuttering on the small stones
and stumbling over the ruts. Below the sound of the wind
and his own panting breath, and the older man's steady,
animal grunts, Innes heard thin ice crackling beneath their
weight as they splashed through puddles. He had no idea
where they were going, and knew only that if Mulholland
had some thought of running him off the area it would not
work. Not until he got Zelda out of that house.

The man pushed him unexpectedly to one side of the
lane, releasing his arm at the same time, so that Innes
stumbled and almost fell over the raised banking. His
attempts to remain upright took him up the slight slope
and down the other side, but just as he managed to regain
his balance Mulholland gave him a hefty push. Innes
staggered, tripped over something and fell, pain jarring
through him as his shoulder glanced off the trunk of a
tree. He only had time to grasp that they were in some
sort of clearing by the side of the lane before Zelda's
father was on him, dragging him up by the jacket with
one hand while he drew the other fist back. Then the

world exploded and everything seemed to vanish for a matter of seconds.

When he regained his wits Innes found himself down on the ground, his body twitching in rhythm to the solid, throbbing pain of booted feet lashing into his sides and his stomach, and his back and his shoulders. His first instinct was to curl himself into a ball in order to protect as much of his body as possible, but realising as his brain cleared that he could not afford to let the fight become too one-sided, he managed to roll off to one side and regain his feet with the help of a sturdy bush.

As he turned, the moon, in a brief appearance between ragged, racing clouds, showed Mulholland facing him, moonlight glinting on the brass studs of the belt he had looped about his neck in order to leave his hands free.

'Have you had enough?' he asked thickly.

'I'm . . .' Innes, wincing at the pain in his jaw, spat blood and tried again, 'I'm not wanting to fight with you, Mr Mulholland. I just want to marry Zelda, and look after her and the bairn the way I should.'

'You keep away from her.'

'If I do that will you leave her alone?'

'That's none of your business. She's my daughter and it's my name she's brought down in shame. I'll deal with her as I see fit.'

'You'll not,' Innes said, and went in fast and low, tucking his chin down so that he could use his skull as a battering ram, well aware that the other man had the weight advantage and that he himself would have to use other tactics. The whoosh of suddenly expelled breath as he connected with Mulholland's midriff cheered him on and gave him added strength. Twisting, he forced his left shoulder into the man's hip, while both hands found Mulholland's left knee. He pulled hard and Zelda's father, already winded, went down forcefully. Innes followed and the two of them grappled, rolling over on the cold, stony ground.

It was inevitable that Mulholland's weight would eventually give control of the situation back to him. Even so, every time he tried to throw the younger man away Innes held on, his hands seeking a good grip. He was fighting for Zelda now rather than for himself. As Mulholland got to his knees, Innes caught hold of one end of the belt and pulled, with some idea of yanking it free and using it as a weapon.

The other end, with the big buckle on it, did not come loose as he had expected; instead, Mulholland's flailing hands slipped away, trying to reach the belt. Innes managed to hold on until Zelda's father, seemingly giving up the fight, fell on to his face, writhing and gurgling. Only then did Innes realise that the buckle had somehow caught in the man's clothing and, with the belt pulled tight beneath his chin, the man was slowly being strangled to death.

'Dear God!' He let go of the belt at once and started tugging at the body, trying to turn it over. 'Mr Mulholland!' For a moment there was no sign of life, then as he dragged on the man's shoulder Mulholland suddenly swung over and his two large hands reached up and clamped themselves about Innes's neck.

'Try to choke me, would you?' the man hissed into his ear as he scrambled to his feet, pulling his victim up after him. A knee jabbed fiercely into the pit of Innes's belly and pain radiated to the very tips of his toes and the ends of his hair. 'Now,' he heard dimly as he sank back on to the ground, 'you'll get the thrashing you deserve!'

Then Innes screamed as the belt buckle scythed viciously out of the darkness and slashed across one cheek. Another blow followed, then another and another, until he was too busy trying to scramble out of reach to count. Mulholland followed him, hauling him back each time he showed signs of hiding beneath a protective bush. Again and again the buckle landed on his head, his face, his arms, legs and back until finally a well-placed blow brought the metal down hard on one temple, and as far as Innes Lowrie was concerned the fight was lost.

Jacob rattled the poker between the bars of the fire, stirring the glowing coals into fresh life. The kitchen was snug and cosy, despite the wind that beat against the door in gusts. 'Your daughter took pity on me today when we met, and invited me in for a cup of tea. She's a fine bonny lass, Jess.'

'She was bonny from the very moment of her birth.' James and Innes had come from the womb red and wrinkled and squalling, but Bethany had been born with skin like porcelain, a silky covering of reddish-brown hair on her small skull and clear, calm grey eyes. Jess had thought as she held her new baby for the first time that a daughter would be special, but as soon as she was on her feet, two months before her first birthday, Bethany had scorned everyone else in favour of James, toddling out of the door after him and the other laddies whenever she got a chance. It was then that it had begun to dawn on Jess that her new baby's calm gaze had reflected a total lack of interest in the woman holding her, rather than serenity.

Jacob dropped the poker, settled his backside comfortably into the chair that had been Weem's and stretched his legs across the hearthrug. 'She's a right mixture of the two of you.'

'You think so? I only see her father in her.'

'She's got his eyes, his strong chin and his nature too, from what I've seen and heard of her so far. But that bonny sheen to her hair, like well-polished mahogany – that's his colouring darkened by yours. And she's got your womanliness.'

'That's something she couldn't have got from Weem,' Jess acknowledged, smiling. 'But I can't say I've seen it in her. She was always a tomboy, and although she makes a good fist of looking after Gil's bairns there's no motherliness about her.'

'That wasn't what I meant. I'm talking of the womanliness that sets a man's heart racing and his mind dreaming of what might be.'

'Don't tell me you've a fancy for her yourself?' She looked at him from beneath raised eyebrows. To her surprise, her teasing ruffled him.

'Not a bit of it! You know fine that there's only one woman I'll ever fancy. I'm just saying that she's got something that not many women have. And she got it from you. To tell the truth, I don't know what she saw in that lump Gil Pate.'

'That's for her to know. None of our business.'

'Aye well, there's no accounting for the world,' Jacob agreed. Then, after a short silence, 'She seems to be bothered about your James wanting to leave the boat.'

'I doubt if it's a matter of wanting. He and Albert just don't see eye to eye. When Weem was in charge of that boat she was always the last into harbour. Many's the day I've spent straining my eyes for a sight of her, and many's the time I almost gave her up for lost before she appeared. I've seen her come in so low in the water with the fish she carried that it was a wonder she didn't sink.'

'He was a good fisherman, was Weem,' Jacob acknowledged.

'James is just like him, but Albert's cautious. He's more likely to scurry back to harbour at the first sign of poor weather with the holds only half-full.' A gust of wind rattled at the door and Jess glanced at the clock. Innes should be back soon, no doubt chilled to the bone after his long walk down from the shepherd's cottage.

'Why did James not take the boat over when Weem died?'

Jess stared down at her knitting, then said, 'Men always think they'll live on for ever and Weem was the same as the rest of them. He made no plans for the future.'

'Will you be as bothered as Bethany if James leaves the Lowrie boat?'

'I'll be sorry about it, but he's a grown man and he must make his own choices. It's none of my . . .' She stopped as someone gave three hefty knocks at the door. 'That'll be Innes. I latched the door against the wind. Let him in, will you, while I make some tea. He'll be frozen through.'

As she busied herself with the kettle a blast of cold air swept around her ankles from the open door. There was a muttered conversation, then Jacob called to her, a note of urgency in his voice, and she turned to see him disappearing into the darkness, leaving the door swinging open. Following, she found him and another man lifting a large bundle from the back of a farm cart.

'What is it?' She wrapped her arms tightly about her body, shivering. Then as the men upended the sack between them she saw, in the light from the open doorway, that it wasn't a sack at all but a man hanging limply from their grasp, head lolling. 'Innes? Innes! Dear God, what happened to him?'

'All I know is that the shepherd brought him to the farm and the master told me to take him home,' the carter said, while Jacob ordered, 'Go on ahead, Jess, and we'll follow.'

Once Innes had been deposited on the bed in the small downstairs room, the carter made himself scarce while Jess and Jacob set about undressing the youth. He came to as they worked on him and feebly tried to fend them off, muttering at them through puffed, bleeding lips.

'What happened to you, son?' Jess asked frantically, shocked by the sight of him. His face was caked with blood and even the hands pushing at her were bruised and cut.

'Zelda,' he said in reply. One of his eyes was swollen beyond opening, but the other was suddenly wide, sweeping round the room. 'I have to fetch Zelda!' He tried to raise himself up, groaning and panting with the effort, but Jacob pushed him back.

'We'll fetch her in the morning. Just be at peace for now and let your mother tend to you.'

As they removed his filthy wet clothes Jess exclaimed again and again over each fresh bruise, while Jacob's hands moved over the younger man's chest, back and limbs, checking for signs of broken bones or internal injury. Then he fetched a towel and began, as gently as he could, to rub warmth into the chilled body, while Jess ran to warm a clean night-shirt before the fire and fetch a basin of hot water and some cloths.

Once washed from head to toe, Innes was a sorry sight. He was covered with welts and bruises, one eye was closed and there were cuts all over his face and hands. Only one of the cuts, from cheekbone to chin on the left side of his face, was still seeping blood.

Jacob applied a cold compress to both it and the swollen eye. 'He's going to be sore and stiff for a good few days to come, but no bones are broken and nothing seems to be hurt inside. He'll recover.'

'But what happened to him?'

'He's taken a good beating; feet as well as fists, and something else that caused those welts. But he fought back . . .' Jacob lifted Innes's right hand and pointed to the bruised, scraped knuckles. 'There were mebbe more than just the one man against him.'

'Who'd do such a thing to a laddie who's never lifted a hand to a living soul?'

Jacob shrugged. 'He's not your wee laddie any more, Jess. What he gets up to is his business, not yours or mine.' He eased the compress back and peered at the cut. 'It's stopped bleeding. Put your hand there, lad.' He lifted Innes's hand and placed it on the compress over his eye. 'It'll help. You'll mebbe have a scar on your cheek to show for the night's business, but that's of no importance,' he said calmly. 'We'll get you into your night-shirt now and I've no doubt your mother'll fetch you some food.'

Innes plucked at the bed-clothing, then peered round the

room.. 'This isnae my bed,' he said, his voice smothered by his bruised, split lips.

'You're in the wee back room, for you're not fit to manage the stairs.'

'Should I mebbe send for the doctor?' Jess asked Jacob when she joined him in the kitchen later, having left Innes to drink a bowl of soup.

'Not at all. I've seen cuts and bruises and broken bones often enough in my time, and I've seen men coughing and spitting blood from hurts inside too,' he added, 'so you can take my word for it that your Innes has nothing like that. We've done all the doctoring that's necessary. Now,' he levered himself to his feet, 'I'd best be getting back to my lodgings.'

'I'm glad you were here,' she said as she saw him out of the door.

'I could always be here, if you just said the word, Jess,' he replied, and went into the night, shoulders hunched against the wind.

23

Zelda arrived early the next morning. 'Where is he? Mrs Bain says their carter brought him here last night. Is he all right?' A livid red welt on one cheek stood out against her white face.

'He'll mend. What hap . . . ?'

'Zelda?' Innes called from the back room and the girl rushed to him, halting in the doorway, her hands flying to her mouth as she took in the sight of his bruised face and swollen eye.

'Oh, Innes, what did he do to you?'

'Never mind me – what did he do to you?'

Zelda glanced over her shoulder at Jess, then went forward primly and sat on the end of the bed, hands knotted together in her lap. 'He was all right after . . . after he came back in, though he'd not tell me what had happened between the two of you, or where you were. It was as if it was all over and done with. Then when I got to my work this morning, the mistress told me that he'd carried you to their door and asked for someone to take you home. Mrs Bain was kind, she let me take time off to see you.'

'Who are you talking about?' Jess asked. Then as they glanced at her, at each other, and then away, like naughty children sharing a secret, she moved to where she could lift the girl's chin and study the damaged face. 'Was it your father, Zelda? Poor wee lass, is this what he did to you?' Turning to her son, her anger mounting, she added, 'And to you . . . all because of a bairn?'

This time they looked at each other, then at her. 'Who told you?' Innes asked.

'I could see for myself. Not because of that, lassie,' Jess added as Zelda's hand instinctively went to her flat belly. 'Because I know my lad here. Three months ago he looked as if he'd been given all the riches of the world, but for the past few weeks he's looked as if he had exchanged those riches for all the burdens. I've been waiting for the two of you to tell me, so's we could make plans.'

'We were going to, once we'd told her parents. But her father didn't take it very well,' Innes said.

'I've brought shame on him,' Zelda explained earnestly, 'and he's finding it hard to forgive me. But I think he's sorry for last night. My mother says he was on his knees most of the night, praying.'

'If I get my hands on him he'll be on his knees again, but only because he'll not have the strength to stand up,' Jess said fiercely, but Zelda had turned her attention back to Innes.

'Are you sure you're all right? Your poor eye looks terrible.'

It did. The area around it was puffed up and coloured dark blue, shot through with yellow streaks. What could be seen of the eye itself was a fearsome sight, since the white was now an angry red.

'I'm fine now that I know you're safe.'

'Oh, Innes!' Tears began to spill down the girl's cheeks. Heedless of Jess, she reached out to stroke her lover's battered face with the tips of her fingers. At her touch, Innes lurched forward on to his knees, pushing the bed-clothes aside, and Zelda went straight into his open arms.

To Jess's irritation, only Stella was in agreement with her desire to see Zelda's father punished for what he had done to Innes.

'It's at such times,' the younger woman said in a low voice, 'that I'm glad I only have lassies. Imagine seeing one of your own in a state like that!'

But when Jess turned to Bethany for understanding all she got was a robust, 'Good for Innes, he's got some gumption after all.' Meanwhile Jacob said, 'I told you, Jess, Innes is a grown man now and he must fight his own battles.'

'A boy who's never fought in his life, up against a big man with a belt in his hand?' Jess had finally got Zelda to tell her what had caused the cuts on her son's face and hands.

'There are no rules in that sort of fighting. Innes has to learn that next time he should make use of whatever comes to hand. I've seen a wee slip of a laddie besting a man twice his size, just because he'd the sense to pick up a length of iron chain from a quay. That was a grand fight,' Jacob recalled nostalgically. 'They ended up in the water and we nearly lost the two of them, for the big fellow cracked his head against the hull of a boat and the wee one wouldn't let go of the chain and got carried to the bottom by the weight of it.'

The following day Jacob called on James. 'You'll know about your brother's wee misunderstanding with his lassie's father.'

'I heard something of it.'

'His poor face is in a terrible state,' Stella chimed in.

'It'll mend,' Jacob assured her, then chuckled as old Mowser said sorrowfully, 'I wish I'd seen it . . . I've not seen a good fight in many a year.'

'Mind the time the new fishing season had to start with blood-letting for good fortune? Fine fights we used to see on the harbourside in those days, eh?'

'You're right there. It was a grand chance for men who couldnae stand each other to do something about it.' Mowser nodded vigorously. 'I got the season off to a good start myself many a time. I mind once when I was a deckhand just made up from being the new lad, and we'd this mate with a right sharp tongue. He'd never let a man get on with his job in peace, that one, and he'd a real down on me, being the youngest. Come the start of the new season, when I was bigger and a lot stronger than I'd been the year before, I made sure the rest of them would keep their hands in their pockets, then I went up to this mate of ours and "Just for the sake of the fishing", I said to him, all polite. Then I took my fist and knocked him arse over tit across the harbour.' Mowser cackled in delight at the memory. 'He made my life even more of a misery after that, but we'd the best damned season in years.'

'That's enough, Da,' Stella cut in, then to Jacob, in a whisper, 'I'd appreciate it, Mr MacFarlane, if you'd not encourage such talk in this house.'

'You're quite right, it's not what I'm here for at all. James, I thought you should be the first to know that your uncle's just agreed to sell his share in the *Fidelity* to me.'

James Lowrie had been sitting at the table, paying little heed to the conversation, but now his dark head jerked up. 'You've bought into the boat?' he asked incredulously, while Stella came to stand behind him, one hand on his shoulder, her face filled with apprehension.

'I have indeed. But it won't make any difference to you or the other shareholders,' Jacob nodded reassuringly to Stella, 'except that I hope you've not promised your services to Davie Geddes, for the *Fidelity*'ll be in need of a good skipper.'

Watching closely, he saw sudden hope spring to James's face, then it was forced out by suspicion. 'Why should you buy into the boat?'

'Because I used to be a fisherman in this district myself and coming back's given me the notion to be part of that life again. Though you need have no worries on my

account,' Jacob added swiftly, 'for I'll not be interfering
with the way you handle her.'

'Oh, James!' Stella, her face radiant, squeezed her
husband's shoulder, but he ignored her.

'You must have offered Albert good money, since he
didn't even have to think about it. Is my mother behind
this? Did she ask you to do it, to stop me crewing for
Davie Geddes?'

'You've either got a very poor idea of me as a businessman or a very good opinion of your mother's powers of
persuasion,' Jacob said evenly. 'Jess might be a good
friend of mine, but I don't seek her advice when it
comes to spending my hard-earned silver. I bought into
your brother-in-law's business because I expect to get a
good return from my investment and I bought into the
Lowrie boat for the same reason. I'm hoping you'll be
her skipper, but if you don't care for the idea I'm sure
I can find someone else.' He rose and picked up his hat,
nodding first to Stella, then to Mowser. 'Mrs Lowrie, my
apologies for having intruded into your home like this. Mr
Buchan, good day to you.'

'James . . .' Stella said again as the door closed behind
their visitor.

'I'll not have my mother using the likes of him to make
up to me for what she did to my father.'

'She did nothing to your father!' Stella spoke out for
once, goaded beyond caution by the way he had just
questioned a good opportunity. 'It was her right to bury
her own man. And she'd never ask Mr MacFarlane to
buy Albert out of the boat just to make you happy.'

'Even if she did,' Mowser said from his corner, 'what
difference would it make? You want the boat and now's
your chance. Don't be so thrawn, laddie!'

James hesitated, looking from one to the other, then
went out of the house. Jacob MacFarlane was walking
briskly away, but he stopped and turned when he heard
the clatter of iron-clad boots at his back.

'James Lowrie. Have you decided?'

'I'd like time to think about your offer.'

'Twenty-four hours and no more. I'd say,' Jacob said with a hard edge to his voice, 'that that should give you enough time.'

'Time for what?'

'To find out for yourself that I do not take my instructions from your mother.'

'You've taken a right beating there,' James said half an hour later. Innes, embarrassed, fingered his swollen mouth gingerly.

'It looks worse than it is.'

'It always does. Next time you'll be more ready, eh?'

'There won't be a next time, please God,' Jess said tartly from the stove, where she was using a large spoon to skim fat from a pot of mutton broth. 'Don't encourage the laddie, he's not a fighter and never has been.'

'He should have learned to use his fists when he was younger. God knows I tried to teach you,' James said to his brother.

'I never thought I'd have the need.'

'You know better now,' James said flatly; then, 'I want you to have a look at the boat's engines on Saturday. I don't think Jocky makes a good enough job of cleaning out the tubes and she needs a proper overhaul since there's a chance she might be doing some line fishing.'

With the advent of better weather some of the drifters had started fishing with long lines for haddock and codling, which were either treated in the smokehouses and sent to the markets or sold locally to housewives, who cooked them from fresh or smoked them on the triangular frames that hung on the outer wall of most cottages.

Innes's stomach muscles, still tender from his beating, twitched uneasily at the prospect, but he said aloud, 'I'll do that for you.' After what he had been through he was sure he could manage to go on board the boat again, as long as she was in the harbour.

'You've talked Albert into going after the white fish?' Jess was surprised. The *Fidelity* had not gone line fishing since Weem's death.

'It's nothing to do with Albert.' James watched her closely as he spoke. 'If she goes out, it's me that'll be taking her.'

'You?'

'Are you surprised? You must know that your friend Jacob's bought Albert out of the boat,' he said, and the spoon slipped from Jess's fingers to disappear beneath the soup's bubbling surface.

'He's done what?'

'He's bought a third share of the *Fidelity* and asked me to be her skipper. You knew nothing about it? And here was me,' James said, 'thinking that the two of you were close.'

She ignored the veiled taunt. 'But why would he do such a thing?'

'He says it's for the same reason he's become a partner in the Pates' business. The man likes to make money,' James went on as the door flew open and his aunt hurried in.

'Jess, wait till you hear . . .'

'I think I just have, Meg.'

'Ach! And here was me running all the way through the town to tell you.' Meg collapsed into a chair, fanning herself with a large scarred hand. 'I just met our Albert with a grin on him big enough to swallow a yacht.'

'So it's true that Jacob's bought his share of the *Fidelity*?'

'So Albert says.'

'How could he do such a thing?'

'You know our Albert – he's never been over-fond of the sea, or of hard work. Now he can be a man of leisure . . . Until he's spent every penny of the money he's getting.'

'Which he'll do as soon as he can,' James pointed out.

'As long as he enjoys the spending . . . You'll be the new skipper now, James?' his aunt wanted to know.

'Mebbe,' he said thoughtfully. Then, straightening his shoulders, 'Innes, I'll see you down at the harbour on Saturday.'

This time, possibly because the cuts and bruises on his face earned him grinning respect from those crew members on board, Innes found it easier to go on to the *Fidelity*. Jacob MacFarlane was there too, watching closely as Innes went over the engine, methodically checking and testing each part before he and Jocky cleaned out the tubes leading from furnace to smokestack. Because sea water was used in the boiler, the tubes salted up quickly and had to be scrubbed out regularly with wire brushes. It was a difficult, dirty job and when it was done both men were filthy and exhausted from working in the cramped conditions.

'I suppose you'll be looking for me to buy you a drink now?' James asked when his brother arrived back on deck.

Innes grinned, wiping his hands on a piece of rag. 'I'd say I've earned one.'

'You surely have, and it's her new skipper who'll be putting his hand in his pocket to reward you, eh, James?' Jacob said, and led the way from the boat. Innes took a deep breath and followed, hiding the panic that quivered deep within him each time he had to step from one boat to another over a sliver of dark harbour water. Knowing that his brother was watching closely, he refused to let his fear show.

'You know your business,' Jacob said admiringly when Innes had slaked the worst of his thirst and cleared the taste of grease and salt from his mouth.

'Each to his own.' Innes looked beyond the older man to

his brother. 'Eh, James?' His cut lip, still healing, smarted from the salt crystals and his bruised body ached from working in the tiny engine room, but he was pleased with what he had achieved.

'I suppose so.'

'It's a pity you didn't become an engine driver,' Jacob went on. 'You'd have been good at it.'

'He would that,' Jocky agreed generously.

'Ach, I much prefer land engines like motor-cars and motor-cycles. I'd not mind working in a wee garage, or mebbe even owning one some time,' Innes said easily. He downed the last of his drink and pushed the glass towards his brother. 'I could manage another.'

When he finally returned home, cheerful but not as drunk as he had been on the last occasion, he announced to his mother's dismay that he was going back to Zelda's home after work the following day to seek permission, once again, for their marriage.

'It's only right,' he insisted when Jess tried to dissuade him. 'I don't want any quarrel to hang over my marriage. Zelda deserves better than that.'

'And what about me having to clean up the blood and tend to the bruises when you're brought back home? Do I not have my rights too?'

'I don't think it'll come to that. From what Zelda says, the man regretted his behaviour almost as soon as it happened. He carried me all the way to the farm, remember, and saw to it that someone brought me home, when he could just have left me lying where I fell. And I still need to know that we've got his blessing and that there's not going be any more trouble for Zelda.'

'If you're going to that house I'm going with you, and that man'll get his head in his hands to play with if he tries to lay a finger on you!'

'For any favour!' Innes protested, horrified. 'Whoever heard of a man taking his mother along with him to ask for a lassie's hand?'

So Jess stayed home, fretting and worrying, and if Jacob hadn't arrived she might have followed Innes at a discreet distance.

As it was, the sight of Jacob pushed her worry about Innes into the background for a moment. 'You never said you were thinking of buying Albert out of the *Fidelity*,' she accused as soon as he came into the house.

'Who told you?'

'James, and Meg right behind him. And a few other folk, when I went out and about. It's a pity,' she said with an edge to her voice, 'that you couldn't come to tell me yourself.'

'I would have, but I'd to go to Aberdeen to sort out the money to pay Albert. I'd thought that he might take time to think about it, but instead he agreed at once, then he wanted the deal done quickly. Mebbe it was as well you heard the news from James, for when I first asked him to be skipper he seemed to think that the idea had come from you.'

'As if I'd ever suggest such a thing. That's men's business, not women's.'

'As a matter of fact, it was your Bethany who first suggested it as a way to keep James with the *Fidelity*.'

'Bethany?' Embarrassment turned Jess's face poppy-red. 'She'd no right to ask such a thing of you! Wait till I get a hold of her . . .'

'Now then, Jess, I'm only telling you because I'd never want to keep secrets from you. I was pleased that your Bethany had the wit to put the idea into my head, for since I came home I've had such a yearning to be part of the fishing again. And now I am, thanks to the *Fidelity*.' He spread his hands out. 'Everyone's content. There's Albert on shore with enough money in his pocket to last to the end of his days if he's sensible, and James running the boat. And even if I'm away in Germany or The Netherlands, or Russia, I'll know that part of me is still here on the Firth where I belong. We're all well satisfied with what's happened,' he said. Then, peering into her face, 'You're not angered with me, are you? You're pleased to know that your James is staying with his father's boat?'

She wasn't angry, but she was disturbed, for events were moving too fast for her. 'Yes, I'm pleased about that, but it seems to me that you're spending altogether too much of your silver on this family, Jacob.'

He leaned across the table and touched her work-roughened hand briefly. 'I'll not make myself into a bankrupt, have no fear of that. And I'm certain sure that James, Gil and Nathan will earn my money back for me, and a bit over besides, once the herring start to move again.'

'Aye well, I suppose you all know your own business best.' Jess got up to re-fill the kettle. 'It's surely time Innes was home.'

'It's early yet and I'm sure that now he's made his protest, Zelda's father won't cause any more bother. Even if he does, Innes has to deal with his own life as he thinks fit.'

'I know, but it doesn't stop me fretting about him, because he's always been the gentle one of the three.'

'I'll tell you one thing,' Jacob said firmly, 'you're right when you say he's not the coward Weem took him to be. That lad of yours is a talented engineer, and after that beating he had from Zelda's father he's gone off to take another, if he has to. He's got his own brand of courage, Jess.'

'I can't help thinking that cowards don't get hurt.'

'And they don't win bonny lassies like Zelda Mulholland, either. Where are they going to live when they're wed?'

'Here, with me, until they can save the money for a place of their own. The sooner that lassie's got a ring on her finger the better, and Innes's room upstairs'll easily take two folk. I'll not mind having Zelda under my roof, for she's got a pleasant nature.' And the thought of having a new-born in the house again, with its mewling cries and its dependency and its sweet, milky baby smell, warmed her heart. But what would any man, especially a bachelor like Jacob, understand of that?

'And I'll tell you another thing. You might say that Innes is the one you worry about, but it seems to me that you fret just as much over James.'

'I do not!'

'I'm glad to hear it, for I don't think he deserves it. I've not forgotten the way he behaved at your table at Ne'erday. He doesn't give you the respect you deserve, Jess . . .' Jacob began, but was interrupted by Innes and Zelda, hand-in-hand, their damaged faces glowing. At the second time of asking Will Mulholland had been gruff and terse, merely saying when Innes faced him with his request for a blessing, 'I suppose she could do worse. And what other man would have her, in her condition, anyway?'

'I could have hit him for that, but I didn't,' Innes assured his mother. 'I suppose when I think of it that he's right enough.' Then he yelped as Zelda dealt him a skelp on the ear.

'That's no way to speak of your future wife,' she said, her eyes bright with laughter and love. Watching them, Jess felt that this, at least, was a union she would not have to worry about.

Come to think of it, it was the only marriage that Weem had not arranged to suit his own purpose.

24

Ever since she had spoken to Jacob MacFarlane, Bethany had been uneasy. It was almost impossible to keep secrets among such a tight-knit community, and since she didn't really know the man well, how could she be sure that he would keep their conversation to himself?

When Gil brought home the news that Albert had sold his share in the *Fidelity* to MacFarlane, and when Stella, bubbling with happiness, confided that James was to become the new skipper, Bethany managed to look suitably surprised, but her unease persisted. When, a week later, she opened the door to find James on the step, glowering at her, she knew why he was there.

'Gil's not in,' she said, and began to close the door. He blocked it with his sturdy boot.

'I know, he's in the public house and likely to stay there for a good while.' He forced the door open again, pushing past her and into the kitchen. 'My business is with you. What d'you think you were doing, running to Jacob MacFarlane to beg favours for me?'

She thought briefly of trying to deny it, then decided that there was no sense in blustering. 'I might have known. Men can never keep their tongues still once they've got a drink in them.'

'Never mind blaming MacFarlane, Bethany, he let it slip without thinking. He believes,' James sneered, 'that you're a fine woman with a fine brain. He was pleased that you put the idea into his head, but I'm not, for I never liked meddlers.'

'Keep your voice down, there's bairns sleeping through in the back room. I only said to the man that it was a shame you had to seek work elsewhere, just because you were unhappy about Uncle Albert.'

'I've always known when you were lying, Bethany, even when you were a wee skelf of a thing. You got in my way then and, by God, you're still doing it!'

The colour that had rushed to her face when she opened the door to him now deepened angrily. 'All right, mebbe I did ask him to buy Albert's share of the boat so that you'd be able to stay on as skipper. What's wrong with that? You know you'd not be happy away from the *Fidelity*.'

'Happy?' He spat the word out. 'What's happiness got to do with it? Folk like us aren't supposed to be happy . . . Though mebbe I'd be a step nearer it if you could mind your own business!' He paced the kitchen like a caged animal while she watched, silent. 'You think I could take the boat now, knowing that you'd arranged it for me?'

'Stella said you'd agreed to it.'

'I've changed my mind and I'll tell Jacob that first thing tomorrow.'

'If you do you're a fool!'

'And if I don't I'd be an even bigger fool, letting a woman interfere in my life! D'you not think my father caused me enough misery, without you putting your neb in as well?'

'Oh, poor wee laddie, was his daddy cruel to him, then? It was you that stood in front of the minister with Stella, not him, so stop girning like a bairn that's dropped its toffee-apple.'

James had never taken kindly to being made a figure of fun; it was a weakness that Bethany had exploited cruelly time and time again in their younger days. 'You're a bitch, Bethany Lowrie,' he said now. 'A conniving, interfering . . .' he sought for more adjectives and, finding none, had to content himself with '. . . bitch!'

'That's better than being a fool. D'you know what I'd give to be in your shoes? It's all I've ever wanted, to be out there on the sea, hauling in the nets with a good boat like the *Fidelity* under my feet, instead of having to clean bairns' backsides, and cook and wash and lie with . . .' She broke off before her tongue gave her away, and began to pace the floor in her turn, wrapping her arms tightly about herself in a vain attempt to hold back the torment within. 'Sometimes the hunger and the longing near drive me out of my mind. It's what I was born to do!'

'Don't be daft, how could a woman ever crew on a fishing boat?' James asked, then stumbled back against the table as she suddenly spun round, the flat of her hand cracking across his cheek with all the force she could muster behind the blow.

In the old days her action would have been the signal for him to launch himself at her. They would have fought tooth and nail with grim, silent determination until one or the other admitted defeat. Now, as he peeled himself away from the table, one hand to his face, she gritted her teeth and set her feet slightly apart for extra balance in readiness. The blow must surely have hurt him, for her hand was stinging and burning with the force of it.

But all he did was examine his fingers, as though expecting to see blood. Then he said, amazed, 'What did you do that for?'

'Because you sound just like the rest of them – just like Gil and Father. I looked for something more than that from you, James. I thought we understood each other.' Tears prickled at the corners of her eyes and she had to struggle to keep her voice level. 'I'll never be at peace, because I was born a woman and can't do what I want to do more than anything in the world. And here's you . . . you've got everything, and you're throwing it away just because you're too thrawn to reach out and take it!'

Then, as he stared, the imprint of her palm and fingers clearly marked in deep red across his tanned skin, the anger drained out of Bethany. He was just like any other man, after all.

'Stay with the *Fidelity*, James,' she said, tired to her very bones now. 'I had to force myself to ask Jacob MacFarlane to help you. I'd to beg for the first time in my life, and the last. Don't let that go to waste.' She gave a shaky laugh. 'We're right miserable souls, aren't we, you and me?'

Then as he continued to stare at her, she swallowed hard and said, 'Come and put some cold water on your cheek. It'll ease the bruising.' She went towards the small sink. 'There's a clean cloth . . .'

'Bethany,' James said in a voice that was part-whisper, part-groan. 'God help me, Bethany, I've not been able to get you out of my mind since that night . . .'

The light in his eyes, hot and hungry, sent a tremor down the length of her. They were on dangerous ground, the two of them.

'You shouldn't have come here tonight,' she said, her voice shaking with the effort of hiding her own hunger.

'Aye,' he said. 'I should. I should have come to you sooner than this. But I'm here now, my lass.' He reached out to her and, tired of fighting her own instincts, tired of trying to do what was right for Gil and Stella, instead of what was right for them – for herself and James – she went into his arms, the tremor shuddering through her again as he bent his head, the red mark on his cheek like a warning flag, to kiss her.

When James had finally gone, slipping out of the front door as silently as a wraith, Bethany hunted out all the pins that had been scattered carelessly across the floor, then brushed her hair and pinned it up neatly. She shook out the rug where they had lain together and, as she laid it carefully back in place, the thought suddenly came to her that if Molly Pate had any notion of what had just taken place on the rag rug she had made, the poor woman must surely be birling in her tidy grave.

A giggle bubbled to her lips at the idea; she pressed them together tightly to smother it, then had to put a hand to her mouth as another followed, then another. She might have become quite hysterical if Ellen hadn't begun to whimper in the back room. She refused to settle down again and finally Bethany picked her up and looked at Rory, on his stomach as usual, with his head twisted at an uncomfortable angle and his pursed mouth making a soft popping noise with each outgoing breath. Carrying Ellen into the kitchen, she gave the little girl a drink, then settled in a chair by the fire with the child in her lap.

When Gil arrived only minutes later Ellen had already fallen asleep again, her thumb in her mouth. At the sight of him Bethany began to struggle up, but he put out a hand to stop her.

'Stay still and don't disturb the bairn.' He sat down opposite, still in his heavy jacket and boots. 'It's grand to come home to such a sight. I'm a fortunate man, Bethany.'

'And a drunk one too.'

'Just a wee celebration of the way things are going for us these days,' Gil said, then, almost shyly, 'I've been thinking, Bethany, would it not be nice to have a bairn of our own?'

'A bairn? But we've already got two.'

'Aye, but I'd like fine to have a wee lassie with your bonny colouring. Or a wee laddie would be even better. And when we move to one of those nice big houses on Cliff Terrace we'll have room for half a dozen more, if we want them. I'd like that.'

Bethany's skin, still tingling from James's touch, James's kisses, crawled at the very thought.

On a crisp, sunny day in February Innes Lowrie and

Grizelda Mulholland stood before the minister and made their marriage vows. Afterwards, both families squeezed into Jess's small kitchen for a wedding breakfast.

Still simmering with rage over the beating her son had taken, Jess had not been happy with the thought of having to entertain Will Mulholland and his wife in her own home. 'If I'd my way of it,' she told Meg hotly, 'that man would have his food thrown over him, instead of put down to him in a civilised way, after what he did to our Innes.'

'What's done's done,' her sister-in-law said calmly. 'The young ones are getting their own way and you'll have another grand-bairn to look forward to. Anyway, I doubt if Innes would thank you for losing your temper on his marriage day.'

Throughout the day the shepherd was remote and expressionless, saying little and keeping himself in the background. His wife, on the other hand, brought a large basket containing fresh farm eggs, a fresh-baked loaf, a pot of home-made jam and a large piece of cold mutton, 'Just to thank you for your hospitality,' she said as she handed them over. Then, removing the clean apron that had been tucked over the top of the basket to protect its contents, she tied it around her waist and added, 'Now then, just you tell me what needs doing and I'll see to it.' In the face of her clear determination to make amends for what had gone before, it was impossible for Jess to bear a grudge.

In any case, there was plenty to do and the more willing hands, the better. The table was swiftly covered with food donated by friends and family: steak pies and yellow fish, trifles and home baking. Most of the china and cutlery had been borrowed, for no housewife ever accumulated enough to supply a large gathering and there were plenty of folk happy to play their part in making the wedding a success. In deference to the Mulhollands' religious beliefs, there was no alcohol at the wedding party, but nobody – other than Albert and Gil – seemed to miss it.

Jess had spread a pretty lace tablecloth over the wall-bed and set out the wedding presents on it for all the guests to admire. There were four lavishly decorated cups and saucers from Bethany and Gil, a beautifully embroidered tablecloth from Stella and James, and a set of dishes from Zelda's parents. Jess had already promised the young couple the few pieces of furniture from Innes's room for their new home when they found it, and had also offered to buy a new bed. Albert contributed some china and Meg gave a pretty set of bed-linen.

'It came from Harry's mother when we were wed, but we werenae together long enough to get the use of it,' she said when she brought it to the house. 'Anyway, ordinary bedding suits me best.'

'It's beautiful!' Zelda marvelled over the pillowcases and sheets, trimmed with crochet so beautifully done that it looked almost like lace.

'Harry's mother did that, God rest her soul. She was grand at the fancy sewing, though I never could do that sort of thing myself.' Meg was delighted with the reception that her gift got, but to Jess she confided in private, 'I doubt if I could ever have slept on fancy sheets and pillows like that, but I never told Harry.'

'Zelda will make good use of it. It was kind of you to give it to her, Meg.'

'Mebbe it should have gone to Bethany, but she married into a house that had everything she needed, and Stella had all her mother's things. Best give it where it's most needed. I met your Bethany on my way here,' Meg added. 'She's looking right bonny these days.'

'She seems to be happier with her life since Ne'erday,' Jess said with relief.

Although it was the tradition that only close family gave gifts, Jacob MacFarlane had bought the young couple a canteen of cutlery, so handsome that Jess had no option but to give it pride of place in the centre of the bed. There were some raised eyebrows when folk realised who the donor was, but Zelda, still slender enough to look attractive in her new blue dress, was thrilled with it.

'I've never had so many pretty things in my life before,' she said to Innes as they inspected their presents. Then, squeezing his hand tightly, 'And I've never been so happy, ever!'

Watching the way Innes was enjoying every moment of his wedding day, Jess wished that the same could have been said for her two elder children. Both had been silent and expressionless during their wedding parties, though Weem had more than made up for them. Remembering how vibrantly alive he had been, how invincible, she had to swallow back a sudden rush of hot tears.

Jacob arrived by her side just then. 'Everyone's having a grand time, Jess. You must be proud of Innes this day.'

'I am that.'

'You women,' he teased gently. 'I never can understand why you cry when you're happy as well as when you're sad.'

It was late when the wedding party broke up and the Mulhollands went off home. Will left without a backward glance, driving his younger children before him as if they were a flock of sheep, but his wife lingered with her daughter.

'I'll see you both at the kirk on Sunday?'

'Of course,' Zelda assured her. It was the custom for the bride and groom to lead the congregation into church on the first Sunday after their marriage for their 'kirkin' – a final blessing on their union.

'And mind and visit us once a week.' Automatically

Mrs Mulholland reached out and smoothed back Zelda's curly hair.

'Ma!' The girl flinched away, embarrassed. 'I'm a married woman now!'

Tears sparkled in her mother's eyes. 'So you are, pet, so you are!'

Innes put an arm about his new wife, who was beginning to snivel a bit at the sight of her mother weeping. 'I'll take good care of her, Mrs Mulholland.'

She gave an almighty sniff and blinked rapidly. 'I know you will, son. She's found a good man and that's all I can ask for her. Here.' She dug into her coat pocket, then thrust something into Innes's hands. 'That's for the two of you. No need to say anything to . . .' she cast a nervous glance at the dark night outside, where her husband and their other children waited for her, then went on, '. . . anybody. Goodnight to you, Mrs Lowrie, and thank you for your hospitality.'

As she closed the door, Jess said, 'I might not be so fond of your father, Zelda, for very good reason, but I like your mother. She's a decent body.'

'So's my da when you catch him in the right mood. Let me see . . .'

Zelda, unable to contain her curiosity, took Innes's hand and uncurled his fingers. Then she gasped at the sight of the two banknotes.

'Look at all that money! It must have taken her years to save it. Oh, Ma!' The tears filled her dark eyes and brimmed over.

Innes held her close. 'We'll put it in the bank, eh?' he suggested. 'Save it towards our own wee house. Then your mam can come and visit us there.' When she nodded, he drew her head in against her shoulder so that she could cry in peace and privacy.

The sight of them together stirred so many memories that Jess's heart turned over in her breast. She had had more than her fair share of loving and being loved and, now that her own day was done, she hoped that for Innes and Zelda the path through life would be just as enjoyable as it had been for herself and Weem.

'I'm ready for my bed,' she said. 'We can clear this place up tomorrow.'

As she unpinned her hair, still long and silky though now well sprinkled with grey, and began to brush it out with long, hard strokes from root to tip, Jess heard the faint murmur of Innes's voice from above, followed by a soft laugh from Zelda. Innes had found the right person and the contentment needed to safeguard a marriage, but it was different, she thought as she brushed and brushed, for James and Bethany.

She had not been overly concerned about James's marriage, for Stella clearly adored him and a man needed to have his own home and his own wife, but she wished she had opposed Weem more forcefully where Bethany was concerned, for it had been clear to her that the girl had no desire to be tied down to domesticity. But he had scoffed at her attempts to remonstrate with him.

'You were mother to two bairns at her age. What makes her so different?'

'I married from choice.'

'And a good choice you made.' He gave her that swift, mischievous glance that had always made her go weak at the knees with wanting him. Even the memory of it more than a year after his death brought a surge of heat to her belly.

'Bethany's not like me.'

'More's the pity. It's time she started behaving like the woman she is. She's been spoiled, that's her trouble.'

'And whose fault is that? You'd never let me scold her when she was wee. She could wrap you round her little finger – and she did, time and again. You made her think she was special.'

Weem had the grace to look ashamed. 'Mebbe I did,

but she was easy to spoil. D'ye no' mind her, Jess, such a bonny wee lass with as much courage in her wee body as James. And a damned sight more than the other one,' he added sourly.

'It's not Innes's fault that he wasn't meant for the fishing life,' she flared, always ready to fly to the defence of her beloved younger son. Weem raised his thick, greying eyebrows and gave her a triumphant smirk.

'Who's doin' the spoilin' now?' he wanted to know. Then as she bit her lip, furious with herself for having fallen into his trap, 'I'll have no more of your fussing, Jess. Gil Pate's desperate to marry with our lass and he'll be a good husband to her. You know what they say: better an old man's darlin' than a young man's fool. Not that Gil's old.'

'Older than her by a good few years. And the father of two bairns already.'

'Carin' for them'll help to bring her round to the ways of a housewife all the sooner, and if Gil's willing to take all the fish the *Fidelity* can catch into the bargain, then that's fine with me. The matter's closed,' Weem said and snapped his newspaper open, always a signal that he wanted to be left in peace.

So Bethany had promised herself to Gil for the rest of her life, and now she and James were both tied to people who, decent enough though they were, could never satisfy their stormy, restless natures and the aching need Jess sensed in both of them. They were still drifting, each of them in danger of finding elsewhere the comfort they hungered for. The very thought of the unhappiness that could cause made Jess shiver.

Before getting into bed she knelt on the cold linoleum, hands clasped together and eyes tight shut against the dark, and prayed for the protection and happiness of her two older children. Then she flicked back the single long plait that kept her hair neat overnight, put out the light and got into bed.

* * *

The wedding was a torment for Bethany, who found it almost unbearable to be in the same room as James for so long, without being able to touch him. Since the night he had come to her door, blazing with rage at the way she had persuaded Jacob MacFarlane to buy Albert's share of the *Fidelity*, James had become the centre of her life. When they were apart it was as though the colour had been leached out of her world; when they were together in company, and unable to touch, she itched with need for him.

They were careful to avoid each other all through the wedding party, afraid of betraying themselves to watchful eyes, but inevitably the moment came when they met in the crowd.

'I'll see you tonight?' he said, low-voiced.

She had managed to get away from the house only two nights earlier to spend precious time with him. It would be hard to find an excuse to go out again tonight. But she no longer had any choice.

'Aye.' She spoke on a soft breath. 'Tonight.'

25

James was already down in *Fidelity*'s cabin when Bethany arrived, waiting at the foot of the ladder to draw her into his arms and kiss her, a deep, strong kiss that made her lips melt against his.

'I can't stay long, for Gil wasnae very happy about me going out again. He thinks I'm seeing too much of my mother these days.'

'I don't know what I'd have done if you hadn't, after being forced to keep my distance from you all afternoon.' He drew her down to sit on the bunk by his side, his mouth mapping out the shape of her face from forehead to eyes to nose to chin with tiny, light kisses. 'I'd probably have come knocking at your door,' he said against the corner of her mouth, 'telling Gil he must let you come to me.'

'I can just see you asking if I could come out to play, like a bairn,' she said, and felt a laugh ripple through him.

'Aye,' he agreed, then drew her closer, lowering her on to the bunk and leaning over her, enfolding her body with his. It was too dark to see his features, but she could feel his breath warm on her face, and when he said huskily, 'Will you, Beth? Will you come to play with me?' she reached up to draw him closer, more than ready to do his bidding.

Lusty though it was, Gil's lovemaking within the comfort of their bed was solely for his own pleasure. Even though she went to him a virgin, Bethany had always found his attentions tedious and unexciting; she had thought the fault was hers, since she assumed that Gil, already once-married, was experienced in the ways of pleasuring women. But with James she had learned that not all men were alike, when it came to knowing how to make a woman catch her breath in delight, and cry aloud, and play her own part in the loving. Just being together was a pleasure, which, had they both had their way, would have gone on for ever, but all too soon her sharp ears caught the sound of one of the church bells ringing the hour.

'I have to go.'

'Not yet . . .'

'And so must you. It's time we were back where we belonged.'

'I am where I belong, with the *Fidelity* and with you. Am I being too greedy, Beth?' James asked against her hair. 'Wanting both of you?'

'Gil must be wondering where I am.' She fumbled in the dark for her clothes, muttering her irritation. 'Put the lamp on.'

'Someone might see it and wonder who's working so late at night.'

'They'll wonder even more if they see me going ashore dressed in your clothes and you in mine. I can't see a thing, James!'

'A match, then, but not the lamp.'

Although they gave only a tiny flame, several matches provided light for long enough to let Bethany sort the scattered clothing into two piles. Once that was done they were able to dress in the dark.

'You go first and I'll follow in a wee while,' James said low-voiced, though there was nobody to hear them. Then as she turned to the ladder she felt his hand on her shoulder, turning her round to face him. 'I'll be here every night, waiting for you,' he said. 'Come to me as often as you can get away.'

Hurrying along the harbour wall towards the town lights, she knew that she would be back as soon as possible. No matter how wicked it was, she had committed herself to James and even if there had been a way to turn the clock back, she would not want to do so.

Once his ring was on Zelda's finger, Innes seemed to grow to manhood before his mother's very eyes. As the son of the house he had rushed in from his work to eat what was put before him before, as likely as not, rushing out again. Now he spent his evenings at home, sitting in the chair that had been his father's with a newspaper in his hands, reading out an occasional item to Jess, who was busy in her usual chair with her knitting wires, and Zelda, perched between them on a stool, stitching away at some small garment for the coming baby. On most evenings Jacob called in to make a foursome.

'When's he ever going back to wherever he lives?' Innes asked his mother after one of Jacob's visits.

'When he's good and ready, I suppose. He's got interests here, now that he's gone into partnership with Gil and Nathan and bought Albert's share of the boat.'

'Aunt Meg says you and him were sweethearts once.'

'Your Aunt Meg's got a long tongue,' said Jess, vexed.

'Were you?' Zelda butted in, eyes bright with interest.

'Mebbe. A long time ago.'

'You don't think . . .' Innes began, but Zelda nipped in sharply.

'Don't be daft, Innes, there'd never be anything like that now,' she said with the amusement that young folk showed towards any suggestion of romance between their elders. She was putting on weight swiftly, and now that she had stopped working at the farm she and Jess were in each other's company for the best part of each day. They divided the housework between them amicably enough and on the surface things worked out well.

'Though I do feel my nose being put out of joint a wee

bit when she tells me what Innes would and wouldn't like for his dinner,' Jess confided in Meg. 'Me that's raised him near on eighteen years.'

'Wives aye like to think that nob'dy knows their men better than they do. It'll not be long before the two of them find their own place.'

Zelda, too, was finding the domestic situation hard to take. 'We need a house of our own,' she told Innes in the privacy of their bedroom.

'I thought everything was working out fine here.'

'Aye, you would, for you're the one that gets the best out of it, with two women to run after you. Innes, you'll never grow up while you're biding in your mother's house. I want us to get a wee place of our own before the bairn comes.'

But when Innes started working longer hours in an attempt to make more money she was still not pleased. 'It's no sort of life, sitting around the house with your mother, waiting for you to come home,' she grizzled.

'If we were in our own house you'd not even have her for company.'

'But it would be different, d'you not see that? It would be ours, just for us. Mebbe we could find somewhere near my mother, or near the Bains' farm. Then I'd be close to folk that I know.'

At his wits' end, Innes went to Stella, who was more domesticated than Bethany, for advice. 'Mebbe you could help me to understand how Zelda feels, for I'm lost,' he said wretchedly, sitting in her kitchen with Ruth on his lap and the twins climbing all over him.

'She's from a big family and she's homesick, just. It's natural,' she assured him. 'I tell you what, I'll take the bairns along to your mother's more often and I'll ask Zelda if she'll start visiting me.'

'I'd not want her to know that I spoke to you about this.'

'She won't. I'll say it's for the company, now that James

is skipper of the *Fidelity*. It'll not be a lie, for even though the line fishing doesn't take him away for long at a time, he spends hours fussing over the boat when she's in harbour. He's like a bairn with a new toy.'

'I'd best be going.' Disengaging himself from the twins and handing Ruth over, Innes took a closer look at his sister-in-law. 'You look a wee bit pale, are you keeping all right?'

'I'm fine, just kept busy with the wee ones. You'll soon know all about that.'

'I'm looking forward to it,' Innes said, beaming.

'It makes a lot of sense,' Jacob MacFarlane urged. 'For one thing, the crew would be sure of a proper wage coming in. You'd not deny them that, surely?'

'But what about the bad seasons?' James, confused, scowled at the figures on the paper that the older man had pushed across the table towards him. 'How could we afford to pay them a set rate then?'

'That would be my problem, not yours. Each to his own strengths, James: you seeing to the boat and me to the money, that's what we agreed. Ask them,' Jacob urged when the younger man chewed on his lower lip. 'Just you ask them what they would rather have, certain money in their hands every week of the season, or having to wait till it's over before they find out how much they'll have to see their families through the winter.'

'I'll think about it.'

'We could tell them together, then I can explain . . .'

'I said I'll think about it. Leave it with me for now,' James said firmly, and Jacob had to be content with that.

'A steady wage to take home to the wife . . . that's somethin' fishermen have never known before,' old Mowser said when Jacob had gone.

'You're right there, Da. It'd mean a lot to the women-folk to know how much money was going to come into their houses, James.'

'I'm not sure, and even if I do agree it won't happen in this house. You heard Jacob proposing that, as the skipper, I would still take my share at the end of the season.'

'We'll do well enough with that. Won't we, my bonny lassie?' Stella cooed to the baby on her lap. 'If your daddy wasn't the fine fisherman he is we'd have nothing to eat at all. Then we'd mebbe have to eat you all up for our dinner.' She grabbed a fat, flailing leg and pretended to gobble it, while Ruth crowed with laughter. 'Yes, we would, and there's enough here to go round the neighbours too, wee fatty-bannocks.' Stella hoisted the little girl into the air, laughing up at her. 'You're a fatty-bannocks, aren't you?'

'D'you have to talk to the bairn as if she's a fool?' James snapped, and the smile was wiped from Stella's face as swiftly as if he had taken it off with the back of his hand. Mowser stared fixedly into the fire while the twins, playing amicably together on the floor, looked up at their father apprehensively.

'It's just the way folk talk to weans. She likes it.'

'How d'you know what she likes, when she's not got the words to tell you?'

'I just know,' Stella said feebly, bewildered by the sudden attack. She laid Ruth down on the wall-bed and began to push the twins into their jackets. 'I'm away along to your mother's to see how Zelda's feeling today. You'll be able to think clearer when we're out of the way.'

'You might as well stay here, for I'm going to the boat.'

'I was going anyway.' Stella wound a long scarf about Sarah's head, crossing it over the little girl's chest then knotting it at her back. Then she began to do the same for Annie. 'I promised Innes I'd keep an eye on Zelda.'

James, hauling on his long, iron-studded sea-boots,

gave her an exasperated look. 'Can Innes not look out for his own wife? And is my mother not capable of it too, since you seem to think that Zelda's in need of special help?'

'It's just that with this being her first bairn, and her own mother not being close to hand . . .' Stella wrapped a shawl about the baby, working quickly, anxious to get out of the house before the tears thickening her throat began to fill her eyes. 'There's a stew cooking, I'll be back in good time to dish it up to you.'

As the door closed behind his daughter Mowser cleared his throat, spat into the fire and made a show of combing his fingers through his luxuriant moustache. 'It doesnae seem right, somehow.'

'What doesn't?' James asked belligerently, wondering why he couldn't keep his tongue off Stella. It wasn't her fault that she wasn't more like . . . He forced his mind away from thoughts of Bethany.

'Now I come to think of it, the idea of a regular wage doesnae seem right for the likes of us. Fisher-folk arenae like factory workers or farm workers. We've our own way of doing things.'

'Times are changing and we need to change with them. I don't know . . .' James stood up, pushing the sheet of paper into his pocket. 'I'll have to think about it.'

Bethany, unable to stay for long in her own home these days, was already in Jess's warm kitchen when Stella arrived.

'You've not been to the house recently, Bethany.' Her sister-in-law loosened the shawl that held Ruth close against her. 'You and James haven't had a falling out, have you?'

'How could we, since we never see each other?' Bethany's voice was sharp and Jess, rolling dough at the kitchen table, saw Stella flinch slightly. Bethany herself must have seen it, for her voice became softer as she said, 'Wee Ellen wasn't herself for a wee while and I thought she might be sickening for something. I didn't want your bairns to catch it.'

Stella cast a doubtful glance at Ellen, who was rolling happily on the floor with the twins, the very picture of health, then she sat Ruth up on her knees and began to play the baby's favourite game.

'Knock at the doorie,' she crooned, tapping lightly with her knuckles on Ruth's forehead; then, touching a fingertip to each of the baby's eyelids in turn, 'Keek in, lift the sneck . . .' Finger and thumb gently tweaked Ruth's snub little nose, then Stella eased a forefinger into the little mouth, wide open in helpless laughter, with a loud 'And walk in!' She bounced Ruth up into the air several times.

'You'll make her sick if you keep doing that,' Bethany told her.

'Ach, she's got a stomach made of iron, her. Everything that goes in stays in, no matter what. Is that not right, my wee birdie? You've got your daddy's appetite.' Stella hugged the baby. 'And she's got his eyes, more than the other two, d'you not think so?'

'I don't see it myself.'

'You must see it, Bethany,' Zelda chimed in. 'She's more like her daddy than the twins.'

''Specially when she's thinkin',' Stella agreed. 'You know the way James goes all quiet when he's puzzling over something, as if he's looking right through you and seeing something that nobody else can.'

'How is James these days, Stella?' Jess swiftly cut the dough into rounds, using the top of a cup, and began to put them on to a baking tin. 'He must be happy to be in charge of the *Fidelity*.'

'He is,' Stella said, then her face clouded and the worry-lines appeared again between her eyes. 'Though it means more work, for it's an awful responsibility. And now there's this new ploy of Mr MacFarlane's for him to think about.'

'What ploy's this?'

'He wants James to pay the *Fidelity* crew set wages every week, instead of giving them a share of the takings at the end of the season.'

'James is surely never going to agree to that!' Bethany said.

'You don't think it's a good idea? It means the men'll get regular money coming in, no matter how the fishing goes.'

'And they'll never get the good big payment if the fishing goes well. They'll never be any more than hired hands, with no chance of ever getting their own boats one day.'

'I never thought of that.'

'I hope James does. If you take my advice, Stella, you'll tell him to think twice about it.'

'Why would he listen to me? I'm not clever when it comes to that sort of thing.'

'You're as wise as anyone else,' Jess assured the younger woman, taking a tray of golden-brown scones from the oven and putting them on the table to cool. 'You're doing a grand job of running a house and looking after two men as well as your bairns.'

'It's not the same, though,' Stella said wistfully. 'James never talks to me about his work, or asks my advice, because he knows I'd not be of any help to him. I wish I was more like you, Bethany.'

Bethany flushed. 'That's nonsense!' The sharp note had returned to her voice. 'You know me and James never see eye to eye.'

'You used to be as close as two peas in a pod. I mind those days, for seeing the two of you together made me wish I was as near to one of my own brothers. And James thinks highly of you even yet. He's always telling me I should be more like you.'

'Is he?' Bethany gaped at her, completely taken aback, as Innes came in, home from work early for once.

All the children greeted him with squeals of pleasure, but just as they were settling down to a rowdy game with him on the kitchen floor, Bethany jumped to her feet. 'Ma, would you keep an eye on these two for a wee while? I've to go to the shops.'

'These scones are cool enough to eat now, and I'm just going to make a fresh pot of tea,' Jess protested, wiping flour from her hands.

'I've my messages to get yet, and the dinner to start. I'll see to that, then come back for the bairns,' Bethany said, and hurried out of the cottage.

Without her in it, the room seemed to Jess to be dimmer than before. There was a glow to Bethany these days, as though a lamp had been lit within her. Briefly Jess wondered if her daughter was expecting at last, but she dismissed the thought almost as soon as it had arrived. A child, Gil's child, would not make Bethany as happy as she was at the moment. Possibly it was because of the partnership between Gil and Jacob, though why that should please her so much was a mystery.

Compared to Bethany, Stella looked wan and worried, but then life with James could not be easy. Jess put an extra layer of butter on the girl's scone, and an extra spoonful of sugar in her tea for added energy.

'Is Mowser in?' Bethany asked as soon as James opened the door.

'He's down at the harbour, and Stella's . . .'

'I know where Stella is, I've just left her there.' Bethany pushed past him and into the kitchen, which was filled with the aroma of the stew Stella had put in the oven earlier. Her knitting and some of the children's toys were scattered about the room, which looked cosy and welcoming.

James closed the door and turned to his sister. 'Is this a good idea?' he asked, though his eyes were burning and his hands already reaching out towards her.

She stepped back, out of his reach. 'Stella tells me that

Jacob MacFarlane has some daft notion about giving the *Fidelity*'s crew a wage instead of a share in the catch.'

'That's right. What's it got to do with you?'

'It's got everything to do with me. I'm a Lowrie, and part-owner of the boat. You're not going to agree to it, are you?'

'I've not decided.'

'Use your noddle, man.' It was something she had said to him on countless occasions over the years, and a smile quirked the corner of James's mouth.

'Jacob's mebbe right when he says they'd be better off with regular money coming in.'

'They might be better off for now, but tell me this – have you ever met a guttin quine who owns her own house or employs other folk?'

'No, but what's that got to do with it?'

'It's got everything to do with it!' Bethany said impatiently. 'Every man who owns a boat here in Buckie got it by working hard, and saving hard, but fisher-lassies never become employers because they're lucky if they make enough to live on. There's no saving from their wages, no money to put behind them so that they can start out on their own. They have to work for other folk all their lives, and the same'll go for the *Fidelity*'s crew if Jacob MacFarlane has his way. If you pay your crew set wages, no matter how the fishing goes, they'll be crewing for the boat for the whole of their lives.'

'That wouldn't be bad as far as I'm concerned. I've got good men there and I'd not want to lose them.'

'That's exactly the way Jacob sees it: fishermen who can't leave one boat to set themselves up with another. That means fewer boats and more fish for the boats already going out. D'you not see that?'

'I suppose I do,' he said slowly.

'Then tell him you'll have no truck with the idea. Why's he telling you what to do anyway, when he only owns a third of the boat?'

'He put in a fair bit of money to buy Albert off and he's really taken to the idea of being part-owner of that boat, Bethany. He's even had a man down on the harbour painting her.'

Bethany tutted. 'Waste of money. *Fidelity* doesn't need painting, she's always been kept smart.'

'I don't mean that sort of painting. I mean he's got someone painting a picture of her.'

'A picture? Why would he want such a thing?'

James shrugged. 'There's some do it.'

'More fool them, wasting good silver like that. And there's another thing,' Bethany suddenly remembered. 'You know that you're making Stella miserable?'

His grey eyes, which had become smoky with desire once the matter of the crew wages was out of the way, suddenly hardened and chilled. 'What's she been saying to you?'

'That you tell her she should be more like me. She says you get impatient with her.'

'She's got no right to talk about me to anyone!'

'For goodness' sake, man, it's what women do. What else do we have to talk about when we get together?'

'I'll not discuss my wife with anyone, Bethany, not even you,' James said stiffly.

'I'm not interested in discussing Stella, I'm just saying you should guard your tongue when you speak to her.'

The anger went out of his face, to be replaced by naked misery. 'She's not you,' he said, low-voiced, 'and that's what's eating away at me every time I look at her, every time I have to touch her. If it could just be us, Beth, me and you . . .'

She swallowed hard and fisted her hands. 'It can never be like that.'

'Why not?'

'For pity's sake, James . . . you know full well why not!'

'I can't think how we happened to be born into the

same family,' James said bleakly, 'for we were meant to
be together, you can't deny it.'

Her eyes prickled and she blinked away a threatened
rush of tears. 'If we were truly meant to be together we'd
not have been born to the same parents,' she said. Then,
dragging her eyes from his, 'I have to go. I shouldn't
be here.'

'I'll see you tonight?' he asked as she stopped on the
doorstep, glancing up and down the empty street.

'Not tonight, Gil's beginning to wonder why I'm going
out so much.'

'As soon as you can, then. I'll be waiting.' The wind
blew an errant strand of her glowing chestnut hair across
her mouth; James reached out to smooth it gently behind
her ear and on an impulse, without thinking where they
were, she reached up and held his hand against her cheek
for a brief, precious moment.

'Oh James,' she said, 'why did we ever let this start?'

'D'you regret it?' When she shook her head silently he
drew his fingers from beneath hers. 'Go away, woman,'
he said, his voice husky, his eyes making love to her. 'Go
away before I pull you back inside and shut the door and
be damned to the consequences.'

26

When Stella prepared to go, Innes offered to walk back home with her. 'You look wearied,' he said when she tried to object. 'I'll carry the wee one.'

'You're not bothered about being seen with a bairn in your arms, then?' she teased as they left the house.

'No, why should I?'

'There's some would think it's not manly.'

'Like our James, you mean?' He set Ruth on his shoulder, one hand balancing her securely, and slowed his usual long stride to accommodate Stella and the twins. 'It doesnae bother me one bit what some might say.'

'You'll make a good father, Innes.'

'I mean to do my best,' he said. 'Thank you for taking the time to befriend Zelda.'

'I enjoy her company.'

'If I could just find a wee place for the two of us before the bairn comes she'd be content.'

'Your mother's very happy to have the two of you under her roof and I know she's looking forward to the baby.'

'She's good to us, but Zelda's impatient for a place of her own. I wish I could earn more money.'

'Have you thought of trying to find work with one of the boat builders? James said you were good with the *Fidelity*'s engines. Better than Jocky, he thought.'

'Did he now?' Innes glowed; he had never been praised

by James before. 'I never thought of working for a boat
builder.'

'You should try it,' Stella said, then as they turned a
corner, 'There's Bethany coming out of our house.'

'She'll be looking for you.'

'But I saw her already today, at your mother's,' Stella
said, then caught at his arm and put out her other hand
to hold Sarah and Annie back, when they would have
scampered ahead. 'Quick, round here.'

Innes, confused, had no option but to follow as she
ducked back round the corner. 'What . . . ?'

'Shush! Bethany was in a right taking with James earlier and I doubt if her temper's improved much. We're
playing hide and seek with Daddy,' she told the twins,
who giggled and hopped about on the cobbles. 'Don't let
him see us, mind.' Then to Innes, 'I told her about some
ploy Mr MacFarlane has for the *Fidelity* and she wasn't
pleased at all. She must have come straight here to lecture
James about it. I don't want to be caught in one of their
quarrels.'

She reached up for Ruth who, unwilling to leave her
exalted position, held tightly to her uncle's hair. 'Let go
of poor Innes, you wee monkey! There now.' She gathered
the little one into her arms. 'Peep round the corner, Innes,
and see if she's gone yet.'

Amused, he eased himself carefully round so that he
could see without being seen. Bethany was still at the
door and she and James were talking earnestly, heads
close together.

'She's still there.'

'Are they quarrelling, d'you think?' Stella's shawled
head bumped against his arm.

Innes stared as James's hand reached out to smooth a
strand of hair away from Bethany's face. 'They don't seem
to be quarrelling,' he said hesitantly. Stella began to ease
herself in front of him and he made a move to block her,
but it was too late. He heard the breath catch in her throat

and felt her stiffen against him as Bethany put her hand over James's, holding it to her cheek. He bent his head closer to hers and said something, then Bethany released his hand, turned and almost ran along the street, fortunately in the opposite direction from where they stood.

James, his head turned away from the spectators, watched until she was out of sight before turning back into the house.

Sarah and Annie were dancing about, tugging at Innes's trousers and Stella's skirt, demanding to know when their daddy was going to get on with the game. 'Daddy doesn't want to play any more,' Stella told them, her voice bleak, all the earlier mischief gone. 'We'd best let you get home for your dinner, Innes.'

'Stella . . .'

'I'll see you again, Innes.' She kept her face averted from him, hugging Ruth tightly and urging the twins ahead of her. 'Thank you for your company.'

As Innes turned homewards he was confused; James and Bethany, once as thick as thieves, hadn't seen eye to eye for a good long while and these days a meeting between them, as his mother was wont to say, was like striking a match in a room full of gunpowder. But for those few moments at the street door they were like . . . like a couple, he suddenly thought. Then as the enormity of what he had just thought hit him, he stopped walking. James and Bethany were not a couple, they were brother and sister; his brother and sister.

He shook his head as though to clear it, and started walking again. He had been imagining things. Of course he had.

But still, he wondered. And when he reached home he said nothing of what he had seen to his mother or to Zelda.

After settling the children Stella began to make the dinner, marvelling at the way her hands and body worked as efficiently as ever, though her head felt as light and empty as a room that had been stripped of its familiar furnishings.

Her father came in, chattering about the men he had met at the harbour and what they had all said to each other. It was a daily ritual and she was able to reply at the right time, ask the right questions and nod when he paused for a response, without actually having to listen to a word he was saying.

While the pots simmered on the stove she fed and changed Ruth. Today, the innocence and trust in the baby's eyes, the smiles that showed four perfect little white teeth, flooded Stella with so much emotion that she had to fight to keep the tears at bay. One day, she thought, wee Ruth would have to find out for herself that the world was a frightening place where nothing – not even trust – could be taken for granted. Stella hoped that when that happened her beloved daughter, at that moment kicking her plump bare legs and babbling to the ceiling, would not hurt as badly as she herself was hurting now.

As soon as Bethany left, James went out the back door to the lean-to wash-house, where he stripped off his jacket, waistcoat and shirt, then pumped cold water into one of the two big stone sinks before dousing his head and shoulders over and over again.

Gasping, he straightened and scrubbed himself with an old towel until his skin glowed and tingled, then put his clothes back on and combed his wet black hair roughly with his fingers, sleeking it down against the shape of his skull.

When he returned to the kitchen it was to find Mowser in his usual chair, a twin on each knee, while the baby chattered to herself in her little crib. Stella, as serene as ever, was ladling stew into some plates. All was calm, all was as it should be.

Apart from the occasional comment from Mowser or

from one of the twins, they ate in silence, James pre-
occupied with thoughts of Bethany and unaware of the
sidelong glances that his wife cast him from time to time.
After a while he pushed his plate away and sat down by the
fire, using an open newspaper to shut himself off from the
rest of the household. Mowser, always hungry for some
man-to-man talk, made several attempts at conversation
before giving up and going off to his bed. Stella settled the
children for the night then sat down opposite her husband,
her fingers busy with her knitting.

'Are you not going out tonight?' she ventured at last.

'No,' he said curtly, then when she stifled a yawn,
'You should go to your bed.'

'In a minute.' The fire had died down and she knelt to
poke it back into life. Looking at her downbent head with
its brown hair sleeked back into a neat bun, James recalled
what Bethany had said about his treatment of Stella. He
leaned forward and took the poker from her.

'Get to your sleep and let me see to the fire,' he said with
gruff gentleness. Startled, Stella relinquished the poker
and rose, but instead of doing as she was told she stood
looking down at him. His hair had curled at the ends, as
it always did when it was drying; she longed to touch it,
knowing that it would feel soft and springy beneath her
fingers. Instead she put her hands behind her back and
said, 'I met Bethany at your mother's today.'

She was sure that her husband's broad back stiffened,
though his voice was casual when he said, 'Oh aye?'

'I told her . . .' Her voice cracked and she had to clear
her throat and try again. 'I said about Mr MacFarlane's
idea about paying wages to the crew.'

He kept his gaze fixed on the fire, the poker rattling
against the bars as he prodded and prodded at the coals.
'I know, she came to see me about it. You know what
she's like, always poking her neb into things that don't
concern her.'

She thought of the way he had smoothed the lock of

hair away from Bethany's face, and of her hand touching his. 'Did you quarrel, the two of you?'

'You know that we always quarrel when we meet up. Nob'dy can reason with Bethany.'

'I'm sorry if I caused any . . .' Stella paused, swallowed, then went on, '. . . any trouble between the two of you.'

James sat back on his haunches so that he could look up at her, his face flushed with the heat of the fire. 'You didn't cause any trouble that wasn't already there,' he said, then his gaze dropped away from hers. 'It's me that should be saying sorry. I've been hard on you lately and it's not been your fault at all. It's . . .' He hesitated and for a terrible moment Stella thought that he was going to say something she didn't want to hear. Her hands instinctively went up, ready to cover her ears, and her body tensed, but he only said, 'It's been a difficult time, with Jacob become part-owner of the boat, but I've no right to take my worries out on you.'

'I'm your wife, James, who else would you girn at?' She tried to make it sound like a joke, but to her own ears it came out as more of a plea. She prayed that he would stand up and take her in his arms and make everything all right, but when he did straighten he turned towards the door, saying over his shoulder, 'Get some rest, I'm just going out for a breath of air.'

'James.'

'What is it?'

'Don't leave me,' Stella said, and he spun round.

'What?'

'I meant . . . it's late to be going out.' It wasn't what she had meant at all.

He stared at her, then said gruffly, 'I'll not be long.'

She had forgotten to put the stone water bottle in earlier, and when she got into bed the sheets were icy against her bare feet. She shivered as much from fear as from cold, wondering where James was going and who he might be meeting. But, true to his word, he returned in a few minutes, blowing out the lamp as soon as he came in.

Stella lay rigid, listening to the rustle of clothing as he undressed in the dark. James Lowrie was her man, her wedded husband, and she loved him even more than she loved the children he had fathered on her. She wanted to sit up in bed, to ask him outright what he and Bethany had been saying to each other when they loitered on the very doorstep she herself brushed every day and whitened every week. 'Nob'dy can reason with her,' he had said of his sister, and, 'You didn't cause any trouble that wasn't already there.' But from what she had seen in that brief peep round Innes's arm, there had been no quarrel between James and Bethany.

When he finally came to bed they lay side by side, silent, for a long time before Stella summoned up the courage to move her hand across the cold, rough sheet to clasp his fingers. She heard a faint catch in his breathing, then after a moment he turned to take her in his arms.

It was what she wanted, and yet it was not what she needed. Even though his body merged with hers, a chasm still yawned between them and, much as she yearned to, Stella could not bridge it.

'Innes Lowrie,' Zelda raised herself on one elbow and peered down at him, 'don't tell me you're asleep already!'

'Of course not, I was just thinking.'

'Thinking about what?'

About James and Bethany, and the way they had lingered on the doorstep together, and the way . . . 'Nothing.'

'You're not here to think about nothing, or to sleep for that matter. I've been in this house all day with your mother, waiting for you to come home to me, and now that we're finally all alone in our own wee bed you're wasting time in thinking?'

The room was dark, her face in shadow, but her long,

loose hair tickled his throat and the dim glow from the
small window highlighted one bare, rounded shoulder.
He reached up and stroked her smooth skin. 'You're
cold.'

'You're my husband, it's surely your duty to do something about that,' she said, and bent to kiss him, her
full soft breasts deliciously cool against his chest. As
he drew her beneath the blanket and wrapped his own
body about her to warm her, it occurred to him that
in the dark, with faces shadowed, a man was a man
and a woman a woman. Even when they were blood-
kin.

'What in the name of God's that din?' Meg cocked her
head. 'It sounds like one of these newfangled motor-cars.'
Then, as the noise stopped, 'Have a keek out the window
and see what's going on.'

'You have a keek, I'm not bothered.'

'You're no' a real woman, Jess Lowrie,' Meg grumbled, levering herself out of her chair. 'You're no' nosy
enough.'

Just as she got herself upright, Zelda came flying down
the narrow stairs.

'For any favour, lassie,' Jess squawked at her in horror, 'will you watch what you're doing! D'you want to
trip and break your neck and kill the bairn into the
bargain?

'I'm fine, I'm fine. It's Innes and Mr MacFarlane in a
motor-car!'

'What?' Jess and Meg reached the window at the same
time. 'What do they think they're doing, giving me a
showing-up in front of all the neighbours? Zelda, pay no
heed to the two of them!'

But the order came too late; Zelda was already opening
the door, and by the time Jess and Meg got to the pavement it seemed that the entire street was already there
to marvel at the gleaming chocolate-brown car. Innes,

beaming so broadly that his face was almost cut in two, jumped down from the passenger seat and hurried round to where his wife hopped about on the pavement like an excited child.

'D'you like it? It's Mr MacFarlane's. I've just been with him to buy it.'

Jacob climbed down from behind the steering wheel, grinning at Jess. 'Your carriage awaits, my lady.'

She cast a horrified glance up and down the street. 'What are you talking about, man?'

'I'm saying fetch your coat and we'll take you for a drive. And you as well,' he added to Zelda and Meg, 'there's room for all of you.'

'I'm too busy.'

'Och, you are not, Jess.' Meg's eyes were gleaming. 'We were just having a bit of a gossip and we can do that any day of the week. I've never been in a motor-car before.'

Betrayed by her sister-in-law, fuming and embarrassed, Jess had no option but to fetch her coat.

'You'll sit by me in the front,' Jacob said, but she shook her head firmly.

'I'm affronted enough without that. What made you bring such a thing right to my front door for everyone to see?'

He looked hurt. 'I thought it would please you.'

'Please me? I don't know where to put my face!'

'Wait till you try it, Jess, it's grand to be able to up and go whenever you feel like it.'

'I already do that,' Jess said, 'only I use my feet. I'll sit in the back with Zelda.'

'I'll go in the front with you, Jacob,' Meg offered. 'How d'you get into the thing?'

After swinging the starting handle until the engine roared into life, Innes joined his wife and mother behind Meg and Jacob, and finally they moved off with a blare of the horn and a cheer from the neighbours. After driving inland for a while they stopped by a pleasant field. While the others found seats on a fallen log, Jacob and Jess strolled towards a stand of trees.

'You're vexed at me – and I thought you'd be pleased with the car.'

'It's got nothing to do with being pleased or not. If you want a motor-car then that's your business. It's just that I didn't like being driven along the street I've lived in all my married life, with folk standing at their doors and keeking through their curtains, and all the bairns too wee to be at the school running alongside.'

'They all wished they could be sitting there with you.' Jacob jerked his head, indicating the gleaming car by the roadside. Innes, too excited to sit still, had returned to it and was busily inspecting one of the wheels. 'Your lad's fair taken with it. He was a great help to me when it came to finding the right motor-car.'

'Innes has an eye for that sort of thing. I've been hearing,' she said, 'that the *Fidelity*'s crew's going to be paid proper wages during the next season instead of a share when the fishing ends.'

'Aye, they were all for it.'

'Not all, surely,' she said. Then when he raised his eyebrows at her, 'Stella tells me that James wasn't best pleased at you speaking to the rest of them before he'd the chance to think it over.'

'Time's moving on and the April herring fishing's almost on us. I began to wonder if the man was going to speak to the crew at all. Someone had to do it.'

'Behind his back, and him the skipper?'

He gave her a sidelong look. 'I felt that he had to be hurried along. Your James is a wee bit old-fashioned, Jess, he spends too much time wondering what his father would want him to do.'

'I hope the two of you aren't going to fall out about this.'

'No fear of that. He cares for the boat too much to

leave it and I know I've got one of the best skippers on the Moray Firth.'

'*We've* got one of the best skippers,' she said tartly. 'Me and Bethany and Innes own a share of her too.'

'Of course you do,' he said heartily, putting a hand beneath her elbow to assist her over the rough ground as they entered the shadows beneath the trees.

27

The new motor-car had certainly made a difference to Innes. He had had the time of his life helping Jacob to decide which one to buy and he was charmed by the way the older man had insisted that he inspect the engine of each model carefully before offering advice.

'He wants me to learn how to drive it, and he's asked me to look after it for him, because he trusts me,' he boasted to Zelda in the privacy of their bedroom.

'Of course he does, who wouldn't trust you? Innes . . .' she said, linking her arm in his. 'It was awful nice, riding along and looking out at all the folk. Could we not have a motor-car of our own one day?'

'Of course we can,' he said confidently, then, remembering the showroom in Elgin with its row of brand-new cars for sale, 'P'raps I'll even set up in a garage of my own. I could sell cars as well as repairing them.'

'We could have a nice wee house beside the garage,' she said at once.

'Aye.' He hugged her, loving the way there was more of her to hug these days.

'But when will it be, Innes?'

'Soon,' he promised rashly. 'Soon.'

James Lowrie would never forget the embarrassment of his brother's first trip on the *Fidelity*. It was no shame to the lad that he had been violently sick, for it was an experience that most new crew members, even James himself, had to go through on their first trip. He could still recall the gut-wrenching spasms and the great thick slice of salt pork that his father had forced him to eat.

'It'll come back up again before it's had time to start spoiling in your belly,' Weem had said candidly as his son, green round the gills, chewed manfully on mouthfuls of the fibrous stuff. 'But it'll cure you and you're better to have something to bring up.'

He was right: once the pork was over the side of the boat James began to feel better, and he had never been troubled with sea-sickness again. The problem with Innes was that he kept on being sick and nothing, including the salt pork, seemed to put an end to it. On the rare occasions when he wasn't hurling his guts overboard, the boy had been of little use and James had had to work twice as hard to make up for him, as well as suffering the jeers and taunts of the other crew members, who seemed to think that it was his fault that he had a weakling for a brother.

And now here was Jocky, his engine driver, flopping in his bed like a netted herring and suggesting that Innes should take his place on the *Fidelity*'s forthcoming trip.

'Are you sure you can't manage yourself tomorrow?' he asked in despair. 'It's only the line fishing and the Firth'll be like a millpond.'

'Can you not hear him wheezing away like a squeakin' gate?' Jocky's wife Nell asked sharply. 'The man's lungs is in a terrible state. He's not fit to walk to the privy, let alone go out on the boat.'

'The sea air'll do you good, Jocky.'

Nell folded her arms beneath her generous bosom. 'What sea air's that you're talking about? The man spends all his time down below with the engine. That's what's given him the bronchitis – all that steam and oil and stinking air. It's all right for you, James Lowrie, up on deck with the wind in your face.'

'D'ye think, lass, ye could fetch a drink of milk to ease my chest?' Jocky asked hoarsely, and when she had gone off with a bad grace he said apologetically to his skipper, 'I'm awful sorry, James, but the woman's right, I can scarce put one foot before the other. The way I am I'd be more of a hindrance to you than a help. I'm sure Innes'll go out with the boat if you ask him. He's a decent lad, and to tell the truth . . .' he broke off to deal with a fit of coughing that shook his skinny frame like a dog shaking a rat, 'he's a better engine driver than I am.'

'You suit me well enough, Jocky. Could you not just give it a try in the morning?'

'And have Nelly chasing me down the harbour, screamin' like a fishwife? No, no. And anyway, I know by the way I feel now that even if the bronchitis is liftin', tomorrow I'll be weak as a babby.'

James chewed his lower lip then said, 'Mebbe I'd be better to just keep the boat in the harbour tomorrow.'

'And hold the rest of the men back from earnin' money on the last trip to the line fishin'?' In his agitation Jocky reared up in bed and clutched at James's sleeve. 'They'll put the blame on me and I'll never hear the end of it! Fetch Innes, he'll do it for you . . .'

He went into another fit of coughing so severe that he couldn't catch his breath at all. As he thrashed about in the bed, whooping and choking and going purple in the face, James yelled for Nell, who rushed in, thrust a cup into his hand and went to sit on the bed, rubbing her choking husband's back.

'There now, there, my wee mannie,' she crooned. Then as Jocky drew in a shuddering breath that sounded like a bagpipe lament attempted by an untalented beginner, she glared up at James. 'Can you not see for yourself the state the man's in? Give me that milk. There'll be no line fishing for him tomorrow, and mebbe no more fishing at all if I can't get him out of this state!'

'Get Innes,' Jocky croaked feebly as James withdrew. 'He'll do it for you. After all, he's your own brother.'

When James arrived at the house to tell him that he was needed on the *Fidelity*, Innes at first thought that his brother was talking about another engine check in the harbour. He agreed jauntily enough, but as James went on, 'Be down at the harbour at five in the morning so's we can catch the tide . . .' his jauntiness disappeared like a puff of smoke.

'You're wanting me to go out with the boat?' He was aware that his mother, washing the dinner dishes, had paused and turned from the sink.

'That's the way we usually do it. We don't just stay snug in the basin and throw the lines across the harbour wall for the fish to catch.' James was as tense as his brother, and when Jess began to speak he tossed a quick, contemptuous look at her. 'The lad's a married man, he can speak up for himself. And if it's that weak belly of his you're worried about, we'll not be away more than twenty-four hours, so he'll not have the time to start spewing.'

'But Jocky Mason . . .' Innes protested.

'Jocky's got the bronchitis and he cannae manage this last trip before the herring fishing. It was him that said I should fetch you instead. He says you'd make a good engine driver, and it'll be a chance for you to see how the engines are running before we're off to Caithness with the nets.'

Innes's mouth had gone dry. 'I've got my own work to do. Surely someone else can go out with you.'

'We're not the only boat short of an engine driver,' James said, his voice taking on a sharp edge. 'There's three or four of them havin' to stay in port for lack of a man this time. But I'm damned if I'll miss out on one more catch of white fish when there's a decent enough driver in my own family. As for your own work, you can surely manage to get a day off. I'll pay you forty-six shillin' for the one trip; I'm sure that's more than the smith gives you for a week's work.'

'You'll do it, won't you, Innes?' Zelda interrupted, beaming. 'I'll go to Mr Gordon myself in the morning and say you're not well. He can surely do without you for one day.'

James grinned at her. 'You've got a good lassie there, Innes. You're a fortunate man.' He gave his brother a hearty slap on the shoulder. 'Tomorrow morning then, and don't be late for we've a tide to catch.'

'All that money for one wee trip,' Zelda gloated when James had gone. 'More to put in the bank, Innes.'

'Aye.' He shot a warning glance at his mother and she folded her lips tightly, waiting until Zelda had gone up to bed before she said quietly, 'You've not told her, have you? You've not told that lassie what you went through the time your father tried to make you into a fisherman.'

'There was no reason to tell her. Anyway, I didn't want her to think me a coward.'

'You're not a coward, Innes! You proved that when you took a beating from Will Mulholland, then insisted on facing up to him again to ask for his blessing on your marriage. The sea made you ill and now here you are agreeing to do it again.'

'James needs me.'

'What's James ever done for you?'

'He's my blood-kin and I can't let him down,' he said doggedly. 'And, Zelda's right, it'll mean more money towards getting a place of our own.'

'You know you're welcome to stay here for as long as you like – the three of you.'

'Aye, and it's good of you to put up with us. But I'm a married man now, Ma. My wife wants her own wee house and it's my job to provide it.'

She seized his arm as he tried to go past her to the stairs. 'Just because you're wed doesn't mean that I can't worry about you.'

'And just because I'm wed doesn't mean that it's easy to keep the peace between my mother and my wife,' he said with the ghost of a smile. 'But it's something I have to do, just like going out tomorrow on the boat.'

'You're a cheeky monkey, Innes Lowrie!' She swiped at him with the dishcloth in her free hand and he ducked away, grinning, relieved to have managed to dredge up some humour to ease the situation.

'I'd best go up to Zelda. Don't worry about me, Ma, and don't you get up tomorrow. I'll see to myself.'

'Innes . . .'

'I'll be back before you know it,' he said, and disappeared up the steep wooden stairs.

Although he was silent as a cat when he crept downstairs at four o'clock in the morning, Jess heard every movement because she was still wide awake, lying as stiff and straight as a poker in the bed. She had put out a good selection of bread and cheese, and scones and pancakes, for him to take with him, and left the kettle on the stove so that he could make himself some tea before going out.

She listened to him moving carefully around the kitchen, heard the soft clatter of the kettle against the teapot and the sound of water being transferred from one to the other. When the street door opened, then closed, she held her breath for a full minute, listening for movement, hoping against hope that he might have changed his mind and was still in the kitchen; but when she finally gave in to her anxieties and got up, Innes had gone, leaving behind half a mug of cold tea. At least, she thought bleakly, he had taken some food with him for later. Unable to go back to bed, she dressed and began to work on her knitting wires.

Several hours passed before Zelda came downstairs, her face still puffed with sleep, her hair tousled. 'I never even heard Innes getting up,' she said, yawning. 'Is there any tea? My throat's parched.'

'Sit down at the table and I'll pour it for you. I heard

Innes going out in good time. He'll be at the fishing
grounds by now.'

Zelda peered through the small window. 'It looks like
a decent enough day.'

'That doesn't mean they'll have good weather at sea.
Innes never spoke to you about his trips on the *Fidelity*
after he left the school?' Jess asked as she set a plate of
porridge before the girl.

'He said his da had wanted him to go to the fishing,
like James, but he didn't take to it.'

'He was awful sick . . . so bad that I knew he'd die if
he tried to keep at it. So I put a stop to his father taking
him to sea again.'

'Surely you can't die from sea-sickness?'

'Mebbe you can. I wish,' Jess said, unable to hold her
tongue any longer, 'that he'd said no to James.'

Zelda, who had always had a good appetite, scraped her
spoon around her plate to catch the last of the porridge.
'Och, he'll be fine. He's a man now, not just a wee laddie
like before. And it's just for the day; he'll be back in no
time at all.'

The moment he arrived in *Fidelity*'s engine room, Claik,
the trimmer, began to talk.

'Can you smell the reek of the fish?' he demanded as
soon as his foot left the ladder. Then when Innes, trying
hard to concentrate on the reassuring, familiar smell of
engine oil, shook his head, 'There must be somethin'
wrong with your neb then. My stomach never gets used
to that stink. The sooner we're at sea, the better, for a
few big seas'll wash the bilges out.'

In an area where most folk were named for their habits,
rather than by the names their parents had given them,
Claik had earned his nickname at school, where he had
been known as a telltale, always running to the teachers
to denounce small, scabbed-knee wrong-doers. Regular
playground beatings had failed to persuade him to mend

his ways and hold his tongue, with the result that he had retained both the nickname and, Innes soon discovered, his fondness for talking, even when he was hard at work shovelling coal into the ever-hungry furnace.

'That's us off, then,' he said while Innes tried hard to ignore the clatter of iron-studded boots on deck and the swinging, lurching movement that indicated *Fidelity*'s turn away from the harbour wall. Then, as the boat began to dip and roll, 'That's us out the harbour now.'

He kept his chatter up on the way to the fishing grounds, seemingly oblivious to his companion's silence. Innes was concentrating hard on convincing himself that James had merely asked him to see to the engines, as before, while *Fidelity* lay in the harbour, but as the boat began to lift and fall to the heavier seas out in the Firth, he quickly discovered that deception was impossible. Despite all the oaths he had sworn and the promises he had made to himself, he was back at sea.

At first, shutting his ears to Claik's babbling, he concentrated hard on the engines, making mental notes of things to be checked when the boat was being made ready for the start of the new herring season. Then he pondered over Stella's suggestion that he should think of trying for a job in one of the boatyards. Every community along the coast, large or small, had its share of yards but until then Innes, because of his fear of the sea, had never thought of working in one of them. The more he thought of it, the more the idea appealed to him. He determined to approach George Thomson of Buckie, and if that yard had no need of him there was Smith's of Buckpool, Herd and McKenzie of Finnechtie, and yards at Cullen or Portessie that any man would be proud to work for. This would be the time to make the change, he decided; a new wife and a new career, all in the same year.

Listing the yards where he might be able to find work kept his mind occupied and kept Claik's voice in the background while the engine, running sweetly enough, carried the *Fidelity* towards the fishing grounds.

When he had run out of boatyards, Innes turned his thoughts to Zelda, which was a mistake since it filled him with a yearning to be with her, or at least to be in his small workshop hard by the smiddy, safe in the knowledge that within a matter of hours he would be returning to her.

He would still be home with her by bedtime, he reminded himself firmly. Boats at the line fishing only stayed out for a day. Just then *Fidelity*, meeting with a steep wave, climbed it with ease before her bows dipped forward and she began the slide down the other side. Innes's stomach suddenly seemed to turn to stone; then, as the boat hit the valley before the next wave with a thud, the stone turned to liquid that boiled up behind his breastbone and into his throat. He had to swallow several times to keep it from reaching his tightly closed lips and splattering between them.

Claik, stripped to the waist and already running with sweat, merely mumbled a curse round the cigarette he had placed between his lips and juggled deftly with the shovelful of glowing coals he had just scooped from the furnace. It was a tricky moment, but he managed to keep the embers balanced on the shovel, and as the boat began to climb the next wave he used them to light his cigarette before tossing them back into the furnace. Then he peered over at Innes, his eyes startlingly white in his soot-streaked face.

'Are you all right? Your face's the colour of a fish floatin' belly-up.'

'I'm fine,' Innes said through clenched teeth.

Claik inhaled a great lungful of tarry smoke, then blew it out in a cloud that filled the small space and returned to the back-breaking work of shovelling coal from the bunker into the roaring furnace.

'Here,' he suddenly remembered, 'did you not have to give up the sea because your guts couldnae take the motion of the boat?' When Innes, unable to trust himself to speak, gave a nod, Claik said comfortingly, 'Ach, that was a while ago. You'll feel different now, eh?' Then, peering again at his engine driver, 'Mebbe no', though. Here . . .'

He put the shovel down for a minute to rummage in a corner, giving a grunt of pleasure when he unearthed a grimy bucket. 'Stick that down beside you just in case. But try not to use it, for the reek in here's bad enough. Would you like a smoke? That always settles my belly when it feels wrong.'

Innes shook his head, convulsively swallowing again and again as the boat started to clamber up the side of another big wave. She began to skim down towards the trough earlier than he had expected, catching him unawares. He staggered, and had Claik not put out an arm to hold him back he might well have fallen against the red-hot furnace.

'Hold on there, man, we don't want you burnin' yourself before we even get to the fishin' grounds,' he said amiably, exhaling another lungful of strong-smelling tobacco smoke. Then, as Innes grabbed at the bucket, the battle lost, 'God,' he went on mournfully, 'just when that stink from the bilges was gettin' washed out, too.'

It was full daylight when they reached the fishing grounds. At James's shouted orders Innes stopped the engine, then the mizzen was set to hold the *Fidelity* head to wind while the lines went overboard. The task was lighter than shooting the nets, but even so it was time-consuming, for there were five lines for each of the seven men in the crew, and each line held about a hundred and twenty baited hooks.

With the engine stopped, Innes at last had a chance to get on deck for some fresh air. 'Not already,' James said when he saw his brother emptying the bucket overboard. 'The water's scarce got a bit of movement on it.'

Innes, his stomach raw with continuous retching and

his entire body aching from the need to adapt his footing all the time to counteract the heavy rolls and pitches of the boat, glared at him.

'You'd be sick if you'd to stay down there, breathing in that poisonous air.'

His brother grinned. 'Am I not lucky being a fisherman instead of an engine man like yourself? We've got good fresh air to breathe up here,' he said. Then, recalling that the boat could not have put to sea without his brother's help, he added in a more friendly tone, 'You can stay on deck while we're putting the lines out, but just keep over there, out of the way.'

The fresh air and the cold wind were both welcoming after the stuffy engine compartment with its obnoxious fumes, but there was nothing stationary, Innes realised wretchedly, to fix his gaze on. The sea rolled and tossed and heaved; the cork float thrown overboard to mark the site of the lines bobbed and bounced in a way that made him feel worse; the horizon swung crazily; and even the clouds overhead raced across the sky, never staying still for a moment.

When the lines were shot and the men went into the galley for their meal he followed them, clinging to the thought that under cover there might be some stability. But in the enclosed space the boat's tossing, lurching motion was made even worse and the smell of the food only added to his misery. Seeing the sense of the adage that it was better to have something in his stomach than nothing at all, he tried to eat a mouthful or two of soup and bread, only to find that he had to rush out on to the deck almost at once, followed by a gust of laughter.

'You've not changed, have you?' James said when he came on deck later to find his younger brother leaning over the side and retching helplessly. 'Da thought you'd grow out of it, but you'll never make a seaman.'

Innes straightened, wiped his mouth on his sleeve and stamped back to the engine room without a word, but even with the engines stopped the place was uncomfortable and claustrophobic. He was soon back on deck, huddled miserably in a corner, yearning with all his heart for land, and home and Zelda.

28

Bethany and the children had almost reached her mother's house when they met Stella and her small family walking in the opposite direction.

'Your mam's not in,' Stella said. 'Mr MacFarlane's taken her out for a run in his motor-car, Zelda says.'

'Are you all right, Stella?'

'I'm fine.'

'You look awful pale. D'you want me to carry wee Ruth for you?' The sleeping baby, plump and rosy, looked far too heavy for her wan young mother.

'Leave her!' Stella said sharply as Bethany reached out to take the little girl. 'And you can leave my man alone, too!'

Bethany felt the colour drain from her face. 'James? I don't know what you're talking about.'

'You know well enough what I mean.' Stella slapped each word down on the air between the two of them; they sounded to Bethany like coins ringing on a wooden counter.

Her mind worked swiftly, desperately. 'James told you about me asking Jacob MacFarlane to buy Uncle Albert out, so's James could be skipper?'

Stella, caught by surprise, blinked at her uncertainly. 'He said nothing about that.'

'I tried to keep it a secret, but he found out and was real vexed with me,' Bethany prattled on, 'but at

least he agreed to stay on with the boat, so no harm
was done.'

Stella eyed her narrowly. 'Not long ago I might have
wondered why you did such a thing,' she said, 'since you
and James quarrelled every time you met up with each
other. But I know now what was behind it.'

'I just felt that he should stay on the Lowrie boat. It's
what Da would have wanted.'

'You're always on about that father of yours, you and
James both. Always on about what he'd want.' Stella's
eyes were burning now, like two red-hot coals. 'And are
the two of you what he'd have wanted, Bethany? You
and my James, brother and sister, sinning together?' she
asked softly, and the blood froze in Bethany's veins.

'Don't be daft!'

'I must have been daft not to have known why he started
spending even more time on the boat, and why he began
to go on about me not being as clever as you. But I'm not
daft any more, not since I saw the two of you together.'

'When . . . where?' Bethany asked in a panic, and could
have bitten her tongue out as the final word left it.

'A week or two past, on my own front doorstep, when
you thought I was safely out of the way at your mam's
house.' Two bright-red blotches were beginning to stain
Stella's sallow cheeks. Red for anger, Bethany thought.
And red for danger.

'Och, that? I only went to see James about Jacob's daft
plan to pay wages to the crew instead of . . .'

'I saw you,' Stella forged on over her sister-in-law's
protestations. 'I saw him touch you and I saw you . . .'
Her voice failed her, but the way she put her own fingers
to her cheek, gently, as though caressing another hand that
had paused there, told Bethany everything. 'How could
you – with your own brother? It's a sin against God and
a sin against nature,' she said vehemently. 'And it's a sin
against me and my innocent wee bairns. I've been lying
awake at nights wondering what to do about it, so I'm

glad I met you today. Stay away from my man, Bethany, and stay away from me.' Her voice was menacing now, her anger so strong that the air about her neat brown head seemed to vibrate with it. 'Stay away, or I swear to God that I'll tell Gil and your mother what I saw. I'll tell the whole coast.'

Bethany attempted a laugh. 'You think anyone would believe such nonsense?'

'Oh, I think they would. I'm not the only one who saw you.'

'Who . . . ?' Bethany's throat was so closed up with shock that the word barely managed to squeeze out.

'That's for me to know and you to wonder about. But you'll know soon enough if you try to come between me and James again,' Stella said and pushed past her sister-in-law, scooping the twins before her. Bethany stared after the woman. Then, sick with shock, she blundered towards the refuge of her mother's house.

Ellen, used to being towed everywhere by the hand and panic-stricken to find herself adrift in the street, followed as fast as she could, bleating like an abandoned lamb until Rory took her arm and pulled her with him. They caught up with Bethany as she fumbled with the latch, so disturbed by the scene with Stella that her fingers were unable to make sense of the simple, familiar mechanism. When Zelda, alerted by the rattling sounds, opened the door from inside, Bethany almost fell into the kitchen.

'You're white as a sheet . . . What's happened to you?' the girl asked. Bethany pushed past her and reached a chair just as her knees threatened to give way beneath her.

'I'm fine, I just took a dizzy turn as I was coming along the street.' Bethany clutched at the edge of the table, squeezing her eyes tightly shut and lowering her head to her knees as the room slowly revolved about her. Dimly, she could hear Zelda talking to the children, settling them down on the hearth rug and giving them something to play with. Then she jumped and gasped as something cold and wet touched her forehead.

'Water, just,' her new sister-in-law said briskly. 'Hold the cloth to your head while I make some tea.'

The cold compress and the hot tea worked their magic, but when Bethany set out for her own home Zelda insisted on going with her.

'You still look awful pale. Mebbe you're sickening for something.'

'I'm never ill.' Now that she was beginning to feel more like herself Bethany was anxious to be on her own, with time to think.

'Mebbe,' Zelda said, 'you've a bairn coming.'

'What? Of course it's not a bairn!'

'You've been wed long enough. I know that when I first fell with this one,' Zelda patted her rounding stomach complacently, 'I fainted once in the dairy at the farm and I was awful sick too. That's how the mistress knew I was expecting. It was her that told me, for I knew nothing about these things. You won't either, since Rory and Ellen aren't your own . . .'

Her voice went on and on; she was as bad as Stella, Bethany thought, and suddenly recalled Stella's face as she had last seen it, ashen apart from the bright-red spots on her cheekbones and the diamond brilliance of her eyes. Stella knew, and according to her someone else knew too, and nothing would ever be the same again.

It was a relief when they reached the house and Zelda, refusing a half-hearted invitation to step inside, hurried away. At last, Bethany thought, she had a chance to think over what had happened. But when she went into the house Gil was there, having finished work early for once and waiting impatiently to tell her that he had just put down the deposit on one of the big houses being built on Castle Terrace, an area in the upper part of Buckie, overlooking the Firth, where the old lighthouse stood.

'You'll feel like a lady there, Bethany,' he exulted.

'Mistress of a fine house, and with a bonny garden as well. I'll plant potatoes and grow kale and neeps for the kitchen. We'll mebbe be able to manage a lassie to help you with the heavy work.'

He kissed his wife soundly, while Rory looked on in shocked disapproval and Ellen jealously clamoured at her father's knee for attention.

'In a minute, henny, in a minute,' he said amiably, then picked Bethany up and swung her round. 'Mr and Mrs Gilbert Pate of Castle Terrace. Does that not sound grand?'

'Aye, it . . .' Bethany said faintly, her head whirling. 'Gil, could you put me down now?'

And when he did she ran out the back and only just got to the privy in time.

At almost the same time Innes – having decided that the fisherman's adage about full bellies emptying easier might be true – was in *Fidelity*'s galley, grimly forcing food down his throat. The place was empty, for the crew, having eaten and rested, were out on deck now, bringing in the lines. Soon they would be turning for home. Soon his ordeal would be over, but as the end approached, Innes, sore inside and out, stiff and bone-weary, decided that it was time for one last attempt to defeat his fear of the sea.

Elbows on the table, he chewed and swallowed, chewed and swallowed, his eyes firmly fixed on the opposite wall. The sea had calmed now and the boat's motion was more even and at first, when he pushed the plate away and leaned back in his chair, he felt better for the food. Energy began to pulse through his body, and he breathed deeply and stretched his arms high above his head. Perhaps he had won, at last. That, he thought with a grin, would make James eat his words.

It proved to be an unfortunate turn of phrase, for within seconds a stirring in the pit of his belly sen him lurching across the small galley to where the bucket waited.

It had been a good fishing, though there was nothing to beat drift-nets glittering with the silvery shimmer of the herring. As the lines came inboard almost every hook carried a fish, and James was exultant as he watched the sea-harvest being emptied into the baskets and lowered down to the hold. This was the last of the line fishing; within the week work would start on rigging *Fidelity* out for the new herring season. There was a lot to be done after the near-inactivity of the past three or four months.

His good nature ebbed at the sight of his brother shambling out of the galley door, staggering slightly as the boat lifted on a wave. James, his own booted feet set firmly on deck and balancing his body easily against the vessel's movements, groaned and then shouted hastily as Innes headed to one side, 'Port, man, port! Can you not tell what way the wind's blowing?'

As Innes turned a pallid face in his direction James stuck one finger in his mouth, then held it up in the air as illustration. 'Empty that bucket against the wind and you'll get it all back to do again,' he roared, and some of the men sniggered.

'Here . . .' Jem, younger and more compassionate than the others, took the bucket from Innes and upended it over the side, letting the wind carry its contents away from the boat. Then he picked up a piece of rope, looped it through the handle, caught both ends in one hand and dropped the bucket down into the waves. Bringing it back up again, he swilled the salt water around before tossing it overboard.

'That's it all cleaned. Best get back into the galley, Innes, or down to the engines,' he said kindly. 'We'll be heading for home soon enough. You'll be glad of that, eh?'

'You might as well stop now, Innes,' James yelled just

then from the bows. 'We've got all the fish we want for this trip, no need for you to go on feeding them.'

As another spatter of laughter passed through the crew, Innes, who had turned towards the galley, set the bucket down again and headed for his brother instead, clutching at handholds as he made his way along a deck slippery with bloody fish-slime. His face was white, but determined, and his voice when he yelled, 'Shut your mouth, James,' was strong enough to be heard along the length of the boat, even above the strong slap of the sea against her hull.

'What?'

Innes came to a stop within arm's length of his tormentor. 'You heard me. Shut your mouth and keep it shut,' he said, a clear, cold rage beginning to bubble up within him. 'You've had your sport with me and it's time to let it be. D'you not think it's bad enough to be spewing up my guts on this . . . this washtub, without you jeering and mocking and making a fool of me for their amusement?' He threw out an arm to indicate the gaping deckhands, then shouted at them, 'Never mind sniggering at me, get on with what you're paid to do, so's we can get off this damned Firth and back to land!'

'Get below,' James ordered his brother as the crew hurriedly turned back to their work.

'No.'

'Do as I say. Start the engines, we're turning for shore.'

'You and me have business between us first.'

'It can keep until we're back in harbour.'

'No,' Innes said. 'It can't. We'll turn for shore when I've had my say, and not before.'

James's expression moved from astonishment to anger. 'I'm master aboard this vessel!'

'Aye, and I'm the engine driver. The boat stays where it is until I choose to take it back to Buckie.'

'You defy me before my own crew, Innes, and I'll . . .'

The boat dropped suddenly beneath Innes's feet and he

clutched at a rope. Fortunately for him it held, allowing him to adjust his balance, but the sudden shudder in the deck beneath him was enough to bring a spurt of bile, hot and sour-tasting, into his mouth. He turned his head and spat it out with enough force to send it flying over the bulwarks and into the surging sea beyond.

'I've just discovered what caused my belly to go bad on me all these years ago, and again on this trip,' he told his brother conversationally. 'It's disgust, James, and contempt; and mebbe a dash of pity as well.'

'Eh?'

'Contempt and pity for you, James, and for our father and the way the two of you kept on and on, all the years I was growing up, about how the only fit place for a man to be was on the sea and how the only decent work was to be found on the fishing boats.'

'Claik!' James thundered. 'Get below and start the engine!'

'He doesnae know how, James. He's the trimmer, not the driver. Claik,' Innes shouted, his eyes steady on his brother's face, 'get everything ready. I'll be with you when I've got this business sorted.'

Stella came into his mind, her small face ashen after the two of them had seen her husband with Bethany, her eyes huge and blank, her voice flat as she told the twins, 'Daddy doesn't want to play any more.' It wasn't just for himself that he was angry; it was for her as well.

'Neither of you ever tolerated the idea of any other life, did you?' he asked James. 'The sea suited you both, but for me there was always more than following the herring. And just because I thought that, the two of you – and Bethany as well – made me feel for all those years that I must be lacking in some way. But all the time, James, it was you who was lacking.'

He spat again and this time the wad of phlegm landed neatly on the deck between his brother's feet.

James looked down at it in disbelief, then in one

movement he snatched at the front of Innes's jacket, twisting his hand tightly in the material so that Innes was dragged towards him. 'Get below and get these engines started right now or, so help me, I'll put you overboard!'

A terrifying memory of being held out by his father over the racing black sea below flickered into Innes's mind, but he found the strength to kick it out again before it could take root. 'Put me overboard . . .' half throttled as he was, he had to jerk the words out between gritted teeth, '. . . and you'll have to stay here until someone comes to tow you in, just like a bairn dangling from its mother's hand. Does that thought not make you wonder just who's the most important of the two of us right now? Anyway, d'you really think that Charlie and Jem and the rest of them would stand by and watch you drown me?'

While talking, Innes had managed to get his fists between himself and his brother and now he pushed upwards with all his might, forcing James to release him.

'Get on with your work,' James yelled at the others. Then to Innes, 'What in God's name's got into you, man?'

'I've had enough.' As the boat shifted unexpectedly, Innes rocked back on his heels, then managed to balance himself. 'Enough of your swaggering and your need to make other folk feel small.'

A sneer twisted his brother's weather-beaten face. 'You're parroting Zelda now, aren't you? If you ask me, she's just what you've been needing, Innes, a nebby wee wife sharp enough to put words into your mouth.'

'Zelda knows nothing of this, though you're right, she would probably say the same thing herself. We're fortunate men, you and me, for we both wed good women, women who love us no matter how many faults we have. I think the world of my wife and I'm determined to make her happy, but I'm heart sorry for yours, for she deserves better than she got.'

'You've not been wed above five minutes and here you are, presuming to interfere between me and Stella? I'll not have that, Innes. Mind your own business and get to the engines!'

'Not until I've had my say,' Innes repeated. He settled himself more firmly on to the decking, for he was beginning to understand the movement of the boat beneath him and recognise a pattern to the sea. 'What's going on between you and Bethany?'

His brother's eyes bulged with sheer shock. 'What nonsense is this you're on now?'

'There's something happening between the pair of you, something that's not right. Something that's not natural. For God's sake, man, she's our sister!'

James's weather-beaten skin had taken on a grey tinge. 'You're haverin'!' he exploded. 'All that vomitin's emptied your skull as well as your belly!'

'I know what I saw, and I saw the two of you on your own doorstep a week or two back. I saw you touch your own sister in the way a man touches a woman when he cares for her.' James opened his mouth to speak, then closed it abruptly when Innes went on, 'Stella was with me, for I was walking her home. She saw it too.'

'She didn't . . . she couldn't!' James babbled. 'She would have said . . .'

'Said what? When have you ever listened to your wife, James? The whole town knows that you only wed her just so's you and Father and Uncle Albert could get your hands on Mowser's boat. You've never cared about the humiliation that caused her, because you've never taken the time to wonder how your wife feels about anything. You don't even see that she's got more self-respect and more pride than you could ever have, do you? Stella would die for you, James, but she'd never allow herself to tell you that, or to beg for the love she's desperate for. Now I come to think of it,' Innes said slowly, coldly, 'I don't want to know anything about whatever's between you and

Bethany, for the two of you disgust me. And now that I've had my say I'll start the engines and get you safely back to harbour.'

He turned away, then turned back to say into James's shattered face, 'I was right when I said that it was the way you and our father treated me that stuck in my craw. All gale-force wind with no substance, James, and now that I've vomited it out all over you it's gone. I feel fine. My mother'll be pleased.'

Zelda and Jess were both waiting on the harbour wall when the Buckie boats came skimming over the dark seas, lining up to come through the harbour entrance one by one, the light on each masthead twinkling. *Fidelity* was one of the last; as her crew took her to her usual place by the harbour wall and the holds were opened, Jess anxiously scanned the deck for Innes. James, setting up the deck derrick and seeing to the removal of the baskets of fish, glanced up once, his eyes raking the ranks of the people waiting above, then looked away without acknowledging his mother or sister-in-law. Gil was there, waiting for the fish to be landed from *Fidelity* and the other boats contracted to him and his brother, but there was no sign of Stella. Given the late hour, with the children and Mowser probably abed, Jess had not expected to see her.

'D'you see Innes yet, Zelda?' she asked, her heart in her mouth.

'He'll be down below seeing to the engine,' her daughter-in-law said comfortably, then her voice soared into a squeak of childish excitement and she clutched at Jess's arm 'No . . . there he is!'

As soon as he came through the galley door Innes looked up. A broad grin split his grimy face at the sight of his wife and mother waiting, and he waved and paused to wipe his face on a large wad of rag pulled from his pocket before making for the iron ladder set in the stone wall. James, busy at the hold, didn't look in his direction and Innes himself paid no heed to his brother. Charlie found a moment to catch at his arm as he passed; Innes listened, then shook his head and gave his cousin a quick slap on the back before climbing the ladder swiftly, though clumsily. The grin was still plastered on his face as he reached the top.

As soon as he was safely away from the drop to the harbour and the boats below, Zelda flew into his arms. 'I missed you!'

'Ach, I wasn't away all that long,' he said casually, winking at his mother over his wife's shoulder. He looked fine, Jess thought with astonishment. Tired, as was to be expected after a long, hard day at sea, but nothing like the ashen, exhausted lad who had twice returned to her from trips with Weem.

'You're all right, son?'

'I'm fine, Ma,' Innes said. 'I hope you've got some food ready for I'm starving.'

'It's being kept hot for you, but are you not wanting to go for a drink with the rest of them first?'

He shook his head and put an arm about Zelda. 'I've got all I need at home.'

'You smell,' his wife said as they set off along the street. 'Fish and oil and goodness knows what.'

'At least you're smelling the reek of it in the open air. Think what it's been like for me, stuck in that tiny engine room most of the day. You've got oil on your face now,' Innes said tenderly.

Zelda insisted on going with him to the outhouse while he washed and changed. A lot of giggling went on, and Jess had to call them three times before they finally came into the kitchen, Innes scrubbed clean and Zelda with her hair damp, both of them tousled and glowing.

They could scarcely keep their eyes off each other during the meal. Jess felt like an outsider in her own home and it was almost a relief when Innes pushed his empty plate away and announced that he was going to his bed.

'You should mebbe go to bed too, Zelda,' Jess suggested to her daughter-in-law. 'You look tired tonight.'

'You're right. I'll just do that.' Zelda bounced up from the table and almost ran up the steep, narrow stairs ahead of Innes. Left alone, Jess washed the dishes, damped down the fire and retired to her own bed with a cushion to put over her ears.

She was asleep long before Zelda, relaxing with a sigh of contentment against her husband's shoulder, said, 'If that's what going to sea does to you, Innes Lowrie, I'll have to send you out on the boat more often.'

'It's what you do to me.' He was drifting off to sleep, but he roused himself enough to kiss the end of her nose. 'And I'm done with the sea. I'll never go back, not for as long as I live.'

29

James stayed behind on the *Fidelity* long after Innes and the rest of the crew had gone ashore. He poured water into the small tin bowl, then stripped and washed himself as best he could before putting on the clean clothes he had stowed in a locker. He needed to see Bethany, to be with her and to talk to her about Innes's revelation, but time passed and there was no footstep on the deck overhead, no voice calling his name quietly from the galley.

He waited in the darkness, chewing at a thumbnail in an agony of worry. Their affair, the wondrous thing that had suddenly made his life worth living, no longer belonged to just the two of them. Decisions had to be made, hard decisions.

Finally he went ashore, heading for the pub and the companionship of the other men. Glancing in at the lit window as he passed, he saw that they were all there – Charlie and Jem and Claik and the others, and Gil was with them. That was why Bethany had not been able to get down to the harbour.

He passed the door quietly and hurried up the hill to Gil's house, keeping to the shadows, although the streets were quiet and many of the houses dark, the folk within already abed for the night.

The door was unlatched; he pushed it open slightly and said through the crack, 'It's me', before sliding in and closing it behind him. Bethany, ready for bed and caught in the middle of brushing out her long, curly hair, spun round, her grey eyes wide.

'James? What d'you think you're doing, coming here at this time of night!'

'It's all right, I've just seen Gil in the pub with a full glass before him.' His limbs went weak at the sight of her in her long white gown, the lamplight mining gold shimmers from the depths of her brown hair. 'Oh God, Bethany . . .' he said, and went to her.

The hairbrush fell to the floor as she melted into his arms, as hungry for him as he was for her. They kissed and kissed again, clinging together as though they had not seen each other for a very long time, or as if they were saying goodbye for ever.

Finally, reluctantly, she drew away. 'You'll have to go.' Her eyes on his face, and her hands tangling themselves in his hair, belied the words. 'He might be back at any minute.'

'I've something to tell you . . .'

'I've something to tell you too,' Bethany interrupted. 'Stella knows about us.'

His arms fell away from her and he felt the blood drain from his face. 'She's spoken to you?'

'More than that, she's told me never to go near you again, or her, or she'll tell Gil and Mother and everyone. And she says someone else knows too.'

'She's right there. It's Innes.'

Her grey eyes widened. 'Innes!'

'He told me when we were out at the fishing grounds. He said . . .' James choked on the memory of his younger brother's anger and contempt. 'Never mind what he said.'

'That's it, then. It's over.'

'No, it's not!'

'See sense, man. Stella and Innes both know about us. We can't go on as we have been.'

'We could go away together, somewhere far away

where we could live as man and wife with nobody knowing any different.'

'You'd leave Stella and your three bairns?'

'For you I would.'

'James, we're brother and sister!'

'But we were never meant to be brother and sister. We
can start again somewhere else – Jacob MacFarlane did
it and so can we. Tonight, before Gil comes home . . .'
Fired with the need to act quickly, he caught at her hands.
'Get dressed, Bethany, and pack some things.'

Her hair swung softly round her ashen face as she shook
her head. Her eyes reminded him, now, of a cold grey mist
on the sea in wintertime.

'No, James, I'm not coming away with you. Fishing's
all we know, the two of us. I don't want to spend the
rest of my life hiding, and wondering if someone we've
met before in Caithness or Yarm'th or Lowestoft'll turn
up on a boat with you, or working the farlins with me.'

'Take a day or two to think about it. I'll be on the
boat every night, same as usual, waiting for you,' he said
desperately.

She reached up to touch his face, her fingers as gentle
as the touch of a moth's wing. 'Best go home to Stella
now, before Gil comes back.'

When he took her in his arms again she clung to him
and kissed him with passion, before pushing him towards
the door. As he left, he heard her latch it behind him.

He had only passed a few darkened houses when he
heard heavy footsteps at the other end of the dark street.
James ducked into a doorway and flattened himself against
the sturdy timbers, listening to a deep voice singing tune-
lessly, mumbling the words and breaking off occasionally
to curse, as Gil – for James recognised the cursing – missed
his footing and stumbled.

When his brother-in-law had passed by he slid out of
the doorway and made his own way home.

*   *   *

Ruth, fed and warm and dry, was crooning sleepily to herself in her little crib while Stella sat by the fire, her hands busy with some darning.

'There's water heating for you.' She nodded at the big pot on the range as she put her work aside and rose.

'I washed on the boat.'

'Was it a good trip?' She wrapped a cloth about her hands before opening the oven door.

'Aye, good enough. Did Gil bring the fish I set aside for you?'

'A while since. You'll have seen him in the pub, surely.'

'I didn't go to the pub, I wanted to put the boat to rights.'

'On your lone?' Was it his imagination, or was there a strange note to her voice? He glanced at her, but her eyes were averted, her head turned from him as she took a plate piled with food from the oven.

'Of course on my lone. D'you think the rest of them would stay on when there's drink waiting for them on shore?'

She said nothing, but the silence roared in his ears. While he ate, the food tasteless in his mouth, he waited for her to say something, wondered if he should speak first, decided that it was safer to hold his tongue, then began to wish that she would say something – anything – to break the terrible silence between them. If only Mowser was still up, filling the void with his usual aimless chatter.

Stella did not seem fazed by the silence. She moved calmly about the kitchen, taking the girls' small garments from the clothes-horse and folding them neatly, calming Ruth when she began to whimper, crooning to her until the baby finally fell asleep, then re-arranging the fancy gilt-edged dishes, presents from Yarmouth, Lowestoft and Grimsby collected by her and her mother and kept on display in a corner cabinet. When she finally spoke it was to ask, 'How did Innes do?'

'He seemed to manage. You've got a right fondness for Innes, haven't you?'

'He's a pleasant lad, and he's always been kind to me and the bairns. There's more if you want it.'

Looking down at his plate, he was startled to find that it was empty, though he had no recollection of eating the great mound of meat and potatoes she had given him. 'No, I'm fine,' he replied, and she put a mug full of scalding black tea before him and said, 'I'll away to my bed then.'

Later, as they lay side by side in the wall-bed, James reached out a tentative hand towards her. 'Stella . . .' he began, but she immediately cut across the words that were about to pour out.

'I'm tired, James. Whatever it is can wait till morning,' she said, and turned away from him.

She had never spoken to him like that before, never turned from him. It was as good an indication as any that all at once things had changed between them, and would never be the same again.

James lay listening to the faint, regular snuffle of Ruth's breathing, waiting for daylight to lighten the window.

'Your mother tells me that you're giving up your work here.'

'Aye, that's right.' Innes's voice was muffled because he was halfway under the bonnet of Jacob's motor-car. He emerged, closed the bonnet and wiped his oily hands on a rag. 'I've been taken on at Thomson's yard.'

'I thought you didn't care for boats.'

'I've no interest in fishing,' Innes was able to say it now without feeling ashamed, 'but steam drifters have engines and that's what I'll be working on. I'll make more money there – but don't you worry, Mr MacFarlane, I'll still be looking after this motor-car for as long as you want me to. You can try her out now.'

'You try her out, since you're the one who's been

working on her.' Jacob climbed into the passenger seat while Innes, flushing with pleasure, started the engine. It ran sweetly and when the motor-car moved off with the younger man at the wheel Jacob suggested, 'You should work in a garage.'

'That's what Zelda says, but there's no work to be had locally and I don't want to be too far away, with the bairn coming.' Innes gave a sudden laugh. 'Zelda's got it into her head that one day I'll have a garage of my own with a nice wee house beside it.'

'It's good to have an ambition ahead of you when you're young.'

'Aye, it is, but right now I'm kept busy enough trying to raise the money for the house, let alone a garage. Though it'll happen one day.'

'I'm sure it will,' Jacob said. 'I know from my own experience that you can do whatever you put your mind to. Well,' he added, with a sidelong glance at Jess's youngest son, 'you can achieve most things, if you put your mind to them.'

To Jacob's annoyance, Jess continued to be uncomfortable with the idea of his motor-car, and on the few occasions when he persuaded her to go for a run in it she insisted on meeting him outside Buckie, rather than being collected from her own home.

'What's the sense in you walking half a mile or more to where I'm waiting, instead of just stepping out of your own door and into the motor?' he wanted to know as they bowled through the pleasant town of Fochabers on their way to Elgin.

Jess, uncomfortably aware of the attention that the smart motor-car was attracting, plucked at the rug he had tucked over her knees. 'I can't get used to the idea of the neighbours seeing me in a contraption like this. Of anyone seeing me,' she added.

'You're an awful woman, Jess Lowrie,' he sighed, and

said it again later as she sat bolt upright on her chair in the hotel where they were having afternoon tea. 'Can you not just relax and enjoy yourself?'

'It's all right for you, Jacob, you've got into the way of these places.' She kept her voice to a whisper, her eyes darting nervously round the fine room. 'But I'm not used to it at all.'

'You could get used to it, same as I had to.'

'I doubt that. Anyway, your livelihood depended on it. I've no such need.'

'But I could show you such sights, Jess.' He leaned across the small table, his eyes taking on an emerald glow. 'You should see Russia, and Germany, and the Niagara Falls in Canada. And the Flemish tulip fields in the springtime, and the windmills . . . you'd enjoy all of those.'

'Mebbe I would, and mebbe the ordinary folk who live there would enjoy seeing the boats coming home in the dark with their lights all twinkling. Mebbe they'd like it on an autumn evening, seeing the sky the colour of an old pewter plate and the wee bit of mist far out on the sea, and the water all the shades of grey and looking like ruffled silk, and the dolphins playing as they go up the Moray Firth. But they'll never see that,' Jess ended briskly, 'just as I'll never see their countries, for people like us don't go travelling all over.'

'I did.'

'I keep telling you, man, that you're different. You've got more courage than I have.'

'It had nothing to do with courage and you know that better than anyone else,' Jacob said with a hard edge to his voice. Suddenly Jess recalled a much younger Jacob, bewildered, asking, 'Why, Jess? Why him and not me?'

'Madam?' A waiter had arrived from nowhere.

'What did you say?' she asked, confused, wrenched from her memories.

'Hot water, madam. Do you require more?'

'No, thank you.'

'Then more tea? It's been standing for a while, it must be quite strong now.'

His hand was outstretched towards the pretty silver teapot when Jess said firmly, 'No, leave it. I like it good and strong.'

As the man bowed and retired Jacob chuckled. 'You're coming out of your shell, woman.'

'I've never been in one, as far as I know, even though the furthest I've ever travelled is the Shetlands and Yarmouth for the fishing,' she told him, picking up another scone. 'And that did me well enough.'

'Aye, well,' he said quietly to her bent head. 'We still have time, you and me. Who knows what might happen yet?'

There had been a time, before the last Yarmouth fishing season, when Bethany and James had rarely set eyes on each other from one month to the next, but now she seemed to see him at the far end of every street she turned into, or passing every shop she was about to leave. She seemed to spend some part of every day avoiding him.

The nights were the worst, when she fidgeted and shifted in her chair, thinking about James, longing to go to the harbour to see if he was alone on board *Fidelity*, waiting for her. Gil, unaware of her misery, spent every evening now talking endlessly about the wallpaper and furniture they would have in each room of the new house, and the bushes he was going to plant in the garden.

Occasionally she was jerked from her own thoughts by some new inflection in his voice, some unexpected comment. Tonight it was, 'Imagine being able to go to the privy without havin' to step outside your own back door.'

'What?'

'You're away in one of your dreams again, aren't you?' He thrust the paper he had brought home with him that night under her nose. 'Look at that: a water closet with a mahogany surround, and a fine big bath, both in the same room. And a sink to wash your hands in, too. Wait till my mother sees it all!'

'She'll not approve. She never approves of anything.'

'That's what she'll say to our faces, but she'll enjoy boasting to the neighbours about us. And she'll not miss the chance to visit, either,' he added, and Bethany groaned inwardly, then forgot all about Phemie Pate as Gil went on, 'We'll be well moved in before the bairn comes.'

'What bairn?'

'The one you're carryin'.' He grinned. 'You thought I didn't know about it, didn't you? It might be your first, but it's my third, don't forget.'

'I'm . . . I'm not even sure that I am expecting.' Bethany's mouth was dry with shock. Zelda's innocent comments the day she had taken a fainting turn near her mother's house had been ringing in her ears ever since, but she had refused to accept them, or pay heed to the slight sickness she felt some mornings. She had never fancied the idea of having a child of her own, and she had more or less made up her mind to try to get rid of it. There were women who could perform that service, but she didn't know of any and she daren't ask anyone about them.

'Ye must be. Ye've not had any of that . . .' even Gil balked at mentioning a woman's monthly cycle, '. . . that business for a wee while, have ye? Ye've had a right struggle to make your belly behave itself when you're cooking my breakfast, and you've been as fidgety as a hen on a hot griddle. And in bed at night, when I touch ye here,' he leaned forward suddenly and took a firm hold of one breast, then grinned as she flinched away from his hand, 'ye're feelin' awful sore, aren't ye?'

'Yes.' It was true, but she flinched anyway whenever Gil touched her. It had been bad enough before James, but now . . . She forced all thoughts of him away.

'When'll it be?' Gil asked, then as she sat and looked at him foolishly, he counted swiftly on his thick, stubby fingers. 'October, I'd say, just before the boats go south. So I'll be here.'

October. Now that she had been forced to look at her pregnancy as definite, rather than possible, Bethany also had to accept that the child could have been fathered by either Gil or James. She shivered, suddenly cold although she was close to the fire.

'I'm right pleased, Bethany,' she heard Gil say. 'It's long past time we had a bairn of our own. Another wee laddie, mebbe, to play with . . .'

His voice faded away behind her as she got up, clapping a hand to her mouth, and rushed to the privy at the back of the house.

A mere week after he started work at Thomson's boatyard Innes came home in great excitement to say that he had just been offered a job at Webster's garage on the High Street.

'Seemingly Mr Webster's heard that I'm a good mechanic.'

'Has he now?' Jess said. Then, turning to Jacob, who had insisted on carrying her shopping home after meeting her in the town, 'Did I not see you talking to Mr Webster today?'

He looked embarrassed. 'The man was just saying what a fine motor-car I had.'

'And you told him that Innes looked after it for you.'

'It's only the truth.' The man looked over at Innes. 'I told him what a good mechanic you are.'

'And you asked him to take me on.' Innes's voice was tight with disappointment.

'I did nothing of the sort. As I said, your name came up in conversation. Anyway, you want to work in a garage, you told me that before.'

'That's right,' Zelda chimed in, her eyes blazing with excitement, 'and here's your chance.'

'I'm promised to the boatyard. What'll they think if I just walk out so soon after starting? Or have you had a word with Mr Thomson, too?' Innes asked the older man levelly.

'Of course not. It's something you'll have to work out on your own, if you decide to take up Webster's offer.'

Innes hesitated, looking from one face to the other, then said, 'I'll sleep on it and I'll make my mind up in the morning.'

Later, when Jacob left after enjoying one of Jess's fine dinners, he had only gone a hundred yards or so along the road when he heard Innes calling his name. He stopped to let the younger man catch up.

'About that job in the garage . . .'

'You'd be a fool to turn it down, when it's what you want and what you'd be best at.'

'I know that, and I'm not daft enough to say no to it just because you put in a word for me. But before I decide what to do,' Innes said, 'I think it's best to warn you that I'm not James.'

'Eh?'

'Just because we're brothers doesn't mean we're alike. You worked things out so's he could become skipper of the *Fidelity*; but I'm not looking for any favours like that.'

'Favours? But . . . but . . .' Jacob knew he was sputtering, but he couldn't help it. He had never known Innes Lowrie to be so coldly determined. Only James had seen that side of Innes, during their confrontation on the deck of the steam drifter. 'You think I bought your uncle's share of the boat just as a favour for your brother?'

'I never said that. You're a businessman, Mr MacFarlane, and I know that you intend to get a lot back from the silver you spent, mebbe even more than money,' Innes said cryptically. 'But I doubt if you'd have bought into any boat other than the Lowrie boat. And you'll benefit from me working at the garage, for now I'll have the proper tools to hand for your motor-car.'

'So you've decided to take up Webster's offer?'

'Probably, if I can leave Thomson's yard without any ill-feeling. I want that job because I know I'll be good at it, but since I minded telling you my dream about having my own garage with a wee house nearby, and since me and Zelda are looking for a house, I thought it wise to tell you that, as far as I'm concerned, your generosity's gone as far as it should. I'll get what I want one of these days, but I'll get it in my own way. Goodnight to you, Mr MacFarlane,' Innes said and strolled back to the house, leaving Jacob with his mouth hanging open.

30

The first thing that James noticed when he went aboard the *Fidelity* was the strong reek of carbolic, even out on deck. When he went into the galley his nose wrinkled and, as he began to descend the ladder to the fore-cabin, the smell became so strong that his eyes began to sting.

'James, stop where you are,' Stella said sharply from below. 'You'll crush the wee one's fingers, for she's trying to climb up. Ruth, will you get away from there!'

As he froze, scared to move in case his heavy boots crushed his youngest daughter's fingers, he heard the splash of a scrubbing brush being dropped into a bucket of water, then a yell of protest skirled through his head.

'No, Ruth, you're not going up there on your lone. Come on now and let your daddy into his own boat! See, here's a liquorice strap for you. And there's one each for you two as well, so let's have some peace here.'

He reached the foot of the ladder to find the cabin filled with his womenfolk. The twins were jammed together on one bunk with their rag dolls, and now Ruth was on another, chewing hard with her new teeth at the thick liquorice strap with which she had just been bribed. Stella, having restored peace, was on her hands and knees, scrubbing the floor. There was no sign of his mother or, he noted with disappointment, of Bethany.

'God save us, Stella, this boat stinks of carbolic!'

'It's a better stink than the one that was here when we

first came.' The words were jerked out of his wife's throat in time to the brisk rhythm of the stiff-bristled scrubbing brush. 'It was a disgrace, so it was.'

'We've been too busy catching fish to do much housework.'

'So I notice. Sit down, man, and get your feet off my clean floor,' she ordered, then as he did as he was told, 'And keep an eye on Ruth for me, she's like a barrowload of monkeys, that one. She should have been a laddie.'

As nineteen-month-old Ruth, taking her mother's criticism as a compliment, beamed at her father, her grey eyes – Lowrie eyes, he realised for the first time – sparkled with mischief. She took the liquorice strap from her mouth and offered it to him, then rammed it back into her smeared little face when he shook his head.

'I'm nearly done.' Stella's head was at a level with her husband's knees. 'The cupboards are cleaned out and the new mattresses are waiting on the deck. You can help me to shake them out then bring them back down.'

'Is my mother not helping you? Or Bethany?' He had not seen her since the night she had refused to leave Buckie with him, and he was sick with longing for a sight of her.

'Your mother was here earlier, but she had other things to do so I didn't let her stay for long. She's not getting any younger and I don't want her making herself ill over work that should be my responsibility now, not hers.' Stella's voice was brisk, and as she sat down on her heels and ran the back of a hand over her damp forehead, her glance about the spotless cabin was proprietary. 'You can help me with those mattresses since you're here. Stay where you are, girls. Sarah, Annie, you make sure Ruth behaves herself. After all, James,' she went on, when she had managed to clamber up the ladder and they were both on deck, shaking out the chaff mattresses, 'you're the *Fidelity*'s skipper now, and I'm the skipper's wife. I should be the one responsible for seeing that she's cleaned out and victualled.'

'Bethany usually helps with the boat . . .'

Stella frowned her displeasure at hearing the name on her husband's lips. 'I thought it best not to ask for your sister's help this year, because she's busy getting ready to move into that fine new house Gil's bought for her on Castle Terrace,' she said in the chilly voice she now used if she had to mention Bethany. 'Anyway, she's probably better not to be doing too much hard work in her condition.'

'Her condition?'

'Oh, did you not know?' The frown vanished and she beamed at him, just as Ruth had beamed earlier, though in Stella's case her face was smeared with dust and not liquorice. 'Bethany's expecting a bairn . . . at last.'

The harbour took a sudden lurch to one side, then almost at once it righted itself again. But it couldn't really have moved, James thought, feeling sick and confused, since Stella seemed unruffled, and work was going on as usual on all the other boats, where the menfolk were busy painting and caulking while their women scrubbed, dusted and polished.

'Expecting . . . Bethany's having a bairn?'

'I thought your mother might have said.' Stella's voice came from a distance.

'I've . . . not seen her for a while. Or Gil.'

The brittle new confidence she had developed since the day of the last line fishing, the day that James had taken Innes to sea as his engine driver, caused her voice to ring out like crystal in the clear, sunny April air. 'Gil's fair pleased, I've heard. That's to be expected, for a marriage isn't a marriage without bairns, is it?' Then, as all the indications of a full-scale battle broke out below, 'Bring those mattresses down, will you?' she said, and fled into the galley.

Bethany – expecting Gil's child. So that was the end of it right enough, James thought drearily as he gathered up the chaff mattresses. She would never go away with him now.

It wasn't until he was halfway down the ladder, several mattresses over his shoulder, that he realised that the child she was carrying might well be his.

He arrived at her house just as she was leaving it. At the sight of him she began to duck back in, but he reached the door in time to put his foot on the step and prevent it from closing.

'Gil's not home and I can't think of any other reason for you to come here,' Bethany said from behind the door.

'I can think of a very good reason.' He pushed the door open with the flat of his hand and marched into the kitchen.

'I'm on my way to Mother's to fetch the bairns home. She'll be expecting me.'

'She can wait. Stella told me about . . .' He glanced at her trim waist, then swallowed hard, but the words refused to come.

Her face, which had been very pale, flushed and she put a hand to her stomach in the instinctive age-old way of women carrying a new life within them. 'What about it?'

'Why did you not tell me yourself?'

'Why should I?'

'For God's sake, Bethany, it might well be my bairn!'

'It's not,' she said at once.

'How d'ye know?'

'I just know. It's Gil's and he's pleased about it, and that's an end to it.'

In his exasperation James wanted to take her by the shoulders and shake the truth out of her. After that, he wanted to hold her and never again let her go. Instead he folded his arms firmly together to keep them from doing something foolish, and took a deep breath before saying as calmly as he could, 'You've been married to Gil Pate for the past two years with no sign of a bairn. We've . . . you and me . . . it's been five months since Yarm'th. And you're certain sure that it isnae my child?'

'I'm sure.'

'I don't believe you. I think it's mine, and that's why I want you to come away with me so's I can look after you, both of you.'

'I've already told you that I'll not do that. What was between us ended when Stella and Innes found out. We knew it was going to have to finish one day.'

'But not yet, not like this! Bethany, I'm sick with wanting you and not even being able to look at you or talk to you.' He had never begged before; had never in his arrogance believed that he would ever have to stoop to such a thing. But now he was driven by sheer desperation. 'Please,' he said, his arms slack by his sides now, his face bleak.

His misery broke her heart but she knew, even if he had not yet accepted it, that there was no going back for either of them. 'James, I have to go and fetch the bairns. Let me go.'

'If I can't have you in my life I don't want anything.'

'You've got a wife, and three bairns. And the boat,' she said with a trace of bitterness creeping into her voice.

Given the opportunity, she would still exchange everything without a backward glance – James, her unborn child, all that she had – for the *Fidelity*. But unlike James, she did not have that option. The thought kindled the old resentment into a little stab of anger that hardened her just enough to propel her forwards, going past him without touching him to open the door.

'I have to go,' she said again. He hesitated, opened his mouth, closed it again, then went past her and into the street.

Bethany followed him out, heading in the opposite direction though it meant taking a longer route to her mother's house. She had not gone far before an elderly neighbour stopped to congratulate her on the coming child.

'You'll be lookin' forward to welcomin' this one,' she said. 'The first's aye special.'

Bethany nodded and smiled and went on her way. She believed that this baby would be special, and that it would be a boy, the one thing that Stella did not have. He would be a fisherman.

Like his father.

When he left Bethany, James went to Rathven grave-yard for the first time since the day he had seen his father buried there. For a long time he studied the stone and the flowers and the neat patch of grass, then he sucked the saliva into his mouth and spat hard on to the grave.

'That's what I think of you, Weem Lowrie,' he said grimly. 'You ruined my life, though I suppose even you couldnae have foreseen what was going to happen, or prevented it. That was down to me and to her. But at least I'll make a better ending than you did. I'll see to that for myself.'

'This,' Jacob said, laying the large square parcel on the table, 'is for you.'

'What is it?'

'A present, just.'

'For me?' Jess, unused to receiving gifts, eyed it with suspicion. 'Why?'

'Because I want to show you how much I value your friendship. Go on,' he urged, 'open it.'

Nervously, unsure how to deal with this unexpected situation, she removed the string and unfolded the brown paper, and found herself looking down at a handsome framed painting of the *Fidelity* at sea, her mizzen sail hoisted and a puff of smoke floating from her stack.

'Goodness,' she said, at a loss for words. Then, realising that Jacob was waiting for more enthusiasm than that, she summoned up, 'Who painted it?'

'A man I heard of in Aberdeen, who does bonny paintings of boats like this.'

She recalled, now, that Meg had mentioned something about seeing an artist on the harbour wall, sketching the boat. 'You paid him to do this?'

'Of course I did.' His eyes crinkled with amusement. 'You didnae think he came all the way here to do it for nothing?'

'It's an awful waste of good money.'

'Not if you like it. Do you?'

'Well, he's got the boat just right,' she said slowly, her eyes on the picture. Time and time again she had seen the boat coming home, looking just like that. 'You'd almost expect her to sail right out of the frame.'

He rubbed his hands, grinning. 'That's what I thought. You could hang it over the fireplace, where you can see it every day.'

'Jacob, I can go down to the harbour and see her every day if I've a mind to . . . unless she's away at the fishing.'

He gave her a long, hard look, then shook his head. 'Jess Lowrie, what do I have to do to get you to change?'

'Nothing, for you can't teach an old dog new tricks.'

'You're not old,' he said, then rushed on as she opened her mouth to argue, 'You're months younger than me and I refuse to be old, so you can't be, either.' Then, on a more serious note, 'We still have a future before us, Jess.'

'You're going away from Buckie.' Now she saw the reason for his gift. She had become used to having Jacob in her life again and she would miss him sorely.

'As it happens, I am, in a week or two, for I'm needed elsewhere. But that's not what I meant about the future.' He took her hand in his. 'Being with you again, Jess, has been like getting the chance to live my life all over again.'

The door was unlatched, as always. Anyone could blunder in and see the two of them standing there, hand-in-hand, Jess thought, embarrassed. Under the pretext of

folding up the brown paper strewn over the table, she
eased her fingers from his grasp. 'That's a chance none
of us ever get.'

'There are ways and means. Marry me, Jess.'

'What?'

'Marry me. We can have the banns called and the
wedding over before I have to leave Buckie. Then you
can come with me and see some of the places I've learned
to call home. I'll bring you back here, don't fret about
that. I know you'd not be happy if I kept you away from
Buckie for too long.'

'I've never heard such a nonsense,' Jess said feebly.

'Where's the nonsense in it? We're hale and hearty
yet, with me still a bachelor and you a widow. What's
to stop us?'

'Weem.' The name was out before she had time to
think. 'Weem,' she repeated, quietly. 'Even though he's
gone, he's still my husband.'

'I'd not ask you to forget him and the years you had
together, but I'm offering you a different life, the like of
which Weem could never give you. You and me, Jess –
together, the way it was meant to be.'

Jess's fingers played nervously with a corner of brown
wrapping paper. 'Jacob, I'm very fond of you, but I'm
still Weem's wife, even though he's lying up the hill in
Rathven and I'm down here in Buckie. I've been a Lowrie
for most of my life and I'll die a Lowrie, with no man's
ring on my hand but his.'

His face tightened, but he kept his voice under control
as he said, 'I've mebbe been too quick with my proposal.
You'll want time to think it over.'

'No, I don't. You've had my answer.'

Now the anger began to show itself as an emerald glitter
in his shrewd eyes. 'So even now he's dead you prefer
Weem Lowrie to me!'

'Is that what it's all been about?' Jess asked, very
quietly. 'I wondered, when you stayed on here longer

than you'd expected to, and when you bought a share in Gil's business.'

'What are you talking about?'

'And then you bought Albert out of the Lowrie boat so's James could be the skipper, even though you don't care for him.'

'There's nothing wrong with your James that a wee bit of maturity can't cure.'

'And Innes . . . letting him help you choose that fine car of yours and look after it for you. Finding work for him in a garage. What was going to be next, Jacob: a wee house for him and Zelda? A nice wee garage of his own?'

The arrogance that had helped him survive and prosper in the years since he had been forced far from the Moray coast, by Jess's love for Weem, now surged to the surface. 'You're haverin'!'

'And then there's me.' Jess indicated the fine painting on the table between them. 'Giving me a picture of the Lowrie boat that's part yours now, asking me to be your wife, offering me a such grand new life . . .'

'Because I love you, I always have. You know that!'

'I know that you once loved me, and that I hurt you. But it's not me you want now, Jacob. Not Jess Innes, that used to bide next door to you. It's Jess Lowrie, Weem's widow. That's why you came back, isn't it? Weem's children, Weem's boat, his wife. You couldn't best him in life, so you set yourself out to best him once he was dead.'

'That,' Jacob said, his face almost purple and his voice thick with anger, 'is the daftest thing I have ever heard!'

'I hope it is, for it's the worst thing I've ever had to say,' Jess muttered wearily.

When he had gone, taking the painting with him, she sat down in her usual chair by the fireside, staring at the larger, empty chair opposite. Even now she could see Weem in it puffing at his pipe, rustling his paper, glancing up to give her the look that always made her weak with wanting him.

She picked up her knitting wires and got on with the tiny jacket she was knitting for Zelda's baby. When it was completed there was knitting to be done for Bethany. Life went on, no matter what.

'Thinking of putting yourself over the side?'

Startled, James spun round to find Jacob MacFarlane standing by his shoulder. 'Why should I want to do that?'

'The way you were leaning out over the water had me wondering if you'd some notion of putting yourself where you thought your father should have gone. Taking his place.'

'You've got a fanciful mind, Mr MacFarlane.' And a shrewd one, James thought uncomfortably, for the man was quite right in what he said.

Jacob chuckled, the strong-smelling smoke from his pipe curling up and away into the grey dawn light, leaving behind only a faint aroma. 'I've been accused of plenty in my time, but nobody ever thought me fanciful. Mebbe it's the fish stew we had for our supper that's done it. It's sitting in my stomach like ballast.' He belched slightly. 'A sleep might have helped, but it's a while since I'd to share a wee cabin with other folk. I'd forgotten how loud snoring can be.'

'That's why I prefer to be the one standing watch when the nets have been shot,' James said, and Jacob chuckled again.

'You'll be hauling the nets soon.'

'When I'm good and ready. We'll let more fish swim into them first.'

The *Fidelity* was off the Caithness coast, on her first trip of the new herring season. Although April was coming to an end, the early morning was chill and sharp, with a wintry feel still to it. The night had been clear and frosty, the sky massed with stars, echoed on the seas by the masthead lights on the great fishing fleet spread for miles around them. It was a fitting time, James had been thinking before he was interrupted, for a man to take leave of the world. Now he wished he had made his move sooner. If his unwelcome passenger would just go below now, before the others woke . . .

But Jacob seemed to be quite settled. 'I came on this trip because it's the last I'll manage before I'm on my way: Holland next, and mebbe Germany after that. I might catch up with you in Yarm'th at the end of the season.' He put the pipe into his mouth, then took it out again to say, 'You know, James, you could be an even better fisherman than your father, if you'd just put your mind to it properly.'

'What d'ye mean by that?'

'I came on this trip because I wanted to get the chance to speak to you before I left Buckie. Married or none, lad, you've had the look lately of a man who's got himself tangled up with some woman he can't have.'

'You're talking nonsense,' James told him roughly.

'I'm entitled to talk nonsense at my age. I was in the same state once over a woman,' Jacob said thoughtfully. 'But I couldnae have her, so I put my mind to other things instead. And d'you know what I discovered? That women age and women can change their minds, but money's aye faithful when it's in the right pocket.'

'I doubt if I'll ever see the proof of that one for myself.'

'Now that's where you're wrong, for I've invested a fair bit in you already, and I intend to see that I get a good return on it. And if I do well, then so will you.'

'I never asked you to put money into this boat, Mr MacFarlane, and I'm not interested in dancing to any man's tune. I thought you'd have realised that by now.'

'You're Weem's son all right. All I'm asking is that you stay with the *Fidelity* and sail her well, and make a fortune for the two of us. And get rid of any romantic nonsense that might be getting in the way,' Jacob said, then he sniffed the air. 'I think your cook's up and about, and I do believe that the fresh air's settled last night's fish stew.'

James glared after the interfering old fool's retreating back. The sooner he made enough money to buy Jacob out, he thought, the better. He cast one final look over the water to where he could see the nearest boats beginning to take in their nets, then went down to the galley for some food. The *Fidelity* would be the last to start hauling and the first to the nearest port to unload her catch, of that he was certain.

Later, as the capstan took the strain and the messenger began to lift towards the boat, water pouring from its length, James dug one boot hard into the angle between bulwarks and deck, and leaned out over the water. At first all was black, apart from flecks of foam, then the first milky tinge appeared far below. It turned to a definite grey stain approaching the boat, and then, as the sun lifted over the horizon and the first net came closer to the surface, it became an unmistakable shimmer of silver.

James let out a yell and leaned even further forward to dig his hands into the mesh breaking through the waves. The herring was there, in abundance. The silver darlings were back, and what more could any man want?

Bibliography

———◆———

Auchmithie Album by Margaret H. King, published by Angus District Council Libraries and Museum Service

Buckie in Old Picture Postcards by Eric Simpson, published by European Library, Zaltbummel, The Netherlands, 1994; reprinted 1996

Collected Poems and Short Stories by Peter Buchan, published by Gordon Wright Publishing, Edinburgh, 1992

Fishermen and Fishing Ways by Peter F. Anson, first published by George G. Harrap, 1932; republished by E.P. Publishing, Wakefield, 1975

Fishing Boats and Fisher Folk on the East Coast of Scotland by Peter Anson, published by J.M. Dent, London, 1974

'The Fishing Industry' by Malcolm Gray, from *The Moray Book*, edited by Donald Omand, published by Paul Harris, Edinburgh, 1976

The Fringe of Gold (The fishing villages of Scotland's East Coast, Orkney and Shetland) by Charles Maclean, published by Canongate, Edinburgh, 1985

How It Was, leaflet by Isabel M. Harrison

Living the Fishing by Paul Thompson with Tony Wailey

and Trevor Lummis, History Workshop Series, published by Routledge & Kegan Paul, London, 1983

The Moray Journal – various newspaper articles

Northern Fishing Ports (From Whinnyford to Portgordon) by James and Liz Taylor, published by Visual Image Productions, Fraserburgh

The Silver Darlings, leaflet by Isabel M. Harrison

'The Story of Buckie', article by Peter Bruce in *The Leopard*, published by the Mill Business Centre, Udny, Ellon, Aberdeenshire, July 1994

That's Fit I Can Mine (That's What I Can Recall) – growing up in Buckie in the 1930s, a collection of poems by Isabel M. Harrison, published and reprinted 1992, second edition, 1995

Women's Contributions to the Fishing Communities of the North East of Scotland, 1850s–1930s, thesis by L.A. McAllister MA, University of Aberdeen